WHERE THE SKY BURNS

THE BLOOD OF EITH, BOOK FIVE

GILLIAN GRANT

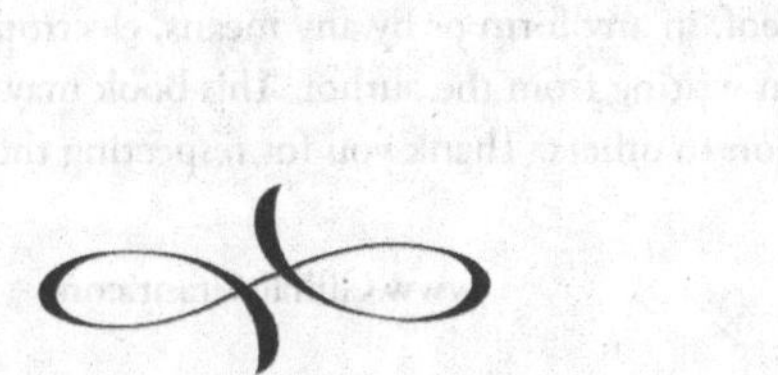

This is a work of fiction. All of the characters, organizations, and events portrayed in this novel are either products of the author's imagination or are used fictitiously.

WHERE THE SKY BURNS
© 2023 by Gillian Grant
Cover Design © 2022 by Stefanie Saw at Seventh Star Art
Eith Map Design © 2022 by Daniël Hasenbos
Formatting © 2023 by Charity Hendry Designs
ISBN: 979-8-9868589-1-3
Available in ebook and print editions.
All rights reserved.

www.GillianGrant.com

DEDICATION

To all the kids who saw dragons in their backyard, and to the
adults who still look for them now.

PRONUNCIATION GUIDE

People and Creatures:
- Sahar Al Fazil: Sa-**har** Al **Fuh**-zil
- Nerezza Quill: Ner-ehz-uh
- Drystan: **Drih**-stan
- Eirunn: **Ai**-roon
- Keres: Keh-**ruhs**
- Mortova: **Mor**-tow-vuh
- Ikedree: **Ike**-dree
- Evren: Eh-v-r-eh-n
- Gyda: **Gee**-da
- Sorin: Sor-en
- Abraxas: Uh-**brak**-suhs
- Arke: ar-**kuh**
- Solri: Soul-**ree**
- Viggo: **Vee**-go

Places and Countries:
- Etherak: Eh-ther-ahk
- Vernes: **Ver**-nes
- Terevas: Ter-eh-vahs
- Boreal Sea: **Baw**-ree-uhl

- Melkarth: Mell-karth
- Gratey: Grah-**tay**
- Orenlion: **Ore**-ren-lee-on

Things:
- Xirstine: Zir-stine

Terms:
- krevas: kruh-**vas** - a dwarven term for dishonored one, coward or traitor
- levenya: lev-en-**ya** - elven word for family, clan, or group
- foya: **foy**-ah - Ikedree term for father

The Banished Faith:

Once a nearly universally worshipped religion, the Banished Faith is now solely clung to by those in Etherak and few others. Once, the Divines were able to give their closest worshippers great power, and their absence has left the once powerful kingdom of Etherak crippled.
- The Banished Divines:
  - Haphion, God of Light and Flame
  - Nutvian, Goddess of Ice and Order
  - Vuhione, Goddess of Honor and Justice
  - Holtia, Goddess of Love and Healing
  - Emion, God of Music and Dance
  - Mandros, God of Knowledge
  - Elos, God of Change and Freedom
  - Eitrix, Goddess of Industry and Money
  - Roania, Goddess of Nature
  - Zelmis, Goddess of Darkness and Chaos
  - Nomien, God of Wrath and Fire
  - Mituna, Goddess of Tempests and Seas
  - Vyone, God of Death
  - Nuris, Goddess of Illness and Envy

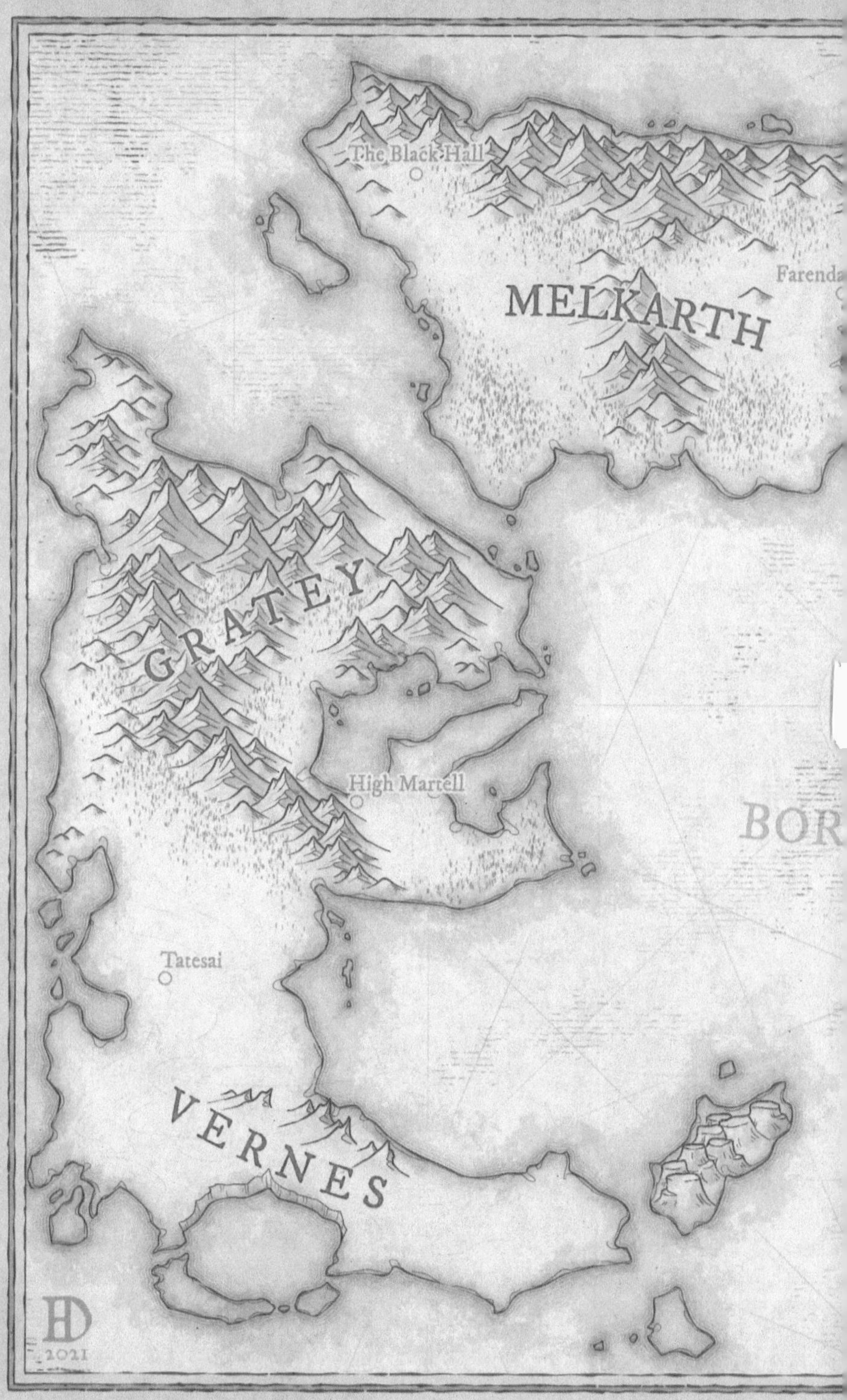

The Black Hall
MELKARTH
Farenda
GRATEY
High Martell
Tatesai
BOR
VERNES
HD
2021

Dirn-Darahl
ETHERAK
Linston
TERERVAS
Rhienwall
SEA
AMRUTHAN
EITH

PROLOGUE

Evren

Heavy, moist dirt clogged Evren's nose and mouth. It caked under her fingernails as she crawled her way up, up, ever upward. It slid through the folds of her armor, chilling her skin faintly like the memories of shadowy tendrils that belonged to someone who'd once been a friend.

Two lost friends. One lost love. And yet she was still living.

Her fingers broke through thick mud first, and then hit open air. She dug them in like claws, meeting slime and gunk of newly wetted earth, and pulled herself up inch by agonizing inch. The soil didn't want to give her up. It kept a loving, cold grip around her torso, around her legs, and tugged her down with every inch she gained.

Peace would not be gained by surrender, not to the earth nor to her own grief. There was work to be done to make up for everything she'd lost.

With a surge of strength, Evren pulled her head and chest free of the ground, gasping and spitting up soil. The sky was dark, and clouds choked away any signs of starlight. The wind was sweet and chilled on her skin as she heaved lungfuls of air.

The gritty taste of dirt caked her tongue, overwhelming the salt and shadow she'd left.

No.

Evren forced those brand-new memories away. She had to focus on the present. She could ignore what happened, if only briefly, to survive this.

Her hands sunk up to her wrists in mud as she heaved herself out of her would-be grave. The mud made wet sucking sounds as her legs pulled free and she crawled away. Every breath that rattled in her lungs she told herself she deserved. Every blink of her eyes made the world clearer. Every beat of their heart—

No.

A few feet away from the hole, Evren collapsed on the ground. The mud eagerly pooled into her armor and hair again. A part of her screamed about her bowstring and how she'd have to clean and replace it. The arrows too. But she couldn't bring herself to care.

There was night. There was air in her lungs. There was an unfathomable ache in her chest. And she was alone.

A cry gurgled from her throat as she sat up. She looked around wildly for holes like hers. She saw nothing but mud and grass. She combed through the mud, torn between wanting to find a hand and terrified of finding one still and cold.

Where were the Wandering Sols? The spell had worked. She *felt* it take her from one place and dump her in another. But what of the others? The spell hadn't forgotten about them. Arke would've made sure they all made it out. He wouldn't have messed it up.

It had to have been a fault of Evren's.

She wasn't sure how long she dug. Hours, perhaps. Her arms screamed with every shove of mud. Her frustration bubbled into a boil when every precious inch she cleared away filled back up in a manner of minutes. She was getting nowhere, and soon her digging became a frantic clawing.

Nothing.

Nothing.

Nothing

Evren's arms gave out just as a sob finally tore free from her chest. She slumped on her knees, cradling her head in her cold, slimy hands as hot tears cut tracks through the crusted earth on her face. There was no primal urge to scream. No need to kick the ground and rage. Her cries left her exhausted. With every new wave of tears, she sank deeper into herself and the knowledge that they were gone, and it was her fault.

Inevitably, her mind returned to the floor of the Boreal Sea. To a palace made of obsidian and a room filling with water. Sorin clutching Sol's unconscious body as tight as he could, wide eyes begging Evren to get them out alive. Sahar still reaching for Nerezza's body, torn and mangled beyond recognition by Divine magic and weapons both. Keres facing off against Abraxas not in triumph and in strength but in desperation as they kept his attention away from Evren. The shattered remains of Gyda's sword glinting in the blue light, winking as blood seeped from the cut on Evren's hand. Soft kisses on Evren's lips. *It was worth it.* Arke pressing the spell into her hands,

I'm sorry, but I left him once. I can't do it again.

Evren had left Arke. That he knew it would happen and prepared for it didn't make it better. If he'd cast the spell, he would've done it right.

Evren tore her hands through her grimy hair, heaving another pathetic sob. It was all for nothing. Nerezza's death. Gyda and Arke's sacrifice. If she hadn't managed to save Sorin, Sol, and Sahar, then she was useless. She'd failed them, all of them.

Abraxas most of all.

Evren hated the guilt that gnawed at her when she thought of him. Even more, she hated the wave of disgust when she remembered how he'd looked having Gyda at his mercy. People changed, she knew that. But she never expected him to fall so far.

When there were no more tears left to shed, no more mud to rake through, and the ache in her chest turned to a dull throb that wouldn't stop beating, Evren forced herself to her feet. In every direction a night-blanketed world spread out before her. Shrouded and still, like it was holding its breath and waiting for something.

Waiting for her.

She could've taken the time to examine the ground and fauna to figure out where she was. But Evren had no energy to do so. A heart that didn't belong to her tugged north, perhaps out of memory or habit, and she followed. Her feet drug tracks across the muddy grave she'd dug herself out of, and the air smelled like death as she left it behind.

~

THE PITCH-BLACK of night didn't lessen as Evren walked for hours. The only spark of light she saw in the distance came from a fire. Many fires, she realized as she squinted. A town, small and rugged. Burning far too bright for a normal night.

Then the screams reached her ears. The clanging of metal. Crackling of burning wood. An attack.

Evren took a deep breath, noting the hint of smoke for the first time. Her hand went to her bow across her back and found it bare, the quiver only holding a few arrows.

Her hand dropped to her side. She'd dropped the bow when she'd gotten to Gyda's side. A relic of her home. Something good that came out of Orenlion that had carried her safely through deadly caverns, hordes of undead, and falling through time. She'd lost it, too.

Absent-mindedly, her hand went to the sheath at her thigh, where she kept the wyvern dagger. Surprise flickered to life in her chest as her fingers met cool metal wings. Gyda must've put it back after she cut Evren's hand. Thoughtful to the end.

Evren swallowed the burning in her throat, drew the dagger, and staggered towards the village.

The closer she got, the less surprised she was. The glint of shining silver against flickering flames. The blaze of green light, like sickening lightning followed by hollow screams and the splintering of wood.

Serevadian troops swarmed the town, beautiful and deadly. Evren stood, ignored, at the edge of town. There had once been a wall that encircled the huddle of buildings, but it lay pathetically at her feet. There were few men and women in black and grey uniforms fighting back against the Serevadians with little success. Farmers guarded their houses with nothing but their tools and determination. They were mowed down.

Blood tinged the air. Evren barely allowed herself to taste it before stepping fully into the battle.

Still, no one saw her. No Serevadian would look behind them for threats when the town was crumbling so easily underfoot. Her wet cloak slapped against her calves as she stepped behind a Serevadian archer and tapped his shoulder.

"Excuse me," she muttered in his language. It felt numb on her tongue.

He turned to face her, the shock registering in his eyes just before her blade sank into his throat. Blood warmed her fingers, but she didn't savor it. She yanked the dagger out and let him crumble to the ground. Stepping over his body, she turned to her next victim calmly.

Calm should've been the last thing she felt at the sight before her. Rage, grief, betrayal, aggravation, those all seemed like normal responses. But her body wouldn't move past the eerie calm. She felt nothing as she slit another throat. More blood to warm her cold hands as she cut tendons, sent soldiers to their knees before cutting off their cries. A slow walk, trailed by bodies. So different from the mad scramble in Vanguard.

Yet another useless sacrifice.

By the time she was in the thick of the fighting, the Serevadians had caught onto her. A cry escaped her last victim before she could stop it, and as his body tumbled to the ground, three of his comrades turned to face her.

"You can leave," Evren said, flicking the blood off her blade. "I wish you would. But you won't."

She was distantly aware of what they saw. A madwoman covered head to toe in mud, her hands soaked in the blood of their friends. Armed with one dagger and a vacant expression. She expected them to laugh. They didn't. The bodies behind her had a lot to do with that.

They all lunged at once. Evren smoothly sidestepped the first blade, glowing so bright she could catch the grime sitting on her cheeks. The second one came at her legs, and she barely jumped over it. The third came at her with reckless abandon, and she batted it aside with her dagger, and darted in closer.

The Serevadian yelped in surprise, then in pain as the blade slid between his ribs. A cry of anger came from behind Evren and, with the dagger still inside him, swung the body around as a shield. It jerked in her grip, blood misting her face where the sword cut a nasty gash where neck met shoulder. She ripped her blade out and kicked the body away from her, sending it careening into her attacker and pinning them to the ground.

Air rustled the hair by her ear, and Evren turned just in time to dodge the third attacker. Their eyes were wide with rage and hatred, both finely focused on her.

I know that feeling, she thought to herself, and settled into a defensive stance.

Truly with just a dagger she should be nothing against a swordsman in full armor. Maybe that was why they hesitated across from her, eyes darting between her and the bodies of their friends.

"You could leave," Evren said again.

"And go where?" they hissed, and swung at her.

Evren backed up one step with every wild swing. She angled her body just enough to avoid the coming swings. Attack after attack, miss after miss. She held onto the cold vacuum of emotionless retreat as more and more the Serevadian became enraged. They put more strength with every swing, the air hissing with every savage cut, but it was an emptier sound than Evren's ripping flesh. The rage built with every missed attack, burning like a wildfire in their grey eyes.

Finally, they screamed in frustration and rushed forward as if to run her through. Evren simply stepped aside, blade up, and caught their throat as they passed. They thudded to the ground as their scream turned into a bloody gurgle.

The second attacker was still wiggling out from underneath her friend's body when Evren circled back to her. Her eyes were wide and frantic, and she kicked uselessly at the heavy body.

"You really should've stayed home." Evren said, and with one more slash the kicking stopped.

Around her, the town still burned. The Serevadians still fought. Villagers died too easily. A handful of deaths by her hand hadn't changed much, only left her with the smell of smoke and blood, and a calm like the center of a hurricane. They raged around her, both sides of this battle, spitting hate and fury. Weeks ago this wouldn't have happened. Weeks ago, that farmer wouldn't have been staring down that Serevadian as he stood between them and his home. Where two worlds collided, ash was left in their wake.

She could've prevented this, too.

Evren turned to go further into the town. She could help that farmer, at least. She froze as a large Serevadian filled her vision, close enough to gut her. She never heard him coming, she'd been so consumed with the carnage around her. Now he was close enough that she could pick out the violet hues in his eyes as they bulged. He opened his mouth and crimson blood poured out. She took a step back as it splattered on the ground, mere seconds before his body followed.

The man that took his place was human. Middle aged, with salt-and-pepper hair and an Etherakian uniform. He wiped his blade on his thigh, leaving smears of blood.

"Who the fuck are you?" he growled.

This man had saved her life. More than that, she knew for sure she was in Etherak now. If the uniform hadn't been clue enough, his attitude and accent were.

"I'm Evren Hanali of—"

Of Orenlion. Of the Deep Wood. Of Eith. Of the Wandering Sols.

She shut her mouth, unable to continue.

The human narrowed his eyes at her, then pointed to the trail of bodies with his sword. "This your handy work?"

"Yes."

"You're here to help?"

"I'm trying."

He looked at her dagger, now completely red, then at her. He didn't look convinced. But another building groaned as fire ate at its supports and collapsed. The cacophony of screams of those it landed on made him wince.

"You need to evacuate," Evren told him. "Get as many people as you can and run. You've lost too many to hold out here."

"They'll just follow us," the man hissed. He broke away from her as he saw one of his own become overwhelmed. He slashed at the Serevadian's calves, spraying bright crimson on silver before cutting them down. Out of the corner of her eye, Evren watched a group of Serevadian's break off and run away. The rest did not. They fought harder.

Not a retreat then.

Evren stepped beside the human and joined the fray. His desperation edged her calm, but both killed regardless. She maimed and then kicked towards him. He finished the job. She went low, knees skidding along the dirt, he went high. Legs buckled and a head flew. Evren got up smoothly and threw her dagger out at a rampaging Serevadian. It caught her just in the eye, and she slumped at the human's feet.

He frowned, bending down and jerking the dagger out. He examined it, and then Evren, with a suspicious eye.

"You're one of them adventurers?"

A twinge of hurt echoed in Evren's chest. She refused to show it.

"Not anymore." She held her hand out for the dagger.

He gave it back, pushing himself back to his feet with his word. "Works for me. So long as you're here to help."

"I am. You should get everyone out. I'll keep them from following."

"Why?" He still didn't trust her, and Evren couldn't blame him.

"Because I need to," she said. "And because I need someone to get a message to the royal family."

He let out a harsh bark of laughter, sparing the time to cut down a passing Serevadian before turning back to her. "What makes you think I can get an audience with the King?"

"You'll be a survivor of this." She swept a hand out to the village. "He'll need to listen. And invoking my name will mean something. They'll listen. You just need to get as many out as you can and tell them that the Wandering Sols failed. The number isn't in the hundreds, it's in the thousands, and they're all over Eith."

The hopelessness that crushed the human's fighting spirit was cruel, but Evren couldn't chance not giving Mei and Barrion a warning. They needed to know that Dirn-Darahl and Vanguard were only the beginning. That Velcros had an army that would bring the world to heel. It didn't matter if she was the one to deliver the message or not.

"You can't hold them all off on your own," the human insisted. "I don't care how damn good you are."

"I assure you that I will be enough of a distraction for you to leave safely."

He opened his mouth to argue, but a low roar cut through the night air. The crackling of fire quieted. The battle slowed to a stop as all turned to see a chained beast lumber into the town, led by the few Serevadians that had broken away.

The beast was easily twelve feet tall, standing on two bulbous feet with legs as thick as tree trunks. The torso was a meaty patchwork of hard muscle and fat, pierced with plates of crude armor that followed up to its chest and shoulders. Long, thick arms with knuckles that dragged along the ground. A collar with chains held by the now small looking Serevadian's leading it. Its head was small, and there were no eyes. Just flaring slits for nostrils and a gaping mouth sucking in the air.

Evren took a step back, her calm momentarily rippled. She hadn't seen a beast like that in Serevadia. Then again, she'd seen very little of the Empire, and none of Xoria. As vast as it was, she shouldn't be surprised to see species she didn't recognize.

It still put a damper on things. A small kink that turned into a noose around her neck that said, *You're really not making it out of this one.* Maybe if she wasn't alone . . .

But she was.

Evren turned back to the horrified human. "That's your cue to leave."

He spared her a pitying glance, accepting that she wouldn't back down even now. His people were already starting to run away. All he needed to do was herd them in the right direction.

"Divines guide you," he whispered. "You'll need it."

"I've seen your Divine's guidance." Evren turned to face the creature. "I neither want nor need it."

She didn't wait to see his reaction, or if there'd be a protest. She stalked towards the creature and the Serevadians holding it. They let go of the chains, stumbling away as it lumbered forward. The surrounding soldiers stopped their fighting to watch, allowing pinned villagers to scamper away.

Evren faced off against the creature. She didn't smile, as her younger self might've at a challenge. She didn't twist her stomach into knots thinking of all the terrible things that led her to this moment. She didn't rage at the fact that this could be her last fight. She stood tall and firm, with her dagger in hand and a monster in her sights.

And then she ran at it.

The Serevadians in her way parted eagerly as she darted towards her death. The creature's nostrils flared again, catching her scent. It slammed its meaty fists into the ground, her legs shaking at the jolt, and threw itself at her.

Evren didn't expect its arms to launch its enormous body so far. It arched through the sky with incredible grace, chains tinkling in the dark air. She skidded to a halt too late. It slammed into the ground mere feet from her, and the force of its landing buckled her knees. She threw herself to the ground, rolling just out of the way as a fist slammed into the ground and left a crater where her body had been.

Adrenaline broke her calm, *finally*. The rush of blood in her ears, the wind in her lungs, it all felt so freeing. Like she'd gotten a piece of herself back.

Evren threw herself to her feet, dancing away from a heavy chain that veered too close to her face. It whistled as it passed her, the creature mouthing the air and tossing dirt. She watched its muscles tense in its arms, a sure sign it was going to strike again, and ran forward. She leapt up, just as its arm started to rise. Her feet caught its ankle, the loose flesh keeping her from tumbling off. She jumped up, dagger raised in a glinting arc to the thick muscle of the creature's bicep. In her mind, the plan was simple. Land the blow, hold on for dear life. Climb up to the head, and stab it. Deal with Serevadia from there.

She should've known better. Evren's plans never did go right.

She slammed into the creature's bicep, dagger and all. But there was no tug, no cut of flesh or resistance. The dagger bounced off the skin the way it would a rock, and left behind not a scratch.

Evren had just enough time to curse before the creature's

other hand wrapped around her legs and flung her off it. She careened through the air for a few gut-spinning moments, lost the dagger, before crashing into a house.

Two walls couldn't stop her speed, but a stone fireplace could. Her side slammed into it, ribs cracking audibly at the impact, and she fell in a heap on the floor.

She groaned, tasting blood on her tongue but none of the power that came with it. Spitting up blood, she forced herself onto her knees. Every breath sent a spike of pain through her body. She couldn't get enough to fill her lungs. Clenching her fists against the rising panic, she wiped the blood from her mouth and got back up.

Of course Serevadia's nasty creature had stonelike skin. Why wouldn't it? Her list of ways to kill it was growing small, and her recovery time was running out.

The hole she'd fallen through was ripped even wider as the whole side of the house was torn off. The creature crumbled the wood in its hands, huffing for her scent. Its bulging foot crossed the entrance, and Evren ran . . .

Towards it.

She clutched her injured ribs, screaming in pain with every jolt of her feet. The creature roared in response, swinging at her. But the house's beams caught its swings. It gave Evren just enough of an opening to push through between the creature's legs and dart out past him.

She didn't stop running. The Serevadians were watching her with stunned expressions. She slammed into the closest one, tossing him to the ground and tearing his crossbow from his hands.

"You don't mind, do you?" she said, slamming her boot into his neck and watching him gasp for air.

Evren turned back to the creature, still fighting and tearing down the house, and fired. A beam of light haloed around the steel bolt as it tore through the air and straight at the creature. It landed true, right between the shoulder blades, and the creature's roar shook the very ground Evren stood on.

It knew that pain. It felt how Serevadian weapons hurt, and it despised them. With no eyes to gauge, Evren was left with just a quivering mass of muscle and rage as it tore away from the house and launched itself at the watching Serevadians.

Screams and torn limbs filled the air. Weapons turned on the creature, enraging it more but barely wounding it. The rest were turned at Evren.

She cursed again, tossing aside the heavy crossbow and bolted. Light-touched bolts whizzed past her by mere inches, embedding themselves deep into the wood of the surrounding buildings. A new idea sparked in her mind; equally terrible, and she ran towards the rampaging creature again.

Her breath hitched with every stride, but she refused to feel it the same way she refused to feel her grief. She dove behind the creature, using its leg as a shield as bolts peppered it and enraged it further.

A Serevadian cried out in alarm beside her. He raised his sword, but she gripped his wrist and twisted until he dropped the blade. She spared enough time to use his own sword against him before jamming it into the creature's thigh.

There was still resistance. The stonelike skin was tough as hells, but the light infused on the metal cut where steel couldn't. It stuck where she left it. The creature swung around, fingers grazing her hair as she darted to the next Serevadian.

It was a strange game she was playing, staying just out of reach of both Serevadian weapons and the creature's grip, but close enough so that they wouldn't stop trying to hurt her. The creature tore through Serevadians faster than she ever could. They whittled its health down with weapons better than her own. Neither party had the luxury of catching on.

The creature's back and torso were riddled with bolts and swords, but it showed no signs of stopping. Serevadian resistance was thin now. There were more bodies than breathing soldiers.

Evren tore the last intact crossbow she could find, biting her tongue until she tasted blood as she fit the bolt onto it.

A burst of hot pain bloomed in her thigh. Evren screamed and buckled, twisting around and firing the crossbow. It barely left the crossbow before tearing a hole through the throat of the Serevadian that stabbed her. He fell backward, his sword tearing out of her leg with him as his death-grip refused to ease.

Blood gushed hotly from her thigh. She blinked back the swarm of black in her vision. Too much blood too quickly. She really didn't have much time left, and she couldn't leave this creature to wander the countryside by itself.

Evren tossed aside the useless crossbow, standing with difficulty. The creature was busy tearing apart a soldier, their innards splayed like a red and grey cobweb between their body parts held in each of the creature's hands. The chains dangled musically, trailing in the blood-soaked dirt.

Evren started limping forward slowly. Then she broke into a halting jog. It was all she could manage between the blood loss and the broken ribs. But it was enough. The creature was too preoccupied with the body it was still tearing apart to notice her until she'd grabbed onto one of the chains and started climbing up.

Immediately it dropped the body and grabbed at her, but Evren swung from one bolt to another to avoid the hands. She kicked off embedded swords she'd placed, climbing up the chest as fast as her ruined body could manage.

She got to the right shoulder, and it scraped off pieces of its own flesh to try and get at her. Gripping the chain, she kicked off as hard as she could, swinging a wide arc across the chest, past the left shoulder and over onto the back. It roared and tried to buck her off as she slammed to a halt on its back. But Evren kept her eyes steady on the stinking grey flesh, crawling up as it jumped and tried to swat her off. Its arms couldn't reach her, no matter how much it contorted.

Evren's head swam as she got up to the right shoulder again.

Her vision was fuzzing out, but she could still see the creature clearly enough. Gripping the chain again, she kicked off and repeated her swing around the neck.

This time when she landed on its back, she used her first crossbow bolt at the shoulder blades to steady herself and pulled with all her might.

Immediately the creature gasped. It stopped clawing at her and turned to the chains wound around its neck. Its nails, dark with its own blood, tore at its throat but did nothing against the iron. Evren gritted her teeth, pulling until her body was almost parallel to the ground, her legs braced against the creature's shoulders. Her grunts of effort turned to screams that tore out of her raw throat. Everything she had left was poured into one final tug, and the creature's strangled cry joined hers in a hellish symphony.

Then, slowly, it stopped fighting. Its arms fell limply to its sides. It tilted from one side, then to another, then began to fall forward.

Evren had barely enough strength to let go of the chain and push herself away, but far too soon. She landed on the ground and her ankle snapped beneath her. She crumbled to the ground, not even uttering a cry. From her spot on her side she saw the village burning, a blur of orange and yellow against the black. She saw flickering Serevadian weapons going dark, and the creature laid next to her, its black tongue lolling out of its mouth.

Then Evren closed her eyes and didn't see anymore.

1

Sorin

Salt was the taste of grief. Sharp and bitter, overpowering and commanding. Through tears or through the sea, it was the one thing in Sorin's life that had stayed the same. The taste of salt meant he'd lost something,

Saltwater was in his blood. It lined his throat, trickled into his lungs, and burned like the sharpest fire. It woke him up to the muffled terror of drowning that wrapped around him like the cold currents caressing his skin.

He was sinking, heavy with his coat and blade. All around him the water swelled. Soft around him, but beyond his touch he could feel the sea rage. Currents lashed out like vipers, swift and deadly. Above him, the surface was an ever-shifting mosaic of black, blues, and white. Waves tore unhindered through the deep sea, large enough that he could feel their pressure deep in his belly.

Sorin didn't panic, although that caged-animal feeling clawed at his mind even as he suppressed it. Panicking would do no good. Swallowing more water would just kill him and he wasn't in the mood to die again. He shoved down his terror and confusion, he forced his mind to focus on one thing—survival.

His mothers hadn't raised him to panic and choke on the very water he loved.

He ignored his lungs. He couldn't have been underwater too long, otherwise he would've drowned. He knew his limit and that he could make it to the surface without passing out.

But he shouldn't be alone.

For one terrifying moment, he almost let the water in. Remembering how he'd clutched Sol's body with his now empty arms, and how his worg's shivering hide had pressed against his back. Water had been climbing up his legs. Shadows had gathered. And he wasn't on the ocean floor, or anywhere near it. The only explanation was Arke's spell, but then—where was everyone else?

The water thrashed around him, and his lungs were demanding his attention. Sorin was running out of time. But the others couldn't survive like him. He had to try. He *had* to.

Sorin wasn't going to lose anyone else.

He blinked his stinging, blurry eyes, looking for telltale signs of his friends. A shock of golden hair, a flash of grey skin, the glint of new armor. The navy depths mocked him with endless blue and swirls of bubbles that flitted around his boots. Navy turned to black, an endless drop before him like a gaping maw. Cold, pitch-black, a grave.

And someone was falling into it.

Sorin didn't hesitate. He tucked and rolled until he was facing the dark and kicked as hard as he could. Pressure built, the steady ringing in his ears turning to little spikes of pain deep within his eardrums. The churning water numbed his fingers and toes. Inside his chest was a wildfire devouring what little air he had left.

He ignored it all.

Sorin grasped Sahar's arm, tugging her away from the black depths. She was limp, the type of almost weightless that only came with water. Her eyes were closed, lips parted. But as he tugged her up, he met resistance far too heavy to belong to her lean frame.

Her alchemy bag, still draped around her shoulders, heavy as a boulder and brimming with components, was dragging her down. Sorin didn't have the strength to save both. He took it off her and let it slide into the black, little bubbles escaping the fine leather as he turned back to her.

The fact that she was likely dead crossed his mind, but he pushed that aside. He swam around, wrapping an arm under her arms and around her chest, pulling her close to him. Her head lolled, long hair tickling his face as it fanned around him like a cloud of ink.

Sorin turned to the surface and swam. Far above the surface raged like the grey clouds of a vicious storm. Bright bursts of orange burned for seconds, a startling color against the heavy blues and blacks, then were swallowed up by the waves. It was a ceaseless churn of black and blue, shapes so fuzzy and indistinct that he couldn't place them even when the bright orange flashed and silhouetted them.

He had no idea what he was swimming towards, what waited for him. But if it was the unknown or death, he'd take the unknown any day.

Sorin broke the storming surface, sucking in air and rain in equal measures as he struggled to fill his lungs.

No longer did the water cradle him. The relative calm of the deep had vanished and he was at the mercy of a raging storm. Thunder rumbled and the black clouds spit out sheets of rain. Waves battered him on all sides, lifting him, trying to pull him under again, letting him fall before repeating to process. He pulled Sahar's limp form against him as much as he could, keeping her head above the water to the point where he went under more than she did. His grip was so tight he was afraid he'd bruise a rib or two.

Better a bruised rib than still lungs, he thought as he was dunked underwater again.

He kicked furiously, breaking the surface and gulping down air before another wave slammed into him, filling his nose with burning salt water.

The sailor in Sorin knew that he should let Sahar go. Even if there was a chance that she'd live after taking on water, being battered by a storm would do nothing for her. And for him, she'd just be an anchor back down to the deep. His chances of surviving in a storm like this were minimal by himself, and down to nothing so long as he kept a hold of her.

Now, more than ever, he wished he'd been blessed with a Stormheart like so many Vasas. At least then he could lessen the weather around him and make some time to gather his thoughts rather than repeat the cycle of gasping for air, keeping Sahar on the surface, and being bullied by waves. Maybe with a Tidemind he could take the water from her lungs or keep the waves off them for a while.

But Sorin had none of those. Just a mind that was too exhausted and panicked to work right and a heart that shouldn't be beating anymore. He'd been so far from the Boreal Sea for so long that he felt like he wasn't a Vasa anymore. Now, as both the sea and the sky tried to drown him, he took that feeling as truth.

The Boreal Sea tolerated only its own, and its message to him was clear; he didn't belong.

Maybe it was the constant weight of Sahar's body dragging him down, or the air that was always laced with more burning salt than he could handle. Or perhaps it was the knowledge of how he got there—through shadow and betrayal that cut deeper than any knife—that finally wore down the last of Sorin's precious resolve. Maybe it was losing the one place he loved, or all the people he considered family.

It was, likely, all of it at once that broke Sorin as the Boreal Sea did its best to kill him.

He turned his head to the storming sky, roiling like the

waves had when he was underwater, and screamed. Every hurt, every resentment, every pain he'd collected since he'd hauled himself out of the water and onto Terevas's shores so long ago, bloody and alone, ripped free from his vocal cords. Salt hummed in his throat as he replayed everything that brought him here.

Fortune's Trinity burning. The screams of his mothers. The gleam of a gold tooth winking in the firelight. Heliodar's cold knife in his heart. The pain of being pulled back into his body. Gail and *Mortova's Maw.* Orenlion and the Eternity Maze. Losing Abraxas.

Abraxas.

The scream turned into a sob he couldn't control.

Abraxas.

His friend. His savior. His pain in the ass, total opposite, aggravating party member. The one he argued with the most. The one he hated himself for despising because staying dead would've been easier but Abraxas couldn't let him go. And now he was suffering more. The two of them, both alive and changed when they were supposed to be dead.

Sorin wanted nothing more in that moment than to be wrong again. He wanted Abraxas, the old friend whose soft smiles hid a world of hurt Sorin couldn't comprehend, to come back.

But that sword in his hand, pointed at Gyda, and that gleam in his eyes. That was not the man Sorin remembered. Sorin hated that man with a passion.

Sorin let that rage overcome his salt-laden grief. He let it burn until he was yelling at the sky again. Scratching noise tearing at his throat, tumbling uselessly into the sky that hurled thunder back at him and drowned him out. The storm was unforgiving, its wrath bigger and stronger than Sorin's. It shook the sky, forking lightning and spitting rain until he was spent and gasping, tasting blood and salt in equal measure in the back of his mouth.

And then, through the crashing of waves and rain, a cry answered him.

Sorin whirled around, wet dreads slapping his face and the water fighting with every turn of his head. At first he saw nothing, only the black of a stormy night. Then there was a flare of orange, of fire, and the silhouette of a vast ship overcame his vision.

The ship's enormous port side was to him. It cut through the water with ease, despite the thrashing waves, and was steadily circling back. Around the ship, the water abruptly calmed, foam and wave settling down under the influence of a Tidemind. The masts speared into the lightning-stitched sky, as black and sharp as Abraxas's blade. But a ship meant Vasa, and a way out. It meant his odds of survival had gone up.

The shout from before came again, undeniably from the ship. Sorin pulled Sahar close to him, waving his other arm in the air.

"Here!" he cried. "Over here!"

He couldn't hear what they said in response. He decided he didn't care, and began the slow, clumsy swim towards the ship. To keep Sahar above the water he had to swim mostly on his side, using one hand to comb through the water as both legs kicked until muscles cramped. But he didn't dare stop. Not when the waves pushed him off course or when Sahar's weight kept dragging him down. He felt like he was swimming through syrup for all the distance he gained, but the ship was getting closer.

When the water stopped fighting him closer to the ship, he nearly wept in relief. Tears were definitely falling when a rope slapped the water next to him. He snatched it up, grateful for something steady to ground him after so much time drifting.

He squinted up against the rain, watching as figures darted around the railing. More flashes of fire illuminated the rigging and tied up sails. A grizzled face peered over the side, frowning at him.

"Ya climbin', son, or are we haulin'?"

The thunder seemed louder closer to the ship, and Sorin had to wait for it to subside before speaking.

"I have a friend," Sorin shouted over the storm. "She needs help."

The man frowned at Sahar's body, likely seeing nothing but the dead in her. But before he could tell Sorin to do the sensible thing and ditch her, Sorin got an idea. A terrible one, but it would get them both out of the water at the same time.

"Pull me up when I'm ready!" he called up, and then sank below the water.

Muffled peace met his ringing ears. He kept a tight grip on the rope, unwilling to lose it even in the calmer waters. Letting go of Sahar's chest, he positioned them both so that he could get her over his shoulder. He hated that she was underwater again, but it was the only way he could keep a grip on her and the rope at the same time.

He surfaced again, Sahar successfully draped over his shoulder and wound the rope twice around his hand.

"All right, pull us up!"

The first three tugs had them out of the water, dripping and heavy, and within those few moments, Sorin knew he was going to lose Sahar. The full weight of both of them dangling with just one arm was killing him. The skin of his palm burned and shredded, and his fingers were losing all feeling from them. No matter how tight his grip around her legs were, he could feel her slipping from his shoulder. His hissed a breath, trying to shoulder her back into position and causing her to slip even more.

He cursed. Straining, the bones of his shoulders popped. They were only halfway up to the main deck. He was going to lose her.

"Now would be a great time for you to wake up," he gritted out as Sahar slipped further. One more heave from above and she'd be dislodged. She'd fall back into the sea, he'd let go and dive back after her, and they'd start the whole mess again until the Vasa gave up on rescuing them or Sorin's body gave out. Which would come quicker—

"Give her to me."

Sorin's head snapped around to find a young, spindly half-elf covered in ropes dangling next to him. A series of intense knot-work kept her weight distributed and steady, so she was less dangling and more standing with one steady foot at the looped end of her rope. She held her arms out to him, balancing impeccably even amidst the waves.

"You'll both fall if you don't," she snapped when Sorin hesitated.

"Fair point," he shrugged Sahar off and the half-elf caught her with ease. She put her over her shoulder in a similar way that Sorin had, but kept a firmer grip. She gave him a small grin as they all began to be hoisted up.

"You from the *Allegiance*?"

Sorin blinked. "No? What is that? A ship?"

She grinned wickedly. "Not anymore."

Another rumble of thunder shook his chest, and Sorin shivered. The thunder, louder closer to the ship, and the blaze of fires made sense now. He'd popped up in the middle of a damned battle and landed on the winning side.

He put aside the fear that they'd hauled him up, thinking him to be a survivor of the enemy ship to likely do nasty things to. They went through a lot of effort to rescue him if they planned to just kill him. Still, he tried to catch a glimpse of the tattoo on the Vasa's hand who held Sahar. She was angled in such a way that all he got was a flash of ink. His free hand went to his sword.

By the time they got to the deck, Sorin was shaking so bad that it took two sailors to pull him over. He collapsed on the wet deck, shuddering from the cold and exhaustion.

The half-elf lowered Sahar down on the deck carefully. She

checked for a pulse, frowning, then looked up at the grizzled man who'd tossed Sorin the rope.

"Get Miks."

The old man blanched. "He's keepin' us steady."

"Get Miks," she repeated. "This one's taken on a lot of water. Unless you want to get Nadine instead."

The man visibly paled, shook his head, and ran off.

Sorin wiped the rain from his eyes. "This Miks can save her?"

"Maybe," she said. "How long has she been underwater?"

"I don't know."

She narrowed her eyes at him. "You don't know a whole lot, do you?"

Sorin laughed nervously, the sounds catching on his raw throat. "You wouldn't be the first to say that. But, in all serious-ness, I'd owe you a great deal if you saved her. She's . . ." He swallowed. "She's all I have left."

"Alive or dead, you'll owe a great deal anyway." She stood up. "We all do."

Before he could press her further, another figure stomped up. Male, human, scowling and crusted with salt along his clothes and long hair. He flicked his long coat back as he knelt by Sahar's side.

"Callin' me for this will earn the captain's ire, Zo." The man, who Sorin assumed was Miks, said.

Zo shrugged, her eyes distant. "He'll be happy to have another body on board."

Miks cursed lowly, fingers running down the column of Sahar's throat and to her chest. He withdrew slightly, pale eyes darting over to Sorin.

"You want her to live?"

"What sort of question is that?"

"Do you want her to live, boy?" he pressed. "I can save her or I can let her go. One will be kinder."

Was this how Abraxas felt when he hovered over Sorin's body? Had he agonized over the choice, knowing one would be more painful than the other? Sahar didn't deserve to die, but maybe she'd wanted to. After watching Nerezza die, knowing that her whole world was crumbling around her and she had no way to stop it, perhaps she'd chosen to drown.

How could he make the choice to force her to live the way Abraxas had with him?

In his hesitation another cannon fired, and the wave of fire lit up the deck. The *Allegiance* was a burning skeleton of a ship, a great beast sinking into the waves with every passing second. This seemed to snap something in Zo, and she turned to Miks.

"Save the girl. You don't have a choice."

Miks scowled, but obeyed. He flattened his palm against Sahar's chest, fingers twitching. Then he slowly slid it back up her throat. Sorin watched, a little sick, as her throat moved with his hand as he pulled the water out her mouth. Ribbons of seawater streamed out between her parted lips, curling around Miks's hand until the last drop was gone from her body. He flicked his hand away, and the water splashed on the deck.

Sahar laid still.

Sorin pulled himself to his knees, but Zo was at his shoulder and kept him from standing. "Relax. Miks knows what he's doing."

Now Sorin could glimpse her tattoo. It wasn't one he recognized, a complex circle of knotwork he couldn't trace to any ship he knew. Looking back at Miks, his tattoo was different. Older and faded, but clearly that of two harpies joined at the claws. That one tugged at Sorin's brain, but he couldn't place the name of the ship to save his life.

Sparks of lightning webbed between Miks's fingers, and the tattoo was forgotten. Sorin blanched at the man. A Tidemind *and* a Stormheart in one body? He couldn't help the swell of jealousy in his chest.

"What are you doing to her?" Sorin asked as Miks lowered his hand to Sahar's chest.

"Restarting her heart," Miks said simply, and laid his lightning fingers against her skin.

The jolt of electricity swarmed her body. Her back arched, shuddering in the night air. Suddenly, the storm didn't register to Sorin. The dying ship faded out of his mind. Thoughts of this cryptic crew of saviors and everything he'd lost were tucked away for later. Right now, all he could do was hold his breath and hope that Sahar came back.

He didn't want to be alone. No matter how selfish or cruel that might be, Sorin couldn't accept the idea of being alone again.

Miks withdrew his hand and Sahar slumped back on the deck. The sparks died from Miks's fingers, and he pressed them gently against her throat. He hummed softly, just as Sorin noticed the rise and fall of her chest.

"She lives." Miks sat back, eyes dark. "Another one for the captain's collection."

Zo's nails dug painfully into his shoulder. "These two are prettier than the last ones. Maybe they'll stick around longer."

Miks looked up at Sorin. "Doubtful."

Sorin's blood ran cold. He reached for his sword, finding the scabbard empty.

"I took it while you were distracted," Zo said flatly. "No use getting yourself killed this early on. Just be happy you and your friend are alive."

Sorin stomped on his rising panic repeatedly, screaming internally until he found something that resembled calm. Looking between Miks and Zo, he found it hard to maintain.

"Why do I get the distinct impression that I was better off drowning?" he asked slowly.

Miks grimaced. Zo was emotionless. Beyond them, the *Allegiance* had sunk fully. Bits of splintered hull floated in the water, some still smoldering with flame. Sorin could see shapes of survivors in the water, although there were few. The sickening dread deepened as the ship steered towards them.

The battle done, the storm began to ease up as if its cue was a sinking ship. The oppressive press of black clouds never left, but the downpour turned to a drizzle, and the lightning reigned back deep into the sky instead of reaching for the ocean. There were no cheers among the crew. Sorin scanned the deck and saw them all waiting silently, like they were holding their breath as they stopped their various jobs. A few glanced his way, but quickly turned their backs. Sorin's unease grew.

A series of heavy footfalls sounded across the silent ship as two figures descended from the quarterdeck. A severe looking woman with matted black hair and a vacant expression in her eyes was behind a man Sorin could only assume was the captain. He held himself as such, with a straight back and a victory-drunk grin on his face. His blond hair was long at the top and tied back, showing off the shaved sides and scars along his scalp. A golden beard dampened to look amber covered most of his face and rings glittered on every one of his fingers.

"Another successful mission!" The captain clapped slowly, rings tinging off each other. None of the crew joined in, but he didn't seem bothered. "Nadine has calmed her storm for us, so I expect us out in the water retrieving survivors within the hour. The *Allegiance* had a large crew. Let's see how many are worthy enough to join us, shall we?"

Something in that rang wrong with Sorin. More than one something. For one, he'd never heard of a Stormheart able to make and control whole storms. The ones he knew could conjure some lightning, maybe some rain, and keep a storm from obliterating their ship. But the storm that had nearly killed him moments ago had all but dissipated. Normal weather didn't behave like that unless it was magically leashed.

And, of course, there was the issue with the rescuing bit, which was sounding more and more like those poor survivors should just dunk their heads in the water and stay that way.

"Captain." The grizzled man who'd saved Sorin stepped

forward, wringing his soaked cap in his hands. "We found two already."

The captain's eyes brightened and swept over to Sorin and Sahar. He lingered on Sahar, no doubt noticing her breaths, before landing fully on Sorin.

His boots sounded like contained thunder as he stepped closer. Zo shrank back, but didn't let go of Sorin's shoulder. The captain stopped a few feet from him and knelt, looking him up and down. He took in Sorin's tattoo, and nothing but a glimmer of glee broke his mask.

"Do you know who I am?" the captain asked softly.

Sorin shrugged. "Can't say that I do. Mind wearing a sign with your name? It'd make things so much quicker."

He snorted a laugh. "Sharp tongue. I find those amusing."

"Well, I'm nothing but amusing." Sorin shifted on his knees awkwardly. Even out of all the evil bastards he'd faced down, this one was making him squirm.

"Oh, I think you're much more than that, Mister Trinity."

Sorin swallowed. The way the captain said his name, like he was savoring a particularly juicy piece of steak, made him want to grab Sahar and dive back in the water. As if it would do any good. He forced himself to meet those eyes, ignoring how cold and gleeful they were.

"You know my name."

"Aye, I do," the captain said. "Which is more than you can say for me, so let's remedy that. My name is Vayne Knave."

"Oh, it rhymes, that's nice," Sorin muttered.

"My ship is the *Red Knave*, and our business is picking up worthy survivors of terrible wrecks. That's how I get this fantastic crew." He swept his hand out. "All survivors, all strong."

Sorin licked the salt from his lips. "Not many wrecks out there, I'm guessing. Have to make some of your own?"

He nodded to the *Allegiance* and Vayne shrugged. "Bad business partners. They crossed me."

"I'm assuming all of your partners cross you at some point."

"So there is a brain in there, good to know," he said, and his eyes fell back to Sorin's tattoo. "I'm not a monster, Trinity. I always leave survivors and I always leave them a place on my crew. We're a big ship, so there's always room. However, there was one ship I missed. Never got to save any of them. Damn tragedy that."

"I'm sure." Sorin tried to wiggle away, image be damned. He didn't like this man. Didn't like how his voice brought back memories of a burning ship and slaughtered family. But Vayne's hand shot out and grabbed Sorin's wrist, trapping his inked hand between the two of them.

Zo immediately backed away, but Sorin couldn't. Vayne's grip was like stone, chafing and immovable.

"I assumed everyone on the *Fortune's Trinity* died," Vayne continued, oblivious to Sorin's struggle. "Combed the water for days. Not much left of that ship when we were done, but I thought that a crew with their reputation could've survived. How did you escape, Trinity?"

"Don't you know kissing a kraken gives you wishes, Vayne?" Sorin hissed between gritted teeth.

A low rumble sounded, and he thought it was thunder again. But it was Vayne, laughing. The deep sound started in his chest and burst out of his mouth like a wave. Sorin didn't shrink back, only stared numbly as Vayne finally smiled wide enough to reveal the wink of a gold tooth.

It made sense now. His mothers's cries for him to abandon them. The sudden attack that left his home smoldering. *Fortune's Trinity* didn't have enemies, only allies. He'd been so confused by the attack all those years ago. He never understood.

"It was you," Sorin whispered. "You destroyed *Fortune's Trinity*."

Vayne's laughter ebbed, but didn't go away. "Aye, Trinity, I did. And you, if I remember correctly, were the little runt with a mouth bigger than your sword."

"*Why?*" Sorin cried. "Why would you do that? We didn't do anything to you! We were peaceful."

"You were valuable," Vayne corrected. "How long has it been? Two, three years?"

"Six," Sorin bit out. "Six years, nine months, two weeks and five days."

"Right, that long," Vayne shrugged. "Anyway, you were young. Not interested in how leadership did things. Never bothered to even meet me and my crew. Maybe if you had you would've stayed in the water and drowned with your friend. But now . . ."

Vayne pulled Sorin in until they were only an inch apart. He could smell nothing but the rankness of Vayne's breath, and could pick out every vein in his eyes. "Now, you're mine. Finally."

2

Solri

Little dwarven girls didn't grow up in Dirn-Darahl and fear the dark. They braided their hair, picked out their piercings. They learned their combat arts and took up a trade. Little dwarven girls conquered little fears and big fears, and became strong dwarven women that made Dirn-Darahl the envy of all other dwarven cities.

But Dirn-Darahl was broken. The little dwarven girls were dead. And Solri Amet was very much afraid of the dark.

She could see well—as any dwarf could—in the murky shadows of the deep. Her rigorous studies made her aware of all the dangers of being underground, such as Guzzlers, cave ins, and choking gasses. But the shadows that had claimed Kleros, that killed Viggo and swallowed her whole, were not the still pools she'd once eyed in her room and begged her papa to disperse with a Luminstone. These shadows moved with purpose and malice. These shadows were monsters in their own right.

They held her for a long time. Searching, cradling, suffocating. Until whatever she'd known before had faded to a strange, fuzzy distance. Memories of a gilded home, of a beautiful woman with jeweled rings and a wheeled chair and a warm smile just for her felt like a dream. Flashes of battles, of blood and desperation through snow, ash, and fire were all nightmares. Mangled dead in a tomb of ice. A crown falling from a dead King's head and resting at her feet. A dark maze cutting through time. A fortress battle in the rain. There were people she knew, people that belonged in her heart. A bellowing laugh. A blinding smile. The smell of ink and parchment and the feeling of coarse fur between her fingers. Soothing bath water that glowed and smelled like spices, the warmth of trusted company even better than the water itself. A nose bled red, a fine handkerchief catching the drop before the beard did.

Shadows.

Shadows and pain.

Shadows and grief.

This was all she knew. This was all Solri Amet was. A corpse bled dry and replaced with oily dark. Whenever she reached for the faded dreams, even the terrifying nightmares, the shadows gently pushed her back. The more she was with them, the more her dreams faded. Tendrils of color bleeding to grey. The shadows held her like an old friend.

Her only friend. After all, her dreams were . . . where were they?

It didn't matter.

She was cold in the black, but not alone. A hand held hers, fingers gentle and callused. And a voice whispered, "I have you Sol. There is nothing to fear. You and I have each other."

Solri couldn't explain to the gentle voice that all her fight had bled out of her when her red blood had left her. All her fear had been washed away by the black that replaced it and stained her bones, her soul.

Those faded scraps of . . . something. Dreams. Visions. Nightmares? They weren't her. All that mattered was the black. She'd never shied away from it before, only tucked it away behind sunshine smiles and soft words.

Little dwarven girls didn't fear the dark. Murderous dwarven women found a home in it.

~

SOL WAS aware of clean sheets against her skin before anything else. She spread her fingers wide, whispering the pads of her fingertips against the soft fabric, warm from her body heat. Next was the smell, woodsy and comforting. Like incense or a candle full of healing herbs. A little sharp around the edges but overall pleasant.

She was stiff, as if she'd been sleeping long and hard like a boulder. It made it difficult to not roll over and pull the sheets over her head. To just fall back to sleep, let the shadows claim her . . .

Sol jolted up, eyes wide open.

The rush of strange dreams and nightmares came back in vivid bursts. Serevadia, Dirn-Darahl, all her adventures, and her friends. Sweet Jalaa, her friends! How could she have forgotten them?

She rubbed her face furiously, trying to force all memories, regardless of how bad they were, to stick. She forced herself to remember what it was like to drown in the icy waters of Myrefall Bay, and how her first sight afterwards was Gyda's weeping eyes. She forced herself to walk the Eternity Maze again and see all that death and destruction. Watch Arke fall to Nerezza. Watch Evren slowly die. Watch Sorin bleed out in her hands by her own dagger. Remember the ache of Abraxas's absence.

Abraxas.

Her heart was thudding in her chest and she tore her hands away from her face. The room she was in was plain. It had no windows, just a door, a bed, a warm lantern, and a smokey haze of burning incense. Where was she? The last thing she remembered was Viggo's body hitting the ground and his light going out. After that, there was nothing but the wretched shadows seeping under her skin and latching on.

She was meant to be saving Abraxas. Stopping a war and saving her people, but most of all seeing that beautiful, haunted face and hugging him again.

"Evren?" Sol called out tentatively towards the door. No answer.

She pushed the sheets back, sparing a glance at her legs just to make sure they were normal. She saw no black veins and gave another silent prayer of thanks. The nightgown was hers too, a simple little shift she'd bought in Orenlion. Their silk really was the softest, but it did little to keep her shivering at bay.

Her bare feet touched the cold stone ground and her legs held her weight fine.

"Sorin?"

Silence. Sol wrung her hands together. Sorin never ignored her. He wasn't a deep sleeper. If she'd been hurt, like she assumed she was, he wouldn't be far. Any time she'd been awake at night he always came when she called his name, so this silence didn't make sense.

Unless he wasn't there.

Sol swallowed down her fear and shuffled to the door. She pressed her ear against it, hearing nothing on the other side. Not Gyda's snores or the murmur of talking.

She was starting to hate silence. Even so, her voice came out as a little squeak.

"Arke?"

Nothing. Her fingers grasped the door handle. She had no weapons, no memory of where she was or what happened to her. She was alone and scared. But that didn't mean she was going to hide under the covers without making sure she couldn't get out. She didn't have her tools to pick the lock, but she—

The handle moved with ease and with no sound.

Sol took a deep breath. No locks were good. This wasn't a

prison. She was fine. Likely her friends were farther away or dealing with another nightmare she'd learn about later.

She pulled the door open just enough to squeeze through and shut it quietly behind her. The hallway was as bare as her room. Sconces dotted the stone walls at regular intervals, shaded but not flickering with flame. She frowned at the warm light, so like the sunlight Sorin loved the bask in. Could they be . . .?

No. She shook her head. If they were Luminstones she'd be back in Dirn-Darahl, then she'd have a serious problem. Then she absolutely would be in enemy hands.

The hallway stretched out before her, no more daunting than her room had been, yet she still had to squeeze her hands to keep them from shaking. She moved away from the door one slow step at a time. The skirt of her slip rustled between her legs. The stone echoed with each pad of her foot. And she controlled her breaths. If there was anything her youth in military training taught her, it was to remain calm in unknown situations. Until she had more information, she needed a weapon. From there she needed to assess the threat, if there was any. She wouldn't feel safe until she had something sharp in her hand, or some truth to keep her imagination at bay.

The first door she came across led to another room like her own, only this one was cold and unused, choked with shadows. She shut the door quickly, and tried to stop shivering by hugging her arms. She wasn't afraid of the dark, no matter what she saw in Kleros. *She wasn't.* And what she saw in her unconscious state was likely very similar to what Evren's mind created when she was dying. Their brains could do the worst things in their final moments.

Sol didn't feel like she'd been close to death, but that was the only explanation she had.

There were three more rooms like her own, all empty and unused. Then, at the very end of the hall, was a spiral staircase leading up. Sol gripped the metal banister and pulled herself up the stairs. Her legs didn't burn much, no more so than they had before. If she'd been seriously injured and bedridden, then she should've experienced some sort of fatigue at this point.

Sol frowned, pausing a few steps up. She looked down at the hand gripping the banister. Her skin was always pale enough to see her veins, and now wasn't any exception. They were the same purplish-blue they always had been. She waited for something black to slither under her skin, or for her skin to shadow and peel like she remembered in her dream. But it stayed the same. Pale, warm, a little drier than she liked but otherwise fine.

She blinked away and continued up the stairs.

The top spilled out into a similar, albeit warmer corridor. The sconces were brighter, and there was a long rug to cover the cold stone floor. Sol wiggled her toes on the plush carpet, absently happy while she looked at the array of doors in front of her. All were closed, except one which was cracked open and spilling out brighter light. Hushed tones whispered through the crack in the door and into her ears.

She padded eagerly over to the door, staying just beside the crack so she couldn't be seen by anyone inside, and tried to listen.

But the words that met her ears were foreign. She didn't understand the language, but she recognized it. She'd heard it as curses, as battle cries, as thoughtful musings between too soft fingers.

Serevadian.

The fear she'd been pushing away gripped her heart like an icy fist and wouldn't let go. She suddenly found it hard to breathe. Her skin itched like hundreds of insects were crawling all over her.

Sol took one step back, and then another. Her mind was racing. No weapons, no armor, in enemy hands with no allies to speak of.

She was dead. She was dead and counting her remaining breaths like they were grains of sand in an hourglass, slipping steadily.

She was alone and afraid and so very—

Her back collided with something warm and hard. She started to cry out, but a hand clamped over her mouth and the noise died in her throat. She was so shocked that she barely computed when the stranger's arm was wrapping around her waist and pulling her up. Carrying her away.

A guard. She was caught and now they were going to do unspeakable things to her. She ticked through everything she'd learned about being a hostage, but it all fell flat. Her guard was much taller than her, likely Serevadian. She felt no armor but that was useless to her if she didn't have a weapon.

They were curving back down the stairs when her training kicked in enough for her to remember elves had the same things between their legs that dwarves did, and they hurt the same when they were kicked. She was reasonably sure her guard was male, and no matter how gentle he was being she would *not* go quietly.

The moment he landed on the final step, she brought both legs up and swung her heels back with all the weight and force she could muster right into his balls.

A wheeze of pain fluffed her hair, and that was all Sol needed as he doubled over in pain. She wiggled free of his loosened grip and jumped away, landing gracefully on the floor.

She needed to go back up as fast as she could. Past the open door there had to be an exit.

Sol turned around, ready to dash around the fallen guard, but was met with someone she didn't expect to see kneeling in front of her.

"Abraxas?" Sol breathed.

It was him, despite the extra gray in his hair and the scrunched-up look of pain in his face. He lifted a shaking finger, asking for a moment that he rightfully deserved as he breathed through the pain.

"Oh, Jalaa's arse I'm so sorry!" she whispered and ran up to him. "I thought you were a guard. I wouldn't have done it otherwise."

Abraxas laughed breathlessly. "You've been busting my balls since the moment we met."

Sol couldn't have helped the smile on her face if she tried. He was hunched over and in pain and looked so damn weary, but it was *her* Abraxas. He was alive and safe and damn it, she was crying.

"Don't do that," he said softly.

She shook her head and wrapped her arms around his neck. The crook of his neck was still the best place for her to bury her head. His shirt still caught her tears and his arms, while shaky, still wrapped around her and held her close.

"I thought you were dead," she sobbed. "I thought I lost you."

His hold on her tightened, and his breath fanned against her skin as he tucked his head on her shoulder as well.

"I'm right here, Sol. You won't lose me again. I swear."

Sol was used to promises, empty or otherwise. But with Abraxas there was no doubt in the weight of his words. She believed him wholeheartedly.

But she still had questions.

Sniffling, she pulled back just enough to look him in the eyes. Oh, those eyes. They looked so worn. There were more wrinkles there than before, but she found they suited him, as did the grey. Elves always aged gracefully, the damn pretty bastards.

"What's going on?" she asked. "Where are we? And where are the others?"

He put his hands on her shoulders. "This is all very complicated, but I swear I'll explain."

"Yes, you will," she agreed. "Now."

He winced. "Preferably not in the hallway. Let me get you to your room, and then we'll talk."

"At least tell me where we are."

"A dwarven outpost outside of Dirn-Darahl. Southern one I believe, although the name escapes me.

"Stone's End," Solri said. It was an old outpost from the ancient wars her ancestors waged. Dirn-Darahl had made no use of it in the centuries since the treaties were signed. "Why are we here? Why are there Serevadian's upstairs?"

"Again, Sol, the hallway?"

"Oh, right. Sorry."

She helped him to his feet, apologizing a few more times if only just to hear him laugh off her attempts. It was good to hear him laugh again. It was good to have him, period. She wasn't alone, and something had gone right. Finally.

She helped him back to her room, which she could now recognize was filled with the scent of Abraxas's herbs. Had it really been so long that she'd forgotten what they smelled like without him here with her?

They settled on the small bed, Sol tucked up as small as she could with the sheets around her lap, and Abraxas sitting gingerly with his feet touching the floor.

"I'm confused, Abraxas." Among other things. "I don't know what happened."

He smiled at her fondly, and that smile alone was enough for most of her worries to melt into the back of her head. "What do you remember?"

She searched through her memories, digging through Vanguard and Kleros up until Viggo's death. After that it was all blank, besides her weird fever dream.

"We were in Kleros," she said. "A strange elf used Blood magic to push us into this pool of shadows. Viggo was able to keep them from hurting us for a little while, but the shadows killed him. After that, they took us. It's all black." She shook her head. "I feel like I'm missing so much. Like I've been out for months but I feel fine."

"That's good to hear." He took her hand in his. "When I found you, I feared you wouldn't make it."

She raised her eyebrows. "Why?"

"The shadows that killed Viggo are under Catarmon's command. They are cruel creatures, uncaring of those around them. Those shadows were meant only to transport, but it seems like you had an adverse reaction. Your body started to shut down because of it. No wounds for me to heal, no magic to banish. It was like an infection of the soul rather than the body."

Sol kept her breathing calm, despite her urge to scream. "But you saved me."

He squeezed her hand. "Another miracle. I'm glad I could."

She squeezed his hand back, smiling a little. It was good to have him back. There was a quiet weight to Abraxas that always calmed her. It could be that he was the one that was always meant to break her out of the prison, before Karas set off Alkimos. But ever since, he'd been a steady friend and she knew better than anyone how few of those were in Eith.

"And the others?" she asked, almost fearing the answer.

His face fell, and he cast his eyes downward. He spoke to their hands. "That is the troubling part. The shadows seemed to have lost them. At least, that's what Catarmon says. Regardless, I can't find them. I believe they're holding them hostage while Catarmon looks for the Eternity Dagger."

"What?" Sol exclaimed. "We don't have it! It was destroyed with . . ."

She faltered and he looked up. "With me?"

Sol nodded.

"I thought as much as well. How else do you think I ended up here?"

"I . . . I don't know," she admitted. "We had no idea you were alive until Viggo told us he saw you in Andovine. We thought maybe you used the dagger to escape at the last minute."

Abraxas nodded, a piece of ink-black hair falling in his eyes. "I did, by accident. It would've been kinder on us all if I hadn't."

"Don't say that," she said. "Abraxas, you can't believe that."

He finally looked her in the eyes. "By living, I found myself chained to the whims of a monster. I have relived my past sins and made them far worse. The things I've done to survive . . . Solri, you would not look at me the same if you knew. I've served Catarmon for nearly a century in the hopes of reaching you in time, but they got you first and I was powerless to stop it."

Sol scooted closer and held his cheek with her hand. She put all the confidence and boldness she had in reserves and poured it from her gaze into him.

"Abraxas Kain, you are no monster," she said. "You are a survivor, and no matter what you have done, you are still my friend. Nothing is going to change that."

Doubt flickered in his face. "I don't know if I believe you."

"I have never lied to you."

"No." He smiled sadly. "You haven't."

"Just because you can't forgive yourself doesn't mean Troll-shit to me, okay? You are my dearest friend and I would walk with you to the ends of Eith if you only asked."

A breath of relief shuddered out of him. He leaned into her palm, eyes closed, as if he'd been starved of friendly touch and was savoring it. When he withdrew she laid that hand, still warm, in her lap.

"Now, tell me who this Catarmon really is and why the hell we're here."

~

Hours passed and Abraxas told her everything from the hell he endured in Vernes, to Nerezza's strange spell, to falling to Catarmon. Catarmon, as he understood them, was something created out of Nerezza's death. A disgusting being that wanted godhood. They had taken over Xoria with ease, and spread to the rest of Serevadia like a wildfire, infecting the minds of Mora first and then more influential people like Velcros. Abraxas explained that Catarmon refused to let him go or kill him, and that he'd remained something of a pet to the creature ever since. Another hell for him to endure while he counted the years to see the Wandering Sols again. He refused to tell her what he'd been forced to do, but that tortured look on his face was all Sol needed to know that he hated himself for doing it.

Serevadia had taken Dirn-Darahl, like Mal and Viggo said. The death toll was enormous, and Sol hadn't the heart to ask about her mother. Abraxas's pained silence on the matter only confirmed her fears.

He'd sacrificed much to keep her close to him. Since she obviously didn't have the Eternity Dagger, Catarmon wanted to discard her. Sol didn't know what Abraxas traded for her life, but she was grateful. She'd make it up to him again, one day, when this was all finished.

"We have to get the others out," Sol said, stretching her stiff legs. "Then take back my city."

Abraxas frowned. "How? We have no army. It's heavily occupied. Velcros himself has taken up residence in the city to keep up with the troops."

She snarled. "Even better. I killed a King. How is an Emperor any different?"

"Killing him won't stop Serevadia. Catarmon will just replace him."

"Then what else can we do?" she asked, exasperated. "Come on, Abraxas. How long do you think we'll be kept alive? We're our friends only chance."

"I know," he said gently. "I'm not trying to discourage you, but I have had a long time without hope. It's somewhat dampened what little rebellion I ever had."

"Trollshit." She poked his chest. "We broke away from Velcros once. We can do it again. Maybe we just need to get out and go to Etherak. Their army could break Velcros's hold on Dirn-Darahl."

"For a time, maybe." He nodded. "But the root of the

problem is Catarmon, and I don't know how we can deal with them with just a mortal army."

"Catarmon isn't a god," Sol said stubbornly.

"Yet," Abraxas amended. "We must make sure that doesn't happen."

"Fine." Sol chewed the inside of her cheek and tried to bring up all her military strategy from when she was younger. It all blurred together, and none of it had anything to do with rooting out an invading army. Dirn-Darahl had never been breached before. Brand-new territory for the history books, assuming the city survived.

She groaned in frustration and put her head in her hands. "I don't know what to do, Abraxas."

His hand patted her back sympathetically. "I didn't expect you to. We'll figure this out, but for now we are two survivors treading dangerous water. We can only dream of when this storm will pass."

"I'm not going to sit on my hands while Eith burns," she muttered to her lap. "You said it yourself, Serevadia's army is all over Eith. We have to do something."

"Or pray for a miracle." He squeezed her shoulder. "I got one with you back in my life. All I need to do is have faith the world will right itself."

"I bet this would be a lot easier if your gods were here to wipe Serevadia away, right?"

It was meant as a joke, a bad one because poor Abraxas was always holding out hope and Sol knew better. But she felt his demeanor shift a little and realized that was *exactly* the type of hope he was hanging onto.

She pressed her lips together before she could crush it. What else had she expected him to fall back on during his time alone? The Wandering Sols were just people. Believing that a higher power could come and save them all was comforting, she had to admit. But Sol's goddess was dead, and Abraxas's were far from the reach of desperate prayers. He knew that, so she didn't say it out loud, but her heart ached for him.

She lifted her head up enough to rest her chin on her fists. "I'm sorry. That was in poor taste."

But he smiled down at her, as gentle as ever. "So is kicking me in the balls."

She laughed a little. "Next time don't sneak up on me like that."

"I wasn't aware anyone could sneak up on you, but I swear to never try again." He stood up, combing his hair back from his face as he did.

Sol sat up. "Where are you going?"

"To talk to our captures about some food and a bath for you. I will have to tell Catarmon that you're awake. They might want to see you. The sight will be . . . unpleasant, so I rather hope not. Regardless, don't worry about your life here. For now, we are safe as we can be in enemy hands."

"We're dogs on leashes you mean," she said.

"Better that then dead. Dogs can always bite back." He winked at her and walked out.

Thirty minutes later she did get food and, despite the rather plain gruel, it was the best meal she'd tasted. Abraxas stayed with her the whole time and when she was done, led her up a flight to the bathing room.

It was a modest room, with a warm pool sunken in the corner. Her clothes, sans armor, were folded next to some towels.

"I'll be just outside," Abraxas said. "Call me if you need me."

She nodded and closed the door. There was no lock, but she didn't need it. She eagerly stripped down and slipped into the warm water, but she didn't give herself time to relax. She scrubbed her skin raw, washed her hair until her scalp tingled. Anything she could do to keep her mind from wandering back to her shadowy dream.

But her mind did wander. To what Abraxas told her and the

hurricane of shit her friends were likely going through. The idea of them suffering only made her scrub harder.

Her friends were taken from her. Her city was in the hands of her enemies, and any allies she might have were likely dead. The world was falling to Serevadia and another would-be god. Well, fuck Catarmon if they thought she would sit idly by. Gail died, and so could they.

Sol got out of the bath and toweled herself off. She slipped back into her familiar clothes and combed her hair. She took the time to carefully shave her beard, which had grown bushy while she slept, and fix her nose ring back in place. When she was done, she recited certain truths to keep herself from falling apart.

She was close to home.

Her friends were alive for the moment.

And Abraxas was lying about something.

3

Sorin

Shame hummed in Sorin's bones long after the metal bars of the brig had shut behind him. He hadn't fought at all. He could blame it on the exhaustion, because he was well and truly burnt out. There hadn't been the time to rest much from Vanguard when he'd been pulled into Kleros, and then into Abraxas's depressing palace. It had been one long fight, starting from the rain-soaked cobblestones and ending with him slumped next to Sahar in a brig that didn't have the decency to stay dry.

An inch of water sloshed back and forth with the swell of the waves, carrying with it pieces of wood, straw and other things he'd rather not think of. Sahar had the only dry spot in the cell, a raised platform where one could sleep without being in the water. Even that was still damp, but it was better than getting soaked all over again.

Sorin sat in the corner, bottom cold and wet, the rest of him sticky and damp, and his mind swimming with enough awful thoughts to drown himself in. His fingers traced the curve of his tattoo, remembering the sting of when he got it, how proud his mothers had been that he'd stayed still the whole time and only offered a few cutting words to the tattooist about how long it was taking.

If he could help it, he tried not to think about the *Fortune's Trinity*. All that did was make him long for a time he couldn't get back, and all *that* did was make him dark in the head again. It hurt when he couldn't smile, when he couldn't force out silver-laced words that made people laugh or angry. When he thought of the *Fortune's Trinity*, of Maria and Hastings and Corliss and Sudie, then he became a shell of himself. Something shadowy where he stayed curled in the back of his mind, wallowing up to his chin in regrets while his body followed through the motions of living.

Sorin hadn't allowed himself to be like that since finding *Mortova's Maw*. He wasn't Gail, and he refused to let grief change who he was. But now he had a name . . .

Vayne Knave.

He rolled it inside his mind, dredging up memories he'd carefully tucked away. Hearing his mothers whispers about the rumors of a captain whose crew was far more powerful than it should be. He could still hear their first mate, Jakoda, snorting into his bottle.

"Ain't no matter 'bout the crew, Captains," he'd said. "If they're loyal, he's good company. Waters bein' as they are, a powerful ally could help us. Never know what kind of storm might be thrown at us next."

Maria, the quartermaster and Sorin's favorite person to shadow, always disagreed. "His offer is too good. It barely has a downside. I don't trust it."

Again, Jakoda snorted. He did that a lot. "You wouldn't trust a barnacle if it was stuck to your arse."

"He would be so lucky as to be that barnacle," Maria said primly, and Sorin remembered everyone but his mothers's at the table had smiled.

He wasn't supposed to be there. He'd earned a hefty punishment of cleaning up the crusted fat of spilled whale oil from his last prank. It'd cost his mothers's two casks of the cargo they were supposed to be delivering to Noxcairn, but the look on Sudie's face when her brand-new pair of shiny boots were ruined was worth the long night of scrubbing ahead of him.

However, last minute he'd been dragged in by his dreads to sit in on the conversation by Maria. To 'fit something useful' in his head for once. Maria wanted him to be in leadership eventually, maybe even take over as captain once his mothers retired. Sorin, as young as fifteen at the time, wanted nothing to do with it.

So he hadn't paid attention. He flipped through the book of maps one of his mothers, Verana, had drawn from her time sailing solo from coast to coast. He traced the lines of her notes, imagining what it would be like to see the world with nothing but the wind and salt to guide him, while across the table, she was biting down her nails in worry. His other mother was proposing that they counteroffer Vayne, to meet him on neutral waters and see if he was trustworthy before accepting anything.

It seemed like a good idea at the time. Even Sorin, bored and dreading the ending of the meeting where a brush would be shoved into his hands, could admit that Elfrieda's patient wisdom hadn't steered them wrong before. Between her and Verana, they'd made the *Fortune's Trinity* a safe haven in the Boreal Sea. A beacon of peace in waters where territory and power mattered more than anything.

Sorin in the present, fighting back sleep and hopelessness, squeezed his eyes shut. He remembered the way the meeting ended and how Verana had plucked her book from his hands and how Elfrieda attempted to talk to him about responsibility and what his punishment really meant beyond split knuckles and sore knees. He didn't hear any of it. He'd just taken his bucket and brush, shrugged off their attempts at a hug, and walked out.

If he could go back, he would've begged for another minute

of Elfrieda's wisdom. Of her kind, knowing smile while she held the hands that cost her more gold than they could repay. He'd lean into Verana's hug, breathing in the sharp scent of sea spray and spices as she laughed and squeezed him until he could barely breathe.

Sorin couldn't go back. He couldn't remember the exact way Elfrieda's calluses felt when they brushed his forehead lovingly, or the precise spice that always clung to Verana like a needy cat.

Vayne had taken that from him. So why did it feel like Sorin had tossed it away and ran because running was easier? Running kept him from hurting. And he'd been running from Vayne for so long without even realizing it, all the while making a long circle back into his net.

There was a hollow inside him. That pit was calling and he didn't have the strength to resist. Not until he heard a change in Sahar's breathing and forced himself out of his wallowing to look her way.

She was sitting up, blinking crusted salt out of her eyes, *alive*. It didn't matter that he'd been subconsciously counting her breaths ever since Miks revived her, Sorin could barely believe it.

She was alive. He wasn't alone.

He flew to her side just as her breathing got too rapid. Panic, that bastard, was hanging around her neck like a noose. Her eyes were so wide, their whites glowed in the dim lantern light.

"Sorin?" she gasped. "I don't . . . where are we? Where's—"

He held her shoulders. "I know. Take a breath, please."

Sahar shook her head. "No—"

"Take a breath, Sahar. With me okay? Slow and sure. In through the nose, out the mouth." He breathed in slowly, then let the air tumble out of his lips, just as Evren had taught him. "Got it?"

She nodded and did the same. It took her a few tries. She breathed too quickly, hiccupped a sob, then tried to do it too fast again. But slowly, with the swaying of the ship to guide them, they breathed in sync. Sorin needed it just as much as she did. With every breath, he shoved away the hollowness, burying it and tucking it away for later.

He couldn't fall apart now, not when Sahar needed him.

He put on a smile. It felt fake. "Better?"

She rubbed her chest, frowning but nodded. "A little. Can you answer my questions now?"

He let go of her shoulders and sat down in the straw beside her. "What I can, yeah. I'm not sure what's going on, really."

Sahar went to work smoothing her hair. She grimaced at every knot her fingers got caught in. They still trembled, but he pretended not to notice.

"We were underwater," she rasped. "Keres and Abraxas . . ."

"Yeah," was all Sorin said. That fight had been ugly. Even uglier was how he'd felt watching it, unsure of who he wanted to win.

"Evren did the spell."

Burning in his throat again. He swallowed it down. "Yeah."

Her dark eyes met his. "Where is everyone else?"

He'd love to tell her that they were only a couple cells down, still passed out and stewing in nasty ship water. That Sol was curled around his worg, both safe and sound in the belly of an enemy ship. That Evren was fretting over Gyda, and Arke was grinching about his spellbook getting wet while Keres made snide comments about mortal ineptitude or whatever.

"I don't know," he said instead. "It was just us in the water, and you were nearly dead. I didn't see anyone else. All I could do was get you out."

Sorin didn't mean for his voice to catch on his words. He didn't mean to imagine the bodies he missed. Evren and Gyda sinking into the abyss together. Sol, who never stood a chance if she was already unconscious. His worg, not even full grown, drowning on the water Sorin loved so much.

And what of Arke? The goblin had left him. Shoved a spell in Evren's hands and left. Could he have made it out with Tolk and an army of goblins? Not likely, with the army of pissed off Serevadians just outside.

Sorin couldn't understand what went wrong between him and Arke. It used to be so simple with them together. If he could count on anything, it was the goblin having his back. And he knew the idea of losing Tolk terrified Arke. Seeing Kleros and those bodies hadn't helped. But Sorin had tried to be a good friend. He'd done everything. He'd stood up to that horrifying elf and he hadn't even begged Arke to stay.

Sorin hadn't asked for a goodbye, and Arke hadn't given him one. Had he done something wrong? What could he have changed to make things better—

Sahar's hand wrapped around his. Slender fingers squeezed lightly, bringing him back to the depressing present. When he looked back at her, she was nothing but ragged understanding.

"I'm sorry," she whispered, and unlike so many apologies he'd heard, he knew she meant this one.

"For what?"

"That you have to be the last one standing."

Sorin breathed in sharply, but didn't let go. She would know better than anyone how it felt to lose one's entire party.

"Now," Sahar said softly. "As far as I'm aware, Serevadia is still planning an invasion, correct?"

"Haven't been enlightened to the contrary."

"Then we have work to do, and it starts with you explaining why we're in a cell."

He winced. "It's not pretty. I don't see us getting out of this one."

"If we are all Eith has, then we have no choice."

She was right, as always. There was a comfort in that. He didn't have to worry about being right with Sahar around. He took another steadying breath, pretending not to notice that Sahar joined in on the exercise, and then told her everything.

It felt wrong that Sahar should know more of his past than the Wandering Sols had, but with Vayne shackling them to the sea, he had no one else to confide in. She listened, her hand never leaving his, and when it was done she started to form a plan.

~

SORIN HAD MAYBE thirty minutes of restless sleep before the door of the brig banged open and Zo sloshed through. In the lantern light, she looked half dead. Sunken cheeks and hollow eyes made him think of Keres, but with far less life glittering in those eyes. He shivered as she looked him over, and Sahar who was struggling to rid herself of sleep as well.

"Good, you're both awake." Zo's eyes flicked to their wrists. "And alive."

Sorin pulled down his sleeves. "That was an option?"

"For the brave, maybe."

Sahar stood up, unsteady as the ship tilted under her feet. Zo made no move to catch her, and neither did Sorin. It was part of her plan. But he still winced as she stumbled to her feet.

"We are ready to negotiate," she said.

Zo's eyebrows raised a fraction. "Negotiate? My, you are a little damaged. Miks said you might be after how much water you took on."

"I assure you, I'm right as rain. Or will be, once we're out of this cell. It's of the utmost importance that we speak with your captain. The fate of Eith depends on it."

Zo huffed. "That's a new one. Well, you're getting your wish, anyway. Captain has requested you meet him for dinner."

Sorin's stomach sank. Food sounded great. Food with Vayne made him want to curl up in a ball and die. And he didn't like the idea of doing anything that Vayne requested.

Sahar barely blinked. "Excellent. We're on the right track then. Sorin?"

He got up, shuffling to stand just behind her. He gave Zo a grim look. "Lead the way."

Following Zo out of the brig and through the rest of the ship did nothing to lessen his nerves. He made a point to count the number of decks, how many rooms they passed, the crew he saw. But it was all a blur. Barely anything was lit beyond the lantern in Zo's hand. Any time he paused to look into a room she snapped at him to keep up, so many times that she eventually stood between him and Sahar, guiding her and keeping an eye on him at the same time.

The *Red Knave* was not a home, and that was all Sorin could gleam from it. It was sterile and cold where even *Mortova's Maw* had been full of life and the memories of those who lived there. The *Knave* was spotless, orderly, with nothing out of place. Sorin had the sudden urge to upend a barrel of whale oil on it to see what came out to scrub it away.

Zo guided them to a room on one of the top decks, blissfully dry and brimming with light as she opened the door. When they stepped inside, Sorin saw nothing but racks of clothes and chests full of trinkets and accessories. There was a slight musty smell to the air that churned his empty stomach and he couldn't remove the idea that he was smelling dozens of different perfumes and scents whittled down to a musty symphony that spoke of neglect.

"Captain wants you dressed for the evening. No good for you to be in your wet clothes anyway." Zo shrugged from the doorway. "He picked out something for each of you. I'll be back in ten minutes to bring you to dinner."

She shut the door and locked it without a word, leaving Sorin and Sahar alone in a room choked with the clothes of old ghosts.

"So, he collects everything," she said. "Not just people."

Sorin didn't respond. He spied the clothes Vayne had picked for them already, draped over two velvet chairs that were falling apart. Sahar picked at the maroon gown with a frown.

"This is a sick game. I hope he realizes that I was raised to play it better," she muttered and snatched the gown up. There was nothing for privacy, so Sorin turned his back on her and looked down at what Vayne had picked for him.

It wasn't as extravagant as Sahar's. Simple breeches and a loose cream tunic, a pair of good boots to match. He picked up the shirt, running his thumb over the stars embroidering the collar.

A memory, unbidden, rose in his mind. Of stopping in Gratey's port city of Vree for a week and watching Hastings fawn over a shirt he would absolutely not be able to wear out at sea. But he'd loved it so much that he'd pooled together all of his coin and bought it. Sorin never saw him wear it, but he remembered the way Hastings put it up in his cabin, admiring the way the constellations were sewn in correctly.

"Like wearing the sky on my skin, Sorin!" he said with a toothy grin. "I'll wear it on my wedding day, I think. That'll be special enough for it."

The golden thread had faded with neglect. Moths had eaten a few holes in the shirt. Sorin couldn't help but think out how upset Hastings would've been to see his shirt in such a state. Then again, Hastings was likely more upset about dying than losing his prized possession. Sorin shoved that dark thought away and got to work changing.

He shucked his boots and sodden clothes off, glowering. Of course Vayne would make him wear something that belonged to his old crew. Just rubbing salt into that wound and grinning all the while.

"What do you think about trading outfits?" he asked over his shoulder. "Vayne never said anything about which one belonged to which."

He lightened when he heard Sahar snort a laugh. "My, that would be an excellent way to begin this mutiny. Cross dressing."

Sorin buckled the dry pants and grabbed Hastings's shirt. "I look lovely in maroon," he grumbled and put it on.

Dry clothes were a blessing, but he couldn't help the feeling of wrongness that came over him as the shirt slipped over his shoulders. It was a little big for him. Hastings had been a wide-built boy, and Sorin found he was dealing with a lot of extra fabric. But he tucked in what he could, rolled up the sleeves and fiddled with the collar until he was sure it would stay still. Even after being stuffed in a dark room for years, the softness of the fabric betrayed its quality. It would've made a great wedding shirt.

"This is ridiculous," Sahar grunted behind him, rustling fabric as she did. "I can't close this bloody thing."

"Need some help?" He asked.

"A lady must look presentable at dinner, so yes, unfortunately, I require your assistance."

He smirked. "Don't sound so put off by it. Could be worse."

Sorin turned around, finding Sahar still with her back to him struggling with the back buttons of the dress. The maroon fabric pooled around her, far too voluminous and formal for a dinner with a pirate. He stepped forward and batted her hands aside as he fixed the row of tiny buttons along the back. The dress fit snugly, almost too much. He could hear her little gasps of breath as she strained against the tight bodice.

"Are you all right?" he asked softly.

"This monstrosity itches like fire."

"Well, that's Etherakian fashion for you," he said. "Uncomfortable, obnoxious and difficult."

Sahar shifted in the dress, struggling for comfort. He was buttoning up the last of it near her neck when she shuddered.

"What's wrong?"

"Nothing." She shook her head. Her damp hair fell over his hands and he carefully put it over her shoulder again. She grabbed it, keeping it from getting in his way as he finished. "I was just imagining the lady this was made for. She probably loved this color and how it looked on her. I can imagine the shoes she picked out to go with it, how she expected to sweep into the room and show it off to her loved ones." Sahar's fingers splayed against the skirt. "She's dead, isn't she?"

"Probably," Sorin admitted.

He stepped back once the last button was finished, and Sahar turned to face him. She didn't look comfortable, but maroon was a good color on her. The sweeping neckline cut deeper than it should've to be proper, but there was nothing proper about a pirate ship, least of all wearing a dead woman's clothes.

"We can do this," she told him, and he wasn't sure if she was trying to reassure him or herself.

He forced another smile, one in a million of fakes he'd been forced to wear. Only now did he wish to give her a real one.

"Yes, we can."

They put on their shoes. Boots that pinched their toes and slippers that slipped on the heels. Then, with seconds to spare before Zo came to get them, they squeezed bravery into each other's hands.

They'd do this for everyone they'd lost, or they'd die trying.

4

Gyda

Gyda noticed two things when she came to consciousness.

One, that she was breathing.

Two, that the air spearing through her lungs was so cold that it was doing more harm than good.

White. White everywhere. It was all she could see. Chilled wetness creaking along her back and thighs. The ground crunched under her palms as she pushed herself up.

Or tried. Her arms shook, weaker than a wisp of hair. Gyda cried out and sank back into the snow. She shivered. *Shivered.* She'd never been cold in her life. Others around her had. She could vividly recall the way Sorin bitched and moaned his first nights in Keld's Outpost about the chill.

"I woke with frost in my eyebrows, Gyda!" he'd cried to her. "My eyebrows! That's not fucking normal."

She'd laughed then, because this weather was how she'd grown up and caused her no discomfort. The ice was like a soothing kiss on her skin, welcome after so much sweltering heat. She couldn't understand how her friends bore the stuffiness of Dirn-Darahl without so much of a sweat, let alone the hot summer months Evren kept promising.

The months after the Long Night, when she'd left behind the Reino Terminan for good, she'd struggled with the rising heat. The campfires at night that felt so unnecessary, the breezes that did little to take away the sun's hot glare. Getting new clothes and armor had helped, but it still made her irritable. How was she supposed to thrive in such discomfort? She couldn't stand the heat of fire anymore, let alone the warmth of her companions' bodies as they walked beside her.

Well, that last one was a lie. Gyda bore the body heat of one with pride. She sank into it the way one might've a blanket during a blizzard. The heat from her fingers didn't bother Gyda. The press of her body at night underneath their shared blanket didn't keep her up twitching with discomfort.

That the heat was there never changed. The fact that it was bearable—no, wanted—with Evren, had.

Now that warmth was gone. Gyda was chilled, frozen. Her fingers were stiff and numb, and she was losing feeling in her back. She hissed between her teeth, her breath fogging up in front of her. She hadn't expected to live, so this problem completely blindsided her. But the fact remained that she *was* breathing, and if she wanted to stay that way, she needed to get moving.

Digging her fingers into the snow—had it ever stung like that before?—she pushed up. Arms trembled, teeth clenched and then clattering. A familiar feeling of frustration curdled in her stomach.

She'd taken on a dragon alone and sent it barreling through time. She'd fought armies, carried stone and wood heavier than herself over long distances. Brought monsters to their knees without so much of a glint of sweat at her temples. And now she was reduced to this? Not even able to scrape together the strength to push herself to a sitting position, much less lift her sword.

Her sword.

Frustration turned to rage, a fire that burned but had no heat. Rage turned to bitter regret, to the sting of betrayal that cut deeper than any wound she endured before.

Abraxas's blade shattering her own. Abraxas's face before he was about to kill her. Kill *her*.

For a moment the tinkling of her blade falling at her feet in a hundred pieces was all she could hear. All she could see was the water rising, Evren's desperate, bleeding hand clutching the spell that would destroy Gyda for good. In that moment Gyda had been so sure of the end, so numb with the only fight she'd ever lost, the only one she'd ever hated participating in, that she'd simply laid down for him.

Because what else was she without her sword? If she didn't have that, she was no match for Abraxas. She couldn't protect Evren, or Sorin, or Sol. If her heart was all that she could give to save them, then that was fine.

But it wasn't enough. Now she was a husk filled with nothing but resentment and anger, struggling in the snow.

Gyda latched onto that anger because it was all she had. It was all she'd been born with. The strength she earned. The sword she fought for. The friends she had been gifted. But that rage was all hers, and for now it was the only strength she had.

Shifting up an inch, Gyda gritted her teeth and thought of Abraxas. Of that smooth, dark blade in his hand, raised to meet her neck. Of the unhinged look in his eyes when she denied him what he wanted.

She never had the fucking Eternity Dagger. She couldn't have given it to him even if she wanted to. The old Abraxas would've believed her. The old Abraxas would never have tried to kill her.

What in the eternal hells had happened to her friend?

Gyda's shout was half a battle cry and half a cry of exertion. It tore from her frosted, raw throat and into the air like a spun cloud, reaching ever upward into a sky that had now darkened to a dull gray. When it was done, when she was spent, she was sitting up and heaving for breath.

Hells, she hated this. Lying in that damn bed after Rhienwall, not knowing if Evren was okay, had been enough to drive her mad. But this was worse. Infinitely worse.

Gyda's hand shook like a dead leaf on a branch as she clutched at her chest. The other hand sank into the biting snow more, trembling with her weight. She didn't have the heart to correct it. She pressed her hand through her cuirass, under her too-thin shirt, and to the scar on her chest. The one that mirrored Evren's. The one that had given her everything. It had taken too, as Evren had warned, but with it came confessions from an idiot too blind to see what was in front of her, and kisses aplenty from that very same idiot.

Their hearts were one. They beat at the same time, as if one-half had never left Gyda's chest for Evren's. It left her weaker, yes, and damn this weakness. This frailty that had her wheezing like child left out to die in the woods, too feeble to survive, pissed her off almost as much as Abraxas's betrayal. But she wouldn't change it. She didn't regret it. In the end, when she'd been staring down at Evren's dying body in her arms, it hadn't even been a choice.

Her heart had already been Evren's from the beginning anyway.

Gyda traced the now familiar lines of the scar. She could feel her half of the heart beating frantically to keep up with her body. The thrum, thrum, thrum, of life. Two lives, hopefully.

Gyda tapped three times on her chest, between the heartbeats. A habit she'd picked up after Orenlion. It wouldn't matter, it wouldn't work, but she had to hope that if Evren was alive and safe somewhere she would get the message.

Her poor heart. Gyda couldn't imagine how badly she must be taking things. She already had a tendency to take blame and heap it onto herself until she was breaking under the weight, regardless if the blame was truly hers to bear. And now Gyda had forced her to use her up, sap her strength, for a spell that spat her out in the middle of nowhere alone.

She squinted. Her eyesight was fuzzier than she remembered. Fuck, did the spell take that too? Never mind, she could still see, it was enough. She was on a mountainside heaped with snow. The sky pressed in close above her, thick with clouds. Not a sliver of sunshine to be found, although this high up, Gyda doubted it mattered. The air was needle thin, the clouds close enough that she would break their cover after an hour of walking up.

She grunted. Maybe two hours. Her legs were as shit as her arms at this point.

And then it came down to a decision. Lay down and feel cold and sorry for herself, which Gyda knew Sorin excelled at and she'd never saw the point. Or, get up and try to keep living. She had plenty to live for, after all.

Gyda tried not to think too much about how long it took her to stand, or the number of times she fell back on her ass, and then her knees, and then back on her ass. Over and over, her legs gave out. Over and over, her arms refused to support her more than a couple heartbeats. But every time she fell, she took a breath, thought of Abraxas, and tried again. She stoked the fires of rage, her constant companion. She thought of Evren, alone and likely mourning her, and hated that she'd left the other half of her heart in such a terrible state.

Gyda would fix things. She'd be fine. She'd regain her strength just like before.

Finally, a sickening amount of attempts later, Gyda swayed on her feet. She grasped for something to steady her and met only air. She staggered through calf deep snow, the struggle to keep her balance rivaling the effort it had taken to get there. When she finally steadied, wheezing through the thin mountain air, she turned slowly and started her descent.

Gyda got three faltering steps in before a cloaked figure appeared before her.

She blinked furiously. It hadn't been there before, but there was no mistaking the now familiar stalker in the torn black cloak. She'd seen it only once, in her bedroom with Evren before Vanguard. That seemed like a lifetime ago. Now it stood in front of her, features irritatingly hidden from the light, motionless and silent.

The amount of energy Gyda would expend going around it made her want to sit back down again.

"Move," she managed. The word felt like a dagger scraping at her throat. She couldn't help the hacking cough that nearly tipped her over. The figure watched her impassively and Gyda, who'd never felt anything other than mild discomfort at the idea of the creature watching her and her friends, now wanted to strangle it.

"Let me pass," Gyda said.

"No," the figure rasped. The finality in its voice shook Gyda to her core. Mostly because she had no idea what the figure was capable of, but whatever it was, it was likely far more than she could afford to do.

Luckily, the cryptic messenger wasn't done. "Fate has need of you. Your road goes up, not down."

Gyda blinked and suddenly they were gone. On a whim she craned her head back. Sure enough, a few feet away the figure watched her, cowled and dark. Waiting.

Gyda scowled. "There's nothing for me up there," she said. "I need to live. I need to go back to her, to all of them."

"The path you seek leads up."

"That will lead to my death. To live is to go down."

"Your job isn't to live anymore," the figure said. "It isn't as simple as that. Come. If you want to save Evren Hanali, and the rest of your clan, your destination lies in the clouds, not at your feet."

Gyda hesitated. Everything the figure had ever said to Evren, while cryptic and vague, had been true. But it hadn't spoken to anyone else. It had ignored Gyda when she saw it last. Its attention felt inevitable, but uncomfortable.

"Why should I trust you?"

The figure said nothing for a while. The wind, biting and cold, tore at its cloak but revealed nothing of what was underneath. Gyda found herself angled up, leaning towards it with bated breath.

"Because I have seen this end and a hundred more," the figure finally said. When that did nothing to persuade Gyda to move closer, its shoulders drooped as if in a sigh. "And because I would see her live. I would see them all live. And it hinges on you."

Gyda had no talent for picking out bullshit. She wasn't like Sol who could read people like a book. But something in the figure's words hit home, deep within her chest. Beneath the scar, the ribcage, to the half a heart frantically beating away. The words had a ring of familiarity, although she'd never heard them before. Not that she could recall.

Slowly, she found herself nodding. With great effort, she turned around and heaved one foot forward. It slid into the crunching snow, which melted into her useless summer boots.

"You have not lied before," Gyda wheezed. "Although you stink of riddles. I will follow you."

She couldn't see the face, but she could feel the smile from the figure.

"Riddles," it said, "are a language time has taught me to speak. Perhaps you will speak some of your own when we are done."

Gyda let those strange words roll off her back and pulled herself up another step. The leg rested beside her other one, and she grabbed her knees to catch her breath. It was going to be a very long, very slow trip to the top.

Gyda stoked her fire, tapped her chest three times, and took another step.

5

Sorin

"Well, well. Aren't you two lookin' finer than sirens in starlight tonight?"

Vayne's voice was the first thing to greet Sorin as he stepped into the captain's quarters with Sahar close behind. The skirt of her borrowed dress swam around his legs, nearly tripping him as the door closed shut behind him.

The quarters were adequately spacious for a ship the size of the *Knave*. That didn't stop Sorin from gawking at the sheer opulence that smothered the room to an almost suffocating size. Crystal lanterns cast rainbows from the candlelight. Tapestries rich with color and detail covered and softened the hardwood of the ship. Plush carpet muffled Sorin's footsteps, and in the middle of the room was a table so laden with food that it sagged in the middle.

It was set for dinner, candlesticks burning, and enough fresh food to make Sorin's mouth water. At the head of the table Vayne lounged, smiling serenely. There were three others seated at the table. Survivors, Sorin realized. Dripping sea water and shaking with fear. Two other places had been set, one opposite from Vayne and the other to the left of that one.

The message was clear.

Without hesitating, Sorin took the seat opposite to Vayne and ignored how his smile grew. Sahar sat beside him, tucking her shaking hands in the folds of her dress. Sorin couldn't tell if it was part of the act or not.

Sorin started heaping food onto his plate. None of the cutlery matched, but it was all obviously valuable. The plates were chipped and cracked, but of high quality. He covered his with piles of tender meat, roasted vegetables, and a healthy pile of red rice he recognized from Gratey. Food this fresh wasn't common at sea, and Sorin chose not to think of how it got to the table, or the fact that the rest of the crew wouldn't be eating as well.

Stuffing his mouth full, he caught the eye of one of the sodden survivors giving him a bewildered look. Sorin just shrugged. If Vayne wanted them dead, he wouldn't poison the food. That's one thing the Vasa had on assholes like the Sovereigns. He'd stab you, but you'd see it coming, and Sorin was too hungry to die on an empty stomach.

It wasn't bravery. Sorin didn't think he had it in him to act brave. Stupid? Reckless? Absolutely. What bravery he might've gained with the Wandering Sols hadn't made it to the surface with him. This was purely hunger, spite, and the need to be someone else. Because all Sorin wanted to do was bang at the door behind him and demand to be let out, not sit across from a murderer and eat his food.

No, Sorin wasn't brave. He was very, very desperate.

But the survivors didn't see it that way. They saw him shoveling food in his mouth without care and slowly started to do the same. Not with the same intensity, for no matter how hard their battle had been, it was nothing compared to what Sorin's body had gone through before being tossed into Vayne's lap. But they did eat, and Sahar was slow to follow.

"You enjoy my food."

Sorin barely glanced up at Vayne. "It's fine."

The captain smirked. "That's one way to describe it. This ship receives the finest Eith has to offer."

"You mean stealing." Sahar forked a flake of fish, the picture of a sophisticated lady despite her damp hair, hollow eyes, and cracked lips.

Vayne's eyes flicked over to her, amusement tinging their blue depths. "A man must make his way in the world, one way or another. My crew benefits greatly from it, as you all will. Think of this meal as a peace offering. I saved your lives, brought you back from certain death. Fed you, clothed you. The least you can do is help me survive out here."

"If it is money you require, then you shall have it," Sahar said. "But I am no sailor, and I will not be kept here."

Vayne shifted in his seat, as if to get a better view and appreciate her more. Sorin chewed slowly, watching the two closely. The other survivors were doing the same, shivering where two opposing wills clashed over candlelight.

"Nobility," Vayne said finally.

"Yes."

He picked up his dinner knife. It flashed gold in the light and the sharp edge reflected on Sahar's neck, as if the light itself could cut the soft skin there. Sorin kept himself from stiffening, for reaching for his own knife. He simply watched as Vayne admired the length of the knife.

"Tell me, my lady. What is a creature as lovely as yourself doing in the Boreal Sea, half dead and clinging to a washed-up Vasa?"

Sahar cut Sorin a sharp look, brimming with disgust, before turning back to Vayne. "My ship was on its way to Vernes when we were attacked. This man is nothing but a thug hired by a rival of mine to kidnap and ransom me off. As distasteful as his actions are, they saved my life until that storm hit."

Vayne didn't skip a beat. "I saw no other ship in the area."

"You wouldn't have. She was a small vessel, meant for stealth and speed, nothing else. We didn't expect an attack, nor the storm that caught us mid-battle. Both ships, mine and his, sank. Although I could hardly call his a ship."

Sorin curled his lip into a sneer. "The *Prancing Worg* was a swift schooner, not the decrepit fishing vessel you claim it to be. She was a solid ship."

"Well, she fell apart rather easily for such a solid ship." Sahar gave him a tight-lipped smile.

Plates clattered against the table as Vayne banged his fist against the surface. Everyone snapped their heads towards him, and Sahar and Sorin's argument was lost. Vayne's actions spoke of anger lingering but his eyes still held that damned amusement, as if this was some sick show he was enjoying.

"I have a few rules, one of which is that there shall be no arguing at my table," he said. "What's done is done. You destroyed each other and came to me. Now I will see how best to use you."

Sahar huffed, setting her fork down. "Use me? I am no pirate and I will *not* be held against my will."

"You will be taught." Vayne pointed at her with the tip of the knife. "There is more to a pirate's life than sailing, and plenty a young, beautiful woman such as yourself can do. You will work your debt off to me, and when it is paid in full, you shall be released."

"I do not have time for your debts." Sahar pushed herself up to her feet, her spine a rod of steel and her hands miraculously still. "Eith does not have time. The mission I was on is one of the utmost import, and if I'm delayed any longer it could mean the fall of civilization as we know it."

Her words shook the survivors from their stupor. They blinked at her standing form, awe coming over their faces whereas Vayne was starting to lose his amusement.

"You're talkin' 'bout them elves," one of the survivors rasped. "You seen them."

Sahar's grief was not faked. "More than seen. I've fought them. I watched Terevas fall to them and I barely escaped."

"Then it's true!" another one of them cried. "Them lights we saw in the water, the fires on the coast. That's them!"

"Which coast?" Sahar asked.

"North. Melkarth, we thought. Don't stay in their waters long enough to know but—"

"Enough," Vayne said softly.

The talkative survivor whirled on the captain. "This is war, this is! You can't keep us. Them elves are gonna kill us all."

"They'll kill those on land." He dismissed the man. "This is nothing new."

"The threat of the Serevadian Empire is not something to ignore," Sahar said. "They are unlike any foe we've ever faced. They don't care about borders and disputes, and you're a fool to think you will be untouched by this slaughter. I do not ask for you to join the fight, only to let me go so that I might give others a chance to live."

An unsteady quiet followed Sahar's words, broken only by the sound of wind and waves outside and the heavy breathing around the table. No one moved. Sorin felt much like a statue holding his breath like this. One last chance for Vayne to redeem himself. One last chance for them to get the easy way out.

Vayne stood up, breaking the illusion of the strange painting. "A fool, am I?"

Sorin couldn't have been the only one to notice Sahar's nails digging into the wood of the table, or how Vayne still had a knife in his hand as he rounded the table to her side.

Sahar lifted her chin. "Only a fool responds to threats of war with indifference."

Gone was the amusement, and it was only then, when Sorin saw the last of it flicker from his eyes, did he fear for Sahar's life.

The talkative survivor bolted to his feet in front of Vayne, eyes wide and desperate but unseeing of the danger he just stepped in front of.

"We're all gonna die! Them grey elves are gonna—"

His words ended in a wet gurgle as Vayne drove his knife into his throat. Blood pattered on the floor, musical when it landed against the goblets of water where red met crystal. It pooled in the white plate, curving around the untouched meal that still sat there, now soaking up life essence.

With a jerk, Vayne took the knife out and tossed the man to the side. Blood now coated his arm and half his shirt and pants, but if he noticed he didn't show it. He flicked the knife clean before stepping over the body towards Sahar.

Sahar couldn't have faked the naked shock that rooted her to the ground. She couldn't have acted the horror that kept her staring at the body as Vayne got closer to her. Sorin's hand went to his own dinner knife.

Vayne stepped until he'd pressed Sahar's back against the table. Her hands fluttered along the table, knocking over her glass of water to keep herself steady. The only part of her that moved was her heaving chest as she was forced to stare Vayne down.

"Now, tell me again." He brought the red knife to her throat at the same spot where the light had shined before. "Am I a fool?"

Sahar opened her mouth to speak, but all that came out was a whimper. Vayne leaned in close, his lips brushing the shell of her ear as if he was a lover whispering secrets. But all heard him.

"That's what I fuckin' thought."

The knife flashed. Sahar screamed. Plates crashed as the blade was buried deep into the table.

Vayne's blood-soaked hand was free now, and he used it to grab Sahar by the jaw. Her lips pressed together, unable to let out more than a few pathetic noises. His fingers left smears of red along her checks, but fresher was the cut on her neck dripping scarlet. Not deep enough to kill, but enough to scar and leave a message.

Sorin couldn't look at her pained face. He focused on the

way her blood matched the maroon of her dress as it dripped onto the once beautiful fabric and was soaked up.

"Here is your first lesson as a pirate, little lady," Vayne hissed at her. "Your captain is as close to a god as you'll get out here. My word is law. My ship is my land. You're just living on it. I take you in, save your life, and you disrespect me? You dare to use your pathetic tricks on *me*? There are consequences. So long as you breathe, you breathe my air. So long as you eat, you eat *my* food. And so long as you're doin' all of that, you belong to me. Do you understand?"

Sahar was struggling to breathe, let alone speak, but that didn't matter to Vayne. He drew back to look her in the eyes, taking note of the gathering tears.

He bellowed, "Do you understand?"

The survivors jumped. Sahar nodded as much as his meaty hand would allow. And once she was done, Vayne tossed her roughly to the ground. She barely caught herself on her elbows, clutching her jaw and caught between Vayne's boots and the body of the sailor.

Vayne turned his raging gaze to the rest of the table. "That goes for all of you! You think I'm runnin' a charity? You think your lives are worth enough that you belong anywhere else but here? I saved you!" He banged his fists on the table again. "*I own you!*"

The remaining survivors nodded quickly. In Sorin's stomach, the food weighed him down. But in his mind he saw his home burning. He saw the shadow of a ship that destroyed it, the glint of a gold tooth in a storm. He saw his family, dead. And his friends, his new family, just as dead.

Sorin saw red.

Vayne continued, his words growing calmer with every passing second. "I ask for very little. Your loyalty and hard work. You will be fed, taken care of, protected. Under my care, you are safe. No army will hurt you. No grey elf will reach us here. All I need is your word. You have a choice. Accept, and live. Deny and die. It's simple."

Vayne was so close. All Sorin had to do was reach out and jab the knife in his throat, and then this would be over. His family would be avenged. He'd save himself and Sahar from this hell. He'd free a ship of slaves.

Sorin's grip on the knife tightened. It wasn't part of Sahar's plan. But none of this was. Surely the crew wouldn't blink if he killed Vayne. They'd see the good he'd done and they'd surrender.

Sahar moved out of the corner of his eye, pushing herself up onto her hands. She was no longer sobbing, but she was still shaking as if pushing herself up was a mountainous task, akin to bearing the weight of the sky, Her fingers, dark and stained, splayed out on the blood-soaked carpet.

And lightning arched between them.

A small flicker. Barely a spark. But Sorin could feel the energy in the air. He could smell it. And if he could, Vayne definitely could.

Vayne twitched towards her, and that's when Sorin lunged out of his chair, knife drawn.

Sorin was used to being fast with a blade. The only one who was faster was Sol. But as his knife arched toward Vayne's exposed throat, and he turned to face him, Sorin knew that this time it hadn't been about speed. It was about noise. The cry of rage from his mouth, the shattering to porcelain and glass from the plates he'd tossed in his hurry to get up, the clattering of his chair against the ground.

It broke his heart that this wasn't a killing blow, just a distraction. But it was what he was good at.

Vayne's hand was around Sorin's wrist before he knew it. He twisted until the pain was enough to cause Sorin to scream. The scream died when Vayne's other hand wrapped around his neck.

He lifted Sorin in the air and then slammed his back into the table. More shattering. Warm food and cut porcelain dug into Sorin's shirt. He gasped for air, struggling under Vayne's grip as the dinner knife was taken from his hand

"I've been waiting all dinner for you to do that," Vayne said. He filled Sorin's vision. There was nowhere to go, nowhere to hide. He squirmed but found that he was just cutting up Hasting's shirt with the remnants of his failure.

"Mister Trinity. Sea brat to kidnapper." He sneered. "And I wonder how you evaded me for so long. You made yourself less than nothing. Weak. Pathetic. I plan on making you more."

The knife was trailing along Sorin's jaw. If he had the ability to speak he might've mouthed off about knife play, but he could barely breathe, let alone joke.

The silver was near his eye now. Sorin refused to look away from Vayne.

Vayne wanted him. It was a matter of pride. He wouldn't kill him.

"Ah, look at that defiance." He tsked. "Your mother had it too. Not the smart one, the other one. She fought until I skewered her with her lover's sword. Kept screamin' until she bled out. You have her spirit, but not her bravery. That's good. That means you can be taught.

"Because I know what that look in your eyes means. You think that because you're valuable I won't kill you. That's not true. A good dog is only worth his salt if he's loyal. If he follows commands. If he knows how to obey. If he fears what his master will do if he breaks the rules."

The knife was gone from the corner of his eye. Vayne pulled up, loosened his grip enough that Sorin could breathe easier. He squeezed once more, a threat to stay put, and Sorin didn't have the strength to fight him. As the hand disappeared from his throat, he thought foolishly that the lesson was done, that he was sufficiently cowed.

When that same hand pinned his left wrist to the table, he knew he was wrong.

Vayne forced Sorin's palm flat against the table, the overlapping rings of his tattoo fresh in the candlelight. The knife was raised above it.

"No!" Sorin bolted up and tried to jerk his hand away, but Vayne's grip was like iron.

"Hold him down," Vayne snapped, and with barely a second for the words to cool down, two sets of hands were grabbing Sorin's shoulder's and shoving him back against the table.

He fought. He kicked. But it was useless. With every struggle, Vayne's amusement returned.

"Please don't," Sorin gasped. "That's all I have left of them. Please!"

Vayne studied the tattoo, tracing the lines with the tip of the knife. "Never had one of these myself, you know. I never much saw the fuss." He looked back at Sorin. "This means a lot to you."

Sorin nodded, that dreaded panic welling up in his throat. The tattoo was his last line back to his family. The pain he'd endured to get it was nothing compared to the warmth and love that came with the acceptance it brought. It was his second choice, the permanent one, that kept him aboard the *Fortune's Trinity*. It was the thing he had in common with all his fellow Vasa, unlike his lack of powers.

It was more than a tattoo. It was his last crumb of home, of his childhood, of a time where he wasn't fighting to survive.

"Boy, I have taken everything else from you. Your ship, your family, your freedom." Vayne paused, as if to let the words sink into Sorin's very pores. "What makes you think I won't take this away too?"

A flash of silver, and then his left hand was speared by pain. Sorin screamed, but Vayne wasn't done. He dug the blade in deep, twisting and cutting tendons as he did. He shredded the skin, calm and collected as the two survivors struggled to keep Sorin's lurching body pinned down. With every stab, the point went clean through to the table. With every cut, the serrated knife ripped through his skin. And with every flick of wrist and blade, Sorin screamed.

It seemed his greatest pains would always be met at the end of knives.

At some point he'd stopped fighting. When Vayne was done and stepped back, there was no one to hold Sorin down anymore. But he didn't move anyway. The pain mixed with shame and loss for a deadly cocktail that made him almost wish Vayne had driven the knife in his throat instead of his hand. Instead, he was left lying there pathetically after begging his family's murderer not to mutilate his hand.

"Now." Vayne tossed the knife to the side and started to clean his hands with a napkin. "I take it you'll remember this lesson from now on, Trinity. Ah!" He caught himself, grinning. "Not anymore. Just Sorin now. Yes, I remember your name. I remember all of them. You don't have a last name. You don't have a ship. If you want one, you'll have to earn your keep here. I'll let you rest tonight and send a healer for the hand in the morning. After that, you get to work. Nod if you understand."

Slowly Sorin nodded.

"Good." Vayne turned back to Sahar, who Sorin could barely see was still on the floor. "You'll be in charge of your old captor until morning. I'm done with you two, Zo will take you back to your cells. Dinner isn't finished for the rest of us."

Vayne turned his back to them and walked back to the head of the table. Sahar hesitated, waiting for the trick to reveal itself. But Vayne started eating and chatting with the remaining survivors as if nothing had happened. She picked herself off the floor then used shaking hands to help him sit up.

"Don't look at it," she whispered in his ear. "Lean on me if you have to. I've got you."

Sorin couldn't have acted in disdain towards Sahar now if he tried. All he wanted to do was melt into her. But whatever unending reserves of strength and willpower she drew from aided her once again. She helped him off the table and kept him stable, but a good distance from her. Hopefully his lapses would be seen as nothing but pain and trauma.

It was almost funny how his mind immediately went to Sahar's plan in an effort to bury the events that just happened. His mangled hand was a throbbing reminder nonetheless, and he found himself torn between the teeth-gritting pain and the scheme, like a rope tugged between two dogs.

Hells, what he wouldn't give to have his worg beside him. To send it after Vayne. It wouldn't erase what had happened but it would make him feel better.

Sorin didn't remember the walk back to the cell, or even Zo leading them at all. It was as if the time after he stood up from the table and the time when the cell door clanged shut had been entirely erased. That might have something to do with him squeezing his eyes shut. He was being herded back to that damn straw bed, if it could even be called that, and sat down by Sahar.

"Is she gone?" Sorin asked, not wanting to open his eyes just yet.

"Yes, we're okay now."

Not safe. They wouldn't be safe ever.

Sorin was content to keep his eyes closed until he heard the sounds of fabric ripping. He blinked them open, watching as Sahar tore strips from her dress.

"Healer be damned, I don't trust him to send one," she muttered. "Give me your hand."

"Pretty silk makes for shit bandages."

"Sorin, please."

He swallowed roughly before slowly moving it so it would hover over her lap. The pit pat of blood on silk was all he could hear. And all he could see was the mangled mess of flesh and bone.

He tore his eyes away, looking instead at the sloshing water at the floor.

"I have nothing to clean this with." Sahar said.

"That's all right, who doesn't love infection?"

"I just need to wrap it. Make sure to stop the bleeding."

"That'd be great, yeah."

"It's going to hurt."

Sorin's good hand balled into a fist at his knee. "So does everything else. Just get it over with."

But it did hurt, and somehow it was worse than when Vayne tore it apart because now the pain was just stacking on top of the old pain. Sahar's gentle fingers could've been swords for all he knew. The silk bandage cutting wire. His nails dug into the palm of his good hand. Sweat dripped in unison to his blood. With each mangled bone tucked in place he muffled his screams. Halfway through he had to shut his eyes, because the water was trailing red and it made him sick to know that it was his.

Sorin was no stranger to suffering. He'd *died*. Of course he knew what it was to suffer. But this, the storm, Abraxas and the army of pissed of Serevadians, it was enough to make him want to scream again.

He didn't, for Sahar's sake. And because he needed the tiny scrap of dignity he had left.

When Sahar was done, it felt like his hand was on fire. Every beat of his heart strained against the bandages. They weren't too tight, but he longed to take them off. It was a bad situation either way, but he wasn't going to be the ass that undid all of her hard work right after she'd finished.

He leaned against the wall, breathing hard. His bad hand was tucked into his lap where it twitched every now and then. He still couldn't bring himself to look at it.

"Sorin," Sahar whispered. "I'm so sorry. I didn't think things would get that bad."

There were a million ways he could respond. Ignoring her, pretending to pass out, snap her head off because *fuck* he hurt and he needed to lash out at something. Instead he rolled his head to the side, eyes open, and gave her the worst smile he'd ever faked.

"Hey, could've been worse, right? He could've just killed me."

Sahar didn't laugh. She looked him dead in the eyes. "Then why do you look like you'd prefer that he did?"

The smile slipped, but he still couldn't be angry with her. "Because however scared of dying I am, I am terrified of fucking up more. Because I don't see how we're supposed to escape this bastard and save Eith all by ourselves. Because all of my friends are dead, including my dog, and I haven't had time to sleep on it much less come to terms with it. But no, don't look at me like that. I don't want to die anymore than I want to take a bath in that sludge down there. It's just an easy way out. And I don't want to leave you at the whims of Vayne. So don't fret. No matter what he does to me, I'm not going to leave you behind."

"Why did you do it?" she asked. "He wasn't worried about you. You would've been fine."

"But you wouldn't have."

She blinked at him, starting to withdraw a bit.

"I saw your hands," Sorin explained. "I felt it. Vayne would have too if I hadn't done something."

"Why does that matter?"

"Because magic is useful and you're only safe if he thinks you're a pretty trophy and nothing more."

She blanched. "I don't have magic!"

"Really? And what was the lightning? Static fairies saying hello?"

"I don't know." She slumped against the wall next to him. "I- I've never felt anything like it before. I was so angry at him for not listening, for killing that man and then hurting me. I wanted to hurt him back and this . . . energy responded. This strange heat in the pit of my stomach just built and built until it was all I could feel."

"Yeah, that would be magic."

"Logically, I guess!" She threw her hands up in the air and let them thump into the billows of silk. "But I have no magic.

None of it is in my bloodline. I could never learn how to use spellbooks. I stuck with my chemicals because they're nature's magic and I always liked that. I've never felt like this before. And magic doesn't just sprout up out of nowhere."

"Kind of does now," Sorin pointed out. "Sorry, but you do remember what happened before we landed in this shitty situation, right?"

She glared at him. "My last remaining friend dying at the hands of your friend and everyone else we loved drowning due to a spell gone wrong?"

"That's it."

"Really? How could I have forgotten?"

She smacked his shoulder lightly, and while it was his left shoulder and it carried some hurt from his hand, he laughed it off. Because if she was being sarcastic, she was living, and that was enough for him.

"Ow! Wounded man over here."

"Sorry."

"Mmm, you don't sound that sorry. I expect compensation when we get out of this. An endless supply of those cinnamon pancakes you had made at your manor."

"Done." She shifted around to face him. "Now, about my new magic. You have a theory?"

"Yeah." He sighed. He hated that this would kill her mood, but she was smart enough to have put it together anyway. "I think that before Nerezza died, she gave Gail's soul to you. Either that, or Keres did. Either way, you've got the soul of one nutty kid with the powers of Mortova knocking around in there. Feel like murdering a bunch of people and creating an army of the undead?"

She scowled. "No."

"Damn. Could be useful."

No matter his joking, he eyed Sahar. It was many kinds of fucked up for her to have this power. Gaining it from Nerezza was like a stab in the heart. Keres was like stubbing her toe, he assumed. Having Gail, the same kid who murdered Vox and Drystan, inside her couldn't be sitting well.

And he knew from experience that people changed after taking souls. The power was great, but how long before Sahar went absolutely off the rails?

"Stop staring at me like I'm going to snap you in half and drink your blood."

"So you *were* thinking about it."

She huffed a little laugh, but that was it. "This is useful, right? We can use this against Vayne."

"Not without help," he said. "Magic is one thing, but you've never been a Vasa. You don't know the storms and sea like we do. If you're not careful, that kind of power could tear you apart." He chewed his bottom lip. "Let's stick to our old plan, you know, when we were both boring and magicless? And we'll develop Gail's little gift to help when we can. Deal?"

She nodded. "Deal. And Sorin?"

"Hm?"

"Thank you. You've saved my life twice now, and you're in what I would consider my worst nightmare. I owe you a lot more than pancakes for that."

"I'll be okay. I always am." He reassured her.

She frowned. "No."

"What?"

"We're going to stop pretending we're okay, understand? We've lost people. We're slaves to a madman. I'm harboring the soul of my friend and lover's killer. And you just had yourself mutilated by the man who killed your family. There's a war going on that Eith has little chance of winning and we are its only hope. Stuck here. In bad clothes and a moldy bed. We are not okay."

Sahar held her arms out. "But we have each other."

Sorin laughed because if he didn't, he'd cry. Because she was right and he hurt so damn much, and he was tired of being strong and plastering a fake smile on when all he really wanted to do was cry himself to sleep.

So he shuffled over and let himself melt into her embrace. He let his head rest on her lap, allowed himself to draw his knees up like he was still a child. He allowed himself to weep, for his family and home, for his friends and his freedom. Sorin wept, and so did Sahar.

They cried, they mourned, and then they fell asleep.

6

Solri

No one in Dirn-Darahl expected Sol to be anything other than a politician. Maybe that was why they so easily overlooked her love of architecture and stone. It was just a hobby at first. She liked to know how the world worked, and that started with the city. From the smallest stairs and doorways, to the massive pillars that held up the ceiling, she wanted to see it all. They were like puzzles for her mind to break apart and put back together. It made sense when she was done, and made her already beautiful city that much more breathtaking.

Her job also helped with that. Good architecture and engineering needed good runes and maintenance, and as the woman in charge of keeping the city running, she was privy to the blueprints of nearly every inch of Dirn-Darahl, as well as things outside city limits.

That meant Stone's End.

In her mind's eye, Sol traced the map of the outpost. Back at the height of the Dwarven Empire, it had been nothing to sneeze at. Neglect, lack of funding, and just general bad leadership had left the space abandoned and crumbling. Sol had never been able to revamp it and turn it into something new, like a research outpost, but she'd poured over the notes of the builders in her free time like she did with every project she had no hope of finishing.

That had been a long time ago, long before she'd been tossed in prison and set off with the Wandering Sols. Stone's End, and the dozens of other abandoned outposts and villages, had been forgotten. Why dream of building great new things on sturdy old bones when she had monsters to slay?

It was fuzzy, her memory of the blueprints, but enough for her to go on. Stone's End was aptly named for being on the edge of a massive subterranean canyon, one which hadn't been explored since the disastrous attempts to bridge across it. It consisted of twenty buildings, three watch towers along the edge of the canyon, and another two on the northern side. Two of those five watchtowers were beyond repair and barely standing, but she couldn't remember which ones. The buildings themselves were split between barracks for the soldiers, equipment and food storage, an old healing house, and officer houses. Stone's End could easily fit three hundred soldiers, making it one of Dirn-Darahl's more armed outposts.

Sol was in one of the officer houses, she was sure of it. The Serevadians had clearly spruced the place up. Running water, Luminstones, repaired walls and fresh beds. Bastards. That was *her* job.

It was surface level stuff, just enough to make the place livable. Sol tried not to let it get to her as she squeezed through the service gaps between the walls of the house.

Three days since she'd woken up and learned her world was in shambles. Three days and she hadn't seen Abraxas, or anyone. She was kept from going past the stairs, this time the door at the top locked. She hadn't even realized it was there the first time, because it was so *elven* to put a door at the top of the stairs. An add on she despised and would burn when she was done with this war.

All her meals were delivered when she slept. All her needs were met in the other rooms on the floor. But she was under no illusions that she was free. A prisoner with no shackles, yes, but a prisoner all the same.

Sol had been a good, loyal dwarf when she'd been thrown in prison, but that was back when she trusted the system and her people to come get her. There was no system anymore, and she wasn't going to sit around and wait.

Sol wiggled another few feet, shaking the cobwebs from her hands. The service tunnels were supposed to be for work that needed to be done on the pipes or runes inside the framework of the house, but these were dwarven houses built in a time of war. These were also used by spies, and those who needed to move unseen from place to place. It had taken her far too long to remember that they existed, and that Serevadians wouldn't know about them.

Dwarven architecture, if anything, was solid and discreet.

That didn't make the journey easy. The space between walls was tight, even for Sol, and choked with rubble, abandoned Guzzler nests, and remnants of other creatures Sol would rather not think about. There was no light, and no matter how good Sol was at seeing in the dark she jammed her toe on every rock and corner. She bit back every curse and hiss of pain by biting her cheek, which was swollen and bleeding before long.

It was worth it. She swallowed copper-tinged saliva and wiggled some more, hands outstretched before her. It was worth it because she was Solri fucking Amet. She was a soldier of Dirn-Darahl, an adventurer of Eith, and she would *not* be contained. She was not raised to be in a cage, and she wouldn't stay in one, no matter what Abraxas said.

He was lying about something, that much she knew. Sol was a good liar, and it took one to know one. It hurt a little that the man who she could always trust to tell the truth was hiding something from her, but she couldn't tell what it was. Likely something to do with their friends. Maybe they were worse off than he'd said, and he was afraid of how that would affect her. Or maybe it was something far worse.

Sol, like every good dwarf, had studied how the mind could change under the stress of being a prisoner of war. It wasn't that Sol didn't trust Abraxas, but she needed information from her own eyes and ears, not those who were used to the way Serevadia had been running things.

Her hands finally grasped the stone cut-outs of a ladder in the wall and she let out a sigh of relief. The climb up to the other floors would be a pain, but she'd get nowhere in what was essentially the basement. So, she dug her fingers and toes into the carved slots, and hauled herself up. Blinking away showers of dust and pebbles, thinking of anything other than sneezing and what was climbing down the back of her shirt. She climbed and reminded herself that she'd been in worse situations.

Direwall had been the worst, hadn't it? With the endless cold and night and an army of creatures that seemed to have no end. But she hadn't been alone then. She'd had the Wandering Sols.

Sol let out a little breath of exertion as she pulled herself past two rungs at a time, growing impatient. She'd see them again, she just had to save them first.

She only felt herself emerge onto the next floor through the rather tiny opening next to the ladder. She had to squeeze her arms together and curse her mother for wide hips as she squirmed out. Once her legs were free, she stepped off onto the floor, shaking her stinging fingers. This floor would have to do.

Leaving the ladder and likely deadly hole to the floor below behind, Sol casually began to grope the wall, as any good dwarf would do in this situation. Although, she wasn't sure any dwarf *had* been in this situation. Surely her ancestors would've died from shock at the mere idea of a dwarven outpost being occupied by elves. Or their city being destroyed by elves.

Sol's fingers skimmed along the wall, memorizing the

increasing familiarity of the makeup of the house. Each architect had their vision, each builder their methods, and through that each building had a personality. Sol could feel it in the way the cracks sat, in the way the stone hummed against her fingers. This was a very old building with many stories to tell, and she was the first one paying any attention to it.

Later, she promised. *I need to get out.*

And so the stone showed her the way, the way every rock in Dirn-Darahl had. Mal used to laugh at her for thinking of the stone as something living, but why not? Trees lived and were revered for it. Soil ached of life, and the sea of chaos. Why couldn't the stone sing for those who listened?

The cracks gave way to a suspiciously smooth section of the wall, just as it had in her room. She smiled, pressing her ear against it with a small push from her hands. The wall gave, just a crack, like a door opening enough to let sound slip through but no light. A little breeze of fresher air hit her, but silence followed it. No one in the room.

She sighed in relief and pushed further to see inside. Warmly lit, a simple room for sleeping and planning, based on the bed and desk being the only furniture in the room. The door on the other side was closed, the bed neatly made. Whoever lived here wouldn't be back for a little while. Hopefully.

Sol slipped out and shut the secret door behind her. The wall perfectly melded back into place as if it was solid stone, its secrets invisible to all those except the ones who listened. She took a moment to clean up the tracks of dust and pebbles she'd trailed with her, using her sleeved hands for a job that needed better but would have to do. Then she rushed over to the window.

Stone's End was as beautiful as she remembered.

A relic of dwarven pride that refused to die all at once, but crumble slowly over time. The watchtowers had new scaffolding that almost covered the angles and brutality carved into their rock. Their light shown over the yawning abyss that fell after the sudden end of ground at their edge. The buildings had been patched and sealed, piles of junk and fresh Guzzler bodies lay on the outskirts to be burned. Leisurely patrols in shining silver armor curved paths between the buildings like snakes.

Sol narrowed her eyes, trying to find Velcros. Abraxas was right, killing him wouldn't solve everything but it would make her feel better. How would an Emperor dress? Velcros always seemed more brute than politician, so she couldn't imagine him in elaborate robes like Viggo.

The minutes ticked by and she shook off her need to see Velcros. He likely wasn't even at Stone's End. Dirn-Darahl would be the best place for him. He would have to wait.

Quick as she could, Sol unlatched the window and pushed it open. Its ancient hinges screamed in protest and she winced as the precious silence was broken. But no alarms tolled. None of the wandering patrols were near the house, nor the window.

She huffed and pushed her hair out of her eyes. "Couldn't oil the damn hinges, you animals?" she muttered, and nimbly climbed out of the window. She shut it behind her, risking more screaming hinges for a chance to cover her tracks. Good soldiers leave no trace.

By then, Sol's body was prickling with discomfort at being out in the open. Or maybe that was whatever got caught in her shirt. Regardless, it was easy to slip into her old habits of sneaking around. Counting breaths between patrols, slinking through pockets of shadows and trying not to shiver, pressing herself against buildings. She'd done this as a little girl, sneaking out to see the lower levels of the city. She'd done this as an adult, slipping out to meet Mal whenever the chance arose. Now the penalty for getting caught wasn't a slap on the wrist or public humiliation, but death. Abraxas wouldn't be able to protect her if she was caught escaping.

Of course, this was a bad escape attempt. For one, she couldn't just leave after finding the first way out. She needed her people. She needed information. More than anything, she needed a plan, and that only came with information.

This wasn't an escape, but a scouting run.

Sol's breathing was calmer than her thundering heartbeat as she crouched behind crates of supplies. Food, she knew with a sniff. Bad, Serevadian food. She wrinkled her nose. How a culture could grow in the same conditions as dwarves and not have a single thing in common with them, such as their cooking, was beyond Sol.

She hadn't picked a direction to go. The canyon was in the west, curving to the south. The north would lead to the road to Dirn-Darahl. Promising, but definitely guarded. Anywhere near the watch towers would be tricky. Stone's End was a bigger prison than she left, but every lock could be picked.

East was louder, pricking her ears. Generally, more noise meant more people which meant easier ways to get caught, but east was also the best chance of getting out. The roads there dipped back into the Yawning Deep. Maybe tunnels Serevadians knew, or maybe not. Either way, untamed wilderness was better than an army.

Sol slipped from shadow to shadow, from corner to corner. She held her breath, and clanking metal turned to marching soldiers walking right past her. But she remained unseen. Stiff, cautious, and quietly scared as she crept ever closer to the noise.

The dull cacophony got clearer as she edged around a newly patched building, the mortar still sticky. Past it were piles and piles of rubble.

And bodies.

Dwarven bodies.

Bile crawled up Sol's throat. They were discarded like trash, their armor shredded like wet paper. Many were missing limbs or had their skulls caved in so badly that she could barely tell where the metal of their helmets ended and the bone of their heads began. Beards were matted with blood. Braids of honor burnt or cut.

The perimeter of this junkyard was lined with Serevadian guards, tall and imposing. They watched coldly beneath their helmets as beaten dwarves picked through the bodies.

Scavenging, Sol realized with horror. They were picking the dead clean for useful weapons and armor to be smelted down and reforged. It was common practice in war, at least to other cultures. But to a dwarf, their weapons and armor were more precious than any gold. They were a part of them. To take Sol's daggers and make them into something else was to like take her bones and make a new body. She'd be losing a piece of herself.

It was so horrifyingly wrong that she had a hard time keeping herself from running out and tearing the stolen pieces out of their hands. They weren't theirs to take. Those weapons and armor should be entombed with them forever. It was blasphemous and—

A cold, long fingered hand clutched her shoulder.

"I remember you, thief." A dark voice whispered. "You're not supposed to be out of your room, are you?"

Sol couldn't have screamed if she wanted to. Everything in her was frozen. That voice dug its claws into her mind, echoing the same things as before when its owner had flipped through her memories as if it was nothing. Sol hadn't thought she'd ever recover from the bone-aching chill of that magic, and when she did, she certainly never forgot it. It was a nightmare brought to reality, one she never wanted to meet again.

She was turned around to face the lean, pale figure of Ainthe, staring down at her with bottomless eyes that rivaled the depths of the canyon.

"There it is," Ainthe grinned, her canines sharp. "I did miss your fear."

7

Evren

There was something cold and metallic biting into the palm of her hand, and that was woke Evren up. That, and the not so gentle rocking of a wagon across bad roads.

One twitch and all the old hurts came back. Broken ribs. Twisted ankle. Bruises and cuts all over. The deep gash in her thigh. Her body was spent and trying to dig itself into another grave-like nap. She sucked in a breath, finding relief only in the fact that she wasn't choking on blood. But her ribs spiked with pain, and she couldn't help the groan that left her lips.

Someone cursed behind her and then there were gentle hands rolling her on her back. She cried out anyway. Everything was stiff, and sudden movements felt like she was breaking skin and reopening wounds barely scabbed over. She gripped whatever was in her hand tightly and forced her eyes open.

"Ah, there she is." A man's face appeared above her, haloed by the grey sky. She blinked until she recognized him—the soldier from the village who'd listened to her when she told him to leave. "I bet you're feeling pretty lucky right now."

"Pretty confused," Evren choked out, and her voice was barely a whisper. "What happened? Where am I?"

The man sat back and Evren's neck didn't hurt too bad so she was able to follow him. Little had changed about him in the daylight. His uniform was bloody and ripped, his hair a mess. He swayed with the wagon with the spine of someone who didn't even feel the bumps and lurches anymore.

"You saved Helmsfirth, that's what happened. Or, well, what's left of it." He shrugged. "No use going back there now. Damn Greys have most of the south. But we got everyone out because of you. Took a leap of faith and went back to find everyone dead and you nearly there."

Evren grimaced. "So you took me with you?"

His eyes twinkled. "You wanted to stay there?"

"Not particularly."

"Then you're welcome. Call our debt even."

It was easy to forget that Etherakians worked through debts. It could bog anyone down who owed their life to an Etherakian with good memory. Luckily, that worked for them as well. Debts were returned, and quickly. That was likely why he went back, and the only reason she was still alive.

Evren's fingers traced the bandage on her thigh. "Where are we?"

"Nearing the Crossroads, west of Linston. Now, before you go hurting yourself, hear me out. Your royal message needs to get to royal ears, right?"

Evren gritted her teeth. "Yes."

"Those tend to be in war camps." He grinned. "At least when our King is more a general than a ruler. We're headed to the biggest one. We should be there by next nightfall."

She sighed and tried to let herself relax. Her head kept knocking on the wood with every jostle, making it impossible. All the while, the soldier watched her.

"Something on my face?" she asked.

"Your broken nose."

"Not the first time."

He shrugged. "Thought so. You remember your name?"

"Evren Hanali. And yours?" It was polite to ask one's savior their name after all.

"Heath Brown."

"Thanks for coming back for me."

He shrugged and wiped an oily strand of hair out of his face. When he looked up at the horizon, his easy façade dropped. It wasn't hard to see that loss of hope as it plummeted to his feet. The darkening of his eyes told all, as did his hand straying to his sword, still caked with dried blood.

"Worlds gone to shit," he muttered. "People like you, well, we need them. All of them. Armies alone are useless now."

The sky was darkening overhead, and it took Evren longer than she liked to admit to notice that it wasn't clouds, it was smoke. Fear lurched in her belly, and she slapped at Heath's ankle.

"Help me sit up."

He winced. "I don't think—"

"Oh please, I've been on the verge of dying twice before and have had my soul ripped from my body. I know my limits. Just help me see."

Heath didn't argue further, although the disturbed look in his eyes only got stronger the more he marinated on her words. He helped her sit up, cursing for her when words cost too much oxygen. Evren reminded herself as her ribs screamed and her body groaned that pain used to be her strength.

She faltered when she realized that hadn't been true since Orenlion. Gyda had been her strength, and now she was gone.

"Whoa, you all right?" Heath asked, when she froze halfway up.

She tried to swallow the icy grief down but it wouldn't leave her. The frost crept down her throat and around her heart. All that was left of the woman she loved.

"Fine." Evren said and made herself sit up the rest of the way and feel everything.

Etherak always felt a little like a massive bowl, with its three mountain ranges and the cliffs to the west. From Linston to the Vanguard mountains was a mixture of green plains and swamplands. Those plains rolled by the color of tarnished gold against the blackening sky, and they spit out the smoke through funeral pyres.

Hundreds of them. Blackened and sizzling, some still roaring an inferno. Evren didn't see the figures that stalked between. Mourners, families, priests keeping the fields from burning. All she saw were bodies and death choking out the sun above.

Beside her, Heath was grim. "Haven't had death like this in centuries, you know? Word is we're supposed to be getting support from the elves in Orenlion. But when I see this, I find it hard to believe anything short of a miracle is going to stop it. The Greys don't care for negotiations or surrenders. They just burn, and we burn whatever bodies they leave behind."

He pressed his palm to his chest and bowed his head. "The Divines will welcome many to their halls before this is done."

He didn't see Evren flinch or the way her face contorted in grief. She was glad for that. She sat back against the wall of the wagon, eyes on the burning horizon. Then she looked down at her hand.

Heath noticed. "That's all you had on you besides the dagger, which is safe. You wouldn't let that go though. What is it?"

The silver moth was bent and broken. Covered in grime, wings crooked from her grip on it. All those long months painstakingly keeping it clean and intact after so many battles and falls, and now it was finally broken. After Viggo broke.

She curled her fist over it. There would be no pyre for him. No one was left to mourn him but her.

"A gift from a friend," she said, not even looking at Heath. Just the billowing black of smoke so like the shadows beneath the sea.

"Who are they? Maybe they can help. If they're anything like you."

"No." Evren shook her head. "He's dead. They all are."

~

The war camp smelled of blood and smoke, coming together for a unique perfume that invoked what grief would be if it was bottled. The air was thick and loud, filled with mumbled conversation, sharp orders, and the screams of the wounded. Jarring to anyone who couldn't tune it out.

Evren hadn't heard anything since she'd passed the pyres.

She was still, finally, settled on the edge of a cot that had just been cleaned. She tried not to think about who was there before her, and why they suddenly weren't. The healers were like bees dressed in graying white, buzzing back and forth with increased anxiety. Evren could hardly blame them for their vacant eyes. The last war Etherak had fought was when magic did most of their healing. Now they relied on potions and the hard way of mending skin back together.

It was a mess.

One of the healers, dirtier and more frazzled than the others, suddenly appeared in front of her with a potion in her hand.

"This is all we can spare," she said curtly. "And you're lucky we've got this. I shouldn't be giving it to you since you're not part of the army."

Evren took the bottle. "Why are you then?"

The healer sniffed. "Brown says you held Helmsfirth enough to get them out, then killed the rest. Never knew the man to be a liar, and you look like you fought an army."

"Wasn't an army," Evren muttered and brought the potion to her lips.

The healer shrugged, watching as Evren choked every drop. She took the bottle back when she was done, stuffing it into the pockets of her skirts.

"Don't matter what it was or wasn't. Etherak's in short supply of good people these days so if I can keep one of them on their feet and in the fight, I will. How's the ribs?"

Evren tested them, bending over, sucking in deeper breaths. They stung a little but the pain was more than bearable. Almost forgettable. And her ankle was visibly less swollen. Her thigh was no longer in danger of bleeding again. There were cuts and bruises that would take longer to heal, but Evren wouldn't push for another potion. She was lucky to get what she got.

She nodded. "Everything feels fine."

"Good. Any more pain in the ribs than normal, come straight to me. Can't ever tell if they healed right in these conditions."

No more conversation, no goodbye. The healer simply buzzed off as someone else was dragged into the large tent. Evren caught just enough of their torn armor and bloodied face before turning away and vacating the cot. Whether the new wounded filled her spot, she wouldn't know. She walked out of the tent and into the war camp.

The potion didn't help the fog in her head. Everything blurred like she was seeing it from underwater. The war camp spread for miles, all soot-stained tents, rattling carts, and nervous horses. Parts of it were as quiet as a crypt, hopeful spouses clinging to the tents waiting for their other halves to come back from distant battles. Most were loud though as soldiers brawled, laughed, and tried to live brighter in what could be their last days.

Mud sucked at Evren's boots as she tromped through, hand on her dagger. No one paid her any mind despite the fact that her armor wasn't part of the Etherakian uniform. They overlooked her like she was just another poor soldier shuffling back to bed.

Evren eyed a few of the older soldiers. Elves that carried old scars and distant stares as they cleaned their weapons. Their armor was older too. Kept clean and well maintained, but had curves and edges speaking of an older time in Etherak.

These elves looked at her with pity when she passed, and it reminded Evren so much of Abraxas that she had to walk away.

In her mind she knew where she had to go. Where the banners of Etherak waved the highest, black-and-gold against a darkening sky. Where guards stood watch more often and the ground wasn't muck. That's where she would find Barrion and deliver the news. She didn't relish destroying what sense of hope the prince no doubt harbored. She also didn't want to see how badly things were turning, and any commander's tent with maps and lists of casualties would surely show her that.

Maybe that's why her feet wandered, and she didn't stop them. It felt good to walk without her body begging her to stop, although her mind was getting to that point. Sleep would be good. Food even better. But the thought of either just reminded her that she would eat and sleep alone for the first time in over a year.

Feet and mind wandered, one aimlessly and the other falling back to the painful place she'd been avoiding since she'd crawled out of her own grave. Back to the black palace filling with water, back to Gyda's hand in her own and Keres standing between them and Abraxas.

That name made her lungs squeeze painfully. Once a source of hope and comfort and now . . . .

She shivered. It was all she could do not to sink into despair remembering how Abraxas had been the one about to kill Gyda. Evren might've been the one to do it, but the black sword in his hand and the gleam in his eyes had set the stage.

Had there been anything left of him? Time changed people, pain too. Evren hadn't been so foolish as to think he'd be the same as before, but she expected something resembling her old friend. To look into his eyes and see nothing she loved, nothing but shadows and a mad lust for power, was another stab in the heart.

How had she let him fall so far?

"Need a prayer, child?"

Evren jolted out of her thoughts, turning to the owner of the voice. She didn't have to look very far. It was a hunched human in priest robes, her brown face wrinkled like dried leather. Behind her was a cleaner tent than the rest. The smells of offerings and incense couldn't mask the stench of the camp, but it reminded her sharply of where she was.

She made a face without meaning to, and the priestess tsked.

"Now, now, don't turn your nose up just yet. The Divines hear us even if they're not here. Preparing yourself to meet them will ease the journey from this world to the next."

"I'd rather not," Evren bit out. Over the shoulders of the priestess she could make out alters and their idols. Soldiers crowded around them silently, offering prayers and wishes to empty air. Haphion's flaming dragon leered at her from its dark corner.

"Your feet brought you here." The priestess pressed. "You mourn like a thundercloud over the mountains. Allow yourself some relief—"

"I said no," Evren snapped, so harshly that the priestess jumped back. Evren immediately regretted it. The old woman didn't know better and was trying her best to ease the pains healers couldn't. But Evren tolerated the Divines from Abraxas many times before, she wouldn't from a stranger.

"I apologize," Evren said curtly. "That was unworthy of me. I have . . . I knew someone who worshipped your gods. I think that's why I'm here."

Damn her feet. She should've gone straight to Barrion.

The priestess only nodded solemnly. "Carrying the burden of the dead is heavy indeed. You brought your friend's soul home."

Evren shook her head. "No, he's not dead."

It wasn't until she said it that she realized how true it was. Even if Keres had succeeded in drowning the palace, Abraxas's shadows could've taken him anywhere just like how Evren had used them. Only, he would actually have control.

Of all those she loved, he was the most likely still breathing. She felt the mud inch up to her ankles as she sank lower.

"Ah, well, then there's still hope." The priestess smiled, missing many teeth. "One shouldn't give up on their friends too quickly. They have a way of surprising us."

Evren didn't know if she was talking about friends or gods again, and decided she didn't want to know. The makeshift temple gave her chills the more she stood in front of it. The stone eyes of Haphion's idol seemed to bore into her soul, and although Evren knew they weren't there to watch her, she still found herself backing away.

So often Abraxas talked about Evren being too young to understand Divinity and how it shaped the world. All she'd ever known was Eith as it was now. She couldn't imagine the oppressive watch of godly eyes, the constant worry of upsetting them and dying painfully. Even being around a place that revered them made her skin crawl as if they could snake through their idols and leap at her at any moment.

Evren was still backing up, the priestess and idols still staring her down, when a strong hand fell on her shoulder and stopped her.

"Finding religion, Xun?"

Her numbness was broken. Before Evren knew it, she was whirling around and facing Song Mei as if she was a vision come to life, sparkling and real enough to burn away the fog of grief that threatened to blanket her forever.

Mei was much changed. Her Khama armor was replaced with Etherakian style plate. Solidly made and beautiful, but very different on the wyvern rider. Her black hair had been braided back from her heart-shaped face, neat and clean, which was a jarring change from the rest of camp and Evren herself. There was a small group of soldiers behind her, all armored like Barrion's personal guards. It almost made Evren laugh to see them protecting Mei of all people.

The one thing that hadn't changed was the sword at her hip. Mei could fight with anything, and when riding a wyvern the Kama favored spears and bows. But she was just as deadly with her sword, and the blood-red tassel hanging off the pommel seemed to be a warning flag to all those who stood in her way.

"You look awful," Mei muttered. Her eyes flicked over Evren's back and she frowned. "Where's your bow? They didn't confiscate it, did they?"

Evren didn't know any 'they.' Heath had gotten her inside.

"No, I lost it."

Evren's voice caught and Mei homed in on that like a bird of prey. Her eyes narrowed and she took Evren by the elbow. Gentle, for her, which made Evren feel even worse.

"What's going on?" she whispered. "Where's the rest of you?"

The rest of her. It really was as bad as that. When Sorin had named them the Wandering Sols, there had been the overhanging promise that they would all drift away from each other one day. But not like this. This left a hole in Evren's chest wildly different than the one she lived with for three years.

"Gone," Evren managed. "It's a long story. Not here, please."

Mei's face didn't fall, but the gloom in her eyes only darkened at Evren's defeated tone. She nodded curtly and, without a word to the guards behind her, steered Evren away from the temple and through the streets.

Mei's was limping. Walking faster than when she'd left Orenlion, but the lurch in her otherwise graceful steps made Evren wince. It reminded her too much of Saros, even more crippled than his rider.

"I didn't think you'd be here," Evren said.

Mei snorted. "Oh, they don't want me here. Barrion's uncle wanted me back in Linston where I'd be safe. The Conclave put up the shield around the city, so no one is getting in. But I refuse to sit and wait for them. I'm just as much a soldier as they are, and a better tactician. If they want me back in that damned castle, they're going to have to tie me up and drag me."

Evren eyed the soldiers passing them by. They gave the women a wide berth, and Evren couldn't tell if that was because of the guards or just the way Mei held herself. Then she had to remind herself that Mei was in line to be Queen. To these soldiers, she was royalty. Of course, they walked around her.

They stared though, as people do to royalty. Mei didn't seem to notice or care. She still walked like a soldier. Elite perhaps, and a little diminished without Saros. But no less powerful.

"I'm glad you're here," Evren said.

Mei eyed her with a small smile. "And I you, surprisingly. Although I worry about the news you bring with you."

Evren did too, but she said nothing as they marched through the camp. Mud turned to packed dirt. Sooty tents became cleaner, and so did the soldiers themselves. Squires and messengers ran back and forth, although plenty stopped and bowed to Mei. Mei always stumbled over the following tilt of the head, or wave of acknowledgment and hissed under her breath in annoyance.

Foot soldiers turned to knights, and knights to generals. A hill rose above them, capped with a couple larger tents flying the black-and-gold of Etherak's flag. The incline wasn't steep, but Mei's hand tightened around Evren's arm and their pace slowed. Her breaths came out in little puffs, her eyes narrowed on the tents above.

Evren would've sooner glued her jaw shut than offer to help the Khama. Wounding her pride as well as her leg would just dig Evren her own grave.

Looking back at the guards, they didn't move to help either. In fact, they fell further back. Evren smiled a little, realizing that the first time they'd made the mistake of coddling Mei was the last time.

"Tell them to keep their eyes on the sky, not on me," Mei hissed under her breath.

"They're looking everywhere but you." Evren said and turned back to the uphill climb.

"Good," Mei said. Then, between breaths, "Took me three weeks to train them to do that. Stubborn asses."

If Evren had been less tired, less hungry, and less prone to doom thoughts, she might've laughed. Instead, she focused on putting one foot in front of the other, always a little faster than Mei so she could use Evren to help her up without it looking bad.

The top of the hill crested soon after, to everyone's relief. Mei let go of Evren and stretched her bad leg, schooling her face into a mask of calm instead of rage. She almost got it right.

"You're one to talk," Evren said. "Stubborn—"

"As the princess consort, I can have you executed now," Mei said crisply.

Evren's grin didn't meet her eyes. "You could've executed me back in Orenlion. Nothing's changed."

"On the contrary." Mei dismissed her guards with a flick of her wrist and they dispersed to the surrounding tents, always within eyeshot. "Everything has gone to shit. I remain steadfast in my threats, is all."

The guards settled behind her, but Evren caught the hints of smirks on a few of their faces. It was difficult to tell them apart with their helms on, but maybe that was the point. They moved as one, guarded as one. And when they looked at Mei, they all had similar expressions on their faces.

Respect.

It'd only been a few months, and Mei was winning Etherak's people over. Granted, soldiers were bound to be easier. Mei could relate to them on a level that even Barrion couldn't, and that went a long way when forging trust. Was it the same with the rest of the country? Did the common people like her? Or the courtiers?

Evren shook herself out of those thoughts. That didn't matter now, and wouldn't until she fixed the problem she helped create.

Evren followed a half-step behind Mei as they walked towards the largest tent in the camp. From the top of the hill, Evren could see the entirety of the army stretching out below her. Even Linston, barely a speck on the horizon and sparkling white against the haze of smoke, winked from a distance. It disappeared as she ducked into the tent with Mei.

The guards stayed outside, but they wouldn't have crowded much. This cavernous tent seemed to be many rooms in one. Dining room, temple, living, and sleeping areas took up the perimeter, and in the middle was a massive war table. The furniture was beautiful and sturdy, but obviously made for travel. The tables had hinges to fold them up, the chairs had runes that Evren assumed made them smaller. The small temple was little more than an altar with an array of statuettes and golden offering bowls. A sword and shield leaned against it, freshly polished. The bed was better than a soldier's cot, but nothing to fit a King, which was who it was made for.

King Loghain Rhys was the furthest from kingly that Evren had ever witnessed, and she'd seen enough. The aging elf was not handsome. His face was a mess of scars that twisted his mouth into a constant sneer. His salt-and-pepper hair was cropped short enough that Evren could see his sweaty scalp, and his armor was not gilded and shining. It was dented, showed signs of constant repair, and was exceedingly plain. Compared to the others surrounding the war table, who wore a menagerie of sashes and medals and gilded robes to show their status, Loghain Rhys stood out.

Evren could see immediately why people whispered he was less a King and more a general.

His eyes snapped up to her the moment she entered. They were the same grey as Barrion's, but held none of the warmth. The King shared nothing else in common with his nephew.

"Your Majesty," Mei said smoothly, and dipped into a bow that Evren hastily copied. "May I present Xun Evren Hanali of the Wandering Sols."

Evren wasn't prepared for how much that hurt. She tried to hide it, but judging by Mei's strange look, she hadn't managed to.

The war table went silent. A few dipped their heads in greeting to Mei, but Loghain didn't bother. He just stared at Evren, something unreadable but achingly familiar passing over the jagged landscape of his face.

"Where is she?"

His voice was a salt-rock rasp, echoing decades of shouted orders and bellowing war cries. Nothing about it was gentle, but Evren knew immediately who he was talking about.

She took a deep breath, her ribs still tender around her lungs. "Divara Rimmel died at Vanguard. She stayed behind to give my party and I time to reach Serevadia, and then used the mountain's fire to destroy what army Serevadia had placed there."

A mage at the table gasped. He wore royal-blue robes edged in grey fur, too beautiful for a war camp. Still, his fingers were stained like Arke's used to be and they pressed against his thin lips.

"Queen Marjorie didn't lie then." He turned to Loghain. "The rumors were true."

"How?" Snapped a woman in sparkling armor and a sour face. "Rimmel was the greatest War Mage of our time. Yet you expect us to believe a small contingent of Greys pushed her to such a violent end?"

Whether it was pride or hurt that smarted at that comment, Evren had no problem biting back.

"A small contingent that consisted of a few hundred," she shot over the table. "There were nine of us. When our plan failed, Divara gave everything up so that we could have a chance at keeping Serevadia at bay."

"Which," the general said, "you failed at."

Evren fell silent. Shame wasn't an easy emotion for her to hide or process, but one she was intimately familiar with. The deadly combination of that and grief threatened to overwhelm her.

That was, until Mei stepped between them, drawing herself up to her full height.

"Take eight men and yourself into an army of hundreds and see how well you come out, Cornell," the Khama snapped.

Cornell's face reddened, and she tried to match Mei's energy. "Divara Rimmel would never—"

"Divara Rimmel barely tolerated your warmongering ass. Stand down."

Cornell's blustering was the only thing heard in the tent. The rest of the table—commanders, advisors, and mages alike—refused to meet her eyes or Mei's. Finally, Loghain lifted his gauntlet clad hand in the air and Cornell fell silent.

"That's enough," the King said weakly. "Leave us."

The human hesitated, face still red, but one pointed look from him sent her into a sharp salute and march out the tent. She clipped Evren's shoulder as she went, but Evren didn't feel it, nor did she smell the sweat and armor polish from her being so close.

Loghain looked around the table frowning. "Did you think that order was just for her? All of you, out. When Hanali is finished with her report I will recall it all back to you. For now, this is a private matter."

Barely seconds later, the tent had emptied and now felt too big for the remaining three. Mei hesitated, casting conflicted looks between Evren and her uncle-in-law. If it was possible, Loghain's face softened.

"It'll be easier if you're not here, Mei," he said. "We both know how taxing these moments can be. However," he looked back at Evren, "if you wish her to stay, she can. The choice is yours."

That more than anything showed her the kind of King he was. Evren wasn't sure what it meant for Etherak, but she liked it enough right now. Having a choice, even as simple as this, made her feel better.

"She can stay."

Mei was Evren's only living connection to a world before . . . before she was just Evren. Mei was the string uncut in a ripped tapestry. She wasn't Evren's closest friend, or someone that Evren could spend hours talking to without feeling embarrassed or guilty. But right now, Evren clung to the idea of not being alone like a drowning woman clung to the idea of air.

Chairs were pulled out. Water was given. They sat at the small dining table, big enough for six but set only for three. Mei across from her and Loghain at the head of the table.

He cast a look at Mei. "Where is Barrion?"

"Gathering intelligence from the recent group of survivors." She wrinkled her nose. "He wanted me to tell you that they were from the coast."

Loghain cursed, and Evren knew what he was thinking. If they lost the coast, they lost Tal-Mashad. The port city was essential for supplies and allies, of which they would get neither if Serevadia cut it off from them.

Finally, he turned to Evren. Not a gentle man, but one who had dealt with people in her position before.

"Tell me everything."

Evren thought when the time came to say everything, she would clam up. That that dam that kept her from feeling too much would catch the words as well. It didn't. They fell from her mouth easily, far too easily. There was so much to tell, starting from the beginning with Heliodar's mission and coup and ending with her crawling from her own grave, but Loghain and Mei heard every dirty piece of it.

Her failure to keep the Ashen Bond together rang hollow in her chest. If she'd done better, could she have saved Drystan and Vox? Could they and Sahar have kept Nerezza in check? Then, none of what happened with the Eternity Dagger would've happened. They wouldn't have lost Abraxas.

What if she'd found a different way into Serevadia? Something quicker. A way to save Kleros and speak to Abraxas sooner.

She should've kept Arke beside her and forced him to do the spell correctly.

She should've seen the lies thrown at her for what they were. From Heliodar, Nerezza, and Viggo.

She should've been smarter. Faster. Stronger.

She shouldn't have been the only one remaining.

Evren didn't know how much time had passed, but when her story was done the lamps in the tent were lit and the light from the sky was gone. Mei sat with a pale, white lipped expression. She hadn't said anything throughout the retelling. Loghain was still, like a statue. And this unnerved Evren more than anything.

After a long moment of silence, Loghain got up and poured himself a glass of wine. He didn't offer any to either of them. He took a long drink, set the goblet on the table, and sighed.

"Mei, I need a moment alone with your friend."

Evren closed her eyes, as if no sight could prevent what was going to happen. She didn't see Mei blanch, but heard the beginning of a protest. Imagined the curt wave that cut her off. Felt the chair clatter to the ground as she stood up abruptly and stalked off. The wind was cool on Evren's neck when she left the tent, and warmed moments later when she was gone.

And then she was alone with the King of Etherak.

"Open your eyes, Hanali."

Evren did so. She was no soldier to follow orders, but she'd be a fool to childishly squeeze her eyes shut. She expected Loghain to be seated in front of her, but instead he was stalking across the tent. She stood up to follow him, falling short by the war table as he stopped at the altar and started lighting the candles there with a gentle reverence unfitting of a man like him.

"When we first got word of strange elves coming from the ground, I thought it was a joke," he said, back to her. "A hoax by a bankrupt city of dwarves who fought themselves into a corner they couldn't get out of. They needed support. Money, I thought, as it normally was with them. The letters from Whitestone did not fully explain the devastation the city of Dirn-Darahl had suffered.

"When Whitestone fell and I had my own people telling me of a foe out of nightmares, I had to listen. But by then it was too late. Rhienwall and Vanguard had been attacked. Across the sea, Gratey and Melkarth suffered similarly. The Vasa made port in Tal-Mashad and spoke of strange lights in the water, stretching from coast to coast, continent to continent. An enemy larger than us in every way. One we had no hope in beating."

He lit the last candle and blew out the long match. He took a few moments to bow to each idol in turn before turning to face her.

Evren took a step back. His voice had been calm, soft even. But the hard rage in his eyes made her want to flee.

He's not a King now, she reminded herself. *This is a soldier losing a war, and it's my fault.*

"We know nothing about Serevadia," Loghain hissed. "We only learned the name last week from Terevas. A name for an enemy who has numbers and advanced weapons we can't match. My people are dying in droves, half of them trying to defend a country that isn't theirs and the other half spread so thin that it's all they can do to evacuate villages before they're burned to the ground. We have *nothing!*"

His fist slammed into the war table and it was all Evren could do not to jump. She worked her jaw, planted her feet in the ground. Somehow it was easier to meet Mortova's eyes than it was to meet Loghain's.

"But you," Loghain sneered. "You knew all along. And you said nothing."

Evren swallowed, her throat dry and scratchy. "We-I made a promise—"

"Damn your promises!" Loghain roared. "You could have saved us! The whole bloody world could've prepared, but you kept the biggest secret in Eith's history to yourself. For what?

One man who betrayed you? You traded all of Eith and its millions of innocents for a dead man."

Unbidden, memories of Viggo crashed over her. The softness of his fingers at her temples. How his mind felt against her own. The look of awe on his face when she showed him the night sky in Orenlion. His fading eyes right before his light died.

Evren took a step forward.

"You have no right to berate me," she said coldly. "I have done my fair share of suffering. Do you not think I regret staying silent? That every night after leaving Serevadia I didn't toss and turn and try not to shout it at the heavens? Everyone I loved is dead because of that secret, and we did everything we could to fix it. It was *our* problem."

"And now it's Eith's," Loghain snapped. "It's mine, as I try to figure out which parts of my country to burn and which of my soldiers will die. You think Etherak is bad? You cannot imagine what horrors are brewing in Gratey as Serevadia tears each city-state apart by the seams. Or in Melkarth, where their isolation traps them in a killing pen instead of saving them. Every survivor brings a new horror that we must swallow and carry. You have suffered greatly, but all that pain is but a drop of rain in a thunderstorm."

Evren's eyes were hot and wet. She blinked them furiously, refusing to look away from Loghain.

"This is not what I wanted," she said. "I never wanted Eith to fall."

"Our actions damn us to the hells before and after our deaths," Loghain said bitterly. "Yours will bring us all down with you."

Grieving, bruised, and numb, Evren took those words and wanted to drown in them. Everything he said was true. This suffering could've been avoided if she'd spoken out, or at least spared her this feeling of gnawing guilt.

And yet, something deeper raged inside her. The part of her that always survived, who dragged herself out of every bloody battle regardless of whether she wanted to live or not. A dark fuel that kept her alive in Orenlion, in Serevadia, in the White Cairn. She'd stopped relying on it, but it was always there. The human part of her that stood against everything that sought to bring her down. Sovereigns, generals, monsters.

Kings.

"This," she said slowly, forcibly. "Is not just my doing."

"You are the only one left alive," Loghain said. "Except for Abraxas."

"Abraxas, yes. That is on you."

Loghain blinked, his rage momentarily gone. Evren snatched her moment between her teeth and stepped up to him until there was only a foot between them. Her fear was gone. He had armor and strength and experience, and he wasn't hurt. But Evren Hanali was a Wandering Sol, and she wouldn't cower to him.

"You say I could've prevented all of this by just speaking out." Evren said, ignoring how he was a head taller than her. "But you could've prevented a hundred years of bloodshed before it began if you'd only stopped your brother sooner."

Loghain's eyes sparked dangerously. "You dare—"

"My blood holds enough magic to grant me the power to snap you in half. Of course I dare." Her finger pressed into the armor of his chest. "You saw Eldridge's madness and did nothing. You crushed kingdoms under your heel, knowing it was wrong. How many people suffered because you were too scared to stand up to him?"

"The Divines spoke through him," he countered.

"The Divines do not rule us!" Evren yelled. "You let them. Because of *you*, the world was forever changed. Because of *you*, thousands suffered, both enemy and allies. Do you have any idea what your war did to Abraxas?"

"It wasn't my war—"

"You led it! It might as well have been you passing judgment if you were carrying out orders. You broke my friend over and over again. You and this fucking country and its fucking gods forced him to be a killer, and when it became inconvenient for you, you banished him.

"How many more Champions are there like him? How many have to endure not only their nightmares but also the waking world that hates them?"

Loghain faltered. Loghain took a step *back*.

"I didn't have a choice," he said, but he was losing his anger. He was more shield than sword now. "I had to choose between them and Etherak. I regret it every day. I knew them. I *was* them. Their battles were mine."

"No longer."

Evren didn't feel like herself. This anger fueled her, but she felt disconnected, like her body moved on its own. Her words were her own, but far harsher than she ever would've wanted them to be. Only now she was too tired to care. She didn't feel the tears on her cheeks. She tasted them on her lips.

"Abraxas Kain was my friend," she said. "And I watched him turn on those he loved and nearly kill us for your fucking gods. So yes, blame me. Serevadia is my burden to bear. But Serevadia would not be the threat it is today if it wasn't for him. If he hadn't been taken from his family and raised to be a killer. If he hadn't been thrown into a holy war that he never truly stopped fighting. If he hadn't fallen . . ."

Evren's voice failed her. She was above the Deep Wood, wind in her hair, smoke in her lungs. Abraxas slipping out of her grasp.

Thank you for the light.

Evren scraped herself together and leveled the King a deadly look. "You failed Abraxas Kain, and he is coming for all of us. The sins of your Divines are catching up to you, and they bear shadows and hate. We could've stopped this, both of us. But there is nothing to do about it now other than fight."

It was not the way to talk to a King, or even a general. But between the two of them Evren saw no power. Just a mass grave of regrets. Corpses rotten in their eyes, and one still pursued. Evren didn't have the heart to hate him, even now.

Loghain slowly walked over to his goblet, but he didn't drink. He stared at the red liquid and Evren wondered if he saw blood.

"Eith will burn yet again for Etherak's sins," The general-made-King said. "And this time I cannot pull away."

Evren shivered. The people outside the tent could be dead by tomorrow, or in a fortnight. There could be no Etherak left for Barrion and Mei to rule.

"Eith will survive," Evren said. "Maybe not its kingdoms, but the land will survive."

Loghain looked over the rim of his cup at her, doubtful. "How do you know?"

"Because I've seen it."

With or without them, the world would survive. What was left was up to them and how hard they fought.

Loghain crossed the tent to her, not a march of a man intent on hurting or scaring her, but the resigned saunter of a man with the weight of the world on his shoulders. He held the goblet out to her, red wine glittering inside.

"I have no right to ask for you to give more to Eith, especially not to Etherak, but I must ask you to stay and fight. If you're able."

Evren eyed the goblet. A simple thing of silver colored metal. She wasn't sure it was true silver. But it gleamed in the lantern light like a beacon. She sucked in a breath, feeling her pains both physical and mental, touching each agonizing memory and lingering on the last one.

Her friend, her partner, her fault.

"Someone's got to try and save the world," she said. "Might as well be me."

She grabbed the goblet and drank, tasting something for the first time since her grave.

8

Solri

Ainthe was dragging Sol away before the words even hit her. Those claw-like nails dug into her shoulder, past her shirt and into her skin. She barely had time to hiss in pain before Ainthe jerked her to the side and into the building.

The shadows were as thick as her dreams, and this time Sol knew they would lash out. They were under Ainthe's command. She kept her mouth shut, breathing sharply through her nose as the smells of wet mortar and dust coated her throat.

Without warning, Ainthe pushed her forward and let go of her. Sol barely kept her footing, freezing mere inches from a writhing mass of shadows. The room got darker as the door shut behind Ainthe.

Sol scrambled for options. Against Ainthe, weaponless, she had about as much as a worm had legs. But she balled her fists anyway, whirling around for a fight.

Ainthe, her white skin glowing with the little light in the room, clucked her tongue disapprovingly at her.

"Enough, daughter of the stone. You know the attempt is foolish."

"Since when has that ever stopped me?"

"You are not the creature whose magic comes with blood and pain. You have a brain between those ears of yours. Try to use it and stand down."

"Fuck you," Sol spat. "If I'm going to die by your hand then I will go down with your flesh beneath my nails."

Sol might've imagined the slight rise of Ainthe's eyebrows. The priestess was ridiculously hard to read even when there was good light. But the idea of surprising her made Sol's anxious heart flutter with pride.

"I wonder how Velcros misses the similarities between our people," Ainthe mused instead of ripping Sol apart with her shadows, which Sol completely expected.

"You and I are nothing alike."

"Are we not? We both live in the dark. We both fight for our kin and way of life."

"I don't slaughter innocents for my own gain."

"Catarmon says otherwise."

Sol froze, her fists lowering without her approval. "What?"

"The creature knows you." Ainthe began to circle her, like a predator. The wisps of her white robes looked like trails of smoke. "It tells a story of you killing your King. I foresaw this."

"No you didn't," Sol argued, whipping her head around to follow Ainthe's movements. "No one can predict the future."

"No, but I saw your ambition. As naked and as sharp as an executioner's blade. Tell me, did your friends react well to such a murder?"

Sol swallowed hard. "It wasn't . . . They didn't understand. They assumed I had my reasons."

"Good, well-intentioned reasons. Like a good, well-intentioned hero ought to have. A shame then, that you committed the dirty work and fled before you could reap the rewards."

"I never . . ." Sol stopped herself. There was no use in lying.

Ainthe had, as she said, looked into Sol's mind. Sol's very angry, very vengeful mind. She'd been angry at the King from the start. An old, foolish man too stupid to see that she was being framed. He never even gave her a chance. The aggravation she bore working for him as he did nothing to grow the city turned to hatred as she rotted in prison.

Oh yes, he was a shit ruler. A weak man unworthy of his crown. Complacent at best to Heliodar's schemes, just like Mal. She didn't have the heart to kill Mal, although she could've. Her aim should've been for Heliodar, like it was meant to be. But one second of hesitation reminded her of who had let things get that bad.

A good King would've seen Heliodar's treachery from miles away. Sol made way for such a King and suffered the consequences.

"You killed your ruler, why?" Ainthe pressed, after her silence.

"I wanted to make sure what happened would never be repeated. I tore out the root of the problem."

"Liar."

Sol narrowed her eyes at Ainthe. "I'm not lying."

The priestess ignored her. "My people choose our leaders brutally. If one is failing, and others see it, it is up to them to destroy that leader and take their place. Just as you should have for seeing your King's weaknesses."

"I didn't want to rule," Sol argued.

"But you loved your people and had a vision to make them better." Ainthe stopped in front of her, eyes boring into Sol's very being. "I saw it. You deny, but you cannot lie to one who has seen every part of you. As I said, your people and mine are not so different. We desire strength above all else. In a place where weakness is crushed by rock and darkness, only strength can build a civilization. I expected such strength when we broke Dirn-Darahl, yet found none."

"Many of our people were killed by a plot by our general."

"So Catarmon has said."

Sol bristled at that. This Catarmon sure knew a lot about her. Then again, every nasty thing aiming for Divinity thought spitting out facts made them sound closer to godhood, so she shouldn't have been surprised.

"Well, this has been just great, but do you mind getting to the part where you flay me alive so we can end this ridiculous conversation?"

This time, Ainthe's eyebrows did go up and Sol couldn't have imagined it. For a woman who looked like she was scowling every waking moment, any other expression just looked comical.

"Why would I kill my weapon?" Ainthe asked, genuinely puzzled.

Fucking Serevadians! Sol never understood them. Ainthe and Velcros and Viggo, they all spoke in circles, never actually touching on what they wanted to say. Couldn't they just skip the fluff and get to the point?

"Just what exactly are you trying to say?" Sol asked. "It's been a long while since I've heard your Trollshit, so I'm trying to get used to it again."

Ainthe scowled, curling one of her boney hands into a fist. "I should think it obvious. I need you to help me kill Catarmon."

Sol waited for more. A 'but' or a 'this is what we Serevadians call a joke.' When she got nothing but uncomfortable silence, Sol waved her on.

"Please tell me you're going to explain to me why you need me to kill the thing you willingly followed in order to topple Serevadia's government and kill us in the process."

"My goal was never to destroy the republic." Ainthe waved her hand. "My goal was to bring my people into the light of the surface, like we were meant to do. It is what I raised my daughters for. It is what I was raised for. But Catarmon . . . this is not what it wanted. This beast wants Serevadia's destruction, and while I do not find myself in agreement with this new Emperor, I will not watch us fall to a monster."

Sol blinked. "Now you're just confusing me. I thought Serevadia served Catarmon. Why would it want to destroy you?"

"A question I asked myself ever since I laid eyes on it. The answer doesn't matter, not now. This war with the surface will destroy us."

"But you're winning." Sol hated the words. "You realize that, right? I know you're not a general, but you realize how big your army is? Your Empire is larger than any of the surface kingdoms."

"It is a false victory," Ainthe seethed. "To placate my people. Now they do not heed the words of the Shadow Dancer, only the stronger voice of Catarmon. Only I see our doom fast approaching, for I have seen inside this creature's mind and know what it plans."

This was strange. Strange enough that Sol found herself pinching the hells out of her arm to try and wake up from this bizarre dream. But Ainthe stayed rooted in front of her. The shadows still snapped at her legs.

Sol took a deep breath. "Say I believe you. Why would I help you? You've done nothing but try to kill me in the past. The only reason you let us go the last time was because of Alkimos."

"The Great Worm defended you. It was my duty to stand down."

"Right, whatever. Why should I help you?"

Ainthe did the same staring thing as before, as if the answer was obvious and Sol wasn't seeing it. Only this time her eyes widened in shock. "You don't know."

"Don't know what?" Sol snapped. Hells, it was like she was back in court again, only this time she had the patience of a rabid worg.

"Catarmon is not easily killed, but you are in a unique position. It does not see you as a threat." She paused, as if pondering how much to share. "I will not tell you what it is. Your Allegiance is fragile enough already."

"What?" Sol exclaimed. "If I'm going to kill it, I need to know what kind of monster it is! Are you afraid to scare me off?"

"Precisely," Ainthe said, inclining her head towards Sol. "You would not believe me. You would turn me in, and then this plan, any hope for our two peoples to coexist in a world where the sky and the rock are not consumed by flame, would fail."

"How, then, am I supposed to know?" Sol asked.

"When the time is right, you will. This is something you must know for yourself."

"Either that, or you're playing me for a fool."

Ainthe said crisply, "Out of all your companions, you are the least foolish. I bring you this because we are alike, whether you see it or not. I do it because I am desperate and running thin on my allies. I do it for my daughters." She blinked rapidly. "May the Shadow Dancer take them into his embrace."

Sol winced. Nerezza, she knew, was dead, but the little girl?

"I'm sorry," she said.

"As am I." The weakness was gone, replaced with a mask of cold cruelty not currently aimed for Sol. "As for your previous question, I have no reason to betray you. If I wanted to, I could've brought you to Catarmon instead of talking to you now. I will offer you this information in order to sate your curiosity—" Ainthe leaned over, white hair falling like a veil over her shoulders. "Your companions are not here. Some of your people, however, are. You have seen them working in the graveyard."

"That's not a graveyard," Sol muttered.

Ainthe ignored her. "Among them is a dwarf you know. An ugly one, by the name of Karas. He has been trying to lead an escape for the past month. If anyone but I had listened, he would be dead."

Sol's heart leapt. She had another friend here. Suddenly the weight of impossibility lifted off her shoulders.

"Karas could help us," Sol said excitedly.

"Perhaps," Ainthe said. "He is of the mind not to trust any

of my kind, so I didn't approach him about this. However, your people's escape should calm your nerves about trusting me. It is something I will help with, so long as you keep your end of the bargain."

"Find out what Catarmon is. Kill it," Sol's mouth twisted into a frown, "and you'll help me free my people?"

"Yes."

"This still sounds like a trap." Sol shook her head.

"Would it matter if it was? Either you try to free your people on your own and die, or you help me."

"And likely die," Sol said flatly.

Ainthe's grin sent shivers down Sol's spine. "What did you say earlier? 'If I die, I go down with your flesh beneath my nails'?"

"Something like that," Sol agreed.

"We are creatures of battle. We die on our own terms. Do your research, daughter of stone, and take this as a sign of good-will." She took something from her sleeve and tossed it at Sol. She caught it easily, looking down at the key with her now usual frown.

"All right, research, snooping, key to somewhere, got it." Sol pocketed the key. "What about Abraxas? He's on my side. Can he help."

"No!"

Sol jumped back at the sheer volume of Ainthe's voice. And the strange sheen in her eyes. If Sol hadn't known better, she would've thought it was terror.

The priestess composed herself. "No. Abraxas Kain is a shell of himself, and much too close to Catarmon. You shouldn't trust him."

This, and the knowledge of Abraxas's lie, made Sol feel sick again. She knew now that he'd lied about the Wandering Sols being close by. But surely that was it.

"He's been through a lot, but this is Abraxas we're talking

about," Sol said. "He's a good man, he's my friend, he'll help me."

"He might. But the end will be the same. Catarmon sees through his eyes. To do so will be to sentence us to doom."

Ainthe's eyes flicked back to the key in Sol's pocket, as if regretting her decision. But she made no move to take it back.

"Abraxas Kain is Catarmon's eyes. If you wish to free your friend from his torment, you must stay silent."

Sol hated this. Every hellsdamned bit of it. Working with Ainthe, not knowing what the hell Catarmon was, and turning her back on Abraxas. But her training told her it wasn't unlikely that Ainthe was right. One hundred years was a long time to be in enemy hands, and Sol shouldn't trust Abraxas so easily. He wouldn't hurt her on purpose, but if Ainthe was right about Catarmon using Abraxas as a spy, especially if he wasn't aware, she couldn't trust him.

Not until she freed him.

"Okay." Sol nodded. "What's our first move?"

Ainthe relaxed. "First, the prisoners. Their escape will draw Catarmon's ire and distract it. From there, we plan our attack."

"Simple." Although it would likely be anything but. "Let's get started."

AN HOUR LATER, Sol had just enough time to sneak back into the house, through the walls, take off her clothes to put on her nightgown, hide the clothes, and slip underneath the covers before a knock came at her door.

"Yes?"

The door cracked open and Abraxas peaked his head in. "Did I wake you?"

She shook her head. "No, I was just about to go to bed."

"Before dinner?"

Her stomach rumbled at the perfect moment. "It's dinner?"

Abraxas laughed and pushed through the door with a tray of food. The same she'd been eating, just army rations but good enough. He kicked the door closed behind him.

"You must still be shaken up if you'd forgotten about dinner."

Sol smiled sheepishly and made room for him on the bed. He sat, putting the tray between them.

"It's hard to keep track of the days down here, you know?" She picked up her fork.

Abraxas nodded solemnly. "I understand. We won't endure this much longer, I swear."

She perked up. "Our friends?"

"I'm working on it, but I think Catarmon is realizing the Eternity Dagger isn't there. Once they lose interest, we'll have a narrow window to get them out before they kill them. I won't let that happen, so we need to be prepared. Here's my plan . . ."

Sol nodded eagerly, shoving food in her mouth without tasting it and listening without really hearing. She nodded when she was supposed to, acted worried when appropriate, but Ainthe's warning kept her from leaning into this plan with her whole heart.

She tied down her pity so it wouldn't show in her eyes. Whatever Abraxas was doing, against his will or without his knowledge, she would endure. She'd save him, just like all the rest.

And then she was going to kill another would-be god.

9

Sorin

"It's going to be sore. Likely won't have complete function back for the rest of your life. But there's no infection and I don't need to lob it off, so count yourself lucky."

This was the most Miks had spoken to Sorin the entire time he'd been healing his hand. The most he did taking off Sahar's bandages was grunt and scrunch his brows together. After that, there was a lot of cleaning, resetting, and overall pain as the weathered sailor prepped the hand for healing potions.

Sorin had choked down what he was given, bitterly missing the one's that Sahar made that somehow tasted better than all the others. Like everything else on the *Knave*, it did the job but made him fucking miserable as it did.

Miks sat back. "Touch your thumb to each finger."

Sorin did so, wincing as a spasm of dull pain shook whenever he stretched his fingers too much. He could touch his thumb, but holding this position made his hand quake. He didn't need Miks to tell him what to do next. He made a fist, sucking air through his teeth. Shitty fist. Weak, shaking, and wouldn't hold up against a solid hit.

He relaxed his hand. "Good thing I never used my left hand."

Miks grunted, apparently satisfied, and started to clean up his workspace. Sorin could hardly call the tiny room a healer's bay. There was room for a table nailed to the floor, one swinging cot, and a cramped shelf full of potions and herbs. And Miks was a damn mess. Nothing was labeled or had any sort of system to it, as far as Sorin could tell.

"So, you're the ship's doctor, huh?" he asked. "Suppose I should try not to see you around too often."

"That would be wise." Miks turned to squint at Sorin. "You don't look very wise, though."

"I've been known to have my moments. I prefer 'cheeky,' however, if we're going for descriptions."

Miks huffed. "Yeah, that won't last long. Enjoy that little flame of rebellion while you have it. Next time I see you, you'll likely lose something more important than a hand."

Sorin didn't mean to look down when Miks said that, but he did. He landed his gaze on his shitty left hand and the mass of scar tissue where his tattoo used to be and tried to keep back the flood of emotions that threatened to overwhelm him. It was just a tattoo, after all. Losing it hadn't erased the memories of his family. But the lack of ink, the constant throb of dull pain, the sharp memory of Vayne's face as he dug the knife into Sorin's hand—that was a wound that would never leave him. No potion or magic could remove it.

Not for the first time, Sorin wondered if it would've been kinder to let the sea take him.

"Back when we first met, when you were saving Sahar," Sorin started, and Miks stiffened. "you offered to let her die."

The man had his back to Sorin, and the only thing that followed his words were the clinking of glass bottles as he put things back in their cupboard. He knew precisely where they went, carefully moving vials out of the way so he could put the used ones back. There was a system, just one Sorin couldn't see.

"Why?" Sorin pressed.

"You ask that now? After your hand?"

"Like I said, I'm cheeky. And stupid, if you hadn't noticed."

Miks blew out a long breath, shutting and locking the cupboard. "At least you recognize it. That's something, I suppose. As for your companion, she could've been spared this if I let her die. Mostly make that decision on my own, but you looked right worried for her."

Miks finally turned around and leveled him with an intense look. "Like no kidnapper and his charge I've ever seen."

Sorin laughed nervously. "What can I say? I was worried about the money."

"I'll bet." But Miks didn't look close to believing Sorin.

Sorin had to force himself not to start jiggling his leg, like he always did when he lied or was nervous. Sol said it was such an obvious tell that a child could see it. Sorin had argued that the children he knew were a lot smarter than him, so her statement was kind of shit. Damn, he missed her.

"You let people die so Vayne can't have them." Sorin lowered his voice. "Surely he catches on."

"Someone always survives, boy. So long as there's at least one breathing soul for him to shackle to this ship, that's enough. The rest I can spare."

Well, what a pleasant way of looking at things. Sorin shivered.

"And he doesn't punish you for that?"

Miks snorted. "Living is punishment enough, and I'm the only one on this ship who has a mind for medicine. Besides that, I've got blessings. Vayne doesn't kill those who are powerful."

Sorin nodded. A man with both a Stormheart and a Tide-mind. It wasn't unheard of, just rare. Any ship would be lucky to have a man like Miks onboard. Obviously, Vayne thought so as well.

Just as he'd started to pose his next question, Miks waved a meaty hand in his direction. "Don't say what you're about to say."

"I didn't say anything yet."

"But you were. Don't take my kindness for weakness, boy. I've been here long enough to know that look in your eye. You think because I disagree with the way things are run that I'll help you get out, is that it? Maybe kill Vayne while we're at it?"

Sorin wasn't going to nod and give Miks the satisfaction of being right, because that was exactly what he'd been about to say. But apparently being perfectly still was just as bad as jiggling his leg because Miks saw right through him.

If possible, the older man scowled further. It deepened the lines in his face, and in the weak light of the small room, made him look like he was melting. He had the timber of a man who'd recited this before, too many times to count.

"All I can do is warn you against it. All I can say is 'no' to your proposal. I won't turn you in, but I won't help you. At some point, if you live, you'll realize that this is the life you've been chained to. There is no outer paradise for us to live in. There are only the storms, the sea, and this ship between them. Vayne is a cruel bastard, but there are crueler. My advice to you is to make yourself useful enough so that you're not disposable, but not so special as to draw his eye. Settle in here, find a routine. One day, a year or so down the line, you're going to find that this life is one to live, and whatever you'd lived before was just a dream."

"No." Sorin surprised himself with how hoarse, how strong his voice was with that one word. Miks blinked at him slowly. "No, I won't."

"They all say that." Miks sighed.

"Well, I'm not them." Sorin stood up, snatching his coat up and shrugging it on. It had been given back to him reeking of blood and salt, but it felt good across his shoulders. "I'm Sorin Trinity."

"No, you're not," Miks said gently. "Not anymore."

Sorin ignored him, ignored the way his name tasted like grief on his tongue, and walked out of the room without looking back.

~

A WEEK of kitchen duty later, Sorin's hand and attitude hadn't gotten any better and he was tired of doing cabin-boy chores. He'd already *been* a cabin boy. This shit was downright demeaning. Scrubbing pots, serving food, scrubbing the floors, running errands, scrubbing food clean, dumping questionable things in the water, scrubbing *again*.

Of course, he knew what it was. This was mind-numbing work meant to put him in his place. To make him complacent. It also kept him from harder jobs that would've torn his body up, likely Miks's idea. Left hands were needed for tying and securing rigging after all. And as pissed as Sorin was at getting handed the dirty jobs, because pirates were filthy people, he was also relieved.

He hadn't been on a real ship in over six years. Sure, there was muscle memory, but it wouldn't have been enough for a ship the size of the *Knave*. And since his cover story was being a bounty hunter who ran a small ship with a modest crew, it would've been damn suspicious if he was tossed into a real job and fumbled his way through it.

More than once, as he was scrubbing away at something foul and slimy, he wondered if Knave would've listened if Sorin had told the truth. Would he have believed the tale of the palace on the ocean floor, and the massive army that was spreading to the different continents? Would he have taken Sorin seriously if he'd only known what he'd done ever since losing the *Fortune's Trinity*?

The answer was no. The risk that posed to himself and Sahar should Vayne ever realize that the two not only cared for each other but were plotting against him was too great. Better to be viewed as a nothing, to pretend to hate Sahar, and make themselves somewhat invisible.

Something large and foul slammed down on the floor next to his leg. Sorin wasn't the praying type but he almost sent a prayer of thanks to the heavens as he turned around.

"A present? For me? Willie, you shouldn't have."

Wilona, the robust half-orc that called the kitchen her home and the poor sobs, himself included, her little worker bees, didn't look amused. She never had, ever since she introduced herself and Sorin promptly gave her a new name instead. Greasy black hair hung in front of her eyes and her tusks, while small, had obviously seen better days. She was perpetually sweaty and stinking of onions, which was fun because at a good foot taller than Sorin he always managed to end up in that cloud of bitterness.

Willie kicked the bucket of . . . yeah, Sorin wasn't going to look at that. He found out the hard way that whatever it was could upend the breakfast he'd been given and keep him from eating dinner later on.

"Needs dumping," Willie huffed. "And scrubbing."

"Must I be both dumper and scrubber today?" Sorin asked, resigning himself to breathe through his mouth. "You wound me, Willie."

The cook just rolled her eyes and lumbered off, her footsteps creaking the floorboards that made Sorin cringe. But he picked up his bucket of horror with both hands, because any bucket Willie carried easily made him think he should've taken up Gyda's offers to train, and waddled out of the kitchen, up the stairs, and into the bright sunlight of a day at sea.

This was easily his favorite part of the day, these few minutes where he got fresh air and sunlight. With the salted wind cooling the sweat on his brow and the spray of sea mist tickling his skin. The *Red Knave* cut through the water like a heavy sword, steady and sure. The cerulean waves lashed out at the crimson hull, but found no purchase.

The deck was busy, as always. It had a large crew that had nothing else better to do than be busy or risk the ire of their captain. Despite the overall coldness of the ship in atmosphere, it's deck never wanted for anything. Broken planks were fixed. Rusted chains were replaced. Ropes and rigging were constantly tended to, as if the riggers thought that climbing to neck-breaking heights would draw Vayne's eye elsewhere.

The sails were a clean cream, full and tight on such a windy day. Sorin cast them a longing look before waddling over to the railing and dumping his bucket's contents into the water. His gaze was fixed on the horizon, so he didn't see it when it slapped the water's surface. The ship was moving fast enough that he didn't have to worry about seeing it floating in the water.

He let the bucket rest on the railing next to him. He found he could steal a few moments in the open air, resting, before he was spotted. He took those moments like a drowning man took air.

It was pathetic, really, that these were the times he looked forward to the most. These little breaks that felt close enough to freedom that he could almost imagine he was somewhere else.

But when he took these moments, his thoughts always drifted back to the Wandering Sols, his anchor. The first day he'd stewed over Abraxas's betrayal, furiously scrubbing and blinking away tears as he heard the echoes of his friend's voice but couldn't believe the words. The second day had been all about Gyda, because he imagined her bonking her head on the kitchen beams once and suddenly she was all he could think about. Tall, surly, terrifying Gyda, who'd made him feel safe on and off the battlefield. He tried to forget how he saw her last, defeated and broken, pressing her lips to Evren's in what could only be a goodbye kiss.

Today was for Arke, and it felt like Vayne was tearing at his hand again.

He'd woken up with a plan to tell Arke what crazy-ass dream he'd had, as he always did before, and found the goblin nowhere.

That was a given, but it still hurt. Maybe not as much as Arke leaving, because nothing had hurt that much.

Sorin replayed that memory in his head again, for maybe the hundredth time, and wondered what he'd done wrong. If he'd been better, would Arke had stayed? Maybe he could've gone with him. Dumped Sol into Evren's arms and ran after him. That was what best friends did, after all.

Sorin didn't get to say goodbye. To any of them, but Arke most of all. Because, with the others being in the middle of Abraxas's tirade, it was a little difficult to tell them that he loved them and would always have them in his heart. But Arke had been right there. No battle to interrupt them, no death on the fringes of their vision. He could've said what he meant and maybe felt better about not following him.

When I met you I was so close to just dunking myself in the nearest body of water and not coming back up. When I met you, I was a sorry excuse for a human just wandering aimlessly from town to town. And you saved me. I know you say often that I saved you from those farmers, and maybe I did. I don't know why, but I did. Stepping between you and them was the best choice I'll ever make in my worthless, pathetic life, because it gave me you. Because your little sullen bits of silence after a failed spell were the only times my brain stopped screaming profanities at me. When you trusted me after sneaking across the border, it was the greatest gift I'd ever received because you looked at me like I wasn't a fuck up. I so desperately wanted you to keep believing in me like that, like I'd always be there to save you. That's why I followed you into Dirn-Darahl and the Yawning Deep and everywhere else. You were my best friend, my only lifeline when my mind was a raging monster trying to tear me down. I don't know when I stopped being your lifeline. I can't pinpoint the day I failed, where you stopped coming to me.

But I'm sorry, Arke. Maybe I leaned on you too much. Maybe I got too invested in the others or our adventures that I failed at being a good friend. Whatever it was, know that you're still my best decision and my best friend.

Know that your memory, not the threat of the world ending, is all that's keeping me afloat.

Sorin was taking too long. Standing at the rail as if he owned the damn ship and could do what he pleased. So he shouldn't have been surprised when something panicked and sweaty bumped into him and knocked Willie's bucket right off the railing and into the water with a loud, ominous plop.

Sorin cursed, whipping around to find the cause of his shitty luck cowering against his legs in a tight little ball. A kid.

Sorin stared at him for a while. "Um . . . can I have my legs back?"

The kid did nothing but whimper and Sorin was really close to cursing again when a dark figure across the deck caught his eye. The woman who'd controlled the storm the night Sorin's whole life got tossed into a pile of steaming worg shit. She wasn't any prettier in the daylight. Matted black hair, skin somewhere between painfully tan and ashen, as if she'd been sitting out in the sun for years. He felt the need to scoop some water up and toss it on her, to see if that relaxed the wrinkles and glower she perpetually wore. She wore the salt-crusted robes of a mage, but no mage he'd ever seen. They were black once, but now were faded grey and spotted with a rust color along the hems. Her withered hands were clasped in front of her, and she was staring right at the kid.

Common sense would be to push the kid away and go off to kiss Willie's slimy boots for losing her bucket. But Sorin never had an overabundance of common sense to begin with.

"Hey, kid, what did you do?" Sorin asked. "Seriously, the witch is looking right at us, I need to know."

Sorin wasn't expecting a response, but a wobbly voice answered.

"She's watching me?"

"Yeah, that's what I just said."

"Is she coming over?"

Sorin frowned. "No, actually, she's . . . Yeah, you're good."

The witch's unblinking gaze was snapped away by Vayne's voice. He was glaring at her on the quarterdeck, and Sorin didn't care to hear what he had to say. Just behind him, Sahar looked like she was counting her breaths to keep calm. She'd been stuck by his side as a pretty ornament until he decided what to do with her, but hadn't laid a hand on her so far. Sorin counted that among their measly blessings.

He caught her eye and she gave him the barest of smiles that lasted as long as it took the wind to get from one end of the ship to the other. Then it was gone.

The witch crossed the deck to Vayne's position, and all those near her made way as if she was the bearer of a deadly plague. Which, she might've been. Hells only knew what was living in that hair.

"She's gone, you're good."

The kid at Sorin's feet melted in relief, uncovering their head. Their hair had been sheared short, almost to the scalp. Pale skin was burnt and peeling along their cheeks and nose, and the little droop of their pointed ears made Sorin's heart ache. Elf kids made him sad for some reason. All that life ahead of them, and they were stuck in the same gangly limbs as any other preteen.

"You made me lose my bucket."

The kid looked up at him, narrowing those large blue eyes against the glare of the sun. "Who the fuck are you?"

"Sorin. Who the fuck are you?"

"Enola," their voice got sharp with attitude until they looked beyond Sorin at the witch and the captain. Then they looked back at Sorin, and all sharpness melted away into a gooey pile of fear and desperation.

"Hide me, please."

Sorin laughed. "Kid, I can't hide you anywhere on this ship. You want me to get my toes chopped off and put into Willie's next creation?"

"Please!" She grabbed his pant legs, because he was fairly sure they were a she now, and balled the cloth in her fists. "Just for a little while. The witch wants my blood for something. I can't give it to her."

Now, normally Sorin would be moved at the pleas of any kid trying to outrun a scary storm witch. It really wasn't difficult to feel sorry for a kid like Enola either, who looked like she hadn't taken to Willie's cooking and was skipping meals. But life just wasn't that simple anymore.

"Well, you look like the same weight as Willie's bucket. I'm sure she could use you as a replacement."

Enola blanched. "*What?*"

But at that point Sorin was already grabbing her by her collar—with his right hand—and hauling her to her feet. She was too stunned to move at first, but then started to lash out with her long-ass legs. Her kicks would've hurt far more if she had any shoes on, but Sorin still hissed.

"Stop it, would you?" he said as he brought her across the deck and pushed her down the dark hole smelling of grease and sweat. "You asked for a place to hide, there you go."

Her big eyes widened like saucers. "I can't be a bucket. Don't turn me into a bucket."

"It's a joke kid, relax."

At that, she stilled her thrashing and he let go of her collar. Nodding to the waiting kitchen, he said "Willie's not going to be happy, so she'll put you to work. But you'll be safe as you can be here, okay? Just stick by my side."

Sorin got halfway down the stairs before she protested.

"Why are you helping me?"

He stopped, sighed, then turned around. She was haloed by the sunlight, a scruffy little elf that was far from the elegant, striking stereotype of her kind. Also, that little sneer made her face scrunch up in the most humorous way. He had to tamp down a smile, because she was easily the type to take offense to it.

"Because you asked, and I have a death wish." He shrugged. "It's simple."

She folded her arms across her thin chest. "You're weird."

He turned back around, clomping down the steps. A second later, she pattered after him. "Yeah, I've been told that a lot. Hey, Willie! This runt knocked your bucket in the water. Captain says she's working with us from now on."

WHEN NIGHT FELL and Willie finally told the two of them that they could stop scrubbing, Sorin took Enola to the crew quarters with him. She wasn't new, at least not newer than him, but stuck behind him as if she didn't know where to go without guidance.

The quarters were pretty large and bare. Swaying hammocks nailed a couple feet above the floor, and then above each other to make room for everyone. The night crew had already gotten up and left the place sparingly empty while the day crew trickled in. Sorin hadn't spent the night in that cell since Miks had fixed his hand, and he was increasingly glad for the lack of nasty water swishing on the floor.

Sorin collapsed in one of the lower hammocks, massaging his hands the best he could. Enola sat opposite to him, kicking her legs up. She eyed the shifting crew with distrustful eyes, but none of them paid her any attention.

"You going to tell me why you sentenced yourself to Willie's wrath?" he asked after a while of silence.

"I already told you. The witch—"

"Was trying to get your blood, I know." He sighed, giving up on his cramping left hand. "Why, though? Why are you so special?"

Enola shrugged. "I dunno, she just needs it. She has vials of it, but likes it fresh. Normally I don't leave her cabin but she left it open today and I ran."

Sorin frowned. "Won't she come back for you?"

Again, Enola shrugged her bony shoulders as if he either should know the answer to that question or those shoulders spoke for herself. At his stare, she worried her bottom lip.

"She's not . . . I mean, she's scary, right? All witches are scary. But she's not mean. She won't hurt you for helping me if that's what you're worried about."

"Then why run away from her?"

"Because! Every time she takes my blood someone gets hurt. I feel really sick and then there's always a storm. There are people crying and it's my fault." She locked eyes with him. "Like you. I was awake when you came on board. I didn't see you, but I heard you."

Before Sorin could say anything, Sahar swept into the room like a lovely dream, tearing her fingers through the knots in her hair and making a beeline for him.

"She's how Vayne's mage is able to call and dismiss storms. Come here, you look dreadful."

Sorin barely had time to stand up before she enveloped him in a hug. He squeezed back, savoring it despite the fact that this was now part of their daily ritual. It was always a blessing to see each other at the end of the day, and they didn't take it for granted, privacy be damned.

She pulled back, and he finally got a good look at her. Thankfully Vayne had given her practical clothes over the dress she'd worn before, but they were frumpy and worn, not suited for how she was trying to present them. Then again, Sahar Al-Fasil could wear a pile of seaweed and still manage to look good, so that was the least of her problems. She was worn and weary, her lips chapped after all day in the sun and her hair a mess.

Sorin had never seen someone so beautiful in his life.

He stepped back, waving her into the hammock and sitting beside her once they were settled. "What's this about controlling the storms?"

"The witch is just a normal Stormheart," Sahar explained. "She was with Vayne all day today, so I could tell."

"Gail coming in handy?"

She grimaced. "Unfortunately, yes. Like you said before, a normal Stormheart shouldn't be able to call and dismiss a storm at will. Control it a fraction, yes, but not command it. This girl's blood must be what she's using to make herself more powerful. Like an amplifier of some sort. There's only one thing we know less about than Soul magic, and that's Blood magic."

"Um, hello?" Enola snapped their attention back to her. "I'm right here."

"Right," Sorin sighed. "Sorry. Sahar, this is Enola. Enola, Sahar."

Enola squinted at them, as she was prone to doing now. "I thought you two hated each other."

"Oh good!" Sahar smiled. "Someone is convinced."

"Yeah, a kid who gets locked up with a witch most of the time. Not comforting."

Enola scoffed. "Well, you two just hugged in front of everyone, so I don't see the problem."

Sorin gestured vaguely to the whole room. "See anyone paying attention?"

She followed his hand in a long sweep before shaking her head.

"That's because everyone is too tired, too depressed, or too pissed to care about us," Sorin explained. "We learned that early."

"Oh." Enola deflated a bit.

Sahar gave her a pitying smile before turning back to Sorin. "We might be able to use this to our advantage, but we need to figure it out quickly."

"Why? Something wrong?"

"I saw the navigation patterns. We're headed towards Etherak, and then curving back to the open sea. Now, I don't know why, but—"

In unison, Sorin and Enola said, "Restocking in Tal-Mashad."

Sahar stared at them. "Right. Okay. So, that's our window."

"Vayne's not stupid. He won't risk docking. It's too easy for us to flee," Sorin said.

Enola nodded along. "He won't. We'll anchor a good ways away, and he sends a landing party for supplies. It's easier in Etherak. Waters around the cliffs make it too dangerous for anyone to swim, so he doesn't worry about jumpers. He can get closer to the port that way."

Sorin filed that information away for later. "And how do we use that against Vayne? Or the kid for that matter."

Sahar hesitated. "I . . . I'm not sure. It seems like she's the key to getting us out, but I'm not sure. I thought maybe we could turn the crew on Vayne, and taking out his witch would be the worst of it out of the way. No one here is working of their own freewill, but no one wants to leave. Its aggravating. The only thing they share in common is—"

"Fear," Sorin finished. "Of him."

She nodded slowly. "Yes. I think taking power from the witch would help, but I don't know how. Many have been here for over a decade."

Sorin got up and started to pace, loudly enough that he saw a few crew members open their eyes to glare at him. He ignored them.

All of them were Vasa. Many where Stormhearts or Tideminds, because who else could survive the destruction Vayne brought to their old crews? It was unnatural to have so much power in the hull of one ship, and yet he'd found no evidence of a single mutiny.

"What the fuck is wrong with all of you?" Sorin shouted, and whoever hadn't been awake was now.

"Sorin," Sahar hissed a warning, but he ignored her too, taking the time to glare at each of them in turn.

"You're all Vasa," he shouted over the din of the waves and creaking of the ship, watching as bleary eyes blinked and focused on him. "You are all powerful survivors. Fuck, that's why Vayne's got you here. Why don't you fight back?"

A couple exchanged worried glances before answering.

"He'll kill us."

"He's one man!" Sorin's scarred hand went up, his finger crooked and quivering where it once would've been straight and still. "He's just a pirate with no powers. Why does he stop you? Don't you know that the might of all of you together would be enough to destroy him?"

"Sorin, stop!" Sahar was up and dragging him away by his shoulders. "You'll ruin this for us."

"No, I won't. Because they won't talk." He glared at them. "Because they're afraid that if they go to him with news of a mutiny in the making, he'll just slaughter them all and start over. Is that it?"

Silence, and a few ashamed heads nodded. A new voice whispered above the creaking hull, "You haven't been here long enough to know who he is, what he's like."

"I know who he is," Sorin spat. "He's a selfish, greedy, ordinary man. He goes against everything our people built. He's stolen our gifts and made us slaves to his will. He is nothing but a man that bleeds, and who has no idea the true might of what he has kept caged for so long. But I do."

Sahar let go of him. Enola watched him with those bright blue eyes, mouth agape.

Sorin didn't move. He kept his jittery legs still. He kept his hands flat against his thighs. And he kept his voice low. Enough to sink into their ears, for the words to nestle in their heads. But not so loud as to be heard anywhere else.

"We are Vasa. We are children of salt and stars, of lightning and sea spray. We do not bow to the wills of lesser men, no matter how brutal and intelligent they may be. I certainly don't. You don't know me, but I have killed monsters far worse than him for far less. He's had this coming for a long time. And it's time for all of us to take a stand against him. For ourselves, for the ones in the future who might find themselves here, and for those who have already failed."

He took a deep breath. Sahar at his back, Enola beside him and a crew of desperate, beaten slaves in front of him.

"My name is Sorin Trinity," Sorin said. "He hasn't taken that away from me. My name is my own. Your names are yours. Take up your name. Take up the spirits of your old crew. And help me destroy this fucker."

The creaking silence that followed his words grabbed at his heart and yanked it down, down, down where the remnants of his hope was. Low, broken, flickering with a half-light. One by one, the crew shook their heads and curled back into their hammocks. A few looked at him with teary, pitying eyes, as if he was some dying dog that they had to watch suffer through his final breaths. These were the few that murmured soft words that hit like knives in his ears.

"Poor boy," they said.

"I don't remember having that kind of fight anymore," they said.

"He won't last the week," they said.

They too turned back into their hammocks, and left Sorin with Sahar and Enola. The two said nothing, did nothing, as he settled down into his hammock. Not until he kicked his boots off and started to lay down.

"Sorin . . ." Sahar was about to plead with him that he shouldn't give up, that this was too much to ask of a crew that hadn't been free in a very long time. But he didn't want to hear it.

He said, "Don't," and made sure to soften the word so she didn't take any harm from it. He laid down and she swayed above him. Enola peeked over the edge of the hammock with every swing. She didn't look surprised, or all that inspired. His words had meant nothing to her either.

Sahar pursed her chapped lips into a thin line, flipping through what to say. Unsatisfied, she blew out a heavy breath.

"We'll figure this out. We always do. There are worse things that have fallen to us, and worse things still ahead."

"That's the problem," Sorin said. "Knowing that we can't fail, that no one is coming to save us. It's us or nothing, and each day it feels like nothing."

"Don't say that," Sahar said, with a lot more fierceness than he expected. "Don't you ever say that. They did not die so we could stay here under the whims of a madman. I won't allow those sacrifices to be in vain, not a single damn one of them. And neither will you. One way or another, we're leaving this ship and we're saving the world."

Sorin almost believed her. Her words held no magic but he clutched them tight inside his aching chest long after she'd crawled into the hammock above his and blew out the lantern.

Across from him, Enola shifted until she laid down. Her wide eyes caught the barest light in the room and were fixed on him.

"You're going to die," she whispered. It wasn't a threat, just an observation. She said it almost like an apology, as if one day of scrubbing foul kitchen junk was enough for her to feel bad for him.

"I've done it once before," he whispered back. "Why not go for a second round?"

10

Arke

"Touch my shit again and I'm gonna turn you into a fuckin' toad and toss you into a desert until you fry." Arke jabbed his finger at the hovering pixie. "*Then* I'm gonna eat you."

The pixie, barely bigger than his finger, stuck their equally tiny tongue out at him. He didn't miss the shark-like teeth the tongue flicked back behind, and he barely jerked his finger back before they snapped at him.

He growled low in the back of his throat, picking up his spellbook from its spot nestled in the roots of the old oak. But the pixie was gone, giggling maniacally as it zipped through the crystalline branches and out of sight.

Arke slumped back against the tree, feeling very much like he had as a child bundled and squeezed in tight with the other goblin kids. Frustrated, hot, and scrunched. But he was also too pissed to move so he sat and glared at the spot the pixie had last been.

Above his head the branches refracted sunlight back to him in shades of blues, purples and pinks. Their faceted leaves shivered in the sweet breeze, crowning golden apples and silver pears. Orange and cherry blossoms sprinkled the air, not as soft as they were back in Eith but smelling even sweeter. They would never turn to fruit, and their petals were sharp enough to cut. As with everything in Unnethen's home, they were as deadly as they were beautiful.

Arke wasn't sure where exactly he was. Unnethen had dragged him here after they massacred enough Serevadians to darken the water with blood. He knew enough about her to know that this wild land was only a small corner of a place she called Sildenior, and the mortals back in Eith called the Brightlands, or the home of the Fey like her. Of course, Unnethen and other Fey wouldn't call it that. All their words made him feel like he was gagging on his own tongue. Terevasans had it right by being simple.

Because everything here was fucking bright. The sun never set. Everything sparkled or glowed and then promptly confused and ate something else that sparkled or glowed. Arke hated every damn minute of it.

It was one thing to be back in Terevas, where the barrier between Eith and the Brightlands was thinner so Fey just marched in there and fucked with everyone and everything. The Wandering Sols had been lucky to stay with Sahar. They didn't notice, but Arke definitely took account of all the hidden iron and wards in their home. Damn rude by both Fey and Terevasan standards, since everyone in the damned queendom had revolved their life around accepting, acknowledging, and surviving Fey visitors in day-to-day life. But the Al-Fasil's were still Vernesian blood, and all the sand and bone-dust sculptures showed their roots better than them parading Keres around like they were a hellsdamned miracle in mortal form.

His friends didn't have to deal with the Fey besides the bard in the parade. Even that one was mostly harmless. He might've had them dancing to near exhaustion, but there were safety measures in place for just that kind of thing. Terevas lived with Fey and knew how to keep their parties death-free.

Arke hated Terevas. The rolling green fields and its black river and the gleaming bronze buildings. Flowers and farms fucking everywhere. Everyone so polite because it could mean death if they snapped at the wrong thing. He could only imagine how damn awful the Queen's court was, all smiling threats and hidden daggers behind fans and sugared lips. It's like they *wanted* to be Fey.

And Arke, being bound to one annoying Archfey in particular, couldn't think of a worse fate.

The roots were digging into his ribs, as if poking him to get up. Which, they very well could be doing just that. He stood up, a string of foul curse words muttered low enough so that the trees couldn't hear him, hugged his spellbook to his chest, and marched away.

If he hated Terevas, then there was no word to describe how he felt about the Brightlands. Mostly he was just frustrated. Occasionally he would dip down into something like depression, but then he just stared up at the sun until his eyes burned and then he was angry again, simple as that. There was no telling how long he'd been there since there was no night and hardly a need to sleep. Unnethen's idea of a gift.

Everything here was a gift, one that he didn't want to accept but had no choice in the matter. Like eating Evren's cooking or enduring Sol's hugs. There was no choice but to grin and bear it, and Arke's cheeks ached from constantly baring his teeth.

Sometimes, when he was particularly low, he wished to go back to the bridge under the sea. A dark palace behind him, heavy water above him, an army at his feet. He hadn't been able to kill them all, just enough to save his brother and the small army of goblins that followed him. But it had been enough for him to forget about the people he left behind, the sacrifices he forced them to make, and the deal he'd made.

Deals weren't anything new to Arke. Unnethen had waited

for him to reach out to her most of his life and had been pestering him with gifts and strings ever since. But back then he'd only had Tolk to worry about. He didn't give a shit about the other goblins or the city he was supposed to rule. Hells, even that had been an accident. He didn't want any of it, so giving it up, leaving it behind, had been easy.

Maybe too easy.

Now he had chains around his heart all tugging in different directions. Ones he'd used just to survive but somehow he'd lost the key to unlock them. Sol and Evren and Gyda and fucking Abraxas all had a claim on him. Sorin had it first, always would be one of the strongest. Arke ignored the dull ache of sadness when he pictured the human's face as he left.

He hadn't even said goodbye to him. Words got caught up in his throat. Didn't want to fuck it up and say the wrong thing so he'd ran. Stupid.

There was Neri too to think about, although he tried not to. He couldn't explain why being with her or talking to her made him feel better. He didn't reach for his spellbook so much with her around. He wasn't so damn twitchy and rude, and even when he was, she didn't seem bothered.

Was she worried that he wasn't on the other side of the mirror? Did Unnethen talk to her and spin a web of lies that made Arke look like an ass for leaving her?

Which, well, he was. He'd given up the mirror and last connection to her with the barest hint of hesitation. Gyda and Evren wouldn't have done that to each other.

Although Gyda was probably dead now, so that was a moot point. Another tally on his 'Arke Fucked Up' list.

Arke glared at the sun for a long while to get the image of Gyda's dead body and Evren screaming in grief over her out of his head. The tears that slid down his face were just from the glare, his eyes watering out of reflex to protect themselves from all the sparkling. That's what he told himself, anyway.

"Glaring at it won't make it flicker out of existence, dear."

Arke scowled, looking away from the sun. His vision burned blue but he kept walking anyway. If he tripped and snapped his neck, Unnethen could fix that.

She fluttered behind him, a wisp of jasmine flowers and mist at his back. Even living with her he didn't dare look at her. He'd lost enough already.

"Sulking still?" she asked. "You have what you wanted. Tolk and his people are safe and back home."

"Yeah, and I'm here," he bit out.

"As per our agreement."

"I know. You don't gotta remind me."

She huffed behind him, sounding quite childish for an ageless Archfey. "Well, the least you could do is pretend to be happy for my intervention. Power like that doesn't come cheap."

He said nothing, the afterimage of the sun fading now to a pale blue orb that he could see around. He wasn't sure where he was going, but walking away felt good. Wasn't like he was in any danger of getting lost. Unnethen's land just repeated itself underneath his feet. Same trees. Same grass. Same flowers. He'd tried to find a way out so many times that he knew them all like the cracks on his favorite claw.

"I don't know why you're pouting." Unnethen kept easy pace with him, even though he heard no footsteps behind him. "You're alive. Your brother is too, and completely oblivious to the destruction you wrought to get him back, something I did free of charge by the way. Your spell worked, and those friends are safe. What more could you want?"

He stopped dead in his tracks, claws raking along the leather spine of his spellbook.

"What more could I want?" he growled. He stared at a swaying topaz daisy as if he could melt it with his mind. He imagined it to be Unnethen. "I want out of here! Obviously! I've been stuck in this glittering layer of hell for who knows how long and my friends are dying. You have the gall to tell me I'm the one that's gotta kill one of them, who's gone off his fuckin' rocker after being alone and tormented by hells know what for a hundred damn years. You promised me that I would be fixin' things but all I've been doin' is walkin' and hatin' myself!"

The last of his rant echoed in the trees. Eyes in the trunks glared at him for disturbing their rest, but they did nothing about it with Unnethen. The scent of jasmine shifted to something a little more sour and Arke forced himself not to tense. Not to let her know he was scared.

"Dear, I was allowing you to rest after your traumatic fights," she said coolly. "Mortals need rest, do they not?"

He gritted his teeth. "Yes."

"And you get so angry at me for dragging you places when you're not ready, so I waited. Wasn't that the *polite* thing to do?"

"*Yes.*"

"Then stop bitching." He imagined her flicking her hair, likely long and free of mortal things like tangles, over her shoulder. "Many mortals would kill to be in your position. You have what you asked for and you're getting more."

"You promised to teach me about the Aether," he said, twitching his ears towards her. "You said it was important."

"It is. It's the veil between all worlds. It is also a source of power to those who know how to manipulate it. Something Abraxas Kain was already practiced at long before you got your grubby little claws on that book."

He hugged it tighter to his chest. "What do I need to do?"

There was no point in skirting around it. He wanted this lesson to be over with as soon as possible. The quicker he got it, the quicker he could get back to his friends. And kill Abraxas. Fuck his watery eyes.

He was trying to get the water back behind his eyeballs where it belonged when something shimmered in front of him. He didn't flinch because when you did that, most things in Unnethen's garden took that as a sign of weakness. But when his vision cleared he wasn't looking at another pixie, but rather a circle of glowing mist haloed by jasmine blossoms. *Not*

Unnethen, he realized after he heard her hum pleasantly behind him.

"This will take us where we need to go."

He squinted suspiciously. "A portal?"

"A tear in the Aether, so yes, a portal. This will let us walk inside it."

Considering that Unnethen used words like 'veil' and 'barrier' and 'strings' to describe the Aether, Arke didn't much like the idea of walking in it. But the choking perfume of flowers threatened to overwhelm him so he discretely covered his nose and stepped into the mist without hesitating.

And immediately fucking regretted it.

When Arke was very young, he'd been just as cranky as he was now. Only then he wasn't allowed to *do* anything. So he stole away after Tolk and did those things anyway. Since his people were no strangers to mixing magic with everyday things, he fell into a lot of situations he shouldn't have.

Like the time he ate more of the purple fungus that grew in the priest's garden walls than Tolk could on a dare.

He hadn't known it then, but that fungus was special. The priests liked to make a lot of things out of it, including spell components. It was essentially chewy magic and he'd eaten half the damn wall. He'd spent the next day and a half in hell. He turned into a plant. He made it rain. He stuck Tolk to the door. He was suddenly terrified of the color green, which was a problem for anyone trying to wrangle his slippery young ass as he ran away screaming through the city.

The magic had been so intense and taxing that Arke hadn't stayed still the whole time it was in his system. Even as a plant he somehow managed to crawl into corners his brother couldn't find. And the whole time his head was spinning. He heard whispers in his ears, flashes of strange lights dazzled his eyes and half blinded him. He was constantly shaking, constantly chilled, and overall having the worst trip of his life.

Being in the Aether felt a lot like that.

Everything was grey around him, yet prismatic at the edges. Like mist catching the sunlight at the first rays of dawn. There was no up, nor down. There just *was*. Which made no sense and perfect sense at the same time, and Arke realized he'd spent too long in Unnethen's company if he was thinking like that.

Just like with the fungus, there were whispers everywhere. Never loud enough to make out, always just on the edge of his understanding. They crept into his ears, tickled them so that he was constantly twitching as if to swat a fly.

And the *magic*.

Arke knew magic well. It took a certain amount of skill and knowledge to spin spells with nothing but ink, parchment and sheer force of will. Even with Unnethen's blessings, he found that calling it on his own was a thrill unmatched by any in the world. Tasting the iron that flooded his tongue with each spell. Watching it spin around him like an eager child ready to show off to its parent. He changed the fabric of the world whenever he made magic, something those who were born with it couldn't fathom.

But the Aether was different. The Aether *was* magic.

Pure. Undiluted. Unhindered by constraints of paper and worldly things like gravity. Arke's teeth ached from being around so much of it. The hairs in his nose shriveled and burned. His head was pounded.

And he was loving it.

He reached his hand out and the mist curled around his fingers. Then it was a hand grasping for his wrist and he jerked back. The mist hand disappeared just as the portal popped out of existence. Unnethen's tickling laugh echoed in the endless space.

"You touch what you don't understand," she said.

He scowled, holding his cold hand. "You wanted me to."

"Hm, yes I did. You know me well. Walk on, dear."

Arke skittered around where the hand disappeared, but it made no difference. Everything looked the same. It was worse than Unnethen's repeating garden, which at least tried to fool him with diversity until he recognized the loop. Here the grey stretched on. And where it did he caught glimpses of hands, yawning mouths stretched in silent screams. The arches of backs. The wisps of hair.

He shuddered.

"Do you understand now?"

There was no color, but Arke was suddenly back in the White Cairn. Flooded with cold and blue light. Trying to hide how much he was trembling as he ran to save Evren and Gyda, not because he was cold but because the ice in the glacier was so choked with magic that he felt like he was going to explode. Getting to Gail made it worse. So close to a knot of so many collected souls, it was all Arke could do to lash out with his own magic in the vain attempt to relieve the pressure building behind his eyeballs.

It had only stopped when the light from the glacier died with Gail and returned to the sky.

"It's people," he rasped. "Souls of the dead."

Unnethen hummed in approval. "Souls hold the most concentrated form of magic, even those who never practice in their lives. They burn with it. It was pure power to create a soul, and that power doesn't diminish when death claims them."

"So, everyone ends up here?" He turned in a circle. Bits of rainbow teeth and flashing skirts caught the corners of his eyes. Unnethen stayed out of sight. "What about the hells? We know they're real."

"The hells are no different than Sildenior," Unnethen replied. "Simply another world full of different beings."

That prey on mortals back in Eith, Arke thought, but didn't say aloud.

Unnethen continued. "For that matter, even the heavens where Divines and their soldiers stay is a different world. It is rare for them to come to Eith physically like myself or the devils of the hell. They haven't done so in a millennia. But they have intense power, and that is enough to influence it."

"Was enough," Arke corrected. "They ain't able to anymore."

"And why is that?"

A hand in the mist crawled towards him and he blew it away, shuffling aside as the leftover tendrils still reached for him.

"How the fuck should I know, Unnethen? I wasn't there."

"Hmm. Pity."

Arke waited for more. A little degradation, some insults, and then a thorny explanation as to why Abraxas's precious Divines were all powerful but couldn't snap through a barrier of misty asshole. Littered, of course, with comments about how wonderfully stupid mortals were, which was him.

Yet nothing came. The scent of jasmine faded and then there was another popping sound of a portal opening.

"Unnethen?" he called behind him.

"You're a fast learner. I'm sure you'll figure it out."

Arke realized what was happening a split second too late. He whirled around, turning half formed ghosts into puffs of smoke as he did. Just in time to see Unnethen's glittering foot disappear into the portal and it close behind her.

11

Arke

"**F**UCK!"

It didn't matter how many times he said it, the landscape didn't change. The misty world of the Aether remained stubborn and buzzing in his molars. The portal really was gone, not some Fey trick like he was used to.

Unnethen had left him in the land between worlds, on fucking soul strings!

"Just figure it out," he muttered in her mocking tone. "Solve the problem of a bunch of necros banishing gods fifty fuckin' years ago, Arke! Never mind that mages past and present have been shittin' themselves to learn the exact same thing and they weren't stuck stepping on people!"

Arke stomped about, dizzy but with nothing to orient himself. No horizon, no glaring sun. No sparkly trees with mouths to devour him. Just an endless, monotonous gloom.

He hated this place too. The way it made his tongue fuzzy and his eyes itchy. He *really* hated Unnethen.

"Hey!" he shouted into the void. "Anyone lookin' to answer questions?"

He stopped when something above him curled out of the mist. A long arm, fingernails broken even in this half-form. Arke could imagine the hand when it was living flesh. Cut up. Fingers broken and bent. Nails missing from their beds.

He hesitated. Maybe he was supposed to get answers from the souls here. Who else better to answer than them?

Arke forced himself to relax and let the mist hand touch his forehead.

Flashes of life assaulted his senses. The stench of blood. A lantern swinging overhead. Shards of needlelike glass being shoved into each of his knuckles. His mouth was full of blood. He couldn't scream, only gargle. His tongue was missing and he kept choking on the coppery liquid running down his throat.

Arke jerked away from the mist hand, scattering it with his spellbook. He ran his tongue over his teeth. Intact. He checked his fingers anyway, the ghost of the shards still stinging underneath his skin.

He shook his hand out. "I ain't askin' shit from you again. Whoever you were."

He paused, suddenly feeling guilty. Whoever they had been, they'd died terribly. That was torture easily recognizable by someone who'd never performed or received it. Maybe even the soul's last moments before they died.

Arke shuddered. What a shit way to go.

"Sorry 'bout your life," he muttered. "Seems like shit. I'd kill the bastards that did that for you but they're probably long dead, huh?"

The broken mist hand didn't come for him again. Arke just nodded to himself and walked, because what else could he do?

He kept away from any more wisps of souls. Touching them and reliving their deaths didn't seem like the way out, just a way to join them.

Could he die in the Aether? There was nothing around. No food or water if he needed them, and certainly no place to rest. Just an endless number of souls. If he could, then he might be the first idiot to join them like that. What a perfect way to go out, eh? Avoiding everybody and stuck with a bunch of dead assholes because of one sparkly, immortal asshole.

Out of habit, he started flipping through his spellbook. There was no origin of light but he saw everything okay. Sorin's little drawings on the front pages had been bleached of color.

Maybe it was a magic problem. He figured out how to transport his friends out of harm. Surely a portal couldn't be so different?

But then he'd been up close and personal to Abraxas's shadows doing the work for him twice. He understood their magic because it abided by Eith laws. Magic laws anyway. It was all about wrestling control from Abraxas to whoever needed the spell, and then the shadows did the work for them. Simple enough, he'd hoped.

But the kicker was that he wasn't on Eith. Maybe closer than he had been, maybe farther away. Magic shuddered through him like wind cut through holey breeches, but it was like trying to grab at air. Nothing was solid enough to latch on to.

Arke flipped through his spellbook and tore out a page. The incantation came easy and didn't even leave his lips before fire burned in his palm. Ash fell on his feet but he couldn't feel it, as if his skin had been numbed to his surroundings.

The orange light put everything into sharp, ugly contrast. Suddenly all he saw were faces gaping in terror, frozen in their death throws. The iridescence disappeared entirely. A shrill sound spiked in his ears until he couldn't hear it anymore, but his head still throbbed with pain and his ear dribbled with blood.

Hissing in pain, Arke shook out the fire in his fist. It fizzled, spark climbing in the air only to be swallowed by mist. The sound stopped; the tortured faces disappeared. Everything turned soft again.

"What," he rubbed his shoulder against his ear to clean the blood, "the *fuck?*"

The souls didn't answer him. No hands reached for him. Or even a wayward foot. But the air had changed. Things felt still.

Arke was small and pissed off enough to know when he was being watched by something bigger. It happened a lot. But the feeling of heavy eyes on him when he saw nothing actually terrified him for the first time since he saw Gyda taking Evren's bloody body from Orenlion.

Goblins, and Arke in particular, were no strangers to being hunted. Tough as they were, they weren't exactly top of the food chain. The big eyes were to see in the dark of their burrows, yes, but also to better make out stalking predators. Their ears were that big to hear anyone creeping up on them.

Arke didn't hear shit. Maybe that was because of the throbbing ache in his eardrums, or possibly because everything was so suffocatingly quiet in the Aether that he was getting sick of hearing his own breathing. Regardless, Arke heard nothing, but he saw plenty.

A shadow just ahead. Something tall. Large. Something that looked big enough to be a giant out of one of Sol and Gyda's stories, but this had six legs and a panther-like body. Its tail was long and curled at its back so it didn't touch the ground. Dozens of red eyes that made his skin crawl stared back at him.

Being left in the Aether was one thing. Being left with a monster made out of nightmares was something else entirely, and there weren't enough curse words in Arke's vocabulary to accurately describe how fucked up that something else was.

Instinct alone tore another page from his book. It was always fire with him. Fire came the easiest. It kept people away, it burned away all the bad shit, was easy to manipulate with emotion and looked the coolest. So the spell came easy. A cluster of burning red glyphs swirling around him. Protecting him, threatening to destroy all those who came too close.

It also sent the souls of the Aether into such a panic that Arke dropped his book and clutched his ears to keep the sound at bay. His glyphs fluttered away and died with his concentration. He snatched his spellbook up, not even bothering to wipe the blood from his ears this time, and ran.

He didn't know why, because there was no place to run. There was nowhere to hide. The monster had six legs taller than Gyda stacked up twice compared to his stumpy little ones. If only he was taller, a wish he'd made since he was young and aware of things bigger than Tolk.

There was no horizon for his perspective to change, but his stomach lurched as suddenly his stride grew longer. He stumbled, looking down to find the mist clinging to his legs like the longest pair of stilts ever. He cackled a laugh that echoed endlessly.

The laugh reached the monster not behind him but directly in front of him.

Arke yelped and threw himself backward. He landed on his back staring up at the monster who hadn't been there before.

Was this a dream?

Hot breath showered him, the realest thing he'd felt since entering the Aether. Jaws opened wide. What kind of monster needed that many teeth?

Definitely not a dream.

In times past, an arrow would sail over him and sink into the mouth of the monster. Or Sorin would be standing between them like a big ol' human wall made of scrawny legs and bottled lightning laughter.

The jaws of the monster started to snap him up, but then the mist rose above him. A wall of gangly limbs and the essence of laughter. He couldn't hear it, but he felt it. The lightning brushing his skin with energy that reminded him of the foolish Vasa.

And then Arke understood.

He got back up on his normal legs, stilts abandoned, and backed up. He was sucking in breaths but that didn't seem to matter. The air didn't help. Maybe he wasn't even breathing—nope, stopping that thought right there.

Aether was pure magic. The monster was not. He couldn't will it away because it would be *gone* now if he could. But the Aether was his to mold, shape, command.

To tear.

The wall went down and the monster shook its snout. All dozens of those burning eyes fixed on him. Seething, searching, *hunting*.

Arke backed up minuscule steps compared to the loping gate of the monster, but it was enough. Enough to send the monster into a dash towards him, mouth frothing. Enough for Arke's hands to flatten behind him and pull at the souls there.

In the split second before the charging beat reached him, Arke couldn't help but think of Gyda and how she would've laughed at such a challenge. Missing her, her strength and her bravery, threatened to overwhelm him.

The popping of the portal felt like a crack of thunder across the silence of the Aether. Arke threw himself to the side before an icy wind from beyond could even grasp his back. The rush of fur, talons and snapping jaws passed over him, unable to stop their momentum. Arke looked up just in time to see the monster hurtle into the portal he opened as wisps of snow fluttered into the grey world in-between. He willed it shut and without hesitation it slammed closed behind the monster, leaving Arke alone.

He laid back, thudding his head against the ground. Or what passed for a ground in the Aether. His heart was trying to punch its way out of his ribcage and he was half tempted to let it. But he waited for himself to calm down and catch up to what he saw, what he'd done. And then a raspy giggle startled him.

His own.

It's been too long since he'd laughed.

Still chuckling, he stood up and dusted himself off. Picked up his fallen spellbook and smiled at the nothing around him.

"Lesson learned, bitch!" he crowed, and his echo joined him across eternity.

One part of it was at least. He could leave, but he was no closer to figuring out how to banish gods the way Vernes did. That was something Unnethen obviously knew but wouldn't tell him. Why she'd continue her games when the world was at stake he didn't know. But he knew two things for certain.

One, he could go anywhere.

Two, he wasn't going back to her.

The world waited. *Worlds* really. He couldn't tell if it was the Aether or himself that hummed with excitement. A year ago, he thought the most amazing thing he could do was spit fire and ice from thin air, but now he was somewhere no living mortal had been, learning what no living mortal ever had before.

Those tall fuckers at the Greyreach Conclave could go fuck themselves. They had nothing on him.

Although it made no difference, Arke picked a different spot to open his next portal. There were a dozen places he wanted to go and numerous faces he wanted to see. But there was only one person who he knew for sure was in one place. Besides, he didn't know how these things worked. Better to stick with imagining a place and meeting someone he knew was there, versus hoping for a person and getting nowhere.

Sorin would have to wait.

Arke waved his hand and the Aether snapped open. The smells of an ancient forest assaulted his nose. Fresh sap, rotting leaves, the tang of something animal and metallic. He smiled and didn't hesitate to step back into the Deep Wood.

12

Gyda

When the figure disappeared and Gyda was left with nothing but the windblown snow and clouds, she stopped thinking of Abraxas and instead mentally wandered back to her youth. She'd tried not to in the past, since even happy memories were tainted with visions of the Long Night that left her alone and frightened for the first time in her life. But the trip up the mountain felt like something out of one of her foya's stories, so it felt fitting to remember them now.

Back when Lostwater was still covered in ice, but lively and bright on the inside. Back when she was very young and small, although still taller than the other children her age by several inches. Back when the fall of the Long Night meant stories galore to keep the children happy and the adults occupied.

The moment the sun went down, everybody gathered in one large house—the largest they had which still fit everyone in their small village with room to spare—and shut the door and sealed it tight to keep out the cold. They heaped on their furs and passed out steaming mugs of milk. Fires were stoked carefully to make sure they could burn evenly through the whole Long

Night. Sweet meats were handed through the furs like secret treats, although all the children knew they were getting some and eagerly waited for their turn.

Gyda, young enough that her hands were smooth and soft, had nibbled on hers and watched with eager eyes as her foya spun a tale about moving mountains. It was her favorite, although if she had said that he would've laughed and said all his stories were her favorite. Which wasn't a lie.

Like her, like she eventually would, he towered a good foot and a half over the tallest adults. His grey skin was uncovered by the furs the others draped over themselves, and his beard clinked with the bone beads he had woven in their course, red strands.

"The mountains have legs," he would say, spreading his large arms in front of the children. They'd gasp, as they always did. Gyda alone could snicker with the adults because she heard this story before.

"A long time ago, the world was so young that there were no clans to wander the ice," he began. "There was only unending wilderness, as far as the eye could see. Farther still. There were no hunters, no prey. In those days, the sun never set and the world only dimmed when the moon danced in front of it. The trees sang, for the world was quiet without us mortals to make a ruckus."

At that, the adults laughed again. A couple of them jeered at a particularly loud couple who'd just been bonded in marriage and had many sleepless nights. But a wave of her foya's hand had quieted them down.

He always had a mischievous twinkle in his eye, as if he knew something very funny he'd share later when the timing was right.

He began again. "The trees sang, and the mountains walked, and the ocean danced so much that it often fell out of its shores and into the forests, muddling the songs of the trees and making them very cross. But in all of that was the first creature. Not born by mother or egg. Not made by the sky or stone. This strange creature crawled from the ground after hearing the singing of the trees and found the world beautiful."

"What was it?" one of the smallest ones cried.

Her foya smiled. "What do you want it to be?"

One of the older kids scoffed. "I'll bet it was a bear."

"Since when do bears come out of the ground, half-wit?" his friend snickered.

"When they're done hibernating for winter, obviously." The boy reddened around the ears. Gyda couldn't remember his name, but she remembered feeling very smug because a bear was the stupidest animal to be the first.

So began the chorus of guesses from the children.

"It's a wolf, I'll bet! They're strong and smart."

"Only in packs. If it crawled from the ground it must be a rabbit."

"Why would a rabbit be the first creature? That's dumber than a bear."

"A bear isn't dumb—"

"It's a fox! They burrow and they're cunning."

"What? A scrawny little fox? No way."

"Bears eat foxes."

"Enough with the bears—"

Her foya's booming laughter sounded through the hall and drowned out the children's arguing. "Perhaps we could listen to the story, and find out for ourselves?"

A chorus of begrudging agreements rose up to meet him, and so the story continued.

"This creature was the first of anything. The first to be able to do all the things the world couldn't do. When the sea danced, the creature did too, and sang a tune for it. When the trees sang, it danced with them and put their still branches to shame. And when it wandered between ocean and forest, it walked with the mountains. While the trees and the sea were put off by something that could do more than them, the mountains found they liked the company. Wherever the creature went, dance and song followed and amused them. They no longer had to rely on the fickleness of trees and water for entertainment.

"The creature saw the world while it was young. And as the ages passed, it watched the sun grow tired and start to dip below the horizon to rest. It always came back up, but now the moon could shine as well. Night was sweet and restful, and soon a world that had known nothing of sleep began to still.

"The ocean settled into its shores for naps. The trees quieted their songs for the shadowed hours. The mountains began to put down roots.

"But the creature wasn't content. Where night fell, it was restless and alone. The world was too quiet, and too still. And very, very lonely. So it decided to wake up one of the mountains, an old friend at this point, and ask it for help."

The bear boy raised his hand. "Couldn't the creature just keep waking the mountains up?"

Her foya grinned at him knowingly. "Have you ever tried to move a sleeping mountain?"

He shrank back, red around the ears again. "No. It's impossible."

"Only because they have slept for so long that there is no waking them," he replied gently. "Our friend had seen them just settle down for a nap, and was much stronger than us, so it was able to wake a mountain.

"After hearing the plea from its friend, the mountain pondered for a long while, then said that it had no worldly idea of how to make the creature's life less lonely. Even mountains couldn't stay awake forever, and they didn't want to. It offered instead for the creature to climb to the very top of its back and ask the moon to bring back the sun so that they would never rest again.

"The creature did that, and it was no small journey. You think our mountains now are large? The ones of young Eith touched the stars themselves! And so new were the stars to the creature that when it got to the top it stared at them with a wide open mouth and swallowed one by accident!"

He made the sound like choking on a piece of fish, and all the necessary moves to it as well that had the children in hysterics.

"By now, the creature couldn't speak to the moon because there was a star in its throat. And stars are tricky, stubborn things that don't like falling into strange mouths. But when the creature hummed, for it couldn't sing, it liked it. When the creature danced, the star liked that too. And walking was something stars couldn't do at all. So they made a deal. The star would help the creature so long as it was allowed to stay. They agreed.

"With a rock graciously gifted by the mountain, a bit of salt left by the ocean, and a handful of pine from the trees, the creature gathered these things together and spat out the star into them. And from this strange mixture, the creature made something like it."

Her foya spread his hands again. "Five fingers, two hands. Five toes, two feet. Legs and arms and a strong middle for the star to rest. A throat for a voice to sing. Eyes to see the world better." He let his hands down. "Can anyone tell me what the creature is now?"

The children shifted in their seats. The answer seemed obvious but that meant it was wrong. The only one still was Gyda, who strained in her seat so she didn't spit out the answer. She knew this story very well and loved it so much that she could almost recite it with her foya.

He caught her eyes and laughed. "Yes, daughter? You look to burst your own star out your throat if you do not speak."

"A giant!" she'd said breathlessly. "The creature was the first giant."

He smiled warmly at her, even though it was no special thing for her to know this. "It was indeed. And after the first giant, and then the second who bore a star, others followed. The stars grew jealous of the fun the two were having during the night, and fell to the earth begging to be given bodies. More came, and soon there was a need for names to help everyone remember who was who. Among the best of them was the youngest, the last star to fall, Jalaa.

"By the time she was made, the sky looked like it does now. Dark and still full of many stars but much fewer than before. The mountains did not wake from their naps anymore. The sea only danced when it felt particularly spiteful, and the trees had all lost their singing voice. The giants spread out to the world, making their best of these new changes. But Jalaa, youngest and brightest, stayed with the first mountain. The mountain that the first giant had climbed to talk to the moon, who's rock made the second giant's skin. She decided that this was a special place, a good place to make her home. And since it was still quite high and treacherous, she helped the giants who were weaker cross.

"So became Jalaa the Watcher. Forever guiding, forever diligent from her spot at the top of the world. She lived through the ages of gods and mortals, helping and hindering both in equal measure. It is said that as the sky grew taller and her mountain shorter, she came to love the funny little creatures that looked like her, but much smaller."

The bear boy perked up again. "Us!"

He chuckled. "Yes, us. Even those who do not carry giant blood. Especially those, she is most fond of. Because they remind her of the days when the world was young, and the sky was full of light even when it was dark. It is said that if you can find that special mountain and climb to the very top, you can find her there still. If you are not worthy of her time, she will lead you safely down. If you challenge her, she will kill you in an honest fight. But if you are worthy, if the soul inside shines as bright as her own, then she will grant you the wisdom you seek to carry on. And then," he sat back, "you won't need her help to get back down. For you will have the wisdom of the Watcher, and know how the world bends to your feet."

Gyda, far older now and having lost her foya, hadn't thought of his stories in some time. The giant ruins beneath Dirn-Darahl had reminded her of him, painfully, and she'd kept him from her memory as best she could after that. His sword was hers, and she'd broken it. She'd served the monster that killed him and had nearly destroyed all the Ikedree in the Expanse because she let fear overcome her. Her foya would've forgiven these things, but Gyda found that he would've forgiven her if she'd slain him herself. He had a soft heart. She missed it terribly.

The little girl in her that longed for stories and sweet meats delighted in the long, aching journey up the mountain. It felt like something out of his tales, like the rock would suddenly open its eyes and start spouting poetry. She decided to think of herself as the first giant making the hard trek up to the stars, alone and miserable.

Because the figure had disappeared and hadn't come back, so Gyda was just left with a sad, slow trudge through snow that seemed to last forever. She was making progress, barely. If her splintering lungs were any indication, the air was getting thinner. Either that, or she was getting weaker. She'd forgotten when she'd last felt her toes.

The dismal grey of the day stretched on. Gyda was thankful because night would bring even colder weather she couldn't survive. As she climbed, rested, struggled, and then rested some more, the clouds got closer. Soon she was breathing them in, moist air chilling her sore lungs. The mountain blurred even further and she could barely see more than a few feet in front of her.

And still, she climbed.

The first color she saw wasn't even color. It just wasn't grey or white, just a shadow. Maybe it had once been plum, or blood-red, or maybe a rich navy. Now it was just black, as far as she could tell, hanging limply off a jagged rock.

Gyda grasped the cloak, half stiff with frost crystals. It was old, thick yet fraying at the edges. It spoke to its quality to have survived intact in such weather. The hood was an extravagant thing she'd seen Etherakian nobles favor, more fabric than could cover the heads of three humans. Whoever had lost it was long gone and even if they weren't, Gyda was taking the cloak.

She shook off as much of the frost as she could and then swung it over her shoulders. The fabric was cool against her skin, but warmed slowly. She burrowed inside, lifting up the ridiculously large hood to cover her head. She would take a tiny miracle to keep her going. The cloak didn't do much, but the extra layer on her raw skin was a blessing she wouldn't let go of even in death.

She stumbled forward another few steps, properly swaddled, and looked up at the clouds. She couldn't see far at all, only a few feet still. The peak could be anywhere, and she wasn't even sure that's where she was going. The figure said up to the clouds, not necessarily above them.

But besides the cloak there was shit-all to see. Rock and snow, wisps of clouds playing with her eyes, and a shadow prowling around her.

Gyda froze.

The shadow was enormous. She couldn't see its exact shape through the fog, but it stretched well over twenty feet long. Six legs she could see, each one so silent that she couldn't hear the snow crunch beneath them. A long neck she imagined ended in a hideous face. Only a whisper of wind alerted her to its movements.

It was circling. Cutting her path off.

Gyda's first instinct was to run away, which did nothing but piss her off. She was not the woman to run away from anything, even if she was weaponless and weaker than a damned kitten.

Fighting wasn't an option, so that left her back to running. Not away, but forward.

She winced inwardly. Running when she could barely walk without losing her breath sounded like a fantastic way to get killed. It also sounded like something Evren would do. Reckless and foolhardy, with a crooked grin on her lips and eyes that seemed to say, *Well, why not at least try?*

Gyda was out of options and feeling both nostalgic and very foolish. So she gathered up her cloak so it wouldn't hinder her legs, watched for the creature's shadow to move just a little more, and then she bolted.

Or, well, she would've at her peak. If she'd had her strength, Gyda would've torn up the mountain with a war cry on her lips and a sword in her hand, no doubt covering her friends as they made the mad dash to safety. But now she was stumbling through snow rather than running, wheezing loud enough that she might as well been screaming, and already her legs wanted to give out on her.

Well, fuck that. No way she lived through Abraxas fucking Kain to die to an oversized monster that wouldn't even show its face.

Making the decision to lose momentum, Gyda scooped up a loose rock the size of her fist and held it to her chest. Her forearm burned with the small effort, and the little added weight seemed to drag her down like she had Arke sitting on the tail end of her cloak instead.

The monster was silent. It was fast. She saw the precise moment its head snapped to her and distantly wondered if she could've snuck around it. Likely not. It could see her better than she could see it and there was nothing to hide behind. Still, there was that moment of flashing white fear when its body angled towards her own with supernatural speed that she regretted her decision to run.

As if it had been any choice at all.

Gyda brought up her memory of Abraxas's blade shattering her own, and that rage was just enough to drive her forward. She turned away from the beast, instead focusing ahead. She put everything she had into her legs to drive her forward. Muscle after fiery muscle that had never failed her before and wouldn't now. She ran for her life, displacing show with each step.

The air was hot and wet near her left leg as the jaws of something nasty almost got her. There was no hiss or growl of frustration, no smashing of rocks as it corrected behind her. The mountain was deadly quiet except for her labored breathing.

There! Just a few feet ahead. The cloud mist parted enough for her to make out staggered stones. Steps, she realized, before something latched onto the edge of her cloak and jerked her back.

Gyda landed on her chest, biting her tongue with her clashing teeth and the rock digging painfully into her ribs. Snow scraped like daggers as she was dragged backwards. All the progress she'd made disappeared in seconds.

That pissed her off too.

Finally, a cry of familiar rage tore through her throat. She twisted around on her back and brought the stone up onto the beast's snout. She couldn't see much beyond its dappled-grey fur and teeth longer than her arm. But the rock hit just right, next to the quivering nose.

A spurt of blue blood on the snow. The creature reared back in a silent scream and the tension in Gyda's cloak vanished. She scrambled to her feet and ran for the stairs.

One foot after the other, closer and closer. The snow beneath her feet quivered with every step of the monster behind her, gaining on her. She could feel its hot breath, smell the metallic tang of its blood like a cloud around her. Be it fear or rage that kept her going, Gyda ran. She ran until her feet hit the first step, and then she tripped and fell.

She dropped the rock to catch herself and the clatter it made echoed across the whole mountain. Panting, Gyda pulled herself up and turned around. If she was to die she would meet it head on.

The shadow grew above her. Pieces of the monster became visible. More dappled fur. A long tail ending in bulbous spikes that reminded her of a war hammer. Feet like an eagle's, with the talons piercing the rock just below the first step.

The face reared back, jaws widening. Gyda tapped three times on her chest again and was halfway to the second tap when it lunged for her.

A howl cut through the air and from behind her a blur of brown fur soared and smashed into the monster's neck. Another silent scream that did nothing but shake Gyda's bones and part the clouds a little. But the small—compared to the monster—brown thing held onto the jowls of the beast with a vengeance. The creature bucked and twisted its head back and forth, backing up all the while. It wasn't until the monster's claws were gone from the stairs that the brown thing dropped from the beast's neck and backed up to Gyda's side.

Gyda almost didn't believe her eyes. It was Sorin's worg. Brown fur crusted with ice and muzzle coated in blue blood. He growled at the beast that prowled at the edge, shaking off blood and sending it spattering on the snow. The blood didn't melt the snow when it hit.

Slowly, with the resignation of someone who'd been beaten but was promising another fight, the beast shrank back into the clouds and left nothing but its blood to prove it had ever been there.

Gyda slumped on the stairs, gasping for breath. Before she knew it a wet, bloody nose was snuffing her face. The worg's tongue smeared blue blood over her cheeks. She scratched its pointed ears and leaned on its broad shoulders, savoring its warmth and familiar smell.

"Don't tell Sorin," she muttered into its fur. "But saving you was the best decision he ever made."

13

Sorin

The days that followed, Sorin saw little of Vayne. Sahar he only saw at night, and she was often asleep by the time he got to her. His constant companion, one he expected to bolt or be snatched up quickly, was Enola.

Enola swearing as her fingers bled all over the newly cleaned pot. Enola dragging something too heavy for her to carry. Enola using crates to get what she needed instead of asking for help. Enola glued to his side to avoid Willie's gaze, although the cook didn't care who she was so long as she was working. Enola listening to his stories and arguing with everything he said.

"No way you killed a sea serpent," she said, handing him fishbones to toss away. She gutted the fish far better than he ever could with his bad hand, so he was stuck leaning against the counter as she fileted and dumped nasty things his way.

He wrinkled his nose and shoved the bones into his pile.

"You keep saying I can't do these things."

"You can't."

"You weren't there!"

Enola groaned long and loud, the way kids always did when

adults were being insufferable and they could get away with it. "Come *on*. A horde of zombies is one thing. But a sea serpent? Impossible."

"I didn't say I did it alone." He scowled. "I had help. A couple of mages, a four-way plan to whittle it down and piss it off. *My* plan, thank you very much. The harpoon was a lucky shot, I'll give you that, and it was the fireball spell that really did him in. But everyone was dying until I figured shit out."

"Still don't believe you."

Sorin threw his hands up in the air, scattering needly bones everywhere. "There's no pleasing you! First it was, 'Oh, there's no lava in the Vanguard Mountains,' as if you've lived there and would know better. The next you're telling me that there's no possible way mermaids exist underground. And now this!"

Enola started giggling, just as he thought she would. It was an awful little laugh, abrasive and loud, but it was the only laughter he ever heard that wasn't Vayne's and he loved it.

He grinned, his theatrics done, and started picking up his fallen bits of fish.

"You know," he mused. "You'd make a great adventurer."

"Yeah, I'd kill more monsters than you." She snickered.

He rolled his eyes. "Yes, yes, you'd be far better than me."

"Double the gold or nothing! No," she paused. "Worse than nothing! I'd befriend the monster and make them my bitch."

"You'd be a menace. Your party would have to put up with you and your antics all day and night."

"Because I'm indispensable!"

Sorin snorted, standing up and making his pile again. He wiped his hands off on his pants. She handed him more guts just as he finished.

He made a face and let the guts slide out of his palm. "Yeah, indispensably annoying. You know, I had a friend like you."

"Bet you didn't."

"Everything that comes out of my mouth is pure truth," he

declared, poking her shaking shoulders with his finger. She started cackling. "Stop—hells, kid, stop laughing at me!"

But she didn't and that awful laugh made Sorin's sad little grin turn into a full-blown, honest smile. It felt strange on his face after so long of careful frowns and scowls. Hells, he barely had the strength to give Sahar anything fake anymore.

But Enola was cackling and he was joining in. And it was the best thing he'd felt since dancing in Rhienwall. The smell of fish, the slime in his hands, the oppressive gloom, none of it left. But for a brief moment he was okay.

He was telling stories by the fire for his friends, enduring their eyerolls at his embellishments. He was dancing to Fey music, free and happy. There was a sunrise above him and a cup of something strong and hot in his hands and his best friend on his shoulders.

Everything was fine. Everything was safe.

For a moment.

When the laughter died, Enola kept up the little humming of laughter in her chest. She kept her grin. But Sorin didn't. He looked at the shards of bone and saw Gyda's broken blade. He looked at the guts and saw rows and rows of Serevadians hanging dead by their feet, bleeding shadows and blood. When Enola's knife flashed, he was reminded viscerally of the flash of Serevadian armor.

"My friend had blood like you," Sorin said after a while. "It nearly killed her, but we helped her get better."

Enola paused, digging at a scale with her knife. "I'm not sick."

"I know. She was. She got better with some help from my other friend."

"How?"

There wasn't any mocking in her voice, just a genuine curiosity.

"They fell in love," he said with a rueful smile. "Gyda gave half her heart to Evren so that she could survive. It was the most dramatic, fairytale-like shit I'd ever witnessed, and I wasn't even there to see it. Just the outcome. But it was obvious that it wasn't a story, that no lie could ever come close to shining as bright as that truth.

"They were insufferable together. Evren on her own had this annoying way of doing things the self-sacrificing way. Gyda was similar, and how we ended up fighting the sea serpent and undead."

"Zombies."

"Whatever." He flicked a bone out of the way. It skittered a shorter distance than it should've. "They loved each other in a different way than they loved us. I don't think that half-a-heart thing would've worked otherwise. I believe in love. I believe in finding people you want to be around for the rest of your life. I just didn't think soulmates were a thing until I saw them."

Enola picked at a scale until it pried free. She set it aside, one side silvery blue and the other coated pink.

"What happened to them?"

"They died."

It was the first time he'd said it out loud, and the words felt as heavy as iron chains on his tongue. He blinked away the responding tears because if he wiped them away he'd get fish guts on his face and it would be all he'd smell all day.

"Our last quest was to save a friend who'd been lost to us for a while," Sorin went on because Enola wasn't interrupting now. "Only he wasn't himself. He hurt us. We were trapped at the bottom of the ocean with no way out except a spell that hadn't been done before. A spell that would kill Gyda if used."

Enola gasped and turned to face him. "Why?"

"All magic comes at a price. Evren's Blood magic used to hurt her when she used it, but with Gyda's sacrifice, it hurt Gyda instead. Gyda and Evren made the choice to lose each other in order to save us."

"You and Sahar?"

"There were more of us," Sorin croaked. "I had a worg I'd

raised. My friend Sol, she . . . she was already hurt when Evren did the spell. And there was Arke. None of them made it."

Enola was unreadable. The way she stared at him made him want to change the subject to something better, but the look in her eyes told him she wouldn't allow it. Like with every kid, once she latched onto something she didn't let go.

"Your friend, Evren," Enola began slowly. "She had special blood like me?"

Sorin nodded. "Kept us alive more than once. Not that she's a model for how best to use it. She was a damn idiot at the best of times. But she was better at it than Nerezza."

"Because she used it to help people."

Sorin nodded. "To help us. Yeah."

Enola started chewing on her lip. "Why do you say I'm like her if my blood hurts people?"

"Because you both have weird laughs and make fun of me. Because you both make that weird face when I do something intentionally stupid, like your eyebrows are about to fuse together." He sighed. "Because Evren thought her blood was a curse too until she learned to call it a gift. She hurt people too. The first things she did with Blood magic were hurt. She learned to be better. A magic like that, that makes you sacrifice yourself and those you love for power? You have to rein it in, make sure you use it on your terms."

"How did she learn?" Enola asked eagerly.

Sorin laughed. "She got lucky. She had us to keep her in check, and if that wasn't enough she had a *really* bad example of what she could become if she didn't get a grip."

Enola suddenly deflated. She folded her legs and plopped down heavily on the crates she was standing on, knife in her lap and chin on her fist. She sniffled once and Sorin settled down beside her.

He set his hand on her boney knee. "Evren also didn't have an evil captain using her against her will."

Enola blinked furiously, refusing to look at him. "My blood hurts people."

"No, it's taken and used without your permission."

"But it's still mine, Sorin!" She shoved his hand off. "It's my fault you're here and not saving the world. It's my fault everyone here is miserable and that Vayne wins every time."

That little chest of hers was heaving hard breaths and no matter how many times she kept batting her eyes she couldn't keep the tears from falling. Her face screwed up as she tried, wrinkling, folding, fusing her bushy brows together.

"I wish I was dead so they couldn't use me."

Sorin was on his knees in front of her faster than he could blink. He grabbed her shoulders and when she struggled to get away he held on hard enough to make his left hand spasm. He ignored it.

"Enola, look at me." She didn't. "Look at me."

Watery blue eyes met his and he loosened his grip. She was shaking, not fighting, now. Tears ran like waterfalls down her gaunt cheeks.

"Don't think like that," he said. "Don't ever wish that. None of what happened to us is your fault. Not a damn bit of it. You are alive because you are meant to be, do you understand? You are bright, and funny, and ridiculously strong for your size. You could have this crew at your beck and call if it was a better ship."

"But it's not," she said miserably.

"No," he admitted. "It isn't. But I'll be damned if I let you think that's because of you. I need you to remember that above all else, you remind me of Evren because you're brave. This is a ship full of people so scared they refuse to look up without permission. You ran at the first opportunity. Evren was a survivor, and so are you.

"I meant what I said, Enola, that you'd be an adventurer that would make this world great if you only had the chance. But dead people don't do that. Your heart has to keep beating for you to change the world."

Enola wiped her nose. "I'm not that brave."

"Braver than me." He offered her a wry smile. "Brave enough to stick by my side and hold onto a knife when Willie tells you to put it back. Brave enough to survive the witch and Vayne every time there's a storm."

He couldn't tell her that he thought about dying all the time. He couldn't tell her that those thoughts were always the loudest unless he kicked them out before they took root. Those weren't fair things to tell children.

"Do you know where every adventurer starts?" he asked.

She shook her head.

"Wanting a better world. It means they start in shit places like this and take matters into their own hands to make them better."

"I can't make this ship better!" she cried, and he rushed to shush her.

"And I'm not asking you to, I swear. Leave that to me. All I want from you is the promise that when you leave this ship behind, you'll do something brave."

"Like what?"

"Like living, Enola. Living is the bravest thing you can ever do in this world."

14

Solri

The mystery key dug into Sol's sweaty hand as she once again took to the walls. Leave it to Ainthe to not tell her *where* the key went. There was nothing quite like a mystery to go along with the threat of their culture's collapsing at the whims of a mad god.

It wasn't to unlock the door at the top of the stairs. That would've been too easy and, frankly, disappointing. So far no one had caught onto her escapes through the walls so she'd keep using them until she couldn't. She had the distinct feeling that every time she stepped into them, that the times she could use them was dwindling down. A foolish fear. If they hadn't found them before now, then the likelihood of them randomly busting down a wall while she was in it and putting her in chains was slim to none.

Regardless, Sol hadn't risked leaving the building like that first time again. The news that Karas was alive and close was enough to give her hope, but she couldn't risk being caught. She needed a way to get him and his people safely out.

She needed to know what Catarmon was, and how to keep it from Abraxas.

Huffing slightly, Sol got to the part of the wall she always used to leave, now marked with a little rune for safety she could feel for when she lost her way. She pressed her ear up against the wall and winced.

Voices. Angry ones.

Not for the first time she longed for Evren. Now, just for translations, but Sol could go for a crooked grin, and some backup anytime. Before that overwhelming feeling of loneliness latched onto her like a nasty tick, she pushed it away. All thoughts of Evren receded. Sol could mourn her, the rest of the Wandering Sols, and all those she lost in Dirn-Darahl later.

The voices were muffled through the stone. Sol could only pick out the emotions in them. Anger boiled at the surface of both voices. Below one was a hint of pleading, of desperation, and a healthy dose of fear. The other was bored, done with the conversation. Their word was final.

Sol couldn't hear the footsteps, but she felt them leave in the vibrations of the rock. One quickly. The other lingering. She imagined this one taking a deep breath to center themselves before following the other, proverbial tail tucked between their legs.

The door hummed with the walls when it opened and Sol slipped out of her hiding spot. The wall shut behind her and as she turned to walk further, she snatched her leg back.

The room was a mess. Whoever made it their home clearly hadn't kept up with it. The desk overflowed with papers and objects, pieces of kohl and melted down candles next to shining pebbles of Luminstones. The blankets from the bed were wadded into misshapen balls in the corner, the mattress bare and cold.

But the floor was worse. The stubs of kohl on the desk must've been the remnants of many others, because the whole floor was choked with drawings in black. Runes she'd never seen before. Magic theories she only recognized based on how they were written, but the language was still far beyond her. Numbers . . . numbers everywhere. At least she could understand them when she stared long enough. Their numeric system wasn't all that different from dwarven.

So many were smudged out. Erased and leaving grey spots on the floor. Some were simply struck out, as if the time it would take to erase them wouldn't be worth it. She saw small numbers, and they were all scribbled out. Bigger ones circled then crossed out. Bigger and bigger, with more agitation in the strokes until the final numbers were so black and jagged that Sol could only imagine the writer digging the stub of kohl into the floor with gritted teeth and a pained expression.

"Over nine hundred," Sol mused. "Of what?"

Troops came to mind, but she knew Serevadian numbers were well over that. This was something else, and without a translator she couldn't figure out what.

Sol made a mental note to ask Ainthe the next time she saw her, cringed at that idea, and then set to picking her way across the room, stepping only on the rare empty spots, or the areas that feet had already smudged before. It felt like child's play, but she still held her breath until she made it to the door.

She swiped a couple Luminstone pebbles and shoved them into her pocket. Pressing her ear to the door, she heard nothing. No whispers of breath or footfalls. Gently prying the door open, she peaked just to be sure. An empty hallway.

Not thinking of her luck in fear of jinxing it, she slipped out of the room and shut the door behind her. To her right was the locked door to the stairs down to her room. To her left was the rest of the hallway. More doors to rooms, and a bisection at the end leading to more of the house.

Sol crept forward carefully, ignoring how exposed she felt as she passed each door. Any minute one of them could open and she would be caught. Or someone could walk through the hallway and she'd be seen. She couldn't even count on the luck of Abraxas finding her if Catarmon really was using him without his knowledge.

She'd just be fucked one way or another.

Voices.

She whipped her head around. Coming from the end of the hall from one of the bisecting hallways. Shadows of two walking figures patterned the walls.

Sol took her chance, slipping into the closest door and shutting it as the voices got louder. She barely had a chance to notice that it was the bathing room, her favorite, before pressing back up against the door.

A little crack, a little peek, and she was rewarded with the vision of two bored Serevadian guards carrying trays of food. They came from the left side of the bisection, and one turned to the right with a groan and a wave. The other laughed and said something short in his language before keeping down the hallway that would lead to Sol's stairs. They always left the food at the top of the stairs just beyond the door, but Sol couldn't help the little spike of anxiety at the idea of this guard being the one to check on her room and finding it empty.

Minutes passed and no alarm was raised. Her food guard waited patiently at the bisection for the other to come back. It took him longer, and when he returned he still had the tray of food. The way he was biting his words could only mean he was cursing. The other guard laughed, patted his back, and they continued to bitch as they went back the way they came.

Sol waited, counting her breaths, before leaving the bathroom behind and darting to the right side of the bisection. Food meant prisoners, and prisoners normally meant locks. Ainthe said her friends weren't there, but maybe someone else was. Someone who could help her with Catarmon.

The winding passage was long and barren. Unerringly quiet, which Sol hated. If she could hear herself breathing, she imaged anyone who might be looking for her could too. There were few doors, and each one she cracked open revealed barren rooms with little light. At the end, a very mirror to her own, was a staircase leading up.

She took the stairs two at a time, gripping the key the whole way, when she got to the top there was a door left ajar. Sol pushed it aside and climbed through into the third-floor room.

It was wide, its ceiling peaked and tall. A generous sized walkway separated two cells made purely of iron bars spaced together so tightly, Sol wasn't sure she could fit her wrist through. The cells were large, one on either side of the room and taking up all the wall space. One was dark and stank of congealed blood and rot. The other was lit only with a few Luminstones and was comfortably furnished with a bed, rug, wide desk scattered with vials and bottles of various brightly colored liquids. Some steamed and bubbles, the smell wafting from them chemical and nearly as bad as the dark cell. But with them came another, better, stroke of luck.

"Temsen?" Sol ran to the cell and pressed her face against the bars.

The dwarf inside jumped, spilling some chemicals. He cried out, taking the time to blot it up with shaking hands. When he turned to look at her she nearly wept in relief.

But it wasn't Temsen. He was built too thick. His beard was far too short and his head too bald. And the burn scar along the side of his head was too distinct.

"Jalaa's sweet tits, you are a sight," Karas breathed.

He was at the bars, clutching Sol's hands. The two had never been close and Sol still found his actions distasteful, but the sight of a friendly face, of hands that were dwarven covering hers, was enough to make her shed a few tears.

"What are you doing here?" she hissed. "I was told you were down in the fields."

"I am during the day. At night they have me makin' shit." He jerked his head back to the desk of chemicals.

"Temsen . . ."

He shook his head no. He looked down at his feet, jaw tight.

"Got him in the first attack. It was an accident. They wanted him alive but he . . . he wasn't gonna go back. Bad explosion. Took him and 'bout a dozen of the grey bastards with him."

Sol let out a heavy breath. "I'm so sorry,"

Karas shrugged his wide shoulders. "Me too. But Temsen had the right idea. I wanted to live and make them pay, so when they came for me I didn't do the honorable thing and fall on my sword." He pushed away from the bars, away from her, and rubbed the top of his head. "They think I can recreate some of Temsen's work."

Sol eyed the vials. "Can you?"

He barked a laugh. "Not anythin' worth using. Simple shit a toddler could mix together. They don't allow me anything that would break me out of here, if that's what you're getting at."

"No need." Sol flashed the key between the bars. "I'm fairly sure this is for you."

He blinked at it, not even having the courtesy to look surprised or grateful. When those eyes flicked over to her face, he said, "Tell me you and your group of idiots are here to break me out."

"I am. Group of idiots, sans one, isn't here." Sol winced. "It's a long story and I'm still figuring out the details, but we have a friend in here that's willing to get us out, and the rest of the dwarves. We just need to know more about Catarmon before we do."

Karas started to say something, but the dark cell behind Sol slithered with sound as something woke up.

"Catarmon?" A slimy voice echoed in the shadows, thin and reedy. "Catarmon the betrayer. Catarmon the *fool.*"

Sol shivered. "What's in there?"

Karas scowled. "Nasty fuckin' elf they slammed in there. Spent the first three days gnawing his own skin off. They sedated him every time he started bleedin. He's been out since. I thought he was dead. Kinda hoped so, anyway."

"I know that voice . . ." Sol said, turning to the dark cell.

The shadows were thick, bulging, reminding her of her dream. But something watched her with heavy eyes within. "You're the creature from Kleros, aren't you? The one draining blood and shadows."

Snickering bounced from the walls to Sol's ears. "So clever, golden dwarf. Clever as a cat. Clever, clever, clever. Those eyes see all, yes? Like the sky. Mistress told stories of the sky. You have such lovely eyes . . ."

Karas grunted. "Charmer, that one."

The elf went on, still unseen. "Pretty eyes see all. Catch the lies, snare the truth. Except . . ." He paused on the high point of his voice. "Within."

Sol was done ages ago. She whirled back to Karas. "Right, that conversation is over. Let's get you out."

"Plan first?"

Sol thumbed along the bars for a keyhole, ignoring the hissing behind her. "Not sure. You know the outside better than I do. I have an easy way out. We'll need to do some digging before leaving, but they just fed us so we should be fine for a little while longer."

Sol finally found the lock, key teeth digging into her hands when she froze. Karas was standing opposite to her and was quiet, looking at the floor. The presence behind her had shifted from something uncomfortable to something powerful.

"Sol, I thought our plan was to wait?"

Sol didn't know what it was that made her hide the key. She didn't know if it was the way her instincts screamed at her to run, like she was faced with a predator, or if it was the way both Karas and the elf went deadly silent that finally triggered her survival. She felt very small, and her skin prickled with raised hairs.

Slowly she turned, tucking her hands behind her between the bars, and faced Abraxas.

He didn't look any different. But the air around him shimmered. The shadows from the cell behind him seem to slither out to seek his hands. Sol blinked rapidly, and they were gone.

"Abraxas," she let out a heavy sigh of relief. "Jalaa, am I glad to see you! You didn't tell me Karas was here."

Abraxas frowned. "Didn't I?"

"No."

"Well." He shrugged. "I was unaware you cared so much for a criminal."

"He was our ally before. He can be again!" she protested. "At the very least, he's against Serevadia."

"I told you this is delicate," Abraxas snapped. "I'm doing everything I can to keep you alive. What of our plan?"

"I can't sit still, Abraxas. I have to do something."

"This something nearly got you killed. What would you have done? Broken him out and then what?"

"We would've figured it out," she snapped back.

"Foolish plans are not how we do things. We aren't—"

"Don't." Sol glared at him. "I know we're not like our friends. But we have to do something."

Abraxas's nostrils flared but that was all that showed how angry he was. He took a step back and Sol heard the elf whimper in the shadows. Abraxas glared behind him, and the whimpering cut off. In that split second, Sol dropped the key between the bars and into Karas's cell. There was a whisper of movement, but no clattering of metal on stone. By the time Abraxas turned back to her, Sol's hands were empty.

"Please," Sol pleaded, and she couldn't even pretend that this part was a lie. "I know you're doing everything you can but let me help. Let *us* help."

Abraxas's eyes flicked over her shoulder and Sol prayed that Karas wasn't openly waving the key about like a fool. She pushed away from the bars and took his hand, shockingly cold in hers.

"Please."

Finally, he looked down at her and the harshness in his features started to soften. There was a little glimpse of the man she knew. The one who chided her as he bandaged her wounds. The one who held her after the White Cairn while she wept for hours. Sol was no stranger to the darker side of her friend, because she knew they all had shadows that lurked with knives. But now more than ever she needed her Abraxas, not the cold soldier he used to protect himself.

"I cannot give you what you ask, Sol." He laid a hand on her shoulder. "Although I dearly wish to."

She didn't have to feign her disappointment, it came too naturally. She longed to tell him about Ainthe, about the plot to get him out and save Eith from Catarmon's wrath. But instinct kept her biting on her tongue. She nodded, hating the conflict so obviously written in the way her body shook and her eyes watered.

Sol let Abraxas wrap his arm around her shoulders and usher her towards the exit. They didn't get very far before Karas broke his silence and banged on the bars. It sounded like bells of mourning tolling for the nameless lost.

"Traitor!" he barked.

Sol tried to turn to look even as Abraxas kept her firmly by his side. She was just able to peak past his arm and see Karas's livid face. She hadn't seen him so angry since the prison. Those eyes burned with a hatred she couldn't fathom in her heart.

And they were directed at Abraxas.

"Says the man who surrendered his people to Serevadian rule," Abraxas said coolly, and continued to walk.

Sol was too numb to resist him. He was a pillar of ice, cold and hard and unyielding as he moved to the door. And behind her, Karas was a wildfire, spitting fury and hate in equal measure.

"Bastard!" he howled. "You sold out your own fuckin' world, and for what? What does a monster like you gain from my cousin's death? Answer me!"

Abraxas didn't. The door shut and Karas's yelling was muffled to the point of incomprehensibility. Deep in the pit of

Sol's stomach, something cold weighed her down. A dread so dark and deep that its weight made her stumble.

She didn't speak as he ushered her down the hall, his arm securely around her. She didn't look at him either, and the silence made the dread worse.

Sol wracked her brain for some semblance of information, a memory that could explain how Karas hated Abraxas. The two didn't start off on good terms but, then again, neither had he with the rest of the Wandering Sols. And after Heliodar, there was a little string of respect strung between the two warriors. Delicate, but visible. The kind of respect that came with putting aside each other's differences to defeat a greater evil. What had happened to those men?

Sol couldn't find the courage to ask.

They cut into the hallway Sol was most familiar with, the one that housed the room she snuck out of and the bath, and she stiffened to see it choked with Serevadians. Some in armor, many not. But Abraxas didn't slow his gate at all, seemingly unphased.

As he drew closer, Sol prepared herself for a flurry of lies to help him. She picked the locks and was looking around for her friends, only a half lie. Or she found the door unlocked? No, that was shit even if it did line up with the guard bringing her food. It all sounded bad, but she had to protect her escape route. If they watched that, she'd be trapped.

But there was no questioning, no lies to be spilled. The Serevadians in the hallway simply moved out of the way. They pressed themselves against the wall, avoiding eye contact. One, an exhausted woman with frizzy white hair, covered her face with kohl smudged fingers as they passed.

It was such a bizarre thing to see that it took Sol until they had descended down the stairs and were halfway to her room before she realized why.

"They're afraid of you."

Sol stopped and wiggled out of Abraxas's arm. He carried on

a step before sighing heavily and turning back to her.

"Sol, please."

"Why are they afraid of you?" she demanded. "Why did they let us pass like that? Why did Karas call you a traitor?"

"Because Karas is a fool!" Abraxas shouted with enough force that Sol took a shuddering step back. His eyes sparked dangerously before he noticed her shuffle backwards. He winced, bringing his hand to his face to smooth out his brow. "Forgive me. That anger was not meant to be for you. Let us not talk of him anymore."

Now Sol was properly scared, and she was damn tired of it. Fear killed her logic. Fear made her words fall flat and her daggers too slow, too dull. And she'd never, ever been afraid of Abraxas.

She shook her head, half to keep herself from staring at him and half to shake away her fear. "I don't understand. What are you hiding from me?"

"I'm not—"

"You are! I know you're lying because I know *you*." He said nothing, and Sol ran her hands through her hair to calm down. Raked her fingernails along her scalp, grounded herself. Turned back to her friend.

Her friend.

"I know the others aren't here," she said.

"You're right, they're not in this building," he said smoothly.

"No, they're not here, period," Sol corrected. "In Stone's End."

He blinked slowly at her. "And how would you know that?"

"Karas told me." A lie.

"And you'd believe a man like him over me?"

Sol squeezed her eyes shut, forcing the dull scarlet of her eyelids to prepare herself for what came next. She could do this. She had no choice but to do it. If she wanted a good chance of leaving with everyone she loved, she needed to stop skirting around the truth.

Abraxas would understand. He was her friend.

She opened her eyes. "You've been on your own for a century. You said so yourself."

He stiffened. "You don't trust me."

"I didn't say that. What I'm saying is that you've been away from us for so long." Sol's eyes were burning now, but he looked unchanged. "You've been alone, with the enemy, for longer than anyone should ever be. That changes people, Abraxas. It changes how you think, so you survive. I'm not blaming you for that. I'm trying to get you to see that you don't have to play by their games anymore. We can do this together."

Sol reached out for him, her hand nothing more than a pale blur in her waterlogged vision. But Abraxas took a step back.

"There is nothing wrong with the way I'm thinking," he responded in what anyone who didn't know him would consider a calm voice.

Sol knew better. She shrunk back.

"Why are they afraid of you?" she asked again.

He drew himself up tall. "Because I have done unforgivable, obscene acts for the sake of our survival. *Ours.* I have a plan, one that will free all of Eith from Serevadia's tyranny, but I cannot do it if I'm chasing after you."

Abraxas held out his hand. "Give me your lockpicks."

Sol's tears slipped down her cheeks, into her lips, salty and warm. She crossed her arms, trying to look strong, but she felt like she was just hugging herself.

"No."

He snarled. "Sol—"

"I won't be a prisoner again!" she cried. "You shove me back in that room with no way out and I'll . . . I'll break. I'll never forgive you."

For the first time, her words seem to hit him. Abraxas, the man who started out as her savior, who'd saved her life, defended her, kept her free time and time again, seemed to wake up and see what he was doing. He looked down at his hand, clenched it into a fist and lowered it to his side.

"I'm not trying to hurt you, Sol," he said quietly, regretfully. "I'm trying to protect you."

She believed him. Out of everything he'd said, she knew that at least was genuine.

"I know." She sniffed, digging her fingers into her arms. "But this isn't just your fight. This is mine too. These are my people and I refuse to sit back, when I've fought for less. Do you understand?"

Something sparked in his eyes. Not like before. This was something she recognized. A little bit of hope in those dark depths. A flicker of possibility where there had once been none.

"I do," he said. "I shouldn't have expected you to wait patiently in the dark. Patience is something none of us were very skilled at, were we?"

He sent a small smile, a peace offering. Sol took it and mirrored it.

"No, we weren't."

He stepped to the side, sweeping his arm to her room at the end. "Please go in and rest a bit. I'll be back within the next few hours, and when I return I swear I'll explain everything."

She raised an eyebrow. "What do you mean?"

"I haven't been entirely truthful, as you've pointed out. There are things I didn't tell you because I was afraid of how you'd react." He hesitated, arm drooping. "The others learned of it in a bad way. They reacted badly, and I wasn't able to rectify it. But you . . . you and I are similar. We share a vision of a better world for our people, but we both know that vision requires sacrifice in order to get it. I think—I hope—you'll understand when I tell you."

Sol's breath caught in her throat. "Everything?"

He nodded. "I swear."

Sol chewed her lip. One at a time, her hands fell to her sides. Her shoulders and neck were as tense as iron-laced rope now, and she couldn't force them to relax if she wanted to. So she just rounded them the way her mother taught her and nodded curtly.

"Okay," she said. "Everything, in a few hours. I'll be waiting."

He smiled and it was like seeing the sun after a devastating storm. Sol loved it. "Good. Thank you. I'll be right back."

He didn't escort her all the way to her room. He left her in the hallway and swept back up the stairs in a rush. Sol couldn't tell if this was a measure of trust or oversight, so she held her breath and waited for the door at the top of the stairs to close and lock.

When it did, she let out the breath and went back to her room. She closed the door because she felt exposed leaving it open and sat heavily on the bed. The mattress creaked underneath her, soft layers beckoning her for a nap. She refused.

She stared at her wall, her secret way out hidden even to her eyes now, and she thought long and hard. She counted her facts again.

Karas hated Abraxas and called him a traitor.

The Serevadians she saw were scared of him.

Ainthe had practically begged her not to talk to Abraxas.

The rest of the Wandering Sols knew what he had done and despised it.

It wouldn't be the first time. Sorin talked to Sol about the time on *Mortova's Maw* where Evren and Abraxas fought about Keres and how to deal with them. And Sorin himself had fought with Abraxas many times. But they were all different people who hadn't lived nearly as long as he had, arguments were bound to happen and when they did, they were gotten over.

What could be so awful that the whole group turned their backs on him and left Sol behind?

"Oh, my friend, what did you do?" she whispered to the wall, to the shadows. "What did you do?"

15

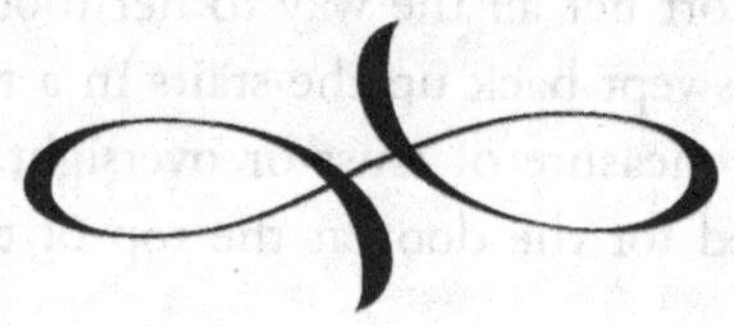

Solri

Precisely an hour and thirty-seven minutes later, because Sol had nothing else better to do than count the minutes, her door burst open.

"Get your soft arse up, Amet," Karas hissed and shut the door behind him. "We gotta go."

Sol bolted to her feet. "What are you—"

"Gettin' you out, what else?" He looked over the room. "Cozy cell."

She rolled her eyes. "Thanks. The wall just there will open. You can get through the rest of the house that way and get out."

Karas took no time dashing to the wall and feeling around until the mechanism caught and it pushed open underneath his fingers. He whistled and tugged it open enough for him to slip through.

"Damn, tight fit for me. But we can make it. C'mon," He turned back to her, watching as she sat back down. "The fuck are you doing?"

"I'm staying."

He shoved away from the wall, stalking back to her. "Hells you are. If I have to drag you out, Amet, I will."

She scowled up at him. "You wouldn't dare. Besides, you couldn't. I don't know how you got down here without being seen—"

"Bashed some heads in."

"—but the moment I start making a ruckus, you'll be caught. Your people don't need that set back. Go."

"Listen here, you spoiled princess," he growled. "I did not risk my life and the lives of my people to come get you only for you to sit here like a good little pet while I do all the work. Get up."

She crossed her arms. "I'm waiting on Abraxas."

Karas's face reddened. "Oh you are, are you?"

"He's going to explain everything to me."

"Why wait?" Karas threw his hands out in the air. "I'll tell you right now. That son of a bitch has been working with Serevadia and helping them. He's the reason Dirn-Darahl fell so fuckin' easily. He's the reason the whole surface has gone to shit. He's got them wrapped around his damn fingers and he's playin' them like Heliodar played us."

"No." Sol shook her head. "Abraxas wouldn't. You don't understand what he's been through. He was forced—"

"You're not that stupid, Amet. You can't think that."

"He's a prisoner of war!" she argued. "Catarmon—"

"He *is* Catarmon!" Karas bellowed, and the name echoed in the small room until it was so silent Sol's gasping breaths could be heard.

The first thing that jumped into her mind was that Karas was lying, but she knew better. He had none of his normal tells, and he was an absolute shit liar. He never learned how to do it properly, so he never bothered with it.

The second thing was how rotten of a truth it was.

"He wouldn't," Sol said, but it was all to convince herself.

Already she could hear Abraxas's voice as he talked not even two hours before.

You and I are similar. We share a vision of a better world for our people, but we both know that vision requires sacrifice in order to get it. I think—I hope—you'll understand when I tell you.

Sol covered her mouth with her hand. "Oh Jalaa, no. He couldn't . . ."

Karas's anger had faded. He knelt beside her on the floor and put a hand on her knee. The touch was hesitant, jumpy. He didn't know how to comfort her.

"I wish I was wrong," he said. "I surrendered the city because he asked, because he promised we would figure a way out together. And the moment I did, our people were slaughtered. The ones that survived were put in chains. I trusted him because he'd fought for me once, and I thought he would again. But that man isn't your friend. Abraxas Kain is gone."

Sol shook her head. Tears flowed again, free and damning because tears meant weakness and she didn't want to be weak in front of him. But he didn't flinch at the sight of them. He didn't move when they pattered on his hand that held her knee.

"My friends?" she asked.

He shook his head. "I dunno. I was hoping to see them since this seems like a mess they would clean up. Ever since you've been in here though he's been agitated. Somethin' must have happened."

Abraxas wouldn't have hurt them, no matter how far gone he was. He just wouldn't. But the more Sol wracked her brain, the more she could see her friends' reactions to the news. If Abraxas had willingly destroyed Dirn-Darahl and more, she couldn't imagine any of them taking it well.

"Why?" She finally looked him in the eyes. "Why is he doing this? There has to be a reason."

"Heliodar had a reason," he reminded her, gently. "A good one. That didn't make it better."

Now it all made sickening, horrible sense. The way Ainthe danced around Catarmon's identity, because she knew Sol wouldn't believe her if it came from her mouth. The way the Serevadians shrank away from him when he passed. The way the elf in the cell opposite to Karas had whimpered and stopped talking when Abraxas came in.

He was their god, forcibly. The flickers of power she thought she imagined were real.

"He's going to destroy Serevadia," she said numbly. "I don't know how, but that's his plan."

"How the fuck does them destroyin' everything in their path factor into this?"

Sol shook her head. "I don't know. Ainthe said that Serevadia's victories were hollow, meant to placate Velcros and the masses. She wants Catarmon—I mean, Abraxas—gone."

Karas sat back on his heels, her knee colder from where he took his hand back to stroke his beard. "So we're trustin' the crazy priestess now?"

It was all wrong. Trusting Ainthe and Karas, two people who had tried to kill her in the past, over the man who'd been her shield for so long. But for the first time since waking up, she had a clear vision.

She stood up, wiped away her tears, and straightened her clothing. "She's all we've got right now. And if there's one thing we learned in strategy, it's that breaking an enemy army's loyalty . . ."

"Can be the key to winning a war," Karas finished and stood up. "You sure you can do this?"

No. Sol had never been less sure about something in her whole life. But she nodded in a way that she knew Karas would take and walked over to the door. The musty smell of freedom beckoned her.

"We need to get your people out first, then find a way out of Stone's End. East?"

"Guarded," he grunted, stepping beside her. "But our people can handle that."

The emphasis on 'our' wasn't lost on Sol. As the dread sloshed and caked her insides, that little word made her smile genuinely. Truly, there was nothing that could hold back a dwarven force working together for a singular goal.

Especially when there was no other choice but submission and death.

Sol didn't look back as she shut the wall behind her. But she did feel guilt, as icy and numbing as the waters of Myrefall Bay, creeping through her veins. Through the thick blackness between the walls, Karas couldn't see her shaking. There wasn't a gleam of light to reflect on the fresh tears tumbling down her cheeks. She had years at court to learn how to cry without sniffling and giving herself away, so there was very little change to her breathing.

Yet, he knew. Somehow Karas knew and Sol could tell by the way he intentionally softened his hands when helping her up the ladder. Maybe it wasn't such a far stretch. Karas was there at the beginning when Abraxas and Sol had first met, when the prison was burning and the world seemed a lot smaller. He was there for Heliodar, and how they fought side by side.

It felt like a lifetime ago since she'd seen her friend. For Abraxas it truly was.

The room Sol escaped out of was quiet and empty, the floor blacker. Karas let out a low whistle before moving to the window. But Sol looked at the markings. Many were fresher, a deep thick black that made her shudder with unwanted memories. Whoever lived there, likely the frizzy haired elf she saw in the hallway, had been busy.

"Amet, let's move."

Sol shook her head. "Karas, what are these?"

"How the fuck should I know?"

"They're important. These numbers mean something."

In the time it took her to let out her breath, he was at her side frowning at the floor. The Solri who lived before the Wandering Sols would've laughed at the idea of lowly thug Goriryn Karas puzzling out complex numbers and theories, but he was a man of many surprises. Still a thug, but there was a sharp brain behind those ice blue eyes.

"Numbers, eh?" Karas muttered. "Could be for troops."

"That's what I thought. But we both know Serevadian numbers far exceed this. And look at these strokes." Sol bent down, running her finger a hair above the kohl smudges. "They're jagged. Thicker than they ought to be. Whoever did this was pressing down hard. But just below it you can see the beginning numbers aren't as bad. They'd be closer to what the normal handwriting of this person was. These are the markings of someone desperate and scared. Whatever numbers they're getting, it's not what they want. And they keep getting bigger, but the way they're underlined . . ."

"Feels like bad news," he grunted. "What's the final number?"

Sol stood up. "Three thousand. I think. Last time I was in here, a little bit before I found you, it was over nine hundred."

"Big jump." He grabbed Sol's arm and pulled her away with a little more difficulty than one would expect from a dwarf his size. "C'mon now, let them worry about big numbers. We have people to save."

"Right." She tore her gaze away and followed Karas out the window. But as she closed it behind them and slinked from one shadow to another, the numbers wouldn't leave her mind. Particularly the way the anger had drained from the kohl strokes, and the etching of three thousand was marked with smears of now dried liquid.

Like tears.

Karas was street smart, but he wasn't as silent as Sol. It took everything she had to keep him from being seen or heard, and that occasionally meant grabbing the waistband of his trousers to keep him from walking straight into an enemy patrol. She anchored him to the shadows, knowing that he couldn't see her scowl so much as feel it, and when it was free to move he'd yank his pants from her grip and skulk away. Sol might have imagined his tenderness about her grief in the walls, but she didn't imagine how red his ears were after every time she saved him by yanking on his pants.

By the fifth time, twenty minutes and half of Stone's End later, he'd come to wait for Sol's signal. He pressed up against a corner, stiff and ready to dart across to the next building. But she caught his eye with a subtle shake of her head. Likely all he saw was the glint of her nose ring, but it was enough to keep him still as a patrol of silver-armored elves marched past, silent as tombs.

"It's a wonder you didn't get caught by Heliodar sooner with the way you sneak around," Sol hissed.

Low light caught the whites of his eyes as he turned to look down at her. For a dwarf he was tall, and had nearly a head of height on Sol.

"Didn't have to sneak 'round, Amet. I paid people off."

She frowned, wondering how many workers she'd interrogated that had kept their mouths shut due to Karas's coin.

"With what money?" She nudged him forward when the coast was clear.

They darted across together, taking a moment to breathe in the safety of darkness.

"Stolen, of course." And that was the voice of a scoundrel winking for sure. Sol rolled her eyes, knowing that he would see it without his eyes. The low chuckle proved her right.

It was strange how easy it was to work with Karas. But Sol supposed after so long being enemies and watching each other, it came naturally to know how to work in tandem. Strange how the man she despised so much in prison would be the one she could rely on the most during her time of need. Then again, it was probably even stranger for Karas. Escaping Serevadia and killing Heliodar was one thing, and they barely spoke to each other then. This was different.

And it wasn't at all as uncomfortable as she expected.

"Here." Karas stopped her, nodding across the street.

They stopped at a large, dark building near the field of corpses Sol had seen. She could even make out the house that Ainthe had dragged her into not too far off. There was only one door, and it was guarded by one, lonely soldier.

"They really don't think much of us, do they?" Sol muttered.

Karas just grunted. "You want him or is he mine?"

Sol worried her bottom lip. "I got him. You can get our people out quicker while I draw him away."

To her surprise, he didn't argue with her. He just nodded. "Don't play with your food, Amet. In and out."

"Oh, please, I know how to do my job. You do yours."

They split up silently, without another word. Sol ran her hands through her pockets. Oh, what she wouldn't give to have her daggers and lockpicks back. She was damn lucky Abraxas had taken her lie about the picks so damn well. But seriously, she felt naked without them. Not that she couldn't fight naked, because she'd done it before, but she missed their familiar weight and it would make her job so much easier.

But Solri Amet hadn't survived the Dwarven Court with things that made her life easier. Sometimes you fight with even odds, daggers in your hands and friends at your back. Other times you were as nude as the day you were born with nothing but a soap bar as a weapon.

One Serevadian guard while she was fully clothed? She had this.

Sol snuck around the side of the adjacent building until the smell of rotting corpses tickled the back of her throat. She didn't gag as she turned back to the guard. He was only a couple buildings away, with a clear view of the field if he bothered to look. Hells, her hair must've shone like a beacon but this lazy bastard wasn't paying attention.

She slipped into the corpse field and intentionally, loudly, kicked a broken helmet. It clattered against the stone like a war drum, and she ducked behind the pile of bodies. She ticked off the seconds, breathing through her mouth. She didn't look at the sightless eyes of the bodies she hid behind, or the way their hair had burned in peculiar spirals leaving blackened chunks against their flesh. She waited and listened.

It took the guard two full minutes to either work up the courage or shake off his boredom enough to get up and walk towards her. He did so slowly, boots scuffing against the ground with every step.

Sol rolled her eyes. *You lazy bastard,* she thought. *I intentionally did my worst just so you could bitch about coming to get me?*

And, just as she predicted, a heavy flow of strange words that could only be curses assaulted her ears as he stepped into the corpse field.

"Missed you, rat?" he said in heavily accented Dwarven. "You not hide in here. Come out. I will kick you."

Sol wasn't sure if that was a giddy threat or something that was supposed to placate her and he'd just butchered the language. She took a handful of gravel in her hands, waited until he was close enough that she could hear his armor clinking against itself with every step, then dashed behind another pile.

This time she was fast, but she let the gravel fall from her hands as she ran, trailing behind her with a clatter of rocks where her feet were silent. The little gasp from the guard was drowned out by the clanking of armor as he whirled around.

Slowly, marked by loud footsteps, he followed.

"Out, rat," he whispered. "Out, and you live. I promise."

Sol wouldn't have believed it even if she hadn't seen him. But from her perch at the top of the pile of bodies, a few feet above his head, she could see that he'd drawn his sword and the gleam in his eye was very much a killing one.

How many escapees louder than her had he slain? How red

had his blade been with the blood of her people before he shined it to such a silver glow?

Questions Sol didn't need answers to. Half a heartbeat after the guard realized the trail of gravel led to nowhere, Sol had leapt from her perch and onto his shoulders. Her knees dug into his armor, smarting at the impact. As he staggered backwards, she gripped either side of his face with her thighs. The ground tilted dangerously as he wavered and tried to hit her with his sword. She didn't even flinch; the blade came nowhere near to hitting her.

The beginnings of a shout gurgled in the back of his throat. Sol couldn't have that. She reached down and snapped his jaw shut. Using that and the strength of her thighs, she twisted her body sharply to the right until there was a loud pop. It echoed in her own body, the snap that meant sudden death. The guard fell limp beneath her and Sol swiftly vaulted off his shoulders and onto her feet before his crooked head even hit the ground.

Sol smiled, despite herself, and picked up the fallen sword. It was made for someone with longer arms than her, and was much bigger than the daggers she was used to. The balance was all off, but a weapon was a weapon. No dwarf could afford to be picky in times of war.

Sol took precious time to search the guard's body. She found keys that she pocketed, but Karas likely didn't need them. Other than that, the guard had little on him besides some bars that looked like they passed for rations. Sol wrinkled her nose but pocketed them anyway. Food was food.

Standing up, Sol finally allowed herself to look at the piles of dwarven corpses. It couldn't be all the army they had left, but the number of piles made her throat tight. There were supposed to be elaborate tombs for those who died in battle. Honors given, days and nights spent in vigil to help the souls return to Jalaa in the mountains. In the days of old, even enemies of the dwarves knew this and would return the bodies with their weapons and armor intact. Only a fool risked the ire of the dead.

But Serevadia didn't care. They'd butchered and tore through Dirn-Darahl's defenses even after surrender. Sol could barely look at the way their braids of marriage, rank and family had been cut off. How their weapons had been stolen, their armor defaced. The Serevadians hadn't defeated them, they had destroyed them.

Sol shivered. They'd tried to break her people and forced them to do the dirty work. Instead of praying over bodies, Karas and the survivors relieved them of the possessions they so desperately needed in the afterlife while a small army of soldiers watched impassively.

Sol froze. Her grip on the stolen blade loosened, and it had little to do with the morality behind it. She looked back at the dead guard.

"Why you?" she whispered. "Why just you?"

The Serevadians she could believe would underestimate them, even if they went so far to degrade them as they did. But one person knew better than to leave a single guard between her and her people. One person knew her better than anyone else.

Sol ran back to the building, now unguarded. The door gaped open ominously, like the waiting maw of an animal. She tore through it anyway, heedless of the way the stolen sword clanged against the door.

"Karas!" She stopped just past the threshold, breathing hard more from panic than the small run.

Panic quelled only slightly at the sight of Karas standing on one side of a massive cell holding at least fifty tightly packed dwarves trying to get the door open. He shot up to look at her, hand going to his belt where his sword should've been.

"What?" he hissed. "What's wrong?"

She shut the door and tossed him the keys. He caught them easily, much to the whispered cries of relief from the mass behind the lock.

"Hurry," she urged him. "This is a trap. Abraxas wouldn't leave just one guard."

Karas's flushed face paled as he came to the same conclusion, but that was the only indication he gave that he was just as scared. He made quick work of the lock, swinging open the door.

"This is an escape, not a damn attack," Karas told the shifting dwarves eager to leap out. "We're headin' east through the tunnels. From there we keep goin' until we find friendly faces or the sun. We don't stop, we don't rest. We push on."

He stepped aside, and the dwarves started filing out obediently. There was a manic stir in each of them, a vibration of energy that threatened to take away the order and send them sprinting into one another to get to the door. But they kept that energy leashed, drawing upon what Sol knew was deeply ingrained training. It was all they had, after all.

But they were a beautiful sight. Underfed, beaten, haggard. A mess in both appearance and souls, but they were alive. Beneath the grime, their eyes glittered like jewels. Their lips were set into firm lines of determination beneath stubble and unruly beards. Their hands were fists shaking at their sides, or wrapped tightly around another hand for strength.

Pride overcame fear, just for a moment, as she stared at them all. Her people. Fighters, all of them, even if this small band was all that was left.

They looked at Karas with hope, but when they saw her there was something else in their jeweled depths. Something more profound. Stronger. Sol couldn't place it because she'd never been looked at that way, and certainly not by so many, but it took her breath away.

One voice came from the crowd.

"You came back," it said, a woman who bore a set of ugly scars marring the side of her face. Her eye on that side was gone, leaving an empty socket. But the remaining one was burning bright. "You came back for us."

It didn't matter that Sol hadn't had a choice in coming back. It didn't matter that not thirty minutes ago it was Karas dragging her out of her prison with the promise to save their people. It didn't matter that the man who had done this to them was someone she loved dearly.

They didn't know that, and they didn't need to.

So, Sol smiled a grim smile. "Of course I did. I always do."

Karas shouldered his way up to her, pressing himself against the door on the opposite side. He breathed words only loud enough for her.

"How much time do we have?"

"I don't know," she admitted. She pulled the door open just enough to peek through and saw nothing but empty streets and piles of the dead. Beyond them, the ring of light around Stone's End faded away, leaving nothing but blackness. There were no watchtowers on this side, as Stone's End had never needed to defend its east side. Sol always thought the idea of leaving one side open to an attack was like bait to an enemy before the outpost could snap its armored jaws around them. Beyond that, the tunnels to the east were as untraveled as the Yawning Deep had been before Temsen Cartack. It would be a long, hard trek if they could make it. But the alternative left no choice.

Sol pilfered through her pockets and pulled out one of the Luminstone pebbles. It was too small to shed much light, but if it was all they had then it would have to do. She shoved it into Karas's callused hand.

"You lead, I'll bring up the rear."

He snorted. "What? No lectures on my shitty sneakin' now?"

"Hard to get caught when there's nothing but darkness, arse." She smirked. "I'm sure you'll manage."

She took her own Luminstone pebble, rolled it between her fingers, and then stepped outside. Karas followed, but where she stayed at the corner of the building watching for signs of patrols and traps, he headed straight to the fields. One by one, the dwarves followed. They uttered not a word. The only sound that came from them were the pattering of their feet against the ground. When the last of them came out in a rush, she was swiftly behind them, sword in one hand and Luminstone in the other.

Sol tried to feel guilty about leaving Ainthe without helping her. She tried to keep the tear-stained number of three thousand out of her head. And she did not think about Abraxas Kain, or the man that had taken his place. For the second time in her life, Sol ran away from a man she trusted, ignoring how it tore at her heart.

The heaps of the dead were mountains to mourn, but the dwarves did not stop. They did not whisper respects or stumble past the eyes of those they knew, forever glazed over and staring at nothing. The desperation for escape, the danger of failing, and the raging promise to come back and avenge those fallen was enough to keep them moving.

Past the field of bodies were guards at the edge of Stone's End. Only ten to watch the never-changing shadows past their light. Sol didn't have to see them to imagine their relaxed body language turning as stiff as stone as the dwarves crested quietly over the small incline towards them. She didn't hear them either, only the snapping of bones and the sounds of flesh meeting fists. By the time she got to the bodies, all ten guards were dead. Three unfortunate dwarves were too, caught by the stray swords. There was only enough time to close their eyes before Karas had everyone on their feet.

The blackness beyond was immense. Sol could feel it humming in her chest—the promise of freedom. The outline of a narrow, natural passage dripping with stalactites became visible to her adjusting eyes.

Karas saw it too. He had everyone up. He had them orderly, hopeful, and quiet. He nodded to Sol in the back, no jinxable smile on his lips but an appreciation that burned through her like a wildfire. It warmed her to her core.

Their people. It had a nice ring to it.

And then Sol felt it. It smothered the fire of pride Karas had sparked. It's cold, leeching fingers were as familiar as Mal's had once been, only this time they kept her rooted to the spot. She opened her mouth to scream and they were there inside her throat, cutting off her vocal chords as if she was a naughty child who couldn't use her toy without apologizing. The shadows of her nightmare emerged from their hidden nest in her chest and Sol was powerless, motionless, and cold.

Sol was theirs.

She could only gasp for breath as the dwarf closest to her, now several feet away, stopped and turned back in confusion. His eyes widened, a lovely amber marred with tearstains that couldn't be washed away.

"Lady Amet!" he cried and rushed forward.

Sol wanted to scream at him to stay away, but instead she saw her sword hand lift. The stolen blade dripped with thick, oily shadows so dark that they stood out in the gloom of the caverns. A flick of her wrist, because the shadows in her veins had taken her bones and muscles and tendons too, had the man's head cut clean off.

Warm blood sprayed Sol's front, and this did bring a cry out of her. Visceral and ugly, and enough to turn Karas and the other dwarves to her. To the body at her feet. To the figure behind her.

Sol didn't know if she turned around or if the shadows did it for her, but before long, Stone's End swam in her vision as Abraxas Kain stood before her. He wore the same face he always did. Soft, understanding, but disappointed.

Sol couldn't help but sob.

"You ran away," he said softly, as if to soothe her, but he didn't make to touch her. He didn't brush her hair away from her face or wipe the tears away. He watched her with cold, dark eyes. "I was going to explain everything."

"You . . ." she gasped through the shadows and the tears. Behind her she was distantly aware of the dwarves's calm running out. Fear and anger in equal measure mingled into a terrifying riot. None came to her aid and she was glad. Blood still dripped down her shirt.

"Tell me you didn't do it!" she cried suddenly. The shadows in her throat jerked back as if shocked, but Abraxas remained the same. "Tell me my home didn't burn because of you. That my mother isn't dead because of your actions."

He stared at her for what seemed like an eternity. "It was never my intention to hurt you, Sol."

"Hurt me?" The tears were cold against her checks, down the column of her throat. "You lied to me! You poisoned me! You made me believe that everything would be okay and then you turned out to be the one who had the dagger to my back the whole time!"

"This isn't about you!" he snapped, the fires of anger finally igniting. "One city burns so the world can be safe. Sacrifices must be made."

"My people aren't sacrifices!"

"They are few of many!" he roared, and stepped closer. In that one step the waiting shadows grew so cold that she was numb. She fell to her knees, her sword clattered to the ground. There was screaming behind her, someone who was throwing words of fire her way, but they all extinguished before they met her ears.

Abraxas took her chin in his hand, as gentle as always. He looked down at her with rage mingled with pity and a dash of disgust. As if he couldn't fathom that she didn't see what he saw.

"You were meant to be the one to understand," he said. "You of all people. You killed your King so that your people could prosper under a stronger rule. You bloodied your hands for a better tomorrow."

"No," Sol gasped. "I did it for me. Because I was angry. Because I could. Because I thought I could be a better King and I wanted control above all else."

Abraxas was blurry with tears. Sol was cold and numb, except for her heart. Every time it beat she felt it tear itself more.

The revelation with Karas in her room had been nothing compared to this pain. Because now she was staring Catarmon in the face and he had eyes she wanted to trust. He had laugh lines that she'd watched crinkle over and over again. He had the chin that used to rest on her shoulder so many times.

"You knew . . ." Sol choked. "You knew I couldn't do this again. You of all people knew that after Mal, I . . ." She finally broke, sobbing into his fingers but unable to hold herself up. She was at his mercy, a puppet on strings. She had been from the very beginning.

"You were my friend!" she screamed. "I trusted you!"

Abraxas's face hardened. He let go of her chin and let her slump on her knees, heaving sobs. He looked over her head to the panicking mass of dwarves.

"No matter what you think of me, this is the only way," he said. "I require not your understanding, nor your forgiveness. Divines know I will get neither."

Sol watched with growing horror as the shadows at his feet leapt past her. Swirls of smoke turned to spikes of obsidian. Death cries echoed in the cavern. She couldn't see, she couldn't turn to look, but she could visualize their individual deaths as if she was the one killing them.

Suddenly she was back in Dirn-Darahl. She was facing the King. She was killing him. There was fighting as her people killed each other, as they tried to kill her friends. Chaos reigned and it was *her* fault. Her greed and anger had led her people to a slaughter. It had killed Sorin. It had driven her from home, where the last memory of her mother was her pressing her weathered hand against Sol's cheek, cool and familiar, as Sol swore to come back home.

A broken promise. A broken home. A broken heart.

And yet this was worse.

Sol was screaming before she knew it. A wordless war cry that startled the very shadows inside her just enough for the numbness to flicker away. Just enough for her to take up her sword and lash out at Abraxas.

All at once the shadows were on her like a trap. The ones inside her froze her muscles and veins, left her gasping as everything suddenly turned to the cold of a body only after it had been long dead. And then the outside shadows were clamoring on her. Sweeping her off her feet and pinning her on her back flat on the ground like a bug to be dissected. The black was all she could see, along with Abraxas above her with wide, hurt, eyes.

Sol craned her head back, looking back at the carnage he'd caused. In just a few seconds he'd killed more than half the surviving dwarves. From her perspective, they laid bloodless and pale on the ceiling, eyes forever wide with shock.

Beyond them, those few that had survived were scrambling away. The shadows had her, they couldn't go for them. Karas was shouldering his way towards her with nothing but a Luminstone in his hand. The others were grabbing him by his broad shoulders, pulling him back. It was taking five of them digging their heels in, and he was still gaining inches.

Someone had to lead them. Someone had to fight, and it was never going to be Solri Amet. Selfish, lying, greedy, manipulative Solri Amet was right where she belonged.

"RUN!" she shouted, and that was all she could manage before the shadows filled her mouth and grabbed her throat with the force of a sucker punch.

She couldn't breathe. The shadows were taking her eyes. But she fought, because as long as she fought, Karas had a chance to get away. Because she was a soldier and that's what soldiers did. Because she was an adventurer, and it was all she could do to save those who needed it.

Because she was Solri Amet, a noble without a city to rule, an adventurer without a party to back her up, and a woman who'd been betrayed far too many times for her heart to handle.

The world went black, and Solri Amet stopped struggling.

16

Gyda

The stairs were slick with ice, one side hanging precariously over the mountain while the other hugged its edge. There was a small mercy in the fact that Gyda couldn't see just how far she would drop if she slipped since the cloud cover was so heavy.

There was another tiny mercy, because Gyda was counting those now, that she was alone besides the worg. No one could see the desperate, slow crawl she submitted herself to. The bit of action she'd had against the mountain beast, while laughable to her past self, had drained her to the point where she felt like the ice was creeping up her limbs and slowing her down. She constantly fumbled with her cloak, numb fingers losing it to the wind more often than not.

And the wind was a problem. The higher she climbed, the more it tried to snatch her from the edge. She was reminded painfully of the first walk back through the Black Pass, with the howling wind and undead tearing at her and her friends. She shoved that memory away before she could linger on faces like Drystan and Vox.

No matter how hard the wind blew, the clouds didn't part. Sharp flecks of snow and ice flung themselves in Gyda's face. She couldn't see more than five stairs ahead of her, and apart from the shifting curve of the path, it could've been the same five stairs she'd been climbing for hours.

The worg walked beside her, never huffing at her slow pace, pressing his warm side against her legs to keep her steady. Between hugging the mountainside and him, Gyda was in no danger of being tossed off the empty side and into the clouds. Not unless the beast suddenly came back.

"Where's Sorin, hm?" she asked the worg idly. "You're never far from the sea rat's side."

The dog huffed and said nothing else. Gyda scolded her own disappointment for expecting him to talk back. But, by all the hells, she was tired. The few hours of sleep after Vanguard had done her little good. To go straight from that to the constant readiness of battle in Kleros to the invasive shadow travel straight into a bloody duel with Abraxas would've been enough to make even her body at its peak beg for a break. But the blood Evren had spilled, that Gyda had encouraged, and that damn spell had left her feeling weaker than ever.

There was an irrational part of Gyda that longed to go back down the stairs and fight the mountain beast. At her best it would've been a glorious battle. And she fucking hated being hunted. Watched. Hiding like some rabbit in the underbrush. She didn't even have her sword.

That hurt worse than it should've. There'd been nothing but the hilt left, but it had been all she had left of her foya. His sword passed down to her. To rebuild it was to forgive herself for surviving when he hadn't. For not being there to protect her clan when they needed her most.

As she took the next five stairs with wobbling steps, she wondered if Abraxas realized he broke more than her blade during the battle. The hilt had been her foya's greatest possession, and he dreamed of completing the sword in whole. The days after she'd lost him she'd gotten a blacksmith to make a blade and fashion it to the hilt. Nothing like what the sword could've been, but it was Ikedree work, which was close enough. The blacksmith had been kind, and gave her the same special attention she'd given the sword. Likely in the hopes of keeping Gyda in Direwall.

The blade was the first thing Gyda had ever did on her own. It was a homage to her foya. A promise to finish what he started one day. Perhaps she'd become too attached to a length of steel, but she felt her father in it. When Abraxas broke it, Gyda felt like she'd lost her foya all over again.

Now the hilt was gone, the last connection back to her old clan. Likely it was churning in the dark depths of the Boreal Sea, or Abraxas had it in his hands—which was worse. Gyda swore she'd had it in her lap when the spell went off . . .

She looked over at the worg.

Gyda had also had Evren beside her. Clutching her hand, kissing her lips, exchanging promises. She should've been there when Gyda woke up in the snow, but the figure didn't seem surprised to find only Gyda. Was she meant to be alone in this journey? Where was the rest of her clan? Sol looked half dead in Sorin's arms, so surely, they'd be together. But, no, the worg had been with them and now he was here with Gyda.

Her head hurt, and she couldn't tell if it was because of exhaustion, dehydration, or confusion over how the fuck that spell had separated them so thoroughly.

Five more five steps, or maybe more, Gyda stopped trying to think about it. She stopped thinking about anything really because there was little good to think about. She could remember the nights wrapped around Evren's warm frame and smile, but as soon as she did she was reminded of how cold and alone she was. Of her lover's resigned grief as the spell consumed her. And then Gyda didn't want to think of Evren at all in the worry that she would taint every good memory with something tragic.

She couldn't think of the Wandering Sols for the same reason. None of Sorin's shanties stuck in her mind, so she couldn't sing them to help her steps march in beat and make the time go by quicker. Memories of Arke just reminded her that Arke hadn't been there to do the spell and made her worry even more about what had happened to the goblin. And Sol was all brightness and sunshine smiles until Gyda remembered how limp and pale she'd been in Sorin's arms.

Had the dwarf been dead? Gyda had been too shocked and numb to check for her chest rising and falling. She'd just been hopeless, overcome, by that despair of having her whole world shattered at the hands of someone she loved.

Maybe there was nothing left of Solri Amet, the same way there had been nothing left of Nerezza when Sahar was clinging to her body.

Maybe Arke had died similarly to Viggo, and all he had left was to pass on a hurried spell that *might* get them all out alive at the expense of Gyda.

Gyda should be dead. With every tenth step she repeated that in her mind.

I should be dead.

Five steps. Five steps.

I should be dead.

Five steps. Collapse. Five steps.

I should be dead.

Five steps, half crawling half dragged by the worg. Five steps with her numbing fingers digging into his coarse fur.

Why am I not dead?

There were no more steps and the sudden flattening of rock made Gyda's stomach flip. The wall of the mountain she'd been hugging disappeared, fell away, and suddenly there was nothing but the stone at her knees, the worg at her side, and clouds. Endless grey clouds swirling around her as the wind screamed. No stone to keep it at bay. It sliced through Gyda's old cloak like a knife and what little warmth she'd taken for granted was snatched away.

She shuddered on her knees. If she stood up she'd surely blow away now. How the worg was keeping so calm and still was beyond her. This was not a place for mortals. This was one for stubborn stars and lonely giants, for the backs of sleeping mountains were home to no others. No singing trees or dancing waters up here. Only isolation, the cold, and Gyda Soul-Dust of the Wandering Sols.

Gyda fell on her hands, choking back a laugh. The ice bit into her palms like sharp teeth. As a little girl she dreamed of climbing to the top of the mountains to find a giant and prove her worth. She'd seen their shadows in the sky, felt their thundering footsteps as they migrated. But that dream of meeting them in their home had died with her foya.

Like all fairytales, the truth was far more bitter than the sugar-sweet story it spun.

Gyda's ragged breaths were stolen by the wind. The worg circled her, whining anxiously. But it took all of Gyda's strength to breathe and blink, much less get back up and keep walking. She was at the top, like the figure asked. She saw no fairytales here, only ice and carved stone and—

She blinked away the snow. Her fingers inched forward, shockingly black at the tips. She didn't feel the carving under her fingers, but she saw it all the same. She hunched against the wind and brushed away the snow as much as she could. She breathed on the ice, trying to melt it.

The moment her hot breath hit the rune it sparked to life. A brilliant blue glow that rivaled the moon in its intensity and nearly blinded Gyda.

She sat back on her knees. The rune was as big as she was.

Slowly, as if they were eyes blinking awake from a long nap, the entire mountaintop came to life. Runes sputtered and held, casting a heavenly glow against the clouds and snow. They spiraled out, one after the other waking each other and burning brighter than any Gyda had ever laid eyes upon. She felt deep within herself the same burning belonging, the same wistfulness she'd felt when she first held the hilt of her sword. The same feeling she'd felt in the giant ruins below Dirn-Darahl. That feeling of homesickness for a place she'd never been, for a people she didn't know, tugged on her harder than ever. Before she knew it, Gyda was on her feet and swaying dangerously in the wind.

The mountaintop was alive with giant runes, each at least as big as Gyda herself. The light from them illuminated strange archways, and shapes between them, circling the mountaintop. And from one of those shapes, something moved.

Something large and powerful. The tearing wind seemed like a breeze for all they flinched at it. Steps like thunder shook Gyda's bones. Runes illuminated large feet, larger than her. Legs that went up until she was craning her stiff neck to see past them and further up. She needn't have bothered. Those legs bent until they were kneeling before her, shaking the ground with a mighty boom. It was all she could do to keep standing.

A beautiful face peered down at her. Skin the color of stone, hair like mist and eyes burning like twin stars. The giant looked down at her with a fondness Gyda had rarely seen, and never with such intensity.

Gyda tried to speak three times before she found her voice.

"You . . ." she managed. "You are Jalaa."

"That I am." The voice was both thunderous and soft, vibrating the bones of Gyda's skull and scattering pebbles at her feet. Yet, Jalaa's mouth didn't move. The voice was the mountain and the air and it was Gyda, too. It was everything.

"And you," Jalaa the Watcher, Stone-Mother and Shepherd of the Lost, said. "Are Gyda. You are lost."

Gyda swallowed the undignified sob that threatened to overwhelm her. This was it. She was living one of her foya's stories.

"I was told to come here," she croaked. The wind drowned

out her words and she worried the giantess wouldn't hear her, but she nodded along.

"YES, WE HAVE BEEN WAITING FOR YOU FOR SOME TIME NOW." She stretched her hand out. The worg went to it eagerly, nuzzling the pad of her thumb before jumping into her palm. He looked at her expectantly, wagging his tail.

Gyda did sob this time. She wasn't sure if it was the wind or the gentle waving of Jalaa that herded her towards her hand, but whatever it was she eagerly crawled into it. The skin was as rough as stone, but strangely warm. Gyda let go all pretenses of strength and honor, and laid down in the giantess's palm.

The worg curled up beside her. The wind moved and the hand rocked and Gyda knew she was being carried somewhere. But as she closed her eyes, she decided she didn't care. She was so tired, so numb yet hurt at the same time. She let the black fog of sleep creep over her and the last thing she heard, like a whisper in her ear, was Jalaa's voice.

"WELCOME HOME, BLOOD OF MY BLOOD. YOU ARE SAFE." And Gyda believed it.

17

Arke

Shao was the first one to find Arke on one of Orenlion's many bridges. The elf narrowed his eyes and looked over Arke's shoulder.

"Where is she?"

Arke grunted. "Nice to see you too."

Shao wasn't fazed. "Wherever you are, Xun is soon to follow. Or causing trouble elsewhere." Then he rocked back on his heels. "How in the hells did you even get in? My men didn't alert me."

"Maybe your men aren't as good as you think."

Shao bristled at that, just like Arke knew he would. He might've earned Sorin's pity and Evren's begrudging trust, but he was still a shit. Easy to poke and make puff up like a pissed off basilisk.

"I'm fuckin' with you," Arke said. "I got in on my own. Magic shit. Didn't even see the guards."

"Magic shit," Shao repeated slowly. He crossed his arms over his chest, armor clanking as he did. He'd changed little since Arke last saw him. Longer hair still tied in that severe knot high on his head. Frown perpetually in place. Always in that damned armor. But he carried his sword now when before he hadn't. It wasn't ornamental, just a plain blade purely for function. The dark circles under his eyes looked like they were weighing him down.

"Is this about Serevadia?" Shao asked. "We've already sent all the troops we could spare to Linston. Aster went with them to make sure there was no miscommunication."

Arke's heart sank, although he should've known this exact thing was happening. While he'd been battling pixies and crystal flowers, Eith was at war.

"No." Arke shook his head. "I'm on my own. Workin' on fixin' this mess."

Shao quirked a brow up. "Seeing as the last time your fixing nearly burned down the entirety of the Wood, I'm only cautiously optimistic." A pause and then, "What do you need?"

Arke could say many things about the old Sovereign, but Shao was at least a quick learner. A sour ass to deal with, but someone he could at least count on to use what was left of his brain.

"Your library still good?"

He scoffed. "Rivaled only by the Conclave in Linston, but you knew that. I'll lead you there."

Turning on his heel, Shao marched off. Arke had no choice but to scramble after him, his smaller legs working overtime to catch up to Shao's long-limbed strides. It was like running from the monster again, only this time he was running *toward* the bastard with too long legs.

Orenlion was a blur in the corners of his eyes as he focused to keep up with Shao. But the rebuilding wasn't lost on him. The city had lost some of its ancient, ethereal nature after the first dragon attack, and the second hadn't made it any better. The newer buildings were made with the same curved rooftops and round windows, but there was a new strength in them that only came from survivors determined never to have to build them again. There was less empty air and more construction. The air was tainted with the smell of fresh-cut wood and sawdust. Hammering and creaking could be heard along with bird song and cries of wyverns.

"Lookin' better," Arke huffed.

Shao looked down at him and slowed his pace just enough that Arke wasn't jogging to keep up. It wasn't a comfortable walk, but he let himself relax. The sun warmed his shoulders and the bridges beneath his feet were sturdy.

"It would be finished sooner, but we've diverted our attention to the city's magical defenses." Shao pursed his lips. "News of this war has left many feeling on edge."

"Serevadia gotten you yet?"

"No, thank the stars. The Wood seems to be a challenge they save for later. However, that might change when they see our troops in Etherak. It is our right and duty to protect our ally, but no one can deny that the sending off a thousand soldiers doesn't make us a threat. How long before Serevadia's ire turns from Etherak to us? Already the messages from Mei speak of destruction in the countryside that rival that of our war with the Hisrachi."

Arke didn't miss the way he hitched at the word, but pride bloomed in his chest anyway. He was making an effort not to call them Weavers.

"Any Hisrachi goin' to Etherak?" he asked. "Since Terevas ain't got an army, it's really the only defense on the continent."

"I'm aware," Shao said. "We all are. No one has been left undisturbed by the loss of Dirn-Darahl. Yes, the Hisrachi have sent some of their own. What good it'll do, I cannot say. Their people have not left the Wood since their creation."

Arke's stomach roiled. "How many?"

"Not quite a thousand. Their leaders don't speak to me, but not all of their forces will head to Etherak. Many will see to the damage near Dirn-Darahl and Whitestone, assuming the common Etherakian farmer doesn't mistaken them for monsters to be slain."

"Wouldn't surprise me," Arke snorted. They turned off another bridge, taking stairs that wound around a massive tree trunk up to the next level. "Why aren't you there with them?"

Shao stiffened minutely, but the sun caught his armor in a way that Arke noticed it. "Someone needed to stay behind for Orenlion's defenses," he said curtly.

Arke winced. "You wanted to go, didn't you?"

"Why wouldn't I?" he snapped. He pulled himself up by the railing as if it was a rope and Arke was a raging fire to climb far away from. "I am still their general, no matter the status I've lost. I should be out there fighting with them. Not sitting here on my hands waiting to be called to action."

"I'd certainly feel better if you were out there."

Shao stopped a couple steps above him and looked down at the goblin with a frown. Arke shrugged.

"What? It's true."

"You need not waste flattery on me," Shao said. "I'm already helping you."

"This ain't flattery." Arke jammed a clawed finger in his direction. "I ain't flattered someone a day in my life. I'm sayin' that for all your stuck-up bullshit, you're a decent general and a good fighter. I would've liked to see you out there."

"Why? You don't even like me."

That was true for a lot of people. "Because my people are out there too, and I'm here. I know what it feels like."

Never a good thing to find something in common with a man that loathed himself to the point of nearly drowning in wine. Shao had yet to outlearn that habit. But he had centuries to do so. And while his admirable qualities were few, they shared more in common than Arke liked to admit.

Being far away from the danger and feeling helpless as their friends fought a war was just the most recent on the list.

Shao didn't say anything. He just nodded sharply and continued up the stairs. Arke followed him, feeling as isolated as he had been in Unnethen's garden, only now the world stretched out in each direction. If he climbed high enough, would he see the armies marching? Would he see the black smoke of the cities burning? If he squinted too hard, would he see the bodies of his friends lying in a pool of their combined blood?

He blinked away those images. He wasn't stupid enough to believe that he would be the difference between their living and dying on the battlefield. He didn't have that much power yet. But he could admit to himself that he'd feel a lot better being at their side feeling hopeless as all hell. That at least was a familiar feeling, unlike the loneliness he felt now.

The library came into view as the stairs ended. A grand and gilded thing, all elegantly stacked stories and archways. The only building that wasn't full of windows or had its doors open to the air. Books and scrolls, even magically protected ones, fell easily to the elements.

Shao stopped short at the doors. "I won't be any help in there. You have free rein of the place, just be respectful."

Arke grinned sharply. "Obviously."

Shao looked like he was regretting letting Arke in with no oversight but didn't take back the offer. "I'll let those in charge know you're here. They'll want to speak with you if you have any information."

Arke hesitated, hand on the red door. He had nothing to tell them about troop movements or enemy weaknesses. They likely already knew about Vanguard. But then there was Abraxas and his role behind everything.

He swallowed the bitter regret in his mouth. It still didn't seem real that Abraxas had turned on them, that every good thing the man had done was eclipsed by this terrible moment in time. Arke still desperately wanted to believe that his friend was in there. They might not have been as close as Abraxas and Gyda were, but they'd fought together, kept watch together, traveled together. That had to count for something.

No. The only thing it counted for was that Arke had to be the one to end him.

Telling Shao and the leaders of Orenlion that the man who'd fought to save them was the very same that was going to destroy them wasn't a good idea. He'd be sending two more armies for Abraxas's head, and that was two more armies for him to obliterate, if he believed anything Unnethen said about Abraxas's strange new powers.

"Arke?" Shao pressed him, hand on the pommel of his sword. The red tassel rested on his knuckles like a trail of blood.

Arke shook his head. "Nah, I've got nothin'. Been stuck in a Fey prison until now so I know less than you now."

Shao nodded slowly and stepped back. "Okay. Thank you."

Arke waved him off and that was all it took to send Shao away. He disappeared down the steps quickly and Arke didn't wait for the loneliness to crash into him before stepping into the library.

He'd been there before when he was helping the old Sovereigns build up the runes of the city after the first dragon attack. Then he'd been bone-tired and pissed about losing a friend to appreciate the beauty of the place. Now? It was the same.

Arke didn't gawk at the swirling wood floors and the fact that there were no cracks in the floorboards at all, just one unending pattern. He didn't care for the paper lanterns and their soft blue glow as he pilfered the shelves. Nor did he stare at the shelves, which covered each and every inch of wall space on five separate floors.

He meandered. He picked up stacks of books after barely reading their titles and came back to his chosen table in a dark corner with bundles of scrolls so high he couldn't see over them. One time he came back and found fresh parchment and ink waiting for him. Not the magical kind, just the normal stuff. Which was perfect for taking notes.

By the time Arke settled into his corner table with three lanterns and books so numerous that the table creaked under their weight, he was already winded. The last thing his body wanted was for him to sit in an uncomfortable chair, hunched over ancient texts and scribbling in the low light.

But that was exactly what he did. His backbone sparked with pain. His ass was numb. Fingers stung from paper cuts and ink. What books didn't work ended up at his feet. The promising ones were held open as he copied passages and his own thoughts onto the spare parchment.

There was nothing on the Aether, which wasn't surprising, and only a little on Vernes. Orenlion had been keeping its nose out of Eith business for centuries, and the war between Etherak and Vernes was no exception. Everything related to Vernes had been marked by the Greyreach Conclave as copies and was sent over as a gesture of goodwill for their new alliance.

The historics they had detailed a few battles, obviously written by someone who wasn't there, and went into the moral complexities behind the war. Arke couldn't give a sparkly shit about why King Eldridge felt himself superior and therefore went on a conquest across Eith. He just wanted clues to how the Aether and Vernes were connected.

"Not even a hello before throwing yourself in here? I'm hurt."

Arke's head snapped up, and his whole neck crackled under the sudden shift. He moved aside some loose scrolls and found the many dark eyes of Neri staring back at him.

It was an odd feeling that came over him every time he was around her. He couldn't do what Evren and Gyda did, which required a lot of mushy confessions and touching. He'd never been one for physical contact—yet another thing that set him apart from every other goblin in Eith.

Yet with Neri he didn't have to. He was all kinds of warm and fuzzy with her, but there was no pressure to be anyone but himself. It wasn't exactly easy. Nothing was when it came to Arke's feelings. But he didn't feel this way towards anyone else. Hadn't ever in his life.

He knew his friends thought it odd that he looked at her

and saw beauty. But how was that any different from the way Gyda looked at Evren when she was covered in blood? *That* was gross, and yet the warrior always looked at her like she was a starving man before a feast.

"I'm sorry," he managed after staring at her for a while. What he was sorry for was anyone's guess. That was another list growing increasingly long.

She chittered and delicately moved the scrolls to the floor. With two of her legs, she started rolling them back up and with another she grabbed for their leather casings.

"Shao told me you were here. Alone." She snapped the leather case shut and set it aside. When she looked back at him her eyes glittered with concern, not anger. *"What happened?"*

It came out in a flood, all of it. Every gruesome detail from the moment they got into Terevas to the moment Arke stepped into Orenlion. She didn't say anything to him the entire time, only settled in on the other side of the table and listened intently. She didn't demand to know why he didn't talk to her about Tolk before when he was brought up. She flinched a little at the mention of Abraxas and what he was doing. And there was nothing in her expression when he got to the part where he traded the mirror shard for his life.

When it was all done, there was no sound but the wind outside. She rubbed her mandibles together in a worried way, and the blue light caught her iridescent hairs the same way the Aether had glimmered.

"You won't find much here," she mused. *"And the Hisrachi keep records by voice alone. Vernes is still a distant dream to us. But maybe we can dig into the real history. There must be someone who was a key figure in this. Someone we can look into for more clues."*

Arke blinked at her. "You're not mad?"

"Why would I be?" she asked honestly.

He struggled for words. "Because I . . . I gave everything to

Unnethen. The mirror shard, myself. I didn't tell you anythin' or try to find you when I first got here."

"*Arke.*" One of her soft legs laid over his hand. "*I will never be mad at you for living. I was worried when I didn't hear from you for a couple weeks, but I knew there was a reason. When war broke out, I knew you'd be fighting in it. I just had to be patient and wait for you to come back.*

"*We both knew that living apart wasn't going to be easy. I couldn't leave, you couldn't stay. We were working through that the best we could.*"

"But I fucked up," he said, his voice catching.

"*You lived,*" she corrected. "*You came back. What happens afterward doesn't matter yet. We'll work this out too.*"

"You can't break a Fey bargain, Neri," he said, feeling more defeated than he had since giving his life to Unnethen.

He'd tried not to think about it before, but now that Neri was there, all he could think about was the fact that if they both lived past this disaster, he'd have to leave her forever. Her and Tolk and Sorin and everyone he'd come to care about despite his best efforts would be cut off from him. He'd be stuck in the Brightlands with Unnethen until he died, or she got bored, whichever came first. The weight of the bargain he made, of what he'd already lost, threatened to drag him to the forest floor.

The only anchor he had was Neri's touch.

"*Maybe not.*" She didn't sound convinced, only humoring him to avoid an argument. "*But that's for later. For now, you have the weight of the world on your shoulders. I may not be able to do much, but I can help ease the load a little.*"

"Okay," he rasped. "Okay."

Because there was nothing else to say that wouldn't make him tear his own heart out and plop it on the cream parchment between them. He tucked the bargain in the back of his mind again, locked it behind several chains of duty and fucks-not-given, and went back to work.

Neri showed him all the books he'd missed. Maps in a

section he hadn't bothered with. They cleared his table of useless tomes and spent a while carefully putting everything back together. It would've gone faster apart, but neither wanted to be parted from the other.

The table was transformed within half an hour. Everything was neat and had its own place split evenly between the two of them. New books were traded back and forth. Passages read aloud to keep words straight. Notes scribbled in shorthand only the two of them could decipher.

There were hidden histories and accounts of the war Arke had completely missed. Soldier's journals, the notes of a general's assistant, even a prisoner of war's recorded words before he was sent back to the other side to trade for a more valuable asset.

The war was as gruesome as it was complex, and Arke tried not to think of Abraxas fighting in it twice. It would've been easier if the elf had shared any of his experiences. Maybe Arke would've had battles and figures to focus on. He found plenty on the War Mage that had helped them, Divara Rimmel. It was all depressing as shit.

"Lots on this Cuskhe battle," Arke muttered. "Vernes won, but it's not even considered a victory."

Neri nodded. *"The cost was too high. I think Abraxas was there."*

"How do you mean?" This was a constant for them. Finding little pieces and rumors of an elf that might've been him. He was never named. Most things barely mentioned him. Like a man tied to a stake to be burned but saved last minute. Or a shadowy elf freeing prisoners with a gang of kids. All useless leads, but tracing his friend's steps might be the key.

"These two accounts from an Etherakian healer and one Vernesian prisoner of war mention someone like him. But . . . it's weird."

"How?"

"There're two separate versions of him, it looks like it anyway. The healer mentions bandaging a Champion of one of

the Divines, saying he never saw such wounds on one so holy. The Vernesian prisoner was delirious with blood loss and went on about an elf in black saving him from a group of knights during the battle. He said that the elf left a trail of bodies behind him, all Etherakian, and fought like death taken mortal form."

Arke worried his lower lip. "Could be they were both him. Same place, two different Abraxas's. I'll bet he beat the shit out of himself too."

Neri had the expression someone might've had if they were frowning. She set down the letters, smoothing them against the table.

"This doesn't look good, Arke. I didn't know Abraxas well, but this would break anyone."

"Docs it say anything about after the battle?"

"No, I don't think . . ." She shuffled through the papers in front of her, her many legs able to flip through them faster. Then she paused. *"Wait, this is Divara Rimmel again. She was at Cuskhe."*

Arke perked up and set aside his book. "What does it say?"

"It's her account of the battle and . . . oh, Arke, she says she died. At the hands of a white-haired necromancer."

"Nerezza," he growled. Everything that happened was because of her, and he wasn't going to take her change of heart for true redemption. Not after the shit she put Abraxas through. "But Rimmel lived. Died at Vanguard."

"Yes, she mentions Divine intervention and Abraxas saving her. But in her notes she said she talked to him—"

"Past Abraxas."

"—and he denied ever being in her area of the city. The stories didn't add up. Divara wrote off the experience and the people she saw as delirium. It meant that her suspicions of a horned people called the Dra'Nacti helping the rebels was never pursued."

"That ain't the first time we heard that name. The fuck are these people?"

"Doesn't say."

Arke shut his book and pushed it off to the side. It smushed up against some of Neri's neat stacks so he took the time to put it in its proper place—the stack of useless books that needed to go up. It was a tall pile.

"This ain't helpin'." He rubbed his eyes. "These are all Etherakian accounts, and if they knew how shit happened in Vernes we wouldn't be in this situation."

"You could go to Vernes."

He scratched his eyebrow. "Yeah, that's what I was thinkin'. Assumin' Serevadia hasn't overrun them. I'd be walkin' through a country I ain't been to before, that's likely fighting off yet another war. And what are the odds anyone there will believe that I'm tryin' to help them? Or even take me seriously?"

Neri busied herself stacking the notes and scrolls, but her hairs quivered with anxiety. *"These people were so desperate to keep their independence that they banished gods, Arke. You need to know more before you go in there and ask them how they did it."*

"Which would be fine, but there's not a lot of people who know enough 'bout Vernes to help me," he said with a sigh. "Sahar's family is from there, yeah, but she wasn't raised there and her parents left while they were young. I remember her sayin' they wished they knew more about their home and history. Keres is probably dead, for good this time, or fuck knows where. Rimmel is dead too. Who does that leave?"

He knew it before she said it, but it didn't stop him from flinching when the name hit him.

"Abraxas would know . . ."

A man who lived a war there twice. Who fought both against and beside the Vernesian rebels. Abraxas would know more than most. Maybe he'd even been there for the banishment the second time around, although Arke doubted that. With all his talk of bringing back the gods, he wouldn't have let them get banished in the first place.

"He won't help me if he knows I'm against him," Arke said, defeated. "And I can't pretend. I can't lie for shit. He'll see right through me."

This was a job for Sol or Sorin. The charming words and silver lies that got the right kind of information. Hells, even Evren had managed it with Viggo. But Arke wasn't like them. He wasn't likable or charming or even passably good at being anyone other than himself. And Abraxas *knew* him.

But what other choice did he have? If Abraxas could tell him one thing about Vernes, one small little detail, that would help him solve this puzzle then it was worth the risk. To give his friends a chance at winning, to save a world he'd been stitching back together one insane quest at a time, there was no risk too high.

He rounded his shoulders. Every part of his spine ached from hunching over books too long. There were no windows, but he knew it had to be well past sundown by now.

"But I know him like he knows me. I can get him talkin'. I can . . ." He forced his voice to be stronger, more for himself than for Neri. "I can do this. Face him. Get what I need. Go to Vernes."

He looked over at Neri for the first time. Her expression was unreadable, and not because Hisrachi facial tics were so different from other races. It was because there was just too many emotions overwhelming her eyes all at once, and they were all potent enough to make his chest hurt.

"I'll come back," he reassured her, although that felt like a lie after everything he said about his deal with Unnethen. He couldn't predict the future. What if he left and the chain of events happened so quickly he couldn't make it back for a final goodbye? What if Unnethen grabbed him before he could get to Orenlion first? And, of course, there was all the dangers along the way. Abraxas, Serevadia, the world collapsing and everyone distrusting goblins on sight.

He had no right to promise her anything. She had every

right to tell him exactly that and force something more reasonable from his lips.

Instead, she looked across the table at him, bathed in blue light. She was everything he didn't know he needed, nothing he could've imagined he wanted.

"*I know,*" she said softly.

A bad lie, a hollow promise, yet she believed it. It was only fair that, in this unfair world, Arke had to try and believe it as well.

18

Sorin

The night was calm when Sorin woke up, for no other reason than his nightmares started to grow jealous of how shit his daily life was and upgraded from awful to terrifying. Nothing new, except for Abraxas's face. And his voice. Calling, pleading, for forgiveness and understanding.

Sorin rubbed his sore eyes, trying to rid himself of the grasping fingers of the nightmare. He spent most of his waking time either cursing Vayne or cursing himself for not doing anything when Abraxas went from mildly insane to full-blown kill friends insane. Not that he could've done anything. Talking wouldn't have helped and Sorin didn't want to fight Abraxas. Deadly sword and beaten Gyda aside, fighting someone he'd once called friend wasn't something he'd call fun. Especially if that same friend had brought him back from the dead.

The scar on his chest didn't hurt, not like his hand. The healing there was as whole as it ever could be. And yet, Sorin couldn't shake the feeling of Heliodar's blade cutting through his chest, of his lifeblood pumping out and trickling through his lips. He'd never forget how cold his body was, how damn scared he'd been. How the last thing he saw was Sol's tearful blue eyes and then . . .

Darkness.

Sorin had never bothered to worry about an afterlife before, but those minutes where his body was still and cooling, and he was somewhere else, he'd panicked. No stars. No welcoming arms of his family.

Just pure, pitch nothing.

Until there was Abraxas's voice. Until there was a light too bright to conceive and he was being dragged back into his body.

Until he was alive again.

Sorin sat up from his hammock, swinging his legs over until they anchored him on the ground. The quarters were dark, save for a singular lantern in the far corner. Those around him slept deeply, but not soundly. Flickers of lantern light revealed their frowning faces even in sleep.

He looked up, content to see Sahar's hand dangling from the edge of her hammock and occasionally twitching. When he looked across the way where Enola had claimed her sleeping spot, he found the hammock empty.

Faster than he could blink he was on his feet and grabbing her blanket. Cold. She hadn't been in bed for a while. It wasn't close to dawn yet, and it was like moving a mountain to wake her up every morning. She wouldn't have gone and stayed gone willingly.

Sorin shoved his feet into his boots, uncaring of how he split his new blisters and how loud he was being. He snatched his coat up, one arm in and the other working its way in as he dashed out of the room.

The *Red Knave* was a labyrinth of shadows at night, but none were like those in his dreams. They didn't nip at his heels or slither beside him as he ran. And he knew where he had to go, so there was little fear of running in the wrong direction. There were places the crew avoided at all costs, and then there were ones they refused to acknowledge existed at all. They would take the long way through the ship instead of taking the same stairs that led them there. They wouldn't even look in its direction.

Sorin grabbed the rope railing and took the stairs down to the belly of the ship two at a time.

Darkness, thick and suffocating, swallowed him but he paid it no mind. He marched forward with no plan, only a wild desperation that raged like a storm in his mind.

There was only one place Enola could be. Only one person who would be so awful as to snatch her out of bed.

Sorin burst into the witch's room with no fear but gained a drop of it once the door shut behind him.

It was lit by a strange blue light coming from a singular lantern that had no flame, and with the lack of windows Sorin felt like he was underwater breathing limited air. The walls were draped with thick, slimy seaweed somehow still wet, as if they'd just been pulled from the depths. Barnacles puckered between the folds, alive and still wriggling for food. The air was damp and smelled thickly of brine.

Water was up to his calves, and Sorin inwardly winced as it soaked his socks. But it didn't move with the ship. It was still and calm, like a tidal pool before high tide came to rescue it and drag the water back to sea.

The room was spare besides that. A table coated in scales and bones, a hammock that looked to be molding, and nothing else. But Sorin had dealt with enough mages to know that he wasn't alone.

"Where is she?" he called out. "Where's Enola?"

The water rippled, sending dazzling reflections on the ceiling. The voice that answered rasped as if her throat was coated with dried salt.

"Enola isn't here, boy."

"Trollshit," he hissed. He dared take another step inside. "What have you done with her?"

"Nothing." The voice came from behind him, close enough that he could smell the foul breath.

Sorin whirled around so quick that he smacked his elbow into the table and yelped. The witch, even more horrifying in the dreary blue light, remained expressionless and immobile as she stood between him and the door.

Sorin massaged his elbow. "Nice place you've got here."

"Sit."

She nodded to the chair beside him, one which looked like it was one Sorin-sized man away from collapsing.

"I'm good, thanks."

"You come into my home after stealing my child, accusing me of stealing her back. You will sit."

Nothing changed in her face, and at this point Sorin was convinced that her features were permanently frozen in a wrinkled frown, but there was a shift in the thick, humid air that prickled at his skin. So Sorin, being the well-behaved man he was, sat down as gingerly as he could. The sodden wood groaned uncomfortably but held. Sorin held his breath too, just in case.

The witch barely disturbed the water as she came around to sit opposite to him. Her gnarled fingers picked at the cleaned scales and bones. It was hard to tell in the light, but they looked like the ones Enola had given him to toss. He was sure they ended up in the ocean.

"I thought you'd find me sooner," croaked the witch.

Sorin let out his breath. "I was busy trying not to die."

"Busy doing the wrong things."

He blinked at her. "What should I—no, never mind. Where's Enola?"

"You've grown fond of the girl." The witch took a shining scale and dipped it in the water at their feet. Her fingers came back empty.

"She ran to me running from you."

"Did she now?" she raised a haggard brow at him, and the beginnings of a smirk might've started to crack that weather face of hers. "I take it you think I keep her secluded in here? That I stole her back?"

"Well, yes!" He shut his mouth. He knew this feeling. When Arke was doing magic things and trying to teach him something that should be obvious but he was just missing it entirely. Or Evren, tracking their dinner and trying to show him the very obvious tracks in the mud that he just couldn't see.

More accurately, when he played cards with Sol and fell for her tricks and lies.

"That's not what happened, is it?" he asked, dread creeping up on him. Shit. *Shit.* He'd told Enola everything. She knew that he and Sahar had plans to get out. She knew that they were lying to Vayne. She knew by now that Sahar was not entirely magicless.

The cackling rasp that came from the witch's throat made him want to curl up in a ball and hide, if doing that didn't mean more water and strangely living sea plants.

"If it had been, would I not have come for her earlier?"

"Oh, I dunno, I figured maybe you wanted a break? Kids, right?" He laughed awkwardly with her, but his died much sooner. He gulped, wishing for a scrap of that reckless energy that brought him down there. "You're going to kill me, aren't you?"

She blinked slowly. "Yes."

"And . . . Enola knows that?"

Sorin didn't think her face could soften, and it didn't. But there seemed to be a twinge of sympathy in those dark eyes.

"No." The witch picked up a thin sharp bone. "She likes you. She would not like this plan."

That was more of a relief than Sorin cared to let show. He fisted his hands on the table, ignoring the spasming of his left hand.

"To be fair, I don't like it either."

"It will be you or the woman." She flicked the bone in the water. "This is how it must be. But you will gain more. I would prefer her on the surface with that boy raging inside her."

Sorin stilled. "That's a lot of words that need further explaining. But first, how did you know?"

The witch's shoulder shrugged. "They are loud. The boy and her are like two forks of lighting battling for the same spot on the ground. She'll burn herself out, eventually."

Simple Stormheart his ass. This witch was something else entirely. Something ancient, powerful, and comfortable with chaos. There were stories of the first Vasa being too powerful, of the sea taking back their powers and giving them sparingly to the Vasa that deserved it or needed it. Sorin never liked those stories because he hated how the sea didn't think *he* deserved power. But his childish mind couldn't help but snatch at those stories and believe that the woman in front of him was an original Vasa, brimming with power that she'd held onto throughout the thousands of years.

"What are you?" he whispered. "Are you an ancient?"

"No, boy," she said. "I am an old woman with magic. I am an old woman who used to be young and fell in love with the wrong man."

"If you're going to say Vayne—"

"I was indeed."

"*How?*" Sorin temporarily forgot that this was the same woman who was going to kill him. "You look old enough to be his mother."

"You still think of him as human?"

"Well, yes," Sorin said, feeling rather stupid. Again.

She waved him off, bone fingers flicking more bones in the water with musical plops. "Hardly your fault. Vayne likes to look normal. And he is, for the most part. Might I tell you a story, boy?"

"Do I have a choice?"

"Indulge an old woman."

"Then please, go ahead." He nodded. Maybe a story would buy him time.

The witch settled deeper into her chair, which he didn't

think was smart given the sounds it was making. She shoved her piles of scales and bones to the center of the table, folded her gnarled hands together and began to speak with the blue light twinkling in her eyes.

"Many years ago, I was a much younger woman. Keep that smart comment in your mouth boy, or I will turn you into a crab and start the story over. Now, where . . . yes, I was a young woman. A gifted Stormheart wanted on nearly any ship. I chose none, for my heart would not be tied to rope and wood. I spent my time in the water with my Bond."

Sorin gaped. "You have a Sea Bond?"

She sighed. "Yes, crab."

"Sorry. Please continue."

"My Bond," she continued, "was not incredibly powerful. Certainly no sea serpent. A simple hippocamp by the name of Oriel."

Sorin kept his mouth shut instead of blurting out something about a horse with a fishtail being her Bond and shortening his lifespan considerably.

"We traveled the waters together. Dangerous, yes, but we kept each other safe. And there are few freedoms as intoxicating as having nothing but the sea and the sky for as far as you can see. I must've been more hippocamp than human with how I lived by her side. Content, young, and thriving. Until we found a ship in need of saving, and decided to help.

"It was in neither of our natures to leave people suffering if we could help. The ship had taken heavy damages, but from what I couldn't tell. Between Oriel and I, we kept it from sinking and brought it to shallower waters. The crew had lost many, including their captain, but a young man was the first to thank us and offer us a reward."

"Vayne?" Sorin asked, and she nodded.

"Make all the faces you would like, boy, he was a different man then." She frowned. "Or maybe he wasn't. I was young and foolish. He was handsome and dashing. And for the first time in all my years, I found myself wanting to leave the water. Oriel was sad, of course, but she enjoyed the boy's company as much as I did and would give me anything I asked. As far as we both knew, this fancy would be short-lived and we could go back to the water."

She tsked, shaking her head. "What fools we were. Vayne was a clever young pirate who knew the stories of the Vasa well. He knew what I was, and what he could gain. But he also knew that I was too flighty to be tied down, no matter how much I liked him. There was only one way to keep me, and that was by catching Oriel.

"Oriel was no fish to be lured, but she knew I was in trouble. When she came for me, Vayne ensnared us both in a net and told us we would be staying on his ship permanently. I take it you have never tried to capture a hippocamp, boy? Good. You have a bit of a brain up there then. They are incredibly wild creatures, and deadly when angered. I had never seen Oriel angry until that day. She fought long and hard, nearly killing Vayne in the process. But he cut her, deeply. The wound sprayed blood on him, and the battle was over. Oriel not dead, but her tail severed. She would never swim again, and that spray of blood brought Vayne power.

"See, man fears nothing more than his own mortality, and Vayne was, at his core, a normal man. Hippocamp blood and meat can halt aging, so long as a piece is eaten once a year. Vayne has survived this long because of that."

Sorin couldn't help it, he gagged. "He's been eating your Sea Bond alive?"

She nodded grimly. "A torturous existence for Oriel. He takes only what he needs to survive. I stay at his side for her, and she stays because she is too weak and crippled to leave."

He paused, trying to wipe the image of Vayne cutting into a hippocamp with a knife and fork while it screamed.

"You've got terrible taste in men."

That salt rasp laughter came back. "Enola says so as well. I would kill Vayne now if I had the strength. But any move I make he is aware of. With that comes the threat of losing Oriel, which I cannot have."

"But he wouldn't kill her," Sorin protested. "He needs her to keep being his immortal, dickish self."

"Who said Oriel needed to be alive for him to benefit?" she asked. "We Vasa have methods a plenty to preserve the meat for decades. That is how we live when the ocean refuses to give us food. You are old enough to know this."

He just grumbled under his breath as she continued.

"Oriel lives as my leash. This is why you must die."

"I was wondering when we'd get to that part." Sorin rapped his good knuckles against the damp table. "Can I ask why?"

"It is what Vayne would ask me to do once I found the boy who's been hiding Enola and plotting against him."

"But you knew that I . . ." He was missing something again. Damn mysterious conversations on three hours of shitty sleep. "You knew. Enola ran to me because of you."

When the witch grinned, her rotted teeth shone like oil. "She ran to you for a reason, boy. How long do you think it'll be before Vayne finds out your friend is harboring the soul of a Vasa more powerful than I? What do you think he'll do to her?"

"I'd rather not know, thanks," Sorin said uncomfortably. "Still don't see how me dying helps her. Unless this is a threat?"

She clucked her tongue against the roof of her mouth and hells, he could've gone the rest of his short and miserable life without seeing that. "You ask all the wrong questions. Better is *how* you will die."

He screwed his face up as if he'd smelled something nasty. Which he had. "Thought I didn't have a choice."

"We all have a choice in how we go. In your case, this will be a show. That is what you're good at, yes?"

She pointed to his mangled hand. Sorin put it back in his lap, but he couldn't deny that she was right. If he was going to die, what better way than making sure he was protecting Sahar and giving the biggest distraction of his life?

"Okay," said Sorin slowly. "I die. You make sure Vayne doesn't see what Sahar is. You get her out?"

"She'll get herself out, don't worry."

"See, when people like you say, 'don't worry,' that tends to be *all* I do."

"There's no reason to worry when you can do nothing to affect the outcome."

"Fine," he bit out. "One last question."

She nodded for him to continue.

"Enola," he began. "Do you really need her blood for your storms?"

"I am a powerful Vasa, but no god. Your friend was correct in assuming that I use Enola's blood to amplify my powers. Enola does hate it, as she's told you. So do I. Vayne isn't aware, however, and will stay oblivious. I knew one day that she would bring me to someone who knew what she was. I knew that when she found that person, they would be the key to ending this hell."

Her eyes were darker than the bottom of the ocean as she bored into Sorin's soul. "I knew she'd bring me to you, Sorin Trinity. The key is set in the lock. It is up to you to see how far it turns."

<h1 style="text-align:center">19</h1>

Arke

Arke got where he was through taking risks. Stealing a spellbook, for one, was something that nearly got him killed but helped with his magic. Following Sorin promised a world of hurt, and delivered, but with a side effect of having a place to belong to. Or people, rather, to belong to.

Magic came with risks. Every new spell he tried, every scratch of ink on his paper could be the thing that kills him if he did it wrong. Going back for Tolk and sticking with Unnethen was his biggest one so far, but he couldn't find the will to regret it.

Getting close to the Wandering Sols, loving them, fighting with them, choosing them, that was once the hardest risk. Now it was easy, second nature. It wasn't even a decision to make.

Maybe that was why, after hours of arguing with Shao about where exactly Abraxas would be, Arke gave up. His old friend could be anywhere. On the surface, below it, fighting, or biding his time. Abraxas had kept stubbornly out of view of any survivors or spies. If Arke wanted to get to him, he was going to have to go the long way, or take a risk.

He told himself that experimenting with magic in a time where he couldn't afford to be ripped to shreds was a bad idea. But there he stood, at the edge of Orenlion with the stars wheeling above him, about to take that very same risk.

Using Aether portals for places was logical, easy. Arke could likely pop up anywhere, although he imagined it was safer to go to places he'd been to before. But trying to navigate to one person? He'd shrugged that off before. Now he didn't have a choice.

"This is gonna stink," he muttered.

Behind him, Shao snorted. "You've said that several times in the past twenty minutes. What are you waiting for?"

"Somethin' like courage, asshole," he snapped. "I can't casually bend the laws of multiple worlds to suit my needs and not shit myself without it."

Before Shao could smart off again there was a whack of something hitting his armor dully. He grumbled at the smack on his leg, taking a few steps away from Neri.

"You've got this, Arke. Just don't think too much."

Easy for her to say. Magic was all about thinking. Spells needed guidelines and rules or else the same fire he wanted to burn his enemies lashed out at him and his friends. But the portals had been different. One born out of fear and survival, the other out of a need for comfort. Maybe she was right . . .

Arke closed his eyes and forced his mind to empty all thoughts except Abraxas. No war, no Serevadia, no Fey and bad deals or Neri behind him for what could be the last time. Just his old friend. The fall of his black hair. The curve of his frown. Pale skin stark against the black of his neck tattoo. Eyes heavy after seeing too much. Shoulders tight from constant vigilance.

Quiet evening watches where neither needed to speak and just stayed content in each other's company. Keeping eyes on each other in strange new towns where either of them could be seen as threats by the locals. Quick glances and checks for injuries after battles. Gentle yet insistent pushes to take care of each other and eat regularly or go to sleep.

The awful moment when he woke up in Orenlion and it was a different healer, not Abraxas tending to him, and he somehow knew he'd never see his friend again.

It was all memory and emotion welling up inside him, yet the rush of power was unmistakable. The portal popped open in front of him and he kept his eyes closed a little while longer while Neri gasped and Shao cursed.

"You could move a whole army across the world like that," the general breathed.

Arke twitched his ears in annoyance and fixed Shao with a glare. "Always about fightin' with you?"

Shao grinned sharply. "Always about magic with you?"

He grunted. "Fair enough."

Arke took the chance to smile at Neri. "Thanks. For everything."

Her eyes shone. Pride? Fear? He couldn't tell. *"Go save the world. We'll be waiting."*

And how could he say no to that? To her? He couldn't in any way. So he turned back to the portal and the still, warm air that wafted from it, took a breath, and stepped through.

He felt himself pass through the Aether. Felt the caress of humming souls and power for the brief second he stepped inside. But it was merely a bridge to the other side, the place he opened himself too. The Aether was gone in a blink, and Arke was standing in a hallway.

The portal closed, and he felt the crushing wave of being alone. Ignored it and forced himself to look around.

Dwarven for sure. The walls had Luminstones illuminating the hallway. Arke felt a sudden, intense ache for his own that he broke in the Yawning Deep. It was like a different Arke had done that to rid himself of the Visha and save Sorin. He hadn't cared much about the group of tagalongs they were traveling with, not then.

It felt like an age ago. An era gone by that he couldn't grasp again. Memories tainted with nostalgia despite the hell it had been to make them.

There was a set of stairs ahead of him, curving and solid like the ones from Dirn-Darahl. But these looked older, worn down. And standing on them, half twisted as if he'd been climbing up until he heard the portal, was an elf in black.

It hit Arke like a boulder to see Abraxas again. Nothing he'd heard about him or imagined had prepared him for that. He looked so much older, so worn down. When he stepped down, closer to Arke, his movements were as measured and cautious as Arke remembered them being in the past. But underneath, there was a power that hadn't been there. Unsettling, otherworldly, ingrained into every part of him.

Arke forced himself not to step away.

Abraxas hesitated at the bottom of the steps. Clenched and unclenched his fists by his side. Looked everywhere but Arke for a while before landing on his face.

"Are you here to kill me, or talk?"

Both, in a way. But Arke couldn't bring himself to say that. The underlying wariness in Abraxas's voice reminded him of a dog that had been kicked too many times and was afraid of every boot that crossed his path.

"Just talk," Arke said. "We didn't get to before."

Before, when the shadows had dragged him under the sea. Before, in a dark palace of endless stairs and hallways, none leading anywhere safe, alone with a teeth-gnashing corpse as he worked out a new spell that would either save or kill his friends. Before, when he made the decision to turn his back on the Wandering Sols for his brother.

"No," Abraxas admitted. His guard let down a little and he swept his arm out to the stairs above. "Come. I'd relish the chance to speak with a friend again."

The last thing Arke wanted was Abraxas behind him. But he went up the stairs anyway, having an easier time with steps built for stubbier dwarven legs than those in Orenlion. At the top was an open door and a Serevadian guard.

Arke immediately bristled and went for his spellbook, but Abraxas stepped around him and waved the guard down. The guard flinched at his hand and pressed himself against the wall with his head bowed. That was nearly enough for Arke to drop his spellbook.

Abraxas remained unfazed, maybe even bored, as he motioned for Arke to keep walking.

"They won't hurt you so long as you're with me."

A threat? Arke's claws dug into the marked leather of his spellbook and followed Abraxas down the new hallway. The elf paused at one room on the left, frowning as if to listen, then shook his head and picked another across the hall. It was a simple room, neatly made bed in the corner and a small desk up against the window, lit only by a single Luminstone on the desk. The view was dark and of an underground cavern and the buildings that scattered the ground. Watchtowers gleamed from where he could see, two of them. No doubt there were more.

Abraxas shut the door behind them but didn't lock it. Arke decided that made him feel worse.

"This your room?" Arke eyed it all. The sparseness had Abraxas written all over it. Arke had never known him to keep anything except what he needed. No useless trinkets or baubles that made him happy. Just the essentials.

"Is it that obvious?" He pulled the chair under the desk out and sat.

Arke stayed standing. "The made bed gave you away."

Abraxas's smile didn't reach his eyes, not by a long shot. In the direct light of the Luminstone, it made him look even colder.

"You weren't with the others in the palace," Abraxas said easily, as if commenting on the weather. "And yet I put you there. You didn't follow them."

"You took my brother."

Abraxas sat up straighter, amusement tinging his expression. "I wasn't aware you had one. You never spoke of him."

Arke gritted his teeth. "You saw an army of goblins marchin' to help us at Vanguard and didn't think to connect two and two?"

"Well, you seem to have such disdain for your own kind, I didn't think you would mind." He blinked at Arke's growing agitation. "Truly, I didn't know. Would an apology suffice?"

"Would it be genuine?" Arke ground out.

"Maybe not. You killed two hundred of my men."

"They were in my way."

"So that makes it reasonable." Abraxas shook his head and leaned an elbow on his desk. His ink-black hair spilled down to frame his face like a curtain. "I wonder what the line between hero and monster is. You massacre for a brother you abandoned, leaving behind our friends, and your actions are deemed worthy. I massacre people for the good of Eith, for a cause greater than myself, and I have been labeled a monster."

"Seems like a debate for people other than us. The unbiased sort."

Arke decided to fuck his fear and hop on Abraxas's bed. It wasn't a comfortable thing, and he had to wiggle to get situated. When he did, his feet dangled above the floor, his spellbook held firmly in his lap.

Abraxas narrowed his eyes at him, and it had nothing to do with the new wrinkles in his bedspread.

"Why are you here?"

"I want to know what happened in Vernes."

There it was, that classic Abraxas stiffness. Gone was the lazy, relaxed nature of someone who had control over the situation. His old friend's eyes sparked with an even older pain twice over. He didn't move, though, and his casual lean got stiffer by the minute.

"Why?"

Arke scowled at him. "Because I'm your fuckin' friend,

dumbass. At least I used to be. I want to know what happened to make you lose yourself."

"I assure you that I haven't lost anything."

"Bullshit." Arke jabbed a claw in his direction. "I know you. I've been there on the nights where you didn't sleep because the nightmares were too bad. I saw your face in Direwall when the fighting looked too much like what you'd left behind. I saw you fight every day to get rid of the memories of Vernes and I know you lost that battle every single day."

"Very perceptive," Abraxas hissed.

"So it ain't a far stretch to say a second time 'round did you in," Arke continued. "You never wanted to go back, and you were forced to. Why?"

"Because Nerezza hunted for things to make herself a god," Abraxas snapped. "That search led her to Vernes, and who else better to show her around than I? As if a hundred years of war wasn't good enough the first time, I endured two years more. Minuscule, in the long tapestry of time, yet an eternity all the same."

Arke before would've stopped there after seeing the obvious pain speaking about it brought his friend. He would've said something vulgar as a way of an apology and then waddled off to distract himself with Sorin or Gyda.

But they weren't Arke and Abraxas of the Wandering Sols anymore. Whatever they were now, walking around each other's glass-sharp emotions wasn't an option.

"What happened?" Arke asked again. "Back in Terevas, we met an old friend of yours, Rimmel. Ringing any Divine bells?"

Abraxas frowned. "Of course. She tried to burn me at the stake, and then died at Nerezza's hand. I brought her back, the same way I did with Sorin, and sent her back to her army. This was not an act of mercy or kindness, Arke. Divara was the reason Loghain was able to stage a successful coup against his brother so we could leave Vernes the first time. She was essential to history, nothing more."

"Liar."

Abraxas sat up straight. "What?"

"Sure, that might've been it. Save her, save Etherak, whatever. But you cared about her. Divara Rimmel and the Abraxas Kain of old were friends."

"She and I, the Abraxas Kain of new, are not."

"Were."

Abraxas stilled even more. It was like looking at a statue. "What?"

"She's dead." Arke let that simmer and rot in the air between them, unblinking and refusing to show he was moved by her death. He hadn't at first when all he could think about was getting to Tolk. But Divara Rimmel could've easily been him, and he couldn't deny that her memory stuck with him.

"How?"

"Vanguard," Arke said crisply. "She helped us take it. If Tolk and his army had come in to help us like they were supposed to, she wouldn't have needed to drown the fort in lava."

Abraxas's jaw was tight and feathered with twitching muscles. He looked down sharply at the Luminstone and stared at it for so long, Arke feared he would blind himself. So focused on Abraxas, Arke didn't realize how dark the room had become until he couldn't see anything but Abraxas and the Luminstone.

Arke fought to keep his fingers from tearing through his spellbook. The shadows coiled close to him, but not touching. Their chill reminded him too much of the salt and black of the palace where everything went wrong.

"A tragedy," Abraxas finally said. "But she lived her purpose. Death finds us all."

"Not at first." Arke focused on Abraxas and not the shadows reaching for him. "You brought her back, how?"

Abraxas laughed mirthlessly. "You know, all this time and I never figured it out. I was told that I'm not entirely elven, that this power I thought belonged to Haphion was not a gift at all, but something inside of me. Divine in nature, yes, it has done more than revive friends from certain death. It brought me to the power I needed. It kept me from succumbing to the same fate Nerezza suffered trying to use the sword."

Arke winced, remembering how far from powerful Nerezza had acted when he saw her last. Veiled and hysterical, on the verge of complete madness. Even almost dying at her hand, he could feel a twinge of pity for what she'd become, although he couldn't deny it was deserved. At least a little.

"I saw her. Some of her. That wasn't pretty."

Abraxas sneered. "It was less than she deserved. Painless compared to the hell I endured through her magic."

Arke sucked in a breath. "What did she do to you?"

"Barely a minute after we survived the dragon, she used my blood to bind me to her will. To disobey and fight her was . . . agonizing. I lost days, weeks, to that pain. I had little choice but to do what she said. The rare moments where I was let off my leash, I was only doing what she knew I would. In the end, when she was killing Divara, I almost died myself to stop her. It was only because of Aushruk that I survived at all."

Arke cocked his head, flicked an icy shadow off his ear. "Aushruk?"

Abraxas's eyes were distant. "Yes. She helped me. Tried to make me a better man. She's the one who told me what I was, or rather, what I wasn't. I suppose in many ways she made me what I am now, although she wouldn't like the man I've become. Much like you don't."

Arke's head spun and he fought to keep looking neutral, or at least pissed off. That was his normal. But inside he clung to that name. Someone from Vernes. Someone who knew more about Abraxas than he did. Who'd tried to save him even.

Perhaps someone still alive.

Arke wanted to press more about who Aushruk was, what she did, what she looked like. He wanted every detail, but he knew that's not where the conversation was heading. Abraxas looked ready to pick a fight. To lash out whenever Arke confirmed his statement or argue when he denied.

What would Sol do? How could she keep this conversation in her control while letting Abraxas feel like he was holding all the strings?

"Maybe she just wanted better for you . . ." Arke said tentatively. "I do. We all do."

"There is no better for me." Abraxas said, but he'd lost his razor-sharp edge. "This is the path I must walk. Do none of you realize this?"

"We just want you back," Arke said and jumped off the bed. The shadows split where his feet touched the ground and he didn't hide his relief. "We lost you and grieved you. I know it's stupid to ask you to come back the way you were before—"

"I will never be that man again," Abraxas said bitterly.

"—but stop bein' such a self-sacrificin' ass for a minute and see it from our perspective! You were gone, and when you came back you have Serevadia burnin' down everything we built. You've murdered people we called allies. You destroyed whole cities. And for what? Gods who didn't care enough to help you when you were with Nerezza?"

Abraxas flinched away like Arke had physically struck him. He stared at him with wide, unreadable eyes, lips parted in surprise.

"You don't understand," Abraxas said. "You and Aushruk both, you don't know the Divines. You haven't lived with them."

"Good! I hope I never fuckin' do!" Arke cried out. "After everything they did to you and all they failed to do, how can you go back? How are they any better than Nerezza?"

This wasn't about Aushruk anymore, whoever she was. These were words bottled up since the moment Arke met Abraxas. They'd softened over time, less cutting and harsh than they'd been in the beginning. Goblins didn't worship anything beyond the occasional Archfey that needed an ego boost, so he never understood religion. He never wrapped his head around how something untouchable, unknowable, could drive decent men and women to commit atrocities.

Men like Abraxas.

"This Aushruk wanted what was best for you, right?" Arke asked.

"What she thought—"

"She saved your life! You look all guilty when you speak of her. That means you cared, just like you did with Rimmel." Arke paused, chest heaving. "Just like you do with us."

Us hung heavy in the air between them. Heavy enough to force the shadows seething into the corner.

Abraxas swallowed, looking down at his hands instead of at Arke. "I know you mean well, old friend, and it means everything to me that you came here to try, unlike . . ." His voice caught and he moved on quickly. "But Aushruk was wrong, as her kind so often are about the Divine. The Dra'Nacti worship nothing but the desert that made them. She could not see why I needed them, or wanted them, and I know the same questions burn through your head. It isn't something I can describe to one who has endured Eith without Divine guidance."

Arke stepped forward and put his hand over Abraxas's. The elf recoiled, as Arke had many times in the same situation, but not enough to pull his hand away.

"You're right." And that drew Abraxas's dark gaze to him. "I'll never understand. I don't want to. Seems to me that the Divine fucks all it touches, and I don't want any part in that. But I'd endure it for you. If you just came back with me, we could fix this together."

Arke couldn't lie. This wasn't a lie. It was a stab in the dark. A hope that flickered to life and was trying so hard to shine. If Arke could bring him home, he could end this. They would be together again, as they should be.

Abraxas laid his other hand on Arke's and it was like nothing had changed.

"I wish it were so simple," Abraxas whispered. "But I have

gone too far and sacrificed too much to walk away now. There is only one way to save Eith from Serevadia's ruin, and I must be the one to do it."

No. No, no, no! He was losing him.

"Please," Arke rasped. "Don't do this. You have a place, Abraxas. You have a home and family with us, if you would just—"

"I have no family but the Divines," he said crisply. How many times had he grown up reciting that lie? How many times did he have to say it to truly believe it?

Arke tried to snatch his hand back, but Abraxas's grip turned to iron. He wouldn't let go and was an elf turned to shackle, although his expression remained the same.

Still, he sounded exhausted and sad when he spoke as Arke struggled. "Join me. I know I have done terrible things, but I tire of being alone. Now more than ever I could use your power and your wisdom."

Arke bared his death. "Let me go."

"You came to me wishing to talk. Did you not see this outcome?"

Arke didn't need to look behind himself to see the shadows rearing back to strike. Abraxas rose from the chair, one hand tightening around Arke's wrist. His eyes remained sad and drawn.

He couldn't rip a spell without both hands. Abraxas had handicapped him better than iron manacles. And Arke had fallen right into his trap like a fuckin' idiot.

"Come on, Abraxas," Arke growled. "Don't do this. I'm your friend, damn it!"

"And as my friend, would you stay out of my way if I let you go?" he asked. The shadows crept up and over his shoulders like a strange cape. "Would you sit idly by while I remade the world?"

Arke pressed his lips together. He couldn't lie.

Abraxas's smile was not one of victory. "I thought not. You

forget that I know you well. I know you all. That has been the most difficult part in this quest—"

Arke bit him.

His teeth sank into the flesh of his hand and hit bone. Distantly, Abraxas cried out. Blood gushed into Arke's mouth and he gagged but held on. Dug deeper. Twisted his hand so that his teeth tore through Abraxas's.

Abraxas let go the same time the shadows jerked Arke away from him. Where only a foot had separated them before, now the whole room did. Shadows seethed and lashed out, binding Arke's arms to his sides. He was barely able to hold onto his spellbook, just as useless as before only now with a mouth full of copper.

Abraxas cradled his hand, mouth drawn tight in pain. A shadow curled towards him and gently caressed the mangled mess Arke had left. In front of his eyes the hand started to knit back together until there was nothing remaining of his bite. Only smooth, pale flesh over long fingers.

Abraxas flexed his hand experimentally and glared at Arke.

"I told you that I was different now." He shook his head sadly. "Why can't you listen? Why can't you understand? Or at least try."

"I did." Arke spat out a mouthful of blood. His eyes stung. "It's you who won't listen. We would follow you anywhere Abraxas."

"No you won't!" he shouted. "You won't follow me now."

"Because you're not you!"

"I am more me than I have ever been!" The shadows darkened around him. The Luminstone started to fade, turning weaker and greyer by the second. "This is what I am, Arke. A Divine's chosen. A Divine's damned. I am the catalyst from which Eith will burn and rise anew. What you think you loved before was nothing more than a husk. This is what I was always meant to be from the start."

Arke struggled to breathe, although whether that was from

the shadows constricting his chest or the stabbing emotions, he wasn't sure.

"Well, I prefer the husk," Arke choked out. "Because the husk was my friend. You are . . . you are everything he would've hated."

Damn the dangers. Damn the man in front of him. Arke poured everything he had into a portal. Every hurt, every conflict, every drop of blood in his mouth. He wanted the grey numbness of the in-between.

The Aether snapped to life just behind his back. The shadows reared away from him. Abraxas's face contorted into shock and pain. Arke didn't want to, but he memorized that expression. That look of betrayal. For a moment he was angry because how *dare* Abraxas look at his actions like a betrayal after everything he'd done.

But it was Abraxas, and Arke felt nothing but a deep, bottomless agony in his heart. He stepped back into the Aether and the portal closed over his once friend's face.

Arke immediately sank to his knees. His spellbook thudded beside him. He put his head in his hands and he wept for the first time in many, many years.

The souls of the Aether responded, curling around him like a cocoon of buzzing voices and fog. He barely felt them. All he could feel was the dagger of betrayal lodged firmly in his heart. A heart that he'd spent his whole life carefully guarding with layers and layers of defenses. It took one stupid Vasa to crack them, and then he was loving so many different people, he couldn't keep up.

But this pain, this hurt, was exactly why he had the walls up in the first place. Because it was always a matter of time until all the good things that love brought soured and made him a wreck.

Arke knew this and let it happen anyway. But try as he might now, he couldn't build up those walls again. He couldn't grasp those bricks even if he wanted to.

Because if he was going to kill Abraxas, he was going to feel everything. The husk deserved that much at least.

"I don't want to," Arke whispered to the dead and gathered souls around him. "I don't want to kill him."

The souls offered no help, for the dead could not comfort the living any more than the living could change their destiny.

20

Gyda

Gyda was finally warm when she woke up, save for something metal and chilled in the palm of her hand. She didn't look at it, couldn't actually, thanks to her using that same arm as a pillow and the worg deciding that her idea was marvelous and he should as well. She woke up with a mouth full of worg fur, his drool in the crook of her numbing arm, and the persistent ache in her hip that she always got when she slept on her side for too long.

She huffed. "Get off."

The worg grunted and seemed to settle down even heavier.

Gyda gritted her teeth and started to wiggle her arm back. With every tug the worg tried to get comfortable on what was left of her arm and did an impressive job of keeping his headrest. Gyda tried her best to ignore the fact that she didn't have her strength back enough to shove him off, which she could've done easily months ago.

"Overfed," she grumbled and pulled again. "Mangy . . . slobbering . . . beast!"

With a final tug she had her arm back against her chest and

the worg flopped down, obviously not thrilled but too lazy to move from his spot. Gyda shifted until she was on her back, letting the pressure on her hip ease up and massaging some feeling back into her arm. She curled it against her chest, working her fingers down from the shoulder to the wrist until she caught a glint of what was in that hand.

An iron dragon, scales speckled with frost and attached to a cord of leather. Evren's most recent gift.

Gyda thumbed away the frost and the scales gleamed. The wings fit perfectly into the curve of her palm. She remembered how the weight felt right on her chest, how she pressed it into her skin when she was alone in bed after Rhienwall, wondering what it would be like to pray for Evren's safe return. Wondering if maybe her old friend had been onto something when she saw her grace her doorway, dirt smudged, weary, and yet so beautifully alive.

Now it made her sick. Her chest was hot and tight, so much so that she could barely breathe around it. When she saw the dragon, she didn't think of Haphion, because he was a god that was beyond her. He hadn't earned her respect, so he didn't deserve her devotion. Like Evren had meant it when she'd given it to Gyda, the dragon made her think of Abraxas. Only now those memories were tainted.

Every good sparring session soured into a battle she'd lost. The *only* one she'd lost. Every quiet talk through complicated emotions curdled into a speech where, with every word, Gyda grew to realize her friend was gone. The hand to pull her up from the ground and get back into the battle turned into a blade at her neck, stopped only by a desperate arrow.

There had been a moment, however brief, that she saw him and thought everything was going to be okay. When he smiled and all she could think about was how much she missed him and there was that overwhelming relief that she didn't have to mourn him anymore.

That relief had turned right back to grief, now tangled with something hot and nasty that made her sick every time she thought of him.

"You are hurt, blood of my blood."

Gyda sat up at the sound of Jalaa's voice, pointedly ignoring the way the blood rushing to her head made her vision go fuzzy. She blinked several times, waiting for the dark blurs around her to become clearer.

When it did, the giant's home made Gyda feel small for one of the handful of times in her life. There was a wave of vertigo, because everything looked familiar. The drape of furs over the bed—although where one got furs that large remained a mystery—were exactly like how the Ikedree warmed their own beds. The firepit sparking big enough that Gyda could feel its heat from across the room. A large kitchen, a chair decorated with more furs and something strangely like knitting, but Gyda was sure that wasn't wool. It glittered like scales, half made into a scarf that could've wrapped around Gyda three times.

And, of course, everything was a lot bigger than she was used to.

Gyda dug her free hand into the worg's fur, and he leaned into her in his sleep. Across the room, Jalaa sat by the fire and stoked its embers. There weren't any logs or kindling that Gyda could see, only the bright red rune underneath the flames that burned brighter each time Jalaa traced it with her fire poker.

On the bed, taking up only a mere corner of it, Gyda felt like a child. So much so that Jalaa had to look back over to her with those starlight eyes and speak again.

"What troubles you? Surely not the metal in your hand."

Gyda glanced down at it, then curled her fingers around the dragon to hide it. She saw Abraxas every time it caught her eye.

"The pendant reminds me of someone," she grumbled.

Jalaa's hum of understanding vibrated in Gyda's sternum. "And this one hurts you."

"Hurt me," Gyda corrected, and winced when she realized she'd corrected a giant of legend. "Sorry."

The giantess simply smiled. "No need for apologies, but you're wrong. This one hurts you still. I can see it in your eyes. What was done?"

"Betrayal," Gyda said hoarsely as she combed her fingers through the worg's fur. "He is—was—one of my dearest friends. I thought him dead but . . ." she shook her head. "It's complicated."

Jalaa stared at her for a while, and a flicker of emotion, possibly resignation as if she'd confirmed something she wished wasn't true, settled in her face. She set down her poker.

"You speak of Abraxas Kain."

Gyda shuddered. Never in her life did she expect to hear his name in the voice of someone like Jalaa. Once, she might've imagined a great quest where all her friends joined her in the journey to the top of Jalaa's mountain. They would be blessed each in turn, and she'd get to share a piece of her culture that wasn't so tainted by undeath and horror. But in that imagining, when Jalaa said Abraxas's name, it was with pride and kindness. The same way she spoke to Gyda.

Jalaa spoke Abraxas's name as if it had the edge of an executioner's ax, too heavy and sharp for her to avoid hurting when she spat it out into the world.

Gyda swallowed. What had Abraxas done to be known by Jalaa with such intense sorrow?

"How do you know his name?"

"Another that knows his story well visited before you did. No, blood of my blood, not the worg. He knows little of betrayal. All he is aware of is that he was alone until now and finds a home in you. He came to me mere hours before you did, and then set off to find you. Such loyalty in animals is not to be taken lightly."

Gyda rested her hand on the worg's head and his pointed ears flicked in her direction, but he didn't open his eyes.

"I don't take him for granted, but he isn't mine," she said.

"He is no one's," Jalaa corrected her gently. "He chose to be with you and those you call your clan."

Gyda frowned and asked, "But why is he here?" when all she really wanted to ask was, *Why aren't they here?*

"You are tied to a strange magic, blood of my blood. A stranger destiny too. These things, as well as the choices you have made, have led you here. You are where you belong, as is he." Gyda opened her mouth to protest, but Jalaa cut her off with a sharp look. "They are all where they belong."

Gyda bit down any arguing her tongue wanted to do. It wouldn't do any good to argue with the legend that saved her and took her in. And who was Gyda to tell her she was wrong simply because she wanted those she loved close by?

"You know where my clan is?" Gyda asked instead.

Jalaa nodded slowly. "The one that came before you told me much, although I wished not to believe it. Their presence is not one I could dismiss lightly. They told a tale of power braided through time, of a man reaching to scar the heavens and set them alight." She closed her eyes with a weary sigh. "Abraxas Kain is not the first to try, but one of few who has those left to love him. The spell your lover performed kept you all from his grasp, save one. Solri Amet, one of my many stone-daughters, is with him."

Gyda's spine straightened with audible cracks. "Sol is with him?"

Jalaa nodded. "She is finding her way through shadows and deceit. The best suited of all of you to do so. Fret not, she is capable."

"I do not doubt that," Gyda said slowly. "Only what will happen when she turns against him."

Jalaa shrugged and offered no comforting words to ease Gyda's frightened imagination. "THE REST OF YOUR CLAN ARE SCATTERED. SORIN TRINITY IS WITH SAHAR AL-FASIL, AND TOGETHER THEY FIGHT A DEVILISH MAN. THE GOBLIN ARKE STALKS BETWEEN WORLDS, UNCOVERING THE KEYS TO ABRAXAS'S PLAN WITH THE HELP OF HIS PATRON."

Gyda put aside the question of Arke and his patron, whoever or whatever they were. He was alive, and that counted for something. But she couldn't help the way her eyes widened just a tad at the last name on the list. Hopeful, breathless in her waiting.

Jalaa smiled knowingly. "EVREN HANALI OF YOUR HEART IS IN ETHERAK, AMONG ALLIES. SHE WAGES WAR IN YOUR MEMORY."

All the breath left Gyda's lungs in a rush. "She doesn't know I live."

"No." Jalaa stood and Gyda's throat closed up at the sudden reminder her of how large she was in person. Gyda had seen giants in the distance, but it was different from being only a handful of feet from her. "THE ONE WHO GUIDES YOUR CLAN HAS LEFT HER BE FOR NOW. IT IS PAINFUL, YOU MUST UNDERSTAND, FOR SUCH A REUNION AT THIS TIME. THAT ONE KNOWS HER PAIN WELL, AND KNOWS THAT WHAT IS NEEDED WILL COME FROM IT."

"You talk of the cloaked figure."

Jalaa nodded again. "THIS ONE PREPARES FOR ABRAXAS KAIN'S PLAN. THAT IS WHY YOU WERE LED HERE. WHY YOU ARE HERE IS BECAUSE OF YOUR STRONG SPIRIT. DO NOT DOUBT THAT."

Strength of spirit Gyda wouldn't deny. Of body? Absolutely. But these were doubts for another time. If Evren's spell had sent her here, and the figure's plan was to help them stop Abraxas, then she didn't have the luxury to doubt. The figure hadn't led them astray so far, and its words to her on the mountain reflected Jalaa's like a mirror's edge.

Gyda stuffed the amulet in her pocket and untucked herself from the worg's side. She slid down the edge of the bed, the fall to the floor making her woozy until her legs hit solid ground. Her knees buckled and she gripped the bed to keep herself standing up. When, finally, her legs stopped trembling, she stood up straight.

"What do I need to do?"

There again was that fondness that made Gyda feel like she was a little girl under her foya's arm again. Gyda hadn't known her mother. It was no secret that she'd been unplanned and that her foya had been more willing to raise her than the woman who'd birthed her. She could imagine that her mother's gaze, if she'd been wanted, could look a fraction like how Jalaa looked at her now.

"OH SWEET, BRAVE GYDA," Jalaa hummed. The worg twitched in his sleep above her. "YOUR PATH WILL BE A BLOODY BATTLE."

She wasn't shy in her sigh of relief. For the first time since waking, Gyda let herself smile. "That is what I'm best at."

Could it be her imagination, or was Jalaa's gaze sad now? As if she knew something that she couldn't say. The thought unnerved Gyda, but she lacked even the strength to ask.

"YES," Jalaa said. "IT WAS WHAT YOU WERE BORN FOR."

21

Solri

It was a truth acknowledge to all but Sol's friends that she wasn't as good and soft as she appeared to be. It wasn't as if she meant to deceive them. Her smiles were always genuine, until they needed to be something else. She loved to joke and make them happy. She loved being with them, fighting for them, and making the world better with them.

But if there was one person who never belonged, never deserved the title of hero, it was Solri Amet.

Sorin was selfless, lovable, and caring.

Arke was intelligent, quick witted, and wanted to do good in a world that viewed him as nothing but a nuisance.

Gyda blamed herself day after day for the horror of the Long Night, but Sol had never met a woman capable of the kindness the warrior was.

Evren, for all her faults, was a product of the Wood that raised her. Brazen and loving with all she had, but deadly to those who meant her harm.

Even Abraxas who sought redemption and forgiveness above all else, was better than Sol.

Because Sol's only guilt for her murder was how it affected those she loved. How it left her mother alone, how it killed Sorin and left him forever changed, and how it forced her away from the only place she'd truly loved.

Sol had seen parts of Eith that few could even dream of. Lands of extremes and magic beyond her wildest dreams. She'd seen the beauty of the sun rising after the Long Night. She'd seen the bronze hued statues in Rhienwall glinting in the summer sun. She'd seen the extent of elven and Hisrachi culture and the beauty in both.

But none of it was home. None of it had the steady heat of Dirn-Darahl or the hum of a thousand runes that kept the city going. There weren't any Luminstones on the surface, lighting everything in the soft but potent glow not as dangerous as the sun. The architecture of the surface, while varied and overall beautiful, didn't have the soul that her city did.

She missed the food, the mingling of friends in the open cafés that dangled at the roof of the caverns. She missed the way the lights were dimmed to mimic nightfall, so that everyone's sleep rhythms stayed similar. The marriage processions that took the new couple from one level of the city to another so that everyone could bless them. The jewels and clothes, all made for her by a tailor who'd clothed her since she could speak and knew all her favorites before she could pick them out.

Warm milk tea in her hands. A city glowing because of her hard work. Clothes that she was proud to wear. A family name she was proud to uphold.

It always came down to pride. At the end of the day, whether by surface sunset or Dirn-Darahl's dimming of lights, Sol was proud. Of her people and what they could become, given the chance. Of her friends and the accomplishments they made under the most dire of circumstances.

But she hadn't been proud of herself since she let that killing dagger fly. And all the forgiveness in the world wouldn't make up for it. Right or wrong, just or unjust, she'd killed for her own gain where the people she loved had killed out of necessity or justice.

And she hadn't even had the courage to take the power she'd left lying there in a pool of blood. If she had, would her city have fallen? Would she have been able to rebuild it before Serevadia came knocking?

Would she have seen through Abraxas Kain's lies?

~

SOL WOKE COLD AND HEARTBROKEN, but she was far from alone.

Her shadows writhed beneath her skin, pulsing with every beat of her heart. She felt them lingering on her bruises, prodding them as a toddler would to see if they'd change color. They were lingering in her mouth, in her lungs, at the very tips of her numb fingers.

Now that she was aware of them, Sol wondered how she ever missed them.

She rolled herself over, looking at the bars of a familiar cell. Karas's old one. The chemicals and table had been removed, leaving nothing but a bed and a blanket. The Luminstone pebble, still clutched in her hand, was as dull and lifeless as the one she'd lost before Kleros. All its glow had been taken, and she let it clatter to the floor.

Sol shivered and pulled the blanket up to her chin. It smelled like Karas, sweaty and tainted with chemicals and the undertone of metal that never seemed to leave him. It was strangely comforting.

Across the room in the other cell, something slithered away. Pale hands curled around the bars. The face didn't show, but Sol closed her eyes anyway.

"You came back."

"Fuck off," Sol muttered. "I didn't have a choice."

"I warned you. Yes, yes I did! I told you to look inside."

She scoffed. "Riddles from a mad Blood mage. As if I would know that meant I had living fucking shadows in my body."

The sound from the other cell could've been a cough, or a laugh, or a sob. Whatever it was, it ended in something wet splattering on the floor and made Sol's skin crawl. It took a while for the thing in the cell to speak again, and all that filled the air was sounds of his labored breathing.

"How did you know?" Sol asked softly.

He paused, like he was mulling the answer over, or he could still be catching his breath. Sol wasn't sure.

"I felt them," he croaked, finally. "I was made to draw them out of blood. Trained for it. Mistress showed me other things with blood. I can feel when it is tainted. When it is wrong." He dissolved into another fit Sol was now sure was coughing, and his throat still rattled when he spoke again. "*I* am very wrong, you see?"

"I don't think I want to," Sol said.

This time, it was a cackle that set her hairs standing on end. "Funny, funny," he wheezed. "Very funny."

"If you say so." After he'd calmed down to the point of ragged breathing, Sol found that if she kept talking she could ignore the feeling of something else in her body. "What's your name?"

"Istnar."

"I'm Sol."

"I know."

She fiddled with the frayed end of Karas's blanket. "Why are you up here? I thought you worked for . . . him."

She couldn't even bring herself to say his name. Either name. Neither fit and she hated that one brought hope still to her heart. Like he would come bursting into the room with the rest of the Wandering Sols, swearing that he'd been impersonated by a shapeshifting monster and that he'd never done those terrible things.

"He killed Mistress. I wanted to kill him." A heavy paused

followed before, "There are debts that I still have yet to pay. Duties I still need to perform."

"So, you're a prisoner as much as Karas was. Why haven't you tried to escape?"

"Who says I have not? Has anyone asked Istnar, 'Istnar, would you like to run away to certain death with us?' 'Istnar, you are not so bad and ugly as Catarmon says, you could come with us!' No. I have tried, yet I have not succeeded. Seeing as I am as stuck as you, I would think that would be obvious. Yes, very obvious."

"You want me to feel guilty about leaving you here after you pushed my friends and I into a pool of shadows that killed one of us and infected me?"

". . . Yes?"

Sol sighed. "Fine. I'm sorry." And she genuinely was, because however demented and creepy Istnar was, he was also pathetic and obviously dying. Hells, he'd been close to bleeding out when Sol last saw him. Tearing two massive holes in his shoulders and kicking his feet bloody and broken. She was glad she couldn't see him.

"Eeeeeeh." He drew out the sound long enough for Sol's ears to ring, then abruptly finished with, "Apology accepted."

"Can you apologize about shoving me in a nightmare hole?"

"Yes. Sorry."

He didn't sound very sorry, but Sol took the strange little apology, because it was the only one she'd get in this damned place.

"Apology accepted."

Quiet descended, but Sol couldn't think of a word to say to Istnar that would make herself feel better. With every passing minute of silence she wanted to tear at her own skin. She wiggled under the blanket, trying to find comfort but only feeling trapped. Suffocated. Every time she closed her eyes she was on the ground again, at Abraxas's mercy. So she kept them peeled and staring at the bars of the cell. Hoping he'd come and talk. Dreading if when he did.

Missing him regardless.

"Where's home, Istnar?"

The elf let out a ragged cough. "Home is . . . small. Not stone. Huts and tents. Mushrooms taller than me. Lived among them."

"That actually sounds nice."

"It was. It is dead. Your home too."

"Thanks for pointing that out."

"You are welcome."

The air was still and cool and smelled of rot. More so every time Istnar hacked up something wet and spat it on the floor. Sol winced each time. Her perception of time between Kleros and now was skewed. There was no telling how long he'd been in his cell, and Sol found herself pitying him despite what she'd seen in Kleros.

Something warmer shifted in the air. Still stale, but smelling of stone and mortar rather than sick. Sol sat up, still cocooned in the blanket. The pale hands on the bars reappeared, as did the tip of a long nose. Both prisoners peered anxiously at the shadows gathering by the door between their cells.

Sol's heart beat rapidly. The shadows wiggled in kind. And stepping out of them was a lady dressed in white and a scowl.

"Fool!" Ainthe shot at Sol. "You have ruined everything with your stumbling."

Sol slumped back into bed. "Nice to see you too. I've got nasty shadows in my body by the way. Thanks for letting me know that. And that my friend is a fucking war criminal!"

"As if you would've believed me," Ainthe said dismissively.

"I wouldn't have. That's not the point. I'm at rock bottom, so I'm brooding."

"Pouting, more like it," the priestess mumbled and walked purposefully up to the lock. "Well, daughter of stone? Do you want out or would you rather work on your impression of a larvae stuck in its shell?"

"What's the point?" Sol snapped. "I can't kill Abraxas, and I won't. I'm drawing my line there. And yes, do point out the fact that I've killed men before for betraying me and shoving me in a cell. It'll make my fucking day. Night. Whatever. Also, unless you can do something about the nasty shit in my body, running away won't make a lick of difference. Abraxas can control me. Hells, he might even be able to track me with them."

Ainthe pursed her bloodless lips. "I did not know about the shadows."

"I'm not sure if I believe you. I've seen you do terrible things with them as well."

"Things I was born with. Catarmon's gifts are kindled by the blade he wields."

Sol frowned and sat up again. "What blade?"

"An artifact of my people," she said. "The very blade that once protected the Elder that made us. In it lies his power, likely all that is left of it. For if he has not come back to reclaim it from Catarmon's unworthy hands, then he is well and truly dead."

"Everyone's gods are dead," Sol said flatly. "That's what started this mess."

"If that is what you believe."

Ainthe cupped her hand, and the ambient shadows in the corner leapt into her fingers like an eager pet. The magic was different than Abraxas's. Smoother and more elegant, but it still made Sol want to retch. The priestess put her shadow-filled hand against the lock, and a series of clicks sounded in the air. From the opposite cell, Istnar shuffled in what Sol thought could be excitement, or envy.

Sol's cell swung open and Ainthe stepped inside, gracefully dismissing her shadows.

"Let me see you."

Sol, by definition of being a stubborn dwarven child who

grew to be a stubborn dwarven woman, sat still long enough for Ainthe's long fingers to start twitching then forced herself up to her feet. She clung to the blanket for a moment before shedding it like a cloak. As it pooled around her feet, Ainthe's eyes widened.

"Oh, what a monster he has become . . ."

Sol looked down at herself and wished she hadn't. It was one thing to imagine the shadows under her skin, but it was entirely different to *see* them. Her veins were as black as ink, pulsing thickly with every beat of her heart. Her fingertips had turned black, as if she'd been digging through charcoal up to her wrists.

She pushed her sleeves back with trembling fingers, noting how the veins never lightened to the normal blue. She was a statue of cream and black marble, shot with gold in her hair and blue topaz for her eyes. All the while still breathing, still screaming on the inside, still stuck between something beautiful and something monstrous.

Sol looked up at Ainthe. "Help me."

Ainthe swallowed and placed her hand at the base of her throat as if she was struggling just to manage that. "I fear I cannot. These shadows aren't mine—they will not obey me. And to use this sacred magic for such a baseless action as to mingle it with flesh . . ." She shuddered. "It is vile."

"You're telling me?" Sol slapped her hands down to her sides. "I'm the one that's fucking mingled!"

A wet wheeze from the other cell drew both of their attentions.

"What is that?" Ainthe snarled.

A terrible idea hit Sol. She shouldered past the priestess, out her cell and towards the smell of rot that lingered like a cloud around Istnar.

She still couldn't see him, and she was sure it was less because of the lack of light and more because of the shadows *he* commanded. Sol had watched him drain it from the elves in

Kleros. She'd watched some leak from his own wounds. Wherever the stink of festering flesh lingered, the black was thicker.

"Istnar," she said gently. "Can you help me?"

The energy of cool power Ainthe always radiated snapped to something more desperate. "Istnar? Impossible. He died with my daughter."

The pale hands appeared again, caked with dried blood and phlegm. The shadows that concealed him slowly parted, just enough so that the two women could see the haggard, broken face of Istnar. His chin and neck were coated in the same dark blood, most of it sticky and wet, but beneath that it was dry and cracking to show bits of dirty skin. Strings of oily hair fell in his face, and the too-large eyes made Sol's heart jump in her throat. They'd been the last thing she saw before she was pushed into shadows, before Viggo's light failed.

And now they looked at her with pity.

"Istnar did not die," he gurgled. "Merely dy*ing*, as it were."

He chuckled at his own joke, trailing off when Ainthe came to stand beside Sol. Those eyes, crusted with gunk and terribly large, stared up at her with the sort of reverence a dog might for the person who gave it food.

"You were with her when I could not be," Ainthe whispered. She put her hand between the bars, trailing her fingers along his face without a care for the blood she smeared. He leaned into her touch, whimpering at the back of his throat. "You were all my Nerezza had at the end of her days."

Istnar's eyes fluttered open again. "I failed her."

Ainthe drew back, fingers bloody. "As did I."

She looked down at Sol, grim with grief that wasn't buried very deeply. Ainthe wore it like her white vestments, diligently but with no pride.

"Is there any hope for this one, Istnar?" she asked. "Could we free her, working together?"

Bones crackled as he popped his neck. He winced. "Perhaps.

It will be painful. I have not done this to keep another alive. And doing so will bring Catarmon's wrath."

"Leave that creature to me," Ainthe said coldly. When Sol started to protest, she lifted her bloody fingers to stop her words. "He killed my daughters. I am aware that their paths, particularly Nerezza's, were my fault. But their ends were his. As a mother, I have every right to challenge him."

"But killing him——"

"I never said I could," Ainthe said softly. "But Nerezza tried. The least I can do is honor her by doing the same. So long as you agree to this operation."

Sol looked back at Istnar. Her veins seemed to smart at the very sight of him, but she clamped down that reaction.

"My friends, the rest of the Wandering Sols, did they live?"

Istnar grinned, teeth black. "Scattered to the corners of the surface. Some hunt for answers. Some build an army. They are where they should be, as the shadows demanded."

Sol uttered a sound of confusion before Ainthe stepped in.

"The shadows could transport people great distances in seconds," she explained. "Your goblin managed to write a spell that changed their allegiances to them, for the time being. As far as new spells go, it was a success. All touched by it lived to see the other side, albeit not together and not where they imagined to be." Her mouth twitched up into a smile. "Something that has kept them from Catarmon's grasping hands for a while now."

"They . . . they didn't leave me?"

She cursed herself for being so vulnerable with Ainthe, but the priestess shook her head.

"Abraxas could've stopped them if he had the concentration to do so. With the creature named Keres occupying his focus, he was able to only keep one. You."

Sol took a breath. They were alive. *All* of them. They were fighting and building and waiting. They hadn't left her. There was still a chance.

"Okay." She nodded to Istnar. "Do it."

He cocked his head to the side so quickly that more bones popped. "You could die."

She shrugged. "Then I die. It's either that or live like this, and that's not going to help anyone."

Ainthe broke the lock on Istnar's door and held it open. They both turned away as he crawled more than walked out of the cell. Ainthe waved Sol back to Karas's bed, as if lying down would help her. Maybe it would, but Sol thought it was the only a comfort in the same way a damp towel was to a dying man. Nothing but a comfort, and a small one at that.

"I'll ward the door," the priestess said. "Try not to scream."

As she turned to go, Sol caught her arm. She was cold and stiff under her fingers, but Ainthe didn't lash out.

"Why are you helping me?" Sol asked. "I'm not going to kill him."

"I know. I always knew." She cut her a look from the corner of her eyes. "But it'll wound him to take you from him. And if I cannot kill, I will inflict many wounds. You harbor love for him that I cannot. This is my way."

"But you should've known when we first met you what he was," Sol pressed. "Back when you saved us from the visha in the lake. You were already serving Catarmon then."

"I knew his voice, not his face. And then, the distinction between Abraxas and Catarmon was clear." She shook her head. "If I had known, I might've killed him then and spared myself the pain. But that isn't what happened, daughter of stone. You landed in my lap and were set free. You brought Alkimos the Great back to us. You uncovered my daughter on the surface. And Abraxas Kain became the monster he is now. There are things in this world that are unchanging, no matter how cruel they are. Surely you know this."

"Better than you think." Sol let go of her arm.

Without another word, Ainthe reached into the folds of her robes and brought out two daggers shaped like twin crescent moons. Sol knew them like her own hands. Sol took them, somewhere between grateful to have them back and terrified that they could be part of what ended her.

Ainthe turned back to the door. Sol doubted that a door, warded or not, could keep Abraxas away. But the priestess knew magic better than she did, so Sol decided that worrying about it would just make her head hurt.

She walked back to Karas's cell, where Istnar sat on his haunches chewing at his long nails. Seeing all of him was worse, even if his shadows trailed him like a wispy cape. The smell carried too. She sat down on the bed, kicking the blanket away.

"What do I need to do?"

Istnar looked up from his biting. "Have something sharp?"

Sol held out one of her daggers and Istnar's boney fingers curled around the hilt. She shivered, ignoring the black blood smudging on the blade she knew so well, and how he caressed it like a lover. She set aside the other dagger.

"Make sure that's clean before you cut me," she said.

Istnar shrugged and took up Karas's blanket to do so. Sol didn't watch to see how good of a job he was doing. She laid back and closed her eyes, counting her breaths as she wondered how she'd fallen so far as this.

She gripped the sides of the bed when Istnar's smell became stronger.

"If I die, will you tell my friends that I tried to—that I tried to get back to them?"

Istnar paused. His breaths rattled and fell wetly on her face. "I will die before I can, even if you do not."

"Well . . . I'm sorry then."

Another wet chuckle, mercifully away from her. "Apology accepted."

There was a stillness between heartbeats where there was an absence of pain, yet she was as tense as stone itself because she knew it was coming. Every moment without it was gone before she could savor it. Sweet blinks of relief that she knew were precious but were slipping through her fingers. She could do nothing but grasp for the next to hold, and then lose it as well.

The pain began with a prick on her forearm, something jagged and sharp pressing deeply into her skin until blood bloomed. When the liquid cooled in the air, the discomfort turned into agony.

The shadows grew sharp under her skin. They shredded and tore, digging into her flesh as they started to slide out from the hole Istnar created. Sol bit down on her tongue to keep from screaming, the buzzing pain nothing compared to what was happening everywhere else.

Her fingernails cracked from gripping the railing so hard. Black turned to hazes of red behind her eyelids. There were other pricks of pain on the surface of her skin, one on each arm and leg, and one down the center of her chest. Shallow cuts, but Sol began to loathe them because with every cut the shadows grew more desperate and wild. They anchored in her bones, cracking them and leaking marrow. They tore at ligaments to rope themselves tighter to her. Squeezed organs, fried nerves.

They were leaking out of her, but they weren't letting go.

And Sol was screaming. She couldn't remember when she'd started. Blood gurgled in the back of her throat, doing little to muffle the cries her ringing ears could barely comprehend.

Her skin was on fire. Gone were the numb stakes that kept her still and obedient. The pain was feral and otherworldly. She felt like she was going to snap in half before it ended.

Cool fingers met her burning temples but this was no relief as seconds later sharp nails dug into her skin again. This time, the pain was brief, and the goal was not the shadows.

Sol blinked her eyes open. She was in a dream. It was fuzzy. The haze of pain still sharp in the back of her mind. A command to not turn back moved her legs.

She was walking down a lush hall, exquisitely built with soaring ceilings and pillars of sweeping designs so delicate they shouldn't be able to hold up the roof. Gorgeous robes fluttered around her legs. A heavy circlet pressed on her forehead. She could feel the swinging weight of her braid behind her back and the coolness of the rings on her fingers.

Sol stopped. "Where am I?"

"Your mind." Ainthe was beside her where she hadn't been moments before. Her voice echoed like it was far away. Which Sol supposed it was. "This was the only way I could keep you from hurting yourself."

Sol frowned. "You did this before. It wasn't quite so pleasant."

The last time Ainthe had forced herself into Sol's mind, Sol had been half dead and delirious, but she remembered the visions vividly. It was impossible to forget the horrors of what she'd been shown. A throne room filled with blood up to her calves. An empty wheelchair rolling slowly towards her. The collapse of one level on top of another through Dirn-Darahl until she was buried in the deepest grave with thousands of her people.

Those visions still stuck, but in the wake of what she'd suffered they seemed smaller.

"I thought you could use something easier," Ainthe admitted. "This is what your mind conjured, not I. A paradise if you will. None of these things can or will exist. Revel in them while you still live."

And then Ainthe was a pale shadow, easy to forget but clinging to Sol's footsteps. Because there was a lovely face in front of her that she hadn't seen in so very long, and Sol missed her with every aching piece of her soul.

"Mama?" She picked her skirts up to walk faster.

Yovena Amet was exactly how Sol left her, except she was standing on her own two legs and her spine was straighter than it had been in years. Her face crinkled into a warm smile as she spread her arms wide.

"My diamond! Oh, look at you." Then she was enveloping Sol into a hug that wasn't frail or shaking as it had been in life, but strong and warm. Sol couldn't find the strength to pull away. The part of her that knew it was all fake kept her from bursting into tears, but the part that had made this fantasy wanted nothing more than to do just that. She shook in her mother's arms uncontrollably, caught between the two warring sides of emotions and practicality.

Yovena pulled back with a slight frown to look at her. She cupped her face in her weathered hands, rings cool against Sol's hot skin.

"What's the matter?"

"I . . ."

It was just a dream. Something sweet to keep her from madness, alerting Abraxas, or hurting herself. But it felt real. The smell of her mother's perfume, the weight of her hands. It brought back every broken promise, every hollow lie she'd ever spoken.

"I couldn't get to you," Sol said. "I'm so sorry, Mama, I didn't know. I should've stayed home with you."

Elegant fingers brushed away her tears the same way they had when she was little. "Solri, there is no reason to be sorrowful."

"I couldn't save you!"

"It was never your job to save me," her mother said. "Just like it was never my job to save your father. There is little we can do when those we love are marked to leave the world. The best we can do is hold their hands and tell them that they are loved no matter where they are."

A sob wracked Sol's body. "I wasn't even there to do that."

"But you are here now." Her mother kissed her forehead. "That is more than enough, my diamond."

There was another hand on Sol's shoulder, and her mother's face crinkled up in the warm way it only did around one other. Sol turned so fast that her skirts caught on her legs, heavy and anchoring. But even they couldn't keep her from throwing herself into the waiting arms of her father.

This was a dream, but the way her father's laugh reverberated in her chest felt real. The way his long beard, clinking with beads and ornaments, scratched her cheek felt real. She was being held like she was as a child, tightly as if she'd fall through his arms at any moment and with her feet dangling off the ground, and when she was set back down again she was face to face with Lothaem Amet.

Like her mother, he was how she chose to remember him. Black hair trimmed with silver. Blue eyes like her own twinkling with barely concealed mischief. He'd died of a wasting sickness in the lungs, but Sol did not see the skeletal corpse they'd buried in the family tomb. She saw him healthy and proud as he'd been in life.

"I've missed you," she said, and grabbed her mother's hand. "I've missed you both."

Lothaem chuckled and took her other hand. "My dear, you have missed us while slaying monsters and saving the world. What a wonderful daughter. I didn't miss my parents at all."

Yovena swatted his shoulder. "Hush, you."

He laughed her off, and Sol did too. Of all the times she imagined meeting her parents again, it always fell flat in her head. The way they talked felt too much like her puppeting them to say what she wanted them to say. This felt like she was seeing them again at the gates of their afterlife.

Sol turned back to Ainthe. "Is this what dying feels like?"

The priestess made a face. "I haven't had the pleasure yet. If you'll give me an hour to challenge the monster that killed my daughters, I can come back to tell you."

"Not necessary." When Ainthe died, the last thing Sol wanted was to be haunted by her. "It just feels so real. Like I could walk with them and never come back."

"You could," Ainthe said. "Your dream will continue until you are dead, and then after that you will be dead, so it will matter little. Perhaps this is what you dwarves see when you die. Happy families in a strange hall—"

"I drew this when I was thirteen. Impossible to build, but I loved it anyway."

"Aside from this hall then." She nodded to her still, smiling parents. "It is a nice way to go out. Better than you'll get dying on the battlefield."

Sol nodded. She squeezed her parents' hands, knowing that they were only quiet because of what her mind wanted them to be. In life, they would've been speaking loudly to voice their own opinions. All in good intention, but she needed them quiet to think.

She stepped back from them, letting their hands drop from her own. They didn't cling to her.

"A dwarf's place is on the battlefield," Sol said. "I won't die before I've done something worth dying for. I refuse to go before I've said my goodbyes to others I love that still live."

She wiped away her tears. It felt like she'd done nothing but that the past several hours. Then she squared her shoulders like her father, brought her chin up like her mother. She didn't think it was her mind that made them smile the way they did.

"I love you both," she said. "I am what you made me, and while I have stumbled, I know you would be proud. I will learn to trust myself again. I will learn to trust others again. But I can't go with you yet."

Lothaem said, "You have more monsters to slay."

Yovena said, "And the world to save once again. We can wait a little while longer."

Her father took her mother's hand, staring at her with the kind of fondness that Sol had only seen in two others. Like he couldn't see enough of her, like she was the most precious thing in the world.

"Longer still, now that we have each other," he said.

The red haze of pain pushing at Sol's back was still there. She moved to be flush beside Ainthe. "Take me back when it's done. I don't care what condition I'm in."

Ainthe nodded and rested her hand on her shoulder. It trembled where Sol knew only steadiness as she watched Sol's parents. Sol didn't look up to see if there was envy in her eyes. She never wanted to wonder what became of Nerezza's father, or if there had been one. Elves were weird, and Serevadians were the weirdest of all. But the fact remained that Ainthe had no one left.

No clan to lead. No daughter to protect. Only the dying elf her daughter had left and Sol herself. Whatever Serevadian afterlife looked like, Sol hoped Ainthe found peace there and a reunion with the daughters she tried so hard to protect.

"It's time," Ainthe said.

It didn't feel like time. There was still pain where she was going. It was comfortable in this paradise. Sol sighed, shaking her head. She relished the feeling of her long hair, in the weight of the circlet on her head. Then she closed her eyes, her last image of her parents smiling proudly.

"Take me back."

It ended abruptly, as all dreams did. Sol was suddenly gasping for breath, her throat raw and sore, her body bleeding sluggishly from many different spots. The floor was black and writhing at Ainthe's feet and Istnar's knees. But the angry shadows made no move to reach for Sol again.

Ainthe stuck her hand in the shadows and gritted her teeth. Sol gaped as they started climbing inside her, blackening her pearlescent skin similarly to the way Sol's had been. Blackened veins and extremities made the priestess that much more terrifying to look at.

The last wisp gone, Ainthe staggered into the wall breathing hard. Istnar scrambled over to her but she waved him away, sweat gleaming on her forehead.

Sol sat up gingerly. She felt like she'd been smacked on a brick wall a few times. "Won't that prevent you from fighting Abraxas?"

"I have control for the time being." Ainthe said through gritted teeth. "I am a vessel, not an instrument. What this will do is draw him to me, not you. From there, I shall do my worst."

Ignoring her stinging wounds, Sol jumped up and took her daggers back, buckling the sheaths around her waist and patting them when she was done.

"Use those well," Ainthe said. "Take your road to the west and do not falter."

"The-the west?" Sol gaped. "There's nothing but the canyon down there."

"And yet Abraxas is here, why?" Ainthe pushed her back none too gently. "Ask yourself that question as you run. We haven't much time now. Istnar?"

The elf wiped the blood from his chin, looking half a corpse and somehow brimming with energy. "I follow you in death where I could not follow Mistress."

Grief fluttered across Ainthe's features. She touched Istnar's forehead once more, tender as if he was her own.

"I will take your loyalty with honor."

The two elves drew themselves up tall, one shaking with exertion and the other hunched. Strange allies, perhaps the strangest Sol would ever have again.

She met Istnar's gaze, covering the cuts he'd made. "Thank you."

He nodded. "You are welcome."

"Run, daughter of the stone," Ainthe said, eyes gleaming dangerously. "Let us die gloriously and well. And do not falter."

22

Gyda

The last piece of her foya that had been taken from her was their shared red hair. Gyda mournfully ran her fingers through the brittle white strands that had replaced them. The lively red, so akin to her foya's, was gone for good. She hadn't despaired over one streak of white, but this irrationally made her want to cry. As if she even had time for that.

She shook her head, pushing the white hair away from her face. Hair was hair. In the end it mattered very little what color it was. Evren wouldn't mind either, although she'd likely fret and blame herself for months afterwards.

Assuming they had months.

Gyda kept forgetting how there might not be an afterwards for them, and that if there was it wouldn't be the same. She couldn't help but imagine an end where things weren't so hard and heart wrenching.

Before, she'd never thought of an end for the Wandering Sols. They had nothing but each other and the cut ties of the lives they left behind. But after this? Who would want to keep adventuring? How many horrors could one thwart before the mere idea of picking up a weapon filled them with dread?

Gyda didn't want to get to that point where she was scared of fighting. But she did want a rest and was damn sure everyone she loved did too. They deserved it.

Maybe they would find some rotting keep in the middle of nowhere. Etherak had plenty of those, or so Barrion had told her. The prince would talk anyone's ears off about the state of his kingdom, and the abandoned keeps dotting the wilderness that no one wanted were a favorite of his. Barrion tried to talk her into buying one before leaving Orenlion. Something about keeping the Wandering Sols close in case of any trouble.

Gyda had refused, obviously. The last thing she wanted to do was settle down after she just lost a friend. But now the idea of the five of them sharing a keep together, fixing it up and going about their lives appealed to her. Arke could have his own library and study and fill it with books no one was allowed to touch but him. And Sorin would get away with it, of course. He's the only one that could, so he'd steal books for the lot of them whether they needed them, or even just because.

Sol would rebuild the keep bigger and better than before, complete with little details in all their rooms that made it uniquely theirs. Likely a large bathhouse as well, because not a day went by when the dwarf wasn't complaining about not having a good bath. And Gyda couldn't blame her.

There would be room on the walls for maps and their trophies, a treasure room for everything they'd earned over their adventures. A kitchen big enough for everyone, but easy enough for someone to herd Evren out when she decided to cook. Lands wild and big enough for her and the worg to hunt. Plenty of space for her weavings, which Gyda secretly wanted to pin up everywhere they went but Evren was too embarrassed to let her.

Gyda braided her hair back, smiling a little at the fantasy. Still, it didn't feel right. Like with everything that had to do with the Wandering Sols, it lacked Abraxas. No matter what he'd become, he'd left a vacuous hole where he used to be.

Gyda wouldn't want a sparring ring without him, even though sparring with Evren was exhilarating and fun. She wouldn't want to put his armor and sword up somewhere she could see, because she'd walk by and think he was waiting silently in the corner for her, like he used to be.

Gyda didn't want to be reminded of her old friend anymore, but she couldn't bring herself to get rid of the pendant.

She tied her hair back, fastened it snugly with her clan-sweave, and did her best not to scowl at the pieces that broke away and fluttered in front of her face. The little white strands tickled her eyes, which she was now sure weren't as sharp as they used to be.

As she had the past three days, Gyda had Jalaa's home to herself. She ate pieces of dried meat, choked down enough water to feel like she was drowning, and then sat still while it all settled in her stomach. When she was sure she wasn't going to make herself sick, Gyda went about the excruciating task of building back up her strength and endurance.

Jalaa hadn't said what to prepare for. She hadn't been home since the first time Gyda had spoken of getting ready for whatever plan the figure had concocted. So Gyda took that as a sign to train without the watchful, pitying eyes of the giantess on her.

Stretches to warm up. Easy things to test how weak her muscles were (very) and to see how much her lungs could handle (little). Then it was on to what she knew best. The sit-ups she used to do with ease she had to get the worg to sit on her feet to help with. And then he wouldn't get off, so Gyda just laid there with an aching abdomen wishing for the end.

Push-ups left her face down on the floor, gritting her teeth until her jaw ached. Simply holding her body weight on her toes and extended arms made her dizzy, as if her body was trying to tell her to fucking quit before she smashed her nose into the floor. She didn't quit, and only narrowly saved her nose at the expense of busted lips.

Using things from around the home, like the fire poker and a couple chairs, Gyda was able to make a place for her pull ups. They went even worse than the push-ups had gone. The iron bar bit into her hands and discouraged her more than her trembling arms. And yet she kept trying. Again and again, pushing herself until her arms trembled when they were relaxed by her side, and her hair was damp with sweat.

When Gyda's chin touched the top of the bar for the first time she was so stunned that she lost her grip entirely and fell flat on her ass. She cursed loudly enough to wake the worg, whose new favorite pastime was napping. He blinked at her a few times before tucking his nose under his big paws and going back to sleep.

"You saw nothing," Gyda murmured. Yet she smiled, because she *could* do this. Maybe her strength wouldn't come back like it had before. Fine. A bigger spell was bound to have bigger consequences. But she'd be damned if she'd go back to Evren unable to pick her up and hold her above the ground for as long as she wanted.

Gyda eyed the bar again. Well, she'd settle for a big sweeping hug that pulled her feet off the ground.

Gyda got back up and tried again.

It went like that for the next three days. Failures were taken as lessons. Bruises were taken as badges of honor. Every time her body was about to give out, Gyda rested, drank more water, and got back up again. If she'd been building this all from scratch she would've been fucked. No one could build strength that quickly. But the memory was there in her muscles, and it only took a healthy amount of coaxing to remind them what they were capable of.

Sword forms were harder. There was precious little in the home to imitate both the weight and size of her sword. Everything was either too big, or the right size but far too light. Gyda took the light pieces of wood over nothing, and even they were enough to send her forearms into a fit the first couple times. She swept through the forms she learned from childhood, feet in all the right places, arms holding position until sweat trickled down her spine. She did it again and again to remind herself as well as her body who in the hells she was.

Gyda knew she was more than a sword, more than her strength. But those were the things she needed more than ever. Eith could have Sorin's silver tongue and Sol's cunning mind. It would have Arke's magic and Evren's willpower. But *they* needed her sword and her power. Every other lovely detail could be admired later, after the fight was won.

On the seventh day Gyda tied her cloak around herself and climbed up one of the chairs she'd pushed next to the door. That alone had been a warm-up for the day to come. With the added height she was able to use the latch on the door and push it open a crack.

Crisp mountain air slithered in. The worg picked his head up, ears pricked hopefully as Gyda hopped down from the chair.

"Well?" She raised an eyebrow at him. "Are you coming or not?"

A happy bark was the only answer she got before he was barreling ahead of her into the day. She followed close behind, closing the door until there was a sliver big enough for her to fit her hand into and left it there. Jalaa wouldn't care about the cold but would likely be cross if Gyda froze to death outside because she was unable to get back in.

Knowing she was at the top of Jalaa's mountain was entirely different from seeing it. A complete opposite of the day she'd fallen into the giantess's hands was upon her. Bright sunlight fell down unfiltered by clouds. Endless blue skies stretched as far as she could see. The peaks of other, smaller mountains pierced through lower cloud cover and sparkled in the sun. The air was sharp and cold, but not cutting. The once blistering winds had settled down to the occasional flurry that teased at the edges of her cloak.

Without the clouds to obscure her vision, she could clearly see what she'd missed that first day. The leveled-out top of the mountain was even and smooth, save for the carved runes, and likely would've made Sol cry for joy. The arches she'd seen were massive things unbent by the weather or time. Snow draped the top of them but didn't obscure the runes glittering bright enough to be seen even in the daylight. Jalaa's home sat in the empty space under one arch, and the top of its roof was at least twenty feet from the top of the arch.

The air was bitingly cold, but Gyda took great lungfuls of it. Ahead of her, the worg ran in circles, skidding on ice and biting on the steam from his own breaths.

From up here there was no war. Eith didn't burn, her friends weren't in mortal danger. It was all frozen and pristine. Gyda could pretend if she wanted to, but she chose to stoke the reliant flames of her rage a little bit more. Better that than to simmer down into cool indifference.

Gyda's boots were still shit against slick ice and mountain stone, so she spent the majority of the day clearing the steps of ice with her stick sword, which was a workout in itself. Aided by the sun and the worg's large paws, she managed to get them all before noon, as there was little else to do and sitting still in the cold would do more harm than good. She gave herself time for a rest in the cabin with a bit of meat for lunch. She stretched out her already sore muscles and stepped back outside.

She stopped at the top stair, breath steaming in front of her. At her feet, the stairs gleamed black under the relentless sun. To her left, the wall of the mountain stood as a reminder of what the stairs had been before they were carved. To the right were clouds and open air.

Maybe it was stupid. Perhaps it was a stretch of her skills and she'd end up a broken corpse halfway down the mountain. But she needed variation, and she needed endurance. This was what came to mind.

With no rails to hold her and no promise that the weather wouldn't turn foul, she descended the stairs at a jogging pace. It took all her concentration to keep her feet from slipping out from under her, or from missing a step entirely and sending her tumbling ass over hair all the way to the bottom.

Feet and breathing. That was all she kept her mind to. Her legs strained against the isolated movement, unable to fly out their full length and take them two at a time. Gyda wouldn't let them. She kept herself steady and in control until she got to the bottom.

The last stair was still marked with the beast's claws. She left that stair alone, turned back and began the hard part. Back up again.

This time was less about control and more about willpower. She had to focus her breathing to make sure she wasn't hurting herself. In through the nose, out through the mouth. Her knees hiked up almost to her chest. Every step sent her legs screaming in a chorus of 'It can't get worse' and then it absolutely did. Every single step felt like a layer of hell. Every time the thought to slow down or stop entered her mind though, she shoved it away. If she stopped, she wasn't going to get back up.

One leg at a time. One step at a time. One breath.

The air was a knife in her lungs. Her cloak was a heavy burden swishing around her burning legs. The only things that burned brighter were her rage and her drive.

If she was hurting, it was only to get strong enough to stand between Abraxas and the world. If she was running, she was running towards Evren.

Over and over that's all she chanted to herself. She wasn't running away anymore. She was running towards something.

Jalaa said it was destiny. So did the figure. Gyda didn't much care for destiny so long as she got a sword and reunion somewhere along the way.

The top of the steps came so suddenly that Gyda stumbled to one knee. Ice bit into her trousers. She settled her forearms on her thigh and tried not to suck in the air too fast. She was quivering. The tie of the cloak hung on her neck in a way that nearly choked her. After a few minutes of gaining her bearings and letting the fire in her legs ebb away, she blew a piece of white hair out of her face and staggered to her feet.

It was a slow march back to the home. The worg waited for her on the porch, head cocked as if to ask, *'You gonna go again?'*

Gyda grinned. "Of course, I'm doing it again." She pulled the door open, wincing at her wobbling legs as they swayed beneath her. "Tomorrow."

And she did. So long as the weather permitted, Gyda began her day with breakfast and sword drills. Then she cleared the steps, ate lunch, warmed up a bit more and then set off to climb up and down the steps. The first two days all she could manage was one trip before she sent herself back home wheezing. By the third, though, she'd finished her first second trip up and down.

The days, though empty without Jalaa, passed quickly like this. Each night she worried until she fell asleep. Each day she worked until that worry was the last thing on her mind. She wondered where the giantess was, what the plan was, but there was no one to ask but the worg, so she stopped wondering and kept working.

The twelfth day came like all the others, only this time the worg marched with Gyda down the stairs. It was the start of her third time down, and while her legs trembled her mouth was set into a firm line. The worg kept pace with her on her right side, keeping her from straying too close to the open edge. If Gyda worried about his safety, she shouldn't have, his feet were far more nimble than her own.

Close to the bottom, they both slowed. A mist was creeping up. Clouds passing higher than normal. Gyda bit back a curse. She'd been lucky these past few days. Weather this high up was as unpredictable as it was dangerous. A storm could roll over them at any moment.

It was sheer stubbornness that kept Gyda from going right back up the steps. Her round here wouldn't count unless she touched the second to last stair. At least, that's what she told herself.

She descended the last few stairs with careful feet, worg pressed tightly against her side. His whole back was bristling. The more the clouds lowered their visibility, the more nervous he got. Gyda rested a hand on his broad shoulders as she came to touch the second to last stair. The marks of the beast were below, as stark as ever.

The worg grew stiff beside her, growling a warning into the clouds. Gyda didn't need to peer into them to know what laid beyond, waiting. Yet she could pick out the silhouette of long legs, of a snout silently gaping. It paced with the grace and ease of the clouds themselves, but didn't come any closer. It knew she was there. Gyda could feel its stare.

What had been fear turned into the thrill she was so used to. She grasped for her sword and met empty air. Narrowed eyes at the beast. Did she imagine its grin?

One thing she knew for certain was that it couldn't come up the steps. Another thing, soon to be remedied, she couldn't take it down.

Yet.

The job back up was easier than before. Easier than ever. It was as if her body remembered what it was like to face a foe again. The excitement, the adrenaline, the pounding of blood in her ears. None of the others knew how it felt, not until Evren had shared her heart. Even then it wasn't quite the same. The battle-song that hummed in Gyda's body when she had her sword in hand and foes against her was unlike any song she'd ever heard before. Uniquely hers. Beautiful.

She was going to hear it again.

Gyda was barely winded when she got to the top. The wind

was picking up and, in the distance, approaching fast, was a swirling storm of angry clouds. Gyda barely paid it any mind because coming through one of the arches was Jalaa.

This arch glowed the same blue as the runes had, and the space between it rippled like water as Jalaa stepped through. She waved her hand and the magic vanished. She didn't look surprised to see Gyda outside.

"The beast below the stairs," Gyda marched up to her. "What is it?"

Jalaa smiled as if she'd expected that question a long time ago. "A PRIMORDIAL HUNTER. A PROWLER OF THE LANDS IN-BETWEEN."

"In between what?"

She stared at Gyda. "WORLDS, BLOOD OF MY BLOOD. THE BEAST, AS YOU CALL HIM, TRAVELS THE SAME ROADS YOUR GOBLIN FRIEND DOES."

Gyda scowled. "Then why is it here?"

"FOR YOU."

Jalaa offered no explanation, and Gyda pressed for none. Monsters didn't always need reasons for what they did.

"I want it gone," Gyda said. The wind picked up, snapping her cloak behind her. She didn't waver. "I want to kill it."

Jalaa nodded, expecting this. "AS HE WANTS TO DO TO YOU. YOU CANNOT LEAVE UNTIL HE IS DEAD."

"Then I need a weapon." The stick she'd been using for a sword wouldn't cut it, and neither would a rock. Gyda had been lucky the first time and she couldn't count on that again.

"A WEAPON YOU WILL HAVE," Jalaa promised. "ONE THAT IS MOST FAMILIAR TO YOU."

Gyda's breath caught in her throat. "My sword? Where?"

Jalaa inclined her head to the stairs. Past them the clouds encroached. She knew without seeing him that the beast was circling at the foot of the stairs. Waiting.

Baiting.

Gyda gritted her teeth. That monster had her sword, or what

was left of it. Steal it back, reforge the blade and then go in for the kill? It was all she could think of. A stupid plan. There was no sneaking up on a creature like that.

And yet the battle-song had begun and Gyda faced the challenge with a grin.

23

Solri

Sol ran.

Body screaming. Blood dripping. Knives gleaming. She ran and she destroyed Stone's End.

Because no one knew dwarven architecture like her, no one could've prepared for the way she took hammers and smashed through supports like butter. No one could've prepared for their weapons to melt and explode with one shattered glass of bottled light. No one could've prepared for the strange fires that ate wood and stone alike that sprang from those bottles.

Because no one in their right mind would've destroyed Stone's End except the woman who loved it.

The ancient outpost burned more than she expected, a dangerous thing underground. Light green flames steadily ate at the stone, taking chunks out of it as elves screamed to get out. Noxious smoke filled the air. From the edges of the outposts, the watchtowers were singing the song of alarm.

Sol jerked her blade out of the neck of a soldier, letting him fall to her feet and then stepped over him. Serevadians ran everywhere in her vision. Streaks of silver and grey amidst the black and green background of Stone's End.

She readied her daggers, the grips warm and just right in her palms. But none of them were running towards her. They didn't seem to see her.

"Count your blessings and run," she muttered to herself, kicking away from the body and jogging forward.

The chaos in her ears was too much to pick apart and identify. Was that scream Ainthe's? Was that snap of energy another wave of light fire or was it Abraxas and his power? No matter how much she itched to look, she had to keep running.

If she died before she escaped, Ainthe's and Istnar's sacrifice were useless.

If she was caught before she escaped, it was still useless.

She had to make it count. For them, for her people, for her friends and for herself.

Sol ducked behind a fallen building, watching another group of panicked elves run by. It had been a desperate trick to start her destruction westward and work her way east, then circle back. She could only hope that if anyone saw the pattern, they would expect her to be going east where Karas had been. It might buy her time. She also might've wasted that time circling back.

A war cry pierced the chaos, familiar and jarring. The smash of something heavy against armor rattled her like a bell. The squish of flesh, the strangled screams cut short. Nothing like the battle she'd been hearing.

Sol looked at the watchtowers aglow over the edge of the canyon. Then she looked back at where the noise was coming from. Someone was fighting. Someone who shouldn't be there.

Someone pissed off.

Sol pushed off the building and ran back into the fray. The watchtowers glared at her back. She'd be back, but she had to make sure her ears weren't deceiving her.

She rounded the corner, daggers ready, and beheld a glorious sight.

The Serevadians were surrounded by dwarves. None of them were armored, and their weapons were crude. Borrowed from corpses, elven, or pieces of stone and wood. But they all fought like devils, tearing through the surprised soldiers like worg's teeth through flesh. Where one dwarf fell, another was immediately there to take their place and avenge their death. Serevadians fell with their beautiful silver armor stained red, crushed, bent, or broken entirely.

And in the middle of it all, wielding a bloody sledgehammer over a pile of dead elves, was Goriryn Karas.

An elf swung behind him, a blow that would've severed Karas's left arm. But Sol was quicker. A flash of steel sent her dagger sailing through the air and into the sword arm of the elf. He staggered back, crying in pain. Sol tore through the battlefield, leaping on him and pushing him to the ground. As he fell, she took both blades and jammed them into his throat. He was dead and silent before they hit the ground.

Sol jumped off of the elf, turning back to Karas. A million things whirled in her head to say. *You came back. Why are you here? You came back. What are you doing? You came back.*

Instead, she said, "Do I have to rag on your fighting as well as you sneaking now?"

Karas stared at her for a minute, eyes wide as if he couldn't believe she was standing in front of him. And then, to add a healthy dose of shock to her already overwhelmed mind, he dropped his hammer and scooped her up into a bone crushing hug.

Sol was so shocked she dropped her daggers. They clattered to the ground next to his hammer and then she was holding onto him as tightly as he was her. His shirt was damp with sweat, his breathing ragged and his shoulder broad enough to feel safe holding. Strange, to be hugging a man she once hated.

But now he was the best thing she'd seen all day, and that included her dream parents.

"You came back," she allowed herself to say. She couldn't tell why her throat felt tight with so much emotion at those words, but she had to fight to keep them steady.

"And you're alive." He pulled back, breathless, but didn't quite let go. He looked her over, at the strange cuts on her arms, legs, chest, and temples. "Right?"

She smiled. "I'm alive. And not carrying deadly shadows, I promise."

"I think I believe you."

He stepped back, and they both grabbed their weapons from the ground. Karas cleared his throat awkwardly, Sol's neck burned. When had they'd become so overwhelmed that they'd thrown down their weapons in the middle of a fight?

A fight that was dwindling, however. The last Serevadian was killed by three dwarves at once. A little overkill, but Sol couldn't blame them. She took in the survivors, and they looked at her with mixed gazes of relief, hope and wariness.

She turned back to Karas. "Why did you come back?"

He hefted the hammer onto his shoulder. "Want me to say somethin' sweet like I missed you?"

"The truth is fine."

He shrugged. "Tunnel's collapsed a ways in. No way out. We had to come back. Figured it was better to take Stone's End or die trying, then we found it, ah, burning." He looked at her knowingly. "Your handy work?"

"A happy accident," she said, as a building collapsed into green flames a few streets away.

"Lady Amet." The one-eyed dwarf from before stepped up, covered in so much blood she might as well have been a red head. "What do we do? Make for Dirn-Darahl?"

Sol shook her head. "That's another death trap. We go west."

Karas's eyebrows rose. "West? It's not a death trap, I'll give you that. It's just death."

"As far as we know" Sol countered. "We've never seen the bottom."

"Only the dead do."

"Dead if we do, dead if we don't." She shrugged. "All I know is that Catarmon is interested in it, which means I'm interested in it. Got any better ideas?"

He scowled, back to normal. "No."

"Then west it is."

A few short commands later and the remaining dwarves, only a few dozen now, marched behind Sol and Karas as they made their way to the burning eyes of the watchtowers.

The buildings cleared behind them. The open space between them and the watchtowers seemed to taunt them, brimming with ambient darkness that flickered against the fire, waiting for a command to snap at them. Sol focused on the three watchtowers, picking apart their structures as best she could. Which could she get to faster? Which one was stronger? Where was the weakest and *why* did she need it?

Simple. She needed light to see the bottom of the canyon, and the watchtowers of Stone's End had been burning for centuries.

It was the southernmost one they'd let slide. Dirn-Darahl they needed to watch in the north. The middle tower served to watch the outpost. But the southern one, last one along the canyon's wide curve, was built up just enough to keep it steady.

"There!" Sol nudged Karas to the south, and he took her direction without a complaint or question as to why. Their jog across the rocky field would've made their old instructors weep with joy, because despite the pain and exhaustion, they were in step with each other. Sol, Karas, and every single dwarf.

They reached the base of the tower, held up by patches of mortar and thick wooden beams no doubt stolen from the surface forest. Sol sheathed her daggers, running her fingers along the stone. Old rock, well loved by its builders. It would be a shame to destroy it.

Sol mentally marked her spots as she walked around the tower, ignoring the sharp descent into black at the edge, and tapping them twice. She ignored the wooden beams, although they would have to come down as well. Serevadians didn't know where to put their supports as well as they thought.

"Here." Sol tapped a spot, then retraced her steps. "Here, and here. Take the beams off, and everyone with hammers hit these areas. Be careful with your blows, we need the tower to fall forward, not to the side or on top of us."

"Why?" someone finally asked.

Sol grinned. "To light the way. Now, let's be quick. I'll deal with everyone in the tower."

Karas took his hammer off his shoulder and gripped it with both hands. "You heard her. To work!"

The beams came down with ease. Those bravest took hammers and edged to the front of the tower where Sol had pointed, and the rest to the sides. It wasn't unlike felling a tree, Sol thought as she remembered her time in the wilds with Evren. Different in that she was relying on the structure's natural weakness instead of driving a notch into it to make a hinge, but the idea was the same. Her tree was bigger, heavier, made of stone and lit like a beacon.

She'd be gorgeous when she came down.

Sol positioned herself idly beside the door, holding one dagger. No sooner had the tenth hammer stroke fell did she hear footsteps coming from the stairs. She waited outside, knives drawn. As the door swung open, she cut upward. The elf gurgled around his cut throat, and she pushed him side. That left two.

The first one darted out of the door quicker than she could slash. He tried flanking her, but Sol darted to the side, kicking up gravel as she did. The gravel caught the slower, second one just as she started to make it out the door. Sol cut at her heels, bringing her down to eye level, then took two daggers into the weak parts of the armor, straight through the ribs.

The first elf yelled in outrage, charging for her. Sol shook the body off her daggers and jumped back just in time to miss his blade. He kept up the fiery act of rage, his attacks swift and hard but easily telegraphed. Sol dodged one after the other, building his frustration until his swings were so sloppy she could've missed them with her eyes closed.

She darted inside his guard, cutting quick and precise in all the areas she needed. Her blades cut deep, but never lingered long. She slid where he stumbled, too light and fast for someone with such bulky armor.

When she stepped away, he swayed on his feet, gushing blood from a dozen different holes. She gave his befuddled gaze a little wave before it went dark and he toppled to the ground.

She sheathed her daggers. "How's it coming?"

Grinding stone answered her. If Karas had answered, the tower had drowned him out. Sol's stomach flipped as she watched it lean forward precariously. Either she was better at her job than she thought or the tower had been ready to give up on life for a while.

Sol ran to the edge. Sheer, unending darkness was just to her left. The air felt thinner, as if it wanted her to know that she was on the edge of nothing. She took the shoulders of the two workers closest to her and dragged them back. On the other side, Karas caught her eye.

"Job well done!" she said. "Move your arse!"

No other explanation necessary. Karas grabbed the rest of the workers and disappeared on the other side of the tower. The two Sol had grabbed managed to get the ones on her side, although they had gotten the idea to leave far before she'd said anything and were scrambling away from the edge to safety.

Sol was last, and it felt fitting. As she staggered back, she watched with an open mouth as the great watchtower shuddered under its own weight. The only thing that remained strong was the beam of light at its top—a Luminstone of greater strength than any mined after it.

Dwarves clumped together, watching as the work of their

ancestors swayed, cracked, and then very slowly began to fall. It was as if the tower itself was savoring the fall, gliding through the air with a grace not normally lent to things as rough as rock. But then gravity caught up with it. It slammed into the edge of the canyon, shaking Sol's knees, and then tumbled over its shining head into the abyss below.

Sol didn't wait long enough to draw breath before she was walking to the edge. A firm hand on her shoulder kept her from going too far, and she smiled at Karas in appreciation. Her toes on the edge, her shoulder anchored, she looked down the dizzying height.

The tower cut through the darkness, getting smaller and smaller with each passing minute. Sol didn't see an end. She saw the light catch jagged sides of the canyon. She saw the tower get small enough that it looked like a torch.

Then she saw something large. Spines of purple, a glimpse of a body larger than Stone's End, and its great muscles twitching upward as the tower passed it by.

Sol, for the first time, saw a true way out. "We're going to make it," she sighed, stepping back into Karas.

He squeezed her shoulder in warning, turning her back to Stone's End. Sol knew what she would see, and the relief was gone in seconds. She squeezed her eyes shut.

"Get everyone behind me," she said. "When you feel wind, jump."

"You're insane—"

"Trust me."

She opened her eyes to look up at him and the look in his eyes wasn't frustration or anger. It was worry. It seemed to be only for her, although Sol trusted her reading of people far less now. She wanted to believe it.

"I do," he said. "Just not him."

"He won't see this coming." Sol took herself out from Karas's hold and marched through the crowd of dwarves. They let her pass with ease, shuffling behind her with whispers of dread and fear. Sol stood proudly between them and the shadow of her friend as Abraxas walked towards her.

He looked unchanged, except for the large sword in his hand. It was pure black, and she couldn't tell if blood or shadows dripped from it.

She put her hands on her daggers and he stopped ten feet from her.

"Sol," he started, and almost sounded like himself.

"Don't," Sol said softly. "You're going to make this harder."

"You don't have to leave."

"You murdered my people, Abraxas," she said without a waver in her voice. "You put those things inside me. You lied and broke my trust. Even if you were to put that sword down now, get on your knees and beg for forgiveness, I don't know if I could trust you."

"Don't know?" he asked slowly. "You know me, Sol. You know I have a reason for this."

"So did Heliodar," she said, repeating Karas's words. "So did Gail, and Mal, and the Sovereigns. So did Nerezza."

"She was a monster," he spat. "You have no idea what she did to me!"

"No," she admitted. "But I know what you did to our friends, to my people, and to me. I know the Abraxas I love wouldn't be capable of any of that."

"I have always been capable of these things." Abraxas lifted his sword and Sol took a step back. There were no warm bodies behind her. They'd jumped so silently that even she had missed them.

Abraxas's eyes narrowed at the empty space behind her. One step at a time, he drove her to the edge. Sol kept the space between them ten feet until her heel met empty air. He stopped when she did.

"Is suicide more preferrable than me?" he asked.

"More preferable to the man who held me after the White Cairn? Who always made sure I remembered to eat? Who bandaged our wounds with no complaints and tried his best to be a good man, despite the horrors he was forced to commit? The man who loved quiet evenings in the wilderness and always forgot to stop his watch so another could take his place? The same man who accepted all of our sins without question, who loved us even when we didn't understand him? Who made his stew too salty and hated elven wine?"

A whisper of air met the Sol's nape.

"I love that man," Sol said. "I'd fight through every hell in existence for him. But you—" She took a step back and watched his eyes widen. "You are not that man. And I'm sorry."

Sol stepped off the ledge, into blackness and heard Abraxas scream. The wind rushed past her and she was sure it was fear in his voice. She was surer those shadows were racing towards her because he thought she was going to die. That made everything worse.

Because an abhorrent monster wearing the face of her friend she could deal with. Seeing the glimpses of him through the darkness gave her hope he was still there. Hope she couldn't afford to nurture.

The shadows raced after her. Gaining on her. The freefall made her feel like she was flying though, and the freedom it gave her was exhilarating. Even if this ended in death, she didn't want to go back. She finally understood Evren's fear of cages.

Sol slammed into something warm and large. Smooth skin rushed underneath her as she slid down, down, down. She clamped down a scream, reaching for something, *anything*, to hold on to.

Her hand brushed spikey membranes, but they slipped through her hands. She let out a cry of frustration, twisting on her stomach. If it moved to the side she would fall off. The curve of its body was just small enough that she could feel the edge curving to more open air.

She grabbed for another membrane and slipped.

Another, and she hit something hard that knocked her off

course. Her feet dangled over open air, a scream in her throat. The shadows darted out for her feet, growing ever closer.

A warm hand snatched her arm and dragged her up. The shadows missed her feet and pierced the flesh of the giant worm. An earsplitting scream rattled Sol's head. She covered her ears, pressed up against a warm body as the curve of the worm changed and dove down.

Falling with nothing around her was terrifying enough, but when Sol was the equivalent to a flea on a dog hurtling through the pitch-black of a never-ending canyon, she could properly allow herself to scream.

The hand that grabbed her turned into an arm around her waist. She found herself clutching the thin membrane of the worm, digging her head into its skin because looking at nothing was better than looking up and still seeing nothing.

She slid and fell and barely held on as the worm burrowed. Through what? She wasn't sure. She just longed for it to end.

She counted her breaths, and soon became aware of the ragged breathing beside her. Of someone holding onto her tighter than the worm itself. Someone who was familiar enough by now that she would know him even without sight.

"Not my best plan?" she cried over the screaming air.

"Fuck you, Amet."

And they laughed. Strangled, half-littered with yelps and screams. But the laugh echoed through the dark anyway, and only settled once the worm stilled to a stop.

Sol sat up, shaky. As she expected, there was nothing to see. Just pitch blackness. She couldn't even see the glow of Stone's End above them, although there was no telling how far they traveled. Sol supposed they could be anywhere.

Light emerged as Karas brought out his Luminstone pebble. He looked a little green, but stood up so the light better hit the worm.

Sprinkled along the back were the surviving dwarves.

Somehow each and every one of them had made it. Although many looked like they had lost what little meals they'd had.

Karas looked down at her. "Ever ask me to jump into the void just to land on a fuckin' juvenile giant worm again, I'm gonna strangle you, Amet."

Sol gave a shaky laugh. "Don't worry, I think I'd strangle myself before I did that again."

One by one, everyone slid off the worm. Many threw themselves on the ground weeping. One lost even more of their meal. Sol stumbled away on shaky legs, giving the worm a pat. It was much smaller than Alkimos, maybe only sixty feet long and five feet wide. Many of its spiky membranes weren't fully grown from what she could tell, as they were still drooping at the ends. It laid perfectly still, breathing softly.

Karas came up beside her frowning at it. "Tell me this ain't the big one's kid."

She grinned. "I think it is. Maybe Ainthe managed to raise it after Alkimos died?"

"And set it free just for us?" He snorted. "I'm waiting for it to eat us."

"Oh, it's not big enough for that," Sol said, hoping internally that she was right. She walked up to its head, nothing the quivering mouth of teeth still coming in and the eyeless face breathing in her direction.

"I don't know if you can understand me, but I knew your papa, kind of." She winced. "I owe my life to giant worms twice over now."

It huffed a foul breath that ruffled her hair, but did little else.

"Hey, Amet," Karas nudged her.

She looked back at him where he was holding his Luminstone up to a cavern opening. Wide enough even for a giant worm twice the juvenile's size. There was nothing particularly welcoming about it. It was another cave tunnel, filled with rocks and stalagmites and dips that would make her ankles sore.

But it meant a way out. Hopefully, it meant the surface.

The survivors gathered behind Sol as she stepped to the entrance. It felt a little like the first time the Wandering Sols embarked on their first quest together. Only this time, the stakes were higher.

This time she had to find them.

"Care to walk with me?" she asked Karas. "I need the light."

He smiled, deeply shadowed in sharp relief with the light between his thumb and finger. "Always."

24

Abraxas

She left him.

Abraxas gripped the sword until he felt his skin start to tear, until the subtle drips of his own blood hit his boots. Then he let go, and the blade disappeared into shadows.

But he couldn't move away from the edge of the canyon. He stared at the spot she'd jumped from, the disturbance of gravel her feet had left, the blackness beyond. The scream that tore through the air hadn't been hers, for it was too large and echoing to belong to her throat alone. It reminded him of Alkimos but that was impossible. The creature was dead, and it couldn't live down there without someone feeding it. Ainthe assured him—

Ah, there it was. His mistake.

Abraxas bid the shadows to bring her to him and seconds later the smell of blood and the sound of wheezing came from behind him. He didn't turn around immediately. He stared at the spot on the ground where Sol had been.

I know the Abraxas I love wouldn't be capable of any of that.

Sol's voice rang out in his ears, still fresh, and for the first time in a long time Abraxas flinched. He stilled himself immediately, and the movement was so quick that many wouldn't have seen it. But he felt it. The shadows saw. And so did Ainthe.

A chilling laugh erupted from behind him, manic and senseless. He turned slowly, taking in the work he'd done to her with an eye calmer than the riot of emotions thudding in his head.

There was little left of her, and what was left wasn't standing. Granted, that had more to do with her lack of legs than anything. Her bloodied stubs leaked onto the stone, the river of blood making its way towards his feet. Below her elbows, her elegant arms were gone. No more boney fingers crooking for her shadows to come. He'd taken them when he'd taken back his own, and the result had left the priestess limbless and broken.

Still, she sat up cackling. Her robes torn to shreds and more red than white. Her hair wild and matted to her bloody face. Her teeth were bared, shining in the burning light of Stone's End. He had the sudden urge to slit her bared throat.

"Are you sore from your loss, *Catarmon?*" Ainthe said mockingly.

Abraxas breathed steadily through his nose. He should've killed her when he saw her again. A century hadn't erased his distaste for the woman. And yet, he'd stayed his hand for no other reason than to have her suffer as he had. Killing her youngest was a little low, perhaps the lowest he'd gone, and it brought him no pleasure. But the girl was another Nerezza. Her head was filled with the lies of her mother, and Abraxas knew first-hand the kind of wretched ambition her bloodline bore.

Yes, keeping Ainthe alive for pain's sake was a mistake. He could've subdued the Mora without her help. He could've killed her with her daughter. He couldn't afford to be that stupid again.

"You got into her head," Abraxas said.

Ainthe spat a clot of blood near his feet. "I told her a few truths. She did the rest. If you had been total in your vengeance, perhaps you would've kept her longer." Ainthe cocked her head to the side. "Karas and I were liabilities. We were never going to be allies to you, and yet you were too weak to kill us and eliminate the threat." Her eyes sparked. "A god should know better."

Yes, he should've killed Karas. The dwarf had given him no favor after the sacking of Dirn-Darahl. It would've been easier to just kill him. Why hadn't he?

Abraxas frowned. Why hadn't he?

"Oh, poor soul." Ainthe tsked. "Even after so much blood and time, you're still conflicted."

"I am clear in my goal," he shot back, unsure as to why he was defending himself. She deserved no explanation. His actions had purpose.

"Which goal?" she pondered, spitting blood. "The annihilation of my people, or the return of your gods? Oh yes, I remember. Don't look so startled. I have been inside your head. I know how desperate you are."

"Desperate." Abraxas stepped over the river of blood towards her and she flinched back. The pleasure that action brought him alone was enough to drown out his lingering doubts. He reached out and she tried to scramble back. But with no arms to hold her and no legs to propel her, all she did was flop uselessly on her side.

Abraxas took a fistful of her white hair, so like Nerezza's that it made his carefully checked rage boil once again. She didn't cry out as he jerked her back up, his face inches from hers.

"If I am desperate, it is because you made me as such," he growled. "If I am desperate, it is because your meddling has left me completely and utterly alone. I am doing the work no other soul could bear and you have the gall to force away the only comfort I had!"

Ainthe didn't smile. She didn't bare her teeth. There was none of her animal ferocity lurking in her eyes. She simply looked tired.

"You," she choked through a crackling voice, "did that to yourself. Solri Amet is no stranger to the darkness of one's soul, nor the regret of one's ambitions and rage. But you fell too far even for her."

"You drove her away from me." If he pulled any harder he would take her hair out, chunks of scalp included. "She fell into a void instead of staying with me. She listened to *you*, trusted *you*, instead of me!"

Ainthe was crying out in pain now. Abraxas didn't even care to see what he was doing. She was a monster, as her daughter had been. And yet, Sol had chosen her evils over his own the same way Evren had chosen Keres and Gyda had . . .

No. He wouldn't think of Gyda anymore.

Abraxas shoved Ainthe's quivering form to the ground, his hands wet with blood. She still lived, barely.

"You accomplished nothing," he bit out. "Your people will still fall. Under my blade and under holy fire, there will be nothing left of Serevadia when I'm done."

The mangled, twitching body of Ainthe gave one last laugh. "They'll stop you. One and all, they'll be the final obstacle you cannot crush."

Abraxas's shadows tensed around him, gathering at his shoulders and ankles. They always waited patiently, humming with need but letting him exact vengeance with his hands if he wanted to. Yet there was something more poetic about letting them finish Ainthe.

"I hope they do," Abraxas said. "But they'll be too late for you and your people. You are fuel for Divine fire, Ainthe. Your soul would be better willing, but I'll take it as I have others before. Everyone else, the people you love so dearly, will fall on their swords quite willingly, and those that don't will fall to Divine justice. Be honored. A righteous sacrifice is a better death than Serevadia deserves."

He stepped over her body. He deafened himself to her screams as he unleashed the shadows behind him. They silenced her quickly, but fed long after. He shivered. Her soul felt as sharp and feral as she'd been in life. But a soul was a soul, and one would grow to many.

Many he needed.

Stone's End burned ahead of him as a figure stumbled forward. Another woman, grey skin streaked with soot and white hair fried. She wasn't pretty in any sense, and her constant startled nature made her seem more like a hunched bird than an elf. But he never needed Halenna to be anything but a mind to work out numbers.

She staggered to a stop, one of her journals tucked against her chest. She bowed deep, never meeting his eyes. It had been like this since the beginning.

"The damage is great, my lord," she said to the ground. "The outpost is lost. We have many wounded, but the bulk of our people have survived."

"And your work?"

She shuddered, her eyes growing wet again. "I need more time. These numbers can't be right. I'm missing something—"

"Halenna," he snapped harshly, and she cringed backward. She almost tripped over her singed robes, and her delicate ribcage heaved under the fabric.

He sighed and stepped forward. She was crying again. Divines, she was always crying. It gave him a headache.

Abraxas took her pointed chin between his bloody fingers and forced her gaze up at him. Tears ran through soot, her eyes were red and puffy, as usual. Thin lips trembled above his fingers.

"Your numbers are correct," he said, and she sobbed. He spoke over her. "You have everything you need. I have gifted you with more knowledge than any other mortal had in thousands of years. What you have done with it has been a gift. It is the key. Now, give me your final number."

"Please," she whispered with watery eyes. "Please, I have made a mistake. Do not take this as truth."

"Halenna, you don't make mistakes. That's why I chose you. Now, the number."

Her lips sucked against her teeth as she tried to breathe through her tears. He didn't let her go and refused to let her break eye contact. He watched as the little barrier of resistance finally broke in her and she squeezed her eyes shut.

"Three thousand," she said. "At the very least. Three thousand souls."

He dropped her chin and she gasped, nearly collapsing on the ground near his feet. Her sobbing picked up in earnest now, and he looked out at the wreckage of Stone's End.

Three thousand. An army. A sacrifice that rivaled even those in Vernes.

"Let us regroup in Dirn-Darahl, then come back here," Abraxas said over her wailing. "Emperor Velcros will need to know that our objective lies west, as well as our final obstacles."

Obstacles over friends. Obstacles over family. He forced himself to forget their faces, their smiles, the way they'd loved him, once. They didn't love him now. They'd all run away and now they were his enemies.

Deep, deep down, a part of Abraxas long buried screamed at that. But that voice was silenced by shadow and a familiar blade in his hand. He stepped over Halenna's sobbing form to gather his troops and march.

His reckoning inched ever closer.

25

Evren

Barrion and Mei waited a blissful and lonely day for Evren to rest, bathe and heal before barging into her tent. It wasn't very big, with only enough room for a cot, armor stand, and a table with a water basin. The three were crowded, but no one cared. Barrion and Mei sat on the cot because Evren was restless and couldn't stay still. It was like after scrubbing away the dirt and blood, she'd opened whatever had locked her into a dull state of stillness. It was still there, lurking in the back of her mind, ready to take over when she was least expecting it. But for now, Evren paced and recounted everything Barrion asked of her.

Barrion scratched at his growing beard. It made him more rugged, and definitely looked older. "I still have a hard time believing Abraxas was behind all of this."

"Is," Mei corrected. "He's alive, which means those little sightings from our scouts about a normal elf amongst the Greys isn't bullshit."

Evren shuddered. "Any idea where he is now?"

Mei shook her head. "Those reports were a surprise. They

happen at random battles all over the continent. Sometimes mere hours from each other. That's why we brushed them off. The scouts had seen a lot, after all. Sometimes the mind plays tricks on us."

"None from the recent batch of survivors," Barrion said. "I thought that might be your next question."

It had been, but his answer was disappointing regardless. Evren needed to find Abraxas the same way she needed to breathe. It was an incessant pull. Like she'd woken up and suddenly knew exactly where to go, only everything blocked her path. She couldn't tell if this pull was made from grief, like she was gravitating towards him because he was the only one she had left, or if she wanted something darker.

"How bad is it?" she asked, nudging at the painful wound they were all avoiding.

Barrion winced. "The coast was all we had. They haven't taken Tal-Mashad, yet. These people were from a few villages to the south. We're sending them to Linston, but we're running out of room. Soon there's not going to be enough space or water for everyone."

Mei nodded grimly. "We can't fit the whole country in one city."

"The Conclave?" Surely the brightest mages in Eith would have an idea of how to help.

But Barrion didn't look hopeful. "We've got most of the mages here in the army. A few stayed behind to keep up the city's defenses. Magic is by far the only edge we have in this fight, but it's not enough."

Evren turned to Mei. "Orenlion?"

Mei straightened. "That's the good news. We're getting fresh troops from both the Hisrachi and Orenlion. To keep things from getting out of hand, Shao and Aster decided to keep the Hisrachi to the east and see if they can weaken the Serevadia's control over Whitestone and Dirn-Darahl."

"Freeing Whitestone would be a boost to moral," Barrion

added. "Many here see the sacking of the holy city as a sign that Etherak is already falling."

Evren and Mei exchanged glances. Whitestone was just a city now, filled with empty temples and massive statues. But to the believers that made up most of Etherak's population, it had once been a place where the gods lived closest to Eith. It was where people like Abraxas were raised. Evren didn't know if Velcros was aware of the blow he dealt the country, or if he was just lashing out at the nearest place after Dirn-Darahl, but his attack still rang throughout the populace.

"Help is good, but I don't see it doing much besides stifling the flow of blood," Evren said. "The simple matter is we don't have the manpower. Even if we managed to free Etherak and Terevas, there's still Melkarth and Gratey to worry about."

Mei's fingers tapped on her knees thoughtfully. "A strike into Serevadia? Take the war to them?"

Barrion shook his head. "We don't know the land, and our easiest way in is Dirn-Darahl. I don't doubt there are other entrances, but our scouts haven't found them yet."

Her fingers drummed faster, a senseless melody and a habit Evren recognized. Mei was running low on ideas, and it was frustrating her.

"We should try," Mei said. "Get to this Emperor, lob off his head, and parade it on a stick like a bloody flag until they surrender."

"Coming from someone who knows Velcros, I'd be glad to lead such a charge," Evren said. "But he'll be protected. He's no fool."

"Neither are we!" she snapped. "Let us show him what it means to attack the surface."

Barrion's hand enveloped Mei's and the drumming stopped, if only because he wound their fingers together and forced them still. Evren expected Mei to wrench away or maybe snap a couple of his fingers off in return. Instead she stilled, stiffened, and . . . softened.

It was such a small, blink and you'll miss it, moment that Evren was sure she'd imagined it. But it didn't go away. Mei let him hold her hand and, maybe, even held his.

Barrion turned back to Evren. "It's something to consider if things get worse. I'd feel better negotiating an end to this suffering, but that's not likely to happen."

Mei wrinkled her nose. "Negotiate?"

"If we win this, there will likely still be a Serevadia below us," he explained. "We can't go back to living like they're not there."

Evren waved them both down. She couldn't think of a time after this. It didn't exist because she wasn't sure *she'd* exist afterwards. Strange that this feeling of creeping death was more comforting than the one back in Orenlion.

"What are the army's plans?" Evren asked. "Surely your uncle has something."

"Tal-Mashad and protecting it."

Mei scowled. "That's a trap."

Evren nodded, "Definitely."

"We all know that," Barrion said. "But there's no other choice. They've already cut us off from Terevas and taken Whitestone. If they take Tal-Mashad, we'll starve before winter sets in."

Evren knew this, knew that Loghain knew this, and hated it even more. Her pacing was doing no good, and she had no one to hold her and force her to calm down. That person was dead. So she forced her boots back on, sheathed her dagger on her hip, and made for the tent flap.

"Where are you going?" Barrion asked.

"To cool off," she said, and left them in her tent as she walked out. Mei and Barrion's guards snapped to attention, but didn't follow her.

It was amazing how quickly Etherak took to frost. It wasn't near winter yet, and still the ground sparkled with it. The evening was drawing to a close, sky painted vibrant reds and purples as the sun dipped away and left them to sleep. Fires lit up the camp, reminding Evren too much of the pyres she saw on the way in. Smoke, cooking meat, and the smell of horses and hounds filled the air. But the camp itself was quiet. People murmured back and forth, horses nickered to the squires brushing them down. But Evren could still hear the bugs and birds, a sure sign that the camp was filled with worried mourners, not hardy soldiers.

Evren barely felt the chill as she walked among them. They avoided her. Some even stepped out of her way as she walked past. By now news had spread about who she was, what she'd done. An adventurer of Eith who'd taken down monsters and helped Barrion secure an alliance that should've saved them. It wasn't enough. Evren knew it, and the eyes that followed her long after she passed knew it, too.

The sky was purple by the time she got to her destination. She wasn't sure why she came back, but the tent filled with godly idols and choked with incense was in front of her before she knew it. The setting sun did nothing to improve the look of the temple. It was still muddy and leaning too far to the left. A few people milled about inside, but as she stepped inside they left quickly. Evren didn't know how to feel about that.

She took a breath, and tried to imagine what Abraxas felt, what Barrion and Loghain and Dagny felt, when they were in places like this. She knew the Elders had existed once, and that still did nothing for her faith. Temples still felt like cold, hollow tombs, unwelcoming to her because she didn't understand blind faith.

There was no doubt that Abraxas's Divines existed. By the way Etherak revered them, they left a massive impression on even the younger generation that hadn't lived to see them. But Evren felt nothing in the temple. No press of awareness at the back of her skull, no overwhelming peace or the prickling of eyes watching her. With the way these people prayed, she expected something. Her gods were dead, but theirs were just banished. If they could watch, surely Evren could feel.

"It doesn't work like that, I'm afraid."

Evren started. Her hand was on her dagger as a shadow next to an alter unfolded itself and strode forward. At first she thought it was Abraxas. But the shadows were just a cloak, muddy and worn, and when the hood was thrown back the man in front of her couldn't be farther from her old friend.

The half-elf was old. Not wizened, for he moved with grace, but his hair was mostly grey and tied away from his square face. He wore a jagged scar along the left side of his jaw, as if someone had tried to cut his face off and failed somewhere near his chin. He didn't look like a priest, but he was definitely Etherakian. At this point, they were almost interchangeable.

Evren forced her hand off her dagger. "I wasn't trying anything."

He shrugged. "Most people come here to pray."

"I'm not here for that."

"Then why are you here?"

Evren hesitated, her eyes flitting along the idols. The stranger had appeared next to the one with a grinning skull. Real, she realized, as the candlelight flashed on the smooth bone. By the imprints in the ground next to that alter, he'd been praying and she'd missed him. Checking off that mystery as solved, she looked at the others, one by one until she landed on Haphion's familiar dragon.

"I guess I wanted to see why so many came here," she murmured.

"For comfort," the stranger said.

"There's no comfort here. It feels like a crypt."

He smiled sadly. "That's because it is. We mourn when we pray. Think of it as . . . visiting a loved one's grave, or their ashes. You know there's nothing there, nothing that can respond to you anyway, but you talk all the same. It does nothing, in the end, but it makes many of us feel better."

Evren made a face and he laughed.

"I take it you don't see it that way."

She shrugged. "Who am I to say? I've never felt comfort visiting dead or vacant things. Mostly just confusion."

"What for?"

"One person tells me that the Divines are little more than things to mourn, and the next one is shrieking about praying loud enough to bring them back." She shook her head. "At this point I can't decide if the Divines are walking corpses or terrible beings straining against a net."

"A little of both."

She looked at him sharply, and the man shrugged one shoulder. "I dedicated my life to them, so I know a little more. The Divines were strange beings not meant to be understood by us. They are beyond, and those that tried to comprehend them fell to madness. If they were lucky."

"So, you're a priest," Evren said, disappointed.

"Worse." He held out his arms, and the cloak fell back to reveal a wicked looking mace. "I'm a Champion. Or, well, was. Fifty or so years gone from that."

Evren's breath caught in her throat. She knew there were others like Abraxas, but she expected them to be like him. Deadly and cold and constantly in a sad, mournful state. This man was near jovial, although all of his actions seemed tinged with melancholy.

He noted her wide eyes with a tilt of his head. "Ah, you've met one of my brothers and sisters, I assume? Which one? Marian isn't so much of a bitch once you warm up to her, I promise. Stefan is just a big baby. And Josephine—"

"Abraxas," Evren interrupted with numb lips.

The stranger's face fell. He tucked his thumbs into his belt, cloak fluttering closed over his shining mace.

"I take it by your tone that the meeting was less than pleasant," he said softly. "I apologize. Abraxas was the best of us when we were younger. After Vernes . . . Well, we all changed. I shouldn't have expected him to remain the same."

"He was my friend," Evren managed to say. "His past . . . it didn't matter in the end. Things are different now."

Could she tell this man what Abraxas had become? Did she dare? What if he saw the genius in Abraxas's plan and decided to join? Or worse, was helping him now? It seemed like an Abraxas move to seek out his old comrades and bring them into his mission.

But the stranger's face only saddened. "Ah, I see. You've got the look of someone who will stab me if I ask further, so I won't. However, you are mourning people. I can help."

She frowned, uncertainty ringing in her bones. "How?"

He swept a hand back to the alter with the skull. "I was Champion of Vyone, God of Death. It sounds much worse than it is, believe me. Mostly it's a lot of helping spirits move on and eliminating undead. I know nearly every funeral rite in Eith, save some of the rare ones from Gratey. But helping families mourn was also part of my duties. The souls of the living need to move on as well as the dead."

"Well, that explains the grave analogy," Evren said smoothly.

The man cracked a smile. The lines on his face showed he smiled a lot, or used to at least. "What can I say? If I can't sprinkle in death analogies and jokes here and there, I'll wither away myself. Vyone used to love my jokes."

Unable to curb her curiosity, Evren asked, "How did you know?"

He turned back to the alter, waving her forward. She crept up slowly, peeking around him as he relit some fresh candles with a light hand. It was speckled with scars and freckles.

"Champions had a deep connection with their gods," he explained. "Starting from birth, actually. We didn't know why. The priests would always have to follow a bunch of vague clues and hints to find us, while the Divines had full conversations with us in our heads. My parents thought I had an imaginary friend. It wasn't until, at age five, I told them how the family hound was going to die, that they took me to Whitestone."

Evren frowned. "The priests didn't find you?"

"Vyone didn't tell them. He's an odd fellow, let me tell you. While the others always had clear commands and rules, Vyone didn't care what I did so long as I was respectful to the dead. He was always there, I could feel him, but most of the time it was just a little buzz at the back of my skull. You grow up with it, you don't feel it."

He shook out his match, laying it in the offering dish with shiny trinkets and straw dolls.

"But when I made jokes, especially the bad ones, I could hear him laughing." He tapped the side of his head with a sly grin. "While my friends groaned and bitched, my god was happy. That's something few Champions felt."

Evren stepped back as he moved to the next alter. Its idol reminded her of a book, or a scroll, if that thing could become something living. It was unnerving to look at, so she watched him start to light the candles again.

"Why not?"

He shrugged. "Other gods were different. I didn't hear them, so I can't say. I was closest to Josephine, whose patron was Emion." He pointed across the temple to an alter that held a golden harp. "God of Music, Dance, and Revelry. And Josephine said he was the most serious voice and personality she ever met. Emion used to scare the shit out of me, because I once saw Josephine make a battalion of soldiers dance themselves to death. The cleanup wasn't pretty, but she helped."

He moved on to the next, which held a strange miniature stone tree. The candles were held in its branches, and he took great care when he changed them.

"My point is, from the people I knew, the Divines were hard to please. Josephine never made Emion laugh, no matter what she did. And Abraxas, well, he was a lot like Haphion was taught to us. Serious and deadly when he needed to be, soft and caring otherwise. I found both sides interesting, but the soft Abraxas was the one who tried not to laugh at my jokes." He paused, candle in hand, to look at Evren. "Did he ever mention me?"

Evren bit her lip. "I don't know. What's your name?"

"Idain. No last name, I wasn't that important."

She shook her head. "No. I'm sorry."

"Ah, figures." He sighed, putting the candle in place. She didn't miss the twinge of hurt in his eyes. "He likely never talked about us at all with you. Too painful, eh?"

"He did, once," Evren said, moving with him to the next alter. "I asked him about the war, and he tried to explain to me why it happened."

Idain sucked on his teeth. "Tough conversation topic."

"It was," Evren muttered, thinking back to that ruin where the campfire glowed between them and their friendship was too young to be called that. "I didn't really understand how Nomien could go about orchestrating a war without the other, better gods, not catching on."

"That's been the question we've asked for decades. Nomien didn't have a Champion at the time, or so we thought. It was Eldridge all along. But how could Haphion, or Elos, or Holtia, or any of them not realize what was happening? There's a simple answer. They did, and they didn't care. For one reason or another, our beloved Divines used us as weapons to destroy each other."

Evren started at his casual tone. "And that doesn't bother you?"

The firelight caught something dark in Idain's eyes as he looked back at her. "Of course it does. I killed as well as buried and burned, despite how much I didn't want to. I didn't think I had a choice, and Vyone didn't tell me otherwise. We learned quickly that unless we were told not to do something, it was our gods' will. It crushed me to know that he let me rot in that war, sifting through battlefields alone day and night, without remorse. Oh, he still laughed. But my jokes became fewer the older I got.

"See, what most people don't realize is that we all questioned ourselves at one point or another. When you're capable of terrible destruction beyond what even a mage can do, and you find yourself in the aftermath of it, the only option *is* to question. But we questioned ourselves, not our gods. Not our missions.

"It wasn't until Vernes took them from us that the blindfolds were taken off. Suddenly the only sure, stable thing in our lives was gone. Everything we'd done didn't have a greater good to back it up. We were just people who had a higher body count than any normal soldier could have nightmares of. Is it any wonder that some of us were driven mad? That a couple killed themselves and others tried in vain to grasp that power again? We were everything, and then we were nothing. Less than nothing, actually. Like temples without gods."

He smiled at her, and it was somehow genuine.

He's moved on, Evren realized. *He loves them still, but he's living his own life.*

But Idain always seemed to have a chance, if his tale about Vyone's lax rules were true. Others, like Abraxas, were not so lucky.

"Idain," she said carefully, unsure of the words but knowing she had to ask them. "Abraxas isn't well."

He made a face. "I'm not surprised, if he's driven a nonbeliever like you to come in and glower at Haphion's ugly statue. Go on, you can admit it's ugly. We all knew it."

Evren let his tone roll off her back and grabbed his shoulder. She turned him away from the alters, and there was little resistance. Soon he was staring down at her expectantly, openly, in such a soft way that it made her long for Abraxas even more.

"Oh dear." He frowned. "Those are tears. Did I say something awful?"

Evren shook her head. She couldn't stop them if she tried, yet she hated the feeling of warmth dripping down her cheeks.

"You don't understand," she whispered. "Abraxas is behind all of this. Serevadia, the war, he's leading it."

Any jovial look was sapped out of Idain. He took her gently by the shoulders, eyes etched with concern.

"Even Abraxas can't fall that far," he said.

"I didn't think so, but he's been hurt." Evren's words felt like a ramble. The pressure on her shoulders, those calm eyes, it was like a sledgehammer to her dam. "He was forced to relive the war in Vernes. He had to do terrible things. They broke him, Idain, and we-I wasn't there to help him. He thinks that he can bring the Divines back."

"Through war?" Idain shook his head, bewildered. "Killing everyone in Eith hardly—oh, I see it now."

"What?"

Rather than elation, Idain was grim. He leaned back on his heels, still holding her shoulders but not pressing so much. He looked distant, thoughtful. And pissed.

"If the gods came into Eith when it was relatively stable, mortals would be irritated. Many outright livid. You're annoyed with how pious this country is? You should've seen it fifty years ago. The Divines would come back to find their followers halved, if they were lucky, and wanting. The world wouldn't accept them with open arms.

"But," he held a finger in the air, "If the world was on the brink of annihilation, and the Divines *saved* us . . . Well, I'm sure you can see where he's going with this."

Evren stumbled out of his grip, which was loose with his own shock. She hugged her arms to her chest.

"It's all about them." She angrily wiped away her tears. "Everything we did to save Eith, to save each other, was pointless. It's like he doesn't care how many people die so long as he gets his way."

"Not his way," Idain said darkly. "Haphion's. Remember, he learned from a god of extremes. Haphion ruled the heavens for a reason. Only one goddess ever defied him, and she was torn to pieces as a result. The God of Light must always cast a large shadow, and he's learned to accept that. Abraxas has stopped trying to be the light, Instead, he's just the darkness, because he thinks that's what is needed."

All at once, Evren was brought back to the giant ruin with Abraxas. Scratchy wool blanket pulled to her nose, the fire crackling merrily. A whispered exchange that ended in a promise.

In the event where I start chasing revenge over justice, I hope someone can talk me back to the light.

We can.

Evren's throat was so tight with emotions it threatened to choke her. She glared at the statue of Haphion, it really was ugly, and barely choked back a sob. He had no idea what he'd done to Abraxas, and he didn't care. Wouldn't, if Abraxas was successful. And Evren hated him for it.

"I have to get to him," Evren choked out, looking up at Idain. "I have to bring him back. I promised I would."

Idain's face was a mask of calm and gentleness, but underneath she saw his sorrow, his doubt. He knew Abraxas's darkness even better than she did. He didn't think she could do it.

"Oaths are sacred things," he said softly. "The one you made to him will be upheld. I can feel it. But at what cost?"

At this point, what else did she have to lose?

"He's worth it," she said. "He fought for me no matter how wrong I was. I have to do the same. I have to try."

He raised his hands in surrender. "I'm not trying to stop you. On the contrary, it's refreshing to see someone fight for us for a change. Simply know that we are different. I hope this ends well, but Abraxas has always been meticulous in his battle plans. He only lost once, and I think I know why now."

Evren started to ask him more, maybe even ask him to stay, when a horn sounded through the air. It rippled the sheets of the tent. The candles fluttered, and some went out. The quiet of the night was broken with the horn, and seconds later, with screams.

"Attack." Idain drew his mace. "They're attacking the damn camp!"

He flew past her and into the night. Evren grasped her knife, all she had, and raced after him. The statues of the Divines bore holes in her back as they watched her dive into battle.

Sorin

The day Sorin was going to die was a miserable, foggy day that bleached all the color out of the world. Even the water looked grey. The air was damp with a constant cold mist, so everyone shivered and was more miserable than normal as they worked. Visibility was so bad that even the imposing black cliffs of Etherak's coast were almost too shrouded to see.

And no one paid Sorin any mind.

He dumped his bucket of nasty in the water and set it on the railing. He stood beside it, hands shaking and heart racing. But his mind was calm, which was new. He always knew something was wrong when his brain wasn't screaming at him to change his mind and rethink the plan.

Not for the first time, he longed for someone to talk him out of it. Or for someone to be at his side and give him a smile of encouragement, a nod, and squeeze on his shoulder that said, *yes you can do this, we believe in you.*

But he couldn't tell Sahar, and she would not encourage him to do this. Enola was hidden, and there were no gods for him to thank so he kept that to himself. And there was no way in all the hells that he was looking to the witch, whose name he learned was Nadine, for encouragement.

Sorin was on his own.

He took a deep breath and shoved the bucket off the side. Then he pushed off the railing and turned to the quarterdeck. As always, Vayne was there. He was talking with his navigator, who was one of the survivors that had held Sorin down. The old one had disappeared. Sahar was behind him, freezing and furious. As usual her eyes skimmed over him with disinterest. Until she saw him advancing up the stairs. Until she saw the stolen kitchen knife in his hands.

He was on the last step, Vayne's back to him, the ship oblivious when she started to mouth 'don't.' And, oh, it wasn't fair to someone like her to see so much death. How many times had he watched grief overcome her? With Drystan, with Vox's body, with Nerezza. As Rhienwall was attacked and she dug furiously through the rubble at his side. As all hope of having a happy ending faded from her mind like a dying star.

It wasn't fair that someone so bright would suffer so much. And it was even less fair that Sorin would be another cause of it.

Oh, who was he kidding? She latched onto him because he was the last one left. It wasn't as if he was as close to her as Evren had been. It wasn't like he shared as many adventures and jokes and stories as she had with the Ashen Bond. The two had nothing in common like she and Sol did. No homeland to tie them together, like her and Arke. No undying love like her and Gyda.

No, Sorin was quite aware that Sahar only looked at him like that because he was all that remained, and that maybe someone better would've been able to get her out of this mess without hurting her.

There was a promise though, and that hurt. A promise to never leave her alone. He was breaking it and doing it willingly. *That* he regretted.

It was unfair to leave the fate of Eith on her shoulders alone, but who else could bear it with such grace and ease?

Sorin didn't say he was sorry. Maybe he should've, but he couldn't get the words to form on his lips even if they were silent. He couldn't even manage a smile.

He turned to Vayne's back as her eyes went wide. He raised his knife. Mist shimmered along the edge of the blade, so carefully sharpened by Willie before being set aside for him to swipe. Careless. Completely unlike her to overlook a knife. He'd thank her . . . well, never.

The blade was raised and falling to meet Vayne's back. The navigator looked on with a wide mouth. Vayne was just starting to turn around. Hells, Sorin could actually land a hit on him.

The wind turned to shackles around his wrist and ankles, yanking him up in the air. The mist was daggers cutting into his skin. He allowed himself to scream in real frustration as he was torn away from Vayne. The knife clattered to the deck, and he was suspended high in the air, at least twenty feet. It shouldn't have made him sick to look down since it was only a tiny fraction of the height of the main mast, but he couldn't help the dizziness that flooded his senses. He had just enough sense to see Nadine emerge from the deck, gnarled hand extended towards him as she kept the winds in check.

If Sorin hadn't gotten everyone's attention, she had. The crew froze to stare at her. Vayne didn't snap at them to keep working. He was grinning. He wanted them to watch.

"Now there is a loyal dog." Vayne swept his hand out to Nadine. The old witch gave him no attention. She focused solely on Sorin. "I know many of you are afraid of our resident witch, but this is what true loyalty looks like. And what does it do to the dogs that bite the hand that feeds it?"

The wind responded in kind, pulling his limbs like they were ropes tied to racing horses. His bones popped, dangerously close to breaking out of their sockets all together. His skin screamed with him, the burning traveling up his wrists and ankles to meet at his core.

The only sounds on the *Red Knave* were the howling wind and his screams.

Black spots danced his vision as Nadine's wind suddenly slammed him into the mast. His ribs splintered, his spine spiked with white-hot pain. Copper flooded his mouth as he bit his tongue.

"I told you, pup," Vayne was saying so very far away. "You only get one chance." To Nadine, his tone was crisp, not condescending. "Finish him."

Sorin closed his eyes and began to sing.

"Take to the stars ye lost souls of water,
Where you salt-laden spirit cannot falter."

Nadine's magic wavered at the sound of his voice. The wind as sturdy as iron turned soft, hardened, and then softened again until it no longer held him. He was falling, stomach clenched between his teeth. Twenty feet was as deadly as Nadine just snatching the air from his lungs, but he twisted just in time to land on his side, head covered, not his legs. He heard another crack, another shooting brand of pain and, yes, that was definitely a punctured lung. At least his bullshitting and singing would keep that from collapsing too soon.

Sorin struggled to his feet, spitting out blood. More crawled up his throat which was just fantastic. Add some color and add to the drama.

He couldn't stand up straight, but he could look up enough to see Nadine's shocked expression, and that of the crew. How long had it been since they heard that song? Was Nadine acting? If so, she was damn good at it for a woman whose face barely moved.

Sorin started backing away from her. No one in their right mind would stay still in front of the witch trying to kill them. The crew stumbled out of his way. He kept singing. It was all he could do.

"Oh, spirits to ash, and bones to the thunder,
We wait for the day our souls meet in wonder,
Leave behind your home of salt in the sea,
Forget the ending of life you didn't foresee—"
When the wind lashed out again, he was ready. The heavy fists meant to slam him into the mast missed him as he danced out of the way. When it curled back around for another go, he hid behind the next mast and felt the scream as it buffeted the wood. He pushed off, hacking more blood. Nadine was advancing on him.

Sorin kept walking back to the bow of the ship, bloody song on his lips and the wind dancing between his legs.

"The Bond that holds us has never been stronger,
I wait for the day our souls meet in wonder."
Sorin gasped for breath, finding the air battling for room amongst the blood. He heaved another breath as he tiptoed around the raging wind. She could tear through the whole ship to get to him, but she'd damage it and the crew. Making his enemies work for him had always been his specialty.

So Sorin danced. He twirled with the sword-sharp air. He felt it skim his back as he spun. He skipped up the ship, feeling for the first time like there was a blade in his hand and the Wandering Sols were at his back again.

"Swim in a sea of stars and ride waves of wind,"
Wind whooshed through his dreads as he skirted around a pile of abandoned rope.

"Your brilliance in life such death cannot dim,"
A hop is all that kept him from the grasp of Nadine's magic, the witch herself a shroud of black death approaching him with slow, even steps.

"Just don't forget who waits for you under,
I cherish—"
His lung gave out, convulsing under his useless ribcage. He stumbled, the song dying with a sickeningly wet wheeze. That was all the window Nadine needed.

The wind lashed out, snatching him up in the air again. Gentler though. No one else would've guessed by the way he cried out.

Blood dribbled down his chin. He looked down to see he'd made it to the bowsprit. Nowhere else to run anyway. This was the end of the line.

Nadine's face was the same, but her eyes, only visible to him, were shining with tears. Beyond her, the crew was watching, transfixed. Some with tears in their eyes, which Sorin could only think as touching but also plainly rude because they didn't know him. Several shook their heads in shame, not looking away but not expecting any less. Miks and Zo were part of them. He could've sworn a few were trying to finish the song, but couldn't bring themselves to.

Vayne was trying to contain how furious he was. His lips were pulled back into a snarl and his knuckles were white, even from where Sorin was he could see them. And just behind him was Sahar, hand over her mouth and eyes overflowing with tears.

He locked eyes with her. He couldn't say sorry. He couldn't say goodbye. But he gave her a bloody grin and this time it was real. Because she deserved a real smile and if she was the last thing he saw then he could die happy.

"FINISH HIM!" Vayne roared.

Nadine reared her other hand back, one that sparked with lightning. Sorin didn't close his eyes. He didn't stare at the weapon that would end him.

Eyes on Sahar, lungs failing, lips slick with blood.

"I cherish the day our souls meet in wonder."

The lightning hit him with the full force of a caged storm finally being set loose. It tore through his ruined chest, carrying over the bowsprit as the wind let go. Bones blackened. Hair sizzled. His jaw was so tight he thought it would snap. He couldn't see Sahar anymore, only the undulating world of black-and-white, black-and-white, desolate black and searing white.

Then there was nothing but black and the last thing he felt was the water dragging him under.

~

~

THERE WERE cold hands on his cheeks. Claws delicately scraping at his cheekbones. Air in his lungs.

Air.

Sorin snapped his eyes open and was face to face with a beautiful, deadly creature. Wide green eyes with a vertical slit instead of a round pupil. Skin a deep grey and patterned with white stripes and spots of black. A mouthful of razor-sharp teeth.

Sorin yelped and scrambled away. Slick rocks cut at his palms, his legs were still in the water. A cave? Didn't matter. He should be dead, and instead there was a fucking *mermaid* about to eat him.

The worst ones were the ones in the caves. Those hadn't even tried the delightful thing of luring their targets into the water. They just tried to kill, which Sorin found both rude and practical. He'd grown up with plenty of stories about mermaids and sirens and harpies. All similar creatures who used song and illusions to lure their dinners to them before brutally tearing them apart. Today was the first day Sorin had ever seen one.

And she . . . was just staring at him.

His leg was *right there*. Child's play for a mermaid. At least, he assumed.

He stared at her, chest heaving. Wait. Heaving? And not in pain? Sorin felt at the spot where the lightning at hit them and there wasn't a mark on him, just his old dagger wound over his heart. His ribs felt fine. And his spine! It was as if he'd been trying to pop it for ages and finally got the right spot.

His hand was still bad. The scar tissue looked uglier in the dim grey light of the cave. He looked up from it to her. She was just staying there, half in the water and leaning on the rocks to watch him.

"Did you . . ." He swallowed, bitter salt making him wince. "Did you heal me?"

"Of course," she purred, and Sorin couldn't help it—he jumped.

Her voice was not the light, airy quality he always imagined. It was a deep tenor, still melodic but reminding him more of a dark tide than a summer breeze.

"I, uh, thought I was dead."

"Almost." She corrected him and tilted her head to the side. Her hair fell over her shoulder oddly, and with a jolt Sorin realized it wasn't hair, but more like long, delicate fins overlapping each other to mimic hair. Her top body mimicked a human woman's at an eye's glance, down to her powerful shoulders and the curve of her breasts, but that was where the similarities ended. Her skin wasn't an array of creams or browns, but that mesmerizing pattern she had on her face all over. Paler on her belly, darker on her back and along her forearms, where tougher fins protruded. Her tail flicked in the water, the same grey, with another, larger dorsal fin tipped white. It surprised him just how shark-like she was, rather than like a fish.

True, there were murdering fish. But Sorin supposed if he had his pick of what kind of sea animal to be like, a shark would be nicer than a mackerel.

"So how does this work?" he asked. "Do I get a head start? Maybe a couple minutes? You're obviously going to catch me, but I figured if you healed me you wanted more of a chase than a weak snack."

The mermaid frowned, which around her mouthful of teeth was almost comical to watch.

"I'm not going to eat you, Sorin."

"Aaand you know my name. Great."

He wasn't freaking out. He *wasn't*, because he was very likely dead and this was some weird afterlife he'd have to deal with because of some preteen fantasies. And as far as afterlives went, this beat unending darkness or putting up with Abraxas's Divines.

But then she laughed and jerked him out of his thoughts. "Of course I do! You gave it to me."

"I . . ." Sorin, not for the first time but definitely for the weirdest time, was at a loss for words.

"And I gave you mine," she continued. "Do you remember?"

It came to him unbidden, like a piece of jewelry buried under years of sediment and silt washed away by a powerful wave.

"Ire," he breathed, and with that name came a memory. Of being too small to be alone but wading in the tidal pools anyway and picking up eels. Of a small white tipped fin, and then a young, round grey face grinning at him and missing many teeth.

"Your name is Ire," he said with more strength. "I met you when I was very young."

"We were just babies then," Ire said. "I don't blame you for forgetting. We weren't even supposed to meet. I broke the rules."

He cleared his throat. Behind her, the water churned in little whirlpools as her tail swished back and forth. "What do you mean? What rules?"

"Oh, bother, you really have nothing behind those pretty eyes of yours, do you?"

"Hey! I'll take that as a compliment and not the insult you meant, thank you." He shifted until he had his legs crossed underneath him. Now that the adrenaline was wearing off, he was freezing and pretty sure he wasn't dead. The sky outside the cave looked as grey and gloomy as he left it, and the waters around Etherak's coast were frigid at the best of times. He struggled not to shiver.

"Please explain," he pleaded. "I don't know what's going on anymore. Up until five minutes ago I thought I was dead. Now you're here, and you saved me, which goes against everything I was taught. Not that I'm not grateful! But, you know, a little background would help things along."

"I thought it would be obvious by now," Ire looked genuinely confused. "Nadine's messages said you'd come into your powers nicely."

"Nadine's messages?"

To answer, Ire fished something out of the water and held her dripping hand out to him. He leaned over just enough to see little bones and scales before sitting back.

"I don't read mermaid, so I'll take your word for it."

She shrugged, putting them back in the water. "I thought you knew."

"I don't have powers anymore," Sorin said. "What little I had died when I did the first time. When I came back, they didn't."

"That's not true." Ire looked sullen. Or as sullen as one could be pouting around that many teeth. *Hells*, that was a lot of teeth. "The only way you wouldn't have power is if I was dead."

"Well that's not—" Sorin stopped as the thought hit him harder than he had hit the main mast. He gaped at her, mouth opening and closing like a dying fish. She watched it with wide, unblinking eyes, bouncing her head up and down slightly to follow it.

"No fucking way."

"Yes!" she said cheerfully.

"That's not possible. I would've known!"

"Nuh-uh. We keep it very secret, my people."

Sorin's hands were on the sides of his head because he couldn't find a place for them elsewhere. The sudden light that shone on him, as if he'd been starved of it for years, felt like the sun after a storm. Renewing and illuminating and damn deserved.

"I have a Bond," he murmured to himself. Then to her, "I have a Bond with you."

"Yes!" Ire clapped and splashed water everywhere. "It's so good to see you again, Sorin! I've missed you."

He swallowed down his protests, the parts of his mind that told him he wasn't worthy enough to have a Tidemind much less a Sea Bond died screaming in the dark corners of his mind.

"I don't understand. Why didn't I know? Sea Bonds are looked for. Claimed by whoever or whatever is Bonded to the Vasa. Why didn't you claim me?"

"Oh, Sorin." She sighed and sank into the water up to her chin. "I wanted to, truly. But answer me this. Have you ever heard of a Vasa Bonded to a mermaid?"

"Uh, no."

"Why do you think that is?"

His hands fell into his lap. With every beat of exhilaration there came that dull cloud of clarity. There was always a catch.

"Because no one fears mermaids more than Vasa," he said.

There were plenty of people smarter than Sorin who had tried to figure out why. Simple superstition taken to the extreme? Was there a war between the two that none had records of? Maybe mermaids held a dark secret that Vasa used to know but was now lost to time. Whatever it was, all that was left was unending fear from both sides.

Ire traced paths in the water with her claw. "A Sea Bonded Vasa's powers come from whatever they are Bonded with. Someone unlucky enough to be Bonded to a kraken would have terrible power of both the storm and sea. Nadine had minimal control of both thanks to Oriel, power that she had to grow with help in order to survive. But Vasa like you who are Bonded to creatures like me get a different power."

"Words, Sorin. Voice. You sway people with what you say. You can make people trust you, or incite a fight. You can lead an army or tear down a kingdom."

Ire blinked at him. "This wasn't lost. It was weak because I had to stay away instead of teach you. Because if anyone found out . . ."

"They'd never trust me again." Sorin shivered. He didn't

think his mothers would've done anything to him, but the rest of his family? He wasn't so sure.

"My voice comes from my anger." She giggled. "Like my name, get it?"

He laughed. "Yeah, I do. Nice play on words."

"Thank you! But yours I think is different."

"How do you figure?"

"Well." She shrugged, and her hair fins plopped into the water. "Nadine says you tried that. It didn't work. When was the last time you remember using your voice?"

That wasn't a hard stretch. He remembered the time vividly. Seconds before a dagger slammed into his heart and changed him forever. A monstrous worm with his friend riding it behind him. An army in front of him.

"I was talking down an army," Sorin said. His words bounced off the cave walls. "I was telling them the truth, but they needed to believe me over their general's lies. My friend Sol was telling me what to say so it would sound right to them, but the words were still mine. I felt them. I knew if they didn't work that there was going to be a war. Either one that would destroy Sol's home or one that would destroy a people we gave our word that we would protect."

He laughed at the irony. "At the time, that moment was everything. It felt like the whole world came down to it, to my words. Then Heliodar . . ." His hand went to his chest and he didn't imagine the fury in Ire's body language. The way her hair fins quivered and her eyes narrowed was more than enough to show him that she lived up to her name. "When I fell, my words did something else. That magic snapped into something differ-ent. Instead of peace and understanding, I just wanted Heliodar gone so I could stop hurting. I wanted her dead for everything she'd done."

"So the army responded in kind." Ire nodded in approval.

"Was that wrong?" he asked. "I forced them to kill. And they did it brutally. They ripped her apart with their bare hands."

Ire bared her teeth. "Kinder than what I would've done. But I'll tell you a secret, Sorin." She leaned in close and softened when he mirrored her. "Our magic only enhances what is already there. We can't make a loving husband butcher his wife. We can't force a mother to abandon her child. Everything we say pulls at what lies within them. *That* is why Vasa fear us. They would rather believe that we are creatures of pure evil before they believe that those people are already capable of such things."

"It's a little terrifying, you have to admit." He winked and she giggled again, all the viscous fury gone. Sorin wanted to revel in this one good thing for a long time. Soak in it like it was a hot bath. He had power, but more than that, he had a Bond, which went beyond power. It was a kinship that he couldn't lose to something as simple as a pirate prone to slavery. It was something he'd had before Vayne, and something he still had.

Thunder rumbled outside the cave. Both Vasa and mermaid looked out to see the grey skies darken to a hideous black, for lightning to fork out of the white capped water. The gusts of wind tossed waves into the cave that made Ire dig her claws into the rock.

As another bolt of lightning struck, it silhouetted a massive ship.

Sorin breathed through his fear, just as Evren taught him. It was useful until it paralyzed him.

"I need to get back there."

Ire hummed musically, just a small inkling of the song she was capable of, and it gave Sorin chills. "I can get you there."

He blinked down at her. "Really?"

She grinned and he saw the same chubby-cheeked child mermaid in the tidepools looking back at him. "Of course! That's what Bonds are for. I've been following Vayne ever since he destroyed the *Fortune's Trinity*, but I wanted us to kill him together. For our family."

Sorin's heart was overwhelmed by the tiniest bit of affection, so her words made it feel like it would burst. There was no Sere-vadian Empire or betraying friends. There was only a vengeance to enact, a friend to save, and a ship to liberate.

"You've waited for me long enough, Ire," he said. "You don't have to wait anymore."

She let out a happy yip and swam in a circle rapidly. When she popped back up, her smooth skin glistened. "Say the words! Please!"

Sorin laughed as he slid into the frigid water next to her. She motioned him to wrap his arms around her shoulders, and he was careful not to rub against her skin. It was smooth one way, but abrasive the other.

"Let's go kill this fucker," Sorin said.

Ire cackled and he kept laughing as they swam out into the deadly storm, hope and vengeance flitting like two leaves in a hurricane in their hearts.

27

Arke

Since time seemed to have no meaning in the Aether, Arke had plenty of time to stew and hate himself before forcing himself to get back to work. He had Aushruk to find, whoever that was, and the prospect of getting to her through portals was looking grim.

He'd known Abraxas well enough that even risking the portal for him had worked out. But Aushruk? He knew her name, her race and that they had the same idea of just how fucked the Divines could get. But he didn't even know what a Dra'Nacti was, let alone how to find one.

Arke wasn't going to ask one of the souls either. Considering how well that went last time, he was completely sure that he didn't want to live through someone else's death.

A wispy hand fluttered by him. He blew it away.

"Fuck off."

It fucked off, and Arke returned to his thoughts. What he knew about Vernes was more now than before. Now he had names of cities. The port city of Mere, the capital of Tatesai, and a handful of others that had been central to the fighting. And, of course, Cuskhe, which he knew from the notes, was abandoned.

It seemed easier to go to a place he'd read countless reports on and had maps of rather than focusing on a person. Still, he kept this strange Aushruk in his mind. What manner of woman had Abraxas befriended in those dark years? Why hadn't she been enough to save him?

Why hadn't *he* been enough to save Abraxas?

Arke forcibly shook his head and scattered more mist as he stood up. His eyes were all swollen and puffy. Every time he blinked he could feel grit stabbing the corners of his eyes, and it never went away no matter how furiously he scrubbed at them.

Tucking his spellbook under his arm, he glared at the Aether in front of him. Already he was grasping for the details of Cuskhe. Maps, notes on how it felt, a soldier's recollection of the walls. Little things that formed a city in his mind. But even as he did, he let it slip away.

What use was Cuskhe? Aushruk wasn't likely to be there. Sounded like no one wanted to be there anymore. Arke was so damn tired, he just wanted answers. He just wanted to get all the horrible shit over with so he could be miserable and with Unnethen for the rest of his days.

So he latched onto Aushruk instead. On the name and the strange way it rolled off his tongue. On the alien idea of what the Dra'Nacti might be, because the only description he had was 'tall and horned,' thanks to Rimmel. And, finally, on the way Abraxas spoke of her. Heavy with guilt, and with a look Arke knew well.

The look of, *I can imagine how my life would've been with this person if I'd stayed and it makes me feel like shit every time I remember them.*

Arke knew that expression well. It was one of many reasons he tried to avoid mirrors.

"All right, let's try this." Arke sighed into the nothing. "Aushruk. Aushruk."

He imagined the Aether tearing under his claw and leading right to her. To the open sea of dunes and the blazing sun above. He'd never been to a desert before, but he could imagine the oppressive heat anyway. The way her horns might look silhouetted against the sun. How she might tower over him. How kind her smile might be, since she'd been kind to Abraxas during a war.

The Aether parted underneath his finger slowly, hesitantly. Arke held his breath as it wavered, almost knitting itself back together before finally giving under his will. Dry, hot air flooded his face, ruffled his hair and ears. He squinted at the reddish-gold beyond and then stepped through.

The portal closed behind him quicker than before, as if it couldn't shut fast enough. As his feet touched sand and his face was shaded by emerald, green palms, he shuddered.

This place felt different. Stained and old. The air, while fresh, carried a scent of mourning with it. Like the smoke of a long distant pyre carried by the wind. Only Arke knew better. Vernes didn't burn their dead.

The oasis was a surprisingly comfortable place to land. A trickling stream on reddish rocks, shaded by groves of trees. There were bushes and grass shooting up along the banks, swaying softly in the desert breeze. Beyond the green was more than he prepared himself for. Desert, but harsh and flat save for strange spires spiking into the sky.

And it was all the color of blood.

Arke took a step back and his neck met the cool kiss of a blade.

Strange hissing erupted from behind him, but not that of a snake. Intelligible, drawn out in some parts and clipped short in others. Pausing where one might pause at the end of a sentence.

"I don't know your language." Arke let his spellbook flop on the ground and raised his hands. "Do you know mine?"

That hissing continued, only now Arke could hear it as laughter instead of strange words.

"Yes, small prey. I understand you."

Core was strange on their tongue. As if they were speaking around a mouthful of teeth not used to the words. Arke used to have the same trouble, even if goblins were raised on Core. Their mouths were meant for a language long since lost.

"Fan-fuckin'-tastic," he muttered. "I'm here for Aushruk. Can you show me to her?"

The blade didn't leave the back of his neck. It was angled in a way that Arke could tell whoever was holding it was tall. He didn't need a shadow from the sun to tell him that it was a Dra'-Nacti, although he desperately wished the sun was behind him rather than in front so he could make out something.

"What would you know of Aushruk?" the voice asked. "You are not one he knows."

"He?" Arke frowned. "I was told Aushruk was a woman."

A soft sigh and the blade was taken away. "Nearly a century ago, yes. But that was a long time. A dark time."

Arke took that as his cue to turn around, although he did so slowly. Like the desert, no amount of preparation would've helped him from seeing a Dra'Nacti for the first time. He barely came up to this one's knee. Covered in ink-dark skin, laced with glittering scales on their shoulders and arms. Lines of gold down their chin, sharp cheekbones and long neck. And the horns were magnificent. Tall and ornamented with clinking charms and bones.

The spear was dug into the ground beside them, and they regarded Arke with curious black eyes. All black and intense.

"I am Aushruk'dien, the one you seek." A coy smile played on their lips, and sharp teeth showed. "And to ease your confusion, I am male now."

Arke blinked up at him. "Right. Ain't helpin' my confusion. You sure there's not another one of you?"

"I assure you there is not." He cocked his head to the side. "And what manner of beast are you to crawl out of thin air like a mirage taken form?"

"I'm a goblin." When Aushruk didn't respond, Arke winced. "I'm from Terevas. Guessin' my kind ain't native here."

"No. Do all goblins," Aushruk's tongue flicked in the air as he tested the word, "appear out of the air?"

"Ah, no. Just me." Arke shrugged. "Magic."

"Hmm, I see."

Aushruk picked up his spear again, all careful grace and power, and walked past Arke deeper into the oasis. Arke scrambled to pick up his spellbook, faltering only when he saw the tail Aushruk whipped behind himself. A tail *and* horns. Made the Serevadians look tame.

Aushruk stopped at the edge of the stream just above where it tumbled into a crystal pool. The air was a dash wetter than the air they'd left, and Arke found himself sighing at the feeling of a little cool mist. His skin already felt like a piece of old parchment left out in the sun.

The Dra'Nacti set his spear down next to a rock where a canvas bag sat. Then he dipped his feet in the water and sighed loudly.

"Come. You wish to speak? In the water."

Arke balked. "Why?"

Aushruk glared. "There are no lies in running water. It is known."

It was very much not known to Arke, but he wasn't going to question someone who looked like he could eat him. So, he set down his book on a flat rock, rolled up his pants and stepped into the water.

Sun-warmed, it was surprisingly relaxing. He flexed his toes, watching their warbled images through the water's surface wiggle. The bubbling of the water eased the tension built in his shoulders. He found himself relaxing like Aushruk had.

"So," the Dra'Nacti murmured over the water. "You came for me. Why?"

"I need your help." Arke gnawed the inside of his cheek. "I

have a friend. Well . . . I don't think we're that anymore. He's tryin' to undo what your country did to banish the Divines."

Aushruk's gasp came out like a hiss. Arke turned to him, startled to see the bare fear on his face.

"Abraxas Kain." Aushruk's eyes were wide. "It is him, is it not?"

Arke nodded slowly. "Thought you'd know him."

The mournful grief on his face was deep enough that it made Arke's stomach twist. This was a creature who didn't hide his emotions, who sought no reason to. And it left Arke feeling everything secondhand. He didn't want that grief, that guilt or bitterness. He had plenty of his own.

"I knew him," Aushruk confirmed. "I knew him as well as one could. He was trapped when I met him. A broken man seeking redemption." His mouth thinned in distaste. "He did not find what he sought through me. I promised, but it was not enough. It never would be, for I am not Divine."

Arke snorted. "You, me, and 'bout four others are in the same boat."

Aushruk had no eyebrows, but the paint along his face lifted. "Oh? How so?"

"He was our friend," Arke said. "But we didn't get to him in time. He's turned against us, and now he's destroying Eith. You gotten any grey elves messin' with you?"

Aushruk sneered. "The ashen plague. They do not do well in this land. Gratey fares worse from what my brethren up north tell me."

"Abraxas is behind them," Arke said. At his startled expression, Arke moved on quickly. "He's made himself their god, but it's not about destruction. Not really. He wants to use them to bring the Divines back. I need to figure out how to stop him, but I can't unless I figure out how you banished them in the first place."

Slowly, Aushruk sat on his rock. Long nails drummed on its surface, clicking a tuneless song with the music and the wind.

His gaze was far away, decades away. Arke could only watch as words formed on shock-numbed lips.

"He saw again what his gods did to my land," Aushruk murmured. "He fought beside us. Against them. I thought maybe he . . ." He shook his head, scowling. "I should have killed him when I smelled the change in him."

Arke hated the pang of anger and protectiveness that overwhelmed him at someone threatening Abraxas. He had to remind himself that Abraxas wasn't his friend anymore, and that if Aushruk *had* killed him, it would've been no different than Abraxas dying over the Deep Wood.

Arke would've been spared the task of doing it himself that way.

Instead, he reigned himself in. He remembered how defeated and lost Abraxas had looked mere hours—days?—ago. Aushruk meant something to him, like a knife kept in the back of a drawer for fear of cutting his fingers.

Aushruk had tried to help him.

"Nah," Arke said, having none of his usual bite. "You shouldn't have. It ain't your fault he's like this."

Black eyes cut to the present and over to him. "Is it not?"

"It ain't. It was Nerezza." Aushruk's face changed in a way that looked like agreement. "And it was his fuckin' gods. I won't ever understand his love for them after what they did."

Aushruk shook his head sadly. "Why does a beaten dog go back to its master? No chain to keep him tied to them, no fence to cage him. And yet, it is all he knows. What passed for love in that temple is all he clings to. The pain is inconsequential."

"So, you get why I'm here?" Arke pressed. He waded through the water until he stood in front of the slouched Dra'Nacti. "I gotta stop him."

Aushruk frowned. "He knows nothing of what I did. He was not there."

"Let's just assume that he's got enough power that he doesn't need to know. But I do." Arke balled his hands into fists. "I got friends dyin' while I go place to place tryin' to stay ahead of him. If I can figure out how to stop him, then they don't gotta die."

"How do I know you are not his spy looking for weaknesses?"

Arke growled from the back of his throat. "Because I can't fuckin lie. Because I put all my faith into him bein' good and now my friends are dyin' for it. Everything we fought for is burnin'. Everything we wanted has turned to shit. And I'm the one that's gotta pick up the pieces. Look at me like that all you want, but the truth is the same. Abraxas Kain was my friend, and it's killin' me to stand against him. I think you know the feelin'."

Aushruk studied him for a long while, and Arke wondered if he found him as strange as Arke found him. It didn't occur to him until this moment that this was likely the first time their people had ever met one another. And what shit circumstances they were.

Suddenly Aushruk stood and Arke backpedaled so fast that he nearly fell in the water. The Dra'Nacti looked down on him, a shadow against the sun. A lot like Arke imagined him to be.

"If Abraxas Kain succeeds in his quest, then everything I have sacrificed will be for naught." Aushruk said. "His Divines will descend on my home with a vengeance so bright and burning that it will turn sand to glass."

"You act like you've seen it."

Aushruk blinked slowly. "It is known."

"Okay." Arke moved past that terrifying thought. "So you'll help me?"

Aushruk nodded stiffly. "I have journeyed to visit the ghosts anyway. They will appreciate another learning their story. Whatever you gather from it, I hope it is enough to stop him."

Aushruk climbed out of the water and Arke scrambled to do the same. He was far less graceful and slung water everywhere, but his new companion didn't seem to mind. They gathered up their respective things, only a spellbook, a spear and a bag between them.

"Where are we goin'?" Arke asked as Aushruk brushed past him. He barely left a print in the sands, whereas Arke's feet dug little dunes as he followed. Out of the trees, a red desert expanded like lungs filling with hot, waiting air. There was no end, and very little to show that there was a change in the scenery. Pale blue sky stretched forever outward, unmarred by clouds.

Aushruk pointed with his spear to the west, where the pillars Arke saw before loomed. The sands seemed darker there, the sky less blue and more grey.

"There," Aushruk said. "This is where we will show you how we banished the Divines from our world."

"Show?" Arke asked hesitantly.

Aushruk grinned like a predator. "The dead in Vernes are not idle, little one. They have stories to tell. And those who suffered at the hands of gods even more so."

28

Gyda

"You do not have to follow me."

The worg didn't answer Gyda, didn't walk back to sit at Jalaa's heels. In the whipping wind of the coming storm, he sat and watched Gyda with squinted eyes. Sometimes Gyda forgot that he was still very young, not yet grown into his massive chest and paws. If his old pack was any indication, he'd reach her hip before he was full grown. What a formidable beast he would make when he did.

But for now, he was still young and staring at her expectantly. Maybe it was because she was the only one he recognized here. Jalaa was kind, but she hadn't raised him. The worg's bond with Sorin was undeniable, and yet the whole of the Wandering Sol had been there for his youngest months and forward. Like they were her clan, Gyda supposed that he would consider them his pack.

If there was one thing Evren had taught her, it was that worgs were fiercely loyal to their own. They wouldn't leave each other behind even in the most dire of circumstances. It went far beyond what nature demanded of them, since a whole pack staying put for the sake of an injured elder was a foolish weakness wolves and other pack hunters shrugged off.

But worgs were different, and those from the Deep Wood even more so. Gyda reached down and scratched behind his ears. He closed his eyes and if a worg could smile with his floppy jowls, then he did.

The stairs back down were at their feet. The windswept snow obscured much, but Gyda knew these steps by heart now. What waited below the claw marks and the clouds stoked a familiar fire in her. Empty hands, unarmored back, and utterly alone save for the worg, she should've shrank back or waited for the storm to pass.

This felt right. Foolish, but right.

Gyda spared a look over her shoulder at Jalaa. The giantess sat under her porch watching Gyda with unchanging starlight eyes. There were no further words of wisdom to give, nothing left for her to offer. For Gyda to get more, she had to prove herself.

Gyda turned back to the steps and rolled her shoulders. She spared just a moment to tap on her chest three times before beginning her descent.

She didn't dare jog like she had before. Not with the wind tearing at her and the beast waiting below. She had to conserve her strength. There was little point to being stealthy, but she found herself trying anyway. None of Sol's natural grace or Evren's dexterity would gift itself across Eith to her. She made do with her own attempts and relished the feeling of needing nothing but her own self to destroy her enemies.

The worg padded behind her silently. If she pretended, she could imagine the others were not far behind. Evren and Arke near the rear, magic and arrows ready. Sorin would be swearing between chattering teeth. Sol would get that quiet stillness that always came to her before battle.

Gyda took their spirits, their memory, as strength as she stepped off the last, marred step.

With nothing to hold on to she clenched her hands into fists. The cold cut through her cloak and she felt every nip and scrape of the icy teeth spinning in the air, yet she ignored it. She focused instead on the insistent drum of her battle-song, mingling with the beating of their heart. The howling of the mountain air faded to nothing in her ears. The choking clouds and snow couldn't blind her. Snow snatched at her calves but was no longer a hindrance as she stepped away from the stairs.

From the clouds a shadow lifted its head. What once could've been mistaken for a rock formation or close mountain peak now bared its teeth in a silent snarl. The gazes of many eyes landed all on her, heavy and numerous, like an army of angry warriors.

Fear was never an option for Gyda. She squashed it under her heel with the snow and the rocks, and charged.

There was the panting and loping gait from the worg beside her. There was her cloak flapping in the wind like a black flag. There was a rushing of thunderous blood in her ears, the battle-song reaching a cacophony that lit her spirit on fire for the first time since Abraxas doused it.

The beast's strides were swift and silent. Nothing but the mountain air to fill the din of battle. Gyda slid low, ice crackling loudly against the silent battle as the beast tumbled over her. In the blink of an eye she was underneath it and then behind it. She caught the glimpse of more striped fur and taloned feet, three pairs of them. They left no print in the snow.

Gyda barely had time to remember the deadly tail the beast had before its shadow was lashing out at her from above. She dove out of the way, snow slithering into her clothes as the spiked club slammed into the ground where her feet had been moments before. A plume of snow rose in the air, coating the cracks of the armored tail. Through that cloud, the worg leapt and latched his jaws around the tail.

No scream, no cry of rage or pain, shook the mountain. The tail flicked up with the kind of breakneck speed that should've sent the worg into the next mountain. But his teeth sank into the armor, splitting it and leaking blood that rained down in cool droplets to mimic rain.

Gyda lurched to her feet as the beast swung around and slammed its tail into the nearest rock. Stone cracked, a muffled yelp shattered the silent battle and when the beast turned back again his tail was dripping blood and empty.

Nothing furry and brave got up from the cracked rock. Gyda couldn't see enough to tell if there was a still body or something limping away.

There was a bonfire in her chest now. The chorus of a thousand battle-hungry ancestors rang in her ears. The beast turned on her and the clouds shifted just enough for her to catch a glimpse of the dozens of glaring red eyes that dotted its almost feline head. Then the clouds descended again, and Gyda's stomach was glad of it.

She charged again.

Snow and rock went flying as talons tore at the earth, seeking flesh and finding only empty rock. Whisps of fur and claws bit into Gyda's cheek, grazed her thigh, tugged on her cloak. Her bonfire spread to her legs, to her arms. She jumped away from another claw attack, landing on the rising foot behind it. The muscles underneath the strange flesh tensed; Gyda had already grabbed fistfuls of fur and was climbing.

The weightlessness of climbing the beast was a whiplash to the brutal kicking and bucking it went through to get her off. Gyda fingers were coated in damp, blue fur with each inch she gained. Out of the corner of her eye she saw the hind leg rear up, claws glinting in the dim light. There was no time to ponder what to do; let go or take the hit. So Gyda did neither.

Arms and core burned as she yanked her whole body up into a tight ball. Her knees caught the thigh of the beast above her. The world lurched in an upside-down view for precious seconds, and in that time the claw slashed into the flesh mere inches from her nose.

More blue blood. The beast staggered away, fury rippling its fur. Gyda's legs fell back down and the world righted itself, blood pounded in her head like war drums.

She grabbed another fistful of fur, and something glowing caught her eye. There! Between the powerful shoulder blades, her beloved hilt was knotted in the mane of the beast.

Rocks reared up in her vision. She had just enough time to realize it meant to smash her before she willed her finger to loosen.

Her legs sparked with pain as she landed. The rock beside her crackled and the beast pushed itself off with a snarl that Gyda felt race down her skin. It jumped back, all grace and misty elegance, and swiped at her with both front claws.

Gyda rolled through the scissor of attacks, and through the next pair as well. The hindlegs stomped in frustration and Gyda skittered on the snow to keep away from the destruction they left in their wake. Just beyond them the bleeding tail lashed back and forth.

Gyda kicked up snow as she ran for it. The mountain trembled as the beast started to turn, its tail twitching as if to impale her. Her legs screamed to run away, but she couldn't hear them over her own blood rushing and the music left only for her.

She slammed into the armor at the end of the tail, the spiked balls of bone digging into her side as the tail jerked up. Gyda was suddenly clinging on to the grooves the worg had left. She dug her fingers into them until she felt the skin break. The world blurred past her in dizzying circles. The tail jerked her to and fro, yanking air from her lungs and startling what normalcy she'd gleaned of heights from living on the top of the mountain for two weeks.

Now it was her or the edge of nothing. Now it was hold on to a creature who would bash her into a pulp against rocks that couldn't hurt it or hurtle down to a very long death through a storm and stone.

Gyda took neither choice.

She rolled to the other side of the tail as it bashed into another rock. Without missing a beat, it swung to the other side. She again flipped just in time and then latched her bleeding fingers onto the gap of armor above her.

It was a desperate climb full of fingernail misses and tongue-biting close calls. Gyda felt nothing but the thrill that barely concealed the fear of failure lurking beneath. Every swing of the tail over the mountainside reminded her of her mortality, but every beat of their heart reminded her of how ageless the fight was.

It wasn't about taking down a monster. It wasn't even about proving that she was once again a predator and not prey. It was about reclamation.

Armor turned to fur and at last Gyda traded one swinging hell for a bucking, spikey hell. The beast's back was long and littered with a spine of spikes that reminded her of the death of the Black Pass.

There was no skirting around these, not unless Gyda wanted a swift, neck-breaking fall below. She dug her feet into the flattened area of the beast's spine and began her mad dash to the mane.

The hilt glittered like a beacon of all that she had lost, of everything she longed to be once again. She weaved between the spines. Every jerk of the beast sent her tumbling into one. Her skin cut like butter against their razor edges. Red blood dappled and dyed the grey fur at her feet, flowing heavier with every foot gained and every spike fated to meet her flesh. Her skin was warm and sticky with it, but her footing was sure, and the spikes kept her from tumbling off the beast's back

Gyda cleared the spikes and slammed face first into the mane as the beast bucked. The hairs were as sharp as steel ribbons, slicing at her face and hands. She squeezed her eyes shut, not seeing the vertigo of how high they jumped but feeling it in the thinness of the air. When her body started to fall before her stomach, she grabbed at the mane.

The hair sliced through one palm. In the other, warm bone greeted her.

Gyda was too dizzy with relief or blood loss to feel them land. She was just up on her knees tearing the hilt free. Her red blood rained down along the ivory hilt, runes greedily drinking the scarlet drops. When it jerked free she landed on her ass, triumph singing in her chest.

And then she was falling.

It was all Gyda could do to tuck herself into a ball, cover her head and neck, and hope for the best. When the ground came the snow did little to soften the bone crunching impact.

But Gyda was up, spitting blood and grinning. The beast rounded on her, dripping just as much blood as it watched her stand up with the hilt.

Gyda paused. Just the hilt. She could run around this thing all day and night to get it to hurt itself, but that would kill her faster. She had what she came for.

A sharp bark, half-panicked and half-proud, pulled at both her and the beast's attention. The worg stood at the stairs, now dusted with inches of snow. And held one paw close to him. His message was clear and Gyda couldn't agree more.

She didn't spare the beast a second glance as she took off towards the steps. As before, the feeling of hot breath and cool blood dogged her steps. The worg tucked his tail and limped as fast as he could up the stairs. Gyda's own injuries seemed as inconsequential as bees to a dragon.

When her foot touched the first step, their heart sang. As if it had all been worth it. The battle wasn't even over and Gyda felt like she'd won. She took the stairs two at a time, seeing the worg's tail around every twist and turn.

Laughter threatened to overwhelm her hardworking lungs. It had been worth it. All those dreadful days barely able to move. All the nights she couldn't sleep without picturing Abraxas's sword cutting into her flesh.

It was worth it. For this feeling alone.

The mountaintop was an eerie mirror of how she first found it. Dark with a snowstorm, windswept and threatening. Gyda's feet were firm, her footsteps bloody. With every step, the runes drank her blood and glittered to life.

The mountaintop sparked to life. The archways shadows against the snow. And the beast's dozens of eyes illuminated the blue back at her.

Gyda took a step back, the shock overwhelming her senses for a moment. Hadn't it not been able to follow? Where was Jalaa?

And then it came to Gyda like a slow, cold tide. The understanding did not douse the flames of premature victory, only emboldened them. The laughter died, tucked away behind her lungs for a safer day when they weren't in danger of being skewered by teeth as long as she was tall.

This was the test. Not just the hilt. She couldn't scream and cry that it wasn't fair that she'd been sent to fight this monster without a weapon. She *had* one, and Jalaa hadn't sent her anywhere. She stepped off the stairs willingly, just as she stepped forward.

The wind snatched at her cloak and her hair. The hilt was warm and slippery in her grip. Beside her, the worg let out a low whine. Gyda didn't spare him a second glance.

"Hide in the stairway," she told him. "If it is quiet, run. If it is not, meet me back here."

Hesitation, then padding away from her.

And then Gyda was walking towards the beast, one hand holding her hilt, the other trailing blood. The silence was gnawing at her. Even the storm seemed quieter, as if everywhere the beast went, a blanket of quiet descended just to piss her off. Gyda needed the pandemonium of battle. The screams and breaking of bone. The cracking of armor and burning of spells. A goblin laughing behind her, a sailor taunting beside her. Arrow whizzing by that brought comfort and relief. A flash of daggers that brought her enemies low enough to stomp on. A shield at her back when she forgot to cover her right side again.

There was nothing like that now. Just the ringing in her ears and the crunch of ice beneath her feet as she picked up the pace of her march. The beast stared her down, unmoving, lips curled into a humanoid sneer that didn't fit its feline face.

Gyda gripped the hilt with both hands as she would've when its blade had made it heavier. The runes hummed into the cuts on her palms, begging to be used. But which one? How could they work now?

Red to spur her to the point where her wounds only made her stronger, where every drop of blood might cost Gyda her life, but cost her opponent's as well.

Blue to slice through armor that wasn't there?

Green to snatch souls?

There was no rune for that, only a sharp sliver of power tucked away from Gail. One that sickened her. One she hated using.

One she reached for now.

She was running now, ice and runes blurring under her feet. The hilt warmed in her hand like it was bone still wrapped in warm flesh. The beast widened its stance, teeth gleaming, claws cutting through runes. It was ready for her, opening its jaws to unspeakable widths as she charged forward.

Gyda's battle cry drowned out the storm. It sang with the song in her body, in her blood. It echoed in the sky as thunder rumbled with her. It shattered the deafening silence that shrouded the beast.

Green light enveloped Gyda. Blinding and sickeningly like the lights of souls Gail saw. But to Gyda it was the most beautiful thing in Eith. It swam around her arms, legs, and cloak. It made her blood, hovering in the air with the whipping snow, glitter as it crystallized.

The gaping maw of the beast descended on Gyda. All she

could see were the four rows of teeth, the razor crested tongue, the ridges along the roof of the mouth.

A breath later, she slipped to the side. Barely moved a foot, the ice did most of the work. The jaws snapped closed where she'd been. She could see the scab where her rock had cut its muzzle. Its throat quivered with a frustration that ebbed into the stone, and as it started to rear back up, the light around Gyda drained away from her. From a cloud of bright vapor, concentrated into a lean blade of pure green light.

She wasted no time driving the new blade up into the soft flesh of the jaw and through the roof of the mouth. There was no blood, no resistance, yet the beast thrashed and echoed its silent scream. Gyda's feet remained firmly on the ground, its head held with nothing but light and her two hands. An impossible strength flooded her body, and she jerked the speared face of the beast closer to her. Nose to large, sweating nose. Those dozens of red eyes reflected her back just as many times.

Smeared with both red and blue blood, white hair falling from her clan weave. She looked monstrous. She looked beautiful.

Later, Gyda wouldn't be able to say why she let one hand stray from the hilt of her sword and into the air. It just came to her, this overwhelming urge to reach into the storm-torn sky. As she did, the fear in the beast's eyes grew.

Good.

Something metallic landed in her hands. Light of metal but heavy with power. Gyda didn't look at the Eternity Dagger until she speared it between two of the beast's many eyes.

The air grew taut and hot, then popped. Gyda had the breath stolen from her but couldn't move. One hand tied to her sword, the other to the lost dagger, she watched with widening eyes as the beast simply melted at her feet. Razor-sharp mane and spines became dust. Fur became smoke. The bones and claw whittled away until there was nothing left but a pile of ash at Gyda's feet, and two destined blades in her hands.

She stumbled away from the ash and then fell to her knees. The light from her sword winked out, as did her strength. She was breathless, bleeding, dazed.

Confused.

The ash parted as the cloaked figure stepped forward. The wind howled a fierce song, grabbing at the hood as if to yank it off. Gyda had no willpower left to tell the wind that its efforts were fruitless; that nothing could reveal a face left so long in the dark.

But then hands appeared from underneath. Just as scarred and terrible as Evren described. They shook in the wind until they latched onto the edges of the hood. Gyda's shared heart was in her throat. Alone, at the top of a mountain, the figure pulled back the hood and revealed their face.

Gyda's world fell away. She wanted to scream, but didn't. Waves after waves of emotion passed through her. Anger, grief, denial, and then another cycle of the three. But in all of that, she saw the story play out in those familiar eyes. A story she despised, but one she knew she had no hope of rewriting.

Gyda blinked away a stray tear, the only one she had left.

"I understand now."

29

Evren

Evren had fought enough large-scale battles to last her a lifetime. She'd defended, she'd attacked. She'd lead armies and a small group of people to something like victory, if not a true win. But that didn't mean the chaos was lost on her.

Battling the undead in Direwall during the Long Night didn't make fighting in the dark with only the sporadic glow of fires any better. The screaming of dying men and women as the Deep Wood burned didn't make her numb to the terror piercing the air now. And facing Serevadia in Vanguard, in Helmsfirth, was nothing compared to how they swarmed the war camp now.

Evren and Idain didn't have a high vantage point with the temple being on the low southern end of the camp. But with the spreading fire and clashing of steel, it wasn't hard to see where the fighting started.

Evren cursed and grabbed a spare bow and quiver from a weapon's rack nearby. The yew short-bow was light, and wouldn't be nearly as powerful as the one she'd lost. But it would have to do.

"They must've followed us from Helmsfirth," Evren shouted over the din.

Ahead, Idain gripped his mace tightly. He had nothing in the way of armor that she could see, and no shield. Yet as they sprinted closer to the fighting, he didn't slow.

"Or they've been waiting for this, for whatever reason." He looked at her just for a moment, the message clear.

They didn't follow the survivors of Helmsfirth. They followed Evren.

There was no time to think on that. The chill of the night was soon overwhelmed by raging fires as Evren and Idain burst into the battle. Tents shriveled under the catching infernos, sparks fluttering into the night sky and catching on other tents, spreading like a glowing cancer. Horses whinnied and pulled against their posts. Some already managed to rip free and darted through the battlefield, while very few bore riders calmer than the chaos below their feet.

Etherak's soldiers were poorly prepared, however. For every one that bore weapons and fought back, another three were wounded or dying. Most had no armor. Many were still in their nightclothes.

Their foe was not so ill-equipped.

Serevadia marched in neat lines of silver armor and keen-edged swords. Bolts of light flew overhead, spearing men mere feet from Evren. Through the tents, the haze of smoke and the darkness of night, she couldn't guess their numbers. But for a moment all the silver blurred together into one large entity, one that threatened to overwhelm her and force her to run away.

Then Idain was standing in front of her, a dark grin on his face. Serevadia faded as the light of the fires caught one-half of his face, illuminating in a hellish light. This was what he was raised for. This was the only life he knew.

No words were exchanged between them, just curt nods. He was a soldier, a veteran of bloody wars in the past. She was a fighter, someone who'd faced down this enemy and came out breathing. There was no choice but to stand and fight, and yet the action of facing the enemy together, bow drawn and mace held high, felt like the rightest thing she'd chosen since she'd woken up.

Evren thought briefly of Drystan, of the way he fought beside her in Direwall, and instead of that pain debilitating her, she found strength. As if he was standing where Idain was, frowning that terrible frown of his and saying,

Well, what are you waiting for? An invitation?

Her first arrow skimmed over the shoulder of a struggling soldier and into the eye of a Serevadian. The survivor looked back at her, breathless and eyes wide. Relief flickered in his eyes, but also something more. Something bigger.

Hope.

Idain's war cry was a prayer to the dead, and each word rang clear in the smoke clogged sky. It was enough to startle the Serevadians, to give the soldiers an edge. It was enough for Idain to ram his mace into one head, two kneecaps, and four separate ribcages without breaking his flow. Evren's arrows picked off those trying to flank him, sending them gurgling into the bloody mud. Idain backhanded them with his mace, then kept up the momentum to nearly take the head of a Serevadian clear off.

Once, just like Abraxas, Evren could see what a force of nature the old Champion had been in the past. A glimmer of his past self, in both robes and armor, wielding a mace and shield and singing a song of death to everyone he laid down at his feet, shone bright in her mind's eye. The song was both a warning and an apology for the destruction to come.

Now, it was neither. The prayer song was a wildfire, igniting fighting spirit in those that heard it. Those fleeing picked up fallen swords, axes, and bows. Those bleeding stood up again.

Idain slew another, standing finally between the line of Serevadia and his people, red mace raining blood as he held it in the air.

"Sons and daughters of Etherak!" he bellowed. "Show them the gates of the hells!"

A bolt of Serevadian light streamed towards his chest, and Evren's arrow was just fast enough to knock it off course. The metal shattered the wood and pierced the mud next to his feet. He looked not at it, but at her, and gave her a salute.

Evren found herself smiling, truly and strangely, as he turned back towards the growing number of enemies and charged. Etherakians joined him, from guardsmen still on duty and fully armored, to squires still in their sleeping caps with knives in the air. Evren's hail of arrows was joined by other archers, lining up behind the chargers to cover them.

The camp was still burning. The dead still littered the ground. Serevadia's force was still overwhelming, but Evren saw what a little faith could do to even the most terrified, and so did the enemy.

It was not a good fight. Too many died under Serevadian blades. Evren's fellow archers were skewered with bolts of metal and light. The mud turned warm and soupy around her ankles. With no high ground to climb to, she was nearly blind to what was being thrown at her. The burning tents and littered corpses of dogs and horses tripped up both sides, costing precious ground.

The line Idain had formed was buckling. Smoke scored deep gouges down her throat, and she was barely choking down her air when a flash of silver erupted in front of her.

Evren lurched back, feet stuck in the mud and back arched painfully as a sword skimmed the empty space where her neck had been. She stumbled back, drawing her dagger just in time to deflect the next attack.

Metal rang loudly as she shoved the Serevadian away. A sneering woman, her helmet torn off to reveal a tumble of midnight-black hair slick with blood. Evren risked a glance beyond her to see that, yes, Idain's line had broken. Serevadia was streaming through.

Evren yelled wordlessly, a rage she couldn't name nearly choking her. She kicked out, spraying mud in her attacker's eyes and scoring a solid kick in her chest. The elf stumbled back, swinging wildly in anticipation of Evren's next rushing attack as she tried to clear her eyes. But Evren didn't step forward.

She threw the dagger away from her attacker, at a nearby Serevadian that caught her eye and cried out in pain when it landed. Faster than she could breathe, her next arrow was nocked, and then landed in the still muddy eyes of her attacker.

Serevadia swarmed like glittering silver ants. She couldn't see Idain, only the muddy, horrified soldiers fighting for their lives. A horse charged past her, saddle empty and eyes ringed with a terror-filled white.

She stumbled towards her dagger, bringing it up to parry an incoming swing while it rattled her bones. Then she dove inside the Serevadian's guard, dagger held before her, and didn't stop until the blade pierced skin, blood spurted on her face, and he was dead on the ground.

Evren got up, fingers slick on her hilt as another Serevadian charged at her. She dropped to her knees, cutting at their tendons and sending them sprawling over the body of their comrade. She cut their life, and their screaming, short with her blade.

Fire dried the blood and mud on her skin. The quiver over her shoulder was too light, but she couldn't afford the time to count what she had left.

The glimpse of a mace right before it crushed a skull caught her eye, and Evren was running towards it without a second thought. As she ran, she took down Serevadians left and right. Arrows and her dagger whizzed through the air, mere extensions of her body. The chaos of battle wasn't lost, the din reaching a crescendo in her ears. But it was that or pick out the individual cries for help. It was the clash of steel or the weeping of the dying, the tearing of flesh and bone, the final breaths into the cool, night air.

Evren's dagger sank deep into the back of a Serevadian, and she twisted until he fell to her feet. Pulling the dagger out, she was breathless and faced with Idain's blood-soaked form.

He was bleeding in a few places, and his cloak was burnt and jagged at the ends, leaving it uneven and trailing ashen embers. Distantly, Evren's own body ached with injuries she hadn't noticed. She shoved them away to deal with later.

"We have to fall back," she cried over the battle.

He shook his head, eyes blazing with a familiar fire of battle. But she grabbed his arm and pulled him back.

"Idain, look!" She nodded to the madness. "We're losing. We need to fall back."

"You think this is the only place they attacked?" he asked. "The rest of the camp will be dealing with the same. We'll just be giving them more ground."

"If we stay, we die."

"And if we flee, we'll die later!" he shouted. "I don't fear death."

"Well I do!" she shot back, then pointed to what was left of Etherak's soldiers. "And so do they."

The veteran's face fell. Evren let him drink in the chaos, let it sink into his bones the way she acknowledged but couldn't fully look in the eye. He didn't flinch, but that battle spirit faded as more of their people were being cut down. He swallowed hard, and she wondered what battle in Vernes mirrored this, if any.

"All right." He nodded and pulled away from her. He spared just enough time to kill a Serevadian crawling towards their weapon before bellowing into the smoke.

"FALL BACK!"

Only once. That was how far his voice traveled. Soon the order was being called further back. Voices ranging from pissed to relieved echoed the same two words. To retreat, to fall to higher ground, to run and pray that their luck changed.

Evren hated it. It was her idea and she wanted to plant her feet and stay. But at Idain's cutting eyes, she turned and ran with him, looking back only to cover their escape with a rain of steel tipped arrows.

She stopped firing and ran when her fingers closed over her last arrow. She left it be, bringing up the rear of the line as they ran through the once peaceful war camp for their lives.

Serevadia pursued like hunting hounds, and the fire leapt with them, just as hungry. What cool relief came from unburning tents soon vanished as flames devoured them and belched smoke into the blackening sky.

In a moment of frightened clarity, she realized she couldn't see the stars, not even through the gaps in the smoke. No moon hung low on the horizon. No cold silver light came from above. Besides the angry orange of the fire, Etherak was draped in darkness and ash.

Bolts of light hummed through the air and took down handfuls of fleeing soldiers. It was all Evren could do not to trip over their fallen bodies as she ran. She saw one with a bolt in his leg crawling into the temple Idain had so carefully maintained. A Serevadian followed him, and blood painted the idols, then fire swallowed the temple whole.

Lungs wheezing, legs cramping, skin stinging, she pushed on. Furiously reminding herself that she outran an army of the undead in Direwall with Drystan in this same body. She'd ridden Alkimos and Saros with the same hands and legs. She helped free Vanguard with the same heart. Once whole, yes, but still beating despite it all. This was not where she was falling.

The flames leapt forward out of the corner of her eyes and for a moment Evren thought they were going to swarm the fleeing soldiers, herself and Idain included. But then they suddenly reared back like horses forced into a grinding halt after a hard gallop. The flames jerked back unnaturally, and then lashed out.

At the Serevadians.

Evren and the others watched, still for the first time and too relieved to be shocked as the flames that once were as dangerous as Serevadia were sucked away from the surrounding tents. They left them blackened and piles of ashes, but turned on the silver armor of the second army as if they were a hated rival. They barely had a chance to scream before the flames were on them, burning and melting armor and flesh alike. It formed a wall of pure heat and sparking rage between the two armies.

Evren whirled around and shoved through the gaping soldiers. At their end, the mage with the frivolous coat stood with his spellbook hovering before him. His thin face was sweaty and smudged with soot, but he spared a feral grin.

"Having trouble, adventurer?"

Evren ignored him. "How's the rest of the camp? Mei? Barrion?"

"The prince and his consort are just fine. The skirmishes around the rest of the perimeter kept us occupied until we realized they were a distraction." He nodded below where his inferno ate at the bodies. "His Majesty thought there would be a bigger assault somewhere else. It seems he was correct."

Great and dandy. But that didn't fix their problem entirely. Once magic was brought into the picture, everything about battle changed. And if Serevadia's warriors were tough, their mages were terrifying.

"Where's the rest of you?" she asked.

He frowned. "What do you mean?"

She gritted her teeth. "Other mages. Troops. We're in the middle of a fucking army camp and you're telling me all they sent was you?"

"The rest of the mages are dealing with the spreading fires and casualties. And I'll have you know that I was top . . ."

He trailed off, and Evren saw why as the orange glow that lit up his face started to fade. She whirled around, last arrow nocked as the barrier of fire was pulled apart like flimsy curtains by large, shadowy hands.

A scorched hill of Serevadians lay where the fire once was, but beyond them were more. Their silver armor glinting red as the fire started to die. As the ground shook beneath her, Evren wondered why she hadn't felt it earlier, but soon realized why.

From the shadowy hands poured three figures. Two large and bulging, their eyeless faces veering left and right as their slitted nostrils flared. They pounded the ground, scattering corpses and embers. Their chains were that of shadow, not metal, and were held by the third figure.

Again, Evren half hoped, half dreaded it was Abraxas. Even Ainthe. But she saw neither. The figure wore black robes that blended in with the surrounding night. Between their skin and hair, they seemed a living shadow themselves, except their eyes. Pure, pale grey so light they were almost white. And they stared right at Evren.

Evren hadn't fought a shadow mage except for Ainthe, and even then she'd only won because of the child and Alkimos. She knew from Abraxas, from Kleros, from Ainthe, how deadly they could be.

She loosed the arrow and it flew true, straight for the chest of the mage. Mere feet from hitting its target, a meaty grey hand swatted it out of the way. One of the giant creatures snorted in her direction.

It happened quickly after that, the deaths of so many all at once.

The shadow mage smiled, teeth white against the black, and flicked a hand out. Shadows surged like two giant scythes and cut through swaths of soldiers. They didn't even have time to scream. Of the ones that survived, just out of range, nearly all began to run.

The mage behind Evren let out a strangled noise before digging through his spellbook. Shoulders jostled them, Idain stood in front of her and the mage. Magic shimmered in the air, brilliant and crisp and controlled as a dozen spears of ice formed in the air. They sparkled for a moment, frozen, then darted forward at such speed that Evren couldn't keep track. All targeted the mage. All were deflected by the shadows. They tore through Serevadian troops, large enough to take down four or five at once. But the failure was sour in the remaining three survivor's mouths.

Evren knew what came next. She gripped them both, bow forgotten at her feet. "Shield!" There was not one among them. None that would've been large enough or strong enough to hold back the great wings of black stretching towards them.

The mage stumbled back. Idain tried to put himself between her and the shadows, but Evren struggled. She didn't know why. Maybe it was the knowledge that his body wouldn't be enough to stop the shadows. Or maybe because she was tired of others dying for her. Regardless, she fought back enough for her hand to slip on his mace, and her palm to catch the jagged spikes along its heavy head.

Pain blossomed, the first she'd truly felt, and without thinking Evren shoved her hand over Idain's shoulder, blood palm facing the galloping shadows.

It was like holding a door closed against a hurricane determined to rip it down, but Evren held. A familiar strength and power surged in her, and when she looked up, she saw the shadows streaming past her hand like water against a rock in a river. Whatever invisible force kept them back, it leaked from the blood in her hand, which trailed warmly down her wrist.

Idain watched with an open mouth. The mage was weeping. Evren paid them no mind. She extracted herself from Idain's arms and forced her power to *push*.

The shadows lurched back, screeching in the air as they fell back to their master. The Serevadian's pale eyes only widened a fraction as they took her in. Beside and behind them, the army waited for an order.

"What are you?" Idain whispered.

Evren drew her dagger with her bloody palm, and pressed it against the other one. The same one Gyda had cut the last time they had each other. She dug her blade into her skin until the physical pain overwhelmed the emotional agony, until blood was pooling in both her palms.

She sheathed the dagger.

"I don't know," Evren said and stepped towards the army. Idain didn't try to stop her, neither did the mage.

The Serevadian army gathered, bristling. If they were afraid, they didn't show it. None seemed to recognize her power, which made Evren sad. All the time Nerezza spent building Serevadia up, and they didn't even know this part of her?

One did. The shadow mage. Their eyes flicked to her bloody palms and they mirrored her. Hands outstretched to their sides, dripping shadows instead of blood. They pooled so thickly that Evren could barely make out the army behind them, or the grunting monsters on either side.

The shadow mage smiled a crescent moon grin and cut their hands through the air. All the shadows streaked towards Evren like a tidal wave, and with it the army and monsters followed its wake. An impossible challenge, even for an adventurer.

And yet Evren planted her feet with her arms wide and welcoming. She faced the army, the monsters, the wave of death, with the same deadly calm as she had back in Helmsfirth. An echo of Viggo whispered in her ears.

We are all the basis of our souls until we are forced to be more.

Evren Hanali was no longer a mere hunter. She wasn't just a bastard half-breed or surly adventurer. She wasn't even sure she was a hero.

Right now she was the bulwark between Etherak and death. And when the shadows came for her, she didn't push.

She pulled.

Evren didn't see the shadow mage's reaction. She felt it through the shadows as she latched onto them and pulled. Her bloody power leaked into the black tendrils, infecting and cleansing all at the same time. Tainting them with her essence. Dragging them tooth and nail to her side.

The shadows tried to pull back as their master tugged their leash, but Evren held firm. Inch by bloody inch she stole ink-black magic until it was spilling from her hands in waterfalls. Every shadow summoned by her opponent was soon wiggling under her control in a matter of seconds.

There was little Evren understood about Blood magic, but Nerezza had made one thing clear. It wasn't like Written or Inherited magic. It couldn't create something out of nothing. But give it a blueprint, give it something to steal, and it was yours just as your blood was your own.

Evren was no shadow mage, yet when the blackness dropped and pooled at her feet, it was at her whim. When it rose with her hands, it was her will. And when it turned on the army, it was her rage that fueled it.

The shadows at her command tore through the charging army with abandon. Finally, fear shone in Serevadian eyes as their weapon was turned against them. Bolts aimed at her were tossed away, the light searing but manageable. The chains around the monsters' necks were tightening until they cut into their skin and their heads were dangling from their bodies.

The tugging of shadows back to their master reared in Evren's mind. She glared at the shadow mage trying to wrangle back control. A pity they weren't stupid enough to try and summon more.

Evren didn't have to move a finger to send the shadows to them and tear them apart. The shadows did so easily, and the mass of black robes were all that was left of her opposition. But she did raise her hands towards the rest of the army.

They wouldn't give up. They wouldn't surrender. Evren bit back furious tears, her hands shaking as she willed destruction and forced the shadows back into the silver armor.

They tore them apart, Evren and shadow. Together with terrible will and power, armor ripped like wet paper. Swords were dulled, flesh destroyed. Shadows sunk into the bodies of the fallen and forced them to keep fighting, and Evren barely kept herself from gagging. She could *feel* the dead flesh as if her fingers were puppeting them instead of the shadows.

As light-laced weapons and shadow turned against Serevadia, Evren wanted to look away. She wanted to block out the screams, but she couldn't. *Wouldn't.* She could hate them as much as her half a heart could bear, but she once fought to protect these people. Sorin had died for them. And now she was demolishing them.

Evren couldn't tell when the fighting stopped. Every second stretched into eternity with the shadows slithering under her thoughts. They weren't inherently evil, but she was wrong to wield them. She wasn't of their kind, and they knew it.

The last Serevadian fell, and Evren was on her knees, gritting her teeth as the mud seeped into her pants. The shadows gathered, just out of reach. Waiting with bated breath for her control to fail.

Idain was suddenly beside her, warm hands reminding her of how terribly cold she'd become. His jaw was tight, and he looked at her, not the gathering wall of shadows.

"It's over," he said gently. "Let them go."

She shook her head. "I can't."

"No power is worth this. What you've done is a miracle but—"

"This isn't about power," she hissed through clenched teeth. Talking and wrangling control was exhausting. She reached for her dagger, slicing her forearm, but the new blood did little in the way of tying down the shadows. It only weakened her further. "They have no master now. I let them go, they destroy us like any other army."

Only this time it would be an army of pure magic. Something they couldn't even fight against. She cursed herself for being too careless. She should've known better than to grab at power she didn't understand, and yet she'd done it from the beginning. A solution to her problem turned into another problem, as it always had.

The shadows lashed out at Idain, and she cried out in her effort to drag them back. They stopped inches from his face, and she shoved them back, seeing spots of black. She collapsed on all fours, heaving.

Strangely, there was no pain. It was like her body was running and tearing itself to exhaustion without moving. With each passing minute she could feel her strength waning, and the shadows growing stronger.

"You need to leave," she told him. "Try to get everyone away. I'll hold them as long as I can."

"A noble sacrifice," Idain said. "But one I won't accept."

"Idain—"

"I don't fear death." His fingers drew her gaze up to him. "And neither, I think, do you. But Eith yet has need for us both. Fight it."

The corners of her vision were blackening. From exhaustion or shadows? She expended energy to keep them back, but it landed like a missed fist. Nothing was there, and she wasted precious strength.

She sobbed. "I can't."

Evren was going to die like her friends. Drowning in a power she couldn't control. She'd never be able to help Mei and Barrion save Etherak, or the rest of Eith. She'd break her promise to Aster to see him again. And her father, all alone in the Deep Wood as the world came crashing down around him.

Her fingers sank into the mud. All Evren could do was breathe. Wretched thoughts of broken promises and the calling of a home she couldn't get back to warred alongside the gnawing shadows. She was a battlefield, and her memories were no match for the darkness that raged across her veins and bones.

Evren Hanali thought of those she lost, and suddenly she felt more like a mass grave. A burning pyre for a group of bodies she loved too much. She was the tinder, the oil, and the flame. She hadn't stopped burning since the first ignition, like a beacon begging them to come home. They lived in her as nothing more than memories, and it wasn't enough. It would never be enough until the fire was out and she had what she lost in her arms again.

Arms that were not Gyda's wrapped around her shoulders, stilling her shaking.

"Tell me what you need," Idain whispered. "Let me help."

She couldn't do that. She didn't know. Every other time she'd been overwhelmed by shadow, her blood had rescued her or she'd submitted until it was through with her.

Evren was so tired of darkness, of being blood-soaked and bone-tired with every sunset. The fighting, the death, was overwhelming her. A yawning chasm of darkness where no light could survive. Had Abraxas felt this way with Nerezza? So utterly alone and broken that he'd sunken to terrible machinations to survive? At this point, she couldn't blame him if he had.

But she could miss the man he was before. The one who grasped for light at every turn. He always looked at the worst places for it, following her to every dark corner of Eith for a spark.

You know, she'd once said carefully. *If you're looking for light, this is a pretty terrible place to do it.*

Abraxas had smiled ruefully. *I say otherwise. In the darkest nights and the blackest shadows, light shines the brightest. If I'm to find it, it'll be here.*

"Light," Evren gasped. It was barely a word, more like a gush of air.

But Idain understood. He gripped her shoulders and yelled over her shoulder. Who was there left to yell at? She wanted to look back but realized with a sickening jolt that she couldn't see. There was nothing but black swimming in her vision. She clung to the feeling of cold mud in her cut palms, of Idain's warm arms around her, of the taste of ash in her mouth.

"Hang on a little while longer," Idain whispered, to which she groaned in response. "I don't know your name, or your funeral requirements. I can't properly lay you to rest."

"Put me in an Etherakian temple as a jar of ashes . . ." she gasped. "And I'll fucking haunt you."

He laughed, the only anchor she had that wasn't mental. She was losing feeling in her hands, like the shadows were sapping her strength for their own.

"Well, that clears that up." He sat in silence, or what Evren assumed was silence. The world had dimmed down to just him. "Don't tell me your name. Don't tell me anything."

"Why?"

"Because I will not bury you, nor will I mourn you. You, my friend, are not dying tonight. None of us are."

Evren choked on her next question. *Who else is dumb enough to be here?*

And then she felt everything.

The burst of warmth, heady against her back. The leftover aches and pains from hard battle. The wind against her ears, Idain's own ragged breathing. She smelled blood, mud, the smell of waste and smoke clogging the air.

And then there was light.

Bright, brilliant sunlight poured from behind her like the sun cresting above the horizon. Golden, rich, devastatingly warm. Evren gasped as her vision cleared, as the light enveloped her and Idain.

The shadows had gathered into a terrible wall in front of her, towering fifty feet high at least. But when the light struck the wall, it burned. She cried out, clutching her ears as ungodly screams tore at her mind. Idain held her but wasn't affected. She alone bore the death-throes of sentient magic, and her tears flowed again.

The shadows burned, died, as the light intensified. So bright was it that Evren was sure the sun was bearing down on them, closer than it had ever dared to venture from its horizon. The heat was nearly unbearable, baking her skin until the mud flaked and peeled and the blood cracked like a mirror hit with a rock.

She smelled burnt hair, heard the whisper of Idain's prayer but understood none of it.

She watched, unblinking, as the shadows died. She witnessed their death, and while there was no prayer she could ever speak for them, she bid them farewell.

Finally, the light winked off and doused them into the pitch-black of night. Evren blinked, half fearful she'd gone blind until embers from a fire flickered in her vision, and glinting armor shone brightly.

Idain was out of breath but helped her to her feet. She clung to his arms, not sure of her strength enough to let go. As her vision started to return, she looked back.

A line of mages threw down their spent spellbooks, sweat beading their brows and their hair, robes singed. The fur on the fancy mage's robes was completely burned off, as were his eyebrows. Considering how little he had, it wasn't a big loss.

Behind them, Evren heard more than saw the rest of the army. A few survivors from the southern battle looked at her with awe. The rest were stuck somewhere between reverence and fear. But there were so many of them staring at her, their eyes a thousand times heavier than that of the imaginary Divines she felt.

They parted for three figures. Loghain, bloody and nursing his arm, and Mei, who leaned on Barrion shamelessly as they both carried used swords. Mei's blade finally matched its tassel.

Evren took a deep breath and whispered to Idain. "I'm going to pass out."

"Well, I should as well. Its rude to leave a hero to faint on their own."

And so they did. Idain first, whether out of actual exhaustion or politeness, and Evren shortly after him. She didn't remember even hitting the ground.

30

Arke

The place Aushruk took him felt like the Aether, only diluted. That same buzzing of powerful souls itched at his ears and bones but wasn't as prickly as before. Like it was pressing against layers of thick blankets to reach him.

"The Aether is thin here," Arke grumbled. The words felt right, but also not. Like someone older and wiser should've said them.

Aushruk frowned. "Aether?"

"Barrier between worlds. Pure power." He paused. "Souls."

That at least made sense. As the pillars rose up around him, he had a sneaking suspicion as to how Aushruk's story would play out.

The pillars were a mix of rock and dark glass. There were hundreds rising up like branchless trees from the rocky ground. The sky above hadn't dimmed, yet the sun didn't reach them. It was colder here, darker. It had nothing to do with the shade.

Aushruk stopped at one pillar. His long fingers trailed on the glass and a low, mournful hum, sounded in the air, coming from the Dra'Nacti.

"There are many souls here, Arke."

Aushruk used his name a lot since Arke told him. He seemed to like how simple and sharp it was on the mouth. Barely a sentence went by without it being hurled into the world again.

"How many?"

"As many as there are pillars, tombs." Aushruk stepped back. "Nine hundred and ninety-nine, to be exact."

Arke balked. Every pillar a tomb. Every body a soul. No wonder he felt like this. So much concentrated souls and power in one place . . . As far as he knew, there wasn't another place in Eith like it.

Suddenly the gloom fit. It was like the desert itself had shrouded itself in mourning veils for the dead. The pillars and their shining glass carried more weight than before. No longer were they strange formations to be wary of, but monuments to respect.

He pressed his hand against one, finding it cool and smooth as all stone. "That many people died here?"

"No."

Arke turned back to him, puzzled. The Dra'Nacti's face was twisted in many emotions warring for a front spot in his void-like eyes. There was nowhere for him to go, no past time to wander in his head. The past was rising up to meet him in the hundreds.

Aushruk's gaze landed on him, older than his seemingly ageless body portrayed. "Nine hundred and ninety-nine souls sacrificed themselves here, Arke. To say they simply died is to remove the duty they performed, the sacred ritual they subjected themselves to so that Vernes, and Eith, could be free of the gods. It is a world none of them could ever touch. No amount of necromancy could bring them back."

Aushruk looked up at the pillars, blinking, and Arke wondered if his people could cry.

"To raise them back to this world would be to unravel what they built," Aushruk explained. "A large net. A chain of power to protect the world. So they remain lost to us, serving so that we might be free. Abraxas Kain would destroy that."

Arke's breaths were sharp in his lungs. Could a sacrifice of that magnitude truly change so much that the gods wouldn't be allowed back in Eith? Aushruk believed so, and Arke knew from experience the amount of power a singular soul could wield. But all of Gail's power had come from stolen souls. Nerezza's consumption of his souls had been the same. Compared to the power wielded here, that was nothing. Minuscule. Child's play.

Could his missing piece truly be the difference between a willing and an unwilling soul?

"Show me," Arke said. "Let them show me. I have to know."

Aushruk's smile was bitter. "You are a fast learner, so willing to accept the different ways of strangers. Not like Abraxas at all."

Arke shrugged. "I said we were friends, not that we were the same. I learn. That's where I get my power. That's how I'm goin' to stop him."

Aushruk nodded and motioned him to follow. Arke did without hesitation. The pillars blurred by with each step, and out of the corner of his eyes he could make out faces in the glass peering back at him.

"One of the spirits will choose you to see their end," Aushruk explained smoothly. "But it will be painful. You cannot pull away. You must endure what they endured, and once they are satisfied, you will return."

Arke thought back to the hand in the Aether and the torture he witnessed, and shuddered. But there wasn't any going back. If he could do this one show of respect, it would be worth the pain.

Aushruk led him through the maze of towering tombs until the ground rose up sharply. Arke had to dig his claws into the rock to follow. When he got to the edge, he was overlooking a massive crater. It was ringed with even more pillars. A graveyard that stretched farther than Arke wanted to see.

"What happened?" Arke asked.

Aushruk picked his way down the slope of the crater, not bothering to help Arke as he slid after him.

"Great power changes the physical world," he explained. "We chose this place for many reasons. Mainly because it was far from where others lived. The consequences of the spell would reach hundreds of miles of desert, and not the cities of innocents. Such private corners of Eith seem made for such magic."

Aushruk stopped at the center of the crater and when Arke stepped beside him he tried not to think about how he was in one massive bowl.

"Sit here," Aushruk instructed. "You will have to clear your mind to welcome one of the spirits inside. By now they must know what you want. Whoever believes they can give you the most will answer, so long as the others are willing. You must understand that these dead do not see the living like others. They are hungry for interaction. Many will want you, so you must stay firm in your resolve."

Aushruk laid a hand on his shoulder. "Keep your question in mind, Arke. The dead are helpful, but they must be guided. If they sweep you away, I cannot call you back, and you could be forced to relive the sacrifices of nine hundred and ninety-nine souls over until your body gives out."

"Fuck." Arke shivered. He hated dead things. What was the point in necromancy when fire was so much simpler? "Just kill me if that happens."

"I cannot." Aushruk stepped back. "You need to stop Abraxas Kain. One way or another, your soul will do so."

Arke hesitated before sitting down. He folded his legs and when Aushruk held out his hand for his spellbook, he only held onto it for a moment before handing it over. It was strange to realize that something that had been so precious and irreplaceable before, something that his life and the lives of his friends had hinged on so many times, suddenly felt useless. There was no need for spells where he was going. Not the ones of paper and ink.

Arke felt a little like he was watching himself outgrow a shirt he loved. How long would he wear it before came to the realization that he had to move on? Was this what growing up felt like? This hollow drumming in his chest that felt neither good nor bad, just waiting for acceptance? Arke thought himself grown. He was getting up in age for a goblin, but he always felt the same. Tolk used to joke that he'd been born an old man. Only now, in the caldera of a crater surrounded by nine hundred and ninety-nine souls, did Arke start to mourn the death of the child he never let himself be.

He closed his eyes. The idea to tell Aushruk what to do if he didn't make it back entered his mind, but he shoved it aside. That felt like giving up, no matter how smart it was. And it wasn't Aushruk's job to take Abraxas Kain down.

He emptied his mind and forced himself not to hear the world around him. The whisper of wind and sand between the pillars. Aushruk's feet shuffling on the rocks. The tinkle of his charms with every shake of his head.

Like with the portal, Arke poured everything he had into one thought.

I need to know how, he thought. *I need to see what happened here.*

And to that thought, all his desperation. The torn strings of his heart still smarting after Abraxas's refusal. The last time he saw Gyda before the shadows, grim faced and determined, her eyes mirroring his need to get to Tolk because she knew better than anyone the feeling of losing family. The way Sorin looked when he walked away, lips parted as if to protest and his golden eyes round with confusion and hurt. Sol's body in his arms, limp and far too pale. Evren's rough, scarred hand taking the spell even as she begged him to stay.

It's for them, he told the spirits. *They are not a country in need of saving, but to me they are everything. They are more. They're why I'm here.*

It was like a cut he knew would happen, yet hurt even more.

There was no preparation for the sudden lurch in power in the world. The Aether washed over him but instead of comforting mist it was hundreds of grabbing hands and wailing voices. His senses screamed, smarted, and then went silent. He couldn't feel his body anymore. He heard nothing over the cacophony of voices all talking at once. Over and over, the same message but different to each soul. They wanted him, nails dragging over his soul like hot coals through snow.

Arke couldn't think. There were no breaths to ground him, no digging his nails into his knees. He was so far from his body. A mindless, wandering soul amidst so many others screaming for someone to hear him, someone to listen—

Gyda's eyes, resolute and understanding. Sorin's mouth forming one word—*stay.* Sol's chest, barely rising with small breaths. Evren's hands around his.

Arke pulled himself together. Literally. He took back the slivers of his soul the others had scraped away. He ignored their moans of protest. Their screams echoed in his ears. So much pain. So much suffering.

But not a single drop of regret.

I need to know how you did it! he shouted. Thought. Whispered. *Show me how you banished the Divines.*

The symphony of voices rose again, each with their own story. Each, their faces pressed against the glass of the pillars watching him with blank eyes. So many all at once that Arke could barely make out words at all. Many he didn't understand. Languages too guttural and foreign for him to comprehend.

And then, out of the chaos, rose one.

None have asked me before. None have cared.

The other voices fell away to the normal buzzing of the Aether. Without his body for it to agitate, the sound was almost soothing, like the wind through leaves.

I care, Arke said. *If what you did is thrown away, Eith will burn.*

No. The soul's voice took on more of a shape and personality. A deep voice. Etherakian accent. Quivering at the fringes of words as if barely keeping back tears. *Vernes will burn. But the rest will live on, as the Divines have no need to destroy what could worship them. But Vernes is enough of Eith to be a tragedy. This is why I'm here, doomed forever to walk this state between living and death, never to return to the arms of my gods and ancestors. The price for such an end was too high even for me.*

Arke floundered. He'd expected a Vernesian to show him. But this man was the opposite. How had he end up being the shield that protected Eith from the Divines that created it?

Why?

The answer pressed into Arke's soul even without being spoken, but it was too much. Too complex, too tangled in doubts and self-loathing even now. It was not something to speak, or feel. It was something to live.

~

~

WHEN ARKE FELT the air on his skin again, saw the world through eyes again and tasted his tongue between his teeth, he was not in his own body. He was taller, his teeth blunter and smaller. He blinked over and over to get his eyes to focus, but found that the world remained golden and fuzzy.

My apologies, the voice sounded in his head. *My eyesight was poor even by human standards. My spectacles are in my pocket.*

Arke reached inside the pocket with longer fingers not hindered by long claws. The nails were bitten down to the nub, making Arke feel everything down to the bed. He grasped the metal awkwardly, unfolding the strange contraption through muscle memory not his own and secured them over his nose and tiny ears. His vision sharpened marginally, but nowhere near to what he was used to.

"Do all humans have such shit eyes?" Arke muttered, although his voice was not his own and made him jump. He sounded like the voice in his head.

Mine was uniquely bad, failing since I was a boy. Although I suspect you have better vision than most species, even if you exclude me.

Arke smirked, thinking of Evren's eyes normally so quick to spot tiny details hidden to everyone else. Unless it had to do with the sword wielding woman she loved.

The world felt real but didn't look like it. Like an artist's interpretation of a place they saw once. Some details stood out, like the sheer purple curtains over the ornate windows, and the incense smoking up the room. Other things, like the walls and the crowd of people around him, were blurry. A few stood out, like faces Arke figured his soul guide would recognize in a crowd. But only one was sharp and clear.

Beside him was a shorter human. Older, much older. Yet, Arke could tell he was beautiful by human standards. His long hair, more silver than black, had been oiled and brailed down his back. His clothes were finer than the rest, and too showy to be practical. Despite the jewels on his fingers and the kohl around his eyes, his face was pulled into a deep frown.

Oshaya, the voice in his head said. *He mourned this ending long before it began.*

As if he heard the voice, Oshaya looked up at Arke sharply. If Arke's face was pulled in worry or pity, the man didn't show it. He grinned wolfishly, in a way that Arke knew wasn't genuine but practiced.

"Don't look so glum, Cullen. I am a feast for even your poor eyes, no?"

Arke didn't speak, but his mouth moved and words not his own came out.

"Leave it to you to dress for your funeral."

Oshaya chucked and ran his hand down the length of his braid. "I will leave this world as beautiful as the day I entered it."

Arke's mouth frowned. Worry not his own knotted in his stomach. "Oshaya, you don't have to do this."

The words were a whisper, and yet the man beside him stiffened as if they were shouted. Oshaya looked around at the massive room. A temple, now that Arke's soul was paying attention. Ancient, unused for centuries, but big enough for the thousand that it held. Now about to be destroyed. It was packed with people. Some meditating. Others whispering to each other. Some drank heavily. Others stared at nothing.

We all face death differently, his soul explained.

Oshaya's face was dark. "I am needed here. You, on the other hand, are not. No one blames you for the destruction of Mere any longer, my friend. You can live to see the end of this."

"I cannot," Arke's mouth said. "I have betrayed everything I stood for, Oshaya. If you saved me five years ago only to set me loose without allowing redemption, what does that say about us?"

Oshaya's lovely lips curled into a sneer. "Redemption. Why is it always about that with your people?"

"Why is it always about death for yours?" Arke nodded to the front of the room, where robed figures looked to be preparing a ritual. "Such a Vernesian thing to do. Death to end a war."

Oshaya said nothing. Arke could feel the years of companionship between the two. Tethers of friendship throughout a war that left them both devastated. He pressed a little more, and the soul gave in. Flashes of his life.

The burning of a beautiful port city. Flames licking at his feet. A stunning spy, heartbroken and reeling, dragging him from the chaos and into the water. Years of work with a dying rebellion in the sands. Frustration, anger, depression. But never resentment.

Oshaya was no stranger to seeing the good in Etherakians.

He was always at their side, feeding information to the rebels. But when we met, there was no more Mere for him to hide in. I set the city ablaze because I couldn't stand to fight for a cause that gave so much suffering. It was meant to be my pyre, but Oshaya changed that.

Vernes should remember Oshaya the spy who saved count-less lives with his intelligence. Only a select few knew the man he became in the final years of the war. And only I knew the love he still harbored for the enemy.

Arke's long, blunt hand reached for Oshaya's shoulder and gently turned him to face him. Reluctantly, the old spy met him in the eyes. He was the only one in the room, Arke realized, that had regret shining in their depths.

"You don't have to do this," Arke's voice said again.

Oshaya swallowed. "My death will bring the end of this war."

"Not like this. Not still hoping for life."

Oshaya scoffed. "What life? I have known nothing but war, and I will know nothing more. You think he will allow me back after what I've done? There can be no life with him, none that doesn't brand me as a traitor to my country."

"And what am I?"

Oshaya flinched. "That's not what I meant."

Arke's mouth smiled ruefully. "I know. But you taught me to be better. I cannot help but think, my friend, that I am trying to pull you out of a fire and you're fighting me."

"Don't," Oshaya rasped. "You big idiot, do not get me to change my mind."

"The ritual won't work if you're not willing."

"I am—"

"You're not," he interrupted. "Because your heart is else-where. With him."

The flood of guilt on Oshaya's face was bright as day and even Arke wanted to turn away. But he couldn't. His soul wouldn't let him. He leaned down closer to his friend, the smell of jasmine filling his nose.

"You told me back then that my heart would lead me to the correct path. For me, Oshaya, this is the correct path. But it isn't for you."

Tears were ruining the kohl, leaving grey smudges down lined, bronze skin. Neither man acknowledged them.

"This isn't right," Oshaya choked. "It should be I who stands so calm before death, and you trembling with fear."

"I am content. My path is here."

"I am the blood of Vernes. My path is . . ."

But Oshaya didn't finish the sentence. A gong rang in the air and everyone's heads snapped up. The robed figures were passing through, anointing everyone with a mixture in bronze bowls. Their faces were already marked. Arke knew Oshaya's time for debate was up.

He pushed the smaller man towards the exit, where a familiar red desert waited.

"Go," he said.

Oshaya stumbled back. Those behind him fell away, their faces neither disgusted nor proud. They didn't look at him at all.

Arke's new body stood proud and smiled genuinely. "You've been away from him too long, Oshaya. You forget that Loghain Rhys would've burned the world for you if you asked for a handful of ashes. Whatever time you have left," he nodded to the silvering hair, "spend it well by his side."

Oshaya opened his mouth as if to say something. Perhaps more arguing or a goodbye. But these things had been said before. Arke knew them without having ever heard them. The old spy just pressed his fingers to his lips and waved them over Arke's head in a strange salute that made Arke's chest tighten.

Then he was gone.

Arke found he could use the body again. He watched the priests come by with the oil. It smelled sweet and coppery. He knew it was blood even before he knelt down and let it smear on his face. It was warm even as it dripped through his eyebrow.

"I don't understand." Arke whispered when they moved on. "Why was Oshaya important?"

He wasn't. He was merely my friend, and I wanted to see him again. Oshaya would've been the thousandth soul in this ritual, but we didn't need him in the end.

"How does it happen? I need details."

Arke used his new height to peer over the heads of the crowd. He couldn't move his feet, and he assumed that was because he only had partial control. This was a memory, and not something he could alter. That he had some control was remarkable and strange, something that pulled on the side of his mind that raced for theories as to why. But he pushed those aside, still scanning for what made this ritual so different.

The temple floors held no diagrams or spell circles. Besides the incense, oil, and blood, there was nothing that stood out. For all Arke could make out this was just a gathering of many hundreds of people.

One by one, everyone knelt. Arke's—Cullen's—body obeyed. The floors were warm on his knees. Oil and blood ran in his eyes.

There wasn't a ritual for manipulating the forces of the world between worlds. The oil, the gongs, the whispers, and priests, those were all for us. Our funerals, if you will. None knew exactly how this would happen. I doubt even those in charge knew much. There was only one clear thing to remember;

Our deaths would bring an end to gods.

Their mouth went dry and Arke couldn't tell whose fault that was when a figure in the center of the room stood up. They were Dra'Nacti, like Aushruk but different. Far older by the length of their horns and the wizen stoop of their back. Their skin was a deep burgundy, and no gold marked the lines of their face and body. Their eyes shone with tears as they looked over the crowd, but the smile shined brighter. More hopeful.

And each hand held an object.

When Arke thought of sacrifices, he thought of blades and fire. Yet, the two objects that would take the souls of hundreds were far from that. One, a diadem made of shining jeweled stars. The other, an amulet with a large black stone swinging ominously in the air.

Arke's breath caught, and Cullen seemed surprised.

You know these things?

He only nodded, unable to speak.

The other two Elder artifacts shone in Cullen's memory like the ones Arke saw shone in his. Vivid, powerful, unforgettable. He could still see the Horizon Walker's likeness in Orenlion, cloaked in the night sky wearing the crown as she wept. The Shadow Dancer's carvings with the sword were everywhere in Andovine. The Eternity Dagger, flashing in the air between his friend's waiting hands. The only one he hadn't seen was the Pale One. No temples to that creature, and yet Arke could feel the sick power radiating from it.

Pieces of the Divine, we were told. Things to manipulate the heavens to our doing. It took forty-five years and many lost souls to find them. More were lost to the power they wielded. That's why they were supposed to be scattered to the corners of Eith when this was done. Whatever remained afterwards, we knew they would survive. I must ask, for my own curiosity, did they stay hidden? If you recognize them, I fear . . .

"I didn't see them. Two others, but not those."

Ah, good. A pause. *Such power should be kept from mortal hands. We weren't meant for it.*

I envied the dwarves of old who told stories of the giants that made them in their image. I envied the Dra'Nacti, who carried the blood of dragons in their veins. Because my Divines are nothing like me, and although I love them fiercely, I cannot see them in my body. My soul carries no trace of them. There is not a Divine ounce in me and I know now that if there was I wouldn't have been the same.

Pity the Divine, Arke. Pity those who love them most of all. We are a sorrowful menagerie reaching for beings that we will never understand. Reaching for beings who cannot be touched ever again.

Arke saw the Dra'Nacti raise the two artifacts together. Before they touched, they closed their eyes, and although Arke was very far away he could hear the clink of precious stone against metal.

And then he heard no more. He saw no more. The world went white and there was a searing silence.

And pain.

Pain unlike anything he'd felt before. And it had nothing to do with his body. That, he knew, had been reduced to glass and stone the minute everything went white. No, this pain was that of a soul being forcibly ripped from its tethers of blood and bone, and then braided together with nine hundred and ninety-nine others. All wailing in pain, all begging for an end, all knowing that there wouldn't be one but never regretting it.

As he was stretched and twisted and broken, Arke realized that there was not a single ounce of regret, every person had died for a cause they believed in. Many had nothing left to live for but everything to give. As their tapestry of souls grew, it spread over Eith. The sun-warmed sands, the salt spray, the misty forests and fragrant fields, they were all far away. Beneath, unseen but felt on the fringes of Arke's soul.

On the other side, Divine's fought.

Arke didn't see them either, but he didn't have to. He *felt* them, like the Eternity Dagger but everywhere. Overwhelming. Beings of so much power and force that they changed Eith on a whim were now being forced out. Hands of sea foam, claws of ice, many necks and faces, and many millions of eyes all burning with Divine rage that made the slivers he'd seen in Abraxas seem tame, tried to pierce through the Aether thickening around them like a shield.

They didn't succeed. The shield held. The creatures that

Cullen described as 'nothing like me' were monsters beyond Arke's comprehension. The glimpses he felt were enough to shake him, burn him, and he couldn't put the pieces together to form what they might've looked like.

Something you should know, should you fail, and the Divines descend back onto Eith, Cullen said softly as souls and gods wailed. *If you meet them, do not look at them. You will not come back whole. You will not come back at all.*

And then it ended. The souls, the Divine, the pain. All of Arke's senses came slamming back into him. His eyes were his, watering and staring up at a bright blue sky. His fingers, small and clawed, were digging into the dirt. And his soul, still shaking, stayed firmly where it belonged.

"Thanks," Arke wheezed, feeling like he'd been trampled by a giant dancing to a jaunty Fey tune.

Cullen was fading, his strange presence slipping away to shield the unfathomable beings from Eith. But his voice echoed one last time.

No, it is I who should thank you. I pray for your success. Live well, while time remains.

Cullen was gone, and Aushruk appeared above him, dark face drawn in worry.

"You are back?" he asked tentatively.

Arke scowled. "What else would I be? Of course I'm fuckin' back."

The Dra'Nacti melted in relief and then leaned down to help Arke up. Normally Arke would've tried to snap one of those long fingers off, but he was exhausted. He let Aushruk help him up and swayed on his feet. He was still blinking sand out of his eyes and trying to reorient himself when Aushruk pushed his spellbook into his hands.

That grounded him. Like an anchor for a ship, as Sorin would've said. He hugged it close and looked at the crater again. Which of the pillars was Cullen's?

"This was that temple before," he rasped.

Aushruk nodded.

"Why weren't you there?"

The Dra'Nacti took a pained step back, fixing his black eyes on the pillars around them. Did he know each of them? Could he name them like they were still fresh in his memory? Besides the obvious grief, Arke couldn't pick out anything else in his expression.

"I wanted to live," Aushruk finally said, sounding defeated. "I wanted to see what a world without gods looked like. But everyone I knew was here. My tribe, my friends . . ." He took a shuddering breath. "I am alone in this world. With no tribe to lead and no war to fight, I stay here. I tend them. Walk among them and mourn them when few in Eith know what they did."

Aushruk's deep gaze landed back on Arke. "Do not make their sacrifice in vain. I would rather live alone until this world fell into oblivion than see all this pain be for naught. Do you now know what to do?"

A plan was forming already. One that might kill him, and even if it didn't, it would leave him feeling just as hollow and lost as Aushruk looked. But it was an end he could see, one peaking over the horizon. One he couldn't fight anymore.

"Yeah." He nodded, turning to the east. "I need to get my people."

31

Sorin

Whatever storm was brewing was devastating. It took everything Sorin had to hold onto Ire as she cut through the frigid northern water. Waves swelled so high that she dove underneath them, their churning rage grasping for Sorin as she shot back to the surface.

The rain was fat and hard, illuminated like drops of silver with every flash of lightning. He choked down more water than air, sputtering after every dive.

Storms like this didn't come from nowhere. It was so dark that if he didn't know better he would've thought it was the middle of the night.

"Why would Nadine do this?" Sorin shouted over the storm.

Ire shook her head as thunder threatened to split the sky. "It isn't her!"

There was only one other who could, and Sorin cursed himself for not realizing it sooner. Someone who had the strength of a Vasa Bonded to a sea serpent, who just watched her last tether back to shore snap and die.

"This is going to kill her." That was all Sorin could manage before Ire was diving again. Her powerful tail propelled them through the water faster than he could ever have dreamed of. The dark hull of the *Red Knave* groaned beneath the sea.

They resurfaced far closer than he remembered being to the ship. Either Ire was an extremely fast swimmer, or the *Knave* was headed straight for the cliffs. Seeing how punishing the water was washing over the deck and pouring over the side, and how the wind was tearing at the sails, he settled on the latter.

There were escape dinghies in the water. Damn dangerous in these conditions, but it warmed Sorin's heart regardless. People were taking the risk and leaving because a deadly storm was preferable to Vayne's reign.

No doubt another cog in Nadine's plan.

"Be careful, I don't want them to hurt you," Sorin told Ire, and she just scoffed. Which, with her head half underwater, was just a lot of bubbles. But she heeded his warning, dipping down low enough so she wasn't seen but he was. A few on the boats shouted when they saw him. Ire ignored all of them except the one still close enough to touch the hull of the *Knave*. Sorin squeezed her shoulder, and she reluctantly swam away from him.

For a handful of terrifying moments, he was untethered in a frothing sea. But before the water could drag him under, he shot his hand out and grasped the side of the closest dinghy.

None of these people he recognized, but the look of shock on their faces was more than enough for Sorin to get the idea that word of his 'death' had spread.

"Hi." He grinned through the rain. He pulled himself up, sopping wet, into the rocking boat. Some froze, others scrambled away. Sorin picked his way over the tangle of limbs to the other side.

The crimson hull was so wet it looked like it was bleeding. Sorin waited until the sea rolled another wave their way, lurching the small boat up to nearly half the height of the ship. He grabbed the rope they'd used to come down, spared another smile, and hung on as the water carried them away.

Dangling over the edge of a ship in the pouring rain. Thunder clapping his eardrums, lightning sizzling the air. Nothing but a hungry sea beneath his feet. This time when Sorin climbed, he knew what waited for him above and the thrill steadied his shaking hand.

The *Red Knave* lurched and groaned under the battering of wind and water. Sorin kept his eyes fixed to the black sky, even as the ship tipped dangerously to the side and he could see glimpses of the deck. Even when a massive wave swept over it and poured enough saltwater on him that he almost lost his grip. He kept climbing, spitting out salt, eyes to the sky, because there was still one person he needed to save.

There was still a promise to keep.

The noises Sorin made as he clambered over the railing of the ship were far from heroic and more like a congested whale. Thank fuck for the dramatic storm to cover that up.

The deck was chaos, as it would be in a storm so bad, but made even worse by the lack of people keeping it from falling to disaster. There were only a few. Sorin spied Zo barking orders as the storm drowned her out. Miks was helping a man with a bleeding arm below deck. And in the middle, surrounded by a whirlpool of flickering lightning, was Sahar.

Down on her knees as if in prayer, her face aimed towards the sky. She mouthed a long silent word, likely just a scream, as flickers of pure energy poured out of her skin. Steam fell from her in waves, casting a ghastly glow on her agonized face. And her eyes . . .

Gone was the warm brown full of wit and understanding. Now they were as white as the core of a bolt of lightning, leaking sparks of power with every gasp.

"Sahar!" He pushed himself off the railing towards her. The deck slid dangerously under his feet, wood slick and shifting with every churn of the waves. But this was yet another dance where he had quicker footwork than his partner.

He dashed forward, only a few quick steps from the bubble

of lightning that surrounded her. The light was blinding, brilliant, all he could see unless he focused on her darker form inside it. The wind-torn black hair. The hands spread out beside her clawing at the air. The shift of her wet shirt in the wind.

A streak of steel flashed through his gaze and Sorin just barely spun out of the way. He caught his balance as the ship tipped to the other side, angling his body just so. When it righted itself, he turned back to Sahar, and was face to face with Vayne instead.

"You just can't die properly, can you?" he sneered. Rain dripped from his mustache into his teeth. That one gold tooth seemed to have lost its luster in the wake of such a storm.

Sorin grinned. "You're not the first to tell me that. Won't be the last either."

"Brave words for a man without a weapon." Vayne's saber glittered at his side. "Braver still for a welp who runs away from every fight."

Sorin Trinity was many things to many different people. Friend, annoyance, storyteller, enemy, really the list went on. But in that one moment he was sure of only one thing he was. As his left hand trembled where his right one was still, yet empty. As the black cliffs drew ever closer and the *Red Knave* buckled against its death throws. As his last remaining friend, who he would've fought for just as hard even if she wasn't, funneled the rage of a serpent into the sky and sea.

This time Sorin didn't smile. He let that careless mask slip away. He felt his mothers in the grim tug of his mouth. He felt Maria in his clenched fists, and Hastings in the spike of adrenaline turning his blood hot in his ears. In the back of his mind, like a welcome pressure now that he was aware of her, was Ire.

"My name is Sorin Trinity," he said. As an affirmation. As a statement. As a massive middle finger to the fucker who took that name and tried to tell him he wasn't worthy of it. "And I am many things. But I'm not a coward, and I'm not running away now."

"So, you're a fool."

Sorin the Fool. Gyda would've loved that title.

Vayne lashed out, his blade slashing through air and water where Sorin had just been. He blinked at the shimmering rain, then over to where Sorin had just sidestepped.

And then it began in earnest. A dance unlike any before because this time, Sorin wasn't just staying alive or drawing attention. He was breathing this fight, relishing it. The teetering of the ship beneath his feet aided him in slipping out of the way of Vayne's vicious blows. The wind tugged him in all the right directions. He could feel the waves when they were cresting, and ducked behind the masts as they hurtled across the deck and Vayne struggled to keep his footing.

The pirate wouldn't be swept away. He was all bared teeth and strong blows that would take Sorin's arms off if he wasn't careful. The *Knave* was his ship, and he knew it well. Sorin got the impression after he dodged a loose cannonball without a sideways glance that the man could fight blindfolded on this ship if he had to and still win.

Sorin leapt aside from another savage swing. Vayne growled, spitting water as he did.

"What's wrong, old man?" Sorin asked. "Can't kill me properly?"

"I'm gonna nail pieces of you across this ship so you never leave!" he roared. His downward slash sent sparks of rain in Sorin's eyes, and the follow-up was so quick it cut into the sleeve of his jacket. "I'm gonna make sure you're here, body, bone, and bloody fucking spirit until the end of the fucking world!"

The flurry of attacks that followed put Sorin on his toes. The saber whispered close enough to itch his skin. He had to fall back, picking around loose rope, boards, and a pissed off pirate all at the same time.

Beyond them, Sahar was getting worse. The lightning that whirled around her lashed out. Bolts left smoldering imprints on the deck, on the wheel, on the sails. Sparks too furious for any rain to put out turned to fire, greedily consuming the sails of the blood-red ship.

The railing hit his back and Sorin grabbed it to steady himself. Vayne in front, that blade between them. Nothing but the ocean and a lot of rock to ruin his day behind him. He could jump. Ire would save him. But he couldn't run away, and there was no guarantee he could make it back to Sahar in time if he did. The only option left was to stay and fight.

"Finally, out of room to run," Vayne snarled, saber drawn back for a killing blow. Sorin could see the path it would take, straight through his scar and into his heart. Heliodar had painted a lovely map for Vayne to follow, only his saber would rip out Sorin's back as well. He'd make for a handsome skewer.

A shrill voice cried out over the storm. "Sorin!"

He turned just in time to see Enola clinging to the quarterdeck and throw a sword, oh his lovely sword, towards him. Vayne's eyes followed it as well, widening a fraction as it turned over on itself, pommel over point, pommel over point, pommel—

Into Sorin's hand.

"Now it's a fight."

Sorin's sword felt as light as air, as quick as lightning, and as deadly as the waters below in his hands. He lashed out, the thinner blade ringing musically as Vayne barely parried the blow.

And took a step back.

If there was one thing you didn't do while fighting Sorin Trinity, it was give him any room to work with.

His blade was an extension of his arm as he pressed Vayne back with nothing more than quick flashes of steel around him. The railing disappeared from his back. Sahar grew closer. From her spot on the stairs, Enola whooped.

"It's just like the zombies!" she cried out.

And Sorin howled with laughter. The wind tugged his feet, and he obeyed. Skimming the water, spinning within Vayne's guard but just out of reach. Untouchable, light and free. The thunder in his heart ached for blood and he obeyed. Steel rang and shook his bones until one blow met soft, tender skin.

Sorin retreated quickly, blade raised to see the blood drip with the rain. Vayne touched the cut on his neck with a pained grimace. Not a deadly wound, but a message. In the back of his mind Ire smelled the blood and her thirst for it nearly overtook him. His shiver had nothing to do with disgust.

He launched into a succession of attacks so quick he could barely keep track of them. They were just a blur of steel in the air, carried through from the past. Vayne could barely keep up. He blocked, fumbled, and got cut, howling with pain. He blocked, blocked, got cut.

Block. Cut.

Cut. Cut. Block.

Cut.

Cut.

Cut.

Sorin flicked his wrist and disarmed the pirate with so much force the saber sang through the air and disappeared into the water. Ire giddily waited for more.

Now Sorin had Vayne against the railing. Etherak's cliffs loomed like a hundred-foot wave too close for comfort. The pirate was bleeding from a dozen different cuts, panting heavily. Behind Sorin, Sahar started to scream.

Vayne's eyes flickered back to her, then to Sorin with a leery grin. "All that covering up for a woman you don't even like. For what? Power?"

Sorin raised the point of his blade until it was under Vayne's chin, forcing the man to swallow with care or risk another, more life threatening, slash.

"You really are the stupidest man I've ever fought," Sorin said. "All this power in your ship and you abused it. All these people, brilliant, tough, beautiful people, and you had them working like slaves."

"I took what the world wouldn't give me and made it mine!" Vayne hissed.

"You abused the gifts we were given, all because you were given none."

"I deserved it!" he howled. "I deserved power over the sea and storms! Over life itself!"

And in that raging pirate Sorin saw a splinter of himself, bitter and broken. Trying to claw some scrap of special out of a world that gave it freely to others. He could only take heart in the fact that when the Long Night closed around him in Direwall and there was no magic to call, that his plans had saved Direwall and gotten them to Gyda in time. He could be proud of making Evren laugh when she looked so miserable back in Orenlion. He could look back on the parade in Rhienwall, on the people he saved in Sahar's manor, on the way he fought side by side with Gyda and Viggo in Vanguard, and know that the way he felt after that had everything to do with *him* and not any kind of power he wielded.

Sorin stepped closer, pressing the tip of his sword into the skin. More blood trickled down his neck. Vayne couldn't get away.

"I have fought terrible people," Sorin said. "Monsters, all of them. And yet, they were all better people than you. Because they did terrible things out of fear for their people, out of survival and madness, out of misguided faith and the need to protect themselves. All their actions I could see why they did it. But you . . ."

Sorin stopped pressing. He let the blade up.

"You are just a man. A horrible, murderous, small man."

Vayne bared his teeth. "Get your vengeance, pup. Be done with it."

Sorin stepped back. "No. No vengeance. Justice."

The pirate barked a laugh. A spray of sea water crashed over him, but that didn't stop him.

"There's no justice on the water! That's why I have lived for so long. Because there's no trial, no executioner. I will always live before the eyes of mortal shits like yourself get their justice."

He spat at Sorin's feet, and when the pirate was done, he grinned.

"The sea has its own justice, Vayne," he explained. "For one so familiar with our ways, you should know that."

He darted forward and gripped the pirate's shoulder, ramming his sword into his gut. Vayne gasped, fumbling to throw Sorin off, but he brought him in close instead until he was sure that all Vayne saw were his eyes and the souls of the *Fortune's Trinity* within them.

"She's been dying to meet you," Sorin hissed, then kicked him off his blade and into the water.

Vayne screamed as he fell, and continued to long after he hit the water. Sorin felt Ire's bloodlust kick in, her predatory drive latching onto her prey. Her satisfaction as she sank her teeth into his neck.

He shook off the feeling, sheathing his sword. The ship was on fire and headed to a rocky death, and he'd be damned if he was dying here.

He turned back to Sahar and saw Nadine standing over her. The old witch was smoking from where the lightning had hit her, but seemed unperturbed as she held Sahar's head between her hands.

"That's it girl, let him out," she crooned. "The boy is not your burden to carry."

Sahar sobbed. Her nails dug into the wood of the deck, leaving shallow scratches. More steam and lightning pulsed from her, and Sorin could've sworn he saw something writhing beneath her skin. He raced forward, stopping just shy of the lightning.

"Sahar—"

"Don't!" Nadine snapped at him. "I needed her emotional to break the barrier she'd put up between herself and him. If she sees you, she'll try to control it again."

"The ship is falling, we need to go," Sorin snapped. "We can do this later."

"She stops now, she dies." Nadine flashed an irritated look at him. "I didn't put up with you only to let her die because you were impatient. Now. Let. Me. Work."

Without waiting for confirmation, she turned back to Sahar starting to convulse as Gail was ripping himself free from her body. Her tears turned to steam as lightning licked them away.

Sorin gritted his teeth until his jaw ached. He gripped his sword with white knuckles, his bad hand shaking until a smaller hand took it. He looked down at Enola, wide eyed and smiling.

"It'll be okay," she told him. "Sahar's a hero. I heard her stories."

Sorin let out a huffed laugh. "You believed them and not mine."

"I believed them all. You're just fun to poke at."

It seemed ridiculous to draw strength from the little elf girl, but that was all Sorin could do as they turned back to Sahar. As she writhed and screamed, and Nadine murmured incoherent things. Her crooked fingers curved up and up, as if drawing a shy cat out of hiding. Only Sorin could see this cat as a monstrous shadow clawing through Sahar, body and soul. With every inch expelled, the storm got worse and she shook more. With every moment passed, Sorin was sure he was watching her die the world's slowest death.

"Come now, child," Nadine said through gritted teeth. "Taste freedom and salty air once again. Warmth and starlight greet you. Cower no more in vessels beneath you. Leave your cage. Leave your cage!"

Nadine brought her arms up to the thundering sky and Sahar went stiff.

"You are free!" Nadine shrieked.

Sahar's screams stopped as something dark erupted from her mouth. A transparent shadow of something monstrous, lithe and long. Frills and spines danced on the burning sails. A long tail whipped around the mast and propelled it into the sky. Against the lightning, Mortova's jaws unhinged into a victory cry.

The next flash, and he was gone. By the following rumble of thunder, the lightning around Sahar had fizzled out and she collapsed on the ground.

Sorin tore his hand out of Enola's as she gaped at the sky.

"The rain is stopping," the little girl murmured.

Nadine muttered something to her, Sorin didn't care to hear. He knelt beside Sahar, pulling her up into his lap. The rain was dying down, but still pattered on her closed eyelids. He brushed the water away, cradling her head carefully.

"Sahar? Hey, I'm here. I'm right here. Just . . . just, please wake up. Come on, I'm sorry for dying. Again. But I'm here now and we really have to go. Please wake up."

The storm was dying, but so was the ship. Gone were the dramatic tilts back and forth, but now it shook and rumbled as rocks from below tore at its underbelly. Enola cried out. There were more voices beyond Sahar, but he tuned them out. Focused just on her, the flutter of her eyelashes against her pretty brown skin, on the little scar next to her nose he never noticed until now, on her slightly parted lips as rainwater dribbled in and they moved.

They *moved.*

"I deserve a lifetime of pancakes for this," Sahar croaked.

And Sorin did the only thing he could do. He laughed because the sudden weight of her dying was lifted off of his chest and felt as giddy and as light as a spring gale. He laughed because of the way she scowled up at him, blinking away the rainwater.

He laughed because finally something was going right.

"You're not dead," she murmured, brow furrowed.

"Nope." He shook his head. "I am very sorry about that."

"As you should be." She poked his shoulder with a weak finger. "I nearly died because of that performance."

"Sold it well, didn't I?"

"Ass."

Someone coughed awkwardly behind them, and Sorin craned his neck around to see quite a few of the crew watching on. Miks and Zo looked particularly worried as the ship cracked underneath them.

"Pleasantries aside, can we leave?" Zo asked.

"I don't know." Sorin helped Sahar sit up. "You have an extra dinghy?"

She frowned. "No."

Miks shook his head. "We wouldn't be able to fit everyone anyway. Not in time."

Nadine straightened up with the help of Enola, beaming as much as a raisin woman could. "Luckily for you lot, I can help. Oriel and I will calm the waters enough for you to swim to shore. These caves will be plenty shallow when the tide drops, and I think you'll find that Etherak's beaches have many ways to get inland."

Sahar leaned on Sorin as they stood and there was another weight off of him that he didn't have to pretend to keep her at arm's length anymore.

"But Oriel is still . . ." He winced. "She can't swim."

"No," said Nadine gravely. "And neither will I. I will stay with her on the ship to clear the way for you, and then we will die together as we should've done many, many years ago."

Enola blanched and started to argue but found a crooked finger over her lips.

"Don't argue, little storm. My life ends here. Yours starts on those shores." Her eyes twinkled. "I recommend sticking with Trinity. He'll need your help."

Nodding numbly, Enola shuffled to Sorin's side. As Miks and Zo started herding people to the side of the ship, the little girl's eyes widened.

"Gimme that." She snatched for Sorin's sword and pulled it out of his sheath enough to cut her palm.

He stepped back, shoving the sword inside the sheath again. "Hey, rude!"

Just like a kid, she ignored him and walked back to Nadine, her bloody palm cupped as an offering. The sea witch smiled, taking her hand and smearing the blood on her own palms.

"Thank you dear. Be sure to wash and bandage that for me."

Enola tucked her hurt hand to her chest. "I will."

Enola darted over to Sorin's other side, and the two of them pretended to ignore how much she was sniffling. They took to the edge of the ship where people were slowly making their way to the calming water below. What had once been frothed and angry, lashing against black rocks, was now almost as still as a pond where they jumped in. Sorin's skin prickled with the magic, both familiar but laced together completely foreign.

As the rope was offered to them, Sorin pressed it into Sahar's hands. "Even with Nadine's help it's going to be a rough swim."

Enola took her rope on the other side, wiping her tears. Sahar smiled wearily at them both, and then at the water knowingly.

"Somehow I think we'll be okay," she said.

~

~

WHEN NIGHT FELL, the survivors made the dangerous climb up Etherak's cliffs to the top. It was a slow process with little talking and no light to guide them but the swollen moon. But the way the sea breeze tugged at Sorin's coat felt good. He ached and was freezing and so damn hungry, but he couldn't stop grinning.

Enola was a good climber, staying ahead of them on the tiny trail cut into the rocks. Sahar and him fared a little worse, but better than the Vasa who'd barely stepped on land more than a few times in their lives, and never land so dangerous as this.

Thankfully, they lost no one. As the moon reached its peak,

they made it one by one to the grassy clifftops. The tall weeds looked silver and swayed high enough to reach Sorin's hips. The exhausted Vasa collapsed on the ground, shaking and crying. Someone vomited. Sorin bet it was Zo.

He fell flat on his ass with a tired groan. Long days deserved long naps. He deserved a hot meal and a soft bed, but this itchy grass would do for the bed. He'd worry about food later. He'd worry about everything later.

"Sorin." Sahar's voice came to him tight with worry.

Never mind.

He blinked open eyes he hadn't realized he closed. She was standing at the cliff's edge looking down. Her face was lit up by soft light and showed every worry line.

Sorin pushed himself to his feet and stumbled over to her. Enola laid just a ways away, passed out already.

"What is it?"

Sahar nodded down to the water. He followed her gaze. Waves crashed normally against the rocky shore. Caves yawned blackly, nestled in the cliffside. The sinking skeleton of the *Red Knave* clawed above the water with blackened fingers.

But below that was the source of light that illuminated all of it. Lines too perfect to be natural lit up a pale green from deep beneath the water. These lines were spread as far along the coast as he could see, and went farther into the ocean until the black waters swallowed them up.

Marching lines, bright and burning with light. Serevadian armor winked vividly from its watery embrace.

The closest one was still miles away, but it was enough to make Sorin sick.

"Almost forgot we had a world to save," he admitted.

"Me too," she said.

They stared at the invading army and resolve settled deep in their bones. War had come regardless of their actions, but they still had each other. That was enough for now and it would be enough until it wasn't.

"Ain't gonna stop it by starin' at it."

Sorin froze at the sound of a familiar rasp. His heart leapt, bruised and eager for more good news. He could hardly breathe as he turned around and came face to face with a familiar green goblin.

Arke smiled, and it was sad, but damn what a great thing to see. "Hey, kid."

Sorin didn't say anything. His eyes were burning and he was stepping over Enola's snoring form before dropping to his knees and wrapping Arke up into a hug. The goblin hissed but didn't wiggle away. Smaller arms patted his back. Sorin squeezed him like he was afraid he would disappear into a puff of smoke.

"I thought you were dead," he mumbled into Arke's shoulder. "I thought . . ."

He didn't need to say what he thought. Arke knew him well enough.

"I know." Arke sighed between his arms. "I'm sorry."

Sorin pulled him back, holding him by his shoulders and looking into those tired yellow eyes. They were a little red, as if he might've cried too. But there was a type of exhaustion in their depths he couldn't name. The kind of stare that came from seeing far too much.

"Where have you been?" Sorin croaked, his throat tight and his cheeks wet.

The goblin hung his head. "I needed knowledge. I figured some shit out."

Sorin didn't know what to do with that shit answer. It wasn't until Sahar stepped up behind him that he realized he didn't have to be the one to pry his friend for clearer information.

"Arke, what kind of information?" she asked, drawing the goblin's eyes upward. "Can it help us with the war?"

"Yeah." He nodded. "It's gonna hurt like a bitch, though."

Sorin scoffed. "Doesn't it always?"

"No. Really, kid." Arke's serious tone killed what little humor simmered in the air. "First thing you gotta know, our people are alive. Gyda, Evren, Sol, all of them."

More good news! Sorin felt like his heart was going to burst with so much happiness. If he didn't hurt so damn much, he might've done a little jig.

"That means Abraxas too."

And there it was. Big foot of bad stomping down the little lightning bug of good.

"We're going to have to stop him, aren't we?" Sorin asked, letting his hands fall from Arke's shoulder to his sides. "Our friend . . . we've lost him."

"I hope not," Arke said. "Its lookin' like it. I can tell you what he's plannin' to do and what we need to do to stop it, but that'll have to be on the way."

Sorin frowned. "The way to where?"

Finally, Arke's eyes twinkled like they had before. "To save the rest of our people. This only works with all of us. That—" he jammed a finger at the lights in the water, "—only stops with all of us."

There wasn't a choice, but Sorin still chose Arke. Sahar still chose to stay with them. They all still chose a path full of pain for the slight hope of relief at the end.

32

Gyda

In Jalaa's home, Gyda and the worg had their wounds healed. The giantess said nothing, and hadn't since Gyda had stumbled back in. She'd known the figure's identity and knew what it would do to Gyda. She knew that it was something she had to see for herself.

Destiny was a bitch like that.

The Eternity Dagger lay on the table, unassuming save for the thrum of power it shed. When Gyda's hands had healed, she hadn't let go of the hilt of her sword. She hadn't even cleaned the blood out of the grooves of the runes.

Jalaa stepped back, frowning down at Gyda the same way a concerned mother would to a sulking child. Maybe sulking was the wrong word, but it felt like Gyda was wading through a bog of the worst kind of emotions. After her high from the battle, it was the worst feeling. A part of her wished she'd closed her eyes. If she hadn't seen that face . . .

No. That face had shown her the key to ending all of this. It had shown her the end, and it didn't include a remodeled keep in the Etherakian wilderness.

"Blood of my blood." Jalaa's soft voice brought her gaze up from her lap. The giantess looked mournful, as if she shared Gyda's heavy feelings. "I wish these things were different."

Gyda swallowed. "Was there ever a chance?" she asked. "Or were we doomed from the start?"

"Only the true Keeper would know," she nodded to the dagger, "and he is dead."

Her eyes were hot, and she shut them to keep back unwanted tears. It was useless to cry now when there was so much left to do. She'd been entrusted with this knowledge instead of Evren for a reason.

"I had it the whole time, didn't I?" Gyda asked. "Abraxas could feel it. Why couldn't I?"

When she opened her eyes again, Jalaa was a blur before her that only cleared after something hot and salty slipped down her cheeks. Starlight was cold and soft in her stare.

"Trust transcends time," Jalaa answered. "And she trusted you most of all."

The worst answer. The only answer. Gyda shouldn't have expected any less. If she thought back to that desolate time right after the flash in the sky, but before Evren came limping back alone, it made sense. She chose not to think too hard though. This grief was different than the one that overwhelmed her in Orenlion. This was as bitter as the sea, made even more so by the life she'd envisioned before.

Some of it might happen. But one key part wouldn't. One person in particular would be missing, and there was no way for Gyda to save her. She'd been shown that much.

But there were people she could save, and she needed to get started.

She sat up straighter. "Do you have it still?"

Jalaa nodded. She went to the shelf where even she had to reach up and pulled a tiny, in her hands, bundle down. She carried it with care and set it before Gyda on the bed.

Gyda unfolded the cloth that covered the mirror shard. She'd asked Jalaa to hide it in case Abraxas could reach her through it. She knew Evren had given her piece to Neri, and Sorin frequently misplaced his. Arke and Sol could have theirs, too. She'd accepted the fact that they were all alive and that she couldn't speak to them until she was strong enough.

Now she didn't have a choice.

Jalaa left the home wordlessly. The worg snored beside Gyda. She picked up the sparkling shard, fingers trembling. The last time she'd used it was before the battle in Vanguard. She hadn't dared touch it since. Didn't need to.

Now she held it up to her face and looked past her reflection. Beyond that she saw nothing but darkness, the flicker of little lights. Not Jalaa's home.

"Hello?" she pressed carefully. "Sol, is that you?"

The blurring lights stopped. Gyda realized that wherever the mirror was it had been walking. She could see the outlines of rocky underground caverns, but nothing else. Not until the mirror moved and she saw a familiar elven face staring back at her.

"So, you live." Abraxas didn't smile.

Gyda, to give herself credit, didn't throw the mirror across the room. Instead she said, "I live, no thanks to you."

"It wasn't me who drained your life for a needless spell."

"It wasn't needless," she shot back. "We would've drowned."

"Not my fault, but the creature's. Tell me, do they still follow you around?"

Gyda tried to school her face to show nothing, but she wasn't sure if it worked. "And if they were?"

That did it. Abraxas was scowling and looking more like the man who had a blade to her neck than her friend. Someone brushed past him, and curt words in what she knew was Serevadian but couldn't make out were passed between them. When he turned back to her, his face was even darker.

"Busy?" she offered.

"In fact, yes." His eyes flickered dangerously. "I had Sol on my side up until recently. Ainthe stole her away and I'm now hunting her back."

She stiffened. "As if I would believe you."

"Believe it or not, but Sol is in danger."

"That I believe."

"I intend to save her."

Gyda sighed. "And that I do not."

"What would you know?" he snapped. "I would've given you everything. All you had to do was trust me, something that came without question before, but now seems beyond even your reach. You were supposed to have my back above all else."

"As were you." Her reply was hoarse. She wouldn't cry.

"I am saving us," he hissed. "All of us. Serevadia is a blight upon Eith and will grow to be even deadlier if we do nothing."

"And that has nothing to do with your fumbling?"

"Better my fumbling than Nerezza's Empire," he said. "You think you know everything, but you have not seen what I've seen."

Wearily, Gyda said, "I have seen enough."

"So, this is it?" He raised an eyebrow. "I chase you through an army of undead, drag our friends through an endless night, defeat a sea serpent, and drag you out of a necromancer's control only for you to turn your back on me? Need I remind you of the number of people who died so you might live?"

"No." She saw them every night before she slept.

"And yet I do something horrific for the sake of our survival and I'm the villain." He shook his head. It was no longer a question, but a statement. "I wished to be soft once. It was all I wanted. I have made my peace with being a monster, if only in the vain hope that the monsters I called friends would find a home beside me once again."

Gyda was a monster. Only a monster could see what she'd seen and remain firm in where to go next. But they were very different monsters.

"Let Sol go, Abraxas," Gyda said.

He glared at her and she could feel the weight through hundreds of miles that separated them. "There is no letting her go, my old friend. She never truly left. These caverns belong to me now. West was once deemed too dangerous unless one found Andovine or Kleros first. No longer. I have seen many wondrous things, and what Sol believes to be an escape will not be for long. I'll make her see truth even if I cannot with you."

"You mean to trap her."

"As one only can for a rogue such as herself." He smiled a little at her tense shoulders. "Worry not, I won't hurt her. I wouldn't dream of it."

"You hurt me."

"You raised your sword first." He shrugged. "Sol won't get a chance. There's only one way out from here, and I have people already there waiting for her. With nowhere to run, she will have no choice but to surrender to keep her people alive, and I will be generous as to do so.

"When we meet again, Gyda, Sol will explain it all. She does have a better way with words than I do."

Gyda let her face fall, contemplated begging some more, then decided to drop the mirror over the bed. It shattered into a hundred little pieces and when she hopped down, she ground all of those under her heel until there was nothing but dust.

Gyda felt very little as she gathered her things. Hilt at her hip, cloak around her shoulders, worg at her side. Dagger hidden with her. She stepped out into the cold without so much as looking back at the place that had offered her peace in a time of chaos.

Jalaa waited for her as the last remnants of the storm fluttered away. It was passing over to the other mountains, the tail end no less threatening than the front of it had been. Gyda ignored the pile of ash as she stepped up to Jalaa.

"Sol is in danger. Abraxas mentioned something about going west. Not so far north as Andovine, but not so far south as

Kleros. There are Serevadians on the surface waiting to trap her. Can you take me there?"

Jalaa nodded. "I know these places. One of my brethren at the southern peaks talks of Serevadians crawling like ants at his base." She paused, cocking her head. "He will help, but not beyond that. We cannot leave our mountains to join your war."

Gyda swallowed back her disappointment. "I understand."

Jalaa walked across the mountain top to one of the arches. She brushed the runes at the top and it sputtered to life. The arch shimmered as if it held water within and she could see nothing beyond the blue.

"This will take you to Ozus, and he will do as you ask. From there on, blood of my blood, you are on your own."

The worg butted his head against Gyda's hand and she let herself smile as she patted him. "No, I won't be. I'll be with them."

Jalaa nodded and stepped back. "Your path is not one trodden by many. I wish you did not have to walk it. Such loss and sacrifice . . ."

"Isn't that what Eith is?" Gyda asked, her smile turning rueful. "There is chaos and destruction, bloody sacrifice until there is hope again. From what I have seen, that is how it works. Since the first sunset there has been change, and with every change comes a destruction of what we know. What emerges from the rubble is the only reason to keep fighting, no matter the loss."

Jalaa hummed in an agreement that was like Gyda's battle-song, only softer. "You speak of Eith with a love not often known by mortals."

"Oh no," Gyda shook her head. "I do not do this for Eith. I do it for them. I do it for her."

～

THE AIR WAS STILL and rank with blood. Gyda had no blade to wipe off, so she shook out her cloak and pushed it over her shoulders. At her feet, the last Serevadian whispered his final breath. The worg, fur wet with blood, snuffled around the battlefield and chewed on anything that looked like it was still moving. Death twitches kept him bouncing across the battlefield, although there were plenty of corpses that were flattened to the point that there was nothing to twitch nor gnaw on. They had Ozus to thank for that.

Gyda looked up at the giant. He was taller than Jalaa and seemed to be made entirely of white granite. Except for his feet, which were now stained red. If she hadn't seen him in battle, she would've assumed the rotund giant too gentle and soft to kill, but he'd been quite happy to wade in after her. The trip down the mountain with Ozus's help took longer than the battle had.

That same mountain was not as impressive as Jalaa's in height, but it was a sturdy thing rimmed with thick forests. The shade was dappled with sunlight and the trees, a little pathetic compared to the ones in the Deep Wood, seemed to lean eagerly over the yawning black hole in the rock.

Gyda would've missed it for what it was if she hadn't been looking. Even with the legion of armed Serevadians, it looked like a normal gash in the earth anyone might find if they hiked too far from civilization. But if the dead elves weren't enough, Ozus's encouragement was.

They didn't have to wait long for noise to erupt from the hole. Ozus was picking arms out of his toes and didn't look up. Gyda was ready near the opening.

"They could be being chased," She called up to Ozus.

The giant nodded and abandoned the limbs in his feet to go search for boulders. He'd barely stepped away before something foul smelling, hairy, and small hurled out of the hole with a sledgehammer raised high.

The dwarf skidded to a stop, blinking his pale blue eyes at the bodies at his feet. Despite the beard and new growth on his head, Gyda picked out the burn scar easily.

"Karas." Her voice startled him. "I'd hate to carry out my earliest threat to kill you."

He barked a laugh. The kind of exhausted, relieved laugh that only came to someone who'd been on edge for far too long.

"Jalaa's sweet arse, it *is* you!" He put his hammer on the ground and called over his shoulder. "Hey! Look who got here and saved our arses from an ambush!"

A huddle of dwarves, only a couple dozen and all equally as filthy and exhausted, pooled out of hole. Among them was a shock of blonde hair that couldn't be sullied with dirt and eyes like the sky themselves.

Gyda knew Sol was alive, but seeing her was something else entirely. Apparently the feeling was mutual because the moment Sol landed eyes on her she burst into tears.

"You're alive!" she cried.

Gyda went down on one knee as she rushed up and scooped her up into a hug. She'd never been one for these, at least not as often as Sol would like. But this time Gyda had a hard time letting go. When she did, Sol didn't go very far. She squealed with delight when she saw the worg who covered her face with plenty of sloppy kisses.

Gyda smiled as she stood, catching Karas's eye as he watched the same scene with a weird expression on his face. It went away the moment he caught her looking and he was back to his normal self.

"You look like you got dragged through worg shit." Gyda said.

"And you look like your mother . . . Bah, never mind." He waved her off. "We're bein' followed if you want to do anything about that."

"No need. Ozus has it."

Sol looked up from scratching the worg's belly. "Ozus? Who . . ."

She trailed off as a shadow lumbered over them. Ozus towered over them, one hefty boulder over his shoulder. With his free hand he made the gesture to move and all the shocked dwarves did just that. All except Sol, who stayed rooted to the spot watching Ozus with her mouth hanging open.

Karas cursed and marched over to her. "If your eyes get any bigger they're gonna fall out. C'mon."

Sol didn't stop him as he dragged her away, her hand clutching his shirt as she craned her head back to watch the giant.

"Goriryn, do you see . . .?"

"Can't miss him, Solri."

Gyda raised her eyebrows. She'd never heard either of them refer to each other as anything other than their last names. What exactly happened between them? Did she even want to know?

Gyda watched Karas herd Sol with the rest of the dwarves and joined them with the worg at her heels. They were used to giants by now so they didn't jump when Ozus shuffled past them and set the rock into the ground with the finality of sealing a tomb. The dwarves weren't so lucky.

Ozus set the rock down so hard that there was a spiderweb of cracks from the mouth of the cave. He shoved it in like one would a cork in a bottle, patted it and then nodded to her. She nodded back. He wasn't a talkative giant, although Jalaa was her only basis for comparison.

Gyda turned back to Sol, still gaping at the giant, and turned her friend until those blue eyes were on her.

"Are you all right?"

She blinked several times. "I, uh . . ."

Karas rolled his eyes. "Physically she's fine. We're all starvin' and exhausted. Haven't drank much either. Wasn't much time to rest with the Empire biting our ankles as we ran."

Sol's eyes cleared and she nodded along with him. "Yes, he's right. Starving, hungry. A few of us have minor injuries that need to be checked before they get worse. Are you . . . alone?"

Oh, how Gyda wished to tell her she wasn't. When she nodded, the dwarf's face fell a little. But brightened again once she caught sight of Ozus walking away.

"That's okay. You're back." She grabbed Gyda's hand. "We're alive. And I got to see a giant. We're the first dwarves in generations to do so! That's got to be a good sign."

Karas grunted, but more than a few nodded behind her. They looked at him with a healthy amount of respect, like one would a general. They looked at Sol like she was made out of fucking gold, which wasn't an uncommon reaction.

Gyda squeezed her friend's hand, bringing her back. "We have to find the rest."

Sol nodded looking upon at her. Taking in the white hair, the new expression, and scars. But she didn't question it.

"We do. Where are we?"

"Northern Etherak."

Sol broke out in a wide smile. "Well, head south until we find someone we recognize? Sounds like a plan."

It wouldn't be as simple as that, but Gyda smiled too. Because one part of four was back with her, and the biggest piece, the half of her heart, was closer than ever.

As was the end she saw in familiar eyes.

33

Abraxas

Glass splintered.

An exit blocked.

A small town to the south with no Serevadian survivors.

Portals to the unknown.

Abraxas thumbed the shard of mirror absently, casting weak moonlight over the frosted ground. His old friends had left marks. Already, news of Stone's End and what Sol had done was spreading to the surrounding containment camps of dwarves. No riots yet, but there were stirrings. Things Abraxas would be worried about if they affected him, which they didn't. The dwarves were Serevadia's problem, and only something they could afford to worry about at the end of the war.

Which, laughably, would leave them with nothing to worry about.

Abraxas chuckled to himself, not even realizing he did so until Velcros snapped away from the scouts reports to glare at him.

"Something funny, Catarmon?" he asked.

Abraxas shrugged and pocketed the mirror and the humor. Staying in a good mood was harder than it used to be, but around Velcros it was impossible. Like a starving void, the new Emperor sucked what little joy Abraxas had out of him with a few curt words.

Still, sharp words and withering glares were all Velcros could manage. He knew all too well what Abraxas was capable of, since it was only by Abraxas's meddling that he could call himself Emperor at all.

"Let me guess," Abraxas drawled. "Your scout is telling you of yet another failure."

Velcros narrowed his eyes but the scout, a round faced Serevadian who's hair was streaked with both black-and-white, shied away when Abraxas looked at him. The scout wouldn't meet his eyes, stared at the ground instead. His chest was rising and falling so fast that, at this rate, he'd pass out.

This was always the case with those he worked with. Nearly all of the common Serevadians were terrified of Abraxas, and those that weren't hated him. That was fine. He could work with fear. He didn't want them to love him, although that would no doubt make his end goal all the more hurtful for them. No, he wasn't that cruel.

"Breathe," Abraxas muttered, turning away. "Deeply. And leave."

Sucking breaths met his ears, slower now. And then the crunch of icy grass against boots as he scurried off. Out of sight, it was easier for Abraxas to think of him as an older elf. To forget that young, terrified face, different from Jado's in every way, but carrying that same look all young in war did. Haunted, confused, trying desperately to be brave.

"He's young," Abraxas said.

Velcros snorted, and rounded to where Abraxas could see him. In the darkness of night, he blended in. All midnight colors and sharp edges. Only the circlet of jagged iron stood out.

"Does it matter? He's not fighting. Besides, you asked for our all to take Eith. That includes the young."

He was right. Not that Abraxas could admit that. The two of them had a dangerous balance to keep. Abraxas's power meant he could easily destroy Velcros, but he needed the Emperor for his ultimate plan, and the bastard knew it. Serevadia feared Abraxas, but they respected Velcros. Only between the two of them could such a large-scale war work.

"What news?" Abraxas asked instead, and watched Velcros's eyes flash with anger. That made him smile. "I was right."

"The assault went as planned." Velcros waved him off. "What little security Rhys's army had is gone."

"But?"

Velcros's jaw tightened. "You were right. The hunter lives, barely. Her interference kept the attack from being utterly successful. What troops were left fell back when our mage was brought down."

Abraxas nodded. Etherak's mages had discipline where Serevadia's had sheer power. Together they would've been able to subdue one lone mage.

"I told you not to ignore Etherak's magic."

"It wasn't Etherak's," Velcros snapped, teeth shining in the moonlight. "It was her and her magic. The same twisted, vile, power that Nerezza wielded. Only she had the decency to use it in favor of our goals. The hunter uses it against us."

Evren. Of course. His smile lingered, although it felt bitter.

Always a surprise, that one. Had she intended her spell to send their friends scattered across Eith just to confuse him? He could admire that choice if it was. Now she was fighting for Etherak, a thought that almost made him laugh again. Oh, how the piousness of his old home must be grating on her, yet she still fought.

His smile slipped.

She fought against him, just as she stood between him and

Keres on *Mortova's Maw*. Just as she had countless times before. He should not be proud.

"You should've killed her." Velcros continued to seethe. "All of them. Word is you nearly had that giant woman, yet you *toyed* with her and allowed the hunter to intervene. The same could be said about the dwarf. If I didn't know better, I would say you were getting weak."

A bad choice of words, and Velcros knew it. He took a measured step back at Abraxas's long stare, but that was the only concession he gave. He lifted his chin, stubbornly meeting the gaze of a man who could kill him as easily as breathing—and *wanted* to.

"What you call weakness was me merely giving a chance to the most powerful people in Eith to join us," Abraxas said coldly. "Together, Eith wouldn't have stood a chance."

Velcros scoffed. "They're just adventurers."

"Adventurers who escaped you once, despite my warning to you. They're the same people who brought down Vanguard and one of your bridges under the Boreal Sea. One of them destroyed Stone's End, almost entirely by herself. Another slipped in and out without ever raising an alarm.

"Your mage and your cave trolls broke under Evren's will. Your army was subdued. I can only pity whoever crosses Sorin's path once he inevitably comes crawling back from wherever he is hiding. And you know full well what *that giant woman* is capable of on her own."

With every word, Abraxas missed them. But he wasn't lying, and it showed with the force of his words. Even Velcros started to become uncomfortable, shifted from foot to foot in a very un-Emperor like way.

The truth was that the Wandering Sols, even only the five of them, had proven to be the only thing that made Velcros nervous. And while they opposed Abraxas as well, he respected them. Velcros simply loathed them.

"Our only advantage is that they remain separated," Abraxas

continued, and looked to the west. Out of the corner of his eye he saw Velcros sigh in relief. *Good.* "There's no tracking Arke. Gyda is likely behind how Solri and the dwarves escaped us. But with Evren in Etherak and Sorin yet to show his face, we have the advantage. We need to move quickly, before they regroup."

Once they did, they'd come for him. Knowing it didn't make it better. It was the only uncertainty that hounded his sleepless nights since Ainthe's last words. Oh yes, he'd always known deep down that it would be him against them. But he could stop that too.

Abraxas had no intention of fighting them. Evren's little trick to keep him from tracking them all down? That would be their undoing. It would take all of them to bring him down, and he would be burning the sky down before that happened.

Velcros, as with every time he was forced to defer to Abraxas, sighed heavily. "Fine. Where do we need to go?"

The sword told him. Whispered every day and night when he was alone and there was nothing but silence to meet his ears. He hadn't been alone, truly alone, since he touched it. Even when it wasn't in his hand, it was in the back of his mind. The primal, otherworldly power scratching along his spine with soft nails.

West. West, ever west. But when he thought of the coast . . . no. Tal-Mashad would be too easy. And the villages and fields atop the cliffs were inconsequential. No, it wanted him to go northwest, to a corner of Eith still so wild and untamed that even the great hunters who dared the Deep Woods shied away from it.

There was nothing there. No city, no small town. Nothing but dark forests breaching the edges of the Reino Terminan. Nothing but an ancient promise tugging at his bones.

Once, Abraxas had been the type of man who wanted answers before he went somewhere new. Now, he learned to trust the sword. If it said to let Gyda bring them the Eternity Dagger, he would wait. He could draw her out on her own with a few idle threats and blows to her ego. If it told him that the northwestern corner of Etherak was a pool of power like the one in Vernes, he would trust it.

The Divine couldn't lie, and he knew the sword was a splinter of the Divine, just as he was. Bigger than him, but similar.

"There's a forest on the foothills of the mountains," Abraxas said. "Northwest, along the very corner of Etherak. This will be uncivilized terrain. Monsters will abound. I'll need three thousand."

Velcros didn't blink, although his face soured with irritation. "I can pull from the assault of Tal-Mashad—"

"No."

The Emperor blinked this time. "Why?"

"They will draw Loghain's army. He won't let the city fall. And with him will be Evren, so you will have her taken care of."

"Fine. We'll draw from High Martell." Velcros shrugged. "Gratey is all but ours anyway. Let them think their city stands a chance before we snatch it back. Assuming you can move that many, Catarmon?"

Abraxas bared his teeth. "Worry not about me. Just make sure your men are prepared."

"Of course," he spit. "What is so special about this forest? Should we not focus on Linston? Or Noxcairn?"

The two cities they'd yet to touch. Linston for its defenses and Noxcairn because it was too far south and waterlogged. The canal city was threatening to sink into the delta it was built on with the weight of all its refugees. It would fall quickly once focused on, as would Vernes, which remained difficult even for Serevadia. That, at least, made him feel better.

"No," Abraxas murmured. "There is a calling. Something is there that will end this once and for all."

"We can win this war."

Abraxas eyed him. "How many more are you prepared to lose? The surface is falling, but it's fighting back. You've yet to touch Vernes. Melkarth continues to turn your own soldiers against you, and we haven't even begun with the Vasa. Let me take these issues away, and the surface will be yours."

Those eyes narrowed again, still as wary as the first time Abraxas presented himself to Velcros. The Emperor was an awful man, but he wasn't a fool. He knew nothing of Abraxas's plans, because any spies of his ended up dead. But trusting someone who wasn't his own people, who'd once stood against him, was a far stretch.

The Shadow Dancer's Blade didn't catch the moonlight so much as swallow it. It was the absence of it, and Velcros's eyes immediately latched onto it as it appeared in Abraxas's hand. Not a threat, a reassurance. Whatever was left of their god had chosen him, and that would have to be enough.

Catarmon was all that was left of the Shadow Dancer, and Abraxas had long since accepted the name as his own.

"Answer me this again, because I'm curious," Velcros said, still eyeing the blade. "Because I love to hear you say it. Why would you, an elf of the surface who once fought so hard for it that you stained a whole kingdom red, turn against them and destroy them?"

The hilt was cool, reassuring in his palms. This was no destruction, as Velcros thought. This was a Divine calling.

"Because," Abraxas said, his words dripping truth like blood from his teeth. "I would see Eith remade in my vision. And Serevadia is a key part of that."

34

Evren

"**Y**ou couldn't even wait until I got here before you started doing crazy heroics?"

Aster's arms were around Evren before she was even out of her cot, and before she knew it the two of them were a mess of tangled limbs and breathy laughter parading as a hug between two best friends. She didn't know how long it lasted, only that the cot started to creak in protest so she had to shove him off, lest she lose the privilege of not sleeping on the ground.

He stood back, letting her get a good look at him. He looked strange in armor, although it was a lighter, leather version of the Khama armor, so it was less strange than the hulking plate so many in Etherak wore. His hair was tied back, and a few loose pieces trailing along his scarred face hinted at the rough ride he'd taken to get there.

It had been a week since the attack on the camp. A week of fussing healers and a slowly recovering army refusing to acknowledge how close they came to being shattered. A week of Barrion insisting she stay in bed to rest and Idain occasionally sneaking in extra rations, although he wasn't supposed to be out of bed himself.

A week where everyone assumed Evren would be bedridden from her blood magic, and she felt fine. Better than fine. And she wasn't sure if that made everything worse or gave her hope that . . .

No.

No, she wouldn't think about her. Today was a good day. Aster was here, and she wouldn't let the ghosts she carried taint this reunion.

Evren swung her legs over the cot and stood up. Aster stepped back, looking her up and down.

"Mei told me of your stunt with the Blood magic." He frowned. "I expected you to look worse. No offense."

"Not nearly as bad as that mess you call hair." She smiled thinly as he tried to pat it down. "Besides, I've been resting. It's all I've been allowed to do. And I think . . ."

No.

She started again. "We don't know what's changed now that . . ."

Stop it. Stop thinking about her.

"It's not as if I don't have a heart again . . ."

Fuck, there it was. Aster's face so drawn in pity. The same was Mei's had been until Evren had told her that she didn't want it any more than Mei wanted it. That same fucking look Barrion gave her every time he mentioned the Wandering Sols, forgetting that there weren't any of them left. Forgetting that Evren was alone, connected only to one who was fighting against her at every turn.

One she had to save, even if he didn't want her to.

"Sorry," she muttered. "I, uh, I guess I'm still working through it."

Loghain needed a soldier. Etherak needed a hero. Evren tried to be those things, but when she was by herself for so long, stewing in what was and what never could be, she was just Evren Hanali. And that was the *last* thing she wanted to be.

Aster didn't move to hug her. He didn't take her hand like Idain did or hold her shoulder like Mei. He waited, and when she fought back those tears he nodded slowly.

"You're right," he said, skipping over the part about her dead friends because she didn't want to dwell. "We don't know enough about Blood magic to know for sure how it affects you now. Still, you should be careful. You're in uncharted waters now."

She shrugged. "Nothing new then."

They could sit and talk more about Evren. She could see him leaning in that direction. More bedrest, more food, more feelings. She'd had enough of that. And while a part of her deep down longed for Aster's familiar comfort, she couldn't give in. She needed to do something, and his arrival meant change. They couldn't keep her in the tent any longer.

She shoved her feet into her boots, lacing them up quickly then snatching her new coat. Her cloak had been ruined, and trading that for a thick Etherakian jacket had been her best decision since arriving. Lined with fur, it'd be hell to wear in battle. Far too constricting. But for walks in the camp, it would do.

"I need air, and you need to tell me everything you know while we walk."

Aster frowned. "Shouldn't you wait for the King to tell you? Once he's decided?"

She looped her arm through his. "I don't even know what he's deciding. That's what you're here for."

He grinned. "I figured you'd take advantage of me like this."

"What are friends for other than trading secrets?"

They left her tent, and the chilly air bit at her cheeks with fervor. She savored it, the bleak grey sky and the mud at her feet. The smells of camp had settled to woodsmoke and horses again, instead of pyres and burnt flesh. She could almost pretend the attack hadn't happened, if not for the chunk of missing tents and soldiers.

Distantly she could hear the cries of hungry wyverns and saw Orenlion's colorful banners. It made her heart soar.

"So," she prodded as they walked. "Spill."

He sighed. "What, exactly? You've missed a lot."

"The basics. Such as why you're here and not Shao."

"Because I'm easier to deal with."

She stared at him until he cracked a smile.

"It's true."

She snorted. "You're leading an army because you have a better temper?"

"Technically because I'm to be the official ambassador between Orenlion and Etherak. I lead in name only. There are Khama in charge of battles and tactics. But I'm Orenlion's voice outside the Wood."

"That's great!"

And it was, because Evren always knew deep down that Aster would find another way to see Mei again. He'd obviously already talked to her, but he would've said it wasn't anything out of the ordinary. Still, she wanted to press. Had he seen Barrion as well? Did the three of them get along? What had been said?

"As for your next questions about Serevadia, I have news."

Never mind, gossip could wait.

"What is it?" Evren asked, ducking her head so her voice wouldn't carry as much. This part of camp was relatively empty, but information spread like wildfire between soldiers. And if it was bad news, moral would plummet to the hells.

Aster's voice was a soft whisper, but his tone was urgent. "We had to go north in order to avoid the bulk of Serevadia, passing Whitestone, Dirn-Darahl and the villages in between. We had Hisrachi help until we left them to harass Whitestone, then we were on our own. Our Khama kept us from any serious battles, but many were unavoidable. Just five days ago, we managed to take one prisoner."

Evren stilled, barely keeping her feet moving in time with Aster's. "A Serevadian?"

"Yes. Any we tried to capture killed themselves first. Rather . . . excessive if you ask me. This one didn't get the chance."

Evren sucked in cold air. "Did you learn anything?"

Aster shook his head. "He only speaks his language."

"I can—"

"I know. That's the first thing Mei and Barrion said as well. Loghain isn't thrilled about it, but has asked for your help."

She snorted. "Asked?"

"You're not a subject of Etherak. He can't order you."

"It's not as if I could say no to him."

Aster stopped, and the absence of motion didn't hit her until her arm was twisted awkwardly and she had to wiggle free to stand in front of him. "What?"

He stared at her. "Evren, do you have any idea what you are to these people? Even if you were a subject of Etherak, Loghain couldn't do anything if you walked away right now."

"But I'm not," she said, growing irritated. Why would she? This was her fault.

"I'm not saying you should." He watched a pair of soldiers walk past them and didn't speak until they were gone. "I'm saying you have a lot of power right now. Do I want you fighting a war? No. I want to pack you on the nearest wyvern and send you to Orenlion where you will make Shao's life hell but will be safe while we save the world. But I know that's not what's going to happen."

"Aster, I don't—"

He grabbed her shoulders and turned her so that all that filled her vision was the camp. "Look, Evren."

And she did. She soaked up the dirty tents, the dogs lounging between the fires. She took in every piece of weaponry that was being sharpened, every suit of armor being polished. The rise of smoke in the air, the waving of flags.

And the gazes of everyone.

Every single person in sight was looking at her. Quick glances, long stares, and everything in between. The whites of their eyes shone against the dull backdrop of Etherak's autumn. With a jolt, Evren realized they'd been staring, waiting, since she left the tent. How hadn't she seen them?

In every one of their eyes, over the fear and depression, was shining hope. Mostly just a spark and nothing more. But when she'd last seen these people, their eyes had been dark and their hands were bloody.

Such a little change, but it was like the sun was peeking through the clouds.

"I don't understand," Evren started.

"They saw what you did for them." He pushed her until her feet began to work and guided her through the camp. Past the people who watched. Towards more that sat up straighter and wacked their neighbor until they too were watching. Many just stared. Some nodded their heads to her. A few bowed, whispered a prayer.

Aster was a constant reminder to keep going. Avoiding the burnt remains of the southern edge of camp and up towards Loghain's tent.

"They know who saved them," he said. "The survivors from the southern edge won't stop whispering about it, and the story gets more ridiculous every day according to Mei. They're calling you Ironblooded."

Evren made a face, then quickly wiped it away when they rounded another corner full of people. "Blood already has iron, that makes no sense."

He laughed a little. "To these people, it means you're a thing apart. Something new, something powerful. Idain even made it clear that you had no gods on your side, and quelled any rumors about you being a Champion reborn. You are Etherak's first hero that hasn't relied on the magic of gods to save them. And, I'll add, the first foreigner to be held in such high esteem."

"So?" she hissed. "That doesn't change anything!"

"For you, maybe not. I know you don't care. But for them it's everything. For them, you're all that's standing between them and destruction."

Evren didn't realize how badly that sat with her until she was halfway up the hill and the fancy mage with no eyebrows bowed to her. Then she nearly choked on the sheer weight of responsibility tossed on her. She already had enough trying to fix Abraxas, which was going to end in pain. But to have a whole army look at her and see her as the only beacon of hope in their entire kingdom? In the world?

She was going to pass out again.

Then Aster took her hand, like he used to when they were kids. Before the betrothal, before her father had disappeared. When it was just the two of them against the Wood and everything felt manageable.

"But you're not alone," he whispered in her ear.

He didn't take her to Loghain's tent. Instead, to one off the side. Not as large, but warm and well furnished. Mei and Barrion's, Evren noted, seeing the larger bed, two sets of armor and weapons, and the pair themselves waiting for her.

"We're not the Wandering Sols," Aster said. "But we're here to help."

Barrion smiled fondly at Aster, giving him a nod of thanks that Aster returned. The prince turned to Evren.

"My uncle is marching to Tal-Mashad by daybreak tomorrow," he said. "As Mei said, it feels too much like staunching an already bleeding wound while turning your back on the raised dagger. But I have nothing to justify this feeling."

"Nothing," Mei added, "but a Serevadian captive."

Her eyes glittered in a way Evren hadn't seen since her injury. Even without her armor, she looked regal. Evren's breath caught realizing that, astonishingly, Song Mei fit the role of future Queen well. If everything turned out all right, she could almost see the couple with crowns on their heads. What a coronation that would be.

Aster squeezed her hand, pulling her to the present. "You're the only one who can translate for us. If there's any chance he has information that could help in Tal-Mashad . . ."

"Or elsewhere," Mei added.

"Then we need to know," Barrion finished.

Evren eyed them all, something unspeakably warm filling her chest. "Why do I get the feeling that you're doing this without Loghain's permission, contrary to what Aster told me?"

Barrion grimaced. "My uncle sees urgency above all else. One captive isn't enough to sway him. We pushed for you to translate but . . ."

Mei sighed. "Loghain didn't think the captive would speak even if you knew his language. There's lies to deal with as well. Trading misinformation to destroy us. He thought it safest to deal with Serevadia with our own wits."

"Orenlion," Aster said, "politely disagrees."

Evren could see Loghain's reasoning. A seasoned general like him had likely dealt with plenty of bad battles hinging on misinformation. And interrogations took time. Time Tal-Mashad didn't have.

"We don't have to worry about lies," Evren said. "I can make sure we get the truth."

Barrion crossed his arms, optimistic but guarded. He learned well from Orenlion. "How?"

Evren's hand went to the moth in her pocket. Still broken, but she'd never get rid of it. "A trick from an old friend."

NIGHT HAD FALLEN by the time they were ready to start. Too many meetings with Loghain where she'd tried to get him to take a chance, but he refused. She couldn't blame him, not really. But age and experience didn't outweigh the truth. He was set on relying on his tactics and his people to win Tal-Mashad. And, of course, her.

Evren gnawed on her lip as she looked at the Serevadian strapped to one of Barrion's dining chairs. Not a mage, but a simple foot soldier. Older too, which surprised her. He had short grey hair, and a weathered face still peeling from the sun. He looked defeated. He hadn't fought Aster and Barrion when they'd snuck him in.

"Has he been like this the entire time?" Mei asked.

Aster nodded, pouring water for everyone. Evren declined hers and he set it aside. "The others in his battalion attacked, slaughtered, then killed themselves when victory wasn't evident. We found him sitting among the corpses. I suppose you could say this was our first surrender."

Mei wrinkled her nose. "Could be a trap."

Barrion sat at the table, eyes fixed on the Serevadian. "I don't think so. No Serevadian has hidden their distaste for us. He's different."

Evren agreed, but didn't know why. This man didn't radiate hate like the others. She pulled another chair out and sat across from him, knees almost touching. He didn't twitch, just stared at his lap.

In Serevadian she asked, "What's your name?"

He flinched but said nothing.

Evren bit her lip bloody. She didn't want to use the Melding on him, mostly because the two times she'd done it she'd been more of a passenger. It also felt wrong. Viggo had told her it was an intimate affair to share information between two trusted parties, and this interrogation was far from that.

"Do you know anything about the siege on Tal-Mashad?" she pressed.

Silence. Stillness.

Evren let loose a frustrated breath. Behind her, Mei's voice was soft but insistent.

"You know what you have to do."

"I know," Evren agreed. She'd made the plan herself. She hated it all the same.

She looked to Barrion, getting his nod of approval, and Aster who tried for a reassuring smile. No, they weren't the Wandering Sols. But they were something, and Evren didn't feel so alone for once.

She lifted her hands until they brushed the Serevadian's temples, and then he thrashed. Evren just barely pulled her hands back to avoid getting them bitten, but now that he was moving he couldn't be stopped. He rocked wildly, legs of his chair creaking as he did. He nearly toppled over until Mei caught him on one side.

"A little help!" she snapped, and Aster shot into action.

He rounded on the other side, grasping the other shoulder and holding him still. Between the two of them it was enough to keep him from rocking, but Barrion stood up, ready to help both of them.

"Do it," Mei said through gritted teeth.

Evren forced down her discomfort and leaned forward, arms raised. She paused when he heard a strange sound. Weeping.

"Hells, he's crying," she whispered.

"Good," Mei said. "That means we're going in the right direction."

"I'm so sorry," Evren said in Serevadian. "I need to know."

"Please!" the Serevadian sobbed. Tears ran through the wrinkles in his skin. "Please, do not. It is a gift. It is a gift!"

"Tell me what I need to know, and I won't have to." Evren lowered her arms.

Mei hissed in alarm, but Evren ignored her.

The Serevadian shook his head. He was missing a piece of his pointed ear. "I cannot. The shadows . . . they'll know. I do not wish to die."

Abraxas had backed her into a corner. How his magic could reach so far she wasn't sure, and didn't like. But it confirmed that he knew something, and he could only tell it by Melding.

Shame coiled hot and disgusting at the pit of her belly. Evren couldn't ignore it this time. She forced herself to feel it, like she would feel everything in the Melding. This was something that, if she lived to see the end of it all, she wouldn't be able to forgive herself for.

"Once again, I am sorry," she told him. "Our people shouldn't have had to be on opposing sides. I don't want it to be us or you, but it is. For that, I'm sorry too."

Before she could change her mind, before he could scream, Evren's fingers were on his temples. He thrashed, trying to get away. But the two elves holding him down didn't budge. Evren felt the familiar pull of strange magic, that sweeping river of mental energy preparing to take her away. With Viggo, it had been calm and slow. This time it was akin to white rapids between jagged rocks, and Evren threw herself in with no care of whether she would drown or not.

The physical world fell away, and she entered a nightmare.

35

Evren

Viggo had guided Evren through his mind, all gentle waves and held hands. Never overwhelming or dangerous.

Ainthe had shown her the worst of her own mind. Evren's fears and past, boiling and bloody as the priestess had torn her apart, memory by memory, to find what she needed.

Evren wasn't gentle. How could she be? She'd never been the one digging before. But she didn't create the nightmare. She knew instinctively the same way she felt Viggo's quicksilver mind that this horror was what lived permanently in the captive's head.

It disgusted her. It made her terribly sad.

There was no order, not like Viggo's. But no void either. It felt more like a mass of pain. A knot of scar tissue that kept breaking, bleeding, then stitched itself back together. Voices from all directions, none of them the captive's, echoed drowning thoughts that brought back things Evren had said to herself long ago. Awful, degrading things. The kind only said in the dead of night when there was nothing but a mirror reflecting back a haggard reflection of what she was.

These weren't her words. She could barely understand them for how layered they were with so many others. Woven together in a blanket of disappointment, loathing, and revulsion. But she felt them all the same, like an arrow had sliced clean through the man in front of her and managed to pierce her as well.

So much pain. Was he showing her this intentionally? Making her uncomfortable enough that she wouldn't see further? Or was this really just him?

Evren concentrated. She blocked out the voices and the hurt the best she could and sifted through her own memories. She was in control. She wasn't as powerful as Ainthe, capable of commanding Evren's own mind to turn against her. But she knew enough from Viggo that crafting a haven from memories was easy.

Underground, to make him more comfortable. She didn't know Serevadia well enough to bring it up. Andovine was a blur of columns and sparkling orbs in her memory. But she could build an in-between area, something easy for both of them.

The stone walls were easy. The bar made of glowing Luminstone shone a little warmer here than it had in real life. The floors were cleaner, the tables weren't sticky. But the stairs would creak if she went up them, the same musical way they did every day Arke and Sorin chased each other up and down the week after beating Heliodar. The corner table was exactly how they left it. Two chairs for Gyda, one for her to use for her feet and another just for her. Arke's horrendous stack of bowls and plates he'd licked clean. The little doodles Evren had carved into the table, still fresh and sharp.

"Why am I here?"

Evren turned to the captive. He was trembling, looking at the empty tavern with wide eyes. The echo of his pain still pressed just beyond the door, hidden for the moment, but always present.

Evren chose a table near the bar and pulled the chair out for him. "I want to talk."

As she sat, he remained standing, regarding her with open animosity.

"You defile a sacred act." His words lost their weakness as anger seeped in. "You are an outsider and you forced yourself inside my head! And then you bring me here! To *talk*."

Evren nudged the chair closer to him with her foot. "Yes."

He glared at her. "I have nothing to say to you."

She sighed and flopped her foot on the ground. It didn't feel right that there weren't any shells underneath to crush.

"Look, I hate this about as much as you do. But we're at war. I'll pay for this each and every day if I live long enough, but can you look me in the eye and honestly tell me you wouldn't do something similar to save your people?"

"It's not the same," he spat. "Sky-touched traditions are nothing compared to our own."

"Really?" Evren frowned. "Because to them, sacking their holy city is the highest form of disrespect. I'll bet anything that you've been burning bodies in Melkarth and Vernes. Do you know that's worse than death for them? It prevents the souls from continuing their natural cycle. Now, I'm not sure about Gratey, but considering how many different city-states there are, I'm sure your people have crossed a cultural line or two in a few of them. This, of course, goes beyond the normal conquering and war since we can both agree that's enough to piss anyone off."

The captive shifted uncomfortably. His eyes took in the architecture, puzzling out where he was.

"Dwarves," Evren continued. "Are a tad different. Besides taking their city, I don't know what you did to them."

"Camps," he muttered. "The survivors were sent to camps to work. We . . . There were many bodies. The Emperor said that we were needed to do greater things so it was the dwarves' jobs to scavenge the bodies and burn them."

"Well, there's your answer." Evren ignored the sick feeling in her stomach. "Dwarves are warriors at heart. Their burials are complicated. Scavenging and burning isn't part of it."

She nudged the chair once more and slowly he sat. Stiff and at the edge, ready to bolt at any moment. He still wouldn't look Evren in the eyes, but this was a start.

"I regret doing this," Evren said. "Just as you regret what you've done so far. Yet we do it for our people. That you must understand."

"I do," he said. "Or I did. Since coming to the surface, everything is complicated. We are all sky-touched now, and more and more I forget what it means to be Serevadian."

Evren blinked. She hadn't expected that. The captive finally caught her look, and his washed-out grey eyes made her shiver. Hollow. If it wasn't for the press of scarred mind-matter against her concentration, she would've thought him a husk.

"There is no use in lying now. You are inside my mind." He shrugged. "I will die anyway, so ask what you will."

"We don't kill our prisoners."

"If you don't, my people will kill me. There is no future for me. But then, I knew that, letting your wyvern riders take me. I have been dead a long time."

There were a million questions Evren wanted to ask, but she kept snagging on his last sentence. Why *had* he let the Khama take him while all others killed themselves first? Every Serevadian seemed steadfast in their beliefs but this one . . .

"What's your name?"

He hesitated before giving in. "Nollo."

"I'm Evren."

He snorted and it devolved into a little laugh. Evren couldn't help but mirror it. As if they were too strangers meeting in a tavern, no war outside where they were slaughtering each other. No conflicting beliefs. Just drinks, strange names, and stranger company.

In another world it could've happened. Not Eith. Not now.

"Why didn't you kill yourself?" Evren asked, and the somewhat light tone soured. A reminder of what Nollo's mind held. Of what the outside world had made of them both. Those empty eyes met hers again.

"Fear," he said simply. "I didn't want to die. Yes, despite what you feel from me, I do not want to die. Not like that. If one of the soldiers had run me through, or one of the wyverns had eaten me, then that would be fine. But I couldn't kill myself."

"Why not?"

His eyes grew distant. "I made a promise."

Like peeking through the door, Evren could see a glimpse beyond her illusion and in Nollo's memories. He kept them locked up tight, jealously guarding them. But this one rose through the scar tissue and blood, delicate and bright unlike the others.

A simple promise amidst a goodbye. A little girl holding his scarred wrists and looking him dead in the eye, far too serious for her age. That was his fault. Raising her by himself, a granddaughter with no other family but him, she'd grown up as cold as him. That wasn't fair. He'd had to stay alive for her. To put away his grief and lust for death because she needed him.

She still did.

"Yes, I put a twelve-year old's promise above a direct order," he said bitterly. "Her words were clear. In no way could I endanger my life knowing it would end in death. Makes battles tricky, but then we mostly win. It's hardly endangering."

"Then why are you fighting?" Evren breathed.

He looked at her sharply. "Because I was told to. Because our god and our Emperor demanded it."

"That's not a reason to fight."

"And why do you?"

Evren opened her mouth to answer but he leaned forward on his elbows, hands clasped in front of him.

"Not this war. Why did you fight before?"

She swallowed. "Money. Survival. Revenge."

He nodded gravely. "And is that so different from me following orders? I believe that I can bring my granddaughter a better life."

"What's wrong with Serevadia? Why do you want to leave so badly?"

"Ask a bird who has known nothing but a cage why he wants to fly," Nollo said, leaning back. "Should we not want the sun? The stars? Perhaps fertile earth to grow with no trouble? Or to feel storms on our skin once again. Should we not want a choice after spending so long living below? Why would we scuttle back into our caves because it is convenient for *you*?

"Serevadia isn't perfect. In many ways, we are just as flawed as the surface kingdoms. But we are stronger than them, united. And we deserve a chance."

"You're taking everything through force," Evren argued. "How is that a chance?"

He smiled wryly. "There is room below, Evren, if you wish to live. The caverns will be empty soon."

Evren leaned back in her chair. She should've known that it was all going to get worse if she debated him. Serevadia *did* deserve a chance, but the way they were taking it was the destruction of modern Eith. How much blood would she let spill before she found the strength to shove them back down and seal their tomb? Did she have that strength, that right, to make that choice for an entire race of people?

"Oh, don't think too hard." Nollo sighed. "You said it yourself, we are on opposing sides. We can see each other's plights, understand them, and then pick our weapons back up. You're not here to convince me to turn against my home, or to soothe your guilt."

"No," she agreed. "I'm not."

It wasn't fair, but nothing in Eith was. She had to remember what side she was on. Aster, Barrion, and Mei depended on it.

She straightened up. "Tal-Mashad. What do you know about it?"

He shrugged. "Ugly port city built into cliffs. Who does that? What got into the minds of Etherakians and told them that was a good idea? Must be terribly dangerous during the winter."

"Serevadia wants it."

"Of course. Cutting Etherak off from the rest of the world is a main goal."

"How many can we expect?"

He frowned. "I was in the northeast. How should I know?"

"No," Evren said smoothly. "You were coming from north, yes, but you weren't part of those in Whitestone. You would've at least recognized this place if you were."

"I . . ." He faltered. "You can't expect me to recognize a random human tavern."

"This isn't human, its dwarven."

His face fell, but Evren hadn't needed that confirmation. The way he looked at the tavern, constantly uncomfortable and trying to make sense of his surroundings is exactly how she'd been in Serevadia the first time. He knew enough about Dirn-Darahl to know what happened to the survivors, but she had a feeling that had nothing to do with the attack on the city, which he hadn't been a part of.

"I let myself slip." He sighed, rubbing his temples. "You're better at this than I expected."

"That's not a compliment."

He narrowed his eyes. "No."

She moved on. "You were near the northwest. Why?"

"I was moving towards Tal-Mashad."

She raised her eyebrows at him, and he heaved a heavy sigh. Was there truly any use lying now when she was inside his head and could feel it? No. He knew it was fruitless.

"We were hunting escaped prisoners," he said. "But were called back."

"Why?" Evren asked. "There's nothing there but mountains. Unless you're adding the Ikedree to your list of people to piss off."

"We'll get there eventually." He rapped his weathered knuckles on the table. "You understand that I know more that I'm letting on. I understand that while you could tear me apart to get that information, you won't. If I tell you, I'm as good as dead. I'm betraying my people, my Empire. But if I don't . . ."

What will you do?

The question could've been his or hers. Neither one of them spoke, but it weighed heavily between them. That neither of them wanted to kill each other, but they had their duties.

"It's not my choice to make," Evren said. "I'm not King of this land."

"Yet you are a King here, in all sense of the title." He waved his hands to the tavern, his mind. "I am but a humble subject living here. So, an offer, if you will?"

She nodded.

"I give you what you need. You give me information that I need. And we both walk away."

"And what would hold me to this promise?"

"You can't lie any more than I can here. Superior as you are for now, I would still know."

"And in the physical world? You're a prisoner."

His smile pulled at his aged skin. "Those that hold me answer to you, whether they realize it or not. Truly, from what I can feel of you, this isn't a difficult request. You feel like the type who has achieved greater goals than smuggling one old soldier out of an enemy camp."

True. Barrion would hate it. Mei would just want to kill Nollo. But they'd still listen to her, and Aster would as well. The only thing holding her back was herself, and the damage she could possibly do with one piece of information.

"All right," she said. "You have a deal."

"Good. Civilized. There might be hope for the surface yet."

Nollo chuckled, and again it was like a strange meeting at a tavern. As if this business deal couldn't destroy one or the other and the biggest risk was shitty food.

Evren leaned forward. "I'll go first. What is Catarmon's plan?"

Nollo's smile slipped, edged with confusion. He'd expected her to ask more about Tal-Mashad, or Velcros. What use would a sky-touched have for his new god?

He swallowed hard. "Catarmon speaks through the Emperor in this. We were pulled away from our hunt to go to the north-western corner of Etherak. If given a map, I can show you. The rest of our army marches on Tal-Mashad, as you know, but he has pulled a large number from Gratey."

Evren felt her mouth go dry. "Why? For Tal-Mashad? Linston?"

Nollo shook his head. "The corner I told you about. A deep forest."

Evren didn't need to get him a map. His mind showed her already. But her puzzlement continued. What use would Abraxas have for monster infested woods? That area of Etherak was unin-habited for a reason. Even the Collective didn't allow its adven-turers to go there. Those that went never came back. Not like the Deep Wood, where its ancient magic and dangers were balanced with two civilizations, or the Reino Terminan which was dangerous but survivable. That part of Etherak was the only one untamed.

"I believe," Nollo drawled. "That is your question answered. I know nothing about Tal-Mashad because I'm not part of the army there. And I've told you what I know of Catarmon's orders. Now, my turn."

Evren nodded, feeling unsatisfied. Like she'd gotten a glimpse of a clue, but it was just out of reach. What was Abraxas playing at?

As she fumed, Nollo's confidence slipped. He stared at her a while, studying both her and the press of emotions he could feel. His confusion deepened, and she saw the very moment his ques-tion changed from something thoughtful and well worded, to the curiosity that nagged at him.

"Your feelings towards Catarmon . . ." He shook his head. "He's not your god, yet you feel keenly. I don't understand. What is he to you?"

There was so much to say, and so few ways to say it. Instead, Evren let him see. What walls she'd put up to keep her memories and thoughts from pouring over Nollo came crashing down, and she let him see all of it. Her life, yes, but mostly Abraxas. Everything they did, everything they accomplished. From saving Gyda and Direwall to the small victories, like getting through the night without any nightmares. Evren let Nollo see Abraxas when he was terrifying, and when he was soft. When he was broken and needed her help and when the tables were turned and she was leaning on him. The grief when he fell with the dagger choked the tavern in a red haze that threatened to overwhelm them. It only thickened when the memory of the sunken palace played out.

Blood on her hand, saltwater at her knees, lips against her own.

And a promise in the center of all of it. Like the eye of the storm, it was steady and calm where everything else roiled and raged. The promise to bring him back to the light, no matter the cost. Because Abraxas Kain, no matter how dark and horrible, was her friend.

Catarmon was, too.

Evren snapped the Melding the instant Nollo's understanding washed over her, piercing through the scarlet grief. In a blink of an eye, they were sitting opposite to each other again. But no table separated them. The tent was colder, darker, and he was still tied and held down.

Nollo's heaving breaths echoed in the tent. Evren felt exposed and pulled the coat tighter as she stood. His hollow eyes followed her. She didn't need the Melding to see the betrayal in his eyes.

One god dead, another a fraud that hated his kind.

"I'm sorry, again," Evren said.

Nollo nodded slowly, casting his eyes downward to the ground as if he could see through the layers of soil and rock to his granddaughter.

"Well?" Mei asked. "Anything?"

Evren put the chair back. "Let him go."

"What?" the Khama hissed.

"I gave him my word. Let him go, Mei."

"That's not your choice to make."

Barrion put his hand on her shoulder, but it did nothing to lessen the Khama's temper. She didn't throw him off, so there was a small victory. Aster watched them, hiding his pain well as he stepped away from Nollo.

"What did you learn?"

Evren took a deep breath. "He doesn't know anything about Tal-Mashad, except that it is being sieged. He wasn't part of that plan."

"And the knife at our backs?" Barrion asked.

"Abraxas's doing." Evren folded her arms across her chest. "He's pulled a large number of troops from Gratey to the north-western wilds of Etherak. Our friend here was part of the effort to go there, but he doesn't know why."

"If Abraxas is behind this, it's for a reason," Aster muttered. "Could Tal-Mashad still be a distraction?"

Barrion shook his head. "Our scout's reports of the army on the coast are very real. If they take Tal-Mashad, it won't matter how long Linston's shield will hold. We'll starve come winter and Etherak will be theirs."

Mei began a limping pace back and forth and tore her hair out of its tight braid. It tumbled free, wild and ink-black as it had been back in Orenlion.

"But what of these new troops?" she asked. "Why take from Gratey when he can crush us easily with what he has?"

"Gratey might be finished already," Aster pointed out.

"A large number," Mei repeated. "Think, Aster, that sort of army occupies once it's done conquering. Even if Gratey has folded, taking so many soldiers away gives them room to fight back. The country is massive. If anything, they should be taking from *Etherak* to cover more ground and secure it before moving on to Vernes."

"Something is happening," Barrion agreed. "But Abraxas knows there's nothing up there. Why station his army in those wilds?"

"To hide them?" Evren offered.

Aster shook his head. "He's got most of Etherak to do that with. No, this is something more. And if Evren and Idain are right about his plans with the Divines . . . Barrion, no matter how much that might help your kingdom, you must see that this is a bad plan."

Barrion nodded stiffly. "I'm aware. I don't agree with it either." At all of their surprised expressions, he chuckled softly. "What? My own father broke the world on the whim of a god, and now Abraxas is doing the same. I can safely say that I both worship the Divines and wish them to stay the fuck away from me and my family. My kingdom. If anything, I know all too well what they're capable of."

Mei stopped her pacing, and the four of them stood in an odd circle around Nollo, who was still staring at the ground. Outside, the camp prepared quietly for their last night before a long march. Frost crystallized and shone with the weak starlight. A King said his prayers to locked-up gods.

And four people who previously had no say in how the world was run suddenly had the weight of it on their shoulders.

Barrion spoke first. "My Uncle won't leave Tal-Mashad to burn. There's too much riding on that city, too many innocents still inside. He'll need every man and woman in this camp in order to break the siege and, even then, the odds aren't good."

"And that's exactly what Abraxas wants," Mei said. "To make us choose between him and the city. We don't know what kind of force is coming from Gratey, but large by Serevadian standards will overwhelm us."

"Splitting the army isn't an option," Barrion agreed. "I can't ask that of these people, especially when we don't know what we're walking into."

Aster's finger trailed along his scar thoughtfully. "But you have another army. Orenlion's."

Evren winced. "That was supposed to support Loghain's assault. They need the wyverns in the air. It's the only advantage we have that Serevadia doesn't."

"A thousand fresh soldiers could be the difference between victory and defeat for Loghain," Mei agreed. "And could add up to nothing but a slaughter with Abraxas."

"Then I'll go alone." Evren shrugged. "Sneak in and do this quietly."

All three managed to curb their disbelief enough not to wound Evren's pride, but it was Aster who disagreed first.

"Assume he's expecting you," he said. "The attack here was for you, likely Velcros's doing but I'd still wager that Abraxas wanted a threat put down."

"All the more reason to go on my own."

Barrion looked like he'd swallowed a lemon. "Forgive me if I don't hinge the fate of my kingdom on one suicidal mission."

Evren threw her arms up in the air, on the verge of picking up Mei's habit of pacing. Already she could feel that tug to the unknown, to Abraxas. She wouldn't last the night before she was saddling a horse and riding off. Not unless they tied her down too.

"We can't split the army," Evren said. "We can't blindly take a handful of troops into the unknown. We can't leave Tal-Mashad defenseless. What choice does that leave us?"

"Orenlion's soldiers are mine to do with as I wish," Aster said firmly. "They're here to support an ally, and you are part of that. As ambassador and voice of Orenlion, I say that Abraxas is the bigger threat than the army at Tal-Mashad."

Mei drew up beside him. "I agree. And as one-half of this alliance, I have a right to say where this army goes. Loghain has enough people to keep Tal-Mashad busy. Orenlion and the Khama go with you."

Aster's fierce look softened when he looked at her, and there was the barest glimpse of what they'd been before. A sliver of a smile from Mei, an acceptance of an apology, relief that poured like a thunderstorm from Aster.

Barrion joined them at Aster's other shoulder, and the three of them cut an imposing figure together. Princely and regal, cunning and elegant, strong and sturdy. Evren's throat constricted.

Barrion spoke softly, but the command was there in his voice. "If what you say is true, then stopping Abraxas is still the key to stopping this war. If we can get to him first, then Tal-Mashad need not be lost."

Evren shook her head. "You won't convince your uncle to abandon the city."

He smiled ruefully, every inch the future King Etherak needed. "Probably not. But I intend to stay behind and try. Aster will ride with you and Orenlion. And Mei," he nodded to her. "Likely already knows what to do."

"Well, I'd rather fly." She huffed. "But that's out of the picture. Horseback will be a bitch, but I'll endure it. If we can't split armies, we can at least split the two of us. I still represent Etherak."

Barrion's smile turned fond and Mei returned it before facing Evren again.

"You don't have a choice, by the way." She shrugged. "We leave tonight. Cut your prisoner loose, get your things. We leave now."

"And Loghain?" Evren asked, not quite believing what was happening.

"Give him time to argue and stop us?" She snorted. "I think not. If he wants to join this mission, he'll have to catch up."

Aster clapped Barrion on the shoulder, surprising the prince. "That's your job, your highness. Otherwise, we might well and truly die. And there goes all that work for an alliance."

Barrion smirked. "I'll keep that in mind. The rest of you simply focus on staying alive and coming home."

∼

∼

NOLLO HAD long since disappeared into the night once Evren got her horse. Borrowed from Etherak's army, of course, as Orenlion's steeds were all accounted for.

The elves were quiet as they took down their tents on the northern edge of Etherak's war camp. Aster had spread the word to all, and any who wanted to take a chance could ride with them. The rest would stay under Loghain's command to Tal-Mashad.

All agreed to ride.

Even the wyverns were quiet, as if sensing the urgency of the mission. They weren't sneaking out but causing a commotion would look bad. If Etherak saw their only allies leaving the night before they marched, hope would plummet. Likely it already would, come dawn.

Evren tried to ignore that as she fixed her saddlebags. She was leaving them after Aster showed her how much hope she'd given them. If she played her cards right, she could even get a good majority of them to come with her. But just like she couldn't ask Loghain to sacrifice Tal-Mashad, she wouldn't ask his people to do the same.

She, Aster, and Mei knew the risks. Orenlion knew the risks. Their home was safe enough now, so they had the luxury of making this decision. Etherak didn't.

Aster's feet crunched on frosty grass when he walked up to her. "Planning on taking down an army with just that knife?"

She laughed, breath fogging in front of her. "I hate the bows here. Planned to steal one from the Khama when they weren't looking."

She patted her horse on the neck and turned to face Aster, who was dressed in his armor again with a thick cloak thrown over his shoulders. In his hands was a wicked looking bow.

"Surprising what relics we can find with Orenlion and the Hisrachi working together." He ran his hand along the arm, which shone like metal. It was thin, light, judging by how he held it. A row of dangerous looking spikes curved down each side of the arms, like the frills of a wyvern. "I saw this and thought of you."

He held it out and Evren took it with gentle fingers. It *was* metal, but none she'd seen before. And it was far lighter than it had a right to be. The spikes were sharp enough to cut, as if it was made to hurt both up close and from afar. As she trailed her fingers across it, her fingers instinctively went for the bowstring.

And found none.

Aster grinned. "That's the best part. No more keeping track of arrows. They fire magically. Just . . . use it like you normally would."

Evren stepped away from her horse and faced the empty fields north of her. Feeling self-conscious but trusting him, Evren tried to draw the bow like she normally would if it already had an arrow. She didn't expect her fingers to catch on humming air, or for a glimmering arrow made of silver light to appear ready to be fired.

Evren hesitated. She was so used to judging her shots by the strength it took to fire them. How could she know with this weapon when it took *nothing* to draw it?

She released the arrow like she would any other, and watched it soar through the air until it was well beyond the range she was used to. Its silver light winked out when it hit the ground, far enough away that Evren had to squint to see where it landed.

She stared, stunned.

"I know it's not going to replace your old bow," Aster said. "But I thought you could use something with—"

"No, no!" Evren turned back, giddy. "This is perfect. Thank you."

He relaxed. "Great, because I was worried. You have a strange tendency to hold onto old weapons."

"Aster," she said seriously. "I would've taken a magical bow over my old one even if it wasn't lost at the bottom of the sea."

He grinned. "Fair enough. It's good to see you with it. It suits you."

Evren beamed, a strange sense of pride overwhelming her to the point where she didn't see a group of figures approaching until they were a foot behind Aster.

Idain inclined his head, chainmail clinking. "It does suit you. Evren, right?"

She nodded, relaxing a fraction. "Yes. Suppose you want to know burial options now?"

"Always a good idea before dangerous missions. We can discuss it on the road. Might I introduce some old friends, and new allies?" He swept his hand out and Evren could see the four figures behind him. All older, greying, but armed to the teeth. Two half-elves, a dwarf, and an elf.

"Josephine, who's lovely red hair is refusing to age." The half-elf woman winked at Idain, gripping a set of daggers at her waist.

"Stefan, who looks uglier than he is, I promise." The next half-elf bowed, and he was horrifying to look at, with half his face disfigured.

"Marian, the fool who refuses to believe the cold won't kill her." The elven woman shot him a dark glare, her platinum hair nearly silver and the telltale scars of frostbite picking at her bare fingers and nose. She wore no cloak.

"And Aeryn! He was our only dwarven Champion, you know. Special one."

The dwarf was the only one who openly carried a Divine

symbol that Evren could see. She made a note to ask about the hammer and coin symbol later, before looking back at Idain.

"And you know me." He smiled. "Hopefully. Your brush with death might've affected your memory."

"I remember you," she said. "What are you doing here?"

"I should think it obvious. We're joining your mission."

She spared looks at all the old Champions. "All of you?"

Marian sneered, although that might just be her face. It was hard to tell. "We wouldn't let Idain drag us here if we didn't plan on following you, girl."

Josephine rolled her eyes. "She means, 'Yes, Mistress Hanali, we would love to help you stop one of our old comrades-in-arms from breaking Eith.' Right, Mari?"

Marian grumbled, but didn't object.

The scarred man, Stefan, gave what should've been a reassuring smile but made Evren's skin crawl. "We Champions know well what our Divines will do if unleashed fully on Eith, and whatever madness has befallen Abraxas is as much our fault as it is the Divine's. As Idain would say, it is a good death to die helping one's friends."

Idain grinned. "I was saving that, you scoundrel."

"You'll find something else to say, likely."

Aeryn the dwarf crossed his arms. "Well? Can we move? We can talk on the road, and I can't pretend not to feel my arse freezing off like Marian."

Josephine laughed musically. "Oh, but she doesn't have an ass! It's all frozen off and flat now."

Marian gritted her teeth. "Thank you, Jo."

"Anything for you, lovely."

Evren was stunned. The half-elves were old, yes, at least in their seventies. They must've been young when they fought. Idain, Marian, and Aeryn would've had longer lifespans, yet they seemed to age with their companions. Whether that was time or the cruelty of all they'd seen, Evren didn't know. But the five in front of her radiated experience and drive.

She'd be a fool to turn them away.

"You have horses ready?" she asked.

Idain tried to mock offense. "I'm hurt that you think us unprepared."

"You are," Stefan grumbled. "The rest of us aren't."

"True enough. Might I ride with you? For old time's sake."

"Of course, but if you snore, I dumping you on the ground."

"I would never!"

The five scattered to their horses, and Aster watched them go with a strange expression.

"They're like Abraxas?" he asked.

She nodded. "I think they know it could've been any of them in his place."

"I think," Aster said, placing the reins of her horse in her hands, "that they want to save him as much as you do, or die trying."

"No one is dying this time," Evren swore.

Aster smiled, but she could tell he didn't believe her. By the time she mounted her horse and stowed her new bow in the saddle, she had repeated the oath so often it burned. She rode at the front of the army, Aster on one side and Mei on the other, marching into the darkness of the north where everything except certain death was unknown.

So many were going to die. Evren knew that. Still, she clung to the sounds of Idain and his friends chattering the night away behind them. She savored Mei and Aster's small talk, and the smells of horse and wyvern.

That and her fragile oath were all that grounded her as she rode to Abraxas for the last time.

36

Evren

The wild forest of Etherak's monsters loomed like a black shadow clinging to the foothills of the mountains and proudly presented a variety of Serevadian corpses at its edge.

There were about thirty, Evren counted from her horse. Behind her, Orenlion's army stilled anxiously at Mei's order. Hard days north had turned the chilly autumn weather to something bordering frigid, and the plumes of white breath from horses, wyvern, and soldiers could be seen like a signal fire. The wyverns weren't doing well in the cold, and it was all the Khama could do to keep them warm enough to fly. It was a concern Evren and Mei had muttered about most of the hard ride, but now seemed insignificant when faced with the litter of bodies before them.

Evren slid off her horse and took her bow with her. Her heavy cloak, now covering her armor, whispered on the frosted grass as she walked forward. Mei's uneven steps soon followed.

"Barrion always told me that Etherak's civility hung by a thread," Mei muttered as they drew up on the corpses. "I didn't think much of it until now. Friendly monsters killing for us, you think?"

Evren knelt beside one of the bodies. Besides the killing wound in his gut, the body was untouched.

"What monster kills without eating?" Evren asked. "No, this was a fight."

Mei nudged a body over on its back, her face impassive as she took in the crushed face and chest. "Different wounds on most. Yours has cuts. This one looks like he was done in with something heavy and blunt."

Evren's eyes hopped to each body in a line, noting the differing wounds on each. Some even had their necks twisted or their throats bruised from strangulation. Most damning and confusing were the ones who had no wounds at all, as if they'd simply fallen dead with no one touching them.

Evren craned her neck up to the forest as she crouched there. It was nothing like the Deep Wood, which was ancient and ominous, but only to those who didn't respect it. This forest was full of thick, black trees. Mostly pine, their green needles darker than she'd ever seen. Mist curled at the edges of their roots, twisting into odd shapes with each brush of the wind.

Unlike the Deep Wood, which had risen tall by being untouched, these trees seemed stooped and gnarled in their age. Tall enough that the horses and their riders would have no issue, but not enough to allow the mobility of the wyverns. It was big enough to hide an army, but it would also be hell to fight in.

"What are you doing, Abraxas?" Evren muttered.

Only a commotion from the army stirred her from her thoughts. She turned to stand as one of the Khama landed his wyvern close by. The young creature was shaking out her wings, hissing at every blade of frosted grass as if they were personally wronging her. Her rider looked just as miserable.

"Your Highness," Khama Gao said breathlessly. "We have, uh, a problem."

"Be more specific, Gao." Mei said. "What kind of problem?"

He winced, reigning in his wyvern before she could snap up one of the corpses. Then he pointed to the west. "A group of survivors from the coast have approached us. They're adamant to speak to whoever is in charge."

Evren and Mei exchanged a look. No Etherakian would mistake them for any other army but Orenlion's. But survivors meant information, and that was something they couldn't afford to turn away.

"I'll handle this with Aster," Evren offered. "Keep an eye out for whoever did this."

Mei pulled a face. "Fine."

Aster was already dismounting when Evren got to him. "Trouble?"

"Probably not," she said, leading him to where Gao pointed. Already the army was settling down, waiting for orders. None looked thrilled at the sight of the forest, but the bodies seemed to give them hope that there was something on their side. "Group of survivors from the coast. Said they wanted to speak to someone in charge."

Aster groaned. "And why did you know before me?"

"Because I was standing next to Mei."

"I don't understand." He shook his head. "I lead them just fine for weeks but the moment she arrives—"

"It's just habit, Aster," Evren said, patting his shoulder. "The Khama answered to her for a long time. And she technically still outranks you."

"Don't remind me."

Aster wasn't angry. Truly, Evren didn't believe he could ever be angry at Mei. She was a natural leader, and while it was a little unfair that the Khama immediately went to her before him, they all knew it wouldn't last. Once this was over, the Khama would likely never see Mei again. Authority wouldn't be an issue once everyone settled back into their respective borders.

That, more than anything, was the reason behind Aster's sullen mood.

Evren didn't have time to talk him through it like she wanted to. As they neared the edge of the army, a commotion was stirring the neat ranks into a thick crowd. She could scarcely see the bronze and jade wings of the wyverns over the helmets in her way. She shouldered her way through, suffering terrible looks until she was recognized and the crowd started to part, muttering apologies. Those apologies were drowned out by a flurry of raised voices from beyond the wyverns.

"I *don't* understand," a small voice was saying, shrill like a child straining to be heard. "They're heroes. You should let them through!"

One of the Khama started to rebuff before another voice, unfamiliar and gruff, piped up.

"Unless they been lyin'."

The shrill voice said, "Why would they lie, Miks? Don't be stupid."

"Honestly," a familiar voice said, crystal clear above all others. "I thought you'd remember me. Dashing, handsome, saved your bloody asses from a dragon *and* an undead army. You should be groveling rather than asking me who I am."

Everyone else faded away. Aster's gasp of surprise, the Khama's retorts, the strange child's laughter. None of it mattered because suddenly the world was a little brighter. As if she'd been wearing a black veil and the wind had tossed it back so she could see the world anew.

He was alive.

Evren dropped her bow. She was aware of Aster reaching for it and calling after her, but she was already gone. Shoving through the soldiers ahead of her with a frantic urgency that threatened to crawl up her throat and spill out of her. She couldn't even feel the cold air in her lungs, the armor beneath her hands.

He was alive.

The last of the soldiers fell away as Evren burst into the

scene. The two Khama startled away and retreated further when Aster's voice ordered them to, miles away it seemed.

And there he was. Standing in the middle of a strange group, sword on his hip and weathered blue coat just a tad more worn than she last saw it. He stood tall, proud, in front of these people. The gangly elven child to his side was yammering to him, but once his eyes found hers he wasn't listening anymore.

His laughter was the best thing she'd ever heard as he scooped her up into a tight embrace. His arms wrapped around her ribs, nearly crushing them as he squeezed her and lifted her off the ground. But she held on just as tightly, somewhere between laughing and crying as she took in the comforting smell of the sea from him.

"You're alive," she croaked in his ear. "You're *alive*."

Her feet hit the ground again, and he let her go just enough so that they could see each other. He was crying too, his golden eyes gleaming like wet coins. He looked a little older, quite a bit more tired, but lighter than she'd ever seen him.

"Of course I am," Sorin said with a brilliant smile. Genuine, blinding, lovely to see. "You got us out."

"I thought I . . ." she shook her head. "You weren't there with me. I thought you were dead. The spell went wrong, or something."

"Well . . ." He shrugged. "You did dump us in the middle of a massive storm in the bloody ocean, but luckily for us, I'm a fantastic swimmer."

Evren's heart leapt. "Us?"

He stepped back and swept an arm out to the crowd. That wasn't who he meant, though, and it was obvious once Sahar stepped forward. Wilder, rougher, but no less beautiful. She gave Evren a tired smile.

"We were stuck together," Sahar explained. "Thankfully for everyone involved."

Her little nod to Sorin sent his eyes crinkling with an even wider grin.

Evren didn't know what to say. She was ashamed that out of all those she grieved, she thought less of Sahar than the rest of them. But now that the last Ashen Bond was in front of her, she felt like she was going to cry again. Was it appropriate to hug her? Were they that close? She wasn't sure where the start.

"Don't forget about me!" the shrill voice piped up.

Sorin rolled his eyes, but it was all for show as he swept back to the elven girl with the shaved head.

"Yes, yes. This is Enola, our most annoying member in this band of misfits we rescued. Plug your ears because they *will* be bleeding by day's end. The rest of us can only pretend to hear normally now."

"Ha ha." Enola kicked at his shins, but missed as he side-stepped her.

"And this," Sorin presented Evren. "Is Evren Hanali."

Enola's entire demeanor changed. Sorin disappeared for a moment in her eyes as she turned to take Evren in with a stare that she didn't know what to make of. She looked at her like she was the answer to every question the little girl had ever had.

"You're the one," Enola said softly, which seemed like a normal talking level for everyone else. "You're like me. Sorin said."

Evren raised an eyebrow to Sorin. "What did you say?"

But Sorin didn't get a chance to speak because Enola was rushing up and pulling at her hands. It took her a moment to figure out the gloves, but once she did, they were tossed to the ground. Cold air prickled Evren's bare hands as Enola shoved hers up as a comparison.

Enola's were smaller than hers, tanner too. But there was no mistaking the scars along their palms. Evren's done by Gyda, and Enola's layered one on top of the other.

Evren's breath caught, and she looked up at Sorin for confirmation. Slowly he nodded.

"She's been dying to meet you," he said. "Wouldn't shut up about it."

Enola scowled, and the expression took over her small face in a comical way. "*You're* the one who wouldn't stop talking about your adventures. You started it!"

Then Enola was back on Evren, eyes bright. "Can you teach me? I want to be just like you! I can help with Serevadia, I swear. Just like I helped Sorin and Sahar."

"Um, I don't . . ."

Thankfully, Aster was there to save her. He picked back up her gloves and handed them to her. "I don't know if an army is any place for a young lady."

"Lady?" Enola drew back and tried to make herself taller. "I'm not a lady."

"But you *are* young." Sorin took her by the shoulder and dragged her back. "I told you to go to Tal-Mashad and wait for me there."

Enola crossed her arms. "Yeah, because that would've gone so well given the bloody army we saw marching in that direction."

"She's got a point," Sahar added

Sorin turned to Evren, exasperated. "I assume this isn't any safer?"

Evren shook her head. "Wildest corner of Etherak. Monsters abound. And an army of unknown number waiting inside."

Sahar shrugged. "Well, it's safer than going in on our own."

"What?" Evren exclaimed.

"Well, we need to go in anyway. Arke told us to."

Too much. It was all too much. Aster's hand on her shoulder kept her from tipping over. "Arke's here?"

"Eh, no," Sorin said. "He said he had to go find Sol in there, for whatever reason. He can magically poof wherever, by the way! I assumed he brought you here. No?"

Aster chuckled. "No."

"Well." He brightened. "I guess we know who waits for us inside. I've never been more excited to dive into a creepy forest before. Say, you don't have any spare rations or cloaks, do you?

This crew wasn't prepared for a cross-country trip into Etherak's frozen ball sack."

Evren spared a look at the survivors gathered behind Sorin. All Vasa, she realized as she took in their tattoos and darker skin. They weren't equipped for the weather, but judging by the set of their jaws, they weren't turning away from him any time soon.

Evren took Sorin's arm and led him a few feet away, the most amount of privacy they could manage.

"Sorin, this is an army," she whispered.

"I know."

"For an assault," she pressed. "There's going to be a massive battle, and I don't know how many are going to make it out."

"I mean, that's with every battle—"

"Those Vasa aren't soldiers!"

"I know." He was strangely firm now, more serious and mature than she was used to. Hells, what had happened to him? "They know too. They had the option to leave a while ago, but there's no place for them to go, Evvie. And I am the unfortunate hero that saved their lives, so they go where I go. And I go with you."

He winked, reminding her that however changed he was, he was still Sorin.

"Besides, are you going to turn away extra hands and some lightning? I thought not."

Evren sighed. More strangers walking into her mess. It would be her fault if they didn't come back out. And little Enola . . .

There wasn't a safe place in Etherak now. Nowhere she could send them that they could get to without running into enemies or monsters before they got to safety. Linston was too far, and likely packed to the brim. And made their choice already. Who was she to take that from them?

"All right," she said. "We don't have an abundance of supplies, but I'll see what I can do."

"Great!"

Sorin's arm was slung around her shoulders, and they walked back to the strange mixing of people side by side. Evren didn't dare hope, not after all that she'd been through. But she let herself sink into Sorin's warmth, let herself relax a little.

Aster was already getting Sorin's band of Vasa cloaked and fed with Sahar's help. The two worked smoothly despite having never met, with Enola trailing loudly behind asking if she could ride the lizards instead of the horses.

It was a strange sight at the edge of the unknown. Evren drank it in, afraid to lose the small smiles of relief and the already budding camaraderie between the sailors and the Khama.

"Can I ride with you?" Sorin asked. "I have a lot to tell you."

She smiled. "As do I. Which is a good thing, because we have no horses to spare. I was going to make you walk."

"HA!" He threw his head back, dreads brushing both of their shoulders. "You say that as if it would make a difference. I can't feel my feet."

Evren smiled wider, leading him through the army and wondering how he and Idain would get along if she locked the two of them in a room together.

~

~

IT WAS NOON, and many of the branches were bare, yet little light reached the army as they picked their way through the forest. Evren rode in the front with Sorin sitting behind her. She didn't need to track, because Serevadia's army left two trails.

One, the obvious trampled underbrush of a large army moving in small quarters.

Two, the trail of increasingly warm bodies they found. Whoever was picking off the Serevadians was doing so without hesitation, and as they drew closer Evren found a strange knot of anxiety and excitement in her stomach. Both she and Sorin suspected Sol.

Dampening that, however, was Sorin's tale of how he got to her.

She let go of his scarred hand, swallowing the fury that hadn't subsided since he explained what happened.

"I should've been there," she murmured. "We all should've been there."

Behind her Sorin shrugged. "I'm glad you weren't actually. I needed to do that on my own, and Gyda would've . . . Shit, sorry. I keep forgetting."

Evren didn't. She couldn't. Because it was a miracle that Sorin and Sahar were alive, and that Arke was getting Sol right now. But there was one person who wouldn't have survived because she fueled the spell. Arke hadn't mentioned Gyda living to Sorin.

Evren tried not to let that bitterness overcome her. She was getting her people back, and it was more than enough. But her half of the heart kept beating, searching for the other half forever missing from her. It was hard to ignore the pain when it came to her every heartbeat.

"She would've killed Vayne for you," Evren finished for him, thumbing the reins. She focused between the horse's ears, the soft rocking of its gate through the trees. "You're right. You needed to do that on your own."

"I had Sahar," he said. "I wasn't completely alone."

Sahar was sharing a stallion with Mei, chatting seriously over the state of things in Terevas. There was a lot of information to go over, and Aster would occasionally pipe up with his own details. It was strange to see them together. Evren spent so long with them on opposite points of her life that it was surreal to watch them talk.

Enola rode with Josephine, and the two hadn't stopped talking since paired together. The other Champions took a shine to the young elf as well, showering her with varying degrees of attention that Enola was soaking up.

The rest of Sorin's crew were scattered around the army. The older and injured rode with other riders, but most preferred to walk. The pace of the army had slowed down enough for that.

Again, it struck Evren that these were two peoples who would never talk in different circumstances. Orenlion hadn't left the Deep Wood since it was founded. Vasa rarely traveled so far inland. Now they were marching together with Etherak's old Champions to what could mean certain death.

"Whatever happens in here," Evren said. "At least we did this."

Sorin hummed in agreement. "Beginning of something like unity, yeah?"

She smiled. "Something like it."

There was nothing but the marching army to break the silence. For all its apparent wildness, the forest seemed devoid of life. Heavy air had no bird song or chattering animals to fill it. There were no prowling predators, although Evren kept her eyes peeled anyway. The silence was oppressive, unnerving, as if the whole forest was a mass grave.

Then something loud and boisterous cut through the air. A voice, triumphant.

Aster's raised hand stopped the whole army, from him to the commanders down to the foot soldiers. He raised an eyebrow at Evren and she nodded. She'd heard it too.

"No chance we could gallop through this forest?" Sorin whispered.

Evren leaned over the saddle. The ground was pretty even. Roots were sparse now, as if the beginnings of a trail were starting to form.

"No galloping, but a little faster. Hold on." She signaled to Aster that she was going to scout ahead and didn't give him a chance to argue before she was kicking her horse into a jolting trot that left Sorin yelping. When she deemed it safe enough, she urged the horse a little faster. The canter was smoother, swifter, but not so reckless as a full gallop.

The previously still air now stung her cheeks. Sorin's arms were tight around her torso as he held on and Evren kept the reins firm to avoid any dips and rising that would put the horse at risk. Amazingly there were few. The forest blurred by in blacks and grays, but a riot of watercolor emotions were mixing inside Evren.

Whatever was ahead could be another piece of her. Another jagged fragment to her broken whole.

The smell of a battle hit first, and Evren barely reined her horse to a stop to keep from tripping over a Serevadian body. Fresh, blood still leaking out. Through all three of their huffing breaths, Sorin's a little louder than the horse's, voices carried.

"Fifteen! Ha! Better than last time, admit it."

"I'll do nothing of the sort. That tenth kill was *mine* before you stole it."

"You want it back? Still won't help you. I got more this time 'round."

"What a gentlemanly offer! Piss off."

Evren and Sorin were scrambling to dismount in a way that made the horse nicker with anxiety. There were more flopping limbs on Sorin's end, but Evren's haste didn't help. It was a miracle they ended up on their feet at all, reins in Evren's hand.

Sorin took off without her, and Evren cursed as she led the horse through the bodies. There were a *lot*. They spanned the gaps of the trees, all in varying states of death. The closer she got to the voices, the more she saw figures moving through the bodies. Dwarves, dirty and bloody, making sure everyone that should be dead stayed that way. They paid her no mind at all.

The arguing ahead was cut off by a squeal of delight, and that was when Evren decided that the horse was well trained enough to be on its own. She dropped the reins and ran forward.

Cutting between two trees she was met with the sight of Sorin practically folded around Sol as he hugged her. Something large and furry circled around them, barking excitedly. Behind them, a familiar burned dwarf shook his head and cleaned off his bloody hammer.

Sol's blue eyes found her and she stretched out her hand. Evren needed no other invitation before crashing into them both, the worg sniffing and licking every face. At some point they were on the ground, and Sorin was a blubbering mess scratching behind the worg's ears and getting his face covered in slobber.

Sol gripped Evren's hand, eyes bright. "I missed you."

An understatement. They both felt it. But those words meant the world, even if Sol looked worse for wear and like she hadn't slept in weeks, she was one of the best things Evren had seen in her life.

"You done cuddlin'?" Came a raspy voice. "Cause I'm not getting' in that again."

Arke picked through the bodies toward them. Evren was on her knees and pulling him into a hug before he could wiggle away.

Claws digging in her arms, grumbling in her ears, yet he didn't pull away. She'd never been happier to see the goblin before now.

Little by little he relaxed.

"You're not mad?" he whispered.

She sniffed back her tears. "No. Not if you're here. Everyone is here, and it was worth it."

Because it was, wasn't it? This was what Gyda would've wanted.

This time Arke pulled away and looked at her seriously. "I need you to do somethin' for me." He pointed into the trees, farther with more bodies. "Walk there for a while. Don't come back until you see it."

"See what?"

Goblin grins were so unnerving until you got used to them,

and then they were as brilliant as the sun itself. "You'll see. The answer to all our problems."

Evren got up reluctantly. Sol nudged her forward with a thumbs up. Sorin was whispering furiously about why he wasn't going to see what was in the woods, both Sol and Arke shushing him. When she passed him, Karas gave her a respectful nod.

"Mutt," he greeted.

"Murderer," she answered.

And then they smiled and parted ways.

Further in, the trees were clearing. The bodies weren't. But with every step they had less blood and more invisible wounds. As if they dropped dead without anyone touching them. As these piled up, she could smell woodsmoke and see the outline of a large house through the trees.

But before that was a better sight. An impossible, beautiful sight.

Gyda stood on the battlefield, pulling her glowing sword out of the last Serevadian. Where the blade had once been was nothing but glowing green energy that dissipated with a flick of her wrist. Her clan weave was bright against the dull grays and blacks of the forest, and she blew a strand of snow-white hair out of her face as she stepped away from the body.

And met Evren's eyes.

The click of two pieces together. The relief. The sigh. The pulling at her heart finally coming to a rest because her feet had finally, *finally* led her back home.

Evren ran to Gyda, like she had after the blizzard. Only this time she didn't stop, afraid of what would happen if she embraced her. This time she leapt into her arms with a cry that meant, 'I have been without you for too long and can't bear it another moment.'

Gyda dropped her hilt and held her. Evren's legs were around her waist and her lips were crashing into Gyda's with the desperate fervor that only came from two souls who thought they would never see each other again.

Their hearts beat in time, separated by scars, bone, and armor, but whole once again.

Evren pulled away to catch her breath, Gyda's lips following hers for a moment. She held her lover's face, blinking away tears for the third time today.

"You're here," she whispered to Gyda, words that not even the closest branches could snatch away.

Gyda carefully brushed away her tears with one hand, supporting her easily with the other arm. She didn't blink, taking all of Evren in as if she was afraid she'd miss a moment and regret it forever.

"I'm here," she promised in a voice that Evren didn't think she would ever hear again. She leaned forward until their foreheads were touching, their breaths mixing in twin clouds of white between them. "And to finish what I was saying before, I love you as well. Never doubt it."

37

Arke

The tavern in the middle of the woods was a surprise to everyone, Arke included. Yeah, he had quite a bit more information than everyone else, but this was weird. Not the normal Etherak weird either, although the two-story building *looked* Etherakian. It also looked warm and inviting, but looks could be deceiving.

"*The Wayfinder's Rest*," Sorin sounded out. "Huh."

The Wandering Sols, whole again minus one member, stood in a tight line as if they were afraid to lose sight of each other. Something Arke wished he could be grumpy about, but he just couldn't find the heart. He'd done it. He'd gotten them back together. The only problem now was what lay further in the forest, and the tavern in front of them.

No one said anything for a while. The army, bolstered with Vasa and dwarves, tittered anxiously behind them.

"Well." Sorin shrugged. "It's getting late. We might as well."

He took a step forward, and in an impressive show of synchronization Arke grabbed the edge of his coat, Sahar took his shoulder, and both pulled him back. Arke snickered under his breath as the human shook them off, scowling.

"What? I'm hungry!"

"Since when do we trust random taverns in the middle of the woods?" Sahar asked.

Arke grunted. Seemed like a Fey trick. Did Etherak have Fey?

"Since the sun is going down and we'll have to camp anyway," Sorin argued, then turned back to Aster and Mei. "Right?"

Mei shrugged. "It would be best to settle down. But the army won't fit in that."

"Oh, well, bummer. We will."

Sol elbowed him. "Sorin, that's rude."

"What's rude is being cold and hungry and not going into the warm tavern. Could it be that bad to go check it out?"

"Yes," said Evren and Gyda in unison.

Aster cleared his throat loudly, pulling everyone's attention away from the tavern and to him. Shao probably would've been better suited to command an army, but Aster wasn't anything like the soft man they met before. More than the scar had roughed him up. Arke just hoped it was enough for the end of everything.

"We'll camp here," Aster confirmed. "Away from the tavern, but I'll have people keep an eye on it. It's getting too dark to find a better place, and we need to set up quickly, lest Abraxas or the forest itself attacks."

Evren nodded, pressing her lips together to hold back what could be another suggestion. Her eyes flicked back to the tavern and Arke wanted to curse. She wanted to go in too.

"We're sleeping in camp with everyone else," Sol proclaimed over Sorin's loud groans of protest.

Almost as if it was at her word, the army started scattering and settling down for the night. Arke could see Mei picking out the watches for the night from the different Khama, rotating the schedule so everyone got rest and kept the wyverns active and warm. Sol's dwarves looked to Karas for instructions but were soon helping clear the ground of dead things so they could pitch tents. The Vasa looked confused and a little useless until one of the elves asked for some help with firewood, and then they set to work. Except for the little girl, who was struggling off the horse of one of the Champions.

The five rode up to the Wandering Sols as Enola bounced until she was between Sorin and Sahar. Evren gave the half-elf riding behind the scarred man a wide smile.

"Trying out the tavern, Idain?"

He shook his head vigorously. "Divines no! Drinking and comfort aren't in my vocabulary. Any of ours, really."

"Maybe not yours," the redhead muttered, but didn't seem upset.

Evren frowned then. "Where are you going?"

"We're scouting ahead." Idain said. "Ah, don't make that face! We just want to see how far Serevadia's defenses go. If our new dwarven friends are to be believed, then they've been pushed back deeper than they expected. This is good. We can discreetly take a peek and report back what we find. Maybe even cause some mayhem while we're at it."

"In the dark?" Sol asked. "Isn't that dangerous?"

Idain gave her a wicked smile that meant it was likely at the bottom of the list of dangerous things he'd done.

"We're veterans of wars like these. We'll manage and be back before sunrise."

Evren hesitated, and the scarred Champion just shook his head.

"Don't try to change our mind, Ironblood. This has already been decided."

The Champions nodded amongst themselves. Arke didn't know how to feel around them. They were all so different, yet when he wasn't looking at them they held the same heavy presence as Abraxas. As if the weight of the souls they'd taken was dragging behind them and compressing all the air. Something he thought was unique to his old friend now radiated from these five newcomers. Were there more like them wandering Eith? Did they suffer like Abraxas did?

"All right." Evren nodded. "You've got more experience than the rest of us. Just be careful."

"We're always careful," Idain said.

The dwarf snorted. "The missing three toes on your left foot say otherwise."

"Please leave my toes out of this."

"Hard not to when you left them back in Vernes."

They bickered, riding away into the shadows. The Wandering Sols watched them until the mists finally ate the last of their cloaks and the hooves of their horses, and their voices couldn't be heard again.

There were maybe five whole seconds of stillness before Sorin exploded.

"I'mgoinginthetavernyoucan'tstopme!"

Before any of them could react, he was bolting off with feet swifter than even Arke remembered. Enola squeaked with glee and took off after him. The worg didn't wait, nipping at her heels while the rest of them were caught between exasperation and anger.

"I forgot," Gyda said slowly. "How quiet things were without him."

The door of *The Wayfinder's Rest* slammed shut behind the three. Sahar started rubbing her temples, a sentiment Arke shared. He loved the boy, but damn his head was throbbing. From the tears? Nah, he didn't cry. Much. It was a long-ass day. When was the last time he slept? Ate? Had it really been all the way back with Unnethen?

Slowly he started trudging towards the door.

"Arke!" Evren called. "What are you doing?"

"I'm fuckin' hungry!"

Also, he wasn't going to lose Sorin. Not again.

He didn't wait for the others to follow him, but as he scowled up at the tall doorknob, contemplating how he was going to get it open, Gyda's hand came from above and twisted it open. He grunted his thanks, shouldering in with the rest of the Wandering Sols and Sahar trailing behind.

Inside was . . . well, a tavern. All warm wood and flickering candles. A roaring fire warmed the place up from the middle, and mostly empty tables sat in clean, if scuffed, condition. Stairs twisted in the back, leading up to the second floor, and to the right was a wide bar. Behind that was a large man that looked like a human sized dwarf. Broad chested, black hair tied away from his face and a long black beard peppered with gray. He had a kind smile hidden behind his beard; Arke could only tell he was smiling by the way his eyes crinkled.

"Welcome!" The man held his beefy arms out. "Your friends mentioned you'd be joining."

Arke spied Sorin and Enola in the corner booth, trying to find a way to get the worg to sit in the chair, and failing miserably.

"Strange place for a tavern," Evren said smoothly.

"Strange place for an army," the man said, picking up tankards and setting them out in a row. "Or two, if the forest tells me correctly."

Sol's hands went for her daggers. "You speak to the forest?"

"As does any sane man who settles down here. Will you listen to my explanation before you stab me, adventurer?"

Sol froze but didn't drop her hands from the hilts. Arke, in turn, narrowed his eyes at the man. He didn't give off bad energy, but he didn't get this far by trusting strangers, especially friendly ones.

"What's your name?" Arke asked, itching for his spellbook.

"Aillard," the man proudly proclaimed. "You types aren't the trusting sort. I serve enough of you to know." He laughed. "*The Wayfinder's Rest* is special. I didn't build it, the forest did. It's a haven for those who wander here. You're safe. And, by extension, so are your allies camped outside."

"Why should we trust you?" Gyda asked the golden question.

"Because you're hungry, thirsty, and tired. Because the old age of Eith is ending, and I can't do anything other than provide a small comfort to those who are fighting through it."

And there it was. Damn, Arke should've seen it earlier. He relaxed a little, waving Gyda down.

"It's all right. He's cursed."

Sahar jumped out of her daze from the fire. "Cursed? How is that good?"

Aillard laughed. "Well, I get to spend my days in constant warmth and comfort, doing what I love and helping people who need it. I don't call that a curse."

"But you can't leave this place," Arke pressed, and Aillard shook his head. "You're bound to it."

"Someone has to keep a fire going at the darkest edge of the world." He shrugged. "I've heard there are more like me. Havens for people like you in dangerous places that would otherwise kill. But my tavern is by far the best. Care for an ale?"

Evren shifted from foot to foot, chewing on the new information. She cocked her head towards Sol, such a common action between the two, yet seeing it again made Arke feel dizzy. Sol eyed Aillard before shrugging.

"He's not lying from what I can tell."

"Could be a good liar," Arke muttered.

"Or exactly what I say that I am," Aillard said. "You don't have to stay here, but no harm will come to you if you do. And, if it does, you're more than welcome to have my head."

"Good enough for me," Gyda said and herded everyone to Sorin's corner table.

It wasn't quite big enough for everyone. The worg had to sit at Sorin's feet, and Enola pulled up an extra chair, her bony elbows propped up on the table, again between Sorin and

Sahar. Evren and Gyda might as well have shared a chair for as close as they were, but Arke couldn't blame them. That gnawing guilt that his own selfishness had forced Evren to kill Gyda was subsiding. No matter the outcome, the choice had been made. But neither woman seemed to care enough to glare at him.

Without being asked, Aillard came out with steaming bowls of hearty stew and crusty bread. There was a platter of cheeses as well, and plenty to drink, be it water, ale, or wine. Aillard mentioned setting food out for those outside, as well as extra blankets and other comfort items. How he had enough for that many people, Arke didn't want to know. Magic was magic, and he was too tired to pick it apart.

So he ate the spicy stew that had been cooked faster than it seemed possible and devoured the cheeses. He tried the different drinks before landing on a dark ale, happily sipping as he was warmed from the inside out. And over the food and drink, in between little breaks of much needed laughter, they all told the stories of how they got back to each other.

Evren's was no surprise. She had brought an army, which Arke hoped they wouldn't need.

Sol's was troubling. Unnerving. He'd been *right there*. He could've gotten her out. But he'd been so wrapped up in Abraxas that he'd completely missed it.

Gyda told her story, and Arke kept the fact that the beast she killed was his accident by downing most of his ale. Still, the fuzzy feeling in his head didn't erase the nagging sensation that she was hiding something. Something important.

Sorin's, of course, made him hurt. All the while he couldn't stop staring at that scarred hand. No matter how much Sorin said he was glad he'd handled Vayne nearly on his own, Arke was pissed. At Vayne, at himself. He should've been there. He should've—

"What about you?" Evren asked him. "Did you get Tolk?"

"And how have you been popping up out of nowhere?"

Sahar asked, a little slurred. Too much wine. Her cheeks were a warm rosy shade.

Arke let go of his tankard, which had scratch marks in it, thanks to Vayne fucking Knave. "New magic. Kind of difficult to explain."

Sol rolled her eyes. "Try us."

He blinked at her, sighed, and then began. "So, souls are power, right? Well, there's an in-between realm that separates Eith from the Divines, the Hells, the Brightlands, and all that shit. It's made up of souls, pure power. And I can manipulate it. Make portals. Learn shit."

Sol sat back. "Okay, I'm so glad I never had any talent for magic. That was simplified, yes?"

"For you dumb ones."

"Right, and I can still barely wrap my head around it."

Arke smirked. "I didn't either, until I got thrown in and had to learn myself. Tough shit, but it got me what I needed."

Gyda raised an eyebrow. "Which is . . .?"

"I know what Abraxas is doing next."

The somewhat jovial tone was bogged down. Sorin slumped back in his seat, eyes distant. Sol fiddled with her nose ring and reached for another piece of cheese. Evren and Gyda just shared looks as if thoughts came with the 'half-a-heart' package.

Evren was the first to speak. "He wants to bring back his gods. We know that."

"But you don't know how." Arke raised a claw in the air and then pointed at himself. "I do."

"Please elaborate." Sol folded her now cheeseless hands together on top of the table.

Arke scooted to the edge of his seat, catching everyone but Sorin's attention. The boy was still staring off into the distance, and Arke hoped he was listening.

"Get ready because I barely understand this shit," Arke warned them. "Essentially, it goes back to Vernes."

"Always Vernes," Evren muttered.

Arke nodded. "They banished the Divines, and I know how they did it. It's a combination of a few things. One, location. Apparently there's places in Eith where the Aether is particularly thin. Malleable. Vernes had a spot, and so I'm guessin' that Abraxas is headin' towards Etherak's."

Evren nodded and motioned for him to continue.

"Two, those weird-ass artifacts we been seein'. Get them to touch and somethin' happens. Somethin' bad. Pretty sure it cleaves a hole in the Aether, the soul realm, to allow for molding, you know?"

"Not really," Gyda muttered.

"Abraxas has one of these things, the sword. He needs two."

Gyda stilled then, her brows furrowing. "That's why he was looking for the Eternity Dagger back at the palace."

Arke nodded. "Yeah."

Sahar frowned. "Well, that's easy to fix. Assuming that the two used by Vernes were either destroyed or locked away, he can't have gotten those in such a short time. And the Eternity Dagger is lost."

"No, it's not," Gyda said. "I have it."

Evren sat straight up. "What?"

"I don't know why," Gyda said. "But I do. Abraxas knew it. I can . . . call it, if I need to. The dagger was passed between us so many times in the Deep Wood, it must've been natural for Abraxas to accidentally send it to me."

"But you never had it on you!" Sol protested. "If you had, we could've gone back for him."

Arke shook his head. "None of us can control that thing. It wouldn't have helped."

"Well, it certainly won't help if we bring it to Abraxas," Sahar said.

Gyda scowled. "I won't give it to him. If need be, we do the same thing we did with Nerezza. Keep it out of his hands."

"He'll focus on you, love," Evren said softly.

"I'm ready this time."

Arke snapped his fingers to get everyone's attention. "I ain't done. Third and final thing goes back to souls. You wanna mess with the existing souls? You're gonna leave gaps in the Aether. Tears where things can come through. So, you need fresh souls to do it properly. Vernes used nine hundred and ninety-nine willing souls to banish the Divines. Emphasis on the willing part. Apparently that makes a difference."

Across the table, Sol's eyes went wide. "Oh, sweet Jalaa, *that's* what the three thousand was for! The number I saw at Stone's End, remember? That has to be what he's planning."

"Fucking hells." Evren rubbed a hand over her face. "He's using his army as fuel. I'd bet gold on the fact that Velcros doesn't know. None of them do."

"I ain't feelin' bad for that asshole," Arke growled.

"Couldn't this affect our army too?" Sol asked. "If, on the off-chance Abraxas does get the dagger from Gyda, and causes this mass event that destroys a massive area, that's everyone. Including our people. Unwilling sacrifices pile up in those numbers to be just as powerful as a smaller pile of willing ones."

"Something he's counting on, I think," Evren said softly. She pushed her ale away, barely touched. "We need to talk about how we're doing this."

Finally, Sorin looked up out of his daze, but only at Evren. "You don't want to kill him."

Evren shook her head and Arke nearly sighed in relief. Maybe he wouldn't have to. Maybe he could fix all of this in some impossible way, and he wouldn't have to drag Abraxas's soul with him forever.

Evren's eyes were wet in the firelight, gleaming and serious. "I promised him, Sorin. At the beginning. Before we were even the Wandering Sols, I swore I could bring him back if he strayed too far."

"Evren," Sol said softly. "We tried. Gyda did, I did."

"So did I," Arke said. "Didn't help."

"But Sorin and I haven't," Evren pressed. "And maybe with all of us he'll see the error in his ways."

All the warmth faded out of Sahar. It was as if the wine had burned out of her, leaving nothing but a cool, calm, anger that made Arke want to shrink back as she leveled Evren a glare across the table.

"You want to give Abraxas a second chance?" she asked. "After waging war on the entire world? How many lives has he claimed? In Terevas, Etherak, and Dirn-Darahl alone? After everything he did to Gyda, you'd still try?"

"We gave Nerezza a chance, didn't we?" Evren asked, not a touch too harsh but the undertone was heard, if not said.

Nerezza started this. Just because she isn't alive to see it doesn't make it any less true.

Sahar stood up abruptly. "I need some air."

Then she was marching out of the tavern, snatching her coat off the bar and heading out into the cold. Sorin started to follow but Enola beat him to it, stuffing more bread in her mouth before scampering out the tavern.

Sorin slumped back in his chair. "She's got a point."

Evren started to protest. "Sorin—"

"I know, Evvie," he said, sounding exhausted. "I want to save him too. I think we might have a chance. But no matter how this ends, we need to understand that he's gone. I hate it, but either he dies on the battlefield or Eith unites to take his head off. And we'll be the people delivering him to them."

"Assuming we can stop him," Gyda said. "If the Divines do come back . . ."

Arke smiled ruefully, feeling the cooler air on his teeth. "Leave that to me."

No one asked what his plan might be. No one asked Gyda why she would risk the dagger or how Sorin planned to talk Abraxas down. Because they'd done this long enough, knew each other well enough, that when the time came they would be ready.

They trusted each other, when all else failed. It was all they had in the beginning, and it was all that mattered now.

The door opened again and they all jumped, even Gyda, expecting to see Sahar. Instead, it was just Karas stomping off the cold.

"Well, don't look so damn disappointed to see me," the dwarf muttered, snagging a drink Aillard held out without question.

Sorin sniffed. "We were expecting someone prettier."

"Everyone pretty is outside freezin' their asses off."

"Oh?" Sol leaned back in her chair. "Everyone?"

Karas, who'd been halfway to the table, stopped in his tracks. He muttered something foul into his cup, and Arke could just see the reddening of his cheeks.

Sol cupped her ear. "Sorry, what was that?"

"Not everyone, damn it," Karas said louder, and Sol's face split into a grin far too warm and bright for Karas.

Arke exchanged bewildered glances with everyone at the table. They were seeing it too, this weird chemistry between the dwarves. Hells, they used to joke about Sol's taste in men, but she really just had *awful* taste.

Or maybe beggars couldn't be choosers. Who was he to judge?

Sol hopped down from her chair, taking her tankard with her. "Well, I don't know about the rest of you, but I plan on living tonight. Hot bath, a soft bed. Good company. Who knows if we'll have the chance again. You have all that, right, Aillard?"

"That's what the second floor is for," the human said with a grin.

"Great!" she chirped, and stepped up to Karas. "I'm going to finish my drink at the bar. You're welcome to join me. And then we can see how the rest of the night goes."

Karas opened his mouth to say something and caught the

rest of the Wandering Sols staring at him. He scowled and turned his back on them.

"Yeah, let's see."

She allowed him to take her to the bar. "Let's see . . .?"

"Let's see, my lady."

Evren nearly snorted up her ale when she heard that and spent the next several seconds trying not to choke while Gyda rubbed her back. Sorin watched the two of them walk off with an unhinged jaw. Arke was seriously considering how Aillard would react to fried dwarf in his tavern. The only thing that stopped him was how pissed Sol would be.

"Leave her to her bad decisions," he said.

"But—"

"Leave it, Sorin."

Evren finally stopped choking and wiped away a few tears. "Oh, hells. The world really is ending, isn't it?"

"Not yet, Evvie. I mean, they haven't done anything *yet*."

Gyda hummed to herself, watching the two at the bar. Karas put his hand on Sol's back and Arke was sure he and Gyda were of like mind, feeling like now was a good time to throw something. If not a fireball, then a tankard or a piece of bread. Instead, she stood up and pulled Evren to her feet.

"She's got the right idea," Gyda said. "A bath sounds excellent."

Sorin thunked his head on the table as Evren hurriedly agreed. They weren't even at the stairs before Aillard was tossing them a key, which Evren caught, and then it was like they couldn't get up fast enough. How *that* was on three of his friends' minds right before a battle that could change Eith forever was beyond him. But that was part of the reason Arke left Tolk and his clan. He just . . . didn't fit. Not like that.

"You're going to leave too, aren't you?" Sorin asked, and Arke didn't miss the edge of bitterness on his words.

Arke hesitated. "For a little bit. I gotta say a few things. To Tolk. I don't know if I'll see him again. But I'll be back."

"Sure." Sorin propped his head up on his chin, and blew a crumb out of his way. "I'll be here."

Arke was leaving him for Tolk, again. But he was coming right back. He swallowed his guilt, now familiar with the taste hurt, never comfortable with it, and hopped down. He waved at Sol, at Aillard, and at Sorin. And before he reached the door, he was already gone.

38

Evren

"This is ridiculous, Evren," Gyda was saying. "You don't have to do this."

Evren rolled her eyes and tested the water one more time. Warm enough for her. Maybe too warm for Gyda? Any colder and those nice smelling bath salts Aillard had left out wouldn't dissolve though. It felt like a weird thing to worry about with what they were about to face, but she latched onto it. Better this than thinking about Abraxas or the Divines.

"Test the water?" Evren asked. "I don't want it to be too warm."

Gyda sighed as she kicked off her boots. "I don't need—"

Evren flicked water on her and the woman shook her head in bewilderment. Good, that kept her from arguing.

"You've been through hell," Evren said. "I thought I lost you. For once in your life, let me take care of you and *get in the tub.*"

Gyda smiled, almost like she was about to challenge Evren, but obeyed. As she started shucking off her layers, Evren busied herself with the bath salts and getting the soaps and shampoos ready. Also, a fresh basin of water, a comb, and a stool. Hells, Aillard really had everything here, didn't he?

Their room was large by tavern standards. The tub was a large thing made of copper and filled with steamy water. A good-sized bed tucked in the corner, a dresser they'd already filled with their weapons and armor, and a worn, but clean rug covering most of the floor. The window by the bed was covered with curtains, which Evren was thankful for. She felt guilty enough sleeping warmly on a bed while soldiers and wyverns shivered outside. Maybe she could get the wyverns inside . . .

The water splashed as Gyda settled into the water, sighing softly. Evren smiled, letting her get settled and watching all her taut muscles start to relax. Her feet were propped up at the end of the tub to let her sink down further, and despite the large size of the tub Gyda was still bigger.

"Better?" Evren asked.

Gyda merely hummed a reply, eyes closed and white hair uncovered, spilling over the lip of the tub.

Evren caught a white strand between her fingers. It was a strange mix of emotions seeing it. She missed the deep red, and the white only served to remind her of how much she'd stolen from Gyda. But, as with every time she let down her hair in front of her, Evren was overcome by the trust, the love, that came with such a gesture. Small, maybe. Ridiculous to some. But to her it was everything.

Evren leaned down to kiss her forehead. "Let me wash your hair?"

Gyda cracked a smile. "Do I have a choice?"

"Not really, no." Evren laughed. "Dunk your head, please."

Gyda peaked open one eye. "When this is done, we get to do something my way, right?"

"As if you don't love this."

"I do." Gyda's eyes twinkled. "Truly."

"Then yes. And dunk."

Gyda obliged, dipping her hair in the water enough to wet it while Evren settled on the stool. She took out the shampoo and managed to contain her sound of surprise as warm water hit her bare feet when Gyda settled back against the edge.

The water did nothing to lessen the tone of the white. If anything, it seemed even more brilliant. The wet strands were warm in her hands as she took them and lathered the sweet-smelling shampoo. Not the scent she would've chosen for Gyda, but it mixed with the steam from the bath perfectly.

She worked her fingers diligently through every strand, massaging the scalp as she went. Soon Gyda's relaxed smirk had slipped into something softer as she leaned into Evren's fingers. The steady rhythm scrubbed away all the oil and dirt from her travels, bit by bit, until her hands were full of more suds than hair.

"We're rinsing," Evren announced, and gently pushed Gyda up from her resting position. She rinsed her hands in the bath before taking the pitcher of fresh water and washing the suds out of every strand of hair. With half the pitcher left, she set it down and pressed Gyda back down. She took up the bottle of creamy rinse, which might help with the brittleness of Gyda's hair. At the very least it would let her spend more time like this.

Evren dumped it in her palms and began smoothing it over Gyda's hair. Only then did she feel the silence.

"Don't," Gyda muttered, not opening her eyes.

"Don't what?"

"Don't apologize."

Evren scowled. "I wasn't."

"You were."

"Fine. But can you blame me?" Evren rinsed her hands again and picked up the wooden comb. Starting from the ends, she started to detangle Gyda's hair. "You nearly died because of me."

"You saved all of us," Gyda corrected. "And you dumped me at the feet of the beginning of my bloodline. Do you know how many Ikedree meet a giant in their lifetime?"

"No."

"None."

Evren sighed. She worked a nasty knot carefully, not wanting tug on her scalp. "I didn't even do that on purpose. If I had control I certainly wouldn't have dropped Sorin in the middle of the fucking ocean."

"He's fine now. Sahar too."

Evren didn't want to think about Sahar. Didn't want to remember the hurt in her eyes, because she couldn't fault her for feeling that way. No one had mourned Nerezza but Sahar. No one would. And yet, there they all were, discussing how to keep Abraxas alive despite the mounting war crimes he was collecting.

Evren wouldn't back down. She had to try to bring him back. After all, he'd done the same for her when she was heartless. And she'd done the same for Gyda. What kind of woman would Evren be if she didn't bloody herself for those she loved?

"I don't know how this will end," Evren said softly. "All I know is that I don't want to have all my words rushed on the battlefield. We've done it before and, frankly, I'm tired of it. I don't want to lose, but more than anything I don't want to lose you. Is it so wrong to want a future for us?"

The water was still, and so was Gyda's face. For a while Evren was afraid she wouldn't speak.

"No, it's not wrong," Gyda said finally. "I want it too."

Evren sighed in relief. But she couldn't imagine her life beyond adventuring. It felt like it consumed her. It was her whole being, her whole reason for fighting. If she wasn't Evren Worm-Rider, the Ironblood, then what was she?

The knot finally came free, strands slippery with the rinse between her fingers. She combed through, making sure it was evenly spread. No, she couldn't picture a future beyond the fight tomorrow, and that irritated her. But maybe that was a good thing. If she imagined a good thing and it was taken away, it would hurt all that much more. And if she lost Gyda again . . .

Gyda's hand wrapped around hers and stilled the comb. She

turned in the water until she was on her side, looking up at Evren.

"We don't talk about the future," Gyda said. "Not now. But we promise each other one thing before tomorrow."

Evren swallowed the sudden dryness in her throat. "One thing."

"Promise me," Gyda squeezed her hand, her eyes harder and more serious than Evren had ever seen. "Promise me that if it comes down between you and him, you choose yourself."

Evren's breath caught. "I can't—"

"You swore to him, I know. But I know you, Evren Hanali. I know you would bleed yourself dry for us. You are a woman of sacrifices, and that is a heavy legacy you shouldn't have to bear. Promise to save a little blood for yourself." She kissed her palm, warm lips against slick skin, her eyes never breaking contact. "For me."

Evren had to force herself to keep breathing, to remember what she was swearing to as Gyda's lips tore any useful thoughts right out of her skull.

"Okay," Evren nodded. "I swear."

Gyda's grin was sharp, playful, a complete switch from the serious tone moments before.

"Good."

In moments she had Evren off the stool and crashing into the water with her. Evren didn't even have time to scream, because if she did she would've ended up with a mouthful of soapy water. She landed in the water on top of Gyda as she laughed. The warm bath seeped into her trousers and shirt, and Evren shook water out of her eyes.

"Gyda!"

She was just laughing, and damn it was a beautiful sound. Evren tried to sit up, but found her hands slipping on Gyda's wet shoulders, their legs tangling together underneath the water.

Gyda sat up, getting Evren out of her awkward position and sliding her into her lap. The water lapped at Evren's torso, tugging at her shirt. Her pants were well and truly soaked now, and her vision was filled with Gyda. Beautiful, enduring, *hers*.

Evren's burning cheeks had nothing to do with the steam as she rested her hands on Gyda's shoulders, staring up into her eyes.

"I wasn't done with your hair," she said.

Gyda's eyes darted to her lips and then back up. "It can wait."

Evren shivered. It meant nothing that she knew this was where the night had been headed. It was always different with Gyda looking at her like that, reminding her of just how close they could become when their hearts beat in sync with their bodies.

A droplet fell from Gyda's eyelash, catching the glacier grey of her eyes before plunging into the water between them. Evren licked her lips, noting the way their hearts picked up the pace, and the way Gyda was staring at her, part adoring, part ravenous.

Evren cupped Gyda's face, tracing her lips with her thumb. "I didn't get an oath out of you, Gyda."

If she expected Gyda to behave, she was wrong. Before she knew it, Gyda's lips were past her thumb and on her neck. Evren gasped, shifting up on her knees unconsciously to give her a better angle as she traced fiery kisses up her neck, her jaw, tracing up to the sensitive point of her ears.

"What do you wish of me?" Gyda whispered before gently nibbling on her ear. Evren bit back her gasp.

She didn't know how long she stayed that way, working through her thoughts as Gyda's lips trailed heat that pooled down between her legs. When it became clear she wasn't going to let up until Evren spoke, she found her voice, just barely.

"Promise me," Evren breathed, and Gyda drew back enough to look at her. "Promise me that you'll stay. When everyone else inevitably wanders away, you'll . . . you'll be there."

Gyda's smile was soft, the kind that only Evren was privy to.

She pressed her lips against Evren's, soft and wanting and burning. They shifted, water sloshing over the sides of the tub as warm metal pressed into Evren's back, and the water covered her chest. Her fingers were slippery from the rinse in Gyda's hair, leaving slick trails over her shoulders and back as she pulled her closer.

"Promise me," Evren begged against her lips.

The warm water, the smell of sugar and flowers, the press of Gyda's body against her own. It was all Evren knew. Everything else fell away. That, and the oath from Gyda's mouth to her own.

"I swear, I'll always come back to you."

39

Arke

Now that Arke knew how the Aether felt, both when it was thin and thick, he shivered as he stepped into Terevas. The Brightlands bled into the very soil here, and he could feel the pressing of the other world against the souls holding it back. Everything had that Fey smell to it, and it only got worse when he went underground.

Goblins were magical creatures, made by a drunk Archfey on a dare. They were jokes even to their creators, and little more than pests to those in Eith. Even so, they were the most innately magical creatures Arke had found in Eith so far. The fact that no one would see that and understand why his people were the way they were irritated him.

But if it kept them safe, he'd take it. Eith didn't deserve the brilliance of goblins just yet. Maybe when this nightmare was done and things changed, they could come out of hiding. But not now.

Now, as Terevas was holding on by a thread with the help of a dwindling Etherakian army, the goblin clans clustered in their cities to wait it out, as Unnethen had told them to. There would be no fighting, no joining the war on the surface. They were to wait until it was over.

Arke didn't want to be seen, so none of his kin so much as glanced at him as he weaved through the crowds. There were more goblins packed into his clan's city than he'd ever seen. Small, floppy-eared kids huddled together, staring at the ceiling as if it was going to come crashing down. Adults watching the tunnels leading in an out with wide, unblinking eyes until their partners took them away. The lights were dimmer, the air didn't smell as sweet. What was worse was how quiet it was. Only a few souls dared to whisper to each other, their hushed tones cracking with stress and anxiety.

Goblins from all clans mingled. They ate without fighting, silently chewing and staring at nothing. Fighters sharpened their weapons, trading whetstones amongst each other. Kings he didn't recognize traveled through the crowds, checking on their people and other clans that weren't theirs. It was an even stranger show of unity than he'd seen on the surface with Orenlion, the Vasa, and the dwarves, however few they were.

None of those goblins mattered. Only one did, and he was blissfully alone in their old home. Technically, it was still their home. Given how complicated kids could be, they normally got to choose their homes, depending on the parent they wanted to live with. Arke and Tolk always stayed in their mother's place with a dozen other kids that were their half siblings. None of them were there now. The large home had lost its warmth and welcome with every dead member, until only the two of them were left.

Arke ignored the memories of sleeping, eating, and living in this place. He put out of his mind how he used to like sleeping with his family, cuddled on top of one another around their mother for warmth. How they would all line up along the roof to eat and throw crumbs at those who passed by. How they were all taught to write using the same wall that the house had been built around.

Tolk sat slumped against that wall, white braids so still that the beads in them didn't clink together. Arke thought he might be dead for one awful moment but saw his chest moving. He was just sleeping.

Arke settled down in front of him, dropping the spell that made him near invisible. Strange how that spell before had taken so much time to prepare, and now it felt like nothing.

Tolk didn't stir, and the longer Arke watched him sleep, the more he didn't want to wake him. Confrontation had never been his strong suit. And what was he supposed to say? That even if he came out of the fight alive tomorrow, he wasn't coming back? Ever? Tolk wouldn't understand, and Arke couldn't tell him without risking the idiot following him. His brother had no fear, no regard for his self-interest. Maybe that was why he'd disliked Evren so much in the beginning. Underneath her half-elven exterior, she was a lot like Tolk, and Arke couldn't stand that guilt.

Arke kept his voice a whisper, knowing it wouldn't wake his brother. He slept like the dead.

"One way or another, I'm dyin' tomorrow," Arke said. "And I wish I could do more for you. I wish I could explain it all. Why I left, why I'm still leavin'. All I can tell you is that it ain't because of you. Never you.

"I won bein' King by accident. I never wanted that damn crown, but you were so proud. I'd never seen you so happy. And I tried, I really did, to be what you wanted me to be. But I never fit here. The only person who ever understood me was you. The last thing I wanted was to rule a clan and never see the rest of the world because I was stuck here until I died.

"Yeah, it was selfish of me to make that deal with Unnethen. I shouldn't have left at all, but I felt like I was suffocatin' here and you . . . I tried to explain, but you didn't understand. Ain't your fault, I know now I'm just different. Unnethen offered me a way out without hurtin' nobody, at a price. Always a price. And you, you got to be King. I thought you'd be happy, thought it would make things better. But you were so damn eager to throw it on me again once I came back. I missed somethin', didn't I? I left you the same crown I didn't want and forced you to take my burden. All without a goodbye, because I was afraid you'd make me stay."

Arke sighed heavily. He'd spent so long trying not to feel guilty for how he left his clan. He didn't regret anything but Tolk, but that was a massive part of his life. The first person who never hurt him, who wormed his way into Arke's heart and never cut him on their way out. The only person Arke's walls never worked on.

Family for goblins was weird. It had to be, with how casual the mating process was. Siblings were close growing up but as adults they grew apart. A goblin child was vastly different to their adult self. The fact that Arke and Tolk had always been inseparable since birth should've been a clue that something was wrong. Different.

Little Arke never understood why his older siblings would act so cold when they saw him again. He didn't understand why his mother insisted he was old enough to sleep on his own instead of with her. Or why their family, so tightknit in the beginning, unraveled like a bad tapestry as the years went by.

That's how goblin minds worked. It was cruel, it was a survival tactic. A flaw in their drunken design. But Arke took too long to realize that. He got hurt too many times as everyone he loved walked away, forgot he existed, and died. The only person who never did was Tolk.

Arke left him twice already, and he was about to do it again. How shit was that? While Tolk had done nothing but try to help Arke fit in with a culture he felt out of place in, Arke just kept hacking at that cord connecting them.

Bad with words. Bad with people. Arke had always been good at one thing—magic. Magic and walking away.

"Unnethen." Arke's voice didn't change in volume or tone. "I know you're watchin'."

Jasmine, mist, the curdling of power as she entered the room. Arke stifled a shiver as she hovered beside him. The strange pink glow that followed her everywhere illuminated the glass beads in Tolk's hair.

"I have nothin' left to give you," Arke said. "But I need a favor."

He imagined her frowning over him. "What for?"

"Make him forget," Arke rasped. "Make him like the other goblins. So that, if he does remember me, it won't mean as much to him."

For the first time since he'd worked with her, he felt waves of sympathy pouring off of Unnethen. Fuck, he didn't need her to tell him how sad this was. It was all Arke could think of to fix this, though. He and Tolk had been different, and it did nothing but hurt in the end. If he could just make Tolk better, then Arke leaving him would only hurt one of them. Arke could live with that.

"You're right, you have nothing left to give," Unnethen said softly.

"I'm yours already—name, soul, all of it. You can make me do whatever you want for eternity."

"I know that. It's not incentive to mess with his memories."

"You did it before," Arke pointed out. "When we saved him. Do it again. You want a cost? Hear it in my voice. Tell me I ain't payin' for this, that I don't hate it."

She sighed, like a breeze through leaves. "I can't tell you that. Is this truly what you want, pet?"

No. Yes. It had to be. Yeah, he was bleeding his damn heart out, but he was finally saving his brother some of the pain. Cutting the cord, severing the connection, never going home again. This time, Arke would pay the price, not the both of them. This time, Arke would suffer instead of someone he loved.

He finally understood Evren. Wanted to hate this feeling, wanted to turn back. But couldn't.

"Do it," he said, because he couldn't say yes without lying, but he was still giving her permission.

He forced himself to watch as the magic shimmered in the air around Tolk. He watched his braids sway, his ears twitch a little, but nothing else moved as Unnethen's magic disappeared into his skin. Arke could almost sense it working, sawing away at that connection between them, as strong as iron, until it finally snapped and everything felt colder.

The shimmering was gone. Unnethen had retreated, her work done. And Arke stood up and walked to the door.

"Hey, whatcha doin' here?"

Arke froze at Tolk's grumpy, just-awakened voice. He grasped the doorway with one hand, feeling the little claw marks of his old family. Arke was a knot of a dozen different strings, all of which had been cut to move him out of the way. Finally, he was free, the last little string heavier than the ones before.

He turned back, ignoring the stab of pain in his chest as Tolk narrowed his eyes at him. He didn't remember, and Arke should've been glad that Unnethen hadn't tricked him. But already he missed his brother's toothy grin and crushing hugs.

Arke breathed through the pain and didn't cry. He forced a shrug. "Wrong house. Sorry."

Tolk shuffled to his feet, ears quivering with irritation. A lone goblin in a house that once housed dozens. "Who are you?"

"To you? Nobody."

Then Arke turned and left. He waited until he rounded the back of the house, tore a portal open and left for good.

HE CAME into *The Wayfinder's Rest* a sniffling mess. Aillard was nowhere to be seen. The only light was the fire where Sorin sat, waiting. He looked up from the flames, took one look at Arke and ran over.

"What happened?"

Arke shook his head furiously. If he talked, he would cry. And he was so damn tired of crying. He was so tired of hurting. He just wanted to be numb and happy again. Content to be alone.

But when Sorin draped his coat over Arke's shoulders and led him to the fire, Arke didn't fight. He plopped down next to the human and unapologetically leaned on him. Sorin didn't push him away; never had. He put his arm around Arke in a way that reminded him enough of Tolk to make Arke's eyes water.

"I hate this," Arke finally said to the crackling logs.

"Me too."

He blinked away the tears. "Why can't we be happy? Why do we gotta hurt ourselves to save the world?"

Arke had nothing left to give. He'd sold everything to Unnethen. His name, his soul, his life, the mirror, and now Tolk. He was so cut off from everything he felt weightless, anchored only by the human next to him. What little things he'd found to love in Eith wouldn't matter after tomorrow. After Abraxas was dead and the world was changed forever. After he had to say goodbye for good this time.

"Because no one else will do it," Sorin said. "Because for some reason or another, we were all taught that the only way to love is by giving ourselves to others completely and now we're doing the same for Eith. Because if one of us fights, we all fight. That's the way we live. Burning too brightly all at once until there's nothing left to give."

Arke thought back to when he met Sorin. He would never have gone to Dirn-Darahl if he hadn't had the human with him. Hells, he wouldn't have made it out of Terevas without him. How different would life have been if he'd picked another path? If Arke had chosen a different spellbook or Sorin had turned a blind eye?

"Do you regret savin' me?" Arke asked.

Sorin squeezed his shoulder, although it was with his bad hand. It wasn't as strong as before.

"Never. Do you regret following me?"

Arke smiled, the fire blinding his eyes. "Nah. Out of all I regret, Sorin, your crazy ass isn't one. You're the best decision I ever made."

Sorin's laugh was breathy, as it always was when he was choked up and didn't want to show it.

"And you're still mine. Always."

Everything hurt just a little bit less. He leaned into his best friend and put tomorrow, the future, out of his mind. He closed his eyes, holding this moment tight in his mind. Memorizing the way the room smelled like smoke and good food, and how scratchy Sorin's coat was around the neck.

"Always."

40

Abraxas

The forest was quieter, much quieter, than Abraxas's head. Even Velcros's army kept as quiet as possible, scattered between the trees. Not a fire in sight, the lanterns glowing a dim green that sent the trees into even more hair-raising shapes. Those lights blissfully faded as he left the army behind him.

Cool, comforting darkness blanketed him with each step. The carpet of pine needles muffled his footsteps. The sword in his hand had a familiar weight as he neared ever closer to the spot where he would change the world.

There was no sign of the monsters rumored in this forest. Nothing seemed to live at all, even the trees seemed subdued. The only prowling monster he was aware of was himself.

He could feel them at the edge of his awareness. Sol and Karas had been hounding his army since they'd entered. But now he felt them all. Sorin and Arke, Evren and Gyda. The Eternity Dagger was with her, just as the sword promised.

How foolish of him to think he could do this without them. A momentary lapse of judgment. He should've known that the only thing that could bring them together so fast was the chance to take him down. To stop him.

It would hurt to have them caught in the crossfire. All he needed was Gyda, however. Maybe Evren as well. He'd have to force her to give up the dagger one way or another, and Evren was the biggest threat besides Arke. Yes, it would hurt. But it would be worth it. After all, what were a handful of once friends compared to the whole of Eith?

The trees cleared and the soft needles turned to something harder. Stone. He scuffed his boot, dislodging some dirt. A floor, even and intact despite the weathering. Looking around he saw nothing else that might indicate a ruin. No rubble or archways draped with frost and leaves. But everything was different here.

He stepped towards the center, shivering. The part of him he didn't quite recognize, the part that was in tune with the sword and the dagger, hummed with excitement. This place tasted familiar, as if he'd been struggling to get here his whole life. Like the doorway to his mother's home, closed now, but what waited on the other side . . .

A twig snapped behind him, and the only indication Abraxas gave that he heard it was the subtle shift of his feet into a fighting position. He knew who it was before he found the willpower to turn around and yet, he found his hands still clammy. Found himself dreading it all the same.

He turned as five figures emerged from the shadows. Familiar weapons glinted in the half moonlight. A spear, a mace, twin daggers, a chain, and a great ax. Armor tarnished as his once was. Scars standing out starkly in the light.

"You should've stayed out of this," Abraxas told them.

They formed a half circle in front of him. They were all so much older than he remembered. Older than they should've been. War had aged them where time couldn't.

It was Stefan who spoke first, which surprised Abraxas. The Champion of Holtia had always been the quietest of them, and completely contrary to everything his god stood for. None could look at his scarred face and picture the Divine of love and healing choosing him.

"Be reasonable, Abraxas," he said in his soft voice. "You've gone too far, even for us. Did you not think we would come?"

He'd feared it. Still, Stefan's words grated him. He'd gone too far? When what he was doing now barely matched what they'd all done in total during their years in power.

"I had hoped you would see this gift for what it is."

Marian scoffed. Her hair looked silver instead of gold now. "Please, this is madness. We all lost them, Abraxas. We all learned to move on."

"Perhaps we shouldn't have," he said.

"We went too far—"

"Who are you to say that?" he roared, and she flinched back. "You were the hand of Nutvian, not the goddess herself. You weren't meant to question her judgment, only obey."

Marian's ice-cold eyes narrowed and her spear winked as she brought it forward. He tensed too, but Josephine was between them like a blotch of rosy color in an otherwise black-and-white world. Her hand pushed down Marian's spear and another was held out to Abraxas.

"It's been so long," Josephine said. "I know how you feel. Hollow. Broken. Like there's nothing in the world that could ever make you feel again."

No. The problem was that he felt too much. He couldn't stop, and it was destroying him.

"But this is not the way," she continued. "You would destroy all of Eith if it meant bringing them back."

"I am saving Eith," Abraxas said. "Why can't you see that?"

Behind her, Idain snorted. "Saving Eith means raising an army from the Yawning Deep?"

Abraxas never liked Idain. There was something unnerving about someone as jovial as him serving death. As if Abraxas didn't miss the gleam in his eye at every new corpse, or the way he smothered his smile at the sight of a battlefield. At least when

Abraxas was done with a kill, he walked away. Idain reveled in it, almost like a necromancer.

"Serevadia was always a threat," Abraxas said. "Sooner or later, with or without my help, they would've done just this. I am simply drawing venom from a wound."

"Burnin' the infection out." Aeryn finally spoke up.

Eitrix had chosen the dwarf when Abraxas was still training. It was odd to see him so unchanged. Greyer, yes, but almost as if he hadn't lost his god at all. The others all looked and felt diminished. He simply wasn't.

Abraxas relaxed a fashion. "Yes. You understand, then?"

Aeryn frowned, tugging on his amulet. "I do miss him."

Stefan whirled on him. "Aeryn!"

The dwarf scowled. "What? You all do. Don't deny it. Life was easier when there wasn't a choice to make. We were soldiers. Now what are we?"

"We are whatever is left over," Idain said. "We make do and live with the consequences. No power is worth what their wrath would bring on the world."

Josephine nodded, prompting Marian to do the same. "We had our chance, Aeryn. Abraxas, it's done now."

Abraxas took a step back. It felt like a retreat. Shouldn't they be grateful? Shouldn't they want the same things as him?

Josephine followed him, keeping her knives tucked carefully in her sheaths. Marian grabbed at her, hissing a warning to bring her back, but the Champion of Emion didn't listen. She walked with the same grace he'd known her to have in the past, more dancer than fighter. She'd been mesmerizing to watch in battle.

The others tensed as well, even Aeryn. Josephine drew close, not even a foot away from Abraxas when she stopped. He could count every freckle as if her skin was still young and smooth. He could get lost counting her eyelashes.

"I miss them too," she said, her voice like a lullaby. "I see the cracks in the world they could fix. I reach for that power whenever I'm scared. But the world has moved on, Abraxas. It needs to keep moving. You alone are holding it back.

"We all know you have suffered. We know that nothing will take away that pain or make you any less broken. No one outside of us will truly understand the depth of your mourning and sacrifice. How could they? They have not wielded Divine magic as you have. As we all have.

"But the time for fighting is done." Boldly, she laid her hand over his, over the sword. He jumped at the contact. "It's time to put down your blade, Abraxas. It's time to rest."

The forest seemed to hold its breath. He could see Marian waiting for a reason to run him through. Idain gripping his mace and looking sick. Stefan counting the links on his chain. Aeryn mouthing a prayer.

What was this cruel trick? That they reminded him so much of the Wandering Sols. Josephine smiled a little like Sorin. Marian was her angry shadow, just like Arke. Stefan was as scarred and reluctant as Evren. Aeryn having that same dwarven stubbornness that Sol had. And Idain was like Gyda, the way he was looking at Abraxas with that same betrayed look in his eyes.

They were like little pieces of the Wandering Sols. The worst of two halves of Abraxas's long life.

A test then.

It was decided even before she'd touched his hand how Josephine would die, yet ripping the sword from her grip and plunging it into her chest was still satisfying. Only because he got to prove that her charm wouldn't work on him.

She couldn't cry out. She couldn't even gasp for air. Blood poured from her mouth as Marian screamed in rage behind her.

"Then rest, Josephine," he said and kicked her off the blade. She tumbled and rolled to a stop at Marian's feet. "I have work to do."

The remaining Champions leapt into action.

Stefan's chain snaked out, whipping through the air in a deadly arch towards his head. Abraxas sidestepped and swept the sword in his direction. The blade was nowhere close to reaching him, but Stefan had fought enough with Abraxas to know the move. The scarred man barely jumped out of the way as a torrent of shadows lashed out along the same path as the blade.

Idain and Aeryn were rushing him in the wake of his shadows, and Marian had finally recovered enough to tear herself away from Josephine's body. She was closer, and her spear had more reach. The cold metal sang through the air, just missing his cheek as he let the shadows tug him out of the way. But she was relentless, her form as immaculate as their days in the sand. Every blow from her was precise, a blur of silvered steel that swung around her in elegant arcs unbefitting of the rage in her eyes.

And Abraxas blocked each and every one. The sword could snap the spear in half, but he held back, relishing the few seconds of clanging metal, of a real fight, before Idain and Aeryn were on him.

Normally this is where the fight would end. Abraxas was caught between all three of them, blocking, parrying and dodging three separate weapons. They circled him as they'd been trained to do, using Marian and Aeryn's reach to press him closer to Idain and his wicked mace.

Abraxas batted the mace aside, steel ringing, and stabbed. Idain was quick, but not enough. The blade grazed his side, cutting through the chainmail like butter and leaving him to fall back, cursing.

Abraxas ducked under one of Aeryn's swings and kicked the dwarf's legs out from under him. Aeryn fell, but before Abraxas's sword could finish him, mace and spear came rushing in from both sides.

A twitch of his fingers and the shadows swallowed him. Only for a second, and he could feel them taking him to safety before dumping him back in the fight behind Marian.

The stiffening of her shoulders, the change in her stance. It was all too late. His sword cut through her back and out her stomach in a kill that wasn't nearly as satisfying as Josephine's, but close enough.

Aeryn was on his feet and charging, rage alight in his eyes. Marian gurgled a warning, but by then Abraxas already had her spear and it was too late. With her hand still on it, he forced the spear through Aeryn and impaled him to the ground.

"Come now, Mare," Abraxas said as she sobbed. "You didn't even like him."

She fell off his blade with no further fight, landing between two unmoving bodies.

There was a tinkling of chains in the air and then cold iron wrapped around his wrist and jerked. Abraxas gritted his teeth, skin pulling and bones creaking. But he refused to let go as Stefan tried to pull the blade from his grasp.

At his other side, Idain came up with a wild swing. Abraxas ducked underneath the mace and with his free hand punched at the bleeding wound in his side. Idain hissed, but didn't retreat. He pulled the mace back for a devastating blow.

"Let it go, Abraxas," Idain demanded.

Stefan's chain was ripping his skin. The shadows hummed at Abraxas's command. He glared at Idain.

"For someone who served death, you're so hesitant to dole it out. That's why you lose."

The shadows erupted from Abraxas's chest, as sharp and as thin as a blade. Stefan cried out as they sliced clean through him. Idain, ever so lucky, dropped to his knees so that they skimmed just above his head.

Chains now slack, Abraxas pulled at them with all his might. Stefan hadn't let go even in death, and his torn half-body came with the chains as Abraxas swung it back and at Idain. Stefan crashed into him, knocking Idain back several feet and pinning him beneath the still bleeding corpse of an old friend.

Abraxas unwound the chains from his hands slowly. Calmly. The shadows came from his feet and licked at the wound, healing it and erasing the pain. They wanted more. They needed more. The blade had only gotten a small taste of blood.

But Abraxas waited. He let Idain push Stefan off of him. Let the man come to the full realization that he was the last person standing. The sobs came first, then the begging for Stefan's return. Not the prayers, strangely. He expected something to send Stefan's soul to its rightful place, but instead Idain was muttering nonsense between his tears.

"Death is always easier when it isn't someone you love, isn't it Idain?" Abraxas asked. Time was up.

He stalked towards the man slowly and kicked the fallen mace far out of reach. Idain hadn't left Stefan's side and was holding that grotesque face in his lap. His wound seeped heavily, pooling on the stone ground like a scarlet pond. Josephine was not the only color in the world now.

As he stopped before him, Idain's face turned up to meet him. No amount of tears could cover the horror, the grief, in his eyes. And the regret.

"Oh, it was you, wasn't it?" Abraxas asked. "You asked them to come and stop me. To redeem me? Yourself? To fight one last time. Has it finally hit you, Champion of Vyone, that you are both their murderer and their death witness?"

Idain's body shuddered, yet there was no fear there. "We were already dead. As are you."

Abraxas's mouth twisted into a frown. "I know."

"She has faith in you," Idain said. "She seeks to bring you back to the light. I tried to spare Evren Hanali that pain, and I failed."

Abraxas recoiled. No. Evren wanted to hurt him. She wanted to kill him. She hated his gods and after what he'd done to Gyda, she would gladly turn her arrows on him.

Right?

"Will you be her death witness, Champion of nothing?" Idain asked. "Will you whisper her name as you bury her and the others. Do you think that even then you could bury your guilt?"

Abraxas's tightened his grip on his sword. "I have no guilt."

Idain grin was bloody and terrible. "We are creatures born of murder and guilt. And you are ripe with it."

Abraxas didn't want to hear anymore. Even as Idain's lips parted to say something else, he was screaming and swinging the sword. The finality of it, of his head rolling on the ground and his body slumping over Stefan's, was not satisfying.

It made him sick.

Abraxas staggered back to the center of the stone clearing. Blood pooled around the bodies. Aeryn's glassy eyes stared up at the sky. Josephine's face was still twisted in shock, and Marian's hand still reached for her even in death.

The shadows grew until the forest was blacked out. Until there was nothing but the stone ground and the bodies and Abraxas himself. He slumped on the ground, sword in his feverish hand. He couldn't stop looking at them. Couldn't stop hearing what they sounded like as they died.

He squeezed his eyes shut, but instead of them, he saw the Wandering Sols. He saw Evren collapsed over Gyda. Arke impaled by shadows. Sorin crawling to him as his blood gushed freely. Sol skewered with her own daggers.

He would do it. He had to do it. For the Divines, for Eith.

But he wept anyway. Not for the bodies at his feet, or the mountain of corpses that haunted him. But for the sacrifice he was using for his own salvation.

He was ripping his own heart out. He was going to bleed out with them. And that was Divine justice.

Evren

Morning came too quickly, as did the ritual of putting on armor. It felt good to have help with the laces on the gauntlet, to have someone there to share in the nerves before battle.

She and Gyda were quiet. All that needed to be said had been said. There was nothing left to do but let the anticipation crawl up their throats and breathe through it.

Evren picked up Gyda's hilt, so much lighter without its blade, and held it out to her.

Gyda gave her a tight smile, fingers brushing hers just as shouting sounded outside. The cries of wyverns joined it. Many voices, pained and surprised, filtered through the window and into their ears.

Gyda snatched her hilt and tossed Evren her bow. She caught it easily, making for the door as Sorin burst through.

"They're attacking us!" he cried. "What kind of sacrifices attack before they can be sacrificed?"

Evren shouldered her way past him, marching down the

hallway as Gyda and Sorin followed. Sol and Karas were already at the stairway, panicked looks on their faces.

"The kind that doesn't know they're sacrifices," Evren shot over her shoulder. With Sol and Karas ahead of her, she took the stairs two at a time. Arke waited at the bottom with the worg, spellbook ready.

"Velcros probably ordered it," Sol said. "He thinks it'll be an easy battle."

Gyda chuckled darkly. "Care to prove him wrong?"

Sol whipped out her daggers. "Gladly."

If Aillard was there, Evren didn't spare a glance at him. He could pick his payment off their corpses if they didn't survive. She wrenched open the door and walked straight into a layer of hell.

The battlefield was right at the doorstep with a Khama choking on their own blood at her feet. Serevadians swarmed the half-dismantled camp like ants over a corpse. Silver armor flashed like lightning. Green bolts tore holes through chests and ripped off arms. A riderless wyvern screamed from the trees and spat a trail of steaming acid. Jaws still dripping, it snapped up another Serevadian, shredding it even as it was peppered with bolts of light.

Evren's arrows were on the archers in seconds, the magical arrows spilling blood as they pierced armor and flesh. The wyvern bled heavily, but leapt from tree to tree, hissing and spitting hate as it went.

Gyda's sword sliced through the air next to Evren where a Serevadian had been seconds before. No wounds, but he fell, lifeless, and Gyda took up her spot at Evren's back.

"Sorin!"

A familiar shrill cry tore through the air. Sorin's cocky posture dropped to one of horror. "Enola? Enola!"

He took off, and the Wandering Sol's ran after him. Arke burnt pages, scattering them and growing thick shards of ice that shot up from the ground and impaled those nearby. Sol's daggers were a mere blur as she and Karas worked in near perfect tandem. Inside Evren's chest, fear was overtaken by the sheer thrill of battle, her heart beating in time with Gyda's as they tore a path through their enemies.

Enola burst from the fighting, hands crimson and running straight for Sorin. He grabbed her with his free arm and pulled her away from a charging soldier. The worg jumped just then, teeth sinking into the Serevadian's throat as he pinned him to the ground.

Sorin pulled Enola back as the Wandering Sols formed a wall around them. Evren spared her hearing to listen to them as she shot arrow after glowing arrow into what seemed to be a never-ending surge of enemies.

"Are you hurt?" Sorin was saying. "No? Just your magic. Okay, where is Sahar?"

The dying cries of the Serevadian Evren just shot nearly drowned out Enola's words.

"I don't know! I haven't seen her all morning."

Sorin cursed, and Evren knew exactly what he wanted to do.

"Cover for me?" she asked Gyda, and stepped back. Gyda easily filled the space Evren left, and her glowing sword cut through any stupid enough to throw themselves at her. The sharp smell of magic curled in Evren's nostrils as Arke eviscerated his enemies.

Sorin was kneeling in front of Enola, tan face ashen with worry.

"Sorin." His eyes snapped to hers. "She's going to be fine."

"You don't know that," he insisted.

"She will be. She survived everything up to this. If we see her, we'll help her. But right now we have to get this under control and get to Abraxas."

"But—"

"I can find her!" Enola piped up.

"Absolutely not." Sorin pushed himself to his feet and nodded to the tavern, not too far away. "You're going in there."

"But I can help!"

"Not this time, kid." Sorin patted her shoulder. "I'll be right back, but I need you safe in there. Got it?"

Enola looked like she was going to argue, but a spray of blood in the air from Karas's hammer caught her by surprise. She stepped back hesitantly, lips pushed out stubbornly.

"You better come back for me." She pushed a finger at his chest. And before he could make a promise he might or might not keep, she ran off to the tavern. Evren watched her go, drawing back her bow and taking down the few who tried to attack her as she ran.

Sorin gripped his sword, looking at her as he pushed down his worry. "Right. Let's go."

The previously quiet forest was a riot of screams and steel. Trees blurred by as the Wandering Sols spread out, always keeping each other in sight. For all the time they spent apart, they fell into the rhythm of battle easily.

Arke hauled himself on top of the worg, slinging spells to cover Gyda, Sorin, and Sol. Evren's arrows cut through enemy ranks, whittling them down or picking off the ones Sol wounded. Gyda's sword blazed a hellish red to match the spilling blood soaking into the ground. Sorin taunted and pulled enemies closer, either taking them down himself or leaving them for Arke and Evren.

No one touched them, and it still wasn't enough.

Evren bit back a curse. They were heavily outnumbered. Even as wyverns flew dangerously close overhead, snatching up enemies with their claws and jaws, there seemed to be no end. Evren had a feeling that Velcros emptied most of Serevadia to make his army, and this small portion was enough to crush the combined forces of three cultures.

Karas stumbled to a halt, leaving himself open to an attack that Sol's daggers barely stopped. But she saw it too as she shook the blood off her daggers. The dwarves were hopelessly surrounded and fighting for their lives. And they didn't have the luxury of armor or good weapons.

"Sol . . ." Karas looked at her, torn. With a jolt Evren realized he'd planned to follow her to the very end, all the way to Abraxas.

"Go," Sol said. "They need you."

Karas hefted his hammer to his shoulder. "And I need you. Come back alive."

She smiled. "You as well. Now, go!"

She pushed him away and Karas was charging through the battle towards his people. Sol itched to go, Evren could see it in her stance. But she turned back to Evren.

"You too," the dwarf snapped. "Let's go!"

And so it went, the chaotic flow of battle. Thrumming of magical arrows at her fingers. Sorin dancing just out of her vision. Him and Sol working in tandem, so much like their first fight in the prison that it nearly hurt Evren's chest.

The worg kept Arke from any serious harm, his snout red. Arke's magic tore the frost from the trees and the ground and hurled it into the air, pinning Serevadians with ice that turned red. Either Gyda would put the suffering ones out of their misery, or she was moving onto the next one.

Evren forgot how breathtaking it was to fight with her. To know that they had each other's back no matter the enemy. The battlefield was where Gyda belonged, thrumming with power and achingly beautiful in a way that Evren couldn't describe.

Over and over, though, it felt like Evren was fighting the same people. All the armor looked the same. She stopped identifying the colors of their eyes when she killed them, stopped hearing what they had to say as they fell. The landscape of black trees and grey ground, the blur of fighting bodies and dead ones.

A never-ending battle. A never-ending forest. And no Abraxas in sight.

A loud war cry was all the warning Evren had before a Serevadian was rushing up on her. Finally, one had gotten the hint to get into her guard instead of her extensive range. He lashed out with twin blades. Evren dodged the first one and parried the second with the metal arm of her bow. The spiked teeth of the bow caught the blade and she twisted, snapping the blade out of his hands, and continuing the arc to his neck. She didn't even feel any resistance. One second she was pulling away, the next he was pouring blood from the slit in his neck and tumbling to her feet.

Evren eyed the bow warily. Who in the hells had made such a weapon?

A chilling roar broke the monotony of the forest. As the ground shuddered with pounding footsteps, large and tree shaking, Evren turned back to her friends.

"Big one!"

That's all she needed to say to get Gyda's attention. The warrior was at her side in seconds, staring eagerly to the north, blade ready. The rest of the Wandering Sols lined up beside her as something massive lurched through the trees.

Chains dangling, knuckles dragging the ground, the massive creature was no less terrible to look at now than the past few times. Evren could tell that it wasn't the only one by the way the ground shook, but she couldn't see any more from where she was. The escorting Serevadians shouted when they saw them, raising their crossbows.

Evren raised her bow in turn. "The skin is like stone. Normal blades won't do anything to it."

"Well." Sorin flourished his sword. "We'll leave the ugly one for Gyda and you, and Sol and I will take the assholes around it. Deal?"

Gyda's sword switched to a sickly green. "Deal."

Gyda paid no attention to the surrounding Serevadians as she charged. Sol and Sorin flanked her, their quick feet and blades lashing out and keeping her from harm just as Evren's arrows and Arke's magic shielded them. Within a minute, the creature's feet were strewn with bloody corpses, Sorin's echoing laughter filling the air. Many of the rushing enemies avoided him now, choosing Sol instead, but she was too quick for them. Her blonde hair was nearly red as she ducked and cut, pulling all of them to her level before she killed them.

Gyda was toying with the creature. With no eyes, the din of battle was confusing it. Every time Sorin laughed it would swing towards him, but Gyda would cut it in the opposite area. She'd dart away as it swatted at her, deadly silent as she poked its defenses, whittled its health down.

It bellowed and tore a tree from the ground. The wyvern resting inside screeched in fury and flew off. The creature swung the tree like a club, taking down large swaths of Serevadians, but not Gyda. Sol and Sorin just managed to get out of the way, shouting curses as they did.

The creature twitched towards them, club raising. But Gyda latched onto the roots and swung herself up. As the tree rose, so did she. Her feet skimmed the bark as she ran down the steepening slope and launched herself at the creature's face.

Her green blade sunk deep into its forehead and it stilled, twitched, and then fell backwards. The fall shook the ground, cascading frost on Evren and Arke. Gyda stood up, taking her sword and looking for the next enemy.

"Fuck, I love that woman," Evren said.

But it wasn't enough. Evren heard more than saw more creatures ravaging through the woods. Trees shuddered and the ground rumbled with every step

Evren eyed the dead creature and where its tree had fallen. It had landed at an odd angle, slumped against another three. With the pines not nearly as sturdy as the oaks she grew up with, it would have to do.

"I'm getting a better look," she told Arke.

He shook fire off his fingers. "Sure."

She handed him her bow and took off. Her feet met the slick bark after she jumped, and she grasped the thin branches to pull herself up. It wasn't a graceful or easy climb, but she reached the upright tree just as thicker limbs were growing and she hauled herself up. One branch at a time, above the chaos of battle, until she had a mostly clear view.

Through the limbs and the needles, she saw a lost battle in the making. Nine more of those creatures tore through Orenlion's defenses. Khama were shot out of the air, their wyvern's wings catching the weak sunlight as they fell like bright petals. She spied lightning arcing from a small corner of the battle, the Vasa storm magic searing through the Serevadians close to them. But it wasn't enough. Even without the creatures to push them back, there were too many Serevadians. The forest was choked with them, and the steadily growing piles of Orenlion bodies.

The battle had been difficult from her eyes, but to everyone she led here, it was hopeless.

Where were Idain and the other Champions? Or Mei and Aster? She saw no signs of them from her perch. And nothing of Sahar.

The reality of it was threatening to push Evren back into her grave. That even if she and the Wandering Sols made it to Abraxas in time, there was no winning this fight.

She locked eyes with Arke below. He could get her to Abraxas. They could end this now. But just as she started to say it, a war horn cut through the air.

From the west, a beautiful sight burst through the trees. Charging horses, glinting armor, banners of black-and-gold raised high. Etherak's cavalry slammed into the still-scrambling Serevadians.

Skulls crushed under hooves. Swords swept through the air, trailing crimson arcs of blood. As the creatures started to turn towards the army, arcs of brilliant magic shot through the air. The mages didn't toy with the creatures like Gyda. They teamed up and eviscerated them, stealing the air from their lungs and choking them, taking command of their chains and binding them until their skin split. Orenlion and its allies were quick to get out of the way, and a ripple of something new hit the battle-field like a wave.

Hope.

At the head of it all were Barrion and Loghain.

Evren scrambled down and took her bow back. "Etherak's here!"

Sol's eyes widened. "They left Tal-Mashad for us."

"Then let's go!" Sorin cried and started to run towards the horn.

Gyda caught Evren's eye and stopped him. "This isn't our fight anymore."

Sorin's face fell. He turned back to Evren and Arke. "Now? Really? They need us."

"And Tal-Mashad needed Loghain," she said. "We have to make this count, Sorin. Or they all die."

"I know that, but—"

Sol cried out a warning of pure terror and Evren was nocking an arrow before she even knew where to shoot. But Sol wasn't worried about a rushing enemy. She was scrambling away from slithering shadows headed straight towards Gyda.

Terror was an ice-cold fist on Evren's spine.

"Gyda!"

The warrior turned, but it was too late. The shadows were already curled around her feet and yanking her off balance. Evren's arrows sank into the inky blackness with no effect, and before Arke's fire could start, Gyda was already swallowed up and gone.

Evren didn't have enough time to process her panic before something frigid slithered around her neck and yanked her back. The last thing she saw before the blackness consumed her was Sol reaching for her.

It was seconds. It was ages. In the darkness, time was mean-ingless. But when it ended, Evren was shivering and sucking in heavy gasps of air. Stone was at her back, the grey sky above her. The sounds of fighting were distant.

She bolted upright. She was in a circular clearing, the forest floor replaced with solid stone. Gyda was just beside her, heaving herself to her feet. She grasped Evren's hand and pulled her up. They both clutched their weapons, looking around the clearing.

"I found the Champions," Gyda murmured, and Evren looked at the pile of bodies. Idain's head was on top, still staring sightlessly.

The shadows hadn't retreated. Instead, they formed a wall encircling the stone clearing to keep them in. And possibly to keep Arke out.

Evren's mouth went dry. As usual, their bad plan was going to shit before it even started.

"I hope the trip here wasn't as uncomfortable as last time."

They whirled to face the center of the clearing, where the shadows parted to reveal Abraxas, sword in hand. His eyes flickered over to the Champions. Did Evren see guilt there? It was hard to tell, because in a second he was looking back on them, his face expressionless.

"I want this to be as painless as possible," he began, and stepped forward.

42

Sahar

Sahar ripped Drystan's ax out of the body and pressed herself against the trunk of a tree. She squeezed her eyes shut, but she couldn't escape the flood of memories. The cold, the screams, the smell of blood and death choking her. It was like Direwall all over again, where everything went wrong.

Only this time she didn't have anyone with her. Nerezza and Drystan were gone. The Wandering Sols and Sorin, who she hadn't even realized she would miss, were caught in the fighting somewhere else.

She should've stayed in the tavern. She should've stayed with them. Even if it felt like she was watching them save the world from the outside looking in, she should've swallowed her hurt and gotten the fuck over it. After all, what did she expect? Of course they'd want to save Abraxas, just like she had fought to save Nerezza.

Sahar failed her friends every single time. It was no wonder she was alone now, of all times.

"Closing your eyes won't make it go away, princess."

Sahar snapped her eyes open, her vision flooded with the

ghastly battle, but mostly the sight of Etherak's future Queen, bloodied and grim. Behind her was Aster, Orenlion's ambassador and Evren's friend. Likely two of the most important people to Etherak's future right now, and they were dragging her out of trouble.

She shook herself. She was Sahar Al-Fasil. She was the Ashen Bond, and she did not shy away from fighting.

Sahar pushed herself off the tree. "I'm not a princess."

Aster shot Mei a look. "Technically, you are."

Mei scowled. "Not something to discuss in the middle of a damn battle."

"Of course not." He turned to Sahar, and she just now noticed the thin stiletto blades in his hands. "Are you hurt?"

She shook her head. "No. Just out of my depth."

"You have a weapon," Mei snapped.

"I'm a bloody alchemist!" Sahar exclaimed. "But I have no tools or serums or anything—"

"You're doing fine," Aster said. "Just stay with us. Or, uh, her. She's doing most of the killing."

As if to prove his point, Mei stalked off with her limping gate towards a group of Serevadians. Barely a minute later they were groaning and dying at her feet. She winced, massaging her bad leg and cutting off one who'd started to scream.

Sahar shivered. If that's what she fought like injured, she couldn't imagine how swift Mei had been before her accident.

Aster ushered her after Mei, and they'd taken all of five steps before a horn cut through the air. The three froze, eyes on the sky. Sahar didn't recognize it, but Mei's face lit up with elation.

"Barrion!" She smiled at Aster. "He did it. He's here."

"Prince Barrion?" Sahar pressed. "I thought he was in Tal-Mashad."

Aster's smile wasn't nearly as bright as Mei's. "He brought an army with him. He chose us. We might make it out of this alive."

Sahar didn't want to be the one to tell him that he likely

jinxed them, and Mei was already racing off towards the sound of the horn. Towards even thicker fighting. Sahar shuddered, but followed, clutching Drystan's ax tightly. More than ever, she was glad for Zo's sticky fingers for taking it and then giving it back. It was all she had left of him, that, and her tattoo. They'd survived this much, they could survive this.

Sahar kept up with Mei and Aster. If she thought her area of fighting had been bad, she was sorely mistaken as they hit what felt like a wall of bodies. The fervor of fighting stung the air. Bodies choked the ground—horse, wyvern and elven alike. Sahar spied the black-and-gold of Etherak's banner seconds before it fell, disappearing into the mass of bodies.

And Sahar fought.

She wasn't as skilled as Mei or as swift as Aster, who gutted his enemies with little blood left on himself. But she kept her swings hard and precise, Drystan's voice in the back of her mind.

You don't have my reach, he'd once told her. *But you're smaller than most enemies. Use that to your advantage. Hit key spots. Their groin, the back of the knees, the neck if you're able. Or all three.*

She remembered laughing and saying. *I won't need all three.*

He hadn't smiled, but the amusement in his eyes was just as nice. *I believe you.*

Sahar's grip was firm but not too tight as she crashed the ax's head into the back of a Serevadian's knee. He cried out as he fell, and she jerked it back out, cutting into his throat and pushing him away. He disappeared into the throng of bodies.

Bright light erupted to her right, and Sahar smelled burnt hair and meat as it cleared. A large swarth of earth had been cleared and charred, all the bodies with it. Sahar looked further, finding the Serevadian much farther back grabbing for a globe brimming with greenish light. She was surrounded by two dozen fighters and had a line of others passing her more globes from a large pile. Sahar watched in growing horror as she launched the next globe in the air. It caught a passing wyvern, and the beast and its rider didn't have time to scream before the light ate them alive.

Mei cried out in rage. Sahar turned to Aster and shoved Drystan's ax into his hands.

"Hold this."

Then she was combing through the bodies, praying that her better equipped escorts would cover her as she searched. She blocked out the sounds of fighting, the feel of cooling bodies under her fingers. There could've been a duel going on above her and she wouldn't have noticed. She pushed aside Orenlion and Etherak bodies, and one that looked Vasa that she pointedly ignored in case she recognized it, and finally found what she was looking for.

She took the still loaded crossbow from the dead Serevadian and stood up so fast her vision blurred. The air smelled like burned hair. The Serevadian had lobbed three more orbs, cutting out swaths of their allies, and Mei was cutting her way through with a vengeance.

"Mei! Get back!" she called.

Mei didn't hear her. She just kept wading through the battle.

Sahar steeled herself, then shouted, "PRINCESS!"

Mei swung around, eyes murderous. Sahar showed her the crossbow and motioned to the pile of orbs. Mei might not have seen the explosions these things caused, but she could guess. Sahar watched her curse, cut down an opponent, and retreat.

"Tell me you can fire that thing," Aster said breathlessly. He *had* been covering her.

"Whether I can or can't isn't relevant." Sahar put the crossbow against her shoulder and lined up the shot. She'd never used a Serevadian crossbow before but, honestly, how hard could it be? The pile was massive. She just needed to hit one for the explosion to trigger. "I'm the Ashen Bond."

She pulled the trigger, and the crossbow kicked into her shoulder hard enough to send her staggering back. Aster caught her and the bolt sailed cleanly through the air towards the orbs.

The Serevadian throwing them noticed too late, and Sahar was able to savor the look of pure terror before the light erupted and swallowed her.

Swallowed much more than Sahar planned, actually. The radius took out a good twenty feet of everything. Trees, Serevadians, and a few unfortunate casualties on her side. It left a burnt circle in the ground, and a yawning gap in the suffocating field that rushed to be filled.

Sahar threw down the crossbow and took back the ax. When Mei rejoined them, they said nothing. They just dove back into the fight.

The more they fought, the more Sahar realized that this was nothing like Direwall. Terrifying, yes, but the scale and tactics were all different. Gail threw everything he had at Direwall, and it overwhelmed them. Serevadia wasn't one entity. They were separate soldiers, commanders with groups to lead and tall creatures that ripped trees out of the ground to wrangle. They cornered Orenlion and Etherak into manageable chunks. They split their forces, found who was causing the most damage, and dealt with them quickly.

But Etherak and Orenlion fought for the world. It was bitter and bloody. It meant every fight was a last stand, and every soldier took down more enemies with them when they fell. The passion and pure fight was something Serevadia, with all its numbers, couldn't match.

It fueled Sahar. It burned her lungs as she heaved breath after bloody breath. Her hands were slick with every swing, her coat ruined and stained. She stopped seeing and just felt the ebb and flow of battle.

Aster and Mei weren't the Ashen Bond. She didn't know how to fight with them, but she managed. They had a rhythm, a cycle of cutting steel that kept enemies at bay.

Sahar was aware that she was running on adrenaline and desperation alone, but she didn't realize how much until two figures in full armor joined their fight. A dozen armed knights flooded behind them, cutting through the growing opposition. And, finally, Sahar let herself breathe.

Hells, she hurt all over. Her shoulder ached like the bone itself was bruised, her wrist spiked with pain each time she moved it, and somewhere along the way she'd gotten a nasty cut on her calf. Nothing serious but it burned fiercely.

Out of habit she reached for her bag of potions and met empty air with a string of curses.

"Careful," Aster panted. "That's the King of Etherak."

Hard-drilled etiquette and manners kept Sahar from making a fool over herself as the taller of the two armored men lost his helmet. The scarred elf was a brute, pure and simple, but that was how King Loghain Rhys was described anyway.

The second one rushed to Mei's side and checked her over. The two exchanged quick words Sahar couldn't hear. Prince Barrion then. Very sweet.

Sahar swallowed her bitterness and forced herself to bow to Loghain.

"Your Majesty."

He grunted. "No need for that. Where's Hanali?"

Sahar and Aster exchanged worried glances. "We don't know. We lost them in the battle."

Barrion lifted the visor of his helmet up, revealing a handsome if sweaty face. "They're going after Abraxas; we just have to hold until they do."

"No amount of holding fixes this army," Loghain growled. "Circling around to flank them helped, but we're still outnumbered. This isn't a fight we can win."

Sahar's heart stuttered in her chest. Even if they stopped Abraxas, how would they defeat this army? It was a field for sacrifice, and Loghain's arrival just gave Abraxas more fuel. But to retreat would leave the Wandering Sols in the middle of Serevadia's wrath. They'd be killing them.

Her or them, essentially. Sahar found it strange how easy that choice came.

She leveled the King her best glare, one that would've made her mother proud. "We're not here to win, Your Majesty. We're here to buy them time. It's us or the world, but you knew that coming in here."

He nodded. "I did. And somehow I don't think anyone would listen if I ordered a retreat."

Fights like this only happen once an era, Sahar thought. *Where life and death are afterthoughts to why the battle is fought in the first place.*

None of them were going to retreat. None of them would turn their backs on the Wandering Sols now that they'd come this far.

For a moment, bloodlines didn't matter. Nationalities, past wars, petty arguments, and differences on how the dead were treated faded away. For a singular moment they were all just people fighting for a chance, not even to live but for others to do so. And it was brilliant, beautiful.

Until it was broken.

The ground thundered in rapid succession as the smoke of the battle parted to reveal one of those massive creatures charging straight for them. Sahar cried out, the guard formed ranks, and Barrion tried to shove everyone away.

But Loghain stood tall as his guards were swept away like dolls and, before their eyes, the King of Etherak was snatched up by a meaty fist. He roared and stabbed into the fingers that held him, but the skin didn't so much as give to his blade.

The creature huffed once, as if annoyed, and threw Loghain away. He hit the tree with a resounding crack and fell limply to the ground. Unmoving, his sword fallen out of his hand.

Barrion yelled in anguish. Sahar had to join Aster and Mei to hold him back as he tried to charge the creature. But Barrion's yell was enough. The creature had heard him and was lumbering forward.

Sahar pushed him back as much as she could. "We need to go!"

He struggled against them. "No!"

"With all due respect, we're going to die!" she cried.

A massive foot slammed into the ground mere feet from where she'd been. The creature loomed over them, sniffing the air.

Mei clamped a hand over Barrion's mouth. Aster had his other arm and was trying to silently maneuver them away. How? Barrion wore full plate. He so much as breathed and they would be heard.

Sahar eyed the swinging chains. Damn it, she wasn't nearly as strong as Evren. She couldn't choke this thing out. Nothing could cut it, but she couldn't just let the new King of Etherak die moments after the previous.

She could run. Draw its attention away from them. A terrible plan that would get her killed immediately, but what choice did she have?

Through the creature's legs, Sahar saw a figure stand up from the bodies. A Serevadian, but he was all wrong. His neck was twisted at a terrible angle and cracked as he righted it. He tore his helmet off, his jaw clicking as he pushed it back into place. His eyes were a bright prismatic color, fathomless and ages old.

Keres's new face split into a grin. "Miss me?"

Sahar nearly sobbed in relief, and Keres took that as a yes. They lifted their arms as if expecting applause, and all the Serevadian corpses around them snapped upright. Sahar jumped back, but they went straight to the creature and swarmed it. It bellowed, throwing them off in chunks. But much in the way living Serevadians never seemed to run out, the undead kept coming.

Sahar and the other three watched with barely bridled horror as the undead pulled the creature to the ground and slowly began to smother it. As it thrashed and died. Keres moved casually to them.

"I assume Serevadian corpses are okay to desecrate?" They

asked. "After all, we can't be picky about what magic aids us, can we, Your Majesty?"

Barrion looked like he was going to be sick, and Sahar remembered vividly how awful it had been to meet Keres for the first time. When you're that old, subtlety is off the table. Even Mei and Aster looked aghast, and Sahar knew Evren had told them Keres had once been an ally.

Slowly, Barrion nodded and Mei let her hand fall from his mouth.

"Where have you been?" Sahar asked.

Keres gave her a sympathetic nod. "Aimless without a body. Abraxas almost succeeded in destroying me. *Almost.* But I'm here now, and I plan on keeping your four and your army, what is left of it, alive."

Aster looked away from the twitching creature. "With . . . the dead?"

"They're helpful, but no." Keres waved dismissively. "Come now, there's a corpse much more important for us to see. And a choice to be made."

They looked pointedly at Sahar. "It's not over yet, dear. One more stand."

Sahar swallowed her doubt, her rising fear. If Keres was here, there was a chance. But what cost it would bring . . .

"Lead the way."

43

Gyda

One moment, Evren was next to her, and the next, she was dripping shadows with Abraxas's hand around her throat. Her bow clattered uselessly to the ground and her hand reached for the dagger at her hip, but Abraxas took that as well, keeping it out of reach.

"Abraxas," Gyda said. A warning, a plea.

He frowned at her. "I made a mistake before. I assumed you would listen and at least try to understand. I now know you both to be too good for that. I respect it. Envy it, even, but I cannot let it stand. Give me the dagger, or I kill her."

A simple threat. An easy one. It sent Gyda's blood boiling and her blade red, but she forced herself to plant her feet. This was always a risk, when love turned out to be a weakness just as much as a strength.

"You won't."

Abraxas's eyes sparked dangerously. "You know me so well, do you? I've killed for less."

Evren gasped, clawing at his hand tightening around her throat. Where she drew blood, the shadows healed him. She kicked furtively at his legs, but the shadows always kept her from hitting. He was as still and unmovable as a statue.

"Not her," Gyda said. "This isn't how this goes."

"It's simple, truly," he said. "You give me the dagger and I'll let her go."

"To die another way."

"If the Divines wish it."

Gyda took a step forward and the entire clearing shivered with anticipation. Did the shadows have their own personality, or did they reflect Abraxas's emotions? They seemed too giddy for him. Then again, she hardly knew him now. The man in front of her wore the face of her friend, but little else.

No, that wasn't quite right. This man had always been there, deep down. He was still Abraxas, and perhaps that was the worst part of it. She couldn't pretend anymore that there was a separation of good and evil in him. That wouldn't do him any justice.

This *was* Abraxas, and that hurt even worse than before.

"I understand," Gyda said. She forced her voice to be soft, like Sol's was when comfort was needed. "I know you think you need to do this for them."

"I don't think I need this," he spat. "I know. This is my path."

"And ours is written to oppose yours, yes? Is that what you believe?"

He pulled his mouth into a firm line. "That's what's happening now."

"We're not here to oppose. We're here to help."

"Liar," he snarled.

"No," she said firmly, and held out her empty hand. A soft shimmer of sand and ash swirled in her palm as the dagger shimmered into view.

The air suddenly changed. Something more charged, more electric. The three of them gasped, and the shadows froze, waiting.

Abraxas stared at the dagger with hungry eyes. Gyda curled

her hand over the hilt. It was warm, as if it'd been sitting in the sun. It felt as tiny and useless as it had in her hand when she faced the Storm of the Wood. How was it that Abraxas scared her more than that beast?

Because she *was* scared. Gyda counted so few things as terrifying. Gail had been one, and the Long Night. But standing in front of Abraxas now was like a nightmare she couldn't wake from.

Her heart was calm. Calmer than it should've been. She met Evren's eyes and found not the absence of fear, but strength from it. Her lover was terrified in his grasp, as if the bodies of the Champions were his way of telling her that he could and would do the same to her. But her heartbeat was calm and her eyes were sure. Placing all her trust in Gyda and her plan.

Gyda nearly choked. There was no plan. Just blind trust.

Abraxas took a step closer, dragging Evren with him, but Gyda drew the dagger to her chest. His eyes flicked up to her and narrowed.

"I thought you were seeing reason."

"If you want it, you fight for it." Gyda raised her sword. The ghostly green blade shone in the light mist she hadn't realized hovered in the air.

"I beat you before," Abraxas said coldly. "I will do it again"

Gyda's heartbeat spiked, but it wasn't her. Again, it was Evren. *That* was what got her blood pumping? That's what made her squirm in terror?

Evren could've fought and kicked some more. Instead Gyda watched as she brought her hand to her mouth and bit hard enough to draw blood.

No weakness came like Gyda expected. Immediately Abraxas's eyes widened. He started to draw back and raise his blade to her. Gyda started to run forward to get between them. But Evren shoved her bloody palm towards him.

And the shadows lashed out at Abraxas.

He surged backwards, slashing his blade to cut them down. Evren ended up on her knees gasping. Her bloody hand curled into a fist and the shadows attacking Abraxas froze.

"Abraxas Kain," she started, her voice hoarse. "I promised to bring you back, and I'll be damned if I don't."

Gyda settled behind Evren, kicking her bow to her. She took it and stood up, her blood following the intricate design of the new weapon.

"Then you'll be damned," Abraxas said. "You can't keep them forever, Evren. You're no mage. Already I can feel you losing control, and you know what happens when you slip."

Evren huffed, her brow beaded with sweat. Gyda wanted to put herself between them, to keep Abraxas's eyes off her. But this was Evren's call and she had to trust her. Even as the dagger hummed in her hand knowingly. Even as visions of the figure haunted her.

"What can I say that hasn't already been said?" Evren asked. "All but Sorin have begged you to stand down, and you refuse. We've appealed to every part of you that we know, and it's not enough."

"It isn't," he agreed.

"Tell me you regret this, at least?" Evren asked. "That you'll think of us down the line."

Abraxas hesitated. He watched the shadows, as if tugging against Evren's willpower, but she didn't break. When he looked back, his jaw was set, his eyes lowered.

"I will regret this until the end of my miserable life. You were like family to me, and I wish it could be different. I wish I was different. But this isn't a choice. I need you to understand that this is far from personal."

Truth. Gyda felt it in the air. Sorrow-tinged and bitter to swallow. It made everything worse, but lessened the hurt.

Evren nodded. "I do understand."

Then she twisted her hands, bloody bow and all, and the

shadows leapt into action. Abraxas was back on the offensive, but the shadows weren't coming for him. They weren't attacking at all. Gyda pulled Evren out of the way of Abraxas's rush as the shadows that surrounded the clearing dissipated and gave way to four ragged figures.

44

Sorin

Seeing Abraxas didn't make Sorin's plan any more sane. Especially when the moment he, Sol, and Arke—riding the worg—entered the strange clearing, Evren cried out and fell to her knees. The shadows suddenly lashed out in all directions and Sorin didn't think, he just let his feet move.

He was quick, just barely getting away from the rush of blackness headed in his direction. Even still, it acted like the wind at the whim of a Stormheart, curling around and coming right back.

A glyph of fire seared the air before Sorin, blocking the shadows before they could get at him. He spared a relieved smile at Arke, who was huddling behind a formation of magical stone he'd just pushed up with Sol and the worg. As the shadows reared back to find a better way, they waved to him. Not that the rock would do a damn thing, but the primal part of him wanted to hide.

He looked back at Gyda and Evren, kneeling at Abraxas's mercy. The shadows were circling them like vultures. When Gyda lashed out, they snapped at her. In a flurry of light and shadow that was over in a blink, they left her hunched over Evren and the small dagger, her sword dull and tossed to the far side of the clearing. They twitched when Evren cut her hand again, but ultimately did nothing. The blade wouldn't be won by blood alone.

And hells, Gyda had the dagger. She was mere feet from him. All he had to do was lash out at one of them and take it from her. Then they'd all be the worst kind of dead and Abraxas would get his Divines back.

Well, fuck all of that.

"Abraxas!" Sorin called. "Don't ignore me. It's rude and I feel left out."

Just as he expected, Abraxas's attention homed right on him. Sorin made a point of dropping his sword, wincing at the tones of warning the steel rang against the stone. His bad hand ached in this cold. He was tired as hell and drenched in blood. In other words, he'd had better days. But as he walked up, he forced confidence into his steps. He forced that fear in his chest to fuck right off, and he met Abraxas's eyes for the first time in months, because Sorin couldn't bear the thought of looking at him in the palace. That betrayal threatened to overwhelm him again, but he didn't have a use for it. He didn't need Abraxas to see how much he hurt because that wouldn't help.

"I suppose you want a turn at appealing to my conscience," Abraxas drawled.

"Me?" Sorin snorted "No. I mean, you know us. We haven't exactly been on the best of terms, have we? You've got no respect for personal boundaries. I have no respect period. That's just us, right? Never seen eye to eye. Never had our moment."

Sorin stopped when Abraxas leveled that black blade at his chest. He didn't look at it though, he kept his eyes on his friend. Hells, he looked awful. Like he hadn't slept in years. More than anything, Abraxas looked confused.

Good.

"You remember what I said in Direwall about people making

themselves gods was evil, right?" Sorin cocked his head to the side.

"I didn't want to be Catarmon," Abraxas gritted out.

"No, but you certainly used the title to your advantage, didn't you?"

Behind Abraxas, Gyda hissed a warning. Sorin ignored her. These things needed to be said.

"You told me that I should be grateful to the Divines for saving me," Sorin continued. "But it wasn't them, it was you. Divara Rimmel knew. I figured it out because I can think for myself every once in a while. And then it got me thinking some more."

"A reason for me not to slit your throat?" Abraxas asked.

"Oh, you don't want to do that, so you won't. Will you?"

Abraxas blinked, bewildered. "I . . ."

Sorin grinned. There it was. "Why kill something you've spent so long protecting? And that goes for all of us. You don't want to kill us, do you?"

He shook his head. "N-no. No, I don't. I don't want to kill anyone. I have—"

"Yes, yes, you have to." Sorin waved his hands in the air, heedless of the sword still pointed at his chest. "We've heard enough of duty and destiny to last another era, so let's move on. Get down to the basics, because I have the pleasure of knowing you, Abraxas. It's not even hard to see, really. You're a man who follows orders. You do as you're told. You don't want to do any of this, you're just following orders."

Abraxas glared at the ground. He seemed smaller now, far less threatening than he was a few minutes ago. He was struggling, trying to bring up those justifications he kept spilling out. Oh yes, he wanted the Divines back. But the cost was too much, even for him.

"I am," he admitted in a choked voice. "I need this. I need them. They can save me and Eith."

"At the expense of three thousand souls and," Sorin

shrugged, "us. But you're not going to do it. Do you know why?"

Abraxas shuddered, refusing to look at him. The blade lowered an inch. "Why?"

Sorin took a step forward. Dangerous, exciting. He could feel his magic working on the tip of his tongue. Not forcing Abraxas to do something he wouldn't, just coaxing out a different outcome.

"You're going to choose not to," Sorin said softly. "You're going to put down the blade, call off your army, and then we're going to fix all of this the right way. Because there's one thing that I've been dying to tell you, Abraxas. Something you've needed to hear that the others can't beat."

Through his eyelashes he looked up at Sorin. "And what's that?"

Sorin held his scarred hand out to Abraxas, pretending the blade didn't exist. "I forgive you."

All the breath rushed out of Abraxas. He stared at Sorin, disbelieving, and all those little cracks Sorin had been chipping away at started to widen. The armor crumbled behind Abraxas's eyes. A hint of the man from before, the first face he saw when he came back from the dead was there.

"For . . ."

"Everything. But mostly me. I forgive you for bringing me back, and I forgive you for everything else. Come home, Abraxas."

Poor, broken, Abraxas. How had Sorin never seen it before? He wasn't strong or menacing. He was just a man made up of jagged traumas, barely held together by oaths to the type of things that could never love him the way he loved them.

Abraxas Kain wasn't a villain, he was just a pawn. And Sorin wanted him back.

Sorin felt the moment something changed. He watched Abraxas's relief turn to horror, then to cold understanding. Sorin realized too late that his words had failed, that the black sword was coming for him.

He was all that stood between Abraxas and Divinity, and far too late Sorin realized he miscalculated just how powerful the Divine influence of the sword was. After all, what was a sea monster to a god?

He was going to accept it because he was too close now. There was no dancing out of the way this time. But then there was Gyda shoving herself between them. There was the Eternity Dagger, risen to block the Shadow Dancer's Sword.

There was his horrible death as they collided, black blade sliding up to the hilt of the dagger as the dagger's blade snapped and the air turned hot and white.

45

Gyda

It played out exactly as she'd seen, but feeling it was different. Feeling the blade snap in half, the chaotic energy pour out and consume her.

Gyda thought she knew pain, but she was wrong.

This energy was overwhelming. All consuming. Biting and cutting as it tore at her flesh. She felt it examine every inch of her, deadly in its curiosity. Every time it sunk into her skin to see how she bled, she screamed. And when it crawled down her throat, cutting that up as well, she could do nothing but sob.

Eternity was madness, and Gyda struggled not to let it take her. She endured the probing cuts because the pain was important. She let it bleed her dry because she hadn't promised not to give her last drop. When she lost her eye to it, she didn't even feel it.

What she did feel was another loss. The shift from warrior to guardian. From fighter to warden. Something new, something quiet and watchful. Something that wasn't her and she wanted to hate. Because her strength was gone. She was hunched and broken, feeble for everything except the Divine power curled inside her. It allowed her to build, to shape, to align. It did not allow for her to fight, to live.

Gyda was dead now, after all.

The first breath of air was a shock. She struggled not to cough, choking on her own blood, and quickly pull the hood over her face. She huddled inside. Made herself smaller. Gyda made herself into what she hoped Evren had seen before.

She was in an unfamiliar room. Bare and black, with imposing walls of unmarred black stone. In the center of the room, floating on a pedestal, was the dagger. Strange, because she'd just broken it for this exact reason; to manipulate time. But time, she was coming to understand, was far from simple.

Then *she* came into the room, choking on ash and the remains of her dress smoking. Gyda's heart lurched at the sight of her, hair freshly cut, her eyes set and determined despite what she'd seen. She wanted nothing more than to go to her and tell her everything.

But that's not what happened.

Gyda said the first thing that came to mind. "It took you longer than I thought to reach me."

Her voice sounded nothing like her. No accent, all raspy and gurgled as she struggled to speak around torn vocal chords. Evren jumped, and the only recognition in her eyes was one of uncertainty, not the warmth Gyda was used to.

Her hand went to her bow. "Where the hells have you been?"

Gyda wanted to laugh and cry at the same time. Seeing that fight made her dizzy with relief. That was her girl.

"Waiting for you," she rasped.

Without thinking, she took a step forward and Evren shrank back. Gyda mentally cursed herself. She couldn't do that. She couldn't reveal anything, because the moment she did, Evren would change it all. And that just wouldn't do.

Gyda glared at the dagger, both savior and tormentor.

Evren was speaking again. "I haven't seen you in months, since you warned me about the Long Night."

Ah, that. She remembered the phrasing.

"I thought you'd come and give me more cryptic messages before I went to Orenlion."

The sudden awfulness broke over Gyda, and she found herself laughing. Hating the dagger, Hating her choice. Hating how any other way would've put someone else in her place, because *someone* had to guide all of this. Someone had to risk it all. Fixed points in time, so long as someone was willing to lose everything for the sake of the world.

"I am bound to that," she spat, gesturing to the dagger. "When I appear to you is up to my own strength and wherever it spits me out in time."

"So you . . . you're not the Eternity Keeper."

"No." *If the bastard was alive I wouldn't have to do this.* "There is no control here. No power. Just a chance in a storm of chaos."

Gyda knew she was in trouble when Evren stared at her as if she could see through the cloak. Gyda hoped not. Wanted to back away but didn't.

"Why me?" Evren asked.

"Because you're my strongest connection to this time." Not a lie. The truth. The only truth. The oath that kept her from dissolving into eternity.

"So . . . I know you."

Hells, Evren hadn't mentioned this part before. She didn't talk about how close they were getting, how Gyda was leaning in, ready to throw it all away for just one more kiss.

No.

Power she didn't understand took her from one side of the pedestal to the other, keeping the dagger between them. This was better. She could focus like this.

"Not anymore." Another truth. She wasn't the Gyda Evren knew.

Evren shook her head, fixated on the dagger again. "I need to take the dagger."

"You don't." *But you do. It's the only way.*

"Okay then, tell me how to fix this without taking it. I'm all ears."

"No." As Evren started to protest, Gyda cut her off. "You don't need the dagger, but you'll take it, anyway."

"Why? If it's safe here and I can fix things on my own, so be it. Give me another option."

"I cannot. Time is fluid and ever changing. Few things are set into the stone of the world, meant to happen. This is one. By taking the dagger, your actions will ripple across Eith for generations to come. Heroes and villains alike will rise and fall because of it."

Evren backed away. "No. No, the futures I saw—"

"—will happen."

"—are terrible!" Evren shouted. Oh, she had no idea. "All I saw for a future in Eith is death. The earth splitting apart and swallowing an army, the Boreal Sea freezing solid, a red moon hanging over a dead city—"

"All fixed points."

"There was so much destruction! So much death and hopelessness . . ."

"Where do you think heroes come from?" Gyda finally snapped. "Tragedy, war, blood and loss, *that* makes a hero."

Evren shook her head. "It shouldn't be like that."

"No," she agreed. Gyda wanted a world where it wasn't like that. "But everything you saw, every terrible moment in time, was fixed by people like you. The sea melted again. The scar in the earth was built over. The blood moon and the plague it brought were cured. That is the nature of this world. Gods or no, the world will break until someone is strong enough to put it back together."

Evren glared at the dagger, torn. Gyda wanted desperately for her to just take it and get it over with. She had more arguing to do with her later. In the past. The future? It was hard to keep track. Hells, she loved this woman, but when the fate of Eith hung in the balance she took her sweet time making decisions.

"Someone takes the dagger out of here," Gyda prompted, softer. "It's needed in the future. If not by you, then someone else."

"How do I fix this?" Evren asked in a hushed tone. "The dagger . . . how do I stop the war?"

Gyda grinned. "There are things in time not set in stone."

Evren frowned at her, but now Gyda was planting the seeds. She saw the battle with the dragon, both bone and flesh. She felt the fire at her back, the undead clawing at her. Evren's lips against her own for the first time.

Gyda leaned forward. "So move them."

Evren looked back at the dagger, breathing sharply. She closed her eyes. "And my friends?"

"Right where they need to be," Gyda whispered. "Always."

The dagger tugged, insistent. Eternity swept her away again and again. And it was all a terrible, magical blur. Gyda saw Evren each time the world became real again, except the times she revealed herself and the horrible plan to her past self and Jalaa. In her bed at Sahar's manor, where she refused to look at her past self, so lucky to have Evren to hold. In the snow with Sol, at the edge of the Long Night. In the alleyway behind the *Bed Rock*, where she turned Evren's would be killer to ash. That was new, fun. Taxing though.

Hells, she was exhausted.

And Evren, younger and not as scarred, watched her warily. Her hair was so long, her face still streaked with soot. Those eyes, unaware of how heavy they would get at the end of an era. Gyda barely felt the words pass through her lips. She knew this was the beginning for Evren, but it felt like the end for her. She didn't want an end, not yet. Not when she still had to say good-bye, to apologize, to beg for forgiveness.

Not when she had time to give her friends.

Young Evren faded out of view, and when eternity dropped Gyda back in the present, she was just as Gyda had left her. Tearful, bloody, shaking.

The clearing was frozen in time. A white-hot bubble was forming between Sorin and Abraxas, and both scrambled away. Arke and Sol peaked out from behind their rock. And Evren stared at her.

Gyda pulled back the hood, grimacing at the gasp that tore through her lover's throat. Evren's hands covered her mouth and she was shaking her head.

"No, no, no," Evren whispered. "What did you do? Love, what did you do?"

Gyda tried to smile and couldn't. "I came back."

Evren sobbed, rushing up and taking her head between her hands. Her fingers smoothed over every scar eternity had carved, over the lips that had spoken to her throughout time. Gyda leaned into her touch, feeling warmth for the first time in what felt like ages.

"I'm sorry," she whispered. "I had to."

Evren hushed her, smoothing away her hair from her face. "Oh, you knew. You knew and you didn't tell me. I want to hate you so much but I can't." She sobbed, resting her forehead against Gyda's. "You came back."

Gyda held her for what could be the last time and looked over at Abraxas. He was staring at the frozen explosion, and then at the sword. He let it clatter to the ground, watery eyes looking up at Sorin.

"Sorin . . . I-I couldn't control it. I'm sorry. Divines, I'm so sorry."

Abraxas made no move towards him, but Sorin held out his hand anyway. His throat worked around the knot of emotion so clearly lodged there. "I told you that I forgave you. Shut up and come here."

Abraxas did. He took Sorin's hand and didn't fight the embrace that followed. He was diminished then in Sorin's arms.

Much less a soldier or Champion, nothing but a broken man who became all too aware of how far he'd fallen.

It should've been over, but it wasn't.

Arke walked up to the explosion, Sol trailing behind him with the whining worg. "It's not over."

Gyda shook her head.

Evren pushed away suddenly. "What do you mean?"

Gyda traced her jaw. "I have kept time frozen for a moment. That hasn't stopped what will happen soon. The ritual is done."

"There's no way to stop it?" Sorin asked.

Gyda shook her head. The dagger was cut in two, its power effectively split. With the blade's own power, that would reach disastrous consequences for everyone around them.

Abraxas pulled away from Sorin. "There is a way."

Arke snapped his head towards him. "No."

"I can do it, Arke. A willing soul should be enough."

"One against a few thousand?" the goblin barked. "You think it's enough for that?"

"What's enough?" Sol asked.

"He wants to sacrifice himself," Arke said. "He wants me to use his soul to hold back the explosion."

Sorin gawked. "No! That's not happening."

"It won't be enough," Evren insisted.

But Gyda knew that it would be. Not enough for everyone, but for them. Someone else had the rest of the army covered.

"It will be," Gyda said. Her one golden eye met Abraxas's, and their shared grief was enough to drown nations. She didn't blame him. How could she when he was her clan? Her family. She loved him more than she could ever hate him.

Sol shook her head. "No. Stop it. There's got to be another way. I'm not losing anyone else!"

"Solri," Abraxas said softly.

"Shut up! I'm not listening, I'm thinking."

She paced, and Evren struggled. But Gyda held her. There wasn't much fight left in her, so she stayed put. Gyda had shown her enough times in the past that she knew what was coming. All Evren could do was accept it.

Abraxas went to his knees and Sol froze, staring at him with wide eyes.

"Stop it," she said again, softer this time.

"I've hurt you. Let me make amends."

"By hurting me again?" she cried. "If I wanted you dead, I would've killed you before! I want to yell at you, Abraxas. I want to scream until I can't anymore and then I want you to tell me that you hated every second of what you did. I don't want you to die."

"I hated every second," Abraxas said. "Except when I was with you. Because for a moment I was just Abraxas again, and I felt whole. What I did to you, to your people, to Eith, was unforgivable. This goes past atonement."

"No . . ." Sol choked on her tears, and Sorin was there to hold her. He was barely holding himself together, breathing hard and staring Abraxas down.

"You are destroying me, Abraxas Kain," Sorin said hoarsely. "I had all these terrible things planned for you. Pastels included. I was going to make you miserable, so long as you were there."

Abraxas laughed a little. "I hate to disappoint you again. Forgive me?"

"Always."

He turned to Evren and Gyda. "There is nothing I can say to make up for what I've done. Let me instead follow your leads. I never meant for it to be like this."

Gyda nodded. "Neither did I. I understand now."

Understood that Abraxas had always touched powers beyond his understanding. Understood that none of them could do it without an outcome like this. To start as mortals with so little understanding of how vast and terrible the universe was, to become something bigger . . . it was something indescribable. A feeling Divine in nature—it was terrible and unknowable, but she felt it all the same.

Abraxas did too. Maybe he always had.

"Evren," he started, then choked on his words. He started again, three different times, before settling on something he'd said before. "Thank you for the light."

Evren sobbed into Gyda's arms. "Not again, please."

"It should've been this way from the beginning, my friend."

And finally, he turned to Arke. The goblin's shoulders were slumped and he dropped his spellbook to pick up Evren's dagger from the ground.

"I hate you for this," he rasped as he stepped up to Abraxas.

"I know," the elf said.

"You and I . . ." Arke took a deep breath. "We're okay."

Abraxas nodded, blinking back his disbelief. "I . . . thank you."

Arke raised the dagger and Sol cried, turning away. Abraxas took it from Arke's hand gently, shaking his head.

"You know what to do," he said softly, and the goblin nodded.

If Gyda had been stronger she would've watched, but she'd run out of strength. She turned away, burying her head in Evren's hair. She closed her eye, embracing the darkness as she forced herself to listen instead. To the blade sinking into skin, to Abraxas's pained gasp. Tears she didn't know she had left fell from her eye and Evren balled her fists into her cloak.

It was always blood and sacrifice for this world. That was all that Eith fed upon.

Arke was grabbing Abraxas's soul, shaping it into a shield when Gyda whispered into Evren's ears.

"I have to go."

Evren held her tighter. "You promised."

"I swore I would always come back, and I meant it. I will. But I can't stay in Eith."

"Where are you going?"

Gyda didn't know. Wherever eternity took her. She was

bound to it now, as she was with Evren. There was nothing that could break that.

"Wherever I go, you'll find me," Gyda said. "You always do."

The shield was done, and eternity wasn't waiting anymore. It tore her from Evren's arms, shoved her somewhere far away and unknowable. She let go of Eith, of the explosion, but never of the people she called home.

46

Sahar

Keres led them to a massive corpse. Nothing but a skeleton, but its finger bones were longer than she was tall. It was half buried under trees, roots, and soil, the gnarled black branches looking like shriveled veins and nerves as they curled around the giant's skeleton. Its ribcage felt like a hollow cathedral as she rushed inside, bloodied monarchs and ambassador in tow.

Sahar turned to Keres. "I don't understand. Are you raising this?"

Keres grimaced. "Would that I could. The soul of this giant is still attached, making it nigh impossible to remove it to make way for an empty corpse. A necromancer's nightmare, to be faced with a body they cannot use. Luckily, it has another purpose."

Leave it to Keres to dramatically explain their plan in the middle of a damn battle. But a voice outside the ribs cut them off, earning a devastating glower. Sahar peaked through the dead foliage to see a Serevadian that looked like he'd been cut from onyx. Even his armor was black and shimmered, as if it had tiny stars winking out of existence within. Sahar didn't know what Emperor Velcros looked like, but one look at the circlet on his head was all she needed.

"The last line of Etherak's kings cowers!" he crowed from beyond and brandished his sword. He wasn't alone, as two shadow mages flanked him and echoed his jeer.

Sahar looked at Barrion, still breathing heavily. His grey eyes were far away, as if he was replaying his uncle's death over and over. His sword arm trembled.

Velcros wasn't done. "Let us end this, little Rhys. They say your father died with hands red from the blood he spilled. Your uncle destroyed entire kingdoms under his command. Do you share their bloodlust? Do you have the same strength?" His smirk was feral. "Or are you the coward they whisper about?"

'They' didn't matter. 'They' likely didn't exist. It was a common tactic to knock an opponent off their feet and get them to do something reckless, and Sahar, who knew verbal warfare far better than physical, saw it for what it was.

But it didn't matter. Barrion was reaching for his helmet—Mei must've taken it off to help him breathe. The Khama snatched it away from him, cold fury lighting up her eyes.

"He's baiting you."

"It's working," Barrion gritted out. "I don't have a choice."

"So you'd walk to your death?" Mei snapped. "And leave Etherak without a ruler?"

Barrion's jaw tightened. Beyond them, Sahar saw Aster weighing the fight outside. None of them knew how good of a fighter Velcros was, but the mages would overwhelm Barrion. Even if Velcros *did* die, this wasn't a fairytale, where cutting the head off the snake magically made the whole army stand down. Going out there would be suicide.

"I can't hide from this, Mei," Barrion said softly. "You know this."

The Khama's grip on the helmet tightened. Sahar was half

afraid it would crumble under her fingers. Instead it just shook as she held it out to him, her face cold but her eyes swimming.

"I know." Armored fingers brushed as the helmet passed between them, but she didn't let go. As Barrion tugged the helmet away, she let it pull her forward. The whole display was so intimate that Aster looked away and Sahar felt like she was intruding by watching.

"I made a vow to you, Barrion Rhys," Mei said firmly. "Your battles are mine. Your enemies are my enemies. Your victories and your losses, your happiness and your grief, they are all mine as well. As your wife, as your Queen, this fight is mine, as well as every other one after this. We do this together, or we don't do it at all."

Barrion stared at her, not quite disbelieving because it seemed like this was common behavior for Mei. But . . . relieved. Grateful.

"Until the stars fall from the sky and the night is eternally black," the young King said.

"Our souls move as one," his Queen finished and let go of the helmet.

There was nothing else to say as they gathered their weapons and marched past Sahar out of the ribcage. Too shocked was she to hear Velcros's laugh, and the icy banter between monarchs before battle. She whirled on Keres, who watched it all with a strange expression.

"Can't you do something? Velcros's mages are nothing compared to you."

"I could," they admitted. "But I need my reserve of power to save the rest of your army. Would you prefer I spend it all on just two people?"

"They'll die," she insisted.

Keres fixed her a fathomless glare. "All monarchs die, Sahar. It is a rare moment that they get to decide how they die."

A warm hand turned Sahar around, and she was face to face with Aster. He looked like he was already mourning the King and Queen outside. One of his blades gleamed crimson in his other hand.

"Whatever you're going to do," he said gravely. "You have as much time as we can give you. Make it count."

Protests stuck uselessly to the back of Sahar's tongue as he turned and walked out, joining the couple on Mei's other side. The three faced off against the might of an Empire, and Sahar, as she had been when Vox, Drystan, and Nerezza had all separately died, was useless.

She turned away from the fighting, the scream of magic, and the clash of blades. She forced herself to keep breathing, to push past the sluggish weight wrapping around her heart as it tried to strangle her into eternal rest. She couldn't—wouldn't—until this was through.

"Tell me what to do." Her words spilled out of her mouth like blood over stone.

Despite the desperate battle separated from them only by bone and roots, Keres seemed unaffected. Too calm and slow as they reached the other side of the ribcage and caressed the bone there, as if meeting an old lover.

Someone screamed in pain outside and Sahar jumped. She refused to acknowledge who it was.

"Keres! Tell me what to do!"

"You have to destroy me," the spirit said simply.

She gawked. "What?"

"We have moments before the Aether is going to rip. If you want to be able to save two armies from being the fuel that burns it all down, then you need something strong enough to protect them." They turned to her. "You need me."

"I don't understand."

"Not surprising. It's complicated magic, you see. It wouldn't work unless you had someone thousands of years old and brimming with power." They gestured to themselves. "My soul has essentially marinated in necromancy long enough to be particularly potent. My magic, when combined with a powerful soul such as this," they swept their hands to the skeleton, "will be enough to hold back what Abraxas unleashes."

Sahar felt sick. The Wandering Sols had failed then. This was all for nothing? It came down to Keres, of all people, to stand between Etherak and its own gods. The thought felt so wrong, so twisted, that she found herself shaking her head.

"No. No, you'll *die*, Keres."

"Oh, sweet Sahar. I've been dead for ages. What I will become next will be different, perhaps even better. Something never seen before." They cocked their head to the side and extended a cold hand. "But I can't do it without your permission."

Sahar started to step back and heard a cry of rage behind her. Mei's. The kind of fury that only something truly devastating can stoke. Sahar almost envied it, because if someone had died and it was rage that Mei turned to, then she was so much stronger than Sahar. Sahar who, time after time, crumbled a little more with each death she faced.

"Why do you need me?" she asked.

Keres frowned, as if it was obvious. "I bound myself to you in the Expanse, Sahar. You are the blood of Vernes, its future. I see home in your eyes. Why do you think I never left your side after the White Cairn? Only for Nerezza? No, my dear. I put myself in your service, and in doing so I cannot leave it without your permission."

The air was stolen from Sahar's lungs. Not just from Keres's words but from the sudden surge of energy that seemed to burn the air right out of her. Bright light erupted in the sky, like the sun itself had fallen. Everything was singeing. Too hot, too bright. Drystan's axe burned at her hip.

Above them, the sky burned a bloody red. Gone was the grey, the light raked its claws through it. Lightning forked hot and deadly, as cracks in the sky slowly opened.

Sahar expected the explosion to consume immediately. To her horror, it didn't. It was a slow, inevitable death that ate everything in its path. She could feel the weight of its hunger pressing on her, and it wasn't even to her yet. The screams of the dying were far away but inching closer by the second.

Keres grabbed her arm. Even they weren't cool anymore. It was almost like a living person was holding her steady. The red light poured through the ribs of the giant, and their eyes looked like rubies. When lightning forked, silent and deadly, they didn't flinch, unlike her.

At the end of everything they knew, Keres was calm.

"Let me go, Sahar," they said.

It should've been an easy order to give. Thousands of lives versus one who'd lived long enough to see it all? Who was *offering*.

But Keres was all she had left of them. Keres was a remnant that remembered. They had Vox's memories. They knew how terribly empty she felt since leaving the White Cairn. Yes, the Wandering Sols knew. They saw and sympathized.

But Keres feasted on loneliness long before Sahar had ever had a taste of it. And now that they were leaving too, she didn't want to bear that alone.

Selfish, she knew, to hesitate before saving thousands of lives at the expense of her own comfort.

Her tears were evaporating before they left her eyes. "What about Vernes? You'll never go home."

They smiled serenely. Their hair had started to smoke. White light was overcoming red and it was almost unbearable to look at them now.

"Such is my fate," was all they said.

A cruel fate, to die to keep back a foe thought long beaten. Cruel to die on the soil of a country that hated you, to dream for decades of home and never get to see it again because you were the only thing able to fix the world.

Sahar knew then that there never had been a choice. Her hesitation was just delaying the inevitable. Keres would die here and no one would remember their name.

The sky burned and Sahar's heart broke as her cracking lips formed the right words.

Keres let her go and she fell to her knees. The ground sizzled beneath her touch and she cowered. She covered her head and closed her eyes and screamed.

Not for pain, because no pain would be equal to holding the bodies of those she loved.

Not for rage, because there wasn't anything left in her to rage. She was spent.

Not for loss, because by now she was intimately familiar with the feeling.

Sahar Al-Fasil screamed to feel. She would not be numb. She would not let ice overtake her again and make her cold, unfeeling, and devoid of life. She would feel, no matter how awful. She'd make the world feel it too.

If the world wouldn't remember Keres, Nerezza, Drystan, or Vox, it would damn well remember her.

When the heat left her skin feeling tight and ready to blister, Sahar was half convinced she was dead. But when she looked up from the smoking ground, the nightmare continued. The sky was still ripping open. The light was still encroaching.

But the skeleton was moving.

Sahar had just enough time to see the body of the soldier Keres had possessed slumped a few feet from her, still forever, before the ribcage started to tear itself from the ground. She pulled herself to her feet, bleeding heart lodged in her throat as she scrambled out of the remains.

Outside was no better. The ground shook and heaved as the giant pushed itself free from its half-grave. Smoldering trees crumbled as its hands combed the ground for support. Against the red sky and the white light, it was a terrible monster rising up to destroy them.

Velcros the shadow was nothing more than an afterthought to her, but she could still savor the look of horror in his face before Barrion ran him through. There was only one mage left, and she fled from the light, the giant, from Mei's bloody blade.

Aster was a crumpled heap on the ground, breathing, but barely, as shadows slithered from his skin. They expelled themselves, as if to run after their mistress, but shrieked and burned under the heat and light. They didn't even leave ash.

Sahar was an outsider again, watching as Mei and Barrion huddled around the fallen ambassador. She was an ant, watching as gods tried to shove through the sky back into Eith. And she was, strangely, hopeful as the giant reached its skeletal hands up to the sky, as if to touch it.

The explosion crashed against whatever shield had been wrought from the giant's magic. Blackened silhouettes of trees and cowering soldiers filled Sahar's vision against the white. It raged to get in, this inescapable death. Its goal was to fuel, to devour, to destroy.

And the giant kept it back. Sahar turned in a slow circle. The air still too hot for her lungs, but her eyes finally producing tears again. The armies were cowering. They were terrified.

They were alive.

All at once the light went out. She stumbled back, blinking rapidly to get used to the darkness. But when her vision bled back into view, it was red.

The scorched forest was red. The armor of three different armies mirrored the still torn sky. The blackened fingers of the trees shied away as cold rushed back in. Not a balm, but another knife in her lungs.

"It's not over," she croaked.

What had she expected? Keres didn't say they could mend the sky, only protect them. The ritual was done, the danger passed. The fighting had stopped, but the worst had already happened.

The giant turned to her, and its eye sockets sparkled the same way Keres's had. That was all that remained of the spirit she knew. This one felt different. There was none of the confidence or flair that Keres always held, no matter the body. They were gone.

"I cannot fix the sky," the giant rumbled, and sounded . . . disappointed. Apologetic even. Sahar had the strange urge to comfort it.

"It's okay," she said, even though it wasn't.

She looked up at the terrible sky and waited for the wrath of the Divines.

47

Solri

When it was done and the sky was as red as Sol's daggers, she knew what she needed to do. What they all needed to do.

She wiggled out of Sorin's arms and pointedly looked away from the black-clad body only a few feet away. She ignored Evren's gasping sobs as she sank to the smoking ground, grasping at empty air and then hugging herself. Sol made her way to Arke, who was shaking, and gently turned him to face her.

He didn't even fight her. He just looked sick. She couldn't fathom what it had been like to handle Abraxas's soul, to use him to live. And if she dwelled on it too long, she would break.

So she didn't.

"This isn't over," she told Arke. "We need to go to them."

Arke nodded numbly, but Sorin made a noise of surprise.

"Go to who?"

"The Divines." Sol turned back to him. He was trying very hard not to look at Abraxas and busied himself by pulling Evren to her feet. Sol had never seen her so empty. She didn't fight him, but leaned on him entirely. It felt wrong to bring her into another fight, but this was different. They needed to see her.

"Sol's right," Arke said. "They're gonna get through, but we need to set the terms."

"How?" Sorin pressed. "How would we even negotiate with them?"

"I got control over the leftover souls right now, I can do with them what I want. Not enough to keep them out, but enough to give us some leverage." Arke bared his teeth in frustration. "They're comin' back, but we get to decide how. I'll get you there." He paused. "For Abraxas and Gyda."

Two they'd lost before, and two they'd lost again. She had to make it worth it.

"Do it," Evren said, her eyes red. "Bring us to them."

Her tone told them everything. What else did they have to lose?

Arke opened the portal with ease and he shuddered. Something told Sol that it was much easier than it should've been, but now that the Aether was tearing under the strain of the gods it shouldn't be surprising.

"Don't look at them," Arke said. "Close your eyes, blind-folds, whatever. Just make sure you don't see them."

They all nodded and huddled together. Then, one by one, closed their eyes and stepped into the Divine Realm.

It was like seeing the sky for the first time and the feeling of pure terror, that she was going to fall into it, grappled at Sol. Only this time she couldn't see, and it made it worse. She had the awful feeling that she was standing on nothing. That the only thing keeping her from an endless tumble was a power full of curiosity. She felt the portal snap shut behind her, and a strange mix of magics all at once. Hot and cold, welcoming and damning. It all fused together into a hurricane that spun around them, and there was no escape.

And the eyes. Sol felt the weight of so many eyes.

Sorin's scarred hand took hers, and with her other one she

grabbed at Arke. He gripped her like she was a lifeline. Far too late Sol worried about bringing Evren here in her state. Would she listen to Arke's warning and keep her eyes closed? Or would her mounting losses override any self-preservation?

Too late to worry now.

"What," a voice boomed from everywhere, "is this?"

"Mortals," replied another that reminded Sol of the way the wind swept across the tundra like shards of knives. "They seek to stop us."

The chorus of voices sent Sol's ears ringing. Too loud. They were everywhere and nowhere. Whispering in her ears and then inside her head. And screaming from far away. She whimpered, and then swallowed back the sound.

Gods they may be, but she would treat them like any other court. Showing weakness would destroy her.

"To stop you would be foolish," she called, and the voices died, blissfully. Her skin seemed to blister under the heat of so many intense gazes. "We can keep the barrier up, but you'd break free in time, wouldn't you? Then we would've sealed our deaths."

Strange how their voices felt more animalistic or symbolic. One sounded like crackling flames and invoked a sense of wrath and vengeance she'd felt before, only much more intense. She found herself squeezing Arke's hand as it spoke.

"Not your deaths," this voice promised. "Something far worse. How sweet to see you think you know the feeling of pain. I have patience to last until the death of this world. I could teach you the meaning of pain, dwarf."

"Nomien, stop," another voice whispered, like a gale of wind. There was power there, but she held it back, as if conscious of how uncomfortable her voice was. "Let them speak."

"So we bow to those less than us, now?" Nomien asked.

"We do not bow, we listen. As we should have before."

A laugh echoed, a thousand voices at once. Each word

spoken was a new voice, from the cry of a child to the croak of an old man.

"My dear sister, you've taken me to heart."

"Change," the gale said bitterly, "is inevitable in mortals, as you've said. So it will be with us as well."

The sting of lightning burned with a shrill voice. "We do not answer to them, nor to you!"

"Be calm, daughter," Nomien said. "We know who is in charge."

Silence. Whoever was in charge wasn't speaking, and Sol took that as her cue to talk.

She could start off pleasant and flowery. Get into their good graces and then make them want to give her what she demanded. But she didn't have the patience for that.

"Never again will you torment Eith the way you did before," Sol said, forcing her voice to remain steady. "We will fight no more wars on your whims. You will not touch Eith, you will not destroy it with your power. The only effect you will have will be what little you can do to influence the weather, the earth, and the forces of magic we cannot control."

A voice that reminded Sol of the way her throat felt when she was sick, tight and slick with mucus, slithered behind her.

"Who are you to stop us?" he asked. "As you said, we will break free eventually."

"If," she said, "we chain you. This is a proposition. A deal."

The metallic smell of gold and silver washed over her. "We're listening."

She took a deep breath. Arke's hand was sweaty, and Sorin's too. Maybe it was just her.

"We have control over the souls sacrificed just now," Sol said. "What we do with them . . ." she prodded Arke.

He swore, then shuffled closer to her. He cleared his throat and spoke loudly.

"I'll thin the Aether in Eith enough to let you back in. As she said, to keep it stable. To control magics like the Elder artifacts. But you will not step foot into our world. You will not force others into your service. And you will *not* touch Vernes."

This made the inferno rage even hotter. Sol's knees buckled and she saw red behind her eyes. The blind need to hurt, to destroy those who'd wronged her. To make Mal suffer until he was begging for forgiveness and at her mercy. To destroy Serevadia and take that throne for herself—

"Those heretics cast us out!" Nomien howled. "I will make them pay."

A voice boomed over him, slick as quicksilver and doused the fire in Sol's body.

"Peace. I think we have listened to your thirst for revenge long enough."

"Having doubts, Haphion?" the God of Vengeance sneered.

"About your loyalties, yes," the god rumbled. "I trusted you after Zelmis. Perhaps too much. Your need for the mortals in Vernes to worship us cast us out. In many ways, this is your fault."

As vengeance started to rage again, Haphion cut him off.

"And mine." He said it in a way that made it clear that he was done talking about it. "Proceed, mortals."

"Right." Arke huffed. "Right. Because I don't trust you—"

"Arke," Sol hissed.

"—I'm gonna make sure the Aether over Vernes and Gratey is unbroken and thick. They don't worship you anyway, so leave them be."

"The rest of the world?" a voice like falling petals asked.

"You can have that," Arke admitted.

A rumbling of content ran through Sol's head and bones. A few spikes of annoyance, but she could feel how badly they wanted back into Eith, even with restrictions.

"We're not done," Sorin said.

The rumbling stopped, and Sol started to sweat for him.

"I get that you people need worshippers, but you're not doing what you did before," he declared. "If you want a Champion, they have to be an adult for their race. They have to be willing and uncorrupted going into this. Their lives are their own, and their choice to serve you will be just that. A *choice*. Never again will you break men and women like you broke Abraxas Kain."

"Abraxas Kain," Haphion sighed sadly. "I did destroy him, didn't I?"

"You did." Sorin's voice shook. "And we paid the price. You twisted him and so many others into what you wanted, and they didn't know what to be without you. He went mad with the quest to bring you back because he thought he was wrong and unloved if you weren't there for him. We had to pick up the pieces. *We* had to love him, even as he hurt us, and *we* had to watch him die for you."

"Never. Again. Your Champions, if you have any, will *choose* you, and they will keep their minds intact."

A moment of pure, ringing silence. "This is agreed."

One by one the gods muttered their own promises to do the same. She couldn't pick out which ones said the names of their fallen Champions. Some didn't care, others seemed to genuinely mourn them, Haphion among them. An anger all Sol's and not Nomien's threatened to overwhelm her.

Who was he to deserve Abraxas? To grieve as if he knew him?

But she pushed that down, imagining Abraxas chiding her for throwing away their chance at peace because she was angry about him. This was the closest the Divines would get to an apology, and she knew with how little Abraxas had been given in life, he would've wept to receive this.

It wasn't enough for Sol, but she forced it to be. For him.

"Is that all?" the petal voice whispered. "Your rules have been met. We can swear upon them now, and fix what was broken."

Sol hesitated. "The Serevadians?"

"Hmm, to displace them would be cruel," another goddess said. "Dishonorable. We cannot kill so many without breaking your rules. But . . . to bring them back to their caverns would be no large task."

A few others agreed, proposing to have Mituna break the bridges under the ocean to keep them separated, and let them stay underground to recover.

"It wouldn't be a solution to last," Haphion warned. "They will be back. But that is a mortal issue. We will fix this because it was immortal magic that drew them to the surface, but whatever comes afterwards will be yours to fix."

Sol let out a breath, her lungs finally relaxing. "Okay. We can deal with that."

In fact, it was more than she hoped for. Fixing all of Eith's problems with a snap of the fingers . . . no wonder Etherak had been obsessed with the Divines. They talked of moving armies like one would pick up a cup of ale and move it to the next table.

Nomien's heat wasn't completely silent. "The Elders . . ."

"Yes." Haphion sighed again. "To bury those artifacts. Mortals should not get their hands on them again. Even though we wished it, we also dreaded it. You have no idea how close you came to unleashing a true evil."

"We didn't do anything," Sorin retorted.

"Separate the pieces of the Eternity Dagger and hide them." Haphion spoke over him. "Take the Shadow Dancer's Blade and bury it where no light will reach it. Only then will you be safe."

Sol found herself nodding. "Okay. Okay, yes. We can do that."

She knew enough about negotiations to know this one was over. She was about to call for their oaths to seal the deal when Evren finally spoke up.

"Who's to keep you in line?"

The gods paused. "What?"

"Who will watch you to make sure you don't step out of bounds?" she asked. "Who will keep you from breaking your oaths a hundred years down the line when we're not here?"

Another ripple of discontent that Haphion quieted. "You have a suggestion?"

Evren's breath was ragged. "I do. Me."

Sol should've seen it coming. Sorin was whispering furiously and asking her to take it back. Arke muttered to himself, feeling the same sense of blame Sol did. And she was just caught between the two, unable to see her friend, unable to do anything.

Evren ignored Sorin. "One of us is part of the magic that will protect Vernes and Gratey. Another is bound to the dagger's magic. Let me join her and walk eternity to keep the Aether in check and to protect Eith."

Sol's heart sank but she didn't have the strength to argue. The gods were eagerly lapping up Evren's painful words as if the blood of her suffering was all that could sate them. Perhaps it was.

It surprised Sol then when the gentle voice of petals came out first.

"Oh, you poor thing," the goddess murmured. "Such strange magic just to keep you alive. You are half of what you're supposed to be. The other is . . . yes, she's gone, isn't she?"

"Holtia!" the sickly voice hissed. "Get away. Let us handle this."

"This is my realm, brother," Holtia said. "I will fulfill this mortal's wish. After all, to leave her to wander with half a heart would be as cruel as we were to our Champions. We promised to do better, did we not? Let us start with her."

Her brother backed off, and Haphion's power joined Holtia as if peering down at Evren.

"We cannot pinpoint eternity's magic, Holtia," the King of gods said gravely. "Do not make promises you cannot keep."

"No," the goddess said. "But I can give her a chance. Listen to this, half-hearted mortal. Whenever eternity strays close to Eith, I will scratch the Aether there. Only for a short time, or else things unseemly will bleed through. Should you find these portals before they close, you may join your other half. And from there you may become our wardens. To watch us, to protect Eith, so long as you both are together. That is the only chance I can give you. Will you take it?"

"Yes," Evren breathed.

Sol bowed her head, fighting back her tears. She was already losing Evren.

"Then it is done." Holtia flitted away. "Our oaths we swear on this day."

All the voices, loud and soft, bright and dark, rose up as one.

"To Eith we will hold, to Eith we will not touch. Let our Champions choose us as worthy and our power flow through them until the day they die or relieve us of duty. Let the darkened part of Eith be uninfluenced by our power, from now until the shield is broken by mortal hands.

"Let the Aether be our guide, not our prison. Let the wardens act with mercy and grace. Let us back into Eith once more."

These oaths carried weight that Sol felt in her soul. As a witness, she would hold them to it until she died. And Evren, who might never die, would hold them to it for eternity.

Arke's portal dropped them back into Eith with such jarring finality that Sol almost puked. Solid ground at her feet. True air in her lungs. Her head was pounding from the absence of so much pressure.

Slowly she let go of Arke and Sorin and opened her eyes.

The sky was healing. The cracks of lightning melded until once again there was a blueish-grey instead of a hellish red. The sun shone again, weak and watery, but it still brought tears to her eyes. From the trees she heard the shouts of confusion as the distant armies watched Serevadia wink away, leaving nothing but scorched earth and bodies as a testament to their battle. The shouts turned from confusion to cheers.

They'd won. It was over.

The remaining Wandering Sols stood in the blackened clearing, now wide enough that she could see the army through the ashes of dead trees. A lumbering skeletal giant hunched over in the distance, a sight that would've been strange once, but Sol just shrugged off.

"We won," Sorin said.

"It doesn't feel like it," Sol said.

Evren said nothing. She knelt beside Abraxas's corpse and smoothed away his hair. She took her dagger back, whispering all sorts of things in Elvish Sol couldn't understand.

They'd have to burn him, Sol realized. Somewhere out of sight and away from everyone else. The people knew Abraxas as a villain. They wouldn't mourn him the way the Sols did.

Sol sniffled and leaned into Sorin, who took her gladly. The smell of ash clogged her nose. Ash and blood and . . . jasmine?

"Oh, for fuck's sake!" Arke growled. "Give me a damned minute?"

They all turned to see the most beautiful woman in existence step onto the ashen stone and stick her tongue out at Arke. She looked vaguely elven, with long ears and a graceful body. But everything else, like her too sharp nails and too wide eyes, spoke of a predator. Her hair was made of constantly flowering jasmine that trailed behind her, her dress nothing but mist that flowed around her legs and bare feet.

When Arke saw them staring at her, he snapped around.

"You told me never to look at you!"

The woman laughed. "I thought it would be funny!"

"You said you'd rip my eyeballs out and wear them on a necklace!"

"It was funny, admit it."

"Uh, Arke?" Sorin laughed nervously. "Who is this?"

The goblin winced. "Call her Unnethen. And for fucks sake, don't tell her your name. She's Fey."

"Oh." Sol felt dizzy. Gods, and now Fey? She needed to lie down, but she tried to remember what Sahar told her about Fey manners. "Is there something you need, Unnethen?"

She smiled. "Not from you. I'm just taking Arke home."

Evren bolted to her feet. "What?"

"That was part of our deal. He got a *lot* on his end. Practically a steal. And it saved all of you, didn't it? Well . . ." she winced. "Most of you. But now he belongs in the Brightlands with me."

"That's . . ." Sorin looked at Arke, who was refusing to meet his eyes. "That's not fair. I thought we were sticking together after this."

Arke smiled sadly. "Me too, kid."

Unnethen rolled her eyes. "Oh, don't be so dramatic. I'm not killing him. He's living with me and delighting in paradise."

"Yeah," Sorin spat. "Alone."

"I never said he would be alone."

Arke froze, half-worried and half-hopeful as Unnethen swept aside and pulled her skirts back to reveal a familiar eight legged form.

Arke gaped at her. "Neri?"

"*You were right,*" the spider said. "*I couldn't break it. But I could amend it.*"

"Yes, yes." Unnethen sighed. "Very sweet. She called demanding that I find a better deal. Do you know how many concessions I've made for you, Arke? If you weren't so beautiful and talented, I'd call this all off. Alas, my pride is at stake now and you *are* beautiful. So, you'll have Neri. You two will live on my lands, free from harm and full of magic. And maybe, *maybe*," she said pointedly. "I allow you to visit Eith from time to time."

Arke brightened. "And the Aether?"

Unnethen frowned. "Why would you want that?"

He looked back at Evren. "I have a feeling I'll have people there, too."

"Fine!" The Fey threw her arms in the air. "Say your goodbyes, please. This place reeks."

She stalked—floated?—off, and Arke waddled up to them.

"It's a long story, and maybe I'll tell you when I see you all again," he said. "But for now, I gotta go. Sorin . . . oh, shit, please don't cry."

"How am I supposed to not?" Sorin asked, wiping away tears. "You're leaving me."

"I'll be back, kid." He tugged on Sorin's coat until the human knelt at eye level. "This ain't forever. Besides, we both know your heart is in the ocean and I'm not the sailin' sort. This was always going to happen."

He turned to Sol, who didn't have to kneel to get the full watery goblin-eye view. "And we all knew that you were gonna have to leave us to help your people eventually."

Sol forced a smile. "I guess we did. Doesn't mean this hurts any less."

"No," Arke agreed. "It hurts like a bitch. Come here, all of you, and savor this while it lasts. Likely won't be another one."

He held out his arms for a hug, and all three of them descended on him. They were a messy tangle of tears, tired limbs, and sniffling noses. They didn't want to let go.

Sol squeezed her eyes shut, taking in this feeling that was perfect and yet still missing two sets of arms. She choked back a sob as Arke broke away, but Sorin didn't let her and Evren go. They stayed holding each other as they watched Arke set his spellbook down next to Abraxas.

He walked up to Neri, and together they went to Unnethen. When she opened a portal, he looked back one last time and gave them a toothy, goblin grin.

Then he was gone, and there were three.

48

Evren

Three Months Later

Linston was a riot of blue ribbons, sparkling snow, and golden sunshine. The richest neighborhoods had their lanterns magically changed to blue flames and their gardens blooming gold and silver. But the poorer districts along the fringes were just as lively. The air was crowded with cheers and the streets littered with fallen decorations. Food, though still scarce, was given out more freely than it had been in months. Pockets of dancing and music could be seen from high above where the Rhys's summer palace, now their official home, overlooked the entire city.

Inside was no small party either, with colorful nobles and mages from all over the continent. But Evren stayed near one of the chilly floor-to-ceiling windows overlooking the city.

These people had a right to celebrate. Many of them would only get this little bit of bliss before trudging back out to the burned husks of their homes to rebuild after winter passed. But even after three months, the weight of what happened wouldn't leave her. Long after the physical wounds had healed and her body had been allowed to finally feel somewhat normal after months of running ragged, she still felt heavy. Exhausted—as if she was struggling to fight her way out of a wool blanket with no end in sight.

A round of vigorous applause erupted from the grand ballroom and pulled Evren away from the view. The end of another toast from Queen Marjorie herself, congratulating Barrion and Mei on their coronation. Hells, that had to make five now. The old woman certainly liked to talk.

Ever polite, Barrion tipped his newly crowned head to her. Evren wasn't used to seeing him as King. The boyish charm was buried, and standing over its grave was a kind but serious man. His black hair gleamed underneath the silver crown, simple and understated. He didn't wear the colors of the old Rhys line, black-and-gold, but instead blue-and-silver. Something he and Mei had decided to do to give Etherak a fresh start.

Mei was on his arm, looking a little bored with the festivities but surprisingly happy. Her Etherakian dress suited her, more silver than blue to match him. Her own crown was a mirror to his, no smaller or less ornate. That was also new, since the old Queen's crown was apparently a lot simpler than the King's.

They were changing a lot already. Barrion planned to make Linston the official capital of Etherak instead of Whitestone, to separate church and state. Their renewed relationship with Terevas was also bearing fruit, and likely the only thing that would get Etherak through the winter. Terevas, with its warmer weather, had food to spare for the armies that had saved it.

Overall, Barrion was doing everything he could to be a different King than his father and uncle. Whether it stuck later in his rule was up for debate, but Evren could hope for a better Etherak under his guidance.

Despite the jovial attitude in the ballroom, none could deny the undercurrent of anxiety. Etherak had its gods back, made apparent by the sudden absence of Serevadian forces and the renewed stability of Eith's weather. There were talks to send forces to Gratey to help clear out any remaining Serevadians, but they didn't want Etherakian soldiers on their soil, helpful or not. The city-states seemed united in one thing, and that was driving out Serevadia by themselves.

Vernes hadn't suffered much at all from the war. Apparently the desert itself had proven too much, and heaps of silver-clad corpses could be found in the desert, weeks from any source of civilization.

Serevadia, now without its Emperor, had been quiet. A beast driven away, for now.

A flash of gold and a waving hand caught Evren's attention. Sorin calling her across the room. She sighed, not wishing to squeeze between the perfumed bodies of nobles but she couldn't deny him. Soon she was pushing herself away from the wall and making her way towards him.

"You wore it!" He beamed, looking over her and the dress he bought for her. It was plain by noble standards, but made of a rich emerald velvet lined with bronze brocade that showed its riches subtly. Sorin was using his reward gold loosely and sported a dashing coat more gold than his normal one.

"It was either this or armor," Evren said. "I doubt they would appreciate that."

"Oh, I don't know, Mei might've liked it." He draped an arm over her shoulder and pushed her towards a circle of well-dressed mages, all dripping with crystal beads and fur from their robes. "Help me out here, yeah?"

The mages parted eagerly to let them in. Morlen, the mage who was finally growing back his eyebrows, bowed deeply to her.

"My lady. Has Captain Sorin dragged you into this mess?"

"No, no, I just enjoy her company." Sorin waved him off with his other hand. "But you can tell her what you told me. She's in a better mood today."

Wrong. Evren was in the same mood, and the mages knew it. They exchanged worried glances before one of them, a half-orc woman with thick black curls and gold capped tusks, sighed heavily.

"We were discussing the use of this teleportation magic," she explained. "Serevadia seems to have a hold on it, although most of their mages were killed in battle from our reports. However. The notes given to us by your partner—"

"Arke," Evren said.

"Yes, Arke. They're enlightening. Aether study is farther behind than we'd like, but the consensus is that casually ripping and mending it to get from one point to another could drastically change how Eith functions—"

Sorin cut her off. "Yes, yes, economic disaster, have to put limits, blah, blah, blah. She knows that. Skip to the part about Arke."

The woman's face soured, and Morlen took over.

"It's not meant to be disrespectful," he said hurriedly. "It's just that we would have to completely rewrite the magic from scratch for it to be used safely. The amount of energy and study would go to the mages in the Conclave—"

"So, you'll be taking the credit," Evren finished coldly.

All the mages shuffled uncomfortably. The half-orc was the only one that would meet her eyes.

"You understand where this is coming from," she said gently. "If we credit a goblin who is no longer here to help us, the lower mages in the Conclave would riot."

"They'd have a fit," Evren amended. "As they do."

Another mage bristled. "It would be their work!"

"Work that wouldn't exist without Arke's knowledge," Evren snapped. "Name the spell after him, list him first in the long line of names that worked to make this happen, or put a massive painting of his ass cheeks on the doors of the tower. Frankly, I don't care what you do, so long as he is credited."

A different mage snorted, a drooping man who looked like melted wax taken human form. "No one will believe that a goblin could do this. It would be seen as a joke. The Conclave would be the laughingstock of Eith."

"Like me, Orsin?" the half-orc asked, and the group fell quiet. "No one thought *I* could be a mage, and here I am about to take your seat as the next High Enchanter. Perhaps we should let the magic speak for itself, instead of the body it comes from."

Orsin retreated into his goblet, muttering darkly, but no one paid him any attention. Morlen sighed as if this was a daily occurrence, which it likely was, and turned to Evren and Sorin.

"Of course we wouldn't dream of discrediting Arke's work," Morlen said. "Painting his, uh, bum would not be my first choice. But we'll think of something. At the very least, he'll be the first name listed. Agreed?"

All the mages, reluctant or not, agreed and soon the conversation turned to how they could tax a magic that would reach countries with different money values and laws. Sorin made a face and quickly withdrew them from the group.

"You didn't need me for that," Evren said as they walked through the crowds.

"No," Sorin admitted. "But you were turning into a statue again and missing all this fantastic information. For example, did you know that Queen Marjorie had been set to marry Loghain in her youth?"

Evren made a face. "No. That seems odd. They're complete opposites."

"The marriage never went through because Loghain was always on the frontlines. But Marjorie, the old gossip, keeps saying that he was secretly married to a lover back in Vernes."

"Worgshit."

Sorin laughed. "I know! Hells, that woman does like her stories though. She spent an hour before the coronation trying to convince Sol to move the dwarves down south. Apparently there's plenty of room!"

Evren scanned the crowds for Sol's familiar form and found the dwarf chatting easily with a crowd of nobles. She too wore a crown, a simple band threaded through her golden hair. Beside her, Karas had cleaned up as well as he could and was talking to what seemed to be the remaining commanders of Etherak's army. Evren had to admit, the two made a good team. She wasn't the least bit surprised when the survivors from Dirn-Darahl elected Sol as Queen.

"Is Sol taking the invitation?"

Dirn-Darahl was still empty. Many feared that Serevadia would take it again, so very few of the three hundred or so dwarves that were freed from other camps like Stone's End were eager to go back. Relocation was one of Sol's biggest issues.

Sorin shook his head. "No. I don't know what she's got planned, but she's got that look in her eyes, you know? Like she's got it all figured out and is just humoring everyone else."

Evren did know, and she was relieved to see that spark in her friend's eye again. The idea of having a whole city of people depending on her would've made Evren crumble, but Sol took it in stride, like she'd been waiting her whole life for it. And maybe she had.

"What about you?" Evren asked. "How's the ship coming?"

Sorin beamed like a sunrise, like he did every time it was brought up. Oh yes, he spent a lot of his gold spoiling himself and his friends, but most of it went into the construction of a new ship in Tal-Mashad's harbor.

"She'll be finished in the next few months," he said excitedly. "Getting a crew together would be hard, but everyone from Vayne's ship that survived is heading out with me on the first voyage. We'll stop at a few *secret* Vasa places to let them get on with their lives if they want. Or they can stay. It's up to them, really."

"And Enola?"

"Still pouting." Sorin shrugged. "To be expected. But she can't go with me. Not yet. She's got to figure out all that Blood magic of hers first."

It was a hard choice for Sorin, Evren knew. He loved Enola,

but knew she wouldn't learn anything out at sea. The best place for her was where she was more likely to find others like herself —in Etherak. Another thing Evren should help with but couldn't.

She had a hunt after all.

Sorin stopped and looked her in the eye. "You're still coming with me, right?"

Evren nodded. "That's where I should go, I think. Besides, I want to see what you named the ship."

"Ugh!" He threw his head back. "I'm terrible at naming things. Fuck, I've got no clue. And it's so important."

"Like the worg?"

"Yes! Shit. He needs a name first. All right, help me come up with something, please? I'll do anything."

But Evren was looking at the crowd again. The mix of dwarves, Orenlion elves, a couple Hisrachi, Terevasan and Etherakian nobility. She caught Sol's eye by pure accident and the dwarf waved excitedly. Then she pointed to Sorin and the spot at her side. The message was clear.

"I think," Evren said, maneuvering them so he was facing Sol. "That Sol can help. Or she's got something she wants to tell you."

Sorin frowned. "Really? Oh! There she is." He waved back at her and started to tug Evren with him.

She held back, slipping out of his arm and Sorin stopped between the two of them, his face falling a little. He recovered, as he always did, with a warm smile.

"Need a moment alone?"

She nodded. "Just some air."

"Okay. Don't be long. If I'm near Karas, we're turning this event into a real party. This time I'll out drink him."

Evren laughed and watched him bounce off towards Sol. The two met with excited chattering and hand waving. Whatever Sol had planned involved Sorin in some way and it made Evren's heart warm to see them still working to keep those ties together. She felt like she was breaking them off one by one.

Evren turned and left the ballroom, taking the now familiar path to the palace doors. The guards there didn't so much as twitch in her direction, although she still felt like she didn't belong. They even held open one of the large double-doors that led outside, and she nodded her thanks before heading out into the cold.

Deep winter wind snapped at her dress as she stood at the top of the wide stairs that led to the rest of the city. Made of gleaming white marble, she couldn't tell the difference between the stone and the frost growing around them. The sounds of a city celebrating their new King was muffled from so high up, and she took a deep breath of cold air to settle herself.

Her heart tugged her west, as it had for weeks now. She tapped a promise into her breastbone and sat at the top of the steps. The velvet didn't hold back the cold, but she endured it, staring out at the city and the lands beyond it. Still scarred from so many funeral pyres, snow refusing to cover them up entirely, still broken from a short but disastrous war. But the slowly setting sun made it all seem golden. As if, when it rose again, everything would be healed and new.

Evren knew who would come for her and wasn't at all surprised when Aster settled down on the steps beside her. He wore his best Orenlion finery, complete with moonstone-studded ear cuffs and beaded robes. But he looked just as dreary as she felt, and it had little to do with almost dying at the hands of shadow mages. Watching the coronation and the obvious comfort Mei drew from being at Barrion's side was still tearing him apart.

Somewhere along the way, Mei had fallen in love with Barrion, and Barrion with her. A good sign for Etherak and their marriage, but Evren couldn't help but share Aster's hurt.

She grabbed his hand, lacing their fingers together and laid her head on his shoulder.

"Is there nothing I can say to convince you to stay?" he eventually asked.

"No," Evren said, and hated it as much as when she proposed the idea to the Divines. Leaving everything on Eith behind with no hope of ever coming back . . . that was selfish. Cutting her ties and saying goodbye, no matter how much her friends understood, was like taking a knife to the chest each time. Telling Aster had brought her to tears, which threatened to come back.

She swallowed them.

"I'm sorry," she said. "I know it's awful to tell you that I'm leaving everything because of Gyda. I know I can live without her, but . . ."

"You don't want to," Aster finished. "I know. Stars, I know that feeling too well. At least you have a chance to see her again. Even if it means that you're leaving us."

"Do you hate me?"

"No. I understand, Evren. I envy you, in a way. But I could never hate you."

The fear that she'd been ignoring ebbed away. He squeezed her hand, as if he felt it and wanted to make sure she knew that she never had to feel that fear again.

"Will you at least come back to Orenlion one last time?" he asked. "To see your father?"

She nodded. She had time, after all. Even if Sorin's ship was done as fast as he promised, they wouldn't leave until the winter ice melted. She had many months to say her goodbyes, and while telling Yuhan yet again that she would never see him would break what was left of her heart, her father deserved to have it come from her.

And she missed the Deep Wood. She'd like to walk it, one last time, with Aster.

"Is it foolish to fear what the world will be like with you gone?" he asked. "Sorin and Sol will have their responsibilities.

Sahar will no longer be an adventurer. Mei is a Queen now. Where does that leave us?"

"Everyone wanders apart, Aster," Evren said. "That's life."

"I thought I'd have more time."

This time it was her squeezing his hand. "I know."

She felt his breaths through his shoulders as he struggled to keep his breathing even.

"Evren, I don't know. This world with the Divines in it terrifies me. What if it all falls apart again? What if we need you?"

To the setting sun and the reveling city, Evren smiled sadly.

"You'll always have me, Aster, even if I'm not there. Besides, I'm not so very special. There's something you need to remember."

"What's that?"

"Every time Eith breaks, there will be someone there to fix it," she said. "This world bleeds heroes."

"There's no one like you."

And for the first time, Evren truly understood Gyda's words back in the Eternity Maze. After seeing all the horrors Eith had yet to suffer, she could take heart in one thing.

"There will always be people like me."

49

Sorin

Seven Months Later

"**A**re you sure you don't want to come with me?"

Sahar shook her head, the wind tugging her black hair free from its bun. She stood on the dock with him, Tal-Mashad rising behind her in the deep grey cliffs. The sun shone warmly down on them, the breeze playful and salt-laden. Over the lapping of waves, there was the sound of voices calling back and forth, the grunting of workers lifting cargo into ships. Into *his* ship.

The Fool's Ire was beautiful, but Sorin was biased. He loved the clean white of her sails as the gulls circled around them. He loved the beautiful bronze sheen that came from the King's Ash used to build her. The snarling worg figurehead was by far his favorite touch. Kain, the model, agreed wholeheartedly.

Her deck was teeming with life as last-minute preparations to set sail were carried out. Familiar faces ran about, mingling with newer ones. Zo scurried back and forth between *The Fool's*

Ire and the two older ships that would be following her, run by two other crews but answering to Sorin and Sol as they ferried the dwarves to their new home.

"*I* could be coming with you." Enola moped to the side, sticking her feet in the water over the dock.

Sahar held her hands up. This was his fight, not hers. He settled beside Enola, watching the water for a familiar face to peek through. Ire grew more and more bold each day they were in shallow waters. He needed to set sail before she nibbled someone's toes off.

"You're mad," he said.

Enola snorted. "Duh."

"You know this isn't forever, right?"

"It could be!" she pointed out. Her hair fell into her eyes. Now that she was growing it out, it just sort of flopped everywhere but softened her forever sharp face. "You don't know what can happen out there. You need me, Sorin."

He tried to choke back a laugh, and didn't succeed, earning him a glower from both girls. He winced.

"You're right, I do."

Enola looked up hopefully, but deflated when he held up his hands.

"I need you strong, Enola." He poked her in her chest. "I need you in control. Right now you're just hurting yourself, lashing out at everything that could hurt you more. That's what almost killed Evren, and I don't know enough to keep it from happening to you."

She twisted her face into a scowl that meant she was going to fight even more, but he wasn't done.

"Why do you think I'm not packing for a long journey?" he asked. "I plan on coming back. Often. Once every couple months, at least, until you're ready."

"Who decides when I'm ready?" Enola protested.

"We do." He nodded to Sahar. "All three of us. We're not against you, Enola. You know that."

She slumped her shoulders, looking down at the water. "I know. I just want to go with you."

He ruffled her hair. "And one day you will. I have a cabin picked out and everything. How fast you get there is up to you."

Finally, it seemed to click in Enola that, yes, she would have to wait. But the more she trained and learned, the faster she could get where she wanted. She jumped to her feet so fast she nearly rammed her head into Sorin's nose.

"Yes! I'll be very fast." She hopped from foot to foot. "By the time you get back, I'll know more about Blood magic than anyone! You bet!"

She didn't give him a chance to respond, she just gave him a strangling hug around his neck and then dashed off into the city. He would be worried, but the people of Tal-Mashad knew Enola well enough by now to stay away.

Sahar sighed as he stood. "Now that's *my* problem."

He shrugged. "Unless you come with me."

She snorted. "Oh yes, that'll make her happy. To know I was allowed to go and she wasn't. Whisk me away somewhere, Sorin, and leave the child alone to fend for herself."

He'd be less ashamed if he wasn't serious. But he was. If it wasn't for Enola, he would be on his knees begging for Sahar to come aboard with him.

And she knew it. That little bit of playfulness left her as she met his eyes, sorrowful in a way that few could understand. But he could.

"I can't," she said softly, regretfully. "It's not just Enola, you know that. I told you Barrion asked me to help with the founding of that city."

He nodded along. Building a city over the spot where Abraxas had torn open the sky and killed hundreds didn't sit well with him. But it was a new collaboration between Terevas and Etherak. A city built together, to help keep an eye over a dangerous spot for rituals. And where one strange skeleton named Vangelis stuck around, refusing to leave.

He'd become a tourist attraction, Sorin would bet gold on it.

Sahar also quietly planned to gather more Ironbloods, as they were calling people like Enola, to the eventual city. A sort of communal training ground to learn. It was their best shot at learning more about Blood magic.

Sahar wasn't an adventurer anymore, able to come and go as she pleased. She had responsibilities and jobs to do. Sorin could respect that, he just wished hers aligned with his.

"Well," he said around the strange knot in his throat. "You can't blame me for trying, right?"

She smiled ruefully. "My first adventure at sea left me bitter, what can I say?"

"One day, Sahar Al-Fasil, I'll change that feeling," he promised, and she let herself laugh, which sounded like music when mixed with the water and the gulls. For a moment her eyes lit up and she looked truly happy. That look lingered, even after she smothered her laugh and returned to her prim, noble face.

Sorin was going to ruin things if he stayed any longer. He'd say something stupid that would make everything awkward between them. And since they shared responsibilities with Enola, he didn't want that. He wanted her happy, and with the ghost of Drystan still clinging to her . . .

Well, there never had been a chance for them.

Still, that didn't mean he couldn't try. After all, he had more charm in his pinky than Drystan ever did, may his scowling soul rest in peace and *not* haunt him.

He swept his coat out behind him, knelt and held out his hand. She humored him, her brown eyes twinkling, as he took her hand and kissed her knuckles. Not necessarily a gentlemanly act when conducted by him, an overdramatic sailor with a high opinion of himself. But it was close enough.

"Until next time, my lady," he said, and slipped in a wink.

She rewarded him with a smirk. "Until next time, Captain."

He swept away, still shivering between the title and the feel of her skin on his lips. But he didn't turn back. He marched down the dock with purpose as a head peaked through the water and swam next to him.

"That was it?" Ire hissed. "You could've swept her off her feet!"

He shook his head. "Sahar loves a ghost, and until the time that she can let him go, I won't force my way into her life."

Ire's groan produced a load of bubbles. "You could make her forget about him, easy."

"I don't want her to forget him," Sorin said, stopping at the plank leading up to his ship. "I want her to choose me when she's ready."

~

~

WEEKS LATER, all three ships circled the empty deep-blue of the Boreal Sea, bobbing with the strangely calm waves in the midday sun. Sorin wasn't yet used to the way the ocean behaved with Mituna's influence, or how some of his crew had started burning offerings to her. He wasn't going to stop them though.

Today he was glad for the calm weather. His stomach was in knots already and he didn't need massive waves to mess him up further.

He made his way down to the main deck, Kain trotting happily at his side. Evren and Sol were leaning against the starboard railing, watching the empty sea in earnest. Sol was dressed simply, no crown on her head today. Evren was in full armor, her bow tucked securely at her waist.

Sorin forced himself to ignore the panic that came with the sight, that he was losing her for good today. This was a good thing. He knew the moment she asked him to sail her that he was leading her to Gyda, and that was perfect. But that didn't make it hurt any less.

"Are you sure this is the place?" Sorin asked, settling on her other side.

Evren nodded, eyes fixed on the horizon. She hadn't slept in three days, and it showed. She was restless, and her prowling spooked his crew more than Kain ever did. He made excuses for her and often tried to get her to rest in his cabin. But the sight of so many mementos from their travels, the maps and trinkets, Abraxas's sword and armor, Arke's spellbook, it all made her worse. He'd stopped calling her days ago.

Sol was right when she whispered that this had nothing to do with him. This was something beyond them that Evren needed to finish, and she wouldn't rest until she did.

Evren stepped away from the railing and looked more normal than she had since the battle. Her façade cracked, as if she was realizing that this was the last time they'd be together.

"I'm sorry," she said, her voice breaking.

Sol shook her head and grabbed her hand. "Don't be. This was how it was going to go. This way we're all safe and together in our own way."

"I . . ." she wavered, her eyes gleaming. "I'm going to miss you both. I need her, but you two . . ."

Fuck, he was going to break down if she said anymore. Instead he pulled her into a tight hug and savored the feeling of her arms around him. He squeezed her tight, memorizing this feeling. Making this something he would remember in vivid detail.

"We'll be all right, Evvie," he whispered. He wanted to say more but found nothing would suffice. He pulled away reluctantly, finding his vision blurry. "I swear we'll be okay. You'll be watching us, after all."

She nodded, wiping away her tears. Then she turned to Sol, who had completely lost her composure and drew the dwarf into another hug. They muttered goodbyes through sniffles and sobs, and when they pulled away, Evren pressed her wyvern dagger into Sol's hand.

"I can't take this," Sol protested.

"It's mine to give," Evren said. "And out of the two of you, only you can use a dagger without hurting yourself."

"Ouch," Sorin muttered but wasn't hurt. He was useless with daggers.

Evren stood up and everything felt different, as if they'd passed under a cloud. Sorin knew they were losing time.

He grabbed Sol and pulled her close, backing away from the railing and leaving Evren there alone.

"Tell Gyda we said hi, okay?" he said. "And we miss her."

Evren smiled, her scars pulling with the genuine expression. There, at the edge of his ship with the world at her feet, she looked like a figure from legend, and his bruised heart swelled. He couldn't help but remember the first time she smiled like that, with longer hair and a different bow, marching towards a burning prison as if the idea of adventure was the most wonderful thing in the world.

Out of all of them, her adventures would continue. She wouldn't be alone, but hells, Sorin was going to miss her.

She turned back as the water near the railing started to mist. From the mist something swirled. A familiar gap in the Aether, soft and blowing in Sorin's eyes. He blinked away, tasting salt on his lips.

Beyond the portal was Gyda. Her scarred hand outstretched, her face grinning and hopeful. Evren's breath audibly caught and then she was climbing up on the railing. Sol sobbed beside him. Sorin tried to wave but even his good hand was shaking.

He could only watch, heart swelling, as Evren jumped into the portal and into Gyda's arms. The portal muffled their peals of laughter, the words tossed between them as Gyda twirled her around. But the kiss needed no words, and Sorin couldn't have described it if he tried.

He blinked only once and the portal was gone, the wide empty sea waiting, nothing else.

The crew jumped to action. They knew what to do, and

Sorin found himself wanting to thank something beyond this world for that but stopped himself.

Sol tugged them to the spot at the railing where Evren had last been. The wood was sun-warmed, but he imagined her hand had warmed it instead. The worg whined and laid at his feet.

"What now?" Sol asked after a while of silence.

That was easy. They found Sol a home. Her people had taken her idea of going to the waves easily, and while he still needed to get her to the hidden Vasa islands, it was a start. A whole fleet of independent dwarven ships, their own floating nation, would soon ride the waves. It would take time to build and work out the details. He and Sol talked endlessly about it over long nights, when dinner had gone cold and Kain was snoring in the bed.

There was also the matter of the Elder artifacts. He and Sol had to bury, hide, and make sure no one else got their hands on the three separate pieces. One sword, and two halves of a dangerous dagger.

But Sorin knew she meant more than that. More than her people's future. Where did *they* go? Him and Sol? Where did they wander next? What would they do?

He breathed in the air, and the salt didn't taste like grief anymore.

"Anything. Anywhere."

THE END

Thank you for reading **WHERE THE SKY BURNS.**

www.GillianGrant.com

ACKNOWLEDGMENTS

Is it odd to thank a book during its own acknowledgments?

I know it's been said a thousand times before, but this book, this series, has been a massive journey. Not only the challenge of getting what's in my head onto the pages, but also the whole process of publishing and promoting and everything required to be an author. It hasn't been easy, and it hasn't gone the way I expected, but it *has* changed me for the better. So, with that I would like top thank the *Blood of Eith* series for not only bringing to life a world that only existed at the D&D table, but also for proving to me that I could be exactly what I wanted to be and more.

To my D&D groups, again, who have been nothing but amazing and supportive throughout this whole process. Eith wouldn't be nearly as interesting without you, although it was refreshing to have an adventuring party whose actions I could predict for once. The Outlanders and the Monster Mash are still my favorites.

To my team who helped take the pile of angst and mush that was *Where the Sky Burns* and turn it into the book you're holding now. Laura, Charity, Stef, Sonia, and Aimee, I can't thank you enough. But I'll continue to try.

To my family, who never blinked when I said I wanted to start this insane journey and only helped and supported throughout it all.

To all the little things that got me through this, because I'm nothing if not a sucker for the little delicacies of life. Arizona

Green Tea (the big cans), every Youtube ambience creator, the Dragon Age games for supporting another comfort playthrough (the 11th, but who's counting?), my extremely dented and overly stickered emotional support water bottle, and all my favorite authors (Becky Chambers specifically for giving me hope for the world and myself).

And finally, obviously, to you. Thank you for coming on journey after journey with me in Eith. This might be the end for the Wandering Sols, but it isn't the end of Eith. There are plenty of stories to be told there. So if you've found Eith to be as much of a home as I have (regular catastrophic events aside), never worry. We'll be back. In the meantime, take you well earned retirement and rest your weary feet, adventurer.

The adventures of tomorrow will be here before you know it.

ABOUT THE AUTHOR

Gillian Grant was born in Texas and grew up enthralled with fantasy stories of all kinds. As she got older she often traveled with her family and imagined wild adventures while exploring the mountains of Colorado and the glens of Scotland. Back home in Texas she took her love of fantasy to the next level and sat a group of friends down to play Dungeons and Dragons. From there, they built the world her first novel, *Where The Shadows Beckon* was set in. When she's not writing Gillian is normally juggling too many D&D campaigns, grooming dogs, and imagining her next adventure. She still lives in Texas with her two cats.

www.GillianGrant.com

facebook.com/GillianGrantAuthor

instagram.com/gilliangrantauthor

bookbub.com/profile/gillian-grant

amazon.com/Gillian-Grant/e/B09J94DBHP